Laurell K. Hamilton is the bestselling author of the acclaimed Anita Blake, Vampire Hunter, Novels. She lives near St Louis with her husband, her daughter, two dogs and an ever-fluctuating number of fish. She invites you to visit her website at www.laurellkhamilton.org.

LAURELL K. HAMILTON

INCUBUS DREAMS

AN ANITA BLAKE,
VAMPIRE HUNTER, NOVEL

headline

First published in the United States of America in 2004
First published in Great Britain by Orbit, an imprint of Little, Brown Book Group in 2004

First published in this edition in 2010 by
HEADLINE PUBLISHING GROUP

3

Cataloguing in Publication Data is available from the British Library

ISBN 978 0 7553 5540 2

Typeset in Monotype Fournier by Ellipsis Books Limited, Glasgow

Printed and bound in Great Britain by
Clays Ltd, St Ives plc

Headline's policy is to use papers that are natural, renewable and
recyclable products and made from wood grown in sustainable forests.
The logging and manufacturing processes are expected to conform to
the environmental regulations of the country of origin.

HEADLINE PUBLISHING GROUP
An Hachette UK Company
338 Euston Road
London NW1 3BH

www.headline.co.uk
www.hachette.co.uk

To J,
companion, best friend, lover,
stick and carrot, true partner,
husband.
Words fail.

ACKNOWLEDGMENTS

To Darla, who is always instrumental in making sure the deadlines get met and the business, all of it, gets attention. Karen, for taking me around to the strip clubs and teaching me never, ever, to sit near the stage. To Sherry, as always, for doing so much to keep everything clean, neat, and as tidy as we'll let her. I do realize that we are the stumbling block. Bear, also for going around to the strip clubs with us, and just being a large and wonderful presence. Robin, for answering my questions and, as always, for being a wise voice. To Marshal Michael Moriaty, for sending me all the nifty stuff on the federal marshal program, and answering some of my questions. All mistakes are mine and mine alone. To Sergeant Robert Cooney of St Louis's Mobile Reserve, for answering questions, for the tour and letting us see all the wonderful toys. His input was invaluable to this book. All mistakes are mine and mine alone. The more I learn about our own Mobile Reserve and all the tactical units across the country, the more impressed I am and the more I despair of ever getting it just right on paper. My writing group, the Alternate Historians: Tom Drennen, Rhett MacPherson, Deborah Millitello, Marella Sands, Sharon Shinn, and Mark Sumner. Fine writers, good friends, and champions of esoteric trivia. To Mary, my mother-in-law, who did grandma day camp with Trinity so that Jon and I could get this rewrite done. If Jon hadn't sat with me and made me do it, you might never have seen this book. To Trinity, who gets more amazing every year, and who I hope someday understands what the heck I was doing all those days and nights up in that room at the top of the house.

I

IT WAS AN October wedding. The bride was a witch who solved preternatural crimes. The groom raised the dead and slew vampires for a living. It sounded like a Halloween joke, but it wasn't.

The groom's side wore traditional black tuxedos with orange bow ties and white shirts. The bride's side wore orange formals. You don't see Halloween orange prom dresses all that often. I'd been terrified that I was going have to shell out three hundred dollars for one of the monstrosities. But since I was on the groom's side I got to wear a tux. Larry Kirkland, groom, co-worker, and friend, had stuck to his guns. He refused to make me wear a dress, unless I wanted to wear one. Hmm, let me see. Three hundred dollars, or more, for a very orange formal that I'd burn before I'd wear again, or less than a hundred dollars to rent a tux that I could return. Wait, let me think.

I got the tux. I did have to buy a pair of black tie-up shoes. The tux shop didn't have any size seven in women's. Oh, well. Even with the seventy-dollar shoes that I would probably never wear again, I still counted myself very lucky.

As I watched the four bridesmaids in their poofy orange dresses walk down the isle of the packed church, their hair done up on their heads in ringlets, and more makeup than I'd ever seen any of them wear, I was feeling very, very lucky. They had little round bouquets of orange and white flowers with black lace and orange and black ribbons trailing down from the flowers. I just had to stand up at the front of the church with my one hand holding the wrist of the other arm. The wedding coordinator had seemed to believe that all the groomsmen would pick their noses, or something equally embarrassing, if they didn't keep their hands busy. So she'd informed them that they were to stand with their hands clasped on opposite wrists. No hands in pockets, no crossed arms, no hands clasped in front of their groins. I'd arrived late to the rehearsal – big surprise – and the wedding coordinator had seemed to believe that I would be a civilizing influence on the men, just because I happened to be a girl. It didn't take her long to figure out that I was as uncouth as the men. Frankly, I thought we all behaved ourselves really well. She just didn't seem very comfortable around men, or around me. Maybe it was the gun I was wearing.

But none of the groomsmen, myself included, had done anything for her to complain about. This was Larry's day, and none of us wanted to screw it up. Oh, and Tammy's day.

The bride entered the church on her father's arm. Her mother was already in the front pew dressed in a pale melon orange that actually looked good on her. She was beaming and crying, and seemed to be both miserable and deliriously happy all at the same time. Mrs Reynolds was the reason for the big church wedding. Both Larry and Tammy would have been happy with something smaller, but Tammy didn't seem to be able to say no to her mother, and Larry was just trying to get along with his future in-law.

Detective Tammy Reynolds was a vision in white, complete with a veil that covered her face like a misty dream. She, too, was wearing more makeup than I'd ever seen her in, but the drama of it suited the beaded neckline, and full, bell-like skirt. The dress looked like it could have walked down the aisle on its own, or at least stood on its own. They'd done something with her hair so that it was smooth and completely back from her face, so that you could see just how striking she was. I'd never really noticed that Detective Tammy was beautiful.

I was standing at the end of the groomsmen, me and Larry's three brothers, so I had to crane a little to see his face. It was worth the look. He was pale enough that his freckles stood out on his skin like ink spots. His blue eyes were wide. They'd done something to his short red curls so they lay almost smooth. He looked good, if he didn't faint. He gazed at Tammy as if he'd been hit with a hammer right between the eyes. Of course, if they'd done two hours' worth of makeup on Larry, he might have been a vision, too. But men don't have to worry about it. The double standard is alive and well. The woman is supposed to be beautiful on her wedding day, the groom is just supposed to stand there and not embarrass himself, or her.

I leaned back in line and tried not to embarrass anyone. I'd tied my hair back while it was still wet so that it lay flat and smooth to my head. I wasn't cutting my hair so it was the best I could do to look like a boy. There were other parts of my anatomy that didn't help the boy look either. I am curvy, and even in a tux built for a man, I was still curvy. No one complained, but the wedding coordinator had rolled her eyes when she saw me. What she said out loud was, 'You need more makeup.'

'None of the other groomsmen are wearing makeup,' I said.

'Don't you want to look pretty?'

Since I'd thought I already looked pretty good, there was only one reply, 'Not particularly.'

That had been the last conversation the wedding lady and I had had. She positively avoided me after that. I think she'd been mean on purpose, because I wasn't helping her keep the other groomsmen in line. She seemed to believe that just because we both had ovaries instead of balls that we should have joined forces. Besides, why should I worry about being pretty? It was Tammy and Larry's day, not mine. If, and that was a very big if, I ever got married, then I'd worry about it. Until then, screw it. Besides, I was already wearing more makeup than I normally did. Which for me meant any. My stepmother, Judith, keeps telling me that when I hit thirty I'll feel differently about all this girl stuff. I've only got three years to go until the big 3-0; so far panic has not set in.

Tammy's father placed her hand in Larry's. Tammy was three

inches taller than Larry, in heels, she was more. I was standing close enough to the groom to see the look that Tammy's father gave Larry. It was not a friendly look. Tammy was three months, almost four months pregnant, and it was Larry's fault. Or rather it was Tammy and Larry's fault, but I don't think that's how her father viewed it. No, Mr Nathan Reynolds definitely seemed to blame Larry, as if Tammy had been snatched virgin from her bed and brought back deflowered, and pregnant.

Mr Reynolds raised Tammy's blusher on her veil to reveal all that carefully made-up beauty. He kissed her solemnly on the cheek, threw one last dark look at Larry, and turned smiling and pleasant to join his wife in the front pew. The fact that he'd gone from a look that dark, to pleasant and smiling when he knew the church would see his face, bothered me. I didn't like that Larry's new father-in-law was capable of lying that well. Made me wonder what he did for a living. But I was naturally suspicious, comes from working too closely with the police for too long. Cynicism is so contagious.

We all turned toward the altar, and the familiar ceremony began. I'd been to dozens of weddings over the years, almost all Christian, almost all standard denominations, so the words were strangely familiar. Funny, how you don't think you've memorized something until you hear it, and realize you have. 'Dearly beloved, we are gathered here today to join this man and this woman in Holy Matrimony.'

It wasn't a Catholic or Episcopalian wedding, so we didn't have to kneel, or do much of anything. We wouldn't even be getting communion during the ceremony. I have to admit my mind began to wander a bit. I've never been a big fan of weddings. I understand they're necessary, but I was never one of those girls who fantasized about what my wedding would be like someday. I don't remember ever thinking about it until I got engaged in college, and when that fell through, I went back to not thinking about it. I'd been engaged very briefly to Richard Zeeman, junior high science teacher, and local Ulfric, Wolf-King, but he'd dumped me because I was more at home with the monsters than he was. Now, I'd pretty much settled into the idea that I would never marry. Never have those words spoken over me and my honeybun. A tiny part of me that I'd never admit to out loud was sad about that. Not the wedding part, I think I would hate my own wedding just as much as anyone else's, but not having one single person to call my own. I'd been raised middle-class, middle America, small town, and that meant the fact that I was currently dating a minimum of three men, maybe four, depending on how you looked at it, still made me squirm with something painfully close to embarassment. I was working on not being uncom-fortable about it, but there were issues that needed to be worked out. For instance, who do you bring as your date to a wedding? The wedding was in a church complete with holy items, so two of the men were out. Vampires didn't do well around holy items. Watching Jean-Claude and Asher burst into flames as they came through the door would probably have put a damper on the festivities. That left me with one official boyfriend, Micah Callahan, and one friend, who happened to be a boy, Nathaniel Graison.

They'd come to the part where the rings were exchanged, which meant the maid of honor and the best man had something to do. The woman got to hold Tammy's huge spill of white flowers, and the man got to hand over the jewelry. It all seemed so terribly sexist. Just once I'd like to see the men have to hold flowers and the women fork over the jewelry. I'd been told once by a friend that I was too liberated for my own good. Maybe. All I knew was that if I ever did get engaged again I'd decided either both of us got an engagement ring, or neither of us did. Of course, again, that not getting married part meant that the engagement was probably off the board, too. Oh, well.

At last, they were man and wife. We all turned and the reverend presented them to the church as Mr and Mrs Lawrence Kirkland, though I knew for a fact that Tammy was keeping her maiden name, so really it should have been Mr Lawrence Kirkland and Ms Tammy Reynolds.

We all fell into two lines. I got to offer my arm to Detective Jessica Arnet. She took the arm, and with her in heels, I was about five inches shorter than she was. She smiled at me. I'd noticed she was pretty about a month ago, because she was flirting with Nathaniel, but it wasn't until that moment that I realized she could be beautiful. Her dark hair was pulled completely back from her face, so that the delicate triangle of her cheeks and chin was all you saw. The makeup had widened her eyes, added color to her cheeks, and carved pouting lips out of her thin ones. I realized that the orange that made most of the bridesmaids look wan, brought out rich highlights in her skin and hair, made her eyes shine. So few people look good in orange, it's one of the reasons they use it in so many prisons, like an extra punishment. But Detective Arnet looked wonderful in it. It almost made me wish I'd let the wedding lady talk me into the extra makeup. Almost.

I must have stared, because she frowned, and only then did I start forward, and take our place in line. We filed out like good little wedding party members. We'd already endured the photographer for group shots. He'd be hunting the bride and groom for those candid moments: cutting the cake, throwing the bouquet, removing the garter. Once we got through the receiving line, I could fade into the background and no one would care.

We all stood in a line as we'd been drilled. Bride and groom at the front of the line, because, let's face it, that's who everyone is really here to see. The rest of us strung out behind them along the wall, waiting to shake hands with mostly strangers. Tammy's family were locals, but I'd never met any of them. Larry's family were all out-of-towners. I knew the policemen that had been invited; other than that, it was all nod and smile, nod and smile, shake a hand, or two, nod and smile.

I must have been concentrating very hard on the people I was meeting, because it surprised me when Micah Callahan, my official date, was suddenly in front of me. He was exactly my height. Short for man or woman. His rich, brown hair was nearly as curly as mine, and today his hair fell around his shoulders loose. He'd done that for me. He didn't like his hair loose, and I understood why. He was already delicate looking for a man, and with all that hair framing him, his face was almost as delicate a triangle as Detective Arnet's. His lower lip was fuller than his upper lip, which gave him a perpetual pout, and being wider than most women's mouths didn't really help. But the body under his black tailored suit, that definitely helped make it clear he was a man. Wide shoulders, slender waist and hips, a swimmer's body, though that wasn't his sport. From the neck down you'd never mistake him for a girl. It was just the face, and the hair.

He'd left his shirt open at the neck so that it framed the hollow in his throat. I could see myself reflected darkly in his sunglasses. It was actually a little dim in the hallway, so why the sunglasses? His eyes were kitty-cat eyes, leopard, to be exact. They were yellow and green all at the same time. What color predominated between the two depended on what color he wore, his mood, the lighting. Today, because of the shirt, they'd be very green, but with a hint of yellow, like dappled light in the forest.

He was a wereleopard, Nimir-Raj of the local pard. By rights he should have been able to pass for human. But if you spend too much time in animal form sometimes you don't come all the way back. He didn't want to squeak the mundanes, so he'd worn the glasses today.

His hand was very warm in mine, and that one small touch was enough, enough to bring some of the careful shielding down. The shielding that had kept me from sensing him all through the cere-mony like a second heartbeat. He was Nimir-Raj to my Nimir-Ra. Leopard King and Queen. Though my idea of the arrangement was closer to queen and consort, partners, but I reserved presidential veto. I'm a control freak, what can I say?

I was the first human Nimir-Ra in the wereleopards' long history. Though since I raise the dead for a living and am a legal vampire executioner, there are people who'll argue the human part. They're just jealous.

I started to pull him in against me for a hug, but he gave a small shake of his head. He was right. He was right. If just holding his hand sped my pulse like candy on my tongue, then a hug would be bad. Through a series of metaphysical accidents, I held something close to the beast that lived in Micah. That beast and Micah's beast knew each other, knew each other in the way of old lovers. That part of us that was not human knew each other better than our human halves. I still knew almost nothing about him, really. Even though we lived together. On a metaphysical level we were bound tighter than any ceremony or piece of paper could make us; in real everyday life, I was wondering what to do with him. He was the perfect partner. My other half, the missing piece. He complemented me in almost every way. And when he was standing this close, it all seemed so right. Give me a little distance and I would begin to wonder when the other shoe would drop and he would stop being wonderful. I'd never had a man in my life yet that didn't spoil it somehow. Why should Micah be different?

He didn't so much kiss me as lay the feel of his breath against my cheek. He breathed, 'Until later.' That one light touch made me shiver so violently that he had to steady me with a touch on my arm.

He smiled at me, that knowing smile that a man gives when he understands just how much his touch affects a woman. I didn't like that smile. It made me feel like he took his time with me for granted. The moment I thought it, I knew it wasn't true. It wasn't even fair. So why had I thought it at all? Because I am a master at screwing up my own love life. If something works too well, I've got to poke at it, prod it, until it breaks, or bites me. I was trying not to do that anymore, but old habits, especially bad ones, die hard.

Micah moved off down the line, and Detective Arnet gave me a questioning look out of her heavily painted but lovely eyes. She opened her mouth as if to ask if I were alright, but the next person in line distracted her. Nathaniel was distracting, no doubt about that.

Jessica Arnet was a few inches taller than Nathaniel's 5' 6", so she had to look down to meet that lavender gaze. No exaggeration on the color. His eyes weren't blue, but truly a pale purple, lavender, spring lilacs. He wore a banded-collar shirt that was almost the same color as his eyes, so the lavender was even more vibrant; drowningly beautiful, those eyes.

He offered his hand, but she hugged him. Hugged him, because I think for the first time she was in a public situation where no one would think it was strange. So she hugged him, because she could.

There was a fraction of a moment's hesitation, then he hugged her back, but he turned his head so he could look at me. His eyes said clearly, Help me.

She hadn't done that much yet, just a hug where a handshake would have done, but the look in Nathaniel's eyes was much more serious than what she'd done. As if it bothered him more than it should have. Since in his day job he's a stripper, you'd think he'd be used to women pawing him. Of course, maybe that was the point. He wasn't at work.

She stayed molded to his body, and he stayed holding, with only that mute look in his eyes to say he was unhappy. His body seemed happy and relaxed in the hug. He never showed Jessica Arnet his confused eyes.

The hug had gone on longer than was polite, and I finally realized what part of the problem was. Nathaniel was the least dominant person I'd ever met. He wanted out of the hug, but he could not be the first one to pull back. Jessica had to let him go, and she was probably waiting for him to move away, and getting all the wrong signals from the fact that he wasn't moving away. Shit. How do I end up with men in my life who have such interesting problems? Lucky, I guess.

I held out my hand toward him, and the relief on his face was clear enough that anyone down the hall would have seen it, and understood it. He kept his face turned so Jessica never saw that look. It would have hurt her feelings, and Nathaniel didn't want to hurt anyone's feelings. Which meant that he didn't see her shining face, all aglow with what she thought was mutual attraction. Truthfully, I'd thought Nathaniel liked her, at least a little, but his face said otherwise. To me, anyway.

Nathaniel came to my hand like a scared child who's just been saved from the neighborhood bully. I drew him into a hug, and he clung to me, pressing our bodies tighter than I would have liked in public, but I couldn't blame him, not really. He wanted the comfort of physical contact, and I think he'd figured out that Jessica Arnet had gotten the wrong idea.

I held him as close as I could, as close as I'd wanted to hold Micah. With Micah, it might have led to embarrassing things, but not with Nathaniel. With Nathaniel I could control myself. I wasn't in love with him. I caressed the long braid of his auburn hair that fell nearly to his ankles. I played with the braid, as if it were other more intimate things, hoping that Jessica would take the hint. I should have known that a little extra hugging wouldn't have done the job.

I drew back from the hug first, and he kept his gaze on my face. I could study his face and understand what she saw there, so handsome, so amazingly beautiful. His shoulders had broadened in the last few months, from weight lifting, or just the fact that he was twenty and still filling out. He was luscious to look at, and I was almost certain he would be nearly as luscious in bed. But though he was living with me, cleaning my house, buying my groceries, running my errands, I still hadn't had intercourse with him. I was really trying to avoid that, since I didn't plan on keeping him. Someday Nathaniel would need to find a new place to live, a new life, because I wouldn't always need him the way I did now.

I was human, but just as I was the first human Nimir-Ra the leopards had ever had, I was also the first human servant of a master vampire to acquire certain . . . abilities. With those abilities came some downsides. One of those downsides was needing to feed the *ardeur* every twelve hours or so. *Ardeur* is French for flame, roughly translates to being consumed, being consumed by love. But it isn't exactly love.

I stared up into Nathaniel's wide lilac eyes, cradled his face between my hands. I did the only thing I could think of that might keep Jessica Arnet from embarrassing them both at the reception to follow. I kissed him. I kissed him, because he needed me to do it. I kissed him because it was strangely the right thing to do. I kissed him because he was my *pomme de sang*, my apple of blood. I kissed him because he was my food, and I hated the fact that anyone was my food. I fed off Micah, too, but he was my partner, my boyfriend, and he was dominant enough to say no if he wanted to. Nathaniel wanted me to take him, wanted to belong to me, and I didn't know what to do about it. Months from now the *ardeur* would be under control and I wouldn't need a *pomme de sang*. What would Nathaniel do when I didn't need him anymore?

I drew back from the kiss and watched Nathaniel's face shine at me the way Jessica Arnet's face had shone at him. I wasn't in love with Nathaniel, but staring up into that happy, handsome face, I was afraid that I couldn't say the same for him. I was using him. Not for sex, but for food. He was food, just food, but even as I thought it, I knew it was partly a lie. You don't fall in love with your steak, because it can't hold you, can't press warm lips in the bend of your neck, and whisper, 'Thank you,' as it glides down the hallway in the charcoal-gray slacks that fit its ass like a second skin and spill roomy over the thighs that you happen to know are even lovelier out of the pants than in. When I turned to the next smiling person in line, I caught Detective Jessica Arnet giving me a look. It wasn't an entirely friendly look. Great, just great.

2

THE HALLOWEEN THEME continued into the reception hall. Orange and black crepe paper streamers dangled everywhere; cardboard skeletons, rubber bats, and paper ghosts floated overhead. There was a fake spiderweb against one wall big enough to hang someone from. The table centerpieces were realistic-looking jack-o-lanterns with flickering electric grins. The fake skeletons were long enough to be a hazard to anyone much taller than I was. Which meant most guests were having the tops of their hair brushed by little cardboard skeleton toes. Unfortunately, Tammy was 5' 8" without heels, with heels she got her veil tangled with the decorations. The bridesmaids finally got Tammy's veil unhooked from the skeletal toes, but it ruined the entrance for the bride and groom. If Tammy had wanted the decorations safe for the tall people, she shouldn't have left it to Larry and his brothers. There wasn't a one of them over 5' 6". Don't blame me. Groomsman or not, I hadn't helped decorate the hall. It was not my fault.

There were other things that I was going to get blamed for, but they weren't my fault either. Well, mostly not my fault.

I'd escorted Jessica Arnet into the room. She hadn't smiled at me as I led her into the room. She'd looked way too serious. When Tammy's veil was safely secure once more, Jessica had gone to the table where Micah and Nathaniel were sitting. She'd leaned into Nathaniel, and when I say leaned, I mean it. Like leaned on him, so that the line of her body touched his shoulder and arm. It was bold and discreet at the same time. If I hadn't been watching for it, I might not have realized what she was doing. She spoke quietly to him. He finally shook his head, and she turned and wove her way through the small tables full of guests. She took the last empty seat at the long table where the wedding party was trapped. The last empty chair was beside me. We got to sit down in the order we'd entered. Goody.

In the middle of the toasts, after Larry's brother had made the groom blush, but before the parents had had their turns, Jessica leaned over close enough that her perfume was sweet and a little too much.

She whispered, 'Does Nathaniel really live with you?'

I'd been afraid the question would be hard. This one was easy. 'Yes,' I said.

'I asked if he was your boyfriend, and he said that he slept in your bed. I thought that was an odd way to answer.' She turned her head so I was suddenly way too close to her face, those wide-searching hazel eyes. I was struck again by how lovely she was, and felt stupid for not noticing sooner. But I didn't notice girls, I noticed boys. So sue me, I was heterosexual. It wasn't her beauty that struck me, but the demand, the intelligence, in her eyes. She searched my face, and I realized that no matter how pretty she was, she was still a cop, and she was trying to smell the lie here. Because she had smelled one.

She hadn't asked me a question, so I didn't answer. I rarely got in trouble by keeping my mouth shut.

She gave a small frown. 'Is he your boyfriend? If he is, then I'll leave it alone. But you could have told me sooner, so I wouldn't have made a fool of myself.'

I wanted to say, You didn't make a fool of yourself, but I didn't. I was too busy trying to think of an answer that would be honest and not get Nathaniel and me in more trouble. I settled for the evasion he'd used. 'Yes, he sleeps in my bed.'

She gave a small shake to her head, a stubborn look coming over her face. 'That isn't what I asked, Anita. You're lying. You're both lying. I can smell it.' She frowned. 'Just tell me the truth. If you have a prior claim, say so, now.'

I sighed. 'Yeah, I have a prior claim, apparently.'

The frown deepened, putting lines between the pretty eyes. 'Apparently? What does that mean? Either he's your boyfriend, or he's not.'

'Maybe *boyfriend* isn't the right word,' I said, and tried to think of an explanation that didn't include the words *pomme de sang*. The police didn't really know how deeply involved with the monsters I was. They suspected, but they didn't know. Knowing is different from suspicion. Knowing will hold up in court; suspicion won't even get you a search warrant.

'Then what is the right word?' she whispered, but it held an edge of hiss, as if she were fighting not to yell. 'Are you lovers?'

What was I supposed to say? If I said, yes, Nathaniel would be free of Jessica's unwanted attentions, but it would also mean that everyone on the St Louis police force would know that Nathaniel was my lover. It wasn't my reputation I was worried about, that was pretty much trashed. A girl can't be coffin-bait for the Master of the City and be a good girl. Most people feel that if a woman will do a vampire, she'll do anything. Not true, but there you go. No, not my reputation at stake, but Nathaniel's. If it got out that he was my lover, then no other woman would make a play for him. If he didn't want to date Jessica, fine, but he needed to date someone. Someone besides me. If I wasn't going to keep Nathaniel forever, like almost death-do-you-part ever, then he needed a bigger social circle. He needed a real girlfriend.

So I hesitated, weighing a dozen words, and not finding a single one that would help the situation. My cell phone went off. As I fumbled for it, to stop the soft, incessant ringing, I was too relieved to be irritated. It could have been a wrong number at that moment, and I still would have felt I owed them flowers.

It wasn't a wrong number. It was Lieutenant Rudolph Storr, head of the Regional Preternatural Investigation Team. He had opted to be on duty during the wedding so that other people could attend. He'd asked Tammy if she was inviting any nonhumans, and when she'd said she didn't like that term, but if he meant lycanthropes, the answer was yes, Dolph had suddenly decided he'd be on duty and not come to the wedding. He was having a personal problem with the monsters. His son was about to marry a vampire, and that vampire was trying to persuade Dolph's son to join her in eternal life. To say that Dolph was not taking it well was an understatement. He'd trashed an interrogation room, manhandled me, and damn near gotten himself brought up on charges. I'd arranged a dinner with Dolph, his wife, Lucille, their son, Darrin, and future daughter-in-law. I'd persuaded Darrin to put off the decision to join the undead. The wedding was still on, but it was a start. His son still being among the living had helped Dolph deal with his crisis of faith. Deal with it enough that he was talking to me again. Deal with it enough that he called me in on a case again.

His voice was brisk, almost normal, 'Anita?'

'Yeah,' I whispered, cupping the phone with my hand. It wasn't like every cop in the place, which was most of the guests, wasn't wondering who I was talking to, and why.

'Got a body for you to look at.'

'Now?' I made it a question.

'The ceremony is over, right? I didn't call in the middle of it.'

'It's over. I'm at the reception.'

'Then I need you here.'

'Where's here?' I asked.

He told me.

'I know the strip club area across the river, but I'm not familiar with the club name.'

'You won't be able to miss it,' he said, 'it'll be the only club with its own police escort.'

It took me a second to realize that he had made a joke. Dolph didn't make jokes at murder scenes, ever. I opened my mouth to remark on it, but the phone was dead in my hand. Dolph never had been much for goodbyes.

Detective Arnet leaned in, and asked, 'Was that Lieutenant Storr?' 'Yeah,' I whispered, 'murder scene, gotta run.'

She opened her mouth, as if she was going to say something else, but I was already moving up the table. I was going to give my apologies to Larry and Tammy, then go look at a body. I was sorry to miss the rest of the reception and all, but I had a murder scene to go to. Not only would I get away from Arnet's questions, but I wouldn't have to dance with Micah, or Nathaniel, or anybody. The night was looking up. I felt a little guilty, but I was glad somebody was dead.

3

STARING DOWN AT the dead woman, it was impossible to be glad. Guilty, maybe, but not glad. Guilty that even for a second I'd found the idea of someone's death an escape from an uncomfortable social situation. I wasn't a child. Surely, to God, I could have handled Jessica Arnet and her questions without hiding behind a murder. The fact that I was more comfortable here staring down at a corpse than at the head table at a wedding said something about me and my life. I wasn't sure exactly what it said, or meant. Something I probably didn't want to look at too closely, though. But, wait, we had a body to look at, a crime to solve, all the sticky personal stuff could wait. Had to wait. Yeah, sure.

The body was a pale glimpse of flesh between two Dumpsters in the parking lot. There was something almost ghostlike about that shining bit of flesh, like, if I blinked, it would vanish into the October night. Maybe it was the time of year, or the wedding scene I'd just left, but there was something unnerving about the way she'd been left. They'd stuffed the body behind the Dumpsters to hide it, then the black wool coat she wore had been opened around her almost naked body, so that you caught that gleam of pale flesh in the bright halogen lights of the parking lot. Why hide her, then do something to draw such attention to her? It made no sense. Of course, it may have made perfect sense to the people who killed her. Maybe.

I stood there, tugging my leather jacket around me. It wasn't that cold. Cold enough for the jacket, but not enough to put the lining in it. I had my hands plunged into the pockets, the zipper all the way up, my shoulders hunched. But leather couldn't help against the cold

I was fighting. I stared at that pallid glimpse of death, and felt nothing. Nothing. Not pity. Not sickness. Nothing. Somehow that bothered me more than the woman being dead.

I made myself move forward. Made myself go see what there was to see and leave my worries about my moral decay for another time. Business, first.

I had to come to the far end of the right-hand Dumpster to see the spill of her yellow hair, like a bright exclamation point on the black pavement. Staring down at her, I could see how tiny she was. My size, or smaller. She lay on her back, the coat spread under her, still securely on her arms. But the cloth had been spread wide, folded under on the side nearest the parked cars, so that she could be seen by a customer walking out to his car. Her hair, too, had been pulled back, combed out. If she'd been taller, that, too, would have been visible from the parking lot – just a peek of bright yellow around the Dumpster. I looked down the line of her body and found the reason that someone had thought she was taller – clear plastic stilettos, at least five inches high. Lying down she lost the height. Her head had been pressed to the right, exposing bite marks on her long neck. *Vampire* bite marks.

On the mound of her small breast was another pair of bite marks, with two thin lines of blood trickling from them. There was no blood at the neck wound. I was going to have to move the Dumpsters to get back there. I was also going to have to move the body around to look for more bite marks, more signs of violence. There'd been a time when the police only called me in after all the other experts had finished with a scene, but that was a while ago. I had to make sure I didn't fuck up the scene. Which meant I needed to find the man in charge.

Lt. Rudolph Storr wasn't hard to spot. He's 6' 8" and built like pro wrestlers used to be built before they all started looking like Arnold Schwarzenegger. Dolph was in shape, but he didn't go for the weight lifting. He didn't have time. Too many crimes to solve. His black hair was cut so short it left his ears exposed and somehow stranded on the sides of his head. Which always meant he'd gotten a haircut, recently. He always had it cut shorter than he liked it, so it would be longer between haircuts. His tan trench coat was perfectly pressed. His shoes shined in the parking lot lights. He didn't care what he looked like, as long as he was neat and tidy. Dolph was all about the neat and tidy. I think it was one of the reasons that murder pissed him off, it was always so messy.

I nodded at the uniformed policeman whose only job seemed to be watching the body and making sure it didn't get messed with by anyone that wasn't allowed to touch it. He nodded back and went back to staring at the corpse. Something about how wide his eyes were made me wonder if this was his first vampire kill. Was he worried that the victim would rise and try to munch on him? I could have calmed his fears, because I knew this one would never rise. She'd been drained to death by a group of vamps. That won't make you one of them. In fact, the act is guaranteed to give the vamps their fun and not to make the vic one of them. I'd seen this once before. I hoped like hell it wasn't another master vampire gone rogue. The last one had purposely left vics where we could find them, in an attempt to get the new laws that gave vampires legal rights repealed. Mr Oliver had believed that vampires were monsters, and if they were given legal rights, they'd spread too fast, eventually turning the entire human race into vampires. Then who would everybody feed off of? Yeah, it would take hundreds of years for vampirism to spread to that degree, but the really old vampires take the long view. They can afford to, they've got the time.

I knew it wasn't Mr Oliver again, because I'd killed him. I'd crushed his heart, and no matter how many times Dracula might rise in old movies, Oliver was well and truly dead. I could guarantee it. Which meant we had a new group of nuts on our hands, and they could have an entirely new motive for killing. Hell, maybe it was personal. Vampires were legal citizens now, which meant they could have grudges just like humans.

But somehow it didn't feel personal. Don't ask me to explain it, but it didn't.

Dolph saw me coming toward him. He didn't smile, or say hi, because one, it was Dolph, and two, he wasn't completely happy with me. He wasn't happy with the monsters lately, which rubbed off on me because I was way too intimate with the monsters.

Still, convincing his son not to become a vampire had earned me brownie points. The fact that Dolph had just gotten off of a leave without pay, with an informal warning that if he didn't shape up, he'd be suspended, had also mellowed him out. Frankly, I'd take whatever I could get. Dolph and I were friends, or I'd thought we were. We were both a little unsure where we stood right now.

'I need to move the Dumpsters to look at the body. I also need to move the body around to look for more bite marks, or whatever. Can I do that without screwing the crime scene up?'

He looked at me, and there was something in his face that said, clearly, he was not happy to have me here. He started to say something, glanced around at the other detectives, the uniforms, the crime-scene techs, and beyond that to the waiting ambulance, shook his head, and motioned me off to one side. I could feel people's gazes follow us as we moved away. All of the detectives there knew that Dolph had dragged me up a flight of stairs at a crime scene. When I said manhandled, I wasn't exaggerating. God knows what the stories said now, probably that he'd hit me, which he hadn't, but what he'd done had been bad enough. Bad enough I could have pressed charges and won.

He leaned over and spoke low. 'I don't like you being here.'

'You called me,' I said. God, I did not want to fight with him tonight.

He nodded. 'I called, but I need to know that you don't have a conflict of interest here.'

I frowned up at him. 'What do you mean? What conflict of interest?'

'If it's a vamp kill, then it was someone that belongs to your boyfriend.'

'It's nice that you said *if* it's a vamp kill, but if you mean Jean-Claude, then it might not be his people at all.'

'Oh, that's right, you got two vampire boyfriends now.' His voice was ugly.

'You want to fight each other, or fight crime? Your choice,' I said.

He made a visible effort to control himself. Hands in fists at his sides, eyes closed, deep breaths. He'd been forced to go through anger management training. I watched him use his newfound skills. Then he opened his eyes – cold cop eyes – and said, 'You're defending the vamps already.'

'I'm not saying it's not a vamp kill. All I said was that it might not be Jean-Claude's people. That's all.'

'But you're defending your boyfriend and his people already. You haven't even looked at the vic completely, and already you say it can't be your lover boy.'

I felt my eyes grow cold and said, 'I'm not saying it couldn't have been Jean-Claude's vampires. I'm saying it's unlikely. Thanks to the Church of Eternal Life, St Louis has a lot of bloodsuckers that don't owe allegiance to the Master of the City.'

'The Church's members are more straitlaced than right-wing Christians,' he said.

I shrugged. 'They do come off as sanctimonious, I'll grant you that. Most true believers do, but that's not why I say it was them, or strangers, instead of the vampires I know best.'

'Why, then?' he asked.

My only excuse for telling the absolute truth is that I was pissed and tired of Dolph being mad at me. 'Because if any of Jean-Claude's people did this, they're dead. Either he'll turn them in to the law himself, or have me do it, or they'll just be killed.'

'You're admitting that your boyfriend is a murderer?'

I took in a deep breath and let it out slow. 'You know, Dolph, this is getting old. Yeah, I'm fucking a vampire or two, get over it.'

He looked away. 'I don't know how.'

'Then learn,' I said. 'But stop letting your personal shit rain all over the crime scene. We've wasted time arguing, when I could have been looking at the body. I want these people caught.'

'People, plural?' he asked.

'I've only seen two bite marks, but they both have a slightly different pattern to them. The one on the chest is smaller, less space between the fangs. So, yeah, at least two, but I'm betting more.'

'Why?' he asked.

'Because they bled her out. There's almost no blood anywhere. Two vamps couldn't drain an adult human being without leaving a mess. They'd need more mouths to hold that much blood.'

'Maybe she was killed somewhere else.'

I frowned at him. 'It's October, she's outside wearing five-inch plastic stilettos, an inexpensive wool coat, and not much else.' I motioned at the building behind us. 'We're in the parking lot of a strip club. Hmm, let me see, five-inch plastic stilettos, naked woman . . . could this be a clue that she worked here, stepped out for a smoke, or something?'

Dolph reached into his pocket and got out his ever-present note-book. 'She's been identified as one Charlene Morresey, twenty-two, works as a stripper – worked, as a stripper. Yes, she did smoke, but she told one of the other girls she was going outside for a breath of fresh air.'

'We know she probably didn't know the vamps.'

'How so?'

'She came out to get some air, not to visit.'

He nodded and made a note. 'There's no sign of a struggle, yet. It's like she came out here for air and just walked over there with them. She wouldn't do that for strangers.'

'If she was under mind control, she would.'

'So one of our vamps is an old one.' Dolph was still making notes.

'Not necessarily old, but powerful, and that usually means old.' I thought about it. 'Someone with good mind control powers – that I'm sure of – age,' I shrugged, 'I don't know, yet.'

He was still writing in his notebook.

'Now, can I move the Dumpster and move the body around, or do you still need the techies to get back in there and do their thing first?'

'I had them wait for you,' he said without looking up from his writing.

I looked at him, tried to learn something from his face, but he was all concentration and business. It was a step up that he'd had the techs wait for me. And that he'd called me at all. Before his time off, he'd tried to get me barred from crime scenes. It was a step up, so why was I still wondering if Dolph was capable of letting his personal life go long enough to solve this case? Because, once you've seen someone you trusted lose it completely, you never truly trust them again, not completely.

4

THERE WAS A matching set of bite marks on the other side of her neck. They were so close to the same size as the ones on the left-hand side, that I wondered if the same vamp had bitten twice. I didn't have my ruler with me. Hell, I didn't have most of my equipment with me. I'd been planning on a wedding tonight, not a crime scene.

I asked if anyone had something to measure bite radius. One of the techs offered to measure for me. Fine with me. She had a pair of calipers – I'd never used a pair of them before.

Measurements do not lie. It wasn't the same vamp. Nor was it the same vamp at each of her inner thighs or her wrists. Counting the bite mark on her chest, that made seven. Seven vampires. Enough to drain an adult human being dry and leave very little blood behind.

There was no obvious evidence of sexual assault, according to a CSU technician. Glad to hear it. I did not bother explaining that the bite alone can be orgasmic both for the vic and the killer. Not always, but often, especially if the vampire is good at fogging the mind. A vampire with enough juice can make someone enjoy being killed. Scary, but true.

After I'd seen every inch of the dead woman, when I knew that her pale flesh might dance through my dreams in their plastic shoes, Dolph wanted to talk.

'Talk to me,' he said.

I knew what he wanted. 'Seven vamps. One has to be good enough at mind control to have made the vic enjoy what was happening, or at least not mind it. Someone would have heard her screams other-wise.'

'Have you walked into the club?' he asked.

'No.'

'Music is loud, lots of people inside,' he said.

'So they might not have heard her, even if she did scream?'

He nodded.

I sighed. 'There's no sign of a struggle. They'll look at her nails, but there won't be any sign of a fight. The vic didn't even know what was happening, or at least not until it was way too late.'

'You're sure of that?'

I thought for a second or two. 'No, I'm not sure. It's my best educated guess, but maybe she's one of those people that doesn't fight back. Maybe once seven vampires surrounded her, she just gave up. I don't know. What kind of person was Charlene Morresey? Was she a fighter?'

'Don't know yet,' Dolph said.

'If she was a fighter, then vampire mind tricks were used. If she wasn't, if she was real docile, then maybe not. Maybe we're looking for a bunch of young vamps.' I shook my head. 'But I'd say not. I'd say at least one, maybe more, were old, and good at doing at this.'

'They hid the body,' he said.

I finished the thought for him, 'And then exposed it, so that someone would find it.'

He nodded. 'That's been bothering me, too. If they had just closed her coat over her body, not messed with the hair, no one would have found her tonight.'

'They'd have missed her in the club,' I said, 'or was she done for the night?'

'She wasn't done, and, yeah, they would have missed her.'

I glanced back at the body. 'But would they have found her?'

'Maybe,' he said, 'but not this quick.'

'Yeah, she's still fresh, cool to the touch, but not long gone.'

He checked his notes. 'Less than two hours since she was on stage.'

I looked around us, at the bright halogen lights. There was no good place to hide in this parking lot, except behind the Dumpsters. 'Did they do her behind the Dumpsters?'

'Or a car,' he said.

'Or van,' I said.

'The serial killer's best friend,' Dolph said.

I looked at him, trying to read behind those cop eyes. 'Serial killer, what are you talking about? This is the first kill, to my knowledge.'

He nodded. 'Yeah.' He started to turn away.

I caught his sleeve, lightly. I had to be careful how I touched him lately. He took so many things as aggression. 'Cops do not use the phrase *serial killer* unless they have to. One, you don't want it to be true. Two, the reporters will get hold of it and report it like it's truth.'

He looked down at me, and I let go of his sleeve. 'There aren't any reporters here, Anita. It's just another dead stripper in Sauget.'

'Then why say it?'

'Maybe I'm psychic.'

'Dolph,' I said.

He almost smiled. 'I got a bad feeling, that's all. This is either their first kill, or the first kill we've found. It was awful damn neat for a first kill.'

'Someone meant for us to find her, Dolph, and find her tonight.'

'Yeah, but who? Was it the killer, or killers? Or was it someone else?'

'Like who?' I asked.

'Another customer that couldn't afford to let his wife know where'd he been.'

'So he opens her coat, draws out her hair, tries to make her more visible?'

Dolph gave one small nod, down.

'I don't buy it. A normal person couldn't touch a dead body, not enough to open the coat, mess with the hair. Besides, that flash of pale flesh was done by someone who knew that it would be as visible as it is. A normal person might drag her out from behind the Dumpster, maybe, but they wouldn't mess with her, not like that.'

'You keep saying, "normal," Anita; don't you know yet, there is no normal. There's just victims and predators.' He looked away when he said the last, as if he didn't want me to see whatever was in his face.

I let him look away, let him keep that moment to himself. Because, Dolph and I were trying to rebuild a friendship, and sometimes you need your friends to pry, and sometimes you need them to leave you the fuck alone.

5

I DIDN'T WANT to go back to the reception. First, I wasn't in the mood to be merry. Second, I still didn't know how to answer Arnet's questions. Third, Micah had made me promise I'd dance with him. I hated to dance. I didn't think I was good at it. In the privacy of our home, Micah, and Nathaniel, and hell, Jason, had told me I was wrong. That I actually danced very well. I did not believe them. I think it was a throwback to a rather horrible junior high school dance experience. Of course, it was junior high, is there any experience except horrible for those few years? In Hell, if you're really bad, you must be fourteen forever, and be trapped in school, and never get to go home.

So I walked into the reception, hoping I could say I was tired, and we could leave, but I knew better. Micah had dragged a promise out of me that I'd dance with him, and he'd gotten me to promise a dance for Nathaniel, as well. Damn it. I don't promise things often, because once I do, I keep my word. Double damn it.

The crowd had thinned out a lot. Murder scenes take so much time out of your night. But I knew that the boys would be there, because I had the car. Nathaniel was at the table where I'd left them, but it was Jason with him, not Micah. Jason and Nathaniel were leaning so close together that their heads nearly touched. Jason's short blond hair seemed very yellow against Nathaniel's dark auburn. Jason wore a blue dress shirt that I knew was only a shade or two bluer than his eyes. His suit was black, and I knew without seeing him standing that it was tailored to his body, and probably Italian in cut. Jean-Claude had paid for the suit, and he was fond of Italian-cut designer suits for his employees. When he wasn't dressing them like they were extras in a high-class porno movie, anyway. For a mainstream wedding, the suit worked. Jason also worked at Guilty Pleasures as a stripper, and Jean-Claude did own the club, but it wasn't that type of employment that let Jason rate designer clothes tailored to his body. Jason was Jean-Claude's *pomme de sang*. Jean-Claude did not think I treated Nathaniel with enough respect for his position as my *pomme de sang*. I had let Micah and Nathaniel go shopping with Jason for dress clothes, and I footed the bill for my two boys. It had been outrageous, but I couldn't let Jean-Claude be nicer to his kept man than I was to mine. Could I?

Technically, Micah wasn't a kept man, but the salary he drew from the Coalition for Better Understanding Between Lycanthrope and Human Communities didn't cover designer suits. I made enough money to pay for designer suits, so I did.

I had time to wonder what Jason and Nathaniel were up to, talking so close together, like conspirators. Then I felt, more than saw, Micah. He was across the room talking to a group of men, most of them cops. He shook his head, laughed, and started across the room, toward me. I didn't get much chance to see Micah from a distance. We were always so close to one another, physically. Now I was able to watch him walk toward me, able to admire how the suit clung to his body, how it flattered the broad shoulders, the slender waist, the tightness of his hips, the swell of his thighs. The suit fit him like a roomy glove. Watching him move toward me, I realized the suit was suddenly worth every penny.

The music stopped before he reached me, some song I didn't recognize. I had a moment of hope that we could just sit down and find out what the other two men were finding so fascinating. But it was a vain hope, because another song came on. A slow song. I still didn't want to dance, but as Micah got close enough to touch, I had to admit that an excuse to touch him in public was not a bad thing.

He smiled, and even with the sunglasses in place, I knew what his eyes would look like with that smile. 'Ready?'

I sighed, and held out my arms. 'As I'm ever going to be.'

'Let's shed the leather jacket first.'

I unzipped it, but said, 'Let's keep it, I'm a little cold.'

His hands slid around my waist. 'Is it getting colder outside?'

I shook my head. 'Not that kind of cold.'

'Oh,' he said, and he pulled back his hands, which had been sliding up my back underneath the leather jacket. He went back to my waist and slid his hands underneath the tux jacket, so that only the thin cloth of the dress shirt separated my skin from his.

I shuddered under that touch.

He leaned his mouth in close to my ear, before he'd finished the long, slow slide of his hands that would have pressed our bodies together. 'I'll warm you up.' His arms pressed me into the curve and swell of his body, but not so tight as to make me uncomfortable in public. Close, but not like we were glued together. But even this close, I could feel the swell of him under the cloth of his pants. The barest brush of touch, which let me know that there was more than one reason he didn't hold me as tight as he could. He was being polite. I wasn't a hundred percent sure whether this politeness was really Micah's idea, or if he'd picked up my discomfort. He was always very, very careful around me. In fact, he mirrored back so exactly what I wanted, what I needed, that it made me wonder if I knew him at all, or if all I saw was what he wanted me to see.

'You're frowning, what's wrong?' He was close enough that just turning his head in against my face allowed him to whisper.

What was I supposed to say? That I suspected him of lying to me, not about anything in particular, but about nearly everything. He was too perfect. Too perfectly what I needed him to be. That had to be an act, right? Nobody was perfectly what you needed them to be, everybody disappointed you in some way, right?

He whispered against my ear, 'You're frowning harder. What's wrong?'

I didn't know what to say. Why was I left so often this night with a dozen things to say and nothing I wanted to share out loud? I decided for partial truth, better than a lie, I guess. 'I'm wondering when you're going to spoil everything.'

He drew away enough to see my face clearly. He let his puzzlement show. 'What have I done now?'

I shook my head. 'That's the problem, you haven't done anything, nothing wrong anyway.'

I looked at him and wanted to see his eyes. I finally reached up and moved his dark glasses just enough to glimpse his chartreuse eyes. But, of course, that was a mistake, because I found myself gazing into those eyes, marveling at how green they looked tonight. I shook my head again. 'Damn it.'

'What is wrong?' he asked.

'Nothing, and that's what's wrong.' Even to me it made no sense, but it was still true. Still how I felt.

He gave me that smile that was part puzzlement, part irony, part self-deprecation, and part something else. Nothing about that smile was happy. He'd come with that smile, and I still didn't understand it, but I knew that he used it less and less, and usually only when I was being silly. Even I knew I was being silly, but I couldn't seem to help it. He was too perfect, so I had to poke at it. Our relationship worked too well, so I had to see if I could break it. Not really break it, but see how far it would bend. I had to test it, because what good was something that couldn't be tested? Oh, hell, that wasn't it. The truth was that if I let myself I could be happy with Micah, and it was beginning to get on my nerves.

I leaned my forehead against his chest. 'I'm sorry, Micah, I'm just tired and feeling grumpy.'

He walked me a little to one side, off the dance floor, not that we'd been dancing. 'What is wrong?'

I tried to think what was wrong. I was taking something out on him, but what? Then, part of it hit me. 'It didn't bother me to see the dead woman. I felt nothing.'

'You have to divorce yourself from your emotions, or you can't do your job.'

I nodded. 'Yeah, but once I had to work at it. Now I don't.'

He frowned down at me, his eyes still peeking over his partially lowered glasses. 'And that bothers you, why?'

'Only sociopaths and crazy people can look at the violently dead and feel absolutely nothing, Micah.'

He hugged me to him, suddenly, fiercely, but was careful to keep part of his body away. It was the kind of hug you'd give a friend in need. Maybe a little tighter, a little more intimate, but not much. He always seemed to know just what I needed, just when I needed it. If we weren't in love, then how did he do that? Hell, I'd been in love with people that didn't even come close to meeting this many of my needs.

'You are not a sociopath, Anita. You have given up pieces of yourself so you can do your job. You told me once, it's the price you pay.'

I wrapped my arms around him, held him tight, rested my forehead in the bend of his neck, rubbed my face against the incredible smoothness of his skin. 'I'm trying not to lose more pieces of myself, but it's like I can't stop. I felt nothing tonight, except guilt that I felt nothing. How crazy is that?'

He kept hugging me. 'It's only crazy if you think it's crazy, Anita.'

That made me draw back enough to see his face. 'What's that mean?'

He touched my face, gently. 'It means that if your life works, and you work in it, then it's okay, whatever is happening is okay.'

I frowned, then laughed, then frowned again. 'I'm not sure a therapist would agree with that.'

'All I know is that since I met you, I've felt safer, happier, and better than I have in years.'

'You said safer; funny, I'd think that would be how Nathaniel would order it, safer, then happy.'

'I may be your Nimir-Raj and a dominant, but, Anita, I spent years at the mercy of Chimera. He was crazy and a sociopath. I've seen the real thing, Anita, and you are neither of those things.' He smiled when he said it and gave a little duck of his head, almost like an old gesture that he'd nearly outgrown. It showed his profile for a moment, and because I was in the mood to pick, I asked something I'd been debating on for weeks.

I traced the bridge of his nose. 'When I first met you, your nose looked like it had been badly broken. I assumed that meant it had happened when you were human, but your nose is getting straighter, isn't it?'

'Yes,' and his voice was soft when he said it. There was no smile now, not even the confusing one. His face had closed down. I'd begun to realize that this was how he looked when he was sad. I'd met Chimera, hell, I'd killed him. He'd been one of the most insane beings I'd ever met. This from a list that included self-deluded would-be gods and millenia-old master vampires, not to mention wereanimals that were both sexual sadists and sexual predators, in the truest sense of the word. So, that I would put Chimera near the top of my crazy-bad-guy list said just how awful he had been. I could not imagine being at his mercy for any length of time. I hadn't enjoyed a few hours. Micah and his pard had been with Chimera for years. I'd avoided this topic, because it was so obviously painful for all of them, but especially for Micah. But tonight, for so many reasons, I needed to know. I needed, almost, to cause him some pain. Ugly, but true.

Sometimes you fight what you are, and sometimes you give in to it. And some nights you just don't want to fight yourself anymore, so you pick someone else to fight.

6

WE ENDED UP standing at the far side of the parking lot, where trees grew in a tall, thin line. Fast-growing maples, with their yellow leaves, dancing in the October wind. My hair was so tight in its French braid that the wind could do little with it, but Micah's hair streamed around his face, like a thick, dark cloud. He'd taken off his glasses, and the streetlights made his eyes very yellow, even with the green shirt on, as if they reflected the light differently than they should have, or would have, if they'd been human eyes.

The wind was cool and held that crisp autumn scent. What I wanted to do was take his hand and walk out into the night until we found some woods. I wanted to go walking out into the darkness and let the wind take us where it wanted us to go. My bad mood seemed to have faded on the cool night wind, or maybe it was the sight of him, his face nearly lost in a cloud of his own hair. Whatever it was, I didn't want to fight anymore.

'You're right, my nose is healing.' His voice held that hint of bitter laughter to it. That tone that matched that confusing smile.

I touched his arm. 'If this is hard, you don't have to.'

He shook his head and put a hand up at his hair, impatient, angry, as if he was mad at the hair for getting in his face. I thought he was probably angry at me, but I didn't ask. I didn't really want to know if the answer was yes.

'No, you asked, I'll answer.'

I took back my hand and let him talk, let him open the bag that I'd wanted opened, so badly, only minutes ago. Now, I'd have let it go to wipe that look off his face.

'Do you know why my hair's long?'

It was such an odd question, that I answered it. 'No, I guess I thought you liked it that way.'

He shook his head, one hand caught in the hair near his face, so he could keep the wind from chasing it across his face. 'When Chimera took over a group of shapeshifters, he used torture, or the threat of torture, to control us. If the head of the group could withstand the torture, then he'd torment weaker members. Use their harm as a way to control the alphas in the group.'

He was quiet for so long that I had to say something. 'I know he was a sadistic bastard. I remember what he did to Gina and Violet, to keep you and Merle under control.'

'You only know part of it,' he said, and his eyes had a distant look, so far away. He was remembering, and it wasn't pretty.

I hadn't meant to bring this on. I hadn't. 'Micah, I didn't mean . . .'

'No, you wanted to know. You can know.' He took in a breath so deep it made him shudder. 'One of his favorite torments was gang rape. Those of us who wouldn't participate, he made us grow our hair long. Said, if we wanted to act like women, we should look like women.'

I thought about that for a second. 'You and Merle are the only men in your pard that have long hair.'

He nodded. 'I think Caleb enjoyed it, and Noah, well,' he shrugged, 'we all did things that we didn't like, just to stay alive. To stay whole.'

I couldn't think much less of Caleb, but it made me think less of Noah. I didn't know what to say out loud. But Micah didn't need me to talk anymore. The story was started, and he would tell it now, whether I wanted to hear it or not. It was my own damn fault, so I listened and gave him the only thing I could at this point – my attention. Not horror, not pity, just my attention. Horror was redundant, and pity – no one likes pity.

'You talked to Chimera, to more than one of his faces. You know how conflicted he was.'

I nodded, then said, 'Yes.'

'Part of him was the ultimate male bully, and that part raped women. Part of him was gay, and the two parts hated each other.'

Chimera had given the idea of split personality a whole new meaning, because each personality had had a different physical form. Until I'd met him, seen it for myself, I'd have said it was impossible.

'I remember that part of him wanted me to be his mate, and part of him didn't seem much interested in girls.'

Micah nodded. 'Exactly.'

I was almost afraid of where this was going, but I'd started it. If he could tell the story, I could hear it, all of it.

'He didn't just rape women,' Micah said, 'but strangely, he would only rape a man if he were already gay. It was as if he only wanted the sex the person enjoyed to be used against them.' He shrugged, but it turned into a shiver. 'I didn't understand it. I was just grateful to not be on his list of victims.' He shivered again.

'Do you want my jacket?' I asked.

He gave a small smile. 'I don't think it's that kind of cold.'

I reached out to touch him, and he stepped back, out of reach. 'No, Anita, let me finish. If you touch me, I'll get distracted.'

I wanted to say, let me touch you, let me distract you, but I didn't. I did what he asked. No one to blame but myself. If I'd kept my mouth shut, we'd be inside dancing, instead . . . when was I going to learn to leave well enough alone? Probably never.

'But somewhere in all that mess Chimera called his mind, he was angry at me. I wouldn't help him torture, wouldn't help him rape. But I wouldn't sleep with him voluntarily either, though he asked. I think he liked me, wanted me, and because his own twisted rules kept him away from me, he found other ways to amuse himself at my expense.'

He touched his face, as if searching it with his fingertips, almost as if he were surprised at what he found. As if it wasn't the face he was expecting to find. 'I can't even remember what it was that Gina wouldn't do. I think he wanted her to seduce an alpha of another pack that he wanted to own. She refused, and instead of taking it out on her, he took it out on me. He beat me bad enough that he broke my nose, but I healed, fast.'

'All lycanthropes heal fast,' I said.

'I seem to heal faster than most, not as fast as Chimera did, but close. He thought it had something to do with how easily we could both go from one form to another. He was probably right.'

'Makes sense,' I said. My voice was utterly calm, as if we were talking about the weather. The trick to hearing awful memories is not to be horrified. The only one allowed to have emotion is the one doing the telling. This listener has to be cool.

'The next time I refused to help him rape someone, he broke my nose again. I healed again. Then he made it a game. Every time I refused an order, he beat me worse, always in the face. One day, he finally said, 'I'm going to ruin that pretty face. If I can't have it, and you won't use it on anybody else, then I'll just ruin it.' But I kept healing.'

He let go of his hair, and the wind whipped it around his face, but he ignored it now. He hugged himself, held himself tight. I wanted to go to him, wanted to hold him, but he'd said no. I had to respect that, had to, but damn, damn.

'He didn't beat me the next time, he took a knife to me. He cut my face up, took the nose, ate it.' He gave a sound that was halfway between a laugh and a sob. 'Jesus, it hurt, and it bled. God, it bled.'

I touched his arm, tentatively, gently. He didn't tell me to go away. I eased my arms around him and found that he was trembling, a fine tremor that went from the top of his head down his entire body. I held him in my arms and wished I knew what to say.

He whispered against my hair. 'When it grew back, but not all the way back, he beat me again. New flesh is more tender than old, and when it broke enough times, it stayed broken. It didn't heal perfectly, and once he'd messed me up, he seemed satisified. Now that Chimera isn't here to mess me up, my nose is healing. It's getting straighter, every time I come back from leopard form.' He leaned in against me, slowly, as if he had to fight to let the tension go. He stayed like that, relaxing by inches, while I held him and rubbed his back in useless circles.

Normal people would have told him lies, like it's alright, I'm here, but he deserved better than lies. 'He's dead, Micah. He's dead, and he can't hurt you anymore. He can't hurt anyone anymore.'

He gave another sound, half swallowed laugh, half sob. 'No, he can't, because you killed him. You killed him, Anita. I couldn't kill him. I couldn't protect my people. I couldn't protect them.' He began to collapse to his knees, and if I hadn't caught him, he'd have fallen. But I did catch him, and I lowered us both to the edge of grass near the trees. I sat on the grass and held him, rocked him, while he cried, not for himself, but for all the people he couldn't save.

I held him until the crying quieted, then stopped, and I held him some more in the windswept silence. I held him and let the October wind wash us both clean. Clean of sadness, clean of that horrible urge I had to tear things down. I made myself a promise sitting there in the grass, with the feel of him wrapped around my body. I promised not to poke at things anymore. I promised not to break things if they were working. I promised not to stir up shit, if it didn't have to be stirred. I said a little prayer to help me keep those promises. Because, God knew, the chances of me keeping any of those promises without divine intervention were slim to none.

7

BY THE TIME Nathaniel and Jason came looking for us Micah was back to normal. Normal for Micah meant that if I hadn't seen him break down, even I wouldn't have guessed. In fact, he was so back to normal that it made me wonder how many other breakdowns I'd missed. Or had I caused this one? Was he able to maintain absolute control as long as no one made him look at it? Of course, even if that were true, that didn't sound very healthy. Oh, hell, maybe we all needed therapy. If I took the entire pard in, maybe we could get a group discount.

Nathaniel sat on the other side of me, putting me in the middle. He sat so that the line of his body touched mine as much as possible. There was a time when I'd have made him give me breathing space, but I understood the shapeshifter's need for physical contact now. Besides, making Nathaniel move over an inch when he slept mostly naked in my bed nearly every night would have been silly. Jason just stood and looked down at all of us. He looked unnaturally solemn, at least for him, then suddenly he broke into a grin. Now he looked like himself.

'It's after midnight, we thought you'd be outside feeding the *ardeur*.' His grin was way too wicked to match the mildish words.

'I'm able to go longer between feedings,' I said, 'sometimes fourteen, or even sixteen hours.'

'Oh, pooh,' he said, and stamped his foot, pouting. It was a wonderful imitation of a childish snit, except for the devilish twinkle in his eye. 'I was hoping to take another one for the team.'

I frowned at him, but couldn't make it go all the way up to my eyes. Jason amused me, I don't know why, but he always had. 'I don't think we'll be needing your services tonight, thanks for offering though.'

He gave an exaggerated sigh. 'I am never going to get to have sex with you again, am I?'

'Don't take this wrong, Jason, but I hope not. The sex was amazing, but what put you in my bed was an emergency. If I can't control the *ardeur* better than that, then I'm not safe to be out in public alone.'

'It was my fault,' Nathaniel said, voice soft.

I turned my head and was close enough to the side of his face to have kissed his cheek. I wanted to make him move, to give me more room, but I fought the urge off. I was just being grumpy. 'It was my fault if it was anyone's, Nathaniel.'

Micah's so-calm voice came from my other shoulder. 'It was Belle Morte's fault, the wicked, sexy vampire of the west. If she hadn't been messing with Anita, trying to use the *ardeur* to control her, then it wouldn't have risen hours ahead of schedule.' Belle Morte, Beautiful Death, was the creator of Jean-Claude's bloodline. I'd never met her in physical person, but I'd met her metaphysically, and that had been bad enough. Micah laid a hand across my shoulders, but managed to put his hand on Nathaniel's shoulder, too. Comforting us both. 'You haven't collapsed since Anita's been able to stretch the feedings out more.'

Nathaniel sighed so heavily that I felt the movement against my body. 'I haven't gotten stronger, she has.' He sounded so sad, so disappointed in himself.

I leaned in against his shoulder, enough that Micah was able to literally hug us both at the same time. 'I'm your Nimir-Ra, I'm supposed to be stronger, right?'

He gave me a faint smile.

I laid my head on his shoulder, curving my face into the bend of his neck, and getting that whiff of vanilla. He'd always smelled like vanilla to me. I'd thought once it was shampoo, or soap, but it wasn't.

It was his scent for me. I hadn't had the courage yet to ask Micah if Nathaniel's skin smelled like vanilla to him, too. Because I wasn't sure what it would mean if I was the only one who found Nathaniel's scent so very sweet.

'You want to ask Anita something,' Jason said.

Nathaniel tensed against me, then in a small voice, he asked, 'Do I still get my dance?'

It was my turn to tense. I couldn't control it, it was involuntary. Nathaniel got very still beside me, because he'd felt it, too. I didn't want to dance, that was true, but I also had a very clear memory of thinking, just minutes ago with Micah, that I'd rather have been dancing. I'd messed up once tonight, I didn't want to do it twice. 'Sure, dancing sounds great.'

That made Micah and Nathaniel pull back enough to look at me. Jason was just staring down at me. 'What did you say?' Nathaniel said.

'I said, dancing sounds great.' Their astonishment almost made it worthwhile.

'Where is Anita, and what have you done with her?' Jason asked, face mock serious.

I didn't try to explain. I couldn't figure out a slick way of saying to Micah, I'd rather have danced, and it's my fault we missed it, without spilling his secrets in front of Nathaniel and Jason. So I just stood, and offered my hand to Nathaniel.

After a second of staring at it, and me, he took it, almost tentatively, as if he were afraid I'd take it back. I think he'd come ready for an argument about the dancing, and not getting one had thrown him.

I smiled at the surprise on his face. 'Let's go inside.'

He gave me one of his rare full-out smiles, the one that made his entire face light up. For that one smile, I'd have given him a lot more than just a dance.

8

OF COURSE, MY good intentions lasted about as long as it took to be escorted onto the dance floor. Then suddenly I was expected to dance. In front of people. In front of people that were mostly cops. Cops that I worked with on a regular basis. No one is as merciless if you give them ammunition, no pun intended, as a bunch of policemen. If I danced badly, I'd be teased. If I danced well, I'd be teased worse. If they realized I was dancing well with a stripper, the teasing would be endless. If they realized I was dancing badly with a stripper, the jokes would be, well, bad. Either way you cut it, I was so screwed.

I felt fourteen again, and awkward as hell. But it was almost impossible to be awkward with Nathaniel as your partner. Maybe it was his day job, but he knew how to bring out the best in someone on the dance floor. All I had to do was let go of my inhibitions and follow his body. Easy, maybe, but not for me. I like the few inhibitions I have left, thank you, and I'm going to cling to them as long as I can.

What I was clinging to now was Nathaniel. Not much scares me, not really, but airplane rides and dancing in public are on that short list. My heart was in my throat, and I kept fighting the urge to stare at my feet. The men had spent an afternoon proving that I could dance, at home, with only people who were my friends watching. But suddenly, in public in front of a less than friendly audience, all my lessons seemed to have fled. I was reduced to clinging to Nathaniel's hand and shoulder, turning in those useless circles that have nothing to do with the song, and everything to do with fear, and the inability to dance.

'Anita,' Nathaniel said.

I kept staring at my feet, and trying to not see that we were being watched from around the room.

'Anita, look at me, please.'

I raised my face, and whatever he saw in my eyes made him smile, and filled his own eyes with a sort of soft wonderment. 'You really are afraid.' He said it like he hadn't believed it before.

'Would I ever admit to being afraid, if I wasn't?'

He smiled. 'Good point.' His voice was soft. 'Just look at my face, my eyes, no one else matters but the person you're dancing with. Just don't look at anyone else.'

'You sound like you've given this advice before.'

He shrugged. 'A lot of women are uncomfortable on stage, at first.'

I gave him raised eyebrows.

'I used to do an act in formal wear, and I'd pick someone from the audience to dance with. Very formal, very Fred Astaire.'

Somehow, Fred Astaire was not a name that came to mind when I thought of Guilty Pleasures. I said as much.

His smile was less gentle and more his own. 'If you ever came down to the club to watch one of us work instead of just giving us a ride, you'd know what we did.'

I gave him a look.

'You're dancing,' he said.

Of course, once he pointed out that I'd been dancing, I stopped. It was like walking on water, if you thought about it, you couldn't do it.

Nathaniel pulled gently on my hand and pushed gently on my shoulder and got us going again. I finally settled for staring at his chest, watching his body movements as if he'd been a bad guy and it was a fight. Watch the central body for the first telltale movements.

'At home you moved to the rhythm of the song, not just where I moved you.'

'That was at home,' I said, staring at his chest and letting him move me around the floor. It was damn passive for me, but I couldn't lead, because I couldn't dance. To lead you have to know what you're doing.

The song stopped. I'd made it through one song in public. Yeah! I looked up and met Nathaniel's gaze. I expected him to look pleased, or happy, or a lot of things, but that wasn't what was on his face. In fact, I couldn't read the expression on his face. It was serious again, but other than that . . . we stood there, staring at each other, while I tried to figure out what was happening, and I think he tried to work up to saying something. But what? What had him all serious-faced?

I had time to ask, 'What, what's wrong?' then the next song came on. It was fast, with a beat, and I was so out of there. I let go of Nathaniel, stepped back, and had turned, and actually gotten a step away, before he grabbed my hand. Grabbed my hand and pulled me in against him so hard and so fast that I stumbled. If I hadn't caught myself with one arm around his body, I'd have fallen. I was suddenly acutely aware of the firmness of his back against my arm, the curve of his side cupped in the hollow of my hand. I was holding him so close to the front of my body that it seemed every inch of us from chest to groin pressed against one another. His face was painfully close to mine. His mouth so close it seemed a shame not to lay a kiss upon those lips.

His eyes were half-startled, as if I'd grabbed him, and I had, but I hadn't meant to. Then he swayed to one side and took me with him. And just like that we were dancing, but it was different from any dancing I'd ever done. I didn't follow his movements with my eyes, I followed them with my body. He moved, and I moved with him, not because I was supposed to, but for the same reason a tree bends in the wind, because it must.

I moved because he moved. I moved because I finally understood what they'd all been talking about; rhythm, beat, but it wasn't the beat of the music I was hearing, it was the rhythm of Nathaniel's body, pressed so close that all I could feel was him. His body, his hands, his face. His mouth was temptingly close, but I did not close that distance. I gave myself over to his body, the warm strength in his hands, but I did not take the kiss he offered. For he was offering himself in the way that Nathaniel had, no demand, just the open-ended offer of his flesh for the taking. I ignored that kiss the way I'd ignored so many others.

He leaned into me, and I had a moment, just a moment, before his lips touched mine, to say, no, stop. But I didn't say it. I wanted that kiss. That much I could admit to myself.

His lips brushed mine, gentle, then the kiss became part of the swaying of our bodies, so that as our bodies rocked, so the kiss moved with us. He kissed me as his body moved, and I turned my face up to him and gave myself to the movement of his mouth as I'd given myself to the movement of his body. The brush of lips became a full-blown kiss, and it was his tongue that pierced my lips, that filled my mouth, his mouth that filled mine. But it was my hand that left his back and traced his face, cupped his cheek, pressed my body deeper against his, so that I felt him stretched tight and firm under his clothes. The feel of him pressed so tight against my clothes and my body brought a small sound from my mouth, and the know-ledge that the *ardeur* had risen early. Hours early. A distant part of me thought, *Fuck, the rest of me agreed, but not in the way I meant it.*

I drew back from his mouth, tried to breathe, tried to think. His hand came up to cup the back of my head, to press my mouth back to his, so that I drowned in his kiss. Drowned in the pulse and beat of his body. Drowned on the rhythms and tide of his desire. The *ardeur* allowed, sometimes, a glimpse into another heart, or at least their libido. I'd learned to control that part, but tonight it was as if my fragile control had been ripped away, and I stood pressed into the curves and firmness of Nathaniel's body with nothing to protect me from him. Always before he'd been safe. He'd never pushed an advantage, never gone over a line that I drew, not by word or deed; now suddenly, he was ignoring all my signals, all my silent walls. No, not ignoring them, smashing through them. Smashing them down with his hands on my body, his mouth on mine, his body pushing against mine. I could not fight the *ardeur* and Nathaniel, not at the same time.

I saw what he wanted. I felt it. Felt his frustration. Months of being good. Of behaving himself, of not pushing his advantage. I felt all those months of good behavior shatter around us and leave us stripped and suffocating in a desire that seemed to fill the world. Until that moment I hadn't understood how very good he'd been. I hadn't understood what I'd been turning down. I hadn't understood what he was offering. I hadn't understood . . . anything.

I pulled back from him, put a hand on his chest to keep him from closing that distance again.

'Please, Anita, please, please,' his voice was low and urgent, but it was as if he couldn't bring himself to put it into words. But the *ardeur* didn't need words. I suddenly felt his body again, even though we stood feet apart. He was so hard and firm and aching. Aching, because I'd denied him release. Denied him release for months. I'd never had full-blown sex with Nathaniel, because I could feed without it. It had never occurred to me what that might mean for him. But now I could feel his body, heavy, aching with a passion that had been building for months. When last I'd touched Nathaniel's needs this completely, he'd simply wanted to belong to me. That was still there but there was a demand in him, a near screaming need. A need that I'd neglected. Hell, a need that I'd pretended didn't exist. Now, suddenly, Nathaniel wasn't letting me ignore that need anymore.

I had a moment of clear thinking, because I felt guilty. Guilty that I'd left him wanting for so long, while I had my own needs met. I'd thought that having real sex with him would be using him; now suddenly that one glimpse into his heart let me understand that what

I'd done to him had used him more surely than intercourse. I'd used Nathaniel like he was some kind of sex toy, something to bring me pleasure and be cleaned up and put back in a drawer. I was suddenly ashamed, ashamed that I'd treated him like an object, when that wasn't how he wanted to be treated.

The guilt hit me like a cold shower, the proverbial slap in the face, and I used it to pack the *ardeur* away, for another hour or two, at least.

It was as if Nathaniel felt the heat spill away from me. He gave me those wide lavender eyes, huge, and glittering, glittering with unshed tears. He let his hands drop from my arms, and since I'd already dropped my hands away, we stood on the dance floor with distance between us. A distance that neither of us tried to close.

The first shining tear trailed down his cheek.

I reached out to him, and said, 'Nathaniel.'

He shook his head and backed away a step, another, then he turned and ran. Jason and Micah tried to catch him as he rushed past them, but he avoided their hands with a graceful gesture of his upper body that left them with nothing but air. He ran out the door, and they both turned to follow. But it wasn't either of them who had to chase him down. It was me. I was the one who owed him an apology. The trouble was, I wasn't exactly clear on what I would be apologizing for. For using him, or for not using him enough.

9

THE FIRST PERSON I saw when I hit the parking lot wasn't any of the men, it was Ronnie. Veronica Simms, private detective, one time my best friend, was standing off to one side from the door. She was hugging herself so hard, it looked painful. She's 5' 8", a lot of leg, and she'd added high heels and a short red dress to show off the legs. She'd once told me if she had my chest she'd never wear another high-neck shirt in her life. She'd been kidding, but when she dressed up, she showed off all that nice long stretch of leg. Her blond hair was cut at shoulder length, but she'd curled the edges under tonight so the hair bobbed above the spaghetti straps on her nearly bare shoulders. It was bobbing a lot, because she was talking low and angry to someone I couldn't see clearly.

I took another step into the parking lot, and the shadows cleared, and I saw Louis Fane. Louie taught biology at Washington University. He had his doctorate and was a wererat. The university knew about the doctorate but not about what he did on the full moons. He was an inch or two shorter than Ronnie, built compact, but strong. His shoulders filled out the suit he was wearing nicely. He'd cut his dark hair short and neat since last I'd seen him. His dark eyes were almost black, and his clean-cut face was as angry as I'd ever seen it.

I couldn't hear what they were saying, only the tone, and the tone was pissed. I realized I'd been staring, and it was none of my business. Even if Ronnie and I had still been working out together three times a week, which we weren't, it still wouldn't have been any of my business. Ronnie had had problems with me dating a vampire, Jean-Claude in particular, but her main objection seemed to be the vampire part. At a time when I'd needed girl advice and a little sympathy, she'd offered only her own outrage, and anger.

We'd started seeing each other less and less over the last few months, until it had gotten to the point where we hadn't talked in a couple of months. I'd known she and Louie were still dating, because he and I had mutual friends. I wondered what the fight was about, but it wasn't my fight. My fight was waiting out there in the parking lot, leaning against the side of my Jeep. All three of them were leaning against the Jeep. It was like a lineup, or an ambush.

I hesitated in the middle of the asphalt, debating on whether to go back and offer to referee Ronnie and Louie's fight. It wasn't kindness that made me want to go back; it was cowardice. I'd have much rather gotten dragged into someone else's fight than face what was waiting for me. Other people's emotional pain, no matter how painful, is so much less painful than your own.

But Ronnie wouldn't thank me for interfering, and it really wasn't my business. Maybe I'd call her tomorrow and see if she'd talk, see if there was still enough friendship left to save. I missed her.

I stood there in the darkened parking lot, caught between the fight behind me and the fight waiting for me. Strangely, I didn't want to fight with anyone. I was suddenly tired, so terribly tired, and it had nothing to do with the late hour, or a long day.

I walked to the waiting men, and no one smiled at me, but then I didn't smile at them either. I guess it wasn't a smiling kind of conversation.

'Nathaniel says you didn't want to dance with him,' Micah said.

'Not true,' I said. 'I danced, twice. What I didn't want to do was play kissy-face in front of the cops.'

Micah looked at Nathaniel. Nathaniel looked at the ground. 'You kissed me earlier in front of Detective Arnet. Why was this different?'

'I kissed you to give Jessica the clue to stop hitting on you, because you wanted me to save you from her.'

He raised his eyes, and they were like two pretty wounds, so pain-filled. 'So, you only kissed me to save me, not because you wanted to?'

Oh, hell. Out loud I tried again, though the sinking feeling in the pit of my stomach told me that I was going to lose this argument. Lately, around Nathaniel, I always felt like I was doing something wrong, or at least not right. 'That isn't what I meant,' I said.

'It's what you said.' This from Micah.

'Don't you start,' I said, and I heard the anger in my voice before I could stop it. The anger had been there already, I just hadn't been aware of it. I was angry a lot, especially when I wasn't comfortable. I liked anger better than embarrassment. Marianne, who was helping me learn to control the ever growing list of psychic powers, said that I used anger to shield myself from any unwanted emotion. She was right, I accepted that she was right, but she and I hadn't come up with an alternative solution, yet. What's a girl to do if she can't get angry, and she can't run away from the problem? Hell if I know. Marianne had encouraged me to be honest, emotionally honest with myself and those closest to me. Emotional honesty. It sounds so harmless, so wholesome; it's neither.

'I don't want to fight,' I said. There, that was honest.

'None of us do,' Micah said.

Just hearing him be so calm helped the anger ease away. 'Nathaniel pushed it on the dance floor, and the *ardeur* rose early.'

'I felt it,' Micah said.

'Me, too,' Jason said.

'But you don't feel it now, do you?' Nathaniel said. His eyes were almost accusing, and his voice held it's own thin edge of anger. I wasn't sure if I'd ever heard him that close to being angry.

'Anita is getting better control over the *ardeur*,' Micah said.

Nathaniel shook his head, hugging himself tight. It reminded me of the way that Ronnie had been holding herself. 'If it had been you, she would have just come out into the parking lot and fed.'

'Not willingly,' I said.

'Yes, you would,' he said, and his eyes held the anger his voice had held. I'd never seen those lavender eyes angry before. Not like this. It was strangely unnerving.

'I would not have sex in the parking lot of Larry and Tammy's wedding reception, if I had a choice.'

That angry gaze searched my face as if trying to find something. 'Why not feed here?'

'Because it's tacky. And because if Zerbrowski ever got wind of it, I would never, ever, live it down.'

Jason patted his arm. 'See, it isn't you she turned down, it's that she doesn't want to fool around at Larry's wedding. Just not her style.'

Nathaniel glanced at Jason, then back at me. Some strange tension that I didn't quite understand seemed to flow away from him. The anger began to fade from his eyes. 'I guess you're right.'

'Well, if we don't want to be fooling around in the parking lot, then we need to get going,' Micah said. 'The *ardeur* doesn't like being denied. When it does come back tonight, it won't be gentle.'

I sighed. He was right. That bit of metaphysical bravado on the dance floor would have all sorts of consequences later tonight. When the *ardeur* rose again, I would be forced to feed. There would be no stuffing it back into its box. It was almost as if, being able to stop the *ardeur* in its tracks, to completely turn it off once it had filled me, pissed the *ardeur* off. I knew it was a psychic gift and that psychic gifts don't have feelings and don't carry grudges, but sometimes, it felt like this one did.

'I'm sorry, Anita, I wasn't thinking.' Nathaniel looked so discouraged that I had to hug him, a quick hug, more sisterly than anything else, and he responded to my body language and didn't try and hold me close. He let me hug him, and step away. Nathaniel was usually almost painfully attuned to my body language. It was one of the things that had allowed him to share my bed for months without violating those last few taboos.

'Let's go home,' I said.

'That's my cue to part company,' Jason said.

'You're welcome to bunk over if you want,' I said.

He shook his head. 'No, since I'm not needed to referee the fight, or for sage advice, I'll go home, too. Besides, I couldn't stand listening to the three of you get all hot and heavy and not be invited to play.' He laughed and added, 'Don't get mad, but having once been included, it's harder to be excluded.'

I fought the blush that burned up my face, which always seemed to make the blush darker and harder.

Jason and I had had sex once. Before I realized it was possible to love someone to death with the *ardeur*, Nathaniel had collapsed at work and been off the feeding schedule for a few days. Micah hadn't been in the house, and the *ardeur* had risen early. Hours early. It had been interference from Belle Morte, the orignator of Jean-Claude's bloodline, and the first, to my knowledge, possessor of the *ardeur*. It only ran through her line of vamps, nowhere else. The fact that I carried it had raised very interesting metaphysical questions. Belle had wanted to understand what I was, and she had also thought it would raise some hell. Belle was a good business-y vampire, but when she could take care of business and make trouble, all the better. So it hadn't been my fault, but my choices had been limited to taking Nathaniel and possibly killing him, or letting Jason take one for the team. He'd been happy to do it. Very happy. And strangely our friendship had survived it, but every once in a while I couldn't pretend it hadn't happened, and that made me uncomfortable.

'I love the fact that I can make you blush, now,' he said.

'I don't.'

He laughed, but there was something in his eyes that was more serious than laughter. 'I need to tell you something, in private, before you go running off, though.'

I didn't like how suddenly serious he was. I'd learned in the last few months that Jason used his teasing and laughter as a shield to hide a rather insightful intelligence that was sometimes so perceptive it was painful. I didn't like his request for privacy either. What couldn't he say in front of Micah and Nathaniel? And why?

Out loud I said, 'Okay.' I started off to the far side of the parking lot away from the Jeep, and farther away from Ronnie and Louie, who even a glance showed were still having a quiet screaming match.

When the shade of the trees that edged the church parking lot lay cool above us, I stopped and turned to Jason. 'What's up?'

'The thing on the dance floor was sort of my fault.'

'In what way, your fault?'

He actually looked embarrassed, which you didn't see much from Jason. 'He wanted to know how I got to have sex with you, real sex, the very first time I helped feed the *ardeur*.'

'Technically, it was the second,' I said.

He frowned at me. 'Yeah, but that was when the *ardeur* was brand new and we didn't have intercourse, and there were three other men in the bed.'

I turned away so the dark would help hide the blush, though truthfully he could probably smell it hot on my skin. 'Sorry I brought it up, you were saying?'

'He's been in your bed for what, four months?'

'Something like that,' I said.

'And he's not had intercourse yet, hell, he's not had orgasm, not real orgasm with like release and everything.'

I couldn't blush harder or my head would explode. 'I'm listening.'

'Anita, you can't keep pretending that Nathaniel isn't real.'

'That's not fair.'

'Maybe not, but I had no idea that you weren't at least doing him orally or by hand, or watching him do himself. Something, anything.'

I just shook my head and looked at the ground. I couldn't think of anything good to say. If I hadn't just had my metaphysical peek inside Nathaniel's head, I would probably have gotten angry, or rude.

But I'd seen too far into Nathaniel's pain, and I couldn't pretend anymore. Couldn't ignore it.

'I thought that by not doing the final stuff that it would make it easier for him when the *ardeur* gets under control and I don't need a *pomme de sang* anymore.'

'Is that still your idea, to just dump him when you have enough control that you don't need to feed?'

'What am I supposed to do with him? Keep him like a pet, or a really big child?'

'He's not a child, and he's not a pet,' Jason said, and the first hint of anger was in his voice.

'I know that, and that's the problem, Jason. If the *ardeur* hadn't come up I'd have been Nathaniel's Nimir-Ra, and his friend, and that would have been it. Now, suddenly he's in this category that I don't even have a name for.'

'He's your *pomme de sang* like I'm Jean-Claude's.'

'You and Jean-Claude aren't fucking, and nobody gets upset about that.'

'No, because he lets me date. I have lovers if I want them.'

'I've been encouraging Nathaniel to date. I want him to have girl-friends.'

'And your not-so-subtly encouraging him to look at other women made him turn to me for advice.'

'What do you mean?' I asked.

'He doesn't want to date other people. He wants to be with you, and Micah, and the vampires. He doesn't want another woman in his life.'

'I am not the woman in his life.'

'Yes, you are, you just don't want to be.'

I leaned against one of the narrow tree trunks. 'Oh, Jason, what am I going to do?'

'Finish what you started with Nathaniel, be his lover.'

I shook my head. 'I don't want that.'

'The hell you don't. I watch the way you react around him.'

'Lust isn't enough, Jason. I don't love him.'

'I'd argue that, too.'

'I don't love him the way I need to.'

'Need to, for what, Anita? Need to for your conscience? Your sense of morality? Just give him some of what he needs, Anita. Don't break yourself doing it, but bend a little. That's all I'm asking.'

'You said the thing on the dance floor was sort of your fault. You never explained that.'

'I told Nathaniel you don't like passive men. You like a little dominance, a little pushiness. Not much, but enough so that you aren't the one that says, Yes, we'll have sex. You need someone to take a little of the responsibility off your shoulders.'

I stared at him, studied that young face. 'Is that all it is for me, Jason? I just need someone else to help me spread the guilt around so I can fuck?'

He winced. 'That isn't what I said.'

'Close enough.'

'Get mad, if you want, but that isn't what I said, or what I meant. Get mad at me, but don't take it out on Nathaniel, okay?'

'I was raised that if you had sex it was a commitment. I still believe that.'

'You don't feel committed to me.' He said it as if it were just a fact, nothing personal.

'No, we're friends, and I was sort of a friend in need. But you're a grown-up, and you understood what it was. I'm not sure Nathaniel is enough of a grown-up to understand that. Hell, he can't even say no to women who are almost strangers.'

'He turned down at least three dance offers while we were talking, and I know for a fact that he turned down the beautiful Jessica Arnet for a date.'

'He did, really?'

Jason nodded. 'Yep.'

'I didn't think he'd be able to say no.'

'He's been practicing.'

'Practicing?'

'He tells you no sometimes, doesn't he?'

I thought about it. 'Sometimes he won't repeat conversations to me, or tell me things. He says I'll get mad at him, and so I should ask the other person.'

'You wanted, no, demanded, that Nathaniel be more responsible for himself. You made him get his driver's license. You've forced him to be less dependent, right?'

'Yeah.'

'But you didn't think what it would mean, did you?'

'What do you mean?'

'You wanted him to be independent, to think for himself, to decide what he wanted out of life, right?'

'Yeah, in fact, I said almost exactly that to him. I wanted him to decide what he wanted to do with his life. I mean he's only twenty, for God's sake.'

'And what he's decided he wants to do is be with you,' Jason said, and his voice was softer, gentle.

'That is not a life decision. I meant like a career choice, maybe go back to college.'

'He's got a job, Anita, and he makes better money as a stripper than most college graduates do.'

'You can't strip for ever,' I said.

'And most marriages don't last for ever either.'

My eyes must have gotten too wide, because he hurried with his next words, 'What I mean is that you treat everything like it's a for ever question. Like you can't change your mind later. I don't mean to imply that Nathaniel wants you to make an honest man of him. That never came up, honest.'

'Well, that's a relief, at least.'

'You'll need a *pomme de sang* for years, Anita. Years.'

'Jean-Claude said maybe in a few months I'd be able to feed from a distance, and not need the up close and personal stuff.'

'You've made progress on going longer between feedings, Anita. But you haven't made much progress on truly controlling the *ardeur*.'

'I controlled it on the dance floor,' I said.

He sighed. 'You shut it down on the dance floor. That's not control, not really. It's like you have a gun, and you can lock it in the gun safe, but that doesn't teach you how to shoot it.'

'A gun analogy? You've been thinking on this for awhile, haven't you?'

'Ever since Nathaniel told me that you hadn't been allowing him release during the feedings.'

'Allow? He didn't ask, and how was I supposed to know he wasn't even doing himself in private? I mean, I didn't tell him not to.'

'You can play with yourself, and it feels good, but it doesn't meet the real need.'

I pushed my back tight into the tree, as if the solid wood could catch me, because I felt like I was falling. Falling into a chasm so deep that I'd never get out. 'I don't know if I can do Nathaniel and still look at myself in the mirror in the morning.'

'Why does doing Nathaniel bother you that much?'

'Because he confuses my radar. I have friends, I have boyfriends, I have people who are dependent on me, people I take care of. I do not fuck the people I take care of. It would be like taking advantage of your position.'

'And Nathaniel falls into the taking care of category?' he asked.

'Yes.'

'You think by having sex that you're taking advantage?'

'Yes.'

'That's not how Nathaniel sees it.'

'I know that, Jason, now.' I closed my eyes and leaned my head back against the roughness of the bark. 'Damn it, I want the *ardeur* under control so I don't have to keep making these kinds of decisions.'

'And if I could wave a magic wand over you and you instantly could control the *ardeur*, what then? What would you do with Nathaniel?'

'I'd help him find a place of his own.'

'He does most of the housework around your place. He buys your groceries. He and Micah do most of the cooking. Nathaniel taking care of the domestic stuff is what allows Micah and you both to work all those hours. Without Nathaniel, how would you organize it?'

'I don't want to keep Nathaniel just to make my life easier. That's like evil.'

Jason let out a big sigh. 'Are you really this slow, or just driving me crazy on purpose?'

'What?' I said.

He shook his head. 'Anita, what I'm trying to say is that Nathaniel doesn't feel used. He feels useful. He doesn't need a girlfriend, because he thinks he already has one. He doesn't want to date, because he's already living with someone. He doesn't need to look for a place of his own, because he already has one. Micah knows that, Nathaniel knows that, the only person who doesn't know that seems to be you.'

'Jason . . .'

He stopped me with a raised hand. 'Anita, you have two men who live with you. They both love you. They both want you. They both support your career. Between the two of them, they're like your wife. There are people in this world who would kill to have what you have. And you'd just throw it away.'

I just looked at him, because I didn't know what to say.

'The only thing that keeps this little domestic arrangement from being perfect for all concerned is that Nathaniel is not getting his needs met.' He stepped in close to me, but the look on his face was so serious that it never occurred to me that kissing was coming, because it wasn't. 'You've set up the dynamics so that you wear the pants in this trio, and that's fine, it works for Micah and Nathaniel. But here's the hard part about wearing the pants, Anita, it means you get to make the tough decisions. Your life is working better than it's worked since I met you. You've been happier, longer, than I've ever seen you. Micah, I don't know that well, but Nathaniel has never been this happy in all the years I've known him. Everything is working, Anita. Everybody is making it work. Everybody but . . .'

'Me,' I said.

'You,' he said.

'You know, Jason, I can't say you're wrong about any of it, but I hate you right this second.'

'Hate me, if you want to, but I'm tired of watching people have everything their heart desires and throw it away.'

'This isn't what my heart desired,' I said.

'Maybe not, but it's what you needed. You needed a wife in that old 1950s sort of way.'

'Doesn't everybody,' I said.

He grinned at me. 'No, some people would like to be the wife, but I just can't find a woman who's man enough to keep me in the style to which I have not yet become accustomed.'

It made me smile. Damn it. 'You are the only one who can say shit like this to me, and not have me pissed at them for days, or longer. How do you get away with it?'

He planted a quick kiss on my lips, more brotherly than anything. 'I don't know how I get away with it, but if I could bottle it, Jean-Claude would pay a fortune for it.'

'Maybe not just Jean-Claude.'

'Maybe not.' He stepped back smiling, but his eyes had that serious look again. 'Please, Anita, go home, and don't freak. Just go home, and be happy. Be happy, and let everyone around you be happy. Is that so hard?'

When Jason said it like that, it didn't seem hard. In fact, it seemed to make a lot of sense, but inside, it felt hard. Inside it felt like the hardest thing in the world. To just let go, and not pick everything to death. To just let go and enjoy what you had. To just let go and not make everybody around you miserable with your own internal dialogue. To just let go and be happy. So simple. So difficult. So terrifying.

10

A CAR SQUEALED out of the parking lot, as Jason walked me back to the Jeep. I only had a moment to see it, before it blasted out into the street, but I recognized the car. Apparently Ronnie was driving them home, but the fight wasn't over. Not my problem. God knew I had enough relationship problems without sticking my nose into someone else's. Of course, sometimes no matter how hard you try to stay out of something, you can't.

'Can I grab a ride home?' It was Louie Fane, Dr Louis Fane, though his doctorate wasn't in the biology of humans, but in the biology of bats. His doctoral thesis had been on the adaption of the Little Brown Bat to human habitation. Actually his work with bats, a different species, had put him in a cave with a wererat that attacked him. It's how he got to be furry once a month.

'Sure,' Jason and I said in unison.

Louie smiled. 'I just need one ride, but thanks.' His eyes, which were truly black, not just darkest brown like mine, didn't match the smile. The eyes were still angry.

'His place is on the way to the Circus,' Jason said.

I nodded. 'Okay.' I looked at Louie and wanted to ask what the fight had been about, and didn't want to ask what the fight had been about. I settled for, 'Are you okay?'

He shook his head. 'Ronnie will probably call you tomorrow and tell you anyway. I guess you might as well know, or maybe you can talk some sense into her.'

I gave a half-shrug. 'I don't know. Ronnie can be pretty stubborn.'

Jason laughed. 'You calling someone else stubborn, that's rich.'

I frowned at him. 'You sure you don't want to ride home with us, instead of Mr Comedy here?'

He shook his head. 'I'm on Jason's way home.' He still hadn't told us what the fight was about. Was I supposed to remind him, or let it go?

'Do you want some privacy here?' Jason asked.

Louie sighed. 'Yes, if you don't mind.'

'I'll say good night to Micah and Nathaniel, and I'll be waiting by my car.' He waved at me and walked away.

For the second, no, the third time that night I was standing out in the cool shadows of the trees getting a heart-to-heart talk with another man. This one wasn't even my boyfriend or occasional food.

'What's wrong, Louie?'

'I asked Ronnie to marry me tonight.'

I'd been prepared for a lot of things, but that hadn't even ocurred to me. Marriage? I just gaped at him. When I could close my mouth and pretend to be intelligent, I said, 'And why the fight, then?'

'She said, no.' He didn't look at me as he said it. He stared off into the dark, his hands plunged into the pockets of his dress slacks, ruining the line of his jacket, but giving him something to do with his hands.

'She said, no,' I repeated it, as if I hadn't heard it right.

He glanced at me then. 'You sound surprised.'

'Well, last I knew you guys were getting along really well.' Actually, the last time Ronnie had confided in me it had been a conversation that had set us both giggling, because it had been mostly about sex. We'd both overshared, which women do more than men, and the sex had been as good between her and Louie as it had been between me and Micah. Which was pretty damned good. Ronnie had had this mistaken idea that dating Micah meant I'd dumped Jean-Claude. When she found out it didn't mean that, she'd not taken it well. She just couldn't seem to cope with me dating the undead. Picky, picky. I could joke, but her last stand on Jean

Claude had been adamant enough that we hadn't talked much since.

'It's all wonderful, Anita. That's what is so . . .' he seemed to search for a word, and settled for, 'frustrating!'

'So, you guys are getting along great?' I made it a question.

'I thought so, maybe I was wrong?' He paced two steps away from me, then back. 'No, damn it, I wasn't wrong. It's been the best two years of my life. Nothing starts my day off better than waking up beside her. I want to start every day like that. Is that so wrong?'

'No, Louie, that's not wrong.'

'Then why did we just have the biggest fight we've ever had?' His dark face was demanding, as if I had the answer and just wouldn't give it to him.

'I'll call Ronnie tomorrow, if she doesn't call me first. I'll talk to her.'

'She says she doesn't want to marry anyone. She says, if she married anyone, it would be me, but she doesn't want to. She doesn't want to.' The pain in his voice was so raw, it hurt to hear it.

'I am so sorry.' I started to touch his arm, thought better of it, and said, 'Maybe you could just live together?'

'I offered that. I offered to just live together until she was ready for more.' He was staring off into the darkness, again, as if he didn't want me to see what was in his eyes.

'She said no to that, too?' I asked.

'She doesn't want to give up her independence. Her independence is one of the things I love most about her.'

'I know that,' I said, and my voice was soft, because it was all I had to offer.

He looked at me. 'You know that, then can you tell her?'

'I'll do everything I can to reassure her that you're not trying to clip her wings.'

'Is that it? Is she just afraid I'll take away her freedom?'

'I don't know, Louie. Truthfully, if you'd asked me beforehand, I'd have said, she'd say, yes.'

'Really,' he said, and he was studying my face now. Studying it as if the secrets to the universe were somehow hidden in my eyes. I preferred him staring out into the dark for his answers instead of in my face. I wasn't sure what the darkness had to offer him, but I knew I didn't have any answers.

'Yeah, Louie, really. Last I knew she was the happiest I've ever seen her.'

'So I wasn't just fooling myself?' he asked, and he was still giving me those raw, demanding eyes.

'No, Louie, you weren't fooling yourself.'

'Then why?' he asked. 'Why?'

I shrugged, and had to say something, because he was still staring at me. 'I don't know. I'm sorry.' It sounded so inadequate, sorry. But it was all I had to offer tonight.

He nodded, a little too rapidly, as he turned away, and stared out into the dark again. I knew he wasn't really seeing the yard that bordered the church. I knew he was just staring to be staring, and not to have to meet anyone's eyes for a while, but it was sort of unnerving. Unnerving to think that whatever he was feeling was so strong that he had to hide his eyes, so I wouldn't see. It reminded me of the way Dolph had turned away at the murder scene. And, in a way, they were both hiding the same thing – pain.

He turned away from the dark and gave me his eyes again. They were raw, and I had to fight to not turn away myself. My rule was always if someone could feel the emotion, the least I could do was not turn away.

'It looks like your sweetheart is coming this way.'

I glanced back to find Micah walking slowly toward us. Normally, he wouldn't have interrupted, but we were on a deadline tonight. Time and the *ardeur* wait for no man. I would have explained that Micah wasn't being rude, that we had to go, but I wasn't sure Louie knew about the *ardeur*, and I hated to explain it to people who didn't know. It always sounded so . . . odd.

'How long have you and Micah been living together?' he asked.

'About four months.'

'Ronnie and you haven't been hanging out much since he moved in with you, have you?'

I thought about it, then said, 'I guess not. She didn't like that I'm still dating Jean-Claude.'

Louie watched Micah walking toward us. His face looked thoughtful. 'Maybe that wasn't it.'

'What do you mean?'

'Maybe it was having someone live with you. Maybe that's what she couldn't handle.'

'She said it was me dating a vamp.'

'Ronnie said a lot of things,' he said, voice softer, less angry, more puzzled. He shook himself like a dog coming out of water, and managed to give me a smile. It left his eyes sad, but it was a start. 'Maybe she just couldn't stand to see you committing yourself to somebody, not that much.'

I shrugged, because I didn't think that was it, but I couldn't blame him for thinking it. 'I don't know.'

He gave me that smile again, his eyes like dark hopeless pools. 'You go home, Anita, and enjoy it.' I caught a glitter of tears before he turned away and looked out into the dark again.

I didn't know what to do. Was I supposed to hug him? If it had been a girlfriend, I probably would have. But it wasn't, he wasn't, and I didn't need any more complications tonight. I did the guy thing, and patted him awkwardly on the back. Whether I would have worked up to a full-blown hug, I don't know, because Micah was beside us.

'Sorry to interrupt, but it's been nearly an hour since we hit the parking lot.' It was his subtle way of reminding me that sometimes an hour was all we got from the time I squashed the *ardeur* down to the time it resurfaced.

I took the hint. With Micah beside me, I felt more secure. If the *ardeur* had risen, he'd have been there to see that nothing disastrous happened. I slid my arm through Louie's arm and bumped my head against his shoulder. 'Come on, Louie, we'll walk you to Jason's car.'

He nodded, as if he didn't trust his voice, and was careful not to look at either of us as we walked him toward the lights of the parking lot. Micah pretended that nothing was wrong. I pretended that there were no tears to see. I kept my hold on his arm all the way to where Jason waited standing beside his car.

Jason opened the passenger side door for Louie, giving me a questioning look over Louie's shoulder.

I started to shake my head, but Louie hugged me. Hugged me suddenly, and fiercely, so tight it took my breath away. I thought he'd say something, but he didn't. He just held on, and I wrapped my arms around his back, held him, because I couldn't not hold him. About the time I thought I was going to have to think of something to say, he stepped back. He'd been crying while he held me, but I hadn't felt a single sob, nothing, but the fierceness in his arms, his hands, and silent tears.

He blinked and gave Micah an odd smile, that was almost a sob. 'How did you talk her into moving in with you?'

'I moved in with her,' he said, voice very quiet, very even, a careful voice, reserved for frightened children, and overly emotional adults. I'd heard that voice often enough aimed at me. 'And she asked me.'

'Lucky,' Louie said, and that one word sounded like it meant anything but, lucky.

'I know,' Micah said, and he put an arm around my shoulders and moved me just a little back from Louie, so there was room for him to get through the open car door.

Louie nodded again, too rapidly, and too many times. 'Lucky.' He slid into the car, and Jason shut the door behind him.

Jason leaned into me. 'What just happened?'

It wasn't my secret to tell, but it felt like dirty pool sending Jason to drive Louie home without warning him. 'It's his secret to tell, not mine. I'm sorry. But let's just say he's had a rough night.'

Louie knocked on the window. The sound made both Jason and me jump. Micah had either seen it coming, or had better nerves than we did. Jason moved back enough so the door could open. 'Don't bother to whisper this close to the car. I can hear you.'

'I'm sorry,' I said.

'Don't be, it's not like he didn't see the fight. Tell him, so I don't have to.' And Louie closed the door again. He leaned his head back against the seat, and more of those completely silent tears began to escape him.

We all looked away, as if it were somehow shameful to watch. I think we'd have been less embarrassed if he'd been undressed. 'What is up?' Jason said.

'He proposed to Ronnie, and she said no.'

Jason's mouth dropped open just like mine had. 'You are joking me.'

I shook my head. 'Wish I was.'

'But they are like one of the happiest couples I know.'

I shrugged. 'I don't explain the news, I just report it.'

'Shit,' Jason said. He glanced back at his car, and at Louie. 'I'll get him home.'

'Thanks.'

Jason gave me a shadow of his usual grin. 'Well, can't send him home with you. Wouldn't that complicate the hell out of things?'

'What?' I asked.

Micah kissed me on the side of the face. 'The *ardeur* rising with Louie in the car. Speaking of which . . .'

'You guys go,' Jason said, 'we'll be okay.'

I kissed him on the cheek, quick and sisterly. 'You're a braver man than I am, Gunga Din.'

He laughed. 'That's not the original quote, is it?'

'Not exactly, but it's still true.'

He looked suddenly serious again. Very unJasonlike. 'I don't know if I'm brave or not, but I'll get him tucked-in.'

'We have to go,' Micah said. He started leading me toward our Jeep.

I kept looking back as Jason went around the car and got in. Louie sat motionless, head back. From a distance, you couldn't tell he was crying.

Micah pulled me in against his body, hugging me loosely to his side. I leaned in against the solidness of him and slid my arm around his waist, so that we finished the walk touching from chest to thigh. I was glad he was with me. Glad we were driving home together. Glad that home meant both of us.

Nathaniel was leaning against the side of the Jeep watching us walk toward him. He was leaning with his hands behind him so that his weight trapped his hands behind him, pinned between his hips and the Jeep. It wasn't just intercourse that Nathaniel hadn't been getting with me. Nathaniel had other 'needs' that I was, if possible, even less comfortable with. It made him feel peaceful to be tied up. Peaceful to be abused. Peaceful. I'd asked him why he enjoyed it once, and he'd told me that it made him feel peaceful. It made him feel safe.

How could being tied up make you feel safe? How could letting someone hurt you, even a little, make you feel good? I didn't get it. I just didn't get it. Maybe if I'd understood it better, I'd have been less afraid to go that last mile with him. What if we had intercourse and it wasn't enough? What if he just kept pushing, pushing me to do things that I found . . . frightening? He was supposed to be the submissive, and I was his dominant. Didn't that mean that I was in charge? Didn't that mean he did what I said? No. I'd had to learn enough to understand Nathaniel and some of the other wereleopards, because he wasn't the only one with interesting hobbies. The submissive had a safe word, and once they said that word, all the play stopped. So in the end, the dominant had an illusion of power, but really the submissive got to say how far things went, and when they stopped. I'd thought I could control Nathaniel because he was so submissive, but it was tonight that I realized the truth. I wasn't in control anymore. I didn't know what was going to happen with Nathaniel, or me, or Micah. The thought terrified me, so I thought about it, really thought about it. What if I found Nathaniel a new place to live? What if I found him a new place to be? A new life?

I rolled it over in my mind as we walked across the pavement. I thought about sending him home with someone else, letting him weep on someone else's shoulder. But more than that, I thought about getting under the covers with only Micah on one side, and no one on the other side. Nathaniel had his side of the bed now. I hadn't realized it until that second, hadn't let myself realize it. The three of us enjoyed reading *Treasure Island* to each other. For Micah and me it was a revisiting of childhood favorites, for the most part, but for Nathaniel most of the books were new to him. He'd never had anyone read to him before bedtime. Never had anyone share their books with him. What kind of childhood is it without books, stories to share? I knew that he'd had an older brother, who died, and a father who died, and a mother who died. That they'd died, I knew, but not how, or when, except that he'd been young when it happened. He didn't like talking about it, and I didn't like seeing the look in his eyes when he did, so I didn't push. I didn't have a right to push if I wasn't his girlfriend. I didn't have a right to push if I wasn't his lover. I was only his Nimir-Ra, and he didn't owe me his life story.

I thought about not having Nathaniel in the bed, not for feeding, but not having him there to hear the rest of the story. To hear what happened when Jim realizes what a soft-hearted villain Long John Silver really is. The thought of him not being there at that moment when we come to the end of the adventure was painful, a wrenching kind of pain, as if my stomach and my heart both hurt at the same time.

He opened the door and held it for me, because this close to the *ardeur*, it wasn't always good that I was driving. He held the door and was as neutral as he could be, as I moved past him. I didn't know what to do, so I let him be neutral, and I was neutral, too. But as I buckled my seat belt in place and he closed the door, I realized that I would miss him. Not miss him because my life ran smoother with him than without him, but I would simply miss him. Miss the vanilla scent of him on my pillow; the warmth of his body on his side of the bed; the spill of his hair like some tangled, living blanket. If I could have stopped my list there, I'd have sent Nathaniel to his room for the night; he did still have a room where all his stuff stayed, all his stuff but him. But I couldn't stop the list there, not and be honest.

He'd cried when Charlotte died, in *Charlotte's Web*. I wouldn't have missed seeing him cry over a dead spider for anything. It had been Nathaniel's idea that we could have a movie marathon of old monster flicks. You have not lived until you've sat through *The Wolf Man* (1941), *The Curse of the Werewolf* (1961), and *The Werewolf* (1956) with a bunch of shapeshifters. They had heckled the screen and thrown popcorn, and howled, sometimes literally, at the movie version of what they knew all too well. The wereleopards had all complained, that at least werewolves had some movies, that once you'd named *Cat People*, the leopards didn't have any movies. Most of the werewolves had known about the 1982 version, but almost no one had known about the original in 1942. We had another movie night planned where we were going to watch both versions. I was sure we'd spend the night complaining, cheerfully, at how far off both films were, and get eerily silent when they hit close to home. Alright, they'd be eerily silent, and I'd watch them watching the screen.

I was looking forward to it. I tried picturing the night without Nathaniel. No Nathaniel coming and going out of the kitchen with popcorn and soda, making people use coasters. No Nathaniel sitting on the floor, next to my legs, half the night spent with his head on my knee, and the other half playing his hand up and down my calf. It wasn't sexual, he just felt better touching me. The entire pard, and pack, felt better touching each other. It was possible to be up close and personal without it being sexual. It really was, just not usually for me.

Which brought me back to the problem at hand. Funny how the thinking led back to it. Tonight when the *ardeur* finally surfaced, what was I going to do? I could exile Nathaniel to his room, legitimately, because I'd need to feed tomorrow, too. I could save him like for dessert. But we'd both know that that wasn't it. I wasn't saving him, I was saving myself. Saving myself from what, I wasn't sure, but it was definitely about saving me, and had nothing to do with saving Nathaniel.

He didn't want to be saved. No, that wasn't true. Nathaniel already thought he had been saved. I'd saved him. I'd been treating him like a prince who needed to find his princess, but that was all wrong. Nathaniel was the princess, and he had been rescued, by me. As far as Nathaniel was concerned, I was the prince in shining armor, I just needed to come across, and then we could all live happily ever after.

Trouble was, I was no one's prince, and no one's princess. I was just me, and I was all out of armor, shiny or otherwise. I just wasn't the fairy-tale type. And I didn't believe in happily ever after. The question was, did I believe in happily for now? If I could have answered that question, then all the worry would have been ended, but I couldn't answer it. So as Micah drove us toward home in the October dark, I still didn't know what I'd do when the *ardeur* finally rose for the night. I didn't even know what the right thing to do was anymore. Wasn't right supposed to help people and wrong supposed to hurt people? Didn't you make the right choice because it was the right thing to do? I always felt squeamish about praying to God about sex, in any context, but I prayed as we drove, because I was out of options. I asked for guidance. I asked for a clue as to what was the best for everyone. I didn't get an answer, and I hadn't expected one. I have a lot psychic gifts, but talking directly to God is not one of them, thank goodness. Read the Old Testament if you don't think it's a scary idea. But worse than no answer, I didn't feel that peace that I usually get when I pray.

My cell phone rang. It made me jump, and my pulse was so thick in my throat that I couldn't answer right away. A woman's voice said, 'Anita, Anita are you there?'

It was Marianne. She lived in Tennessee and was the vargamor for the Oak Tree Clan. It was a very old-fashioned title and job, basically she was the witch that helped them deal with their metaphysical problems. Most packs didn't have one anymore, too old-fashioned. Maybe the New Age stuff would bring it back into vogue.

She was also helping me cope with my abilities. She was the only psychic I knew, and trusted. She knew the shapeshifters almost as well as I did, in some ways better, in some ways not. But she was the closest thing I had to a mentor of late, and I needed one.

'Marianne, it's great to hear your voice. What's up?' My voice sounded breathy even to me.

'I just got this overwhelming urge to call you. What's wrong?'

See, she's psychic. I wanted to explain everything, but Nathaniel was behind me in the car. What was I supposed to do, make him put his fingers in his ears and hum while I talked? 'It's a little awkward right now.'

'Should I guess?'

'If you want.'

She was quiet for a few moments, and she wasn't guessing. She was using either her own gifted intuition, or she was drawing a card, a tarot card that is. 'I'm looking at the Knight of Cups here, that's usually Nathaniel's card.' I'd been skeptical, to say the least, when Marianne first got out a deck of cards to do a 'reading,' but they were eerily accurate, at least in her hands. When she'd first started, Nathaniel's card had been the Page of Cups, a child's card, or at least a very young person, but of late he'd been promoted. Knight of Cups.

'Yeah, that's it.'

Silence, and I knew she was laying a spread. She'd actually tried to get me to use the cards, to see if I had any abilities for divination, but they were just pretty pictures to me. My gifts lay elsewhere.

'King of Wands, Micah is with you, too.' It wasn't a question.

'Yes.' I could picture her with her long gray hair tied back in a no-nonsense ponytail, probably in one of her loose, flowing gowns, sitting cross-legged on the bed, which is where she'd have been this late. She was slender and strong, and her body didn't match her hair, or the fact that she was closer to sixty than fifty.

'The devil, temptation. You haven't fed the *ardeur* yet, have you?'

It used to creep me out that she could do this, but I'd gotten used to it. It was just something Marianne could do. She didn't hold it against me that I raised zombies, and I didn't hold it against her that she could tell what was happening hundreds of miles away. In fact, sometimes, like now, it came in handy.

'Not yet.'

'The Priestess, you have a question for me.'

'Yes.'

'You're not doing something silly like trying to choose between Micah and Nathaniel, are you?'

'Thanks a lot.'

'You can't blame me, Anita, you do tend to complicate your life.'

I sighed. 'Fine, true, but sort of, and not exactly.'

'Fine, be cryptic.'

'Not in the way you might mean,' I said finally.

'So not dumping one for the other,' she said.

'No.'

'Well, that's good.' She was quiet for longer this time. 'I'll stop guessing. I've laid a reading.' She preferred to do a reading without knowing anything about the problem. Marianne felt that if you talked too much you influenced the person doing the reading.

'I put you in the center, Queen of Swords. The past is the five of pentagrams, being left out in the cold, not getting your needs met.

Deity is the six of cups, which can be someone from your past coming back into your life, someone you felt a strong connection with. Future is the Knight of Cups, Nathaniel's card. The mundane is the four of pentacles, the Miser, holding on to things that no longer help your life run smoothly. Now we'll do the connecting cards.' She was quiet for a second or two, while she thought, or prayed, or whatever she did to make the cards talk to her. I understood everything but the six of cups so far. 'Connecting the mundane to the past is the Lover's card. Something happened in your love life that made you be afraid of being hurt, or giving up something, or someone. Connecting the past to deity is the King of Wands, usually Micah's card, but it could be energy, a male prescence in your life. Connecting deity to the future is the two of swords; you have a choice to make, and you think it's difficult, but if you take off the blindfold, you can see, and you have what you need to do it. Connecting the future to the mundane is the Knight of Wands, another man in your life. You do draw a lot of male energy to you.'

'Not on purpose,' I said.

'Hush, I'm not finished.'

'Overlaying the Miser is the six of swords, help unseen, or help from a spiritual source. Overlaying the Lovers is the four of rods, the marriage card. Overlaying the out in the cold is the ten of pentacles, happy prosperous home. Hmm. The King of Rods and the six of cups stand on their own, but the two of swords has crossed with the Queen of Wands. Nathaniel's card is crossed with the ten of cups, a happy home, true love. The Knight of Wands is crossed by the Devil, temptation.'

'Okay, I get most of it, but who is the Knight of Wands, and why is he covered by temptation? And who is the Queen of Wands?'

'I think the Queen of Wands is you.'

'I'm always the Queen of Swords.'

'Maybe that's changing. Maybe you're coming into your power, into yourself.'

'I'm already myself,' I said.

'Have it your way.'

'I'm trying to.'

'I'd say the Lovers and the four of rods are your old fiancé in college that dumped you. That experience led you to be the Miser with your emotions. You need to let that go. Your home was the five of pentacles, cold, but now it's a happy prosperous home. You're going to be offered up some difficult choices soon; that has something to do with someone from your past. I think Micah's card is the message that he's helped you heal some of those old wounds, because he bridges the past with deity.'

'He's a gift from deity?'

'Don't be cheeky. When the universe, or God, or Goddess, or whatever you choose to say, gives you someone in your life that comes in and makes so much right, so quickly, be grateful. Be grateful instead of picking at it.' Marianne knew me too well.

'And the Knight of Wands?'

'Someone new, or someone old, but you'll be seeing them in a new light. It will be a temptation, but the wands represent power, so it could be a temptation to use power or gain power, rather than anything relationshipwise.'

'I don't need more temptation in my life, Marianne.'

'Did you start a case tonight?'

'Why?' I asked.

'Because I felt compelled to draw another card. It's the eight of swords, a woman bound and blindfolded, surrounded by swords. A woman died tonight.'

I try to avoid calling Marianne in the middle of a murder case, for a lot of reasons, this was one of them. It creeped me out, and gave her nightmares.

'Five of rods, there will be a lot of conflict on this one, and more to die. But the Justice card says the guilty will be punished, and it will work out, but not without loss. The eight of pentacles? That's odd. Someone will be involved that was once your teacher.

Someone older. Do you know who that would be?'

I thought about it being Dolph, but that didn't sound right. 'I don't know, maybe.'

'They haven't come into the situation, yet, but they will. They will help you.'

'How sure are you that there will be more killings?'

'Aren't you sure of it?' she asked, and she had that tone in her voice that said she was listening to voices I couldn't hear.

'Yeah, I got that feeling.'

'Trust your feelings, Anita.'

'I'll try,' I said.

'You must be almost home by now.'

I didn't ask how she knew we were turning into the driveway. She wouldn't really have been able to tell me. Psychic stuff wasn't big on A, B, C logic. It was more like A to G, leaps of logic, with no road map as to how we got to G.

'Yeah, we're home.'

Micah blew me a kiss and got out of the Jeep. I heard Nathaniel get out of the back. They both closed the doors and left me in the suddenly dark car, alone with the phone.

Marianne spoke into the sudden silence. 'Oh, one more thing, the message I just got was, 'You know what you need to do. Why are you asking me?' That's not my message to you, you know I never mind you asking my advice. I actually kind of like it. Who else have you been asking advice from?'

I opened my mouth, and closed it. 'I prayed.'

'What I'm getting is that you usually only pray when you're out of other options that you like. It might be nice if you prayed as something other than a last resort.' She said it so matter-of-factly. Nothing big, you prayed, God can't talk to you, so he left a message on your machine. Great.

I licked my suddenly dry lips, and said, 'It doesn't bother you that you just took a message from God for me?'

'Well, it wasn't from him directly. He just sent it.' Again, utterly matter-of-fact, no big deal.

'Marianne.'

'Yes.'

'Sometimes you creep me out.'

She laughed. 'You raise the dead and slay the undead, and I frighten you.'

Put that way, it sounded silly, but it was still true. 'Let's just say that I'm glad you have your have psychic powers, and I have mine. I feel guilty enough without knowing the future.'

'Don't feel guilty, Anita, follow your heart. No, it was the Queen of Rods, not of Cups. So follow your power, let it take you where you need to go. Trust yourself, and trust those around you.'

'You know I don't trust anybody.'

'You trust me.'

'Yeah, but . . .'

'Stop poking at it, Anita. Your heart is not a wound to be poked at to see if the scab is ready to come off. You can be healed of that very old pain, if you'll just let it happen.'

'So everybody keeps telling me.'

'If all your friends are saying one thing, and your heart is saying the same thing, and only your fear is arguing, then stop fighting.'

'I'm not good at giving up.'

'No, I'd say that is the thing you are worst at. Giving up something that no longer serves a purpose, or protects you, or helps you, isn't giving up at all, it's growing up.'

I sighed. 'I hate it when you make this much sense.'

'You hate it, and you count on it.'

'Yeah.'

'Go inside, Anita, go inside, and make your choice. I've said all I have to say, now it's up to you.'

'And I hate that most of all,' I said.

'What?' she asked.

'That you don't try and influence me, not really, you just report, tell me my choices, and let me go.'

'I offer guidance, nothing more.'

'I know.'

'I'm hanging up now, and you're going inside. Because you can't sleep out in the car.' The phone went dead before I could whine at her anymore. Marianne was right, like usual. I hated that she just gave me information and helped me think, but wouldn't tell me what to do. Of course, if she'd tried to boss me around, I wouldn't have tolerated it. I made my own choices, and when someone pushed me, it just made me more determined to ignore them, so Marianne never pushed. Here's your information, here are your choices, now go be a grown-up and make them.

I got out of the Jeep and hoped I was grown-up enough for this particuliar choice.

II

THE LIVING ROOM was dark as I entered the house. The only light was from the kitchen. One or both of them had walked through the pitch-dark living room and only hit a light switch when they went to the kitchen to check messages on the machine, which was on the kitchen counter. Leopards' eyes are better in the dark than a human's, and Micah's eyes were permently stuck in kitty-cat mode. He often walked through the entire house with no lights, just drifting from room to room, avoiding every obstacle, gliding through the dark with the same confidence I used in bright light.

There was enough light from the kitchen, so I, too, left the living room dark. The white couch seemed to give off its own glow, though I knew that was illusion, made up of the reflective quality of the white, white cloth. I was pretty sure the men had both gone to change for the night. Most lycanthropes, whatever the flavor, preferred fewer clothes, and Micah didn't like dressing up. I walked into the empty kitchen not because I needed to, but because I wasn't ready to go to the bedroom. I still didn't know what I was going to do.

The kitchen held a large dining-room table now. The breakfast nook on its little raised platform with its bay window looking out over the woods still held a smaller four-seater table. Four had been more chairs than I needed when I moved into this house. Now, because we usually had at least some of the other wereleopards bunking over due to emergency, or, often, just the need to be close to more of their group, their pard, we needed a six-seater table. Actually we needed a bigger one than that, but it was all my kitchen would hold.

There was a vase in the middle of the table. Jean-Claude had sent me a dozen white roses a week after we started dating. Once we had sex, he'd added one red rose, so it was actually thirteen. One red rose like a spot of blood in a sea of white roses and white baby's breath. It certainly made a statement.

I smelled the roses, and the red one had the strongest scent. Hard to find white roses that smelled good. All I had to do was call Jean-Claude. He was fast enough to fly here before dawn. I'd fed off of him before, I could do it again. Of course, that would simply be putting off the decision. No, it would be hiding. I hated cowardice almost more than anything else, and calling on my vampire lover in this instance was cowardice.

The phone rang. I jumped back so hard that the roses rocked in their vase. You'd think I was nervous, or guilty of something. I got the phone on the second ring. The voice on the other end was cultured, a professor's voice, but it wasn't a professor. Teddy was over six feet, and a serious weight lifter. That he also had a very fine mind and was articulate had surprised me the first time I'd met him. He looks like dumb muscle and talks like a philosopher. He was also a werewolf. Richard had allowed the wolves that wanted to help to join the coalition. 'Anita, this is Teddy.'

'Hey, Teddy, what's up?'

'I am fine, but Gil is not. He will be, but right this moment we are in the emergency room of Saint Anthony's.'

Gil was the only werefox in town. So he depended a great deal on the 'Furry Coalition,' as the local shapeshifters and even the local police had started calling it. The coalition had orginally been designed to promote better understanding and cooperation among the various animal groups, but we'd branched out to dealing with the human world, to try and promote better understanding with them, too. One great big love fest.

'What happened?' I asked.

'Car accident. A man ran a red light. We've got other victims in the emergency room that are still ranting at the man. If Gil had been human, he'd have been killed.'

'Okay, so he called the answering service and got your cell phone number, and . . .'

'A policeman at the accident site noticed that Gil was healing much faster than he should have been.'

'Okay, why do I think this is going somewhere bad?'

'Gil was unconscious, so someone called the number in his wallet marked in case of emergencies. He has no family, so it was the answering service number. By the time I got to the hospital, Gil was handcuffed to a bed rail.'

'Why?'

'The policeman, who is still by his side, says he's afraid Gil will be dangerous when he wakes up.'

'Shit. That is illegal,' I said.

'Technically, yes, but the officer can, at his discretion, prevent harm from coming to the citizenry.'

'That's not what the cop said.'

'Actually, he said, "until I know what the fuck he is, I'm just playing it safe."'

I nodded, even though he couldn't see me. 'That sounds more like it. So you're there to make sure he doesn't put Gil in a safe house.' Safe houses were really prisons for lycanthropes. They'd been designed originally for new lycanthropes, so you had someplace safe to go during your first few full moons. It was a good idea, since the first few moons could turn into a killing spree, unless you had other shapeshifters to watch over you. The newly furry spent a few full moons with no memory of what they'd done, and very little human in them while they were in animal form. The safe houses were a good idea in theory, but in practice, once you went in, they never let you out. You never had enough control to pass their tests and get out. You were dangerous and would always be dangerous. The ACLU had begun the legal battles on grounds of illegal imprisonment without due process, but so far they were still bad places to be sent.

'The hospital seems worried that Gil is dangerous and has mentioned that.'

'Do you need a lawyer down there?'

'I have taken the liberty of calling the law firm that the coalition has on retainer.'

'I'm surprised it's gone this bad, this soon. Usually, you need an attack to get them handcuffing people and talking safe house. Is there something you're not telling me?'

He hesitated.

'Teddy?' I said his name the way my father used to say mine when he suspected I was doing something I shouldn't have been.

'The emergency room staff are wearing full hazardous material gear.'

'You're joking,' I said.

'I wish I were.'

'Is everyone just panicking?'

'I believe so.'

'Is Gil still unconscious?'

'In and out.'

'Well, stay with him, wait for the lawyer. I can't come down tonight, Teddy. I'm sorry.'

'That is not why I called.'

I had one of those uh-oh moments. 'Okay, then why did you call?'

'There is another emergency that needs someone right now.'

'Shit, what?'

'One of the pack called. He is at a bar. He has had far too much to drink, and he is fairly new.'

'Are you saying he's going to lose control in the bar?'

'I fear so.'

'Shit.'

'You keep saying that,' he said.

'I know, I know, profanity doesn't solve anything.' Teddy had started commenting on how much cussing I did. Him and my step-mother.

'I can't come down, Teddy.'

'Someone must. The lawyer is not here, and you know there is that little law on the books that they can sign an unconscious shapeshifter into a safe house if they deem him a danger. I do not understand why everyone is panicking this badly, but if I leave Gil alone, I think we will be trying to get him out of a place that has no bail.'

'I know, I know.' I was really happy that Richard had allowed the wolves to join the coalition. They were the largest shifter population in town, so the wolves came in handy to help man the phones and the emergencies. The downside was that Richard felt that if the pack were going to help, then the pack could take advantage of the emergency service. It sounded fair, but since there were nearly six hundred werewolves in the area, it had quadrupled our emergencies. The wolves gave us enough person power to meet the demands. It was a blessing and a problem all in one.

'Did the wolf call his brother?' *Brother* was slang for the older more experienced werewolf that all the new wolves got. They carried their number for emergencies.

'He says he did and got no answer. He sounded very fragile, Anita. I fear that if he changes in the bar, they'll call the police . . .'

'And they'll shoot him,' I finished it for him.

'Yes.'

I sighed into the phone.

'I take it you can't make this one, either,' Teddy said.

'I can't, but Micah can.'

Micah came into the kitchen about that time. He looked a question at me. He'd already changed out of the suit, and knowing him, hung it up. He was wearing a pair of sweat pants and nothing else. Just the sight of him shirtless and padding barefoot across the floor made my heart go pit-a-pat. He'd tied his hair back in a loose pony-tail, but I could forgive that, when I could see the fine muscle of his chest and stomach. His arms and shoulders looked like some weight lifting had gone into them, but truthfully, most of it was natural. Not all, but most. He was just shaped nicely.

'Anita, are you still there?' I realized that Teddy had been saying something and I hadn't heard him.

'Sorry, Teddy, can you repeat that?'

'Do you want me to give you the address of the bar, or wait to talk to Micah?'

'Micah is right here.' I handed him the phone, and he took it with raised eyebrows.

I explained as briefly as I could.

Micah put his hand over the phone. 'Are you sure this is a good idea?'

I shook my head. 'Almost sure it's not, but I can't take the run. Not with the *ardeur* about to surface sometime in the next minute or the next two hours. I'm stuck here until it's fed.'

'I know, but maybe Nathaniel could go?'

'What? Go down to a bar in maybe a bad section of town and arm wrestle a werewolf so new he can't drink safely?' I shook my head. 'Nathaniel has many fine skills, but this isn't one of them.'

'You're not really good at it either,' he said, with a smile to soften the harsh truth.

I smiled back, because he was sooo right. 'No, I could have done the hospital run and kept Gil out of a safe house, but I couldn't talk down the werewolf. I could shoot him, but not talk him down. Not if I don't know him.'

Micah got on the phone long enough to take the address and name of the bar down, then hung up. He looked at me, face careful, neutral with an edge of concern. 'I'm okay with you and Nathaniel being here alone for the *ardeur*. The question is, are you okay with it?'

I shrugged.

He shook his head. 'No, Anita, I need an answer before I leave.'

I sighed. 'You need to get there before the wolf loses it. Go, we'll be alright.'

He looked like he didn't believe me.

'Go,' I said.

'It's not just you I'm worried about, Anita.'

'I will do my best for Nathaniel, Micah.'

He frowned. 'What does that mean?'

'It means what it says.'

He didn't look happy with the answer.

'If you wait around for me to say, Oh, yes, it's fine that I'm going to feed the *ardeur* and fuck Nathaniel, the wolf in question will have shapeshifted, been shot by the cops, and maybe taken some civilians with him before you even leave the house.'

'You're both important to me, Anita. Our pard is important to me. What happens here tonight could change . . . everything.'

I swallowed hard, because I suddenly didn't want to meet his eyes.

He touched my chin, raised my face up to meet his gaze. 'Anita.'

'I'll be good,' I said.

'What does that mean?'

'I'm not sure, but I'll do my best, and that is the best I can offer. I won't really know what I'm going to do until the *ardeur* rises. Sorry, but that's the truth. To say anything else would be a lie.'

He took a deep breath that made his chest rise and fall nicely. 'I guess I'll have to settle for that.'

'What exactly do you want me to say?' I asked.

He leaned in and laid a gentle kiss against my lips. We rarely kissed so chaste, but this close to the *ardeur*, he was being careful. 'I want you to say you'll take care of this.'

'Define take care of it?'

He sighed again, shook his head, and stepped back. 'I've got to get dressed.'

'Are you taking your car or the Jeep?'

'I'll take my car. You might get a call from the police for another body, and your gear is all in the back of the Jeep.' He smiled at me, almost sadly, and left to go get dressed. He made a soft exclamation as he went around the corner. He spoke in low voices with another man. The cadence was wrong for Nathaniel.

Damian glided around the corner. 'You must be very distracted not to have sensed me sooner.' He was right, I was good at sensing the undead. No vamp should have been able to get this close without me knowing, especially not Damian.

Damian was my vampire servant, as I was Jean-Claude's human servant. The *ardeur* was Jean-Claude and Belle Morte's fault, something about their line had contaminated me. But Damian as my servant, that was my fault. I was a necromancer, and apparently mixing necromancy with being a human servant had some unforseen side effects. One of them was standing across the kitchen staring at me with eyes the color of green grass. Humans didn't have eyes like that, but apparently Damian had, because becoming a vamp doesn't change your original physical description. It may pale you out, lengthen some of the teeth, but your hair and eye and skin color remain the same. The only thing that was probably more vibrant was his hair. Red hair that hadn't seen the sun for hundreds of years, so that it was almost the color of fresh blood, a bright, fresh scarlet. All vamps are pale, but Damian started life with that milk and honey complexion that some redheads have, so he was even paler than the norm. Or maybe it was the quality of his paleness, like his skin had been formed of white marble, and some demon or god had breathed life into that paleness. Oh, wait, I was that demon.

Technically, my power, my necromancy made Damian's heart beat. He was over a thousand years old, and he would never be a master vampire. If you aren't a master, then you need a master to give you enough power to rise from the grave, not just the first night, but every night. Sometimes people rise by accident with no master near, and that is how you get revenants. Walking corpses little better than zombies, but they take blood instead of meat, and they don't rot. Little problems like that is why there are vampire laws about how you attack humans and how you don't. Break the laws, and the vamps will kill you for it. And that's in countries where vampires are still illegal. In the United States where they have rights, the vamps are more civilized, if the police find out about the crime. If they can keep it secret they take care of their own. Even if it means killing their own.

Damian must have come straight from work, because though he, like most of the vamps fresh over from Europe, almost never wore jeans and tennis shoes, he also didn't like dressing up as much as Jean-Claude insisted on.

He was wearing a coat I'd seen before. It was a deep pine green, a frock coat like something out of the 1700s, but it was new, designed to gape open to expose the pale gleam of his chest and stomach. Embroidery nearly covered the sleeves and lapels of the coat, putting a little glitter of color near all that white skin. The pants were black satin, poofy, like there was way more cloth there than was needed for Damian's slender legs. He wore a wide green sash for a belt and a pair of black leather boots that folded over just above the knee, so that the outfit was very pirate-y.

'How was work?' I asked.

'Danse Macabre is the hottest dance club in St Louis.' He kept walking toward me, gliding rather. There was something about the way he looked at me that I didn't care for.

'It's the only place where people can go and dance with vampires. Of course it's hot.' I looked at him, concentrated, and I knew he had fed tonight, on some willing woman. Willing blood feeding was considered the same as willing sex. Just be of age, and you could feed the undead and have bite marks to show your friends. I'd ordered Damian to only feed from willing victims, and because of our bond together, he could not disobey me. Necromancers of legend could boss around all types of undead, and they had to do your bidding. The only undead I could boss around were zombies and Damian, and frankly, I found even that unsettling. I didn't like to have that kind of control over anyone.

Of course, there was one kind of control that Damian had over me. I wanted to touch him. When he entered a room, I had an almost overwhelming urge to touch his skin. It was part of what it meant to be master and servant. This attraction to your servants, this need to touch and tend to them was one of the reasons that most servants were treasured possessions. I think it also kept even the craziest, most evil of vamps from killing their servants out of hand. For often a vamp didn't survive the death of his servant, the bond was that close.

He walked around the table, fingers trailing on the backs of the chairs. 'And I am one of the vampires that they have been pressing their bodies up against all night.'

'Hannah is still managing the club, right?'

'Oh, yes, I am merely a cold body to send into the crowd.' He was around the table now, to the island that separated the working area of the kitchen from the rest of the room. 'I am merely color, like a statue, or a drape.'

'That's not fair. I've seen you work the crowd, Damian. You enjoy the flirting.'

He nodded, as he came around the end of the island. Nothing separated us now but the fact that I was still leaning against the far cabinets and he had stopped at the end of the island. The urge to close that distance, to wrap my hands around his body, was almost overwhelming. It made my hands ache with the need, and I ended with them pressed behind me, pinned by my body the way Nathaniel had leaned against the Jeep earlier.

'I enjoy the flirting very much.' He traced pale fingers along the edge of the island, slowly, tenderly, as if he were touching something else. 'But we are not allowed to have sex while we work, though some of them beg for it.' The emerald of his eyes spread and swallowed his pupils, so that he looked at me with eyes like green fire. His power danced along my skin, caught my breath in my throat.

My voice started out a little shaky, but I gained firmness as I talked, until the last was said in an almost normal voice. 'You've got my permission to date, or fuck, or whatever. You can have lovers, Damian.'

'And where would I take them?' He leaned against the island, arms crossing over that expanse of pale chest.

'What do you mean?'

'I have a coffin in your basement. It is adequate but hardly romantic.'

He could have said a lot of things that I'd expected, but that wasn't one of them. 'I'm sorry, Damian, it never ocurred to me. You need a room, don't you?'

He gave a small smile. 'A room to use for my lovers, yes.'

Then I realized something. 'You mean like bring strangers here. People you've just picked up, and have them like sleep over, be at the breakfast table in the morning?'

'Yes,' he said, and I understood the look on his face now; it was a challenge. He knew I wouldn't like the thought of strangers coming into the house, much less facing a strange woman that he'd simply brought home to fuck, first thing in the morning.

I had a tiny spurt of anger, and that helped me think. Helped push back that need to touch him that had nothing to do with the *ardeur*, and everything to do with power. 'I know you had a room at the Circus. Maybe we could arrange something with Jean-Claude, so you could take lovers back there.'

'My home is here, with you. You are my master now.'

I cringed a little at the master part. 'I know that, Damian.'

'Do you?' He pushed away from the island and came to stand just in front of me. This close the power shivered between us. It made him close his eyes, and when he opened them, they were still drowning emerald pools. 'If you are my master, then touch me.'

My pulse was jumping in my throat like a trapped thing. I didn't want to touch him, because I wanted to touch him so badly. In a way, this was part of the attraction between Jean-Claude and me, as well. What I'd taken for lust and new love was also partly vampire trickery. A trick to bind the servant to the master, and the master to the servant, so that both served the other willingly, joyfully. It had bothered me when I first realized that part of what I felt for Jean-Claude was somehow tainted with vampire mind games, though it wasn't on purpose from Jean-Claude's point of view. He couldn't help how it worked on me any more than I could help how it worked on Damian.

He was standing so close I had to crane my neck backward to see his face clearly. 'I want to touch you, Damian, but you're acting awfully funny tonight.'

'Funny,' he said. He moved in so close that the edges of his coat, the poofy satin of his pants brushed the thick cloth of my tuxedo pants. 'Funny, I don't feel funny, Anita.' He leaned his face close to mine, and whispered his next words, 'I feel half-crazed. All those women touching me, rubbing themselves against me, pressing their warm,' he leaned in so that his hair brushed my cheek, 'soft,' his breath felt hot against my skin, 'wet,' his lips touched my cheek, and I shuddered, 'bodies, against me.'

My breath shook on its way out, and my pulse was suddenly loud in my ears. It was hard to concentrate on anything but the feel of his lips against my cheek, though all his lips were doing was resting lightly against my skin. I swallowed hard enough that it hurt, and said, 'You could have gone with any one of them.'

He laid his cheek against mine, but it meant he had to bend over more, which moved his body farther from mine. Compromise. 'And could I trust that their windows were proof against sunlight?' He stood up and put a hand on either side of the cabinet behind me, so that I was trapped between his arms. 'Could I trust that they would not harm me, once the sun rose and I lay helpless?'

I tried to think of something to say, something helpful, something that would help me to think about something other than how much

I wanted to touch him. When in doubt be bitchy. 'I'm getting a crick in my neck with you standing this close.' My voice was only a little breathy when I said it. Good.

Damian put his hands around my waist, and just the solid feel of his hands around me stopped whatever else I meant to say. It stopped him for a moment, too. Made him bend his head down, eyes closed, as if he were trying to concentrate, or clear his mind. Then he lifted me, suddenly, and sat me on the edge of the counter. It caught me off guard, and he had put his hips between my knees before I could react. We weren't pressed together, except for his hands on my waist, but we were one step away from it.

'There,' he said, voice hoarse, 'now you can see me better.'

He was right, but it hadn't been what I meant him to do. I wanted breathing space, and instead my hands were free, and he was a hard thought away. My hands came to rest on his arms, and even through the heavy material of his coat I could feel the solidness of him. It was as if my hands had a mind of their own. I traced up the line of his arms, found his shoulders, and ended with my hands on the broadness of those shoulders, with his hair tickling along the back of my hands. There was something about my hands on his shoulders, or the silk of his hair on my skin that made me bend toward him. I wanted a kiss. Simple as that. It seemed wrong to be this near and not touch him.

He bowed his head toward mine. His eyes were like deep green pools, deep enough to drown in. He whispered, 'You have but to tell me stop, and I will stop.'

I didn't say stop. I slid my hands to the smooth pale line of his neck, and the moment I touched his bare skin with mine, I was calmer. I could think again. That was his gift to me, as my servant. He helped me be calmer, more in control. When I was touching him, it was almost impossible for me to lose my temper. He lowered my blood pressure, helped me think.

I cupped his face between my hands, because I wanted to touch him, but what I gained from his centuries of controlling his own emotions, was that when he put his lips against mine, I was not lost. Not overwhelmed unless I wanted to be overwhelmed. It wasn't that I felt nothing, because it wasn't possible to be enfolded in Damian's arms, pressed against his chest, have his lips caressing mine, and be unmoved. You'd have had to be made of stone not to melt into that embrace, just a little. But, as I'd gained calmness from him, he had begun to gain back the passion that he'd lost over the centuries. A passion not just for sex, but any strong emotion, because the master that made him tolerated no strong emotion, save fear. She'd beat everything else out of him over more centuries than most vampires ever survived.

He drew back enough to see my face. 'You're calm. Why are you calm? I feel crazed, and you give me peaceful eyes!' He grabbed my upper arms, and dug his fingers in until it hurt, and I still felt calm. 'It is cruel fate that makes you calmer and calmer the more we touch, and drives me more and more wild.' He gave me a small shake, his face raw with emotion. 'I am being punished, and I have done nothing wrong.'

'It's not punishment, Damian,' and even my voice was low and calm.

'Jean-Claude says that if you wished, you could gain calm only when you needed it. That you could touch me and enjoy touching me, but not be trapped behind this mask.' His fingers were digging in so hard, I was bruising.

'You're hurting me, Damian.' My voice was still calm, but there was an edge of heat to it, an edge of anger.

'At least you feel something when I touch you.'

'Let go of my arms, Damian.' And just like that, he released me, let me go as if my arms had grown hot to the touch, because he could not disobey a direct order from me. Whatever that order might be.

'Take a step back, Damian, give me some room.' I was angry now, even with the rest of his body touching me. When he did what I told him and was no longer touching me at all, the anger filled me up and spilled over my skin like heat. God, it felt good. I was used to being angry. I liked it. Not the most positive thing to say, but still true.

I started to rub my arms where he'd squeezed, then stopped. I didn't like letting anyone know how much they'd hurt me.

'I didn't mean to hurt you,' he said, and he was holding his own arms. I thought for a moment he was feeling my pain, then realized he was hugging himself to keep from touching me.

'No, you just want to fuck me.'

'That's not fair,' he said.

He was right, it wasn't fair, but I didn't care. Without him touching me, I could be as unfair as I wanted to be. I wrapped my anger around myself. I fed it with every petty impulse I'd fought for days. I should have remembered that one control is much like another. That if you throw away one kind of control, it makes other kinds harder to hold on to.

I unleashed my anger like you'd unleash a rabid dog. It roared through me, and I remembered a time when my rage had been the only warmth I allowed in my life. When my anger had been my solace and my shield. 'Get out, Damian, just go to bed.'

'Don't do this, Anita, please.' He held his hand out to me, would have touched me, but I moved back, just out of reach.

'Go, now.'

And with that he couldn't help himself. I'd given him a direct order. He had to obey.

He walked out, tears glittering in his green eyes. He passed Nathaniel in the doorway. Nathaniel gave me neutral eyes, a careful face. 'Micah had to go.'

I nodded, because I didn't trust my voice. I hadn't let myself get this angry in so long. It had felt good for a few moments, but I was already beginning to regret how I'd treated Damian. He hadn't asked to be my servant. The fact that I'd done it accidentally didn't make it any more right. He was an adult person, and I'd just ordered him to bed like he was a naughty child. He deserved better than that. Anyone did.

The anger pulled back, and even my skin felt cooler. The term *hot with anger* was very real. I was ashamed of what I'd just done. I understood why, in part. I so did not need another man tied to me by metaphysics that demanded a piece of my bed, or at least my body. I didn't need that. I especially didn't need a man who might not even be capable of feeding the *ardeur*. Because even in the middle of the worst of the *ardeur*, Damian's touch could cool that fire. With him holding my hand, the *ardeur* could not rise, or at least it could be put away for hours. So why didn't I paste Damian to my body? Because of how much more he wanted from me than I was comfortable with giving. I could not use him to help me fight the *ardeur* if I wasn't willing to give in to that skin hunger we both felt for each other.

Nathaniel padded into the room, wearing nothing but a pair of silky jogging shorts. They were his version of jammies. He'd taken his braid out, so that his thick hair spilled around him like some kind of cape. 'Are you alright?'

I started to say, I owe Damian an apology, but I didn't say it, because in that one breath, the *ardeur* rose. No, not rose, engulfed, drowned, suffocated. I suddenly couldn't breathe past the pulse in my throat. My skin felt thick and heavy with it. I don't know what showed in my eyes, but whatever it was, it stopped Nathaniel where he stood, froze him like a rabbit in the grass that knows the fox is near.

The *ardeur* spilled outward, like invisible water, hot, wet, and suffocating. I knew when the power hit Nathaniel, because he shivered. Goose bumps broke on his body, as his very skin reacted to the power.

I'd shoved the *ardeur* down once tonight, and that had a price. I'd refused the touch of my servant, and that had a price. I'd embraced my anger, and let it spill out onto someone I cared about. That had a price, too. I didn't want Nathaniel to be the one who paid that price.

12

I DIDN'T REMEMBER crossing the room, but I must have, because I was standing in front of him. His eyes were wide, so wide, his lips half-parted. I was close enough to see the pulse in his throat beating against the skin of his neck like a trapped thing. I leaned in toward him, leaned just my face until I could smell the warm vanilla scent of his neck. Close enough to taste his pulse on my tongue like candy. And I knew this candy would be red and soft and hot. I had to close my eyes so that I didn't lean my mouth down to that point, didn't lick over his skin, didn't bite down and free that quivering piece of him. I had to close my eyes so I wouldn't keep staring at that pulsing, jumping . . . My own pulse was too fast, as if I would choke on it. I'd thought that feeding the *ardeur* on Nathaniel was the worst I could do, but the thoughts in my head weren't about sex. They were about food. Thanks to my ties with Jean-Claude and Richard, I had darker things inside me than the *ardeur*. Dangerous things. Deadly things.

I stayed perfectly still, trying to master my own pulse, my own heartbeat. But even with my eyes closed, I could still smell Nathaniel's skin. Sweet and warm and . . . close.

I felt his breath on my face, before I opened my eyes.

He had moved in so close that his face filled my vision. My voice came soft, half-strangled with the needs I was fighting. 'Nathaniel . . .'

'Please.' He whispered it as he leaned in, whispered it again as his mouth hovered above mine, he sighed. 'Please,' against my lips. His breath felt hot against my mouth, as if it would burn when we kissed.

His lips this close to mine had done one thing. I wasn't thinking about ripping his throat out anymore. I understood then that we could feed on sex, or we could feed on meat and blood. I knew that one hunger could be turned into another, but until that moment, where I could almost taste his lips on mine, I hadn't realized that there would come a point where *something* must be fed. I did not feed Jean-Claude's blood lust, though there was a shadow of it in me. I did not feed Richard's beast, with its hunger for meat, but that lived in me, too. I held so many hungers in me, and fed none of them, except the *ardeur*. That I could feed. That I did feed. But it was in that heartbeat, as Nathaniel kissed me, that I understood why I hadn't been able to control the *ardeur* better. All the hungers channeled into that one hunger. Jean-Claude's fascination with the blood that ran just under the skin. Richard's desire for fresh, bloody meat. I had pretended I didn't carry their hungers inside me, not really. But I did. The *ardeur* had risen to give me a way to feed, a way that didn't tear people's throats out, a way that didn't fill my mouth with fresh blood.

Nathaniel kissed me. He kissed me, and I let him, because if I drew back from it, fought it, there were other ways to feed, other ways that would leave him bleeding and dying on the floor. His lips were like heat against my skin, but part of me wanted something hotter. Part of me knew that blood would be like a scalding wave in my mouth.

I had a sudden image so strong that it made me stumble back from him. Made me push away from that warm, firm flesh.

I felt my teeth sinking into flesh, through hair that was rough and choking on my tongue. But I could feel the pulse underneath that skin, feel it like a frantic thing, the pulse running from me, like the deer had run through the forest. The deer was caught, but that sweet, beating thing lay just out of reach. I bit harder, shearing through the skin with teeth that were made for tearing. Blood gushed into my mouth, hot, scalding, because the deer's blood ran hotter than mine. Their warmth helped lead me to them. Helped me hunt them. The heat of their blood called me to them, made their scent run rich on every leaf they passed, every blade of grass that brushed them, carried that warmth away, betrayed them to me. My teeth closed around the throat, tore the front of it free. Blood sprayed out, over me and the leaves, a sound like rain. I swallowed the blood first, scalding from the chase, and then the meat that still held the last flickering of pulse, a last beat of life. The meat moved in my mouth as it went down, as if it were struggling, even now, to live.

I came back to the kitchen, on my knees, screaming.

Nathaniel reached out toward me, and I slapped at his hands, because I didn't trust myself to touch him. I could still taste the meat, the blood, feel it going down Richard's throat. It wasn't horror that made me slap at Nathaniel. It was that I had liked it. Gloried in the feel of blood raining down on me. The struggles of the animal had excited me, made the kill all the sweeter. Always when I touched Richard, there had been hesitation, regret, revulsion about what he was, but there had been no hesitation in that shared vision. He had been the wolf, and he had brought the deer down, taken its life, and there had been no regret. His beast had fed, and for this one moment, the man in him had not cared.

I shut down every shield I had between him and me, and it was only then that I felt him look up, felt him raise his bloody muzzle, and look as if he could see me watching him. He licked his bloody lips, and the only thought I had from him was good. It was good, and there was more, and he would feed.

I couldn't seem to cut myself off from him. Couldn't shut it down. I did not want to feel him sink teeth into the deer again. I did not want to be in his head for the next bite. I reached out to Jean-Claude. Reached out for help, and found . . . blood.

His mouth was locked on a throat, fangs buried into that flesh. I smelled that flesh, knew that scent, knew it was Jason, his *pomme de sang*, that he held clasped in his arms, clasped tighter than you hold a lover, because a lover does not struggle, a lover does not feel their death in your kiss.

The blood was so sweet, sweeter than the deer's had been. Sweeter, cleaner, better. And part of that better was the feel of his arms locked around us, holding us as tight as we held him. Part of what made this more was the embrace. The feel of Jason's heart beating inside his chest, beating against the front of our bodies, so that we could feel the franticness of it, as the heart began to realize something was wrong, and the more frightened it got, the more blood it pumped, the more of that sweet warmth poured down our throats.

All I could taste was blood. All I could smell was blood. It spilled down my throat, and I couldn't breathe. I was drowning. Drowning in Jason's blood. The world had run red, and I was lost. A pulse, a pulse in that red darkness. A pulse, a heartbeat, that found me, that brought me out.

Two things came to me at once. I was lying on cool tile, and that someone had me by the wrist. Their hand on my wrist. I opened my eyes, and found Nathaniel kneeling beside me. His hand on my wrist. The pulse in the palm of his hand beat against the pulse in my wrist. It was as if I could feel the blood running up his arm, smell it, almost taste it.

I rolled closer to him, curled my body around his legs, laid my head upon his thigh. He smelled so warm. I kissed the edge of his thigh, and he opened his legs for me, let my face slip between them, so that the next kiss was against the smooth warmth of his inner thigh. I licked along that warm, warm skin. He shuddered, and his pulse sped against mine. The pulse in the palm of his hand pushing against the pulse in my wrist, as if his heartbeat wanted inside me. But it wasn't his heartbeat that he wanted inside me.

A roll of my eyes, and I could see him swollen and tight against the front of his shorts. I licked up the line of his thigh, licked closer and closer to that thin line of satin that stretched over the front of his body.

I tasted his pulse against my lips, but it wasn't an echo from his hand. My mouth was over the pulse in his inner thigh. He let go of my wrist, as if now we didn't need it, we had another pulse, another, sweeter place to explore. I could smell the blood just under his skin, like some exotic perfume. I pressed my mouth over that quivering heat, kissed the blood just under his skin. Licked the jumping thud of his pulse, just a quick flick of my tongue. It tasted like his skin, sweet and clean, but it also tasted of blood, sweet copper pennies on my tongue.

I bit him, lightly, and he cried out above me. I slid hands over his thigh, held it tight, so that the next bite was harder, deeper. His meat filled my mouth for a second, and I could taste the pulse under his skin. Knew that if I bit down, that blood would pour into my mouth, that his heart would spill itself down my throat as if it wanted to die.

I stayed with my teeth around his pulse, fought with myself not to bite down, not to bring that hot, red, rush. I could not let go, and it was taking everything I had not to finish it. I reached down those metaphysical cords that bound me to Jean-Claude and Richard. I had a confusing image of meat and viscera, and other bodies crowding close. The pack was feeding. I shoved that image away, because it wanted me to bite down. Richard's muzzle was buried deep into the warmth of the body, buried in the sweet things inside. I had to run from those feelings, before I fed on Nathaniel the way they were feeding on the deer.

I found Jason lying pale on Jean-Claude's bed, bleeding on the sheets. Jean-Claude's blood thirst was quenched but there were other hungers. He looked up at me, as if he could see me. His eyes were drowning blue, and I felt it, the *ardeur* had risen in him. Risen in a wave of heat that left him staring down at Jason's still form with thoughts that had nothing to do with blood.

He spoke, his voice echoing through me, 'I must shut you out, *ma petite*, something is wrong tonight. You will force me to do things I do not wish to do. Feed the *ardeur*, *ma petite*, choose its flame, before another hunger comes and carries you away.' With that, he was gone. Gone as if a door had slammed shut between us. I had a moment to realize that he'd slammed a door between not just himself and me, but between Richard and me, as well. So that I was suddenly cut adrift.

I was alone with the feel of Nathaniel's pulse in my mouth. His flesh was so warm, so warm, and his pulse beat like something alive inside his skin. I wanted to free that struggling, quivering thing. I wanted to break it free of its cage. To free Nathaniel of this cage of flesh. To set him free.

I fought not to bite down, because some part of me knew that if I once tasted blood I would feed. I would feed, and Nathaniel might not survive it.

A hand grabbed mine, grabbed mine and held on. I knew who it was before I raised my face from Nathaniel's thigh. Damian knelt beside us. His touch helped me get to my knees, helped me think, at least a little. But the *ardeur* didn't go away. It pulled back like the ocean drawing back from the shore, but it didn't leave, and I knew it would come back. Another wave was building, and when it crashed over us, we needed a plan.

'Something's wrong,' I said, and my voice shook. I held on to Damian's hand like it was the last solid thing in the world.

'I felt the *ardeur* rise, and I thought, great, just great, left out again. Then it changed.'

'It felt wonderful,' Nathaniel's voice came distant and dreamy, as if all he'd been having was good foreplay.

'Didn't you feel it change?' I asked.

'Yes,' he said.

'Weren't you afraid?'

'No,' he said, 'I knew you wouldn't hurt me.'

'I'm glad one of us was so sure.'

He raised up onto his knees, from where he'd half swooned. 'Trust yourself. Trust what you feel. It changed when you tried to fight it. Stop fighting it.' He leaned in toward me. 'Let me be your food.'

I shook my head, and clung to Damian's hand, but it was as if I could feel the tide rushing back toward the shore. Feel the wave building, building, and when it came, it would sweep us away. I didn't want to be swept away.

'If Jean-Claude told you to feed the *ardeur*, then feed it,' Damian said. 'What I felt from you just now was closer to blood lust.' His face was very serious, sorrowful even. 'You don't want to know what blood lust can make you do, Anita. You don't want that.'

'Why is it different tonight?' It was a child asking someone to explain why the monster under the bed has grown a new and scarier head.

'I don't know, but I do know that for the first time when you touch me, I feel it. A dim echo, but I feel it. Always before, Anita, when you touched me, it went away.' He made a movement with his fingers like putting out a candle, 'snuffed out. Tonight . . .' He leaned over my hand, and I knew he was going to lay his lips across my knuckles. One of the gifts of the *ardeur* is that it lets you look inside someone's heart. It lets you see what they truly feel. When his lips touched my skin, I felt what Damian was feeling. Satisfaction. Eagerness. Worry, but that was fast fading under the feel of his lips on my skin. He wanted. He wanted me. He wanted to feed the hunger of his skin. The hunger of his body not so much for orgasm but for that need to be held close and tight, that need we all have to press our nakedness against someone else's. I felt his loneliness, and his need, even if it was only for one night, not to be lonely, not to be exiled down in the dark, alone. I saw how he felt about his coffin down in the basement. It was not his room. It was not his in any way. It was just the place he went to die every dawn. The place where he went to die, alone, knowing that he would rise as he had died, alone. I saw the endless stream of women that he had fed on, like pages in a book, a blonde, a brunette, the one with a tattoo on her neck, dark skin, pale skin, the one with blue hair, an endless stream of necks and wrists, and their eager eyes, and grasping hands, and nearly every night, it was in public view, as part of the

floor show at Danse Macabre. So that even his feedings were not private.
Even that was not special. It was eating so you wouldn't die, with no
meaning to it.

In the center of his being was a great emptiness.

I was supposed to be his master. I was supposed to take care of
him, and I hadn't known. I hadn't asked, and I'd been so busy trying
not to be tied to another man through some weird metaphysical shit,
that I hadn't noticed that Damian's life sucked.

'I'm sorry, Damian, I . . .' I don't know what I would have said,
because his fingers touched my lips, and I couldn't think. His fingers
held heat and weight that they'd never had before.

His eyes widened, surprised, I think, as surprised as I was at the
sensation. Or did my lips give heat to his skin, too? Did my lips
suddenly feel swollen and eager as his fingertips did to me, as if both
mouth and fingers were suddenly more?

I moved my lips against his touch, barely a movement, just enough
to press my mouth against the ripeness of his fingers; barely enough
to call it a kiss, but it wasn't his skin I tasted, or not the skin I was
touching. It was as if I laid my mouth against the most intimate parts
of him. There was the hard, solid press of his fingers, but the taste,
the smell of him, was the perfume of lower things, as if I were a
dog on the scent of where I wanted to be.

He drew his breath in with a shaking gasp, and when I rolled my
eyes up to see his face, the look in his eyes was one of drowning, as
if I already touched what I could taste. His eyes filled with emerald
fire, and just like that there was a line of desire carved from my
mouth down his fingers, his hand, his arm, his chest, his hips, to the
center of his body. I could feel him thick and rich and full of blood.
Could taste the warmth of him as if my mouth were nestled against
his groin. I could taste him, feel him, and when I slipped my mouth
over the tips of his fingers, slid something so much smaller, harder
into my mouth; his green eyes rolled back into his head, ginger lashes
fluttering downward. His breath sighed out in one word, 'Master.'

I knew he was right, in that one moment, I knew, because I remembered being on the other side of such a kiss. Jean-Claude could push desire through me as if his kiss were a finger drawn across my body, down my very nerves so that he touched things that no hand or finger could ever caress. For the first time I felt the other side of such a touch; felt what Jean-Claude had felt for years. He'd tasted my most intimate parts, long before he'd ever been allowed to touch them, or even see them. I felt what he'd felt, and it was wondrous.

Nathaniel touched my hand. I think I'd actually forgotten about him, forgotten about anything but the sensation of Damian's flesh against mine. Then Nathaniel touched me, and I could feel his body through the palm of my hand as if a line ran from the pulse in my palm down his body in a long line of heat and desire and . . . power.

I felt that power flare outward from my mouth and hand to their bodies. It was my power, the power Jean-Claude had woken in me by his marks, but it was also my power, my necromancy that burned like some cold fire through Damian's body, but when it hit Nathaniel's body, the power changed, shifted, became something warm and alive. In the blink of an eye, the power flared through me, through all of us, but it wasn't sex that I felt anymore, it was pain. I was trapped between ice and fire; a cold so intense that it burned, and the fire burned because that was what it was. It was as if half the blood in my body had turned to ice, so that nothing flowed, and I was dying; and the other half of my body held blood that was molten like melted gold, and my skin could not hold it. I was melting, dying. I screamed, and the men screamed with me. It was the sound of Nathaniel and Damian, their screams, not my own, that dragged some part of me above the pain.

That one blinded, aching part knew that if I let this consume me, we would all die, and that was not acceptable. I had to find a way to ride this, to control this, or we would be destroyed. But how do you control something that you don't understand? How do you ride something you can't see, or even touch? I realized in that moment that I touched nothing. That somewhere in the pain I'd let go of both of them. My skin was empty of their touch, but the link between us was still there. One of us, or all of us, had tried to save ourselves by letting go, but this was not a magic so easily defeated. I knelt alone on the floor, touching no one and nothing, but I could feel them. Feel their hearts in their chests as if I could have reached out my hand and carved those warm, beating organs from their bodies; as if their flesh was water to me. The image was so strong, so real, that it made me open my eyes, helped me ride down the pain.

Nathaniel was half crouched, his hand reaching out to me, as if I'd been the one who pulled away. His eyes were closed, his face screwed tight with pain. Damian knelt, pale face empty; if I hadn't been able to feel his pain, I wouldn't have known that his blood was turning to ice.

Nathaniel's hand touched mine, like a child groping in the dark, but the moment his fingers brushed me, the burning began to fade. I gripped his hand, and it didn't hurt anymore. It was still hot, but it was the beating pulse of life, as if the heat of a summer's day filled us.

The other half of my body was still so cold it burned. I took Damian's hand, and the moment we touched that, too, ceased to hurt. The magic, for lack of a better term, flowed through me; the chill of the grave and the heat of the living, and I knelt in the middle like something caught between life and death. I was a necromancer; I was caught between life and death, always.

I remembered death. The smell of my mother's perfume, Hypnotique, the taste of her lipstick as she kissed me good-bye, the sweet powdery scent of her skin. I remembered the feel of smooth wood under small hands, my mother's coffin, the clove scent of carnations from the grave blanket. There was a bloodstain on the car seat and an oval of cracks in the windshield. I laid a tiny hand on that dried blood and remembered the nightmares afterward, where the blood was always wet, and the car was dark, and I could hear my mother screaming. The blood had been dry by the time I saw it. She had died without me ever saying good-bye, and I had not heard her screams. She'd died almost instantly, and probably hadn't screamed at all.

I remembered the feel of the couch, rough and nobbly, and it smelled musty, because after Mommy went away nothing got cleaned. In that moment I knew it wasn't my memory. My father's German mother had moved in and kept everything spotless. But I was still small and hugging the side of that musty couch, in a room I'd never known, where the only light was the flickering of the television screen. There was a man, a huge dark shadow of a man, and he was beating a boy, beating him with the buckle end of a belt. He kept saying, 'Scream for me, you little bastard. Scream for me.'

Blood spurted from the boy's back, and I screamed. I screamed for him, because Nicholas would never scream. I screamed for him, and the beating stopped.

I remembered the feel of Nicholas spooning the back of my body, stroking my hair. 'If anything happens to me. Promise me, you'll run away.'

'Nicholas . . .'

'Promise me, Nathaniel, promise me.'

'I promise, Nicky.'

Sleep, and the only safety I ever knew, because if Nicholas watched over me, the man couldn't hurt me. Nicholas wouldn't let him.

The images broke then, shattering like a mirror that had been hit; glimpses. The man looming up and up; the first blow, falling to the carpet, blood on the carpet, my blood. Nicholas in the doorway with a baseball bat. The bat hitting the man. The man silhouetted against the light from that damned television, the bat in his hands. Blood spraying the screen. Nicholas screaming, 'Run, Nathaniel, run!' Running. Running through the yards. A dog on a chain, barking, snarling. Running. Running. Falling down beside a stream, coughing blood. Darkness.

I remembered battle. Swords and shields, and chaos. And try as I might, chaos was all I could see. A man's throat exploding in a bright gush of blood; the feel of my blade hacking so deep that it numbed my arm; the force of running headlong into someone else's shield with my own; being forced back down narrow stone steps; and over all that was a fierce joy, an utter contentment; battle was what we lived for, everything else was just biding time. Familiar faces swam into view, blue eyes, green, blond and red-haired, all like me. The feel of a ship under me, and a gray sea, running white with the wind. A dark castle on a lonely shore. There had been fighting there, I knew that, but that was not the memory I got. What I saw was a narrow stone stairway, that wound up and up into a dark tower. Torchlight flickered on those stairs, and there was a shadow. We ran from that shadow, because terror rode before it. The gate crashed down, trapped against it, we turned and made our stand. The crushing fear, until you could not breathe. Many dropped their weapons and simply went mad, at the touch of it.

The shadow stepped out into the starlight, and it was a woman. A woman with skin white as bone, lips red as blood, and hair like golden spiderwebs. Terrible she was, and beautiful, though it was a beauty that would make men weep, rather than smile.

But she smiled, that first curve of those red, red lips, that first glimpse of teeth that no mortal mouth would hold. Confusion, then the feel of small white hands like white steel, and her eyes, her eyes like gray flames, as if ashes could burn. The images jumped, and Damian was lying in a bed, with that terrible beauty riding him. His body was filling up, about to spill over and into her; riding the edge of pleasure, when she changed it, with a flex of her will, as a flex of her thighs could give pleasure; a thought and he was drowning in fear. A fear so great and so awful that it shriveled him, tore him back from pleasure, threw him close to madness. Then it would pull back like the ocean pulling away from the shore, and she would begin again. Over and over, over and over; pleasure, terror, pleasure and terror, until he begged her to kill him. When he begged she would let him finish, let him ride pleasure to its conclusion, but only if he begged.

A voice broke through the memories, shattered it. 'Anita, Anita!'

I blinked, and I was still kneeling between Nathaniel and Damian. It was Damian that had called my name. 'No more,' he said.

Nathaniel was crying and shaking his head. 'Please, Anita, no more.'

'Why are you blaming me for the tour down bad memory lane?'

'Because you're the master,' Damian said.

'So it's my fault we're reliving the worst events of our lives?' I searched his face, while I kept a tight grip on his hand. It wasn't erotic anymore, it was more like their hands were safety lines.

'You are the master,' Damian repeated.

'Maybe it's over, whatever it was, maybe it's finished.' He gave me a look that was so like one of Jean-Claude's that it was unnerving. 'What's with the look?' I asked.

'I can still feel it,' Nathaniel said, and his voice was hushed, thick with fear.

'If you would stop arguing and start paying attention to what's happening, you'd feel it, too,' Damian said, and he wasn't talking to Nathaniel.

I shut my mouth, it was the best I could do for not arguing, but even silence was enough. Into that brief silence I felt power like something large had pushed against a door in my head. A door that would not hold for long.

'How did you break us free of it this much?'

'I'm not a master, but I am over a thousand years old. I've learned some skills over the years, just to stay sane.'

'Alright, Mr Smartie-Vampire, what's happening to us?'

He squeezed my hand, and something in his eyes said plainly that he didn't want to say it out loud. I realized that I couldn't feel his emotions.

'You're shielding us all, aren't you?'

He nodded. 'But it won't hold.'

'What is it? What's happening to us? Why are we sharing memories?'

'It's a mark.'

I frowned at him. 'What?' Marks were metaphysical connections. I shared them with both Jean-Claude and Richard.

'I don't know what number, but it's a mark. It's not the first, maybe not even the second. Maybe the third? I've never had a human servant, or an animal to call. I've never been part of a triumvirate. You have, so you tell me.'

'Us,' Nathaniel said, in that breathy, scared voice.

I looked into those wide lavender eyes. He was waiting for me to make this better. The problem was, I didn't know how. I didn't know how it had begun, so how could I end it? I turned away from the utter trust in his face, because I couldn't think looking into his eyes. I tried to think back to the third mark. There had been a sharing of memories, but it had been benign. Glimpses of Jean-Claude feeding on perfumed wrists, sex with women wearing way too many undergarments; Richard running in wolf form in the forest, the rich world of scent that he had in that form. They had all been sensual, but safe memories. It had never occurred to me to ask either of them what memories they'd gotten from me. I probably didn't want to know.

'Third mark, I think. Though with Jean-Claude in charge it was just flashes of memory; mostly sensual, nothing too serious. Why are we trapped in therapy hell?'

'What did you think of just before the memories began?' Damian asked.

'Death,' I said, 'I was thinking about death, I don't know why.'

'Then think of something else, quickly.' His voice held a hint of panic, and I could feel why. I could feel that door in my head beginning to bow outward as if it were melting. I knew that when it went, we better have a plan.

'I didn't try to mark anybody,' I said.

'Do you know how to stop it?' he asked.

'No,' I said.

'Then think of something else, something better.'

'Think happy thoughts,' Nathaniel said.

I gave him a look. 'Who do I look like – Peter Pan?'

'What?' Damian asked.

'Yes, I mean no, but think,' Nathaniel said. 'Think happy thoughts. Think like you need to fly. I survived what happened after . . . after Nicholas died. But I do not want to live through it twice. Please, Anita, think happy thoughts.'

'Why don't one of you think happy thoughts?' I asked.

'Because you're the master, not us,' Damian said, 'your mind, your attitudes, your desires, are what will rule how this goes, not ours. But for God's sake, stop thinking about the worst things that ever happened to you, because I don't want to see the worst that I remember. Nathaniel's right, think happy thoughts.'

'Happy thoughts,' Nathaniel said, and he wrapped both his hands around one of mine. 'Please, Anita, happy thoughts.'

'I am fresh out of pixie dust,' I said.

'Pixie dust?' Damian said, but he shook his head. 'I don't know what you are talking about. Just think of something pleasant, happy, anything, anything at all.'

I tried to think happy. I thought about my dog Jenny, who had died when I was fourteen, and crawled out of the grave a week after she died. Crawled out of the grave and into bed with me. I remembered the weight of her, the smell of fresh-turned earth, and ripe flesh.

'No!' Damian screamed. He jerked me to face him, his eyes wild. 'No, I will not see what comes next in my story. I will not!' He grabbed my upper arms and turned me to face him, shaking me. Nathaniel wrapped himself around my waist, huddling around my body. Damian said, 'Don't you have any good memories?'

It was like one of those games where they tell you not to think of something or to think of something. I was supposed to think of good things, and for the life of me, everything ended badly. My mother had been wonderful, but she'd died. I'd loved my dog, but she'd died. I'd loved Richard, but he'd dumped me. I thought I'd loved someone once in college, but he'd dumped me. I thought about the feel of Micah's body, but I was waiting for him to dump me, too. Nathaniel hugged me tighter, his face buried against my back. 'Please, Anita, please, happy thoughts, fly for me, Anita, please, God, fly for me.'

I touched his arm, his hand, and thought of the vanilla scent of his hair. Thought of his face alive and listening as Micah read to us. I still thought Micah would go from Prince Charming to the Big Bad Wolf (no anthropomorphic bias intended), but Nathaniel would never dump me. There were moments when the thought of having Nathaniel with me forever panicked the hell out of me, but I forced that worry down. Pushed it away. I concentrated on the feel of him, and as if he felt my thoughts, he began to relax against me. He came to his knees behind me, his arms still around my waist, spooning our bodies together. He leaned his face over my shoulder, and I caught the sweet scent of his skin. I had my happy thought. I wouldn't fly because Nathaniel had asked me to, I would fly because of Nathaniel.

I laid a kiss against his cheek, and he wound himself around the back of my body, rubbing his cheek against the side of my face, my neck.

Damian still held my arms in his hands, but loosely now. He stared down at both of us. 'I take it you found a happy thought?'

I breathed in that clean vanilla scent and gazed up at Damian. 'Yes.' My voice was already thick with the scent of skin and the sensation of Nathaniel's body against mine. I thought, *It's like he's a living comfort object, like a teddy bear or a penguin*, but even as I thought that, I knew it was only partial truth. My stuffed toy penguin, Sigmund, had never kissed my neck, and never would. It was one of Sigmund's charms. He didn't make many demands on me.

That door in my mind was melting, like a block of ice left in the sun. Panic fluttered in my chest, and I knew that panic would be a bad emotion to take behind that melting door. I pulled Damian down to us and whispered, 'Kiss me.'

His lips touched mine, and the door vanished. But we didn't get memories this time, we got the *ardeur*. For the first time, I embraced it, called it pet names, and did the metaphysical equivalent of saying, come and get me. Come and get us.

13

I'D NEVER EMBRACED the *ardeur* before. I'd been overwhelmed by it, conquered by it, given in to it, but never lowered my flag and surrendered to it, not without at least a fight. Jean-Claude had told me that if I could only stop fighting it wouldn't be so terrible. That once a little control was gained, you needed to 'make friends' with the power. I'd given him a look, and he'd dropped the subject, but, he was right, and he was wrong. For him I think it would have been a seduction, but it was me, and the fact that I could still think while it was happening was a problem more than a blessing.

I was okay with my tuxedo jacket going bye-bye. I was okay with Damian's green coat sliding to the floor, even if it did leave his upper body pale and naked, with the fine muscles gliding under skin the color of fresh, white sheets. Nathaniel was the problem, or rather my confusion about him. I ran my hands up the unbelievable warmth of his skin, but the look in his lavender eyes was too much. I did not love Nathaniel, not the way I needed to, but the look in his eyes left no doubt how he felt about me. This was wrong. I could not take this from him, if he were in love with me, and I was not in love with him. I could not do it.

I pulled my hands away, shaking my head. Damian was molded against my back, but the moment I pulled away from Nathaniel, his eager hands slowed. 'Shit,' he whispered, and leaned his face against the top of my head.

Nathaniel's eyes went from shining with love, to something darker, older. He put his hands on either side of my face, cradling me. 'Don't pull away,' he said.

'I have to.'

'If it's not sex, it will be blood, Anita, can't you feel it?' Damian asked.

I could feel something. It was as if this time it was I who put up the shields. But there was still something large and frightening on the other side. Something that I had put in process, but not on purpose, something that was hungry. It didn't care what it fed on, but it would, eventually, feed on something.

Damian's hands were still on my shoulders, but he'd leaned his body back enough so we no longer touched anywhere else. 'Anita, please . . .'

I turned in Nathaniel's hands, so that I could glimpse Damian's face. 'It's wrong, Damian.'

'The sex, or who the sex is with?' he asked.

I took a breath to answer him, but Nathaniel's hands closed round my face. He turned me back to look at him, and I was suddenly almost painfully aware of the strength in his hands. A strength that could have crushed my face rather than cradled it. He was so submissive that he rarely reminded me of how very strong he was, how dangerous he could have been, if he'd been a different person.

I started to say, Let go of me, Nathaniel, but only got as far as, 'Let go,' before he kissed me. The feel of his lips on mine stopped my words, froze my mind. I couldn't think, couldn't think about anything but the velvet feel of his mouth on mine. Then something seemed to break inside of him, some barrier, and his tongue thrust into my mouth as deep and far as it could go. The sensation of him thrusting that much of himself that deeply into me tore my shields away, and since no one else was fighting, the *ardeur* roared back to life. It roared back to life on the edge of Nathaniel's lips, his hands, his need.

There was a confusion of ripping cloth, buttons snapping and raining down on us. Hands, hands everywhere, and the sound of clothing ripping. My body jerked with the force of my clothes being ripped away, and my hands were ripping at their clothes. It was as if every inch of my skin craved every inch of their skin. I needed to feel their nakedness glide over mine. My skin felt like a starved thing, as if I hadn't touched anyone in ages.

I knew whose skin hunger I was channeling. It wasn't just sex that Damian had missed. There are needs of the body that can be mistaken for sex, or lead to sex, but it isn't sex that they are about.

There was one leg left of my pants, pooled around my ankle. My vest flapped open, and the shirt was in shreds. It was Damian's hand from behind that grabbed a handful of my panties and pulled, ripping them off my body, leaving me nude from the waist down. I might have turned around to see how much clothing he still had on, but Nathaniel was in front of me. His shorts had been shredded. By me, I think. He knelt on the floor in front of me, naked. I almost never let Nathaniel be nude around me. It had been one of the reasons I'd been able to resist taking those last steps with him. Just keep your clothes on and nothing too bad will happen.

Now, he knelt in front of me, and all I could do was gaze up the line of his body. His face with those amazing eyes, that mouth, the line of his neck spilling into the wide, hard flesh of his shoulders, the chest that showed the weight lifting he'd been doing, the curve of his ribs under muscle leading my gaze to the flat plains of his stomach, the slight dimple of flesh that was his belly button, the rich swell of his hips, and finally the ripeness of him. I'd seen him totally nude and excited only once before. I didn't remember him being this wide, not quite this long; of course he hadn't been pressed this tight to his own stomach, as if the very ripeness of his flesh was almost too much to contain. He seemed thick and heavy with need, as if the lightest touch might make him spill that ripeness out and over me.

I started to reach for him, but Damian chose that moment to brush the head of his own ripeness against the back of my body. The movement made me writhe and lower the front of my body, raising myself upward to him like an offering, like something in heat. The thought helped me swim back up into control, at least a little. I'd never even seen Damian nude, and now he was about to plunge that nudeness into my body. It seemed wrong. I should see him first, shouldn't I? There was no logic to the argument. No logic left to anything, but it made me turn my head, made me look at him.

The blood red of his hair spilled over his shoulders so that it framed the unbelievable whiteness of his body. He was narrower of shoulder, of chest, and his waist seemed to go on forever, smooth and creamy, like something you should lick down, until you found the center of his belly button, and just under that, the length of him. He rode out from his body, so it was harder to judge length. He seemed carved of ivory and pearl, and where the blood ran close to the surface he blushed pink like the shine inside a seashell, delicate and shining. I realized in that moment that he had been paler in life than any vampire I'd ever seen nude, and his body was almost ghostlike in its coloring, as if somehow he wouldn't be real.

Nathaniel's face brushed mine, brought my attention back to him. He had knelt down so low that his face, like mine, was almost touching the floor. He pressed his cheek against mine and whispered, 'Please, please, please,' over and over, and between each *please* he kissed me, a light touch of lips; please, kiss, please, kiss. With his kisses and his voice warm against my face, he brought us both up to our knees again. I'd been so aware of his face, his mouth, his eyes, that I hadn't thought what kneeling this close would do until his nude body pressed against the front of mine. Until the thick, solid length of him pressed between us, pinned against my stomach by the push of our bodies. He was so warm, so unbelievably warm, so warm, almost hot, and the push of him against my body was so solid, as if he were fighting not to push himself through the front of me. To make a new opening, anything, anything, just to be in the warm depths of my body. It took me a second to understand it was Nathaniel's need I was feeling. That he did want that badly, but it was my wanting, too. My wanting and denying that want, that helped make this moment what it was. Over all that, was Damian at my back, his body one huge piece of need. Nathaniel and I were being drowned in Damian's skin-hunger. So lonely, so terribly lonely. And under that was Damian's fear. Fear that this would not happen, that he would be exiled back to his coffin, with all this undone. His loneliness was like a theme underneath his lust, and I had a glimpse of a room high in the castle. A room that overlooked the sea. Silver bars upon the windows, heavy with runes, and the sound of the surf always through the windows, so that even if he turned away, he could still hear it. She'd given him one of the best rooms in the castle as his prison, because she had a way of knowing what things meant to you. A way of knowing what would hurt the most. It was her gift.

Someone kissed me, hard and fast, forcing my mouth open, pushing his tongue so far in I almost choked, but it brought me back, brought us all back from that lonely room and the sound of the sea on the rocks below.

Nathaniel drew back enough to say in a harsh whisper, 'Happy thoughts, Anita, happy thoughts.' Then his mouth was on mine, tongue, lips, even teeth light against my own lips, so that it was more eating than kissing, but it brought a whimper from my throat, a small helpless sound of pleasure.

My hands were on his body, following the flow of his shoulders, his back, and the smooth silken curve of his ass. The back of his body filled my hands, and the front of him was like heat wrapped in flesh, as if we'd burst into flame.

Damian's hands were on the back of my bra; somehow it had survived that first rush. He snapped it open, and the front of it fell against Nathaniel's chest. Hands spilled over my breasts; one from behind, and one from the man pressed against the front of my body. Damian's touch was delicate, stroking. Nathaniel wrapped his hand around my breast and dug his nails into my flesh. It was Nathaniel's hand that bowed my back, tore my mouth away from his, and forced a scream from my mouth.

Damian hesitated, pulled back from that scream, as though he had to feel that it was pleasure and not pain. He didn't like to hear women scream. And just like that we were back in his memory. There was a room underneath the castle, torches, darkness, and women, any woman that she thought was prettier than she. No one was allowed hair more yellow than hers, eyes more blue, or breasts larger. These were all sins, and sins were punished. A rush of images; piles of yellow hair, wide blue eyes like cornflowers, and the spear that put them out, a chest as pale and fair as any he'd seen, and the sword . . .

Nathaniel screamed, 'Noooo!' He reached past me and grabbed a handful of red hair. He jerked Damian so hard against me, that just feeling the hard length of him made me writhe between them. 'Happy thoughts, Damian, happy thoughts.'

'I don't have any happy thoughts,' and on the heels of that statement were other dark rooms, and the smell of burning flesh.

I was the one who screamed this time, 'God, Damian, no more. Keep your nightmares to yourself.' The memory that had gone with that smell, had dampened the *ardeur*. I could think again, even pressed between both their bodies.

'Tell him to fuck you,' Nathaniel said.

I stared at him. 'What?'

'Order him to do it; then he won't be conflicted.'

It seemed almost ridiculous to be huffy, kneeling pretty much nude between two nude men, but it was still how I felt. 'Maybe *I'm* conflicted.'

'Almost always,' he said, and smiled to soften the words.

Damian's voice came, low and heavy with something like sorrow. 'She doesn't want to do this. She wants me to help her stop the *ardeur*, not to feed it. That's what she really wants, I can feel it, and that's what I have to do.'

'Anita, please, tell him.'

But Damian was right. He was the only port in a storm of sexual temptation. I valued his ability to make me not feel the *ardeur*. I valued that more than anything his body could do for me. And because I truly was his master, and that was my true wish, he had to help me do it. The coolness of the grave rose between us, and it wasn't frightening this time. It was soothing, comforting.

'Anita, no,' Nathaniel said, 'no.' He put his face against my shoulder. The movement put his body farther away from mine, and that helped me think, too.

I turned to look at Damian, though I didn't need to see his face to feel the overwhelming sadness. The sense of aching loss that seemed to fill him, like some bitter medicine. But the look on his face drove the sorrow home like a blade thrust through my heart. It hurt to see anyone's eyes full of such pain.

I turned to face him, still held lightly in both their arms. Nathaniel put the top of his head against my naked back, shaking his head. 'Anita, can't you feel how sad he is? Can't you feel it?'

I looked into Damian's cat-green eyes, and said, 'Yes.'

He turned his face away, as if he'd shown me more than he was comfortable with. I touched his chin and brought his face back to me. 'You don't want me,' and there was a world of loss in those words. A loss that tightened my throat, made my chest hurt. I wanted to deny it, but he could feel what I was feeling. He was right, I didn't want him, not the way I wanted Nathaniel, let alone the way I wanted Jean-Claude or Micah. What do you say when someone can read your emotions, so that you can't hide behind polite lies? What do you say when the truth is awful, and you can't lie?

Nothing. No words would heal this. But I'd learned there were other ways to say you're sorry. Other ways to say, I'd change it, if I could. Of course, even that was a lie. I wouldn't lose the cool reserve that Damian could give me, not for anything.

I kissed him, and meant for it to be light, gentle, an apology that words could not make, but Damian thought he'd never get this close to me again. I felt a fierceness rise up through him, a desperation that made him tighten his grip on my arms, made him thrust his tongue into my mouth, and kiss me hard and eager, and angry.

I tasted blood and assumed he'd nicked me with his fangs. I swallowed the sweetish taste of the blood without thinking. Then I could smell the ocean, smell it like salt on my tongue. We drew back enough to look into each other's faces, and I saw the trickle of blood trailing over his lower lip. Nathaniel had time to say, 'I smell seawater.' Then the power flooded up and up and smashed us against each other. It ground us against the floor like a wave cracking a boat against the rocks. We screamed, and writhed, and I could not control it. If I'd been a true master, then I could have ridden it, helped us all, but I'd never meant to mark anyone. Never meant to be anyone's master. The fourth mark was crushing us, and I didn't know what to do. The inside of my head exploded in white star bursts and gray miasma. Darkness ate at the inside of my head. If I'd been sure we'd wake up again, I'd have welcomed passing out, but I wasn't sure. I didn't know. But it didn't matter; darkness filled up the inside of my head, and we all fell into it. No more screaming, no more pain, no more panic, no more anything.

14

I WOKE TO early morning sunlight. It left me blinking, and only after I could see through the warm dazzle of it, did I wonder, *Where am I?* and *Why am I on the floor?* Why was I naked on the floor? Without turning my head, I saw the chair legs and the little raised area that was my breakfast nook. Okay, I was in the floor of my own kitchen, naked. Why?

I heard the soft sounds of movement before I felt a hand brush mine. It seemed to take a lot of effort to look to my right, down my body, and see Nathaniel lying on the floor, more nude than I was. I still had the remnants of my tuxedo clinging to my legs. The tuxedo made me remember the wedding. I remembered talking to Micah after we got home. I remembered Micah had had to go out and save one of Richard's wolves. I remembered the *ardeur* rising and that something had gone wrong. I remembered that Damian had been there. He must have woken before we did and dragged himself down to his coffin. Trust the undead to recover quickest.

Someone groaned, and it wasn't Nathaniel, and it wasn't me.

I suddenly found I could turn my head, a lot quicker than I had before. Adrenaline will do that to you.

Damian lay on the floor, his upper body bathed in golden morning light, as if his white skin had been dipped in honey. Part of my mind registered the beauty of him, lying there in a pool of blood-red hair and golden light, but most of me was terrified. I was on my knees and grabbing for his leg before my body could argue. Nathaniel was beside me, and we jerked Damian out of the sunlight.

He was awake now; awake and screaming. He was out of the direct sunlight, but the kitchen faced east and north, and the room was bright with early morning light. Damian had backed into the cabinets, pressing his body into them as if he thought he could melt into them, and hide in the dark. I tried to take his arm, to get him to his feet, to get him out of the light, but he fought me. His hands were beating at his skin like someone covered in spiders, trying to bat away their darkest fears, when those fears are crawling on their body. But sunlight isn't spiders, and you can't brush it off of you.

I grabbed a flailing wrist and held on. I yelled above the screaming, 'Nathaniel, help me!'

Nathaniel fought for a grip on the other arm, and we pulled the vampire out of the light and into the curtained dimness of the living room. He didn't stop screaming. Even when we put him up against the wall, in the cool near-dark, he still shrieked. The moment we let go of his hands, he started beating at his skin again, as if he were putting out invisible fire.

But it shouldn't have been invisible flame. I'd seen a vampire burn in sunlight, and they flash burned, hot white flames, like magnesium. There was nothing invisible about it. They burned, and if they didn't get out of the light, they melted, even bone. It takes a hot fire to melt bone, but vamps in sunlight burn good.

Nathaniel was kneeling, trying to comfort Damian, to hold him, to just get him to stop swatting at things we couldn't see. I stared down at Damian and tried to think past the fear that was choking me. I was choking on Damian's terror. I couldn't think past it. I could barely breathe past it. I threw up shields, put metal in my mind against his fear, and tried to think. I looked down at Damian's white skin, and there was not a blister, not even a red spot. He wasn't burned. He wasn't burning. I didn't know why not. He should have burst into flames the moment the sunlight touched him, but he hadn't, and if he hadn't burned with the sunlight drowning him, then he wasn't going to burn here, in the dark.

I could hear the phone ringing in the other room, but it was dim over the sound of Damian's screams. For once I let it ring. If it was the police, they'd call back. If it was a friend, they'd call back. If it was another emergency, it could wait. One disaster at a time.

I knelt in front of him and tried to talk over the awful screaming. 'Damian, Damian, you're safe. You're okay. You're not burning.' I put my hands on either side of his face and screamed back at him, 'Safe, you're safe!'

His eyes stayed wide, the pupils like pinpoints. He wasn't hearing anything. It was like shock, but worse. If it had been an old movie, I'd have slapped him, but I wasn't sure that would help. What do you do with a hysterical vampire? What do you do with a hysterical anybody?

The front door burst open behind us. My eyes were dazzled by the sunlight that spilled over us. Gregory, one of my leopards, stepped out of that blaze of light. I don't know what I would have said, because Damian let out a sound that was beyond a scream. It was a sound that should never have come from a human throat. He was up and moving like a white and red blur, darting farther into the house, out of the warm blaze of light.

Nathaniel followed him in that faster-than-the-eye-can-see speed that shapeshifters have, and they'd both turned the corner before I got to it. I expected to see the basement door open, but it wasn't. Movement up the stairs caught my eye, and I saw Nathaniel clear the last step and vanish down the hall. In his panic, Damian had run up, not down, up into the part of the house where the vampires rarely went. Up into the part of the house where the drapes were open and the morning light streamed in. Shit.

15

I WAS NEARLY to the top of the stairs when I heard Gregory behind me. He called up after me, 'What's going on?'

I didn't know how to answer the question, so I ignored it. The upper hallway was a blaze of light, the big window at the end open to the risen sun. The hallway was empty. I thought, *Where are they?* and I knew. I could feel them, both of them in the smallest room to the left, our guest room. I had made one step toward the doorway when Damian came running out as if all the demons of hell were chasing him. He ran screaming into the room across the hall, which was the bathroom. Unfortunately, it had a window, too. All the rooms up here had windows. If we could get him into a closet, maybe.

He came running out of the bathroom and fell, and scrambled on all fours like an animal toward the next open door. He vanished inside, only his piteous screaming coming back out to tell us he'd found another open window, another wash of sunlight.

'Was that Damian?' Gregory asked.

I nodded.

Nathaniel came to the first door Damian had run out of, blood ran down his shoulder, and he was cradling his arm. He looked at me, and his eyes held all the sorrow in the world. 'He's gone crazy again.'

The last time Damian had gone mad, he'd killed several people, butchered them, not just fed. But that had been because I was his master, and I'd left town. I hadn't known I was his master then. I hadn't known that leaving him alone without the touch of my magic, or whatever you want to call it, would make him a revenant, a mindless killing thing.

If it had been my fault before, somehow it was my fault again. I was his master now more than ever; I had to be able to fix this.

'Gregory, close the drapes. Start with the ones at the end of the hall.' His blue eyes were wide, and his face held a dozen questions, but Gregory could follow orders when he wanted to, or you made him. He didn't argue, just started down toward the end of the hallway.

I went for the room that Damian had gone into, but I never made it, because he came tearing back out of it and nearly ran me down. I grabbed him, but my touch didn't calm him, and his didn't calm me, not today. He slammed me into the wall, and if I'd let go of his arm, he'd have run again, but I didn't let go. I hung on and got slammed into the wall on the other side of the hallway. Shit.

I yelled, 'Damian, stop it!' But either he couldn't hear me, or I'd lost the power to make him obey me. Either way, it wasn't good. When he tried to slam me into the wall again, I braced my legs and used his own momentum, turning him into the wall, so that his own strength drove him into it so hard, the plaster gave under the impact.

He came off the wall snarling, fangs bared, his face thinning down, his humanity folding away, until what pinned me to the floor wasn't Damian. The only thing that saved me from having my throat torn out was that little extra bit of speed I'd gained from all the metaphysical shit. It gave me the time to throw one hand across his throat and one hand into his chest. I held him off of me by an arm's length, my fingers curled around his throat. Normally, I'd have thrown an arm into his throat and not trusted that I could get a hand there in time, but the last two times I tried that manuevuer with a vampire, they'd torn up my arm. So I set my fingers in his throat and my palm against his chest, and tried to hold him off me.

His teeth snapped and snarled at me, like a dog on the end of its chain. Saliva splattered my face, trailed from his mouth as if he were a rabid animal. He struggled mindlessly to reach me, to sink those teeth into my flesh. If he'd been thinking like a person he'd have used his hands, his arms to overwhelm me, but he wasn't thinking like a person. So he fought my hands, pressing his body against the force of my hands, as if that were all that mattered. He pressed the strength of his madness against the push of my hands, and he began to press my arm inward. I don't know if he'd been sane whether my new metaphysics would have helped more, but he wasn't sane, and crazy anything is stronger than sane. It was like trying to bench-press pure muscle, a snarling, breathing force of nature. My arms began to bend, and I knew that if he got close enough, he'd tear me apart. His eyes had bled to green, and there was nothing in them but a mindless ferocity.

I had no weapons on me. I might have been able to tear his throat out. I didn't know if I was that strong now, or not. But he wasn't a master vamp, and I didn't know for certain that he'd heal if I pulled his throat apart. If he'd just been a bad guy, I'd have torn into him and done my best to take him out before he took me out, but Damian wasn't a bad guy, and whatever was wrong was somehow my fault. I couldn't kill him, because I wasn't master enough to handle him.

He pressed himself into me, and I put everything I had into keeping him away from my face and throat. My arms started to shake with the effort, and my elbows were bending. His face filled my vision, and his saliva dripped on my face. I did the only thing I could think of, I yelled for help.

Gregory was there, his hands on Damian's arm and shoulder, trying to use supernatural strength against supernatural strength. He slowed Damian's push toward my face, but only slowed it. Damian was like a human on angel dust, stronger even than he'd been, because there was no one home to help him regulate his force. He was all about that force, and his goal in life seemed to be my face.

Nathaniel grabbed Damian's other shoulder. Blood was still dripping down his arm, but it had slowed. Which meant Damian had found a way to injure him that didn't include teeth or nails, those wouldn't have started healing, yet. I think with the two of them pulling and me pushing, we might have made it, but Nathaniel's bloody arm was next to Damian's face. He was enraged, but all vampires, even revenants, react to fresh blood.

His neck turned in my hand, and I'd been so intent on pushing him away, that it surprised me. He would have sunk fangs into Nathaniel's arm, except Gregory was a fraction too quick, and a fraction too slow. He managed to get his arm halfway around Damian's neck, which put his wrist almost in the vampire's mouth. Damian did what any animal would do, he bit him.

Gregory screamed and tried to pull away. It worked, and it didn't. He pulled away from us, but the vampire went with him. They moved so fast, that Nathaniel fell against me, smearing blood down my skin. He was on his feet and moving toward the sounds of fighting farther down the hallway, before I'd gotten to my knees.

Damian had Gregory pinned on the floor, worrying at his arm like a dog with a bone. Even over Gregory's screams I heard the bone crack. Nathaniel was there, wrapping his arms around Damian's waist. He lifted him into the air, but the teeth stayed in Gregory's broken arm, so that Gregory was pulled to his knees by the pain and the fangs locked into his arm.

I was almost to them, when Damian remembered he could fly. He pushed off from the floor and smashed Nathaniel against the ceiling hard enough that plaster dust rained down on them, and when Damian touched ground he rolled out of Nathaniel's loosened grip. Damian had been a warrior once, and though Nathaniel and Gregory had the strength, they didn't know how to fight. Strength without training was no match.

I was suddenly the only one standing in the hallway, except for Damian. He came for me in a blur of movement. I got one foot planted and had a heartbeat to see him, think what I'd do, and do it. Years of practice in judo, and my body remembered, before my mind had caught up. I used his own momentum against him, one arm and his hip as the pivot points, and I threw him, as far and as hard as his own motion would let me.

He ended at the top of the stairs, crouched, and turned toward me, before I had time to marvel at how far I'd thrown him. Let's hear it for not being human anymore.

But a figure rose above him, coming up the stairs. It was Richard Zeeman, local Ulfric, Wolf-King, ex-fiancé, and in the wrong place at the worst time. I had a few seconds to see that his hair had grown out just enough to give some curl to his woefully short locks, that the white T-shirt made his fading tan summer-dark with contrast, that he was still one of the most handsome men I'd ever seen. Then the vampire turned, noticed him, and launched himself at Richard. He balanced them both for a second, then the other man's weight took them both, and Richard fell backward down the stairs, with the vampire riding him. They vanished from sight, and over the sound of their bodies falling down the stairs, I heard a woman start to scream.

16

I WENT TO the stairs, expecting to see them struggling on the steps, but the stairs stretched empty. I ran down the stairs toward the sound of fighting. Richard had taken the fight out into the living room, so he had room to use his long legs and arms.

He kicked Damian in the face hard enough that the vampire staggered backward. I got a profile glimpse of Damian's face; blood ran from his mouth and the right side of his face. Richard took the extra seconds that the vampire gave him to do a beautiful roundhouse kick to the other side of Damian's face. This one was hard enough that blood flew in a thin arc. Damian staggered, and I think would have gone down, but he bumped into the wall. He hesitated long enough for Richard to get set up for another kick. Back foot set, front foot, set but loose, body partially turned to give that pivoting strength, the way when you land a fist you turn the fist into the skin for that extra little bit of harm.

Looking at Richard with all his attention on the vampire, his body tensed and ready, hands held in loose fists, even though he was setting up for a kick, I was reminded that here was someone with preternatural strength that did know how to fight. There was blood on his left hand, and I couldn't tell if it was Damian's blood or his own.

A small sound jerked my attention to the far side of the living room. A woman I didn't know was standing near the television set. She was pale, dark-haired, and scared. I didn't have time to notice more. I was standing too close to the fighting to sightsee.

If Damian had just been a big bad vamp in my house, I'd have gotten my gun and finished him, but he wasn't a villain. It was

Damian, and somehow it was all my fault. I couldn't get a gun and just shoot him. For one of the few times in my life I was frozen, overwhelmed by my choices, or the lack of them.

Damian had been against the wall for so long – fifteen, thirty seconds – that I thought the fight might be over, that Richard might have actually kicked some sense into him; I was wrong. The vampire came off the wall in a white and red blur. Richard met the charge with a kick to Damian's chest. It wasn't a pretty kick, not like the roundhouse, but the sound of its impact was thick and meaty. If he'd been human it would have dropped him, but he wasn't human, and it didn't.

He staggered backward, and I could have almost reached out a hand and touched his back. Damian went very still, like the old vamps can, as if he were some beautiful statue. Then I knew, knew that he was about to move and not toward Richard.

I had an extra few seconds to react, when he turned in a whirl of white skin and red hair, turned so fast that the colors blurred so he looked like a whirlwind of snow and blood.

I threw myself to one side, rolling over the back of the couch. I ended up on the other side of it, on the area rug. I had a heartbeat to stand, and Damian was on me.

I braced for it, but it was like trying to brace for a freight train. There was no stopping it, or fighting it. I was just suddenly falling backward with Damian on top of me. I didn't fight the fall, I used it. When my body met the floor I had one foot in Damian's stomach and two hands on his arms. A tome nage throw is the only throw in judo where you commit your whole body to it. Most throws have variations you can do at the last minute if they don't work, but the tome nage either works or it doesn't. You fail, and your opponent is on top of you in a perfect position to pin you. But I hadn't chosen the throw, it had been the only move Damian's attack left me. I had seconds to do it right or have him eat my face. So when I kicked up with my feet, I gave it all I had. I'd forgotten that all I had was more than it used to be.

Damian flew through the air again, but it wasn't his supernatural powers this time. I rolled over in time to see Damian hit the wall yards away. He hit hard enough to crack the paint and leave a partial imprint of his body on the wall, when he slid to the floor.

I heard someone behind me say, 'wow,' and it wasn't Richard, because he was nearly up beside me, rounding the couch. I didn't have time to glance behind me to see if it was Nathaniel or Gregory, because two bad things were happening at once.

The first bad thing was that Damian was getting slowly to his feet. Slowly enough that I think I'd hurt him, but he was still getting up, still not unconscious. The second bad thing was the woman had started screaming again, and thanks to me throwing Damian across the room, she was the closest person to him. She'd backed up when he sailed through the air, otherwise she'd have been almost where he landed, but when he turned around, she'd be a yard away. Not good.

Richard made a move toward her, but she was already backing up, and not toward us. She was backing up toward the open front door. There was something about the way she was moving that made both Richard and I say something. Richard had time to say, 'Clair, don't...' I had time to say, 'Don't run.' But it was too late. She ran, just as Damian turned to see her. It was like putting a cat into a room full of mice; they'll chase the running one first.

Richard was moving, but even with his speed there wasn't time to get ahead of Damian and block the door. All Richard had time for was to rush Damian, to crash into him and take them both to the floor.

He had the vampire down but not pinned. Richard screamed. His shoulders blocked my view, and I had to move around to their heads to see Damian's mouth buried into Richard's upper chest.

I knelt to help pry Damian's mouth from his flesh, but Richard made the preternatural rookie mistake. He grabbed Damian by the hair and pulled him off of him. Vampire bites are like snake bites;

if the snake has a good grip, you don't just yank it off. Yanking it off causes more damage than letting the snake let go on its own, or prying it loose. I guess the exception would be a venomous snake, if you go on the asumption that the longer it bites you the more poison it pumps in, which may or may not be true, but vampires aren't venomous. It was an impressive show of strength, tearing the vampire's mouth away from his flesh, but impressive shows of strength have their price. Richard's shirt ripped away from that entire side of his body, and a great, bloody hole showed in his upper chest, almost to the shoulder. His hand, which had been pushing against Damian's shoulder, suddenly went limp, and all that kept Damian from sinking teeth into Richard again was Richard's grip on his long red hair.

I put a hand on Damian's shoulder and pressed, and unlike every other time I'd tried to hold down a rampaging vampire, this time it worked, at least a little. Let's hear it for preternatural strength.

A gobbet of flesh fell out of Damian's mouth as he tried to turn and sink fangs into me. Richard yanked on his hair and kept those straining fangs from me. He tried to use his left arm again, and it moved, but he couldn't push with it. Something important had gotten torn up. Super strong or not, he was suddenly fighting with only one arm.

Between the two of us we could keep Damian from sitting up completely, but we couldn't keep him pressed to the floor. He kept straining upward, teeth slashing the air, sounds coming from his throat that were more animal than human. We weren't losing the fight, but we weren't winning either. We needed a different plan of attack.

I moved off of his shoulders enough that he raised up more, and Richard's eyes were wide. 'I can't hold him one-handed, not alone.'

'I'm going to put an arm around his neck to control his head,' I said, 'but I need him higher off the ground.'

'A choke hold won't work on a vampire. They don't breathe.'

That was half true, but I let it go. We could argue later. 'I'm just trying to control his head, that's it.'

He gave a small nod. He didn't look convinced, but he didn't argue about it, and that was good enough. I slid in behind Damian, and he was so busy straining after Richard, that he didn't seem to notice. I knelt behind the vampire, and for the first time was very aware that I was nude. The fight had sort of made it unimportant. What made it important now, was that Richard's hand was still in Damian's hair, and his hand had to stay there until I had my arm wrapped around the vampire's neck. I needed to have one arm wrapped around Damian's neck and the other arm holding my wrist, and I needed to be squeezing like a son of a bitch, while my face was buried against the back of his head, so he, theoretically, couldn't reach me. Only Richard's grip and the vampire's desire to bite him would keep him from tearing into me during the process. So Richard had to keep his hand there, but now, suddenly, my bare breasts were going to be pressed into the back of his hand and arm. The fact that that bit of knowledge froze me for a second tells you how badly I behaved around Richard, or how screwed up about him I was. A life and death struggle and I was worried about pressing my breasts against his hand. Focus, Anita, focus. Survive first, be embarrassed later.

'Hurry,' Richard said, and there was strain in that one word. Super strong doesn't mean you don't get tired.

I took a deep breath, let it out, and moved into both Damian's body and Richard's hand. I had to move fast and firm, no hesitations, because Richard's grip wasn't perfect control. If Damian noticed me before my arm was under his chin, I wasn't sure there was anything Richard could do to save me some damage. My hand touched Damian's blood-slick skin, and I had to follow through. I had to ignore the almost electric reaction I had when my bare breasts brushed the back of Richard's hand. One small touch and my skin ran with goosebumps. But it was more than just physical attraction. It was as if the world held its breath. Even Damian went still for that frozen moment. I felt Jean-Claude wake. Felt his eyes open, knew he woke in a welter of silk sheets in the sunless dark of the underground in Circus of the Damned. He turned in that nest of silk and darkness and touched Asher's body, found it still cold, still hours from waking.

Jean-Claude's voice echoed through my head. 'What have you done, *ma petite*?'

I don't know what I would have answered, because in that moment the world came back into focus. I could still feel Jean-Claude all those miles away, but I was back to the here and now.

Damian helped me concentrate on the here and now. He twisted in Richard's desperate grip and lunged at me, mouth wide, fangs straining like a striking snake. I suddenly had my own grip on his hair and helped Richard hold him away from my skin by fractions of an inch. I snugged my right arm under his chin, tight against the front of his neck. And he reacted like the only danger was the arm sliding in from his right, so that he never tried to turn in against mine and Richard's grip on the other side. There was no human thought to him in that moment. No human. No vampire. I wasn't even sure *animal* was the word. I had no word for what Damian had become. In a different century it would have been *demon, possessed, damned*.

Jean-Claude's voice in my head again, 'He will be damned if you cannot bring him back.'

I had to shake my head, like his voice was an insect buzzing inside my skull. It distracted me. I thought very hard, *stop talking*. I don't know if he heard me or figured out on his own that he was distracting me, but he stopped.

I let go of Damian's hair and used my arms to close around his neck in what would have been a choke hold, if he'd needed to breathe. Vampires do breathe, but they don't have to. My arm slid into place more easily because of all the blood, but the blood also made it harder to hold him still, harder to maintain my grip. I put my head down, tight against the side of his head, using all my upper body to simply control his head.

Richard let go of Damian's hair, and the vampire sprang up off the floor. I tightened my grip around his neck, but was along for the ride. I could control his head from moving side to side, but I couldn't choke him, and I didn't weigh enough to slow him down.

Damian was on top of Richard, pinning the bigger man to the floor. Richard had his good arm pushing out against Damian's chest. I got my feet under me on either side of them. It was awkward, because I just wasn't tall enough to do it comfortably, but I began to fight to pull Damian's neck backward. I could feel that I could snap his neck. I was almost sure I could, but I could not simply fight him backward. I knew if you decapitated most vamps, they died. I'd never had the strength before to snap a neck this easily, so I'd never tried. If I snapped his spine would he die? Would he be crippled? Would spinal damage cripple a vampire?

Richard's arm was beginning to shake and collapse at the elbow. I pulled backward, and felt Damian's windpipe begin to give. I was going to crush his neck before I broke his spine. I looked past us and found Nathaniel bent over Gregory at the foot of the stairs. Gregory wasn't moving, but one problem at a time. I screamed, 'Nathaniel!'

He turned, and there was blood all over the front of his body. I didn't think most of it was his. His face looked surprised as if he had lost track of our fight, but he came to me. He grabbed Damian's arm, and it was as if he'd given the vampire another target. Damian leapt off of Richard and was suddenly on top of Nathaniel. I was beginning to feel positively useless. If I couldn't choke him, wasn't heavy enough to slow him down, wasn't willing to break his neck, I was useless. I used what weight I had to stagger him, throw him off balance so that Nathaniel had time to get his arms up and a leg into Damian's stomach. If Nathaniel had known how to fight, he'd have been able to do more, but at the moment just keeping the vampire from biting him was good.

Jean-Claude's voice, soft, in my head, 'You have done something to damage the bond between yourself and Damian. You must reopen it, *ma petite*.'

'A little busy right now,' I said.

Richard wrapped his one arm around Damian's waist and helped me pull him off of Nathaniel. The three of us rode him down to the floor. I changed my grip on his neck to a choke hold that wouldn't have worked at all, if Nathaniel hadn't been pressing on his shoulder and chest and Richard sitting on the rest of him. My body was curled around his neck, using my own weight as an anchor to make it harder for him to rise and strike. But I'd tried this hold on large human males in judo class before, and it wasn't effective, not if they had the upper body strength to sit up with me dangling from their neck. I did it now, only to control his head, his mouth, those fangs, and because I had Richard and Nathaniel to help me.

He fought us, but three on one, we had some control. Not much, but some. My voice came breathy, but clear, 'What do you mean I've damaged the bond between Damian and me?'

'Who are you talking to?' Nathaniel asked, through gritted teeth.

'Jean-Claude,' Richard answered for me.

'Can you hear him, too?' I asked.

'Sometimes.'

I wanted to ask, 'like now?' but Jean-Claude was answering me. 'You have put up shields specifically against Damian, why?'

'He woke up in a flood of sunlight. It seemed to terrify him. He was so afraid. The fear was choking Nathaniel and me.'

'Both you and Nathaniel?' Jean-Claude asked. I could see him lying on the white silk sheets, his black hair spread out like a dark dream across the pillow. One hand idly touching Asher's bare back, the way you'd drum your fingers on a desk or pet a dog, if you were thinking about other things.

'Yes, both of us.'

'I asked you when I woke, what had you done. Now, I may know.'

For once I was at least up to speed on the metaphysical disasters in my life. I got to say, 'We know already.'

'Know what, *ma petite*?'

Damian gave a particularly violent movement, bucking me up off the floor, slamming me back down only after I felt, rather than saw, the other two men force him back down. I thought it, because I didn't have breath to speak at the moment, *That we're a triumvirate.*

'I heard that,' Richard said, and there was a sullen note under his breathless exertion as if he'd thought I'd only thought it to keep it from him, or maybe I was just projecting. I was always willing to believe that Richard was being difficult. As he was always willing to believe I was being bloodthirsty.

Jean-Claude didn't ask stupid questions or try to discuss metaphysics. If we all knew that somehow I'd managed to forge a second triumvirate, then we could move on. 'When you shielded from Damian's fear, you shielded too well. You have cut him off from your power, as you did by leaving once.'

'I'm right here,' I said, trying to turn my face away from the blood that had decided to trickle down Damian's face and onto mine.

'There physically, but not metaphysically, and your servant needs both.'

'How do I fix this?' I asked.

'Drop your shields,' he said, and even in my head, his voice was matter-of-fact.

It sounded so simple, so obvious. I remembered shielding from Damian's fear. I had thought of metal, hard, cold, solid, impenetrable. Not a metal wall, or door, but truly just the essence of metal. It had taken me months of work to understand how to shield not with an imaginary door or wall or building, but just to think, rock, water, metal. Block the things you don't want to get through, or drown them. Marianne could also shield with air and fire, but I didn't get that. Air just wasn't strong enough for shielding, and fire, well, fire's fire. I used the tools I understood.

How do you unshield? Once I'd had to picture the wall crumbling, or the door opening, but very lately, I'd understood something that Marianne had been saying, but I hadn't been understanding. I simply stopped thinking about metal. I stopped. It went away. Poof, gone. One second I was safe behind my thought of metal, the next I was drowning in Damian's rage. No, not rage, rage implies anger, human emotion, and that wasn't what roared through my head. I'd thought more than once that I was going crazy in a detached sort of sociopathic way, but I'd been wrong. That hadn't been being crazy – this was.

I forgot about holding Damian down. I forgot about why I'd dropped my shields. I forgot about everything. There were no thoughts. No words. There was just sensation, and impulse. The smell of fresh blood. The taste of our own blood in our mouths, bitter. Hands pushing us to the floor, crushing us. Hunger, hunger like fire in our gut, like something that would eat us alive if we didn't feed, and feed, and feed. The smell of fresh blood, the warmth in their hands pushing on us, all that was maddening. Pain, my body was just pain. Like a fire that was burning me up from the inside. I screamed, and the sound was loud and not loud enough. It didn't help. Only one thing would quench that fire, fill me up, stop the pain. Blood. Fresh blood. Warm blood.

My hands touched warm skin, and if it hadn't been Richard, I'm not sure I would have stopped. But the feel of Richard's muscled arm under my hands called something of me up through the hunger. I was staring into Richard's solid brown eyes from inches away, almost as if I'd moved in for a kiss, but it hadn't been his mouth I'd been aiming at. Even now, the long solid line of his neck beckoned to me. The smell of fresh blood overwhelmed the subtler scent of the blood that pulsed under his skin, but somehow lapping at the bloody wound wasn't enough. It needed to be fresh. I needed my teeth in flesh. I needed to make my own hole to tear at. Only that would satisfy. Only that would be enough.

I forced my gaze up to Richard's face. I looked into his wide eyes, made myself look at his face, trace the line of his jaw, the fullness of his lips. I looked on the face of someone I'd loved once, and I had to work harder than I'd worked at almost anything ever, to see him as something other than food.

Damian bucked, and Richard had to pay more attention to the vampire he and Nathaniel were still pinning to the floor than to me. A cool voice flowed through my mind. 'I am helping you shield, *ma petite*. Forgive me, I did not understand what dropping your shield would do to you.'

'He's a revenant,' I said, and I don't think I said it out loud.

'*Oui.*'

'How do I help him?'

'You must rebind him as you did when he came out of the coffin. Let him taste your blood and say the words over him.'

'Are the words really important?' I asked.

I felt him shrug, where he sat on his silk-covered bed. 'They are the words that masters of the city have spoken over their followers for thousands of years. I would not want to chance that the words are not part of the magic that will bind master to servant, by leaving them out.'

I nodded. 'Did Richard hear this?'

'*Non.*'

'Tell him.' A moment after I said it, I was still cool and a little distant from what was happening, but I could hear it again, see it. I was sitting on my living-room floor, not too far from the door, and Richard and Nathaniel were still trying to keep Damian on the floor. They were mostly succeeding, though it was hard to tell through the blood if there were any new wounds. They were all three covered in blood.

I stared down at myself and realized that the front of my body was covered in it, too. I didn't remember getting that messy. For a moment I wondered if I'd done something that I didn't remember, but I pushed the thought away. Time later for too much truth. Survive, keep moving, worry about what you did later. Yeah, that's the ticket. But after a peek inside Damian's mind, a ticket to the situational sociopath express didn't look half bad. I knew now, for dead certain, that there were worse things.

17

DAMIAN BUCKED SO hard that he threw Nathaniel to one side. Richard's weight alone wasn't enough. Damian sat up, and Richard rolled off of him to keep the vampire from sinking fangs into him again.

I waved my arms and yelled, 'Damian, here, I'm here!' I don't think it was his name that attracted his attention, I think it was the movement. I'd been in his mind, I knew he was past words.

He rushed toward me, so fast he was a blur of white and red, and his eyes like green streaks. Nathaniel ran for him. I yelled, 'No, let him come!'

Richard hesitated still on the floor but with his hand outstretched toward the vampire's legs. They could have caught him again, but why? It was my blood he needed. I was calm, peaceful, it was like that quiet place I went when I killed. No fear. Nothing. I watched the vampire come at me like a comet streaking across the heavens, something elemental and otherworldly.

To say he smashed into me didn't come close to the impact of flesh on flesh. I was on the floor breathless, sightless, and only years of training on how to fall kept me from smacking my head against the floor, or breaking a bone. I caught my breath in time to scream. Damian plunged his mouth low in my neck, just above the shoulder. It had been a long time since I'd been vampire bit without head games or sex. It hurt.

A wereleopard appeared over us, standing on crooked, almost-human legs. He was yellow and pale gold and white, with beautiful black rosettes scattered over a body that was more than a foot taller than he was in human form. The color told me it was Gregory, because Nathaniel was black in leopard form. Gregory's chest was broader, his arms were longer, muscled, and tipped with talons like frightening knives. The face was leopard, but with something strangely different around the muzzle and the neck. He towered over us, snarling and reaching down for the vampire's pale back. He was going to pull Damian off of me, like Richard had pushed the vampire off of himself.

I wrapped my arms around Damian's shoulders and back, got one leg free to wrap around his waist. I held him to me and said, 'No, Gregory!' If he pulled him off I'd end up hurt as bad as Richard. 'You'll tear me up worse.'

The leopardman hesitated, growling. He said in that thick voice they all had in half-human form, 'He's hurting you.'

Damian snuggled his mouth deeper into my flesh, forced a sound that was not happy out of my mouth. But I said, in a breathy voice, 'When I need your help, I'll ask for it.'

I could tell Gregory was puzzled even through the fur. I wasn't always good at facial expressions once my friends went furry. But this one even I could read.

'Damian,' I said, my voice was soft. I wanted to see that he was in there before I said the words. His eyes were closed, but he relaxed against me by inches, until he wasn't so much pinning me to the floor as lying on top of me. It was more my arms and leg that held him pressed to me. 'Damian,' I said again.

I felt him come back into himself as if a switch had been thrown. One moment, monster, the next, Damian. Even before he opened his eyes and looked at me, I knew he was in there again. He was back from wherever he'd gone. Relief flooded through me until my arms and leg started to slide off of him. Weak with relief wasn't just an expression.

He was still sucking at the wound, but it was gentler now. It had stopped hurting. He drew, slowly, from the wound, his mouth crimson with my blood. I was suddenly aware in a way that I hadn't been before that we were both nude, and he was male, and he had fed. His body was thick and heavy against my thigh, where a moment ago it hadn't been. Blood pressure is a wonderful thing.

If I had not put a leg over his body to help hold him against me, it wouldn't have been quite so compromising. If Gregory hadn't tried to help me, I wouldn't have . . . oh, hell. I was suddenly afraid in a very different way. Afraid to move, afraid of making things worse, or better. Afraid of how my body pulsed in his arms. It was as if all the blood in our bodies was pulsing in time. It was hard to breathe. I was almost choking on . . . power. Magic. I'd bound him once before and it hadn't been like this.

His hand slid slowly, tentatively down the side of my body, and it wasn't so much a caress for sex, as just for touching. He used his whole hand, getting as much of his skin against mine as he could. I felt him marveling at the grace of our bodies so close, so completely without barriers. His skin hunger was there like some new kind of beast. A need so intense and so long denied that it was a kind of madness of its own.

I felt his loneliness like a great echoing thing. It brought tears to the edges of my eyes and made me want to fix it.

I moved my hands along his back, so that I was no longer holding him, but closer to an embrace. 'Blood of my blood,' and he moved upward to bring his mouth to mine for the kiss that would seal the words, but that small movement slid his body against the front of mine, so that the swell of him brushed against me, and that brief touch made me writhe underneath him, and it suddenly wasn't a kiss I wanted to seal this bargain with.

The thought helped me pull back. Helped me realize that what I was thinking was not entirely me. I gazed up into his emerald eyes and knew who was doing the thinking.

Nathaniel knelt beside us. I reached out a hand, and the moment he touched me, I could think a little, and Damian's pull was a little less. Damian snarled at him, and those green eyes wavered, as if sanity wasn't permanent in them, not yet.

Jean-Claude was in my head, and I felt a tiny thread of fear from him. 'You must finish binding him, *ma petite*, and you must start from the beginning of the words.'

I wanted to ask, 'Why are you afraid?' And I must have thought it very hard, because he answered, 'If he goes insane now, *ma petite*, your lovely throat is very unprotected. Finish it.'

Maybe Richard was hearing the interior conversation, because he came to kneel on the other side of us. Suddenly, it couldn't have gotten more awkward. 'I'm here,' he said, and he said it like it should have made things better, as if he didn't understand how horribly embarrassing it was to have him kneeling there.

Damian gave him an unfriendly look, and a sound that was more growl than anything trickled from his mouth. I was losing him. 'Blood of my blood, flesh of my flesh,' and he gazed back down at me, and with each word, sanity filled his eyes, his face, him. He slid his body against mine, and I felt him pushing against me. And again I felt that almost overwhelming need. That certainty that it was not a kiss we needed to seal this with. The need roared over me. I thought for a heartbeat we'd raised the *ardeur*, but then I could hear it – them. Two needs. I turned my head and found Nathaniel gazing down at me with those lavender eyes. It was there in his eyes, his face, but I could have told you what was there without using my eyes, because I could feel it. Feel him. Them. Both of them, pushing at me, not just physically, but in ways that hands could never hold you down, or bodies pin you to the floor. Their need undid me more easliy than any physical strength or threat. Their need undid me because I cared for them, and if you could feel another's pain, as if it were your own, wouldn't you do anything to stop that pain? Wouldn't you?

My voice was breathy, and it was Nathaniel's gaze I held when I said, 'Breath to breath, my heart to yours.' Damian slid inside me in one long push of his hips. The sensation made me writhe underneath him, made me grip Nathaniel's hand hard enough to dig nails into his flesh. My hips ground upward to meet Damian's thrust. It was as involuntary as the next breath I took.

A sound drew my attention away from Nathaniel, and it wasn't a sound from above me. The sound came from the other side of us. Richard had pushed himself away from us, until his back met the side of the white couch. I don't know what I expected to see on his face, lust, disgust, anger, jealousy, maybe, but what I saw was fear. A fear so raw and naked, that it hurt to meet his eyes.

Damian grabbed my face, turned me back to look up at him. 'It's me I want you to be thinking about,' he said, and he began to pull himself out of me, slowly. For a second I thought that would be it, but part of me knew better. He'd raised himself up, almost in a push-up, the tip of him barely inside me, and gazing full into my face, his eyes pinning mine as surely as his body pinned the rest of me, he said, 'Blood of my blood,' and thrust into me. I cried out underneath him, and Nathaniel echoed that cry, while his hand gripped mine. His lavender eyes were wild when I turned to look at him. Damian touched my face again, but a touch was enough to turn me to face him, to feel his body sliding out of mine, to hear his whisper, 'Flesh of my flesh,' before he married our flesh as close, as fast, as he could. I felt Nathaniel convulse hand to hand, and I felt his pulse like a second heartbeat against my palm, but I kept my eyes on Damian's face, my gaze on his as he drew his body out of me, almost, and, said, 'Breath to breath,' and slammed himself inside me. I screamed and Nathaniel's voice echoed mine. I finally realized that Nathaniel was getting if not the full ride, a shadow of what I was feeling. Damian drew himself out, out, until . . . 'My heart to yours,' and he slid himself inside me.

He stayed frozen above me, body as deep inside me as he could get. His breathing was harsh and shallow. A shudder passed down his body from head to toe, and I writhed underneath him from it. Nathaniel moaned, jerking on my hand, as if it were his body being explored. Damian's voice was shaky, 'Oh, don't do that. If you do that again, I won't last.' He buried his face against my hair, and another shudder rippled down his body and made me dance underneath him, crying out, and that was it. He was suddenly above me, his upper body arched, and he shoved himself into me, deep, hard, and it was partly his body inside me, partly watching his body above mine, his eyes closed, his head thrown back, his hair like a bloody waterfall around the pale candle of his body, and knowing that he was thrust as deep inside me as he could get that tore a scream from my lips. And Nathaniel's voice screamed with me, our hands convulsing around each other, our nails biting into each other's skin. I felt Nathaniel's body thrust against the carpet, felt him let go, and that orgasm traveled back up my arm and into Damian. It was his turn to scream, and that made him writhe with his body still plunged inside of mine, which made me move underneath him. It was like being caught in an endless loop of pleasure; one body's release, bringing the other, until we ended in a sweating, bloody pile on the floor.

Damian let out a shaky laugh. And I felt, heard, knew, that underneath the lust was sorrow, and an almost certain knowledge that he might never get to do this again, once my head cleared. For some reason that made me think of something I had forgotten. I turned my head and found that Richard was still there, but it wasn't fear on his face now, but a sort of wonderment. I realized in that moment that, though Richard wasn't getting all the sensations that Nathaniel was getting, he could still hear inside my head. So could Jean-Claude, but it was Richard's thought that came the clearest. 'You've never fucked either of them.' On the heels of that thought came another, that he'd assumed I was screwing everything in the house, because he'd pretty much been doing the same down at the lupanar.

I was naked in the middle of sex with one man, maybe two, depending on how you counted things, yet, suddenly, I had the moral high ground. Weird.

18

GREGORY CRAWLED TO us on all fours, sniffing just above our bodies. He said in that growling voice, 'Me next.'

I had to look up and back over my shoulder to give him the look he deserved, but looking back with him on all fours gave me a sight line down his body, and suddenly I was more embarrassed than I had been. Shapeshifters look sort of like they do in the movies in half-man form, but there is one big difference. They have genitalia, and right at that moment Gregory was very, very happy to be here. I think what bothered me more than the erection was that he'd gotten it from watching me have sex with Damian. For some reason, unfair probably, it bothered me that Gregory had enjoyed the show.

'Back off, Gregory,' I said, and my voice sounded harsh and like I meant it, even while I blushed.

He did his kitty-cat impression of a smile and backed off, literally. He put his head down, and crawled backward, abasing himself. It was a gesture closer to a real wolf than a real leopard, but were-animals are people at heart, and some gestures just translate better to our human brains. Abasing yourself by going low is one of those gestures.

Damian was looking down at me, and the look was not one that I'd ever seen on a man's face just after finishing sex. He looked sad, and I remembered the burst of emotion at the end. Sorrow covering the pleasure like evil chocolate ruining your ice cream.

But it was more than the look on his face. I realized that I could feel his sadness. Feel it, not like it was my own, but like it was a coat that clung to my skin. I was still hooked up to him emotionally, well, not just emotionally. I could feel him plunged deep inside me, his weight still pinning my lower body. Touching made any sort of meta-physical intermingling worse. I needed to stop touching him. And not just him.

Nathaniel lay beside us, his fingers still tangled in mine. The side of his body pressed up against me, so that our bodies touched from shoulder to hip. He must have scooted closer when Damian finished. I think I would have remembered if Nathaniel's body had been touching mine during the act. Wouldn't I?

His lavender eyes were unfocused, almost sleepy. What came through his skin was contentment. Contentment like a great warm ocean that filled him, floated him, held him, rocked him. Maybe I stared at him too long, or maybe he sensed my own growing unease, because his eyes focused, sharpened, and the look in them wasn't the least bit sleepy. It was almost an anticipatory look, as if he were already thinking about next time. Since I didn't think he'd had a first time yet, it helped clear my head. Anger always did.

'Everybody off, out of the pool,' I said.

Damian's sorrow was almost like rain on my skin. Nathaniel wasn't sad. He went straight to panic, afraid he'd done something wrong. 'It's alright, Nathaniel, you're alright. We're all alright.' I wasn't sure I actually believed that down to my toes, but the panic subsided, and everybody got off of me. Yeah. Though Damian's sadness clung to me like I'd walked through some metaphysical cobweb.

While we were getting untangled, Micah came through the splin-tered door. I'd been found in compromising positions by boyfriends before, but never with less embarrassment. He didn't ask stupid ques-tions or make me feel like a slut. In fact he concentrated on the most important thing. 'Wow,' he said, and the wow seemed to take in the blood scattered here and there on the floor and the walls, the injuries that he could see on most of us, the broken door, all of it, but what he said outloud was, 'Is everybody alright?'

I started to get up off the floor, and Damian offered me a hand up. I wouldn't have taken it normally, but we'd just had sex, and it seemed odd to slap away his hand. The moment my hand touched his, I realized it was more than that. That need to put my skin against his was still there. One moment of good sex didn't take away centuries of need. Sex was like some kind of fuel like food – you burned it up and needed more.

I got my hand out of his and took a slightly shaky step away from Nathaniel and Damian. A little distance would be helpful, I hoped. 'We'll all live,' I said.

'Good.' He cocked his head to one side and said, 'I didn't know that Damian could walk around this early in the day.'

'He can't,' I said.

'Do I say the obvious, "but he is walking around during the day," or do you want me to just stop asking questions?'

I was suddenly tired, and I probably wasn't the only one. 'Have you been to bed at all?'

He shook his head, and as if I'd reminded him, he rubbed his chartreuse eyes, his sunglasses already tucked into the front of his shirt. 'When I drove the guy home from the bar, he had a live-in girlfriend and a child. Girlfriend started a fight about his drinking. Anger does not help you fight the change.'

'Did he shift?' I asked.

'No, but it was close, and he's so new . . .' Micah shook his head again. 'I'd feel better if the girlfriend was a little more understanding about how dangerous he could be. She just didn't seem to understand.'

'She didn't want to understand,' Richard said.

Micah turned and looked at him. I realized that of all the people in the room, Richard had been the only one that Micah hadn't really looked at. 'Then you've met Patrick's girlfriend.'

Richard started to shake his head, stopped in mid-motion, and winced. 'No, but I've seen it. The human spouse just doesn't want to understand that they're married to a monster.' I think he meant it to sound matter-of-fact, but it didn't. It sounded bitter.

I'd never made Richard feel like that, that I knew of; no, he'd spent a great deal more time making me feel like a monster. So I let it go. I let it go because I didn't know what to say, or if there was anything to say. Okay, I had one thing to say. 'The coalition is offering a monthly meeting for family members. I thought we'd given flyers out to the werewolves.'

Richard got to his feet, cradling his arm. 'This is my Patrick, Patrick Cook?'

Micah said, 'Yes.'

'And you've been baby-sitting him all night?'

'Yes,' Micah said, again.

Richard looked down at the floor, then back up. He met Micah's gaze, but his face wasn't completely happy about it. 'Thank you for looking after my wolf.'

'The wolves are part of the coalition, too,' Micah said, 'I'd do the same for anyone's people.'

'All the same, thank you.'

'Don't mention it.'

There was one of those awkward silences. I hated to leave everybody alone, but I really needed a shower. The shower would hurt the wound on my throat, but I'd just had sex without a condom, which meant all the mess had gone into me, but it wouldn't stay there. So I needed to clean up. Truthfully, I'd have preferred a condom, but it hadn't occurred to me until afterward. Tammy had gotten pregnant on the pill. Yeah, she had fallen afoul of the fact that antibiotics don't mix well with the pill, but still. That one percent chance suddenly seemed like it wasn't good odds. Damian was a thousand-year-old vampire; chances were he was infertile, but still ... It was one thing getting pregnant by a boyfriend, but pregnant by someone who wasn't even that ... well, that seemed somehow worse. 'I'm taking a shower.'

They all looked at me. I guess it was abrupt. 'I'm sorry, but I just can't stand here like this anymore. So everybody behave themselves. I'll be as quick as I can.'

'I'll call for a doctor,' Micah said.

I nodded. 'Good, good.' I suddenly had to not be there, naked, smelling of fresh sex, with Richard and Micah in the same room. Having Damian and Nathaniel naked didn't help my comfort level. I was fairly comfortable around nudity in general now, but specific nudity, that was still a problem. For more reasons than I was comfortable with, I needed to leave the room.

'By the way, there's a woman crying in your car in the driveway,' Micah said.

'My car?' I asked.

'No, Richard's, or at least I assume it's Richard's. I know Gregory's car, and that's not the one she's in.'

Richard cursed under his breath, something he rarely did. 'Clair, I forgot about Clair.'

'Who's Clair?' I asked.

He hesitated, then said, 'My girlfriend,' then he was walking to the door holding his arm like it hurt to walk that fast.

His girlfriend, and I'm buck naked the first time she sees me. Great. Well, at least she hadn't seen me fuck Damian. That helped. Sure, great. Just great. I was shaking my head as I went toward the bathroom.

It was Gregory, in his growling voice, who said, 'I guess it's none of my business, but should Richard really be in front of the house where cars could see him? He is covered in blood.'

I turned and looked at the leopardman and said, 'Shit, no.' I started for the door, and Micah stopped me. 'I'll go. I'm the only one that they wouldn't call the cops on right now.' He squeezed my shoulder and smiled at me.

I realized that I hadn't kissed him hello, I always kissed him hello. Of course, I was still covered in blood and other bodily fluids, and none of them were his, but he might not understand that that was why I hadn't wanted to get too close. Some of my confusion must have shown on my face, because his smile widened. He turned me around by the shoulders, gave me a little push toward the bathroom, and slapped me on the ass. 'Get cleaned up, I'll take care of things here.'

'I can't believe you just did that,' I said.

'Did what?' he said, and he was grinning at me.

I could probably count on one hand the number of times Micah had grinned at me. His eyes were sparkling with laughter as if it were all he could do not to let it out. I was happy to see him having this good a time, really I was. But I wasn't sure what was funny, and I didn't have the courage to ask. It was probably something that would be at my expense, or something I'd just done that he found cute. I was not cute. Confused, fucked-up, bruised, but not cute. Nathaniel and Damian knew better, but as I passed Gregory, I had to say, 'If you touch my ass, I will rip you a new one.' I said it as I moved past him, not even pausing.

'You're no fun,' he growled.

I looked back just before I turned out of sight of him. 'Oh, I'm a lot of fun, just not for you.'

He snarled at me. 'Bitch.'

'Woof, woof,' I said, and finally made it into the bathroom.

19

I TRIED NOT to think in the shower. Thinking bad; hot water good. I turned the shower head to as hard as the water would go and the let the water beat against my body, finding bruises I didn't know I had. Once I would have been hurt, really hurt, by the beating that Damian had given me. Thanks to Jean-Claude's vampire marks I was just a little stiff. The bite would take the longest to heal, and even that would be gone in few days, a week at the outside. The healing was great, the rest of it . . . well, let's just say the jury was still out.

I heard a noise over the pounding water. It took me a minute to realize that someone was knocking at the door. I tried to ignore it. The knocking stopped for a second, and I thought, oh, good, but it started again, louder, as if whoever was knocking thought I hadn't heard the first time.

I sighed, turned off the water, and called, 'What?'

'Damian isn't doing well,' Nathaniel said through the closed door.

I stood there a second water dripping into my eyes, and said, 'What do you mean, Damian's not doing well?'

'Can't you feel it?'

I thought about it. I thought about Damian, and suddenly fear was like a crushing weight on my chest. It staggered me for a second, and I was glad there was a safety bar in the shower to grab on to. It was a shadow of what had driven him to run screaming through the house. I wasn't sure we'd all survive him doing it twice. 'I'm coming.'

I squeezed out my hair, wound a towel around it, and was trying to towel off enough for a robe, when the door sprang open. Gregory came first in his fur suit, one clawed hand under Damian's arm. Richard had the other arm. They half-dragged, half-carried him through the door. They carried him toward me, and his fear rode before him. I'd felt fear before, but not like this. It crushed my chest so that I couldn't breathe, closed my throat. The fear had weight enough to slam me to the floor, as if something had smashed into me. It wasn't my pulse I was choking on, it was as if the terror itself were wet silk, and I was trying to swallow it. Slick, wet, suffocating, more real than any fear I'd ever felt. Not real the way an emotion is real, but real the way a rock, a chair, or an animal is real. Fear had become something . . . more.

They dropped Damian into my lap, and it was as if every part of my skin ran with chills, and then every inch of my skin tried to crawl away. Tried to crawl away and leave my body to die. My skin would have saved itself if it hadn't been trapped against my body. The rest of me would have gone with it, but we were trapped under Damian's weight. Trapped in his fear, frozen in it. If I could have breathed, I would have screamed, but all I could do was drown. Drown in Damian's fear.

Someone touched my shoulder, but it was distant. As if no one's skin were as real to me as Damian's. Someone shook me, sharp and hard. My breath came in a huge gasp, as if I hadn't been breathing for a long time, when my breath came out, it was a shriek.

I was staring up into Richard's startled face. It was his hand on my shoulder. Him kneeling beside us. 'Anita, Anita, can you hear me?'

I grabbed Richard's arm, my other hand clutching Damian to me, as if I were afraid if I let him go he'd be lost. As if the fear were some horrible beast that could literally eat him up, and destroy him.

Richard shook me again. 'Anita, say something.'

'God, it's so . . . awful.'

Damian nodded his head against my stomach. He'd been lying almost limply against me, but now he grabbed me around the waist and hip, his hands holding on as if I were the last solid thing in the world. I felt a burst of emotion from him, and it was gratitude. He was grateful that I could share his fear. Sharing it seemed to make it less, or make it more bearable.

That thought, that sharing fear made it easier to bear, brought a memory. It wasn't my memory. It was a face that I had never seen before, but one that Damian knew as well as his own. All high angles and strong lines, a scar from his forehead to his cheek, where he'd been cut in the first raid we'd gone on. She-who-made-us said once that the scar saved his life, because without it, his hair was more blond than hers, his eyes more blue. That scar ruined his handsomeness enough for her to leave him whole. For even men who were too fair were not safe from her envy. The only name I heard in my head was Perrin, but I knew that wasn't right. That hadn't been his name, anymore than Damian had been mine, ours, his.

I smelled vanilla and felt something thick and warm glide over my skin. I blinked awake, if *awake* was the right word. Nathaniel was kneeling beside us. He'd undone his braid so that the vanilla scent of his hair had perfumed around me. His hair cascaded around him and spilled over the side of my body, pooling into my lap, covering Damian like a blanket, if a blanket could flow like liquid over a body. Nathaniel had covered us in his hair, but had very carefully avoided touching our skin with his. He was so close to us that not touching took effort, so close it was as if a sigh would have pressed the line of his body against mine. But he stayed that near painful inch away, letting only scent and the furred glide of hair reach us. The only thing he gave me of his skin was the warmth of it, which even from a distance I could feel. Heat trembling against my skin, as if the warmth of him breathed outward and wanted to touch me. Maybe it did.

It had been such a smart way to bring me out of Damian's memory without risking Nathaniel being dragged into it himself. So smart, but a plan is only as good as everyone in it. Damian moved in my lap, and I had a second to realize what he was going to do. I drew a breath to warn Nathaniel, but didn't have time to breath out. It was that quick.

Damian grabbed Nathaniel's arm, and that one touch was enough. It was like drowning in light. As if the world had caught fire and become heat, and heat was golden like the color yellow had spilled out and covered everything. Yellow warmth, golden heat. Our eyes were dazzled by it. We were blind in the light. There was nothing but the light and the touch of her small hands, and Perrin's hand in mine. His hand so large, firm, an anchor in the nightmare of the light. Her hands caressed, but it wasn't real. She'd dragged us into the light to drink our fear, not our sex.

She tore his hand away from mine, and her voice, which once I'd thought beautiful, sounded like an evil whine in my head, poisonous, because I could not tell her no. 'One to burn, one to keep.'

Perrin turned, framed for a moment in the light. His hair as yellow as the light itself, his eyes like the sky beyond the window. He was tall, his shoulders so wide that he filled most of the window. He'd always been a big man even among big men. Some of the towns we'd raided, people had run screaming, 'Giant!' or their word for it.

Perrin stood, covered in the light. Covered in the light, but not burning. The words that had begun this folly came back, 'Perhaps the reason they can walk out with you in the sun, Moroven, is not you sharing power with them, but that they have gained power of their own, to sun walk.' A messenger from the council had said the evil words and left it as a poisonous flea in she-who-made-us's ear. For a heart's beat we thought the messenger had spoken true. We thought Perrin stood in the light on his own power. For one glorious second, we believed. But the look on his face wasn't triumphant, it was frightened. That one look was enough. Something was wrong.

The smoke began to curl off his skin, just like in the movies. The part that was still me, still Anita, thought *but that's not right*. All the vampires that I'd seen die by sunlight just burst into flames. No smoke, no waiting, just instant inferno, poof. My puzzlement helped drag us back from the edge of terror. It helped us watch smoke rise from Perrin's skin, kept the horror from choking us. Flames burst along his skin, and for the blink of an eye he was haloed by rich orange and gold flames. His long yellow hair fluttered in the wind of the heat. A moment to think, *how pretty*, then the flames ate over him and his skin crawled with fire.

Perrin shrieked. *Shrieked*, for scream did not describe that sound coming from a man's mouth.

We screamed because we had to. All the horror, the sorrow, the fear had to come out of our mouths, or it would have burst out of our skin and shattered our minds. We screamed because it was all that kept us from going mad.

I suddenly smelled forest, that rich green smell of the deep woods – half Christmas tree pine and half fresh-turned earth. I stared at the burning vampire, my lifelong friend, my brother, but I was calm. All I could smell was forest, not the salt of ocean, not anything, then there was something else – wolf. The sweet musk of wolf. Richard.

The thought of him made the scent of forest and fur override everything else. The memory began to fade. Literally, the images became misty, and we began to draw away from that awful room. Perrin's voice floated down all those years, his scream turned distant by the fading. He began by screaming her name, the name I'd heard used for she-who-made-them, 'Moroven, Moroven,' but the screams changed, became another name, 'Nemhain!' I had enough left of Damian's mind in me to understand that Nemhain was her secret name, her true name. Over and over again, Perrin screamed her name, and Damian echoed it, his screams, which were louder now as the memory faded, his screams were her name, 'Nemhain!'

We spilled back into the now, into the floor of my bathroom, into Richard's hand on my arm. I started to look into his face, but Damian came to his knees, as if he would run toward something I couldn't see. I wrapped my hands around his waist and chest. Nathaniel had a death grip on Damian's arm. We held him, as if he could still run to Perrin's fire and destroy himself. He was still screaming, 'Nemhain, Nemhain, curse you!' He collapsed so suddenly that I'd have fallen back into the glass doors of the shower if Richard hadn't caught me with a hand across my back. Nathaniel caught Damian around one shoulder, slowing his fall. Damian was still talking in a voice that was more sob than whisper, 'Curse you, Nemhain, curse you.' He curled into a ball in my lap, pushing me hard into the curve of Richard's arm. Nathaniel stroked Damian's hair, over and over, the way you'd comfort a child.

He was still muttering her name, and literally cursing her, when the world suddenly drowned in fear. It was as if terror could become air and you had to breathe it in or you would die, but breathing it in was dying, too. It was all death. All fear. It roared through my head, thoughtless, formless, fear so pure that it stopped my heartbeat for a second, a hesitation, as if my heart would simply stop from fear. Dying of fright wasn't just a saying. There was a breathless moment where I waited for my heart to decide whether it would beat again, or whether silence was better, anything to escape. Anything.

The support of Richard's arm vanished, and I was left with the cold press of glass behind me, as if he'd closed the door to support me, so he wouldn't have to touch me anymore.

My breath came out in a rattle, and my heart leaped in my chest, and hurt as if it had bruised itself against my body. My chest hurt, my throat hurt, and still the air was fear made real. Every breath seemed to draw her in deeper. Because it was a her. It was Nemhain, Moroven, Damian's maker, and Perrin's. It wasn't just a superstition that you did not speak her name. Her name had conjured her power, brought us to her attention. I expected a voice to match the terror, but there was silence, a silence so loud that all I could hear was the beating of the blood in my veins. My heart thundering inside my body. Then I heard another heartbeat, faster, more frightened even than mine. How could he live so afraid?

I turned my head slowly, because I couldn't do anything else. I made myself turn through the fear and look at Nathaniel. His eyes were so wide they flashed white, and he was gulping at the air as if he was having trouble breathing it down. As if he would choke on the fear.

Damian lay like the dead in my lap. His eyes were closed, and he wasn't breathing. There was no heartbeat to hear. The thought came, *She's taken what she gave him*, but on the heels of that thought came another. *He's mine. I make his heart beat. I make the blood move in his veins. He's mine. Not yours. Not anymore. Mine.*

Nathaniel's fingers dug into my arm, and he was gasping as if some invisible hand were choking off his air. I didn't think that was really happening, but he was choking on the fear. Choking on her power. I met his terrified gaze and tried to say his name, tried to say anything, but no sound came out. I tried to call power, anything, but I couldn't think. Fear had stolen my thoughts, my logic, my power. No, no, some small part of me knew that wasn't true. She was just another vampire. Just another vampire. I was a necromancer. She could not do this to me. Part of me believed that, but most of me was fighting too hard to breathe to think at all.

If I'd had air enough, I'd have screamed. Not my fear, but my frustration. I didn't know how to fight this. She wasn't trying to mark any of us as servants, or seduce us, or control us. She simply had sent terror like some invisible wind to kill if it could, or not. She didn't care. There was no malice here, no strong emotion of any kind, except the fear, and the fear was a sending. She felt nothing. Absolutely nothing.

I didn't know how to fight against nothing. I didn't know what to do. We were dying, and I didn't know what to do.

20

JEAN-CLAUDE CALLED IN my mind, '*Ma petite*,' but the fear swelled upward and covered his words. I knew he was talking in my head, but I couldn't understand what he said. The fear was drowning him out like one radio station overwhelming another. His words were like the ghost sound of a distant station, just under the sound of the terror, but all I could hear, all I could feel, was Moroven's fear.

Nathaniel collapsed against me, mouth still open, gasping as if the air were too thick to breathe. Me dying was one thing, but it wouldn't just be me. Nathaniel and Damian lay across my lap, their hair mingling like bright and dark ribbons.

Gregory knelt in front of me; I'd almost forgotten he was there. I usually had trouble reading his face when he was in half-leopard form, but this face, this face I could read. Even under spotted fur and yellow kitty-cat eyes, the hunger showed through. Not lust, hunger. He said in that growling voice, 'They smell like food.'

'I know.' Richard's voice, and it turned me to him. I stretched my hand out toward him. He'd dragged us out of Damian's memory, maybe he could drag us out of this.

He looked . . . unhappy, angry. I let my hand begin to fall, but he took it, at the last minute, he took my hand in his. Instantly there was the sweet scent of forest and the musk of fur. The fear receded a little, like a wave of the ocean pulling back, but there was another wave just off shore, and you knew it was coming.

I could talk now, and what I said was, 'Help me.'

Jean-Claude's voice swelled inside me, pushed back the fear enough so I could hear his words. 'You must raise the *ardeur*, ma *petite*, you must. She does not understand a clean lust, free of pain and terror. Use our Richard, and I will be able to join my powers to yours, and we can defeat her.'

I stared up into the face of the man that Jean-Claude had so casually called 'ours,' and knew he wasn't. I could smell that wonderful musk, the calm of pine and leaf mold, but the look on his face was anything but calm. His brown eyes were full of a fine, shimmering anger. Touching his hand like this, I should have felt that anger dance over my skin, but I didn't. All I could feel was Moroven's power like a storm hovering over me. The only emotion left in me was terror.

'*Ma petite*, can you hear me?'

'Yes,' I managed a whisper.

'Then what is wrong?'

I wanted to ask him, What am I supposed to do, wrestle Richard to the floor and ravage him? But all that came out was, 'Can't, I can't.'

'Can't what, *ma petite*?'

'Can't feed off Richard.' It seemed silly to say that out loud while staring up into that handsome, angry face, but I couldn't concentrate enough to say it silently in my head. Talking was hard enough.

'Richard has agreed to this, *ma petite*.'

I shook my head. 'Don't believe it, he's angry.'

Richard looked even angrier, but he said, out loud, 'Jean-Claude's telling the truth, Anita, I agreed to feed the *ardeur*.' His face was dark and frowning with his rage. He'd agreed, but he didn't want to do it. Come to think of it, neither did I. I did not want to go down this metaphysical path again. We'd worked so hard to separate ourselves out, and sex with Richard would bind us close again. I didn't want that, wasn't sure my heart would survive being broken again. There's only so much emotional super glue in a person's soul, after that everything just stays broken.

'I cannot hold Moroven's fear off forever, *ma petite*, you must act before my strength fails us all.'

'Easy for you to say,' and it almost sounded like my own voice, not breathy with terror, but nicely sarcastic. Good. 'It's not your lily-white ass on the line.'

'If I could fly to you, I would, but it is broad daylight, and I cannot. You and Richard must do this, for already I am losing against Moroven. I can feel her nightmare coming closer, and when it comes close enough, I will flee and save myself, in hopes that when darkness falls there will be something left to rescue. But if you and Richard do what I fear you will do, then darkness will come too late, too late for Damian, too late for Nathaniel, and if you do not survive the deaths of your servant and your animal, then Richard and I may never see moonrise again. Is it so horrible to feed from our Richard, *ma petite*, is that a fate worse than death?'

Put that way, no, but . . . damn it. Why did it always come down to sex? Why wasn't there ever another way to fight?

Jean-Claude answered inside my head, 'Because we can only fight with the tools at our command. I am an incubus, *ma petite*, and seduction is both my curse and my greatest power. If I had another magic to offer you, I would, but it is what I know. It is almost all I know.'

'If the only tool you've got is a hammer, every problem looks like a nail,' I said.

Jean-Claude started to ask something, but he was swept away. Everything was swept away by terror. My heart was in my throat like I'd swallowed a fish. I was choking on my own heart. My skin was cold with the iciness of her power. So afraid, so very afraid.

Richard jerked away from my hand, stepped back from me, and I couldn't read his face now. It wasn't anger.

Gregory knelt closer to us and stretched his upper body out, over Nathaniel and Damian, stretched out until his half-leopard face was only inches from mine. He sniffed the air in front of me. 'Smells, so good, so yummy. Fear and flesh,' he let out a long sigh that tickled his breath along my skin, 'fear and flesh.'

I wasn't afraid of Gregory, I knew that, but I was afraid, and the fear was formless, but it didn't want to be. When Gregory drew his lips back from his teeth in what was supposed to be a smile, I gasped. The fear coalesced around that flash of fangs, that hungry gleam in those eyes. I was suddenly not just afraid, I was afraid of Gregory. Afraid of the claws, the teeth. I was afraid in a way that I'd never been of him, or any of my leopards. He licked my face, one quick movement.

I yipped, a small, high-pitched, frightened sound.

Gregory growled next to my skin, 'Hmm, do it again.'

Richard grabbed him and pulled him away from me. 'Stop playing with her.'

Gregory stayed crouched on the floor, as if he were half-thinking about springing up and turning it all into a fight. But what he said was, 'Alright, I won't play with her.' He turned and put his face next to Nathaniel's. Gregory snapped his teeth just short of his skin, and Nathaniel screamed. Our fear had found a cause to wrap itself around. There was no logic to it. Anything fearful would have done, we just happened to have a leopardman so conveniently at hand.

Gregory laughed.

Richard jerked him back and dragged him as far away as the bathroom would allow. 'I said stop playing with them.'

'You said, stop playing with her. I did.'

'Leave them all alone,' Richard said.

Gregory stood, and in leopardman form he was as tall as Richard. 'Don't tell me you don't want to play with them, too?'

'Yes, yes, I want to play, but I'm not going to.'

'Why not?' Gregory asked.

'Because you don't torment your friends, Gregory,' Micah said from the doorway with Richard's newest girlfriend beside him. She was about my size with dark brunette hair cut just above her shoulders. She was wearing a pale blue skirt and a white blouse with little blue flowers all over it. Sandals and carefully painted toenails completed the outfit. She was clinging to Micah's hand and arm with both her hands. You didn't usually hang on to someone like that unless they were your boyfriend. I realized there was an emotion I could feel through the fear – jealousy. What the hell was she doing hanging on to Micah?

She shivered in the doorway, and her eyes lost focus, as if she was hearing things no one else could hear. She whispered, 'What is that?'

'Fear,' Gregory said.

'Oh,' she said in a small voice, and she pulled away from Micah and walked into the room. She stopped staring down at us, then looked away. She blushed and met Richard's eyes, and blushed harder.

Gregory came to stand beside her, his furred form towering over her. 'You want to play, too, don't you?'

She looked down at us again, and this time her eyes weren't human. I'd seen that particular trick a thousand times, but this time I screamed. Screamed like a tourist, and Nathaniel pressed himself against me as if he were trying to push himself out the other side. Damian just lay in my lap, like the fear had already killed him.

'Get Clair out of here,' Richard said, and his voice held that first edge of growl. 'She's too new, if you bring her beast like this, she'll bleed people.'

I made a small sound in my throat, a helpless sound.

Micah took Clair by the arm and started leading her toward the door. She didn't fight him, but she made him pull a little, while her animal eyes in that pretty face stared at us. She wasn't embarrassed anymore, there was nothing human enough left in her to be embarrassed about nudity.

'What's happening to them?' Micah asked.

'Damian's first master is trying to kill them,' Richard said.

'How?' I wasn't sure if he were asking how she'd kill us or how it had happened.

'Scare them to death.'

Micah almost had Clair to the door. 'How can you stop it?'

Richard looked at Micah then. 'I let Anita feed on me, and Jean-

Claude comes riding to the rescue.' The growl had left his voice, and all that remained was tiredness and a sort of world-weariness, as if he'd seen too much, done too much, and didn't want to do it anymore.

Micah and Richard stared at each other for a moment, then Micah gave a small nod. 'Keep everybody alive,' he said, and he pulled Clair through the doorway.

She grabbed the door frame. 'They smell so good.'

Micah threw her over his shoulders, and the movement startled her enough that she let go of the door and he carried her out of sight. Her words floated back, 'No, I don't want to go.'

Richard tried to get his jeans unfastened one-handed, and it wasn't working. 'I need some help here Gregory.'

The leopardman looked at him. 'Going to fuck while you have the chance?'

Richard growled at him, and I made a small sound. Nathaniel whimpered. I knew in the front of my head that this was stupid. That Richard would not hurt me, not in that way, but the fear had a mind of its own. Nathaniel was a wereleopard, but he was terrified, too. No logic, just fear.

'If I shift, the pants will shred, and I don't have extra clothes over here anymore,' Richard said.

'I thought your control was better than that, Ulfric,' Gregory growled.

Richard turned some of that anger loose and yelled, 'I can taste their fear on my tongue, down my throat, as if I've already swallowed them.' He balled his good hand into the torn front of his T-shirt and pulled. He was suddenly standing over me naked from the waist up, with a look in his eyes that would have frightened me even if I'd been myself. It was a wild, fierce look, made up of hatred and lust. Hatred and lust in a man's eyes is a bad combination.

It seemed to take physical effort for him to turn away from me and look at Gregory again. 'Did you feel that?'

Gregory's only answer was a low growl that made Nathaniel whimper again.

'God help me, she's afraid to see me nude, and I fucking love it. I love that she's afraid of me, and I hate myself for loving it. The *ardeur* will rise, but God alone knows what we'll do before it does. With this much fear, with her, I don't trust my control. And whatever happens I want clothes when it's over, because I'm going to want to get the hell out of here.'

He undid his belt with one hand and squeezed the top button of his pants. The button popped open, and, still gripping the top of the pants, he made a rolling motion with his hand and the buttons snapped open in a long rolling line. The front of his pants spilled open, and he spilled out. Either he wasn't wearing any underwear, or it couldn't keep him contained.

I'd seen Richard nude enough times to lose track. The sight of him nude had excited me, made me nervous, afraid in that oh-my-god, where-am-I-going-to-put-it-all sort of way, envious when I'd lost my naked privileges, angry when he was being shitty, or trying to rub my face in the fact that I still found him handsome, but he wasn't mine anymore. All those emotions, and lust, and love, but never fear. Never that feeling that he was physically so much larger than I was, so much stronger, so much . . . he'd never hurt me physically, and I'd never been afraid of him physically, but I was now. I was afraid the way virgins are supposed to be afraid when white slavers snatch them away. Afraid of being ravished. Afraid of him using that body in mine. Afraid in a way that I'd never been afraid of anyone that I loved.

I put my hands over my eyes like a child. If I couldn't see him, he couldn't hurt me. Stupid, silly, but I couldn't stop the way I felt. Couldn't change the way I felt. I felt a scream growing in my throat. A scream that was waiting to be touched. I knew I was going to do it, and I couldn't stop it.

But it was as if he felt that scream waiting to come out, because he didn't touch me. I felt his face on the other side of my hands like heat, a moment before I felt his breath against the back of my hands. If he'd touched me, the fear would have spilled out my mouth, but he didn't touch me, not with his body.

His breath was hot against my skin, so hot. I felt Damian being lifted out of my lap. I wasn't sure how I knew he hadn't crawled out on his own, but I did.

'Anita, look at me.' His voice was very soft, and very close, each word breathing out against my hands. 'Please, Anita, please look at me.'

His voice floated through the fear, eased the tightness in my throat, relaxed the muscles along my shoulders.

'Anita, look at me, please,' he whispered.

I could breathe past my pulse again.

'Please,' he whispered, and he touched fingertips to the back of my hand. The lightest of touches, and my hands lowered an inch, two inches, and I could see his face from between my fingers. His eyes were pure chocolate brown, and at that moment, they were gentle. There was no trace of anger, or lust, nothing but patience and gentleness. This was the part of him I'd fallen in love with once.

He touched my wrists, gently, and lowered my hands away from my face. He smiled and said, 'Better?'

I started to nod, then Damian grabbed my leg, and the fear roared back, and the scream ripped out of my throat. It wasn't just Moroven's power, it was Damian's fear of that power, and the fact that I couldn't shield against it.

21

I SCREAMED, AND Richard's mouth was suddenly on mine. He kissed me, a gentle press of lips. Fear thrilled through me, all the way to my fingertips, as if terror were an electric current. I shoved him away from me.

I waited for the anger to come rushing through me, to ride over the fear and everything else, but it didn't come. In fact the fear blossomed into panic. Panic that freezes your body, numbs your mind, makes you forget everything you've ever learned about how to make your body a weapon, and all that is left is a small screaming voice inside your head that makes you a victim. If you can't think and can't move, then you are a victim. That's why panic will get you killed.

Richard knelt in front of me, only as far away as my arms had moved him. There was nothing gentle in his face now. He looked eager, anticipatory. He was on one knee, the other leg turned so that he shielded himself from my view. The body language was modest; the look on his face was not.

He leaned in toward me and sniffed, drawing the air in deep, so that his chest rose and fell with it. His eyes closed as if he'd smelled the sweetest of flowers, his head thrown back, just a little. When he opened his eyes, they weren't brown, they were amber, dark orange wolf amber. There was a moment where seeing those eyes in the tan of his face was breathtaking, then Damian's fingers dug into my leg. A fresh wave of panic poured through me, tore a scream from my throat, and Damian echoed it. I had a confused image of bodies, hands, being held down, cloth ripping, the weight of a body pinning us to the table and . . .

A hand wrapped around my wrist and jerked me up and away. Damian's nails ripped through my skin as he tried to hold on. Richard tore me away from Damian's hands, his horror, his memories, and his fear.

The moment Damian couldn't touch me, the panic faded, a little. I could breathe again. The fear was still there, pulsing through me, but it was diminished some. It was like the difference between drowning in the ocean and drowning in a fish pond. Better, less frightening, but just as dead.

I looked back at Damian, and he lay on the floor, his hand outstretched, and even from a distance, I reached back for him. I could feel his need.

Richard pulled on my arm, sharp, sudden. It threw me off balance, and he used that momentary stumble to swing me in against his body, my arm behind my back with his hand still on my wrist. I should have been more interested in the pain, but it was the sensation of being suddenly pressed against his naked body that overwhelmed me. It was not just being pressed against a man's body, even a lovely body, that unnerved me, it was as if my body remembered him. Remembered what it was like to be pressed against this flesh, these arms, and with the skin memory . . . it was as if the emotional scars tore open and spilled my heart out into my skin. You fight so hard, so long, to cut someone out of your heart, but it's not always your heart that betrays you.

But in among the emotional debris I felt Moroven pull back. We hadn't needed the *ardeur* to confuse her, all we'd needed was how Richard and I felt about each other. Just as Moroven didn't understand pure lust, she didn't understand love, no matter how broken. I don't know if the emotion frightened her, or if she simply couldn't understand it. She wasn't the only one.

We were touching, and the triumvirate was working just fine. We'd both thrown down our shields to help Jean-Claude raise the *ardeur* and save us, but shields protect you from so many things. What is love? What does it feel like in its rawest form? Lust, need, desire, and that aching want, as if the center of your body was carved out and hollow, and the only thing that can fill it is the person that you're touching.

I loved Richard. I couldn't hide how I felt, couldn't deny it. I was laid bare in his arms in every way. For a moment, I felt him feel the exact same way, then I felt something else . . . shame. He was ashamed, not that he loved me, but that part of him was angry that Moroven had fled. He'd wanted to drink my fear while he fucked me. That was the thought that came, not in words, but in confused images. I felt that to him my terror was almost the same as the terror of the deer he'd chased down and killed. Fear, even a little fear, made everything better – food and sex.

He let me go, stepped away so we wouldn't be touching. He clanged his shields tight into place and left me standing alone. I was shaking and couldn't understand why.

Richard's face got that angry look he used to hide what he was thinking. He grabbed his pants and went for the door. 'You're as horrified by it as I am,' he said, and was gone.

I wanted to say he was wrong, but in a way he was right. I wasn't horrified by the fact that he liked a little fear with his sex, a little rough play, most of the shapeshifters did. I think it had something to do with them being programmed to chase animals and kill them. If they didn't get off on the fear, their human sides might come to the forefront and cripple them for the kill. Or maybe, that wasn't it. Maybe it was something else. Maybe it was that Raina and Gabriel had been attracted by latent talent. I don't know, but I wasn't horrified with what Richard had wanted. The fact that he thought of taking me while Moroven's fear rode me hadn't bothered me. It was mild compared to some of the things that my wereleopards liked. Just because I didn't participate didn't mean I was blind.

No, that wasn't the problem. I dropped to my knees and stayed there. I'd felt that he loved me, still, but I'd also felt that his hatred for everything he was, was stronger and more important than his feelings for me. I'd thought he loathed his beast, but it was more than that. He hated what he liked in the bedroom. We'd been lovers for months off and on, and I'd never known that he was a closet sadist. How tight he must have to hold his own leash for me not to have known.

A hand touched my shoulder, and I jumped. Nathaniel was staring at me with those lavender eyes. 'Are you okay?'

My eyes felt hot, and my throat tight. God, I didn't want to cry. I shook my head, because I didn't trust what would come out if I opened my mouth. No sobbing, no screaming, no hysterics. I hadn't realized until moments ago that somewhere in the depths of my soul, I'd held out hope. Hope that Richard and I would work out, somehow. I thought I'd moved on – stupid. I hadn't moved on, I'd just hidden it away. I couldn't give myself completely to anyone, because I was still in love with Richard. How fucking stupid was that?

He did love me, but he loved his shame more. He hadn't run because I could accept his beast. He'd run because living with me, he couldn't pretend. He couldn't pretend to be normal. I'd never been much on pretending to be something I wasn't, and lately, I'd gotten even worse at it. Could you pretend to be someone else and truly be happy? I don't think so.

Nathaniel put his arms around me, slowly, as if he were afraid I'd stop him, but I didn't. I needed to be held right then. I needed to be held by someone who wanted me, wanted all of me, the good and the bad, the nice and the scary. Richard had been pressed naked against my body, and even the promise of that hadn't been enough.

Micah appeared in the doorway. 'Dr Lillian is in the kitchen looking at Richard's wound.' He looked from Nathaniel to Damian, then to me. 'Richard looks shaken, what happened?'

I held out my hand, and he came to me without me having to say a word. I buried my face against his shoulder, and that hot, hot tightness spilled out of my eyes, and my lips. I balled my hands into his shirt and cried.

Nathaniel was at my back rubbing his hands over and over my skin, making soothing noises.

'What happened?' Micah asked again.

It was Damian who answered, and his voice let me know that he was close before his hand patted my shoulder. 'Richard hates himself more than he loves anyone else.' It was only in that moment that I realized that Damian and Nathaniel had still been connected to me when Richard and I had had our moment. My first thought was, *He would hate knowing that they know his big dark secret*. My second thought was, *Who the fuck cares?*

I clung to Micah, with Nathaniel at my back and Damian patting me awkwardly on the shoulder.

Gregory growled in his leopard voice, 'What just happened? I thought you and Richard were going to fuck.'

Micah saved me the trouble of saying anything. 'Get out, Gregory, now before you say something even more stupid.'

'I didn't mean . . .'

'Now!' Micah's voice held that edge of growl to it. Enough that it sparked his beast awake inside him, and I felt it curl inside his body, like brushing up against a cat in the dark. A cat that you've shared a bed with, until the feel of that fur, that small body is like your pillows, or your sheets, just a part of a safe night's sleep. Comfort, companionship, warmth, and the knowledge that there are claws in the dark in case things go wrong. His beast flared mine, and it felt so warm, so comfortable, as those two invisible bodies rubbed against each other. The feel of his neck against my face, his skin wet with my tears, our beasts resting against each other, his arms around me, and I had one of those moments, where I understood that if I let him close enough, his arms could be home.

Nathaniel kissed me, very lightly on the shoulder. 'Don't be sad, Anita, please don't be sad.' I turned my head enough to see his face.

There were tears on his cheeks. I opened one arm so that I could wrap it around his waist and hug them both. I let myself sink in against them, let them hold me, let myself cling to them both. What is love? Sometimes it's just letting yourself be who and what you are, and letting the person you're supposed to love be who and what he is, too. Or maybe, what and who they are.

22

WHEN I FINISHED having hysterics and everyone had rinsed enough blood off them to be presentable, or at least not make my neighbors call the police, I got dressed. Micah had pointed out that we'd probably all be going to bed, so why bother getting dressed, but I needed clothes. Black everything from the skin out, including the shoulder holster, Browning Hi-Power, and hidden under my hair the hilt of a really big knife. It sat in a custom-made sheath along my spine that attached to the shoulder holster, though it could be worn without, but not as comfortably. Micah tried to point out that I probably didn't need that much weaponry to go into my own kitchen. I looked at him, and he stopped. No one else complained.

Have you ever tried to get dressed with three men watching you? I wanted Micah, and it seemed shitty to kick Nathaniel out, and Damian . . . we were all afraid what might happen if the vampire was separated from me by a room and a door. He and I had had sex, and he'd seen me very naked, and even walked behind me into the bedroom, but I still made him turn and face the wall while I dressed. Maybe the wereanimals were finally affecting my view of nudity. It just seemed, strangely, more intimate to dress in front of someone than to be naked. Or maybe my modesty had just had all the shocks it could handle for one day.

Speaking of which, if I hadn't thought it was cowardly and childish, I'd have hidden in the bedroom until Richard left, but it was cowardly, and it was childish. Damn it. Besides, Nathaniel promised he'd make coffee. I hated eating before ten o'clock, but coffee before ten was a necessity.

Damian had done one thing that made me feel better, he'd asked for a robe. His request made me realize something. None of the vampires I knew did casual nudity. They'd be naked for a good cause, but wouldn't just walk around nude like the shapeshifters did. Funny, I'd never thought about it before.

Nathaniel had fetched Damian's very own robe from the basement and had taken a side trip to put on a pair of jeans himself. He got brownie points for dressing without me having to ask.

Damian's robe looked like something straight out of Victorian England, and maybe it was. It was a dark, rich blue velvet, and heavy, almost more like a coat than a robe. There were worn places at the elbows, and the cuffs and hem were beginning to fray. But the whole robe screamed expensive. Damian wrapped it around himself like it was his favorite teddy bear. Once he belted it in place it covered him from neck to ankle, only his hands peeking out.

'That's not a robe, is it?' I asked.

He shook his head, as he pulled his hair free of the collar, so it spilled like a surprised red splash against all that blue. 'It's a dressing gown,' he said.

I nodded as if I understood exactly what that meant, then I offered him my hand. Not because I wanted to touch him, though that was there, but because of the lost look in his eyes and the way his hands kept rubbing the thinning velvet, as if touching it made him feel safer. He took my hand and gave me the first smile I'd seen since she-who-made-him had reared her vicious head. The smile was shaky 'round the edges, but it firmed up when he touched my hand.

I'd been afraid that when I touched him again that it would change. That there'd be lust, or love, or something else I couldn't deal with, but that wasn't what came through the touch of his hand. What came through was a sense of safety. Relief that I'd reached out to touch him first. If I touched him first, I couldn't be that angry.

'I'm not mad,' I said.

His eyes widened just a little. 'You know what I'm thinking?'

'Don't you know what I'm thinking?'

'No.'

'Ask him if he knows what you're feeling,' Nathaniel said.

'I just asked that.'

'No, you didn't.'

I thought about it for a second. He was right. 'Okay, what am I feeling?'

'Nothing,' Damian said, 'you are very carefully feeling nothing.'

I thought about that, too, and just nodded. He was right. I felt numb, at most relieved that Damian's need for safety overrode other complications, but really, truly, I felt nothing. I felt like one of those shells that washed up on the sand, so pretty, so clean, so white and pink, and so empty. That place inside me where Richard had been meant to fit, to fill, was empty, but not empty like a wound. Empty like that seashell, all slick and wet and waiting. Waiting for someone else to come along and slip inside and make that emptiness into their protection, their shield, their armor, their home.

Even thinking it that clearly, I still felt almost nothing. I realized it was close to that static emptiness where I went when I had to kill, but it wasn't staticky. It was a peaceful emptiness, like gazing out to a horizon of just water and sky. Peace, quiet, but not empty, just waiting. Waiting for what?

Damian squeezed my hand. I smiled at him but knew it didn't reach my eyes. I smiled because he smiled at me, more reflex than emotion. Inside was nothing. It was a little like being in shock. Shock is nature's insulation, the thing that shuts you down so you can heal, or sometimes so you can die without hurting, or being afraid.

Well, I wasn't going to die. You didn't die of a broken heart, it just felt like you were going to. I knew from personal experience that if you just kept moving, acting as if you weren't bleeding inside, you didn't die, and eventually you stopped wanting to.

Micah came to stand in front of me. Once it had seemed odd to have such serious intelligence out of kitty-cat eyes. Now, they were just Micah's eyes. He touched my face, and his hand was so warm that I wanted to rub my cheek against it, but I didn't. I don't know why, but I didn't. I just stood there with Micah touching my face and Damian clinging to my hand. I could feel that my face was as empty as I felt inside.

'You don't have to go in there,' Micah said.

'Yes,' I said, 'I do.'

He put his other hand up, so that he framed my face between his warm, warm hands. 'No, Anita, you don't have to.'

Damian was rubbing his fingers across my knuckles the way he did when he was worried that I would be angry with someone. I wasn't angry, or maybe he was worried about another emotion all together. Damian could help me be calmer, help me control my temper, and be less ruthless, or less quick to kill, but your servant can only give you what they have to share. Damian could not help me fight fear, or loneliness, or sorrow, because he carried too much of it inside himself. Today, the only real comfort he could offer was the touch of a friendly hand. But there are worse things to offer.

I closed my eyes, not to hide from Micah's serious face, but to bask in the warmth of his hands. I had to close my eyes so I could feel his hands and not be distracted by the color of his eyes. I let myself do what I'd wanted to do since he touched my face. I rubbed my cheek against first one of his hands, then the other. His hands moved with me, so that it was like a dance, his hands against my face, my hair, and me rubbing against him cat-like.

He kissed me somewhere in all that movement, with my face writhing between his hands. His lips were soft and full, and he pressed them against mine, firm but gentle. I opened my eyes to his face so close I couldn't focus on his eyes.

He drew back enough so we could see each other, but kept my face between his hands. 'I would spare you this, if you'd let me.'

I put my hands over both of his, so that we held each other. 'You mean make my apologies for me, and Damian and I go hide out in the bedroom?'

Someone had propped the front door back into place. The door hung crooked in the frame, and a little light leaked around the edges, but it wasn't bad. Damian had grabbed at my shoulder at the first line of light that crawled across the floor. I'd patted his hand, but didn't know what else to do. Micah informed us that he'd shut the drapes in the kitchen, so it was as dim as he could make it. I'd smiled at him for that. He always seemed to anticipate my wants. Sometimes it bugged me, but not today. Today, I'd take all the help I could get.

Damian would have been the perfect excuse to hang out in a darker part of the house. Unfortunately, almost as much as I didn't want to see Richard, I didn't want to be alone with Damian. Men can be sort of funny after you've had sex with them, some get downright possessive, others get emotional, and still others just want a chance to do it again. None of that sounded like something I wanted to deal with right that minute. Sure he felt calm against my skin, but that didn't mean that once we were alone he'd be able to stop himself from being male. After all he was one. I just wasn't willing to risk it.

'If you have to look at it that way, yes.'

'It's not that I have to look at it that way, Micah, it's the way it is. It would be hiding out.'

'She won't hide,' Nathaniel said, voice soft and full of sorrow that I couldn't understand, and just the sound in his voice made me glad at that moment that we weren't touching. Whatever he was feeling didn't sound fun in the least.

'Isn't discretion ever the better part of valor with you?' Micah asked, and there was a look in his eyes that was close to pain. But strangely, of all the men in my life, he was one of the few whose mind and emotions I couldn't read. I could read his face, his eyes, his body, but his mind and internal emotions were his own.

'No,' I said, 'never. Well, almost never.' I patted his hands and stepped back just enough so that he had to let me go, or hold on when he knew I didn't want him to.

He let his hands fall away from me, and the first hint of anger trickled into his eyes. 'I don't like seeing you hurt.'

'I don't like seeing me hurt either,' I said.

That almost made him smile. 'Trying to make jokes, I guess that's a good sign.'

'Trying, only trying? I thought it was funny.'

'No,' Nathaniel said, 'no, it wasn't.' He squeezed my arm as he walked by. 'I'll get the coffee started.'

'You're not going to wait for us?' I asked.

He turned back just short of the kitchen doorway. He was smiling. 'I know you'll get in here, eventually, because you couldn't stand yourself if you chickened out. But, by the time you talk yourself into it, I could already have coffee made.'

I frowned at him, and just a tiny thread of anger came with it.

Damian grabbed for my hand again, and I didn't fight it.

'Don't get mad at me,' Nathaniel said, 'I'm about to grind fresh coffee beans for you and use the new French press Jean-Claude got you.'

I frowned harder.

'I know how much you hate to admit that you like the French press, but you do like it.'

'It doesn't make enough coffee at one time,' I said. Even to me it sounded churlish.

'I'll tell Jean-Claude that you would like a really, really big French press.' He said it completely deadpan, and only the faintest of smiles and the tiniest gleam in his eyes let me know he was going to add something. 'Size queen,' then he was through the door, before I could close my mouth and decide whether to yell at him, or laugh.

23

NATHANIEL'S ATTEMPT TO make me laugh accomplished one thing; it made me feel better, though I have to admit the smell of freshly ground coffee helped lure me through the door. I couldn't let one ex-fiancé stand between me and my coffee, could I? Not and keep my self-respect, so in we went.

Richard was sitting at the kitchen table on the side nearest the door. Dr Lillian was standing over him finishing the bandaging of his entire right shoulder and arm. She glanced at us as we came through the door, but most of her attention stayed on her patient. The first time I'd met her she'd been gray and furry, but now she was a woman of about fifty, slender, with hair as gray and white as her fur was when she was in rat form. There was always something neat about Dr Lillian, as if her clothes never got too dirty and she always had medical supplies when she needed them. She never seemed to panic. In the human world, she was head of one of the few local emergency trauma centers that had survived the cutbacks. But she spent more and more time helping the semi-permanently furry. Since Marcus had died, we were really short on doctors.

Which explained why there was a bodyguard leaning on the other side of the doorway watching us move into the room. He was slender, a little shy of six feet, though something about the way he stood made him seem shorter. A tangle of black hair fell into his eyes, and they glittered like black jewels from that fall of hair. His graceful hands caressed the edges of his leather jacket, and I caught glimpses of at least four knife hilts before he let the jacket fall closed. There might have been six hilts, but I was sure of four, and that was plenty.

I'd been told the wererats were here, plural, but I hadn't thought about it. Hadn't really heard it. I'd been so busy not seeing Richard, that I hadn't really looked at the room. I'd strapped on a knife and my gun, but I might as well have been unarmed for all the good they would have done me, if Fredo had meant me harm. I hadn't seen him. He'd been standing just inside the door, opposite the side I came through, and I hadn't seen him. Shit.

I managed to keep it off my face. I nodded to Fredo; he nodded back. I wanted to say something, but I didn't trust my voice. I was thinking, *Stupid, stupid*. And that kind of stupid could get me killed.

Nathaniel was at the back of the kitchen by the sink, under the window that we'd once had to replace because of shotgun damage. The window was fine now, but I wasn't. I lived in a world where I had to see the bad guys. Fredo was on our side, but he was definitely a bad guy. Not a bad guy that would kill me, but one that could, and I'd walked into the room right past him. It was a rookie mistake that let me know just how badly I was doing.

I kept walking until I stood beside Nathaniel with our backs to the room. Damian trailed me like a lost puppy that had found a likely handout. I'd let go of his hand when I realized I hadn't seen Fredo, when I'd felt the movement of Fredo behind me. I wanted my hands free. I knew that Damian needed to touch me, but I needed my hands free. I was feeling claustrophobic. The kitchen's a good-sized room. When the curtains are open it's bright and shiny, but with the curtains shut and the overhead lights on, it was dim and shadowy, and I wanted light. I wanted to step out on the deck and watch the trees with the morning light on them. I didn't want to stand here in the dark and hold the vampire's hand. I wanted a choice, and I didn't seem to have any. I was suddenly so angry, and it wasn't Damian I was mad at.

The far drapes moved, and Clair came back in from the deck, all smiles. 'It's a wonderful view.'

'Thanks,' I said, and went back to watching Nathaniel make coffee.

If I just kept not looking anywhere else, maybe I wouldn't let my anger get the best of me. I wanted to rant at Richard, to scream and accuse. And I so did not want to do that in front of his new girl-friend or my *boyfriends*. Did I just say boyfriends?

I put my hands on the coolness of the counter, closed my eyes, and just tried not to think again. Not thinking was good. Not feeling was better.

A hand laid itself over mine, and the moment it did, I was calmer. I knew without opening my eyes who it was, because only one man's touch calmed me. Calmed me because he'd spent centuries perfecting his calmness. I opened my eyes and met Damian's green gaze. I wanted to hate him. I wanted to be furious at being trapped with him, tied, but I couldn't be. With him touching my hand, with his eyes so ready to fill with pain, I couldn't be angry, not with him. Shit.

I couldn't breathe, not a good solid breath. He took my anger, but he couldn't take the fear. I jerked away from him. 'I need to be angry right now, Damian, it's all I've got.'

A hand touched my arm, and I jerked away from it. Nathaniel's eyes were cautious rather than hurt. 'What's wrong?'

I moved back from both of them, bumping up against the island hard enough that the dishes rattled in the cabinets.

'Anita.' Micah's voice. He was at the end of the island looking at me with his serious kitty-cat eyes.

I couldn't seem to get a deep enough breath. It was as if the room was getting smaller. Nathaniel was in front of me, and either side of the island was blocked by the other two. I felt cornered, trapped in so many ways.

'Boys,' Dr Lillian said, 'I think Anita needs a little air.'

'I can't leave Damian alone,' I said, but my voice sounded choked.

She came and moved them all away from me, shooing them back. 'Come on, a little fresh air and some open spaces, doctor's orders.' She held out her hand to me, but was careful not to touch me, as if she knew what I was feeling better than I did. She eased me to the drapes and pushed me through them onto the open deck.

The light was dazzling, and I was blind with it for a moment. When I could see again, she was as far away as the wraparound deck would allow her to be and still be on it. She didn't say anything, just looked out at the view.

I started to say something, then thought, *Fuck it, she's right*. I went to the rail and looked out at the trees. The trees were a kaleidoscope of color. The wind stirred all that gold and orange, and a cascade of leaves like an upturned bag of gold showered down around me. The sky was that flawless blue that only happens here in October, as if the sky were closer, fresher, newly minted blue, as if all the clear skies until now had been practice for these few weeks of blue, blue sky. I breathed in the heavy gold of the sun, like pale syrup on the leaves. It smelled like autumn, that crisp, clean, sharp smell, that is made up of dying leaves, chill nights, and the warm breath of the day before night falls. You could taste fall on your tongue like some kind of bread or cake, something thick and nutty and sweet. I took in as much air as I could and let it out slow, as if my body didn't want to let it go.

I stood there leaning on the railing, drinking in the sunlight, the colors, and the rich scent of autumn woods. I was smiling and calm all on my own by the time Dr Lillian spoke. She stayed on her end of the deck, as if she wasn't sure how much room I needed. 'Feel better?'

'Yes,' and I smiled at her, though I felt a little embarrassed. 'Sorry that I lost it in there.'

'You've had some big changes in a very short space of time, Anita.'

'How much do you know?'

'That you've somehow tied yourself to Damian and Nathaniel, somewhat the way that Jean-Claude tied you and Richard to him. That you did it by accident. That it's a miracle no one's dead.'

I sighed, and the smile was gone. 'Yeah, I could have handled it better.'

'No one could handle all that you handle, Anita, better or worse. You keep surprising all of us.'

'Us, who?' I asked.

She smiled. 'All of us, the shapeshifters, the vampires, all of us. I can't really speak for everybody, but I know you are a constant amazement to the wererats. We never know what you're going to do next.' She leaned against the rail with her arms crossed over her clean white shirt.

'Neither do I, not anymore.'

'That loss of control issue again, isn't it?'

'You know, I really don't want to psychoanalyze myself right now.'

'Fine,' she raised her hands as if to show she was unarmed, 'but the next time you start getting claustrophobic, and you need some air, get some air, okay?'

'It was that obvious?' I asked.

'If I say yes, you won't like it, because you hate for anyone to be able to read you. If I say no, I'd be lying, and you hate that, too.'

'I'm just impossible to get along with, aren't I?'

'Not impossible, but not exactly easy either.' She gave a small laugh to soften it, and said, 'Do you feel up to going back inside?'

I took another deep breath and nodded. 'Sure.'

She nodded, too. 'Good, be careful when you move the drapes. Don't want to flash too much of this beautiful sun onto Damian.'

I nodded and felt the good air leaving me. Before I stepped back through the sliding glass doors, I was wondering, what was I going to do with him? I couldn't keep touching him all day. Could I? I was willing to do it up to a point, but all day would drive me mad. Especially if it was not just today, but every day. I suddenly saw an endless stream of days with Damian permanently attached to me. It was claustrophobic.

I half expected him to leech onto me when I came through the door, but he didn't. I stood there in the sudden dimness of the curtained kitchen, letting my eyes adjust. My eyes automatically turned to where Richard had been, but I forced myself to look for Fredo first. He'd moved closer like a good bodyguard, leaning against the small two-seater table in the breakfast nook. The white roses that Jean-Claude sent every week framed Fredo's darkness. His fingers were tracing the edges of his jacket again. I'd never seen Fredo use his knives, but something told me that he'd get to his blades faster than I'd get to my gun, not to mention my knife. The back sheath was really an emergency backup, not a main weapon. If I'd wanted a blade as a main weapon, I'd have put on the wrist sheaths.

I eased into the room away from Fredo, not because he meant me harm, but simply on principle. I wasn't at my best, and he was the only professional bad guy in the room, so I treated him with the caution he deserved. Besides, I had to redeem my earlier stupidity somehow, and the days when I would have picked a fight just to reassure myself I was still tough were long ago and far away. Being a girl, that phase had been shorter anyway. We are much more practical creatures than men, as a general rule.

Richard was still at the table. Clair was beside him now. She had a hand on his good shoulder, her small hand very pale against the darkness of his skin. She was watching me. Her eyes were blue, a dark sort of gray blue, but blue nonetheless.

Micah stood at the side of the island closest to the table. He seemed tense, but it was a flicker of his eyes that helped me find Damian and Nathaniel.

The vampire had wedged himself into the corner between the cabinets and the sink. He was holding his knees tight to his chest, his face resting on them, so that he could hide his eyes. He'd managed to hide almost all of himself in the blue velvet dressing gown and the fall of his own hair. Nathaniel was beside him on the floor. He was touching Damian's hands, but that was all.

Nathaniel looked up at me, and there was something in his violet eyes, pain, helplessness, something. I wasn't mad anymore, and I didn't feel claustrophobic as I crossed the kitchen to them. I knelt on the other side of Damian and looked a question at Nathaniel. 'I thought my touch might help him until you got back inside.'

I nodded. It sounded logical.

'He didn't want me to touch him much.' He wasn't hurt when he said it, it was just a fact.

I touched Damian's bowed head. His hand suddenly wrapped around my wrist. The movement had been too fast to see, which didn't happen often to me with vamps, and shouldn't have happened with this one. The speed of it, and the strength in his hand made me gasp.

He raised up and gave me the full look of those emerald eyes. I was suddenly struck by the sheer beauty of him. It was almost a physical force. As if beauty were a hammer and I'd taken a hit directly between the eyes.

'My God,' Nathaniel whispered.

It took more effort than was pretty for me to tear my glance away from Damian. Once I saw Nathaniel's face it was easier, and I could breathe again. 'Do you see it, too?' I asked.

He nodded. 'It's like a really good face-lift, not much change, but the changes are just right.'

'What are the two of you talking about?' Damian asked.

His talking made me look at him again, and I was held spellbound. He'd always been handsome, but not like this. 'It's vampire powers, somehow. I thought as my servant he'd be less able to do that, not more.'

'I don't think it's mind games, Anita,' Nathaniel said. He reached out to touch Damian's face.

Damian pulled back. 'What? What's wrong with my face?'

'Absolutely nothing,' I said, 'Richard beat the shit out of you, but there's not a mark left.'

He raised his own hand up and touched his mouth. 'It's healed,' he said.

I nodded, and it was as if I was mesmerized by him. Was it mind tricks, or had more than just the damage healed? I couldn't tell, and I wasn't sure whether Nathaniel was a better judge than I was. 'Micah, can you look at him?'

Micah came to stand at the end of the island closest to us. The look on his face was enough, before he said, 'Wow.'

But was it mind tricks? That's what I wanted to know. I reached up to touch his face, and he didn't lean away from me, as he had Nathaniel. I'd seen part of his memory of what had happened to him at the hands of other men, men that she-who-made-him had given him to, so she could feed off his pain and fear. So I understood some of the homophobia, but Nathaniel wasn't a threat to him, not in that way. In other ways, he was a threat to everyone who saw him. Oh, well.

I touched Damian's cheek, and it was solid. But it was all solid. Nathaniel was right, it was like a really good face-lift; there wasn't that much difference. What was it about his face that was different? What had kept Damian's face from being this heart-stopping before? I'd never made a study of his face, I wasn't sure I knew him well enough to know what had changed. Maybe my confusion showed on my face, because Nathaniel said, 'His mouth, his lips were too thin for his face, now they're full and . . . they match.'

Now that Nathaniel had said it, I could remember Damian's mouth, and this wasn't it. Was it just mind glamour? It had to be, didn't it? I closed my eyes and touched his mouth, but I'd never run my fingers over his lips. I didn't remember them. I kept my eyes closed and used my hands to guide me. I kissed him, soft but firm. I'd kissed this mouth less than two hours ago, and it wasn't the same mouth. The lips were fuller, as if he'd gotten a collagen injection while we weren't looking. I drew back just enough to see his face clearly. There was a slight up-tilt to his eyes, and they were bigger, not much, but just a little, or was it that his eyebrows had a wider arch to them? Were his lashes thicker, darker? Shit.

'What's wrong?' Damian asked again, and this time there was a thread of fear in his voice.

'I'll get a mirror,' Micah said, and turned and went for one.

'This isn't possible,' I said.

'Is there anything I can do?' Dr Lillian was at the far end of the island. Damian looked up at her, and she said, 'Oh, my.'

'What?' he asked, and his voice was frantic.

I patted his hand. 'You're fine, in fact you're . . . beautiful.'

The fear spread from his voice to his eyes. 'What are you talking about?'

Micah came back in with a hand mirror. He simply held it out toward me. I took it, but Damian shut his eyes tight, as if he were afraid to look. 'It's okay, Damian, I promise, you look wonderful.' But I sort of understood the fear, because even if it was an improvement, how weird would it be for the face you've had for a thousand years to suddenly change. I'd have had trouble with changes to the face I'd only had for part of a lifetime.

He was shaking his head over and over again.

'Please, Damian, just look. It's good, not bad. I promise.'

He opened his eyes a little at a time, but once he saw enough, his eyes went wide, and he took the mirror from me. He moved it around so he could see his eyes, his mouth, and there was some change to his nose that he could see and I couldn't. Like I said, I hadn't made a study of his face, but he had.

He touched his face tentatively, as if he expected it to feel different than it looked. He dropped the mirror, and Nathaniel caught it before it hit the floor. 'What is happening to me?'

I opened my mouth to say, I don't know, but Micah said, 'I think we need to call Jean-Claude. We know he's up.'

Good idea, I thought. 'Yeah, I think so.'

I actually got up to go for the phone, but Richard was at the end of the island, across from the phone, and I suddenly didn't want to be that close to the phone. His right arm was taped to his chest, completely immobile, like Lillian had started to mummify him and stopped. He wasn't looking at me. He was looking lower, at Damian.

'Healing and a little facial reconstruction, you are good,' he said, and his tone made it not a compliment.

'I didn't do it on purpose.'

'I know,' and those two words just sounded tired. 'Jean-Claude told me once that he couldn't remember what he and Asher looked like before Belle, but he'd seen others before and after. Belle never chose people who weren't pretty, but some afterward were more beautiful than before. It wasn't a common thing even in her bloodline, but it happened often enough to start the legend that it always happened to her blood.'

I looked at him. 'And when did you and Jean-Claude find time for all this information sharing?'

'When you deserted us for more than half a year. We had a lot of time to talk, and I had a lot of questions.'

I couldn't argue with the 'deserted us' part, so I ignored it. 'I asked him once if his body and face were vampire tricks, and he said no.'

'Vampire tricks aren't real,' Richard said, 'this,' and he motioned at Damian with his good arm, 'is.'

'But Damian's been a vampire for a long time; if this kind of change was going to kick in, then it should have done it by now.'

'I'm not of Belle's line,' Damian said. He was touching his face with just the tips of his fingers, as if that made it less awful, or something.

'But Anita is,' Richard said. 'Through her ties to Jean-Claude, she is a part of Belle's line.'

'I'm not a vampire,' I said.

'You feed like one,' he said.

Anger was finally rearing its ugly comforting head. If I could get mad, I'd feel better, and Richard's presence wouldn't bother me so much. 'You're as tied to Jean-Claude as I am. It's only luck that's kept the *ardeur* from you, Richard. Next time we get an extra special treat, maybe it'll be your turn.'

'I can't heal with sex, and it looks like you can.'

'Did you raise the munin when you were with Damian?' Dr Lillian asked.

I shook my head. 'I'd have noticed Raina being around. She's sort of hard to miss.' I heard a distant echo in my head, Raina's 'ghost' saying, so glad you noticed. I shut that particular metaphysical door tight, locked it, and bound it with silver chains. All metaphorical, or metaphysical, but all real just the same. A part of Raina lived inside me, and nothing I could do seemed able to rid me of her completely. I could control her to a point, but not exorcise her from me. God knows I'd tried.

'If it wasn't Raina, then one of you was able to heal during the sex,' Dr Lillian said. She said it like it was just logical. Two plus two is four, that kind of thing.

I was shaking my head long before I realized I was doing it. Shaking my head over and over. 'I didn't do this.'

'Then who did?' Richard asked. His face wore the arrogance of his anger. When he looked like that, he was both more handsome somehow, and less approachable. It was one of the few times I was sure that Richard was aware of just how handsome he was, when he was angry enough to want to strike out and cause someone pain. Why does anger make people pretty? Rage doesn't. Rage makes you ugly, but a little anger, that just seems to add spice. One of nature's cruelties, or maybe it's to keep us from killing each other more often.

'I don't know, but he didn't look like this after the sex. He didn't look like this in the bathroom when Mor . . . she-who-made-him popped up. He didn't look like this in the hallway,' I took a step closer to Richard, 'or the bedroom,' another step, 'or the living room.' Another step, and I was as close to him as I could stand and still see his face comfortably. He was almost a foot taller than I was, there were angle issues.

'The closest person connected to Jean-Claude in this room at that moment wasn't me.'

He looked down that perfect profile at me. 'I didn't go near him.'

'Jean-Claude might know the answer to this,' Micah said. He was behind me, not too close, but close enough that if I'd done something stupid, I wondered if he'd planned on interfering.

'Micah is right,' Dr Lillian said.

'Yeah, Micah is always right,' Richard said, and his voice held emotions the words didn't even hint at. It was the first real sign of jealousy I'd seen. Part of me was happy about it, and the moment that tiny glad spark reared it's ugly head, I knew better. I was ashamed of myself, and I hate that.

'Most of the time he is right,' but my voice wasn't angry. We needed answers, not temper tantrums. I made a motion with both hands. 'If you'll let me get to the phone.'

He moved, but looked puzzled. For a second, I wondered if he'd been picking a fight on purpose, and if he had been, why? Picking fights was more my thing than Richard's. Later. I'd worry about it later.

I had my hand on the phone, when it rang, which scared me. 'Shit!' I picked up the receiver and must have sounded at least a little angry, because Jean-Claude said, 'What has happened now, *ma petite*?'

I was so relieved to hear his voice, I forgot to be mad. 'You have no idea how glad I am to hear your voice.'

'I can hear the relief in your voice, *ma petite*. Again, I ask, what else has happened?'

'How do you know anything happened?' I asked, and was already willing to be suspicious.

'I felt Damian's master flee from your and Richard's emotions. Only the two of you could turn such a simple thing as lust into something so –' he seemed unable to find a word and finally settled for – 'disappointing.'

'You're talking to the wrong third of the triumvirate, Jean-Claude. I can put him on, if you want to talk to him.'

'*Non, non*, tell me what is happening.'

'Can't you read my mind? Everyone else seems to be able to.'

'*Ma petite*, do we have time for childishness?'

'No,' I said sullenly, 'but Richard tells me that some vamps in Belle's line turn prettier after a while. Is that true?'

'The change from human to vampire can bring on small changes to the appearance. It is rare even for Belle's line, but *oui*, it does happen.'

'So you really weren't this beautiful once.'

'As I told our inquisitive Richard, I do not know. I know that many acted as if I were this beautiful, but I have no paintings of my old face. I have no way to remember after centuries. I honestly do not know for certain. Belle never made much of any of us that changed, because she enjoyed the false rumors that her touch beautified all. If she fussed about those who did become more lovely, then it would tarnish her legend. You have met her, *ma petite*, she likes her legend.'

I shivered. I'd met Belle, secondhand, through a metaphysical possession or two. She was scary, and not just because of how powerful she was. She was scary because of her character flaws, a certain blindness to anything she didn't understand, like love, friendship, commitment as opposed to slavery. She didn't seem to see much difference between the two.

'Yeah, Belle likes her legend so much, she's beginning to believe it.'

'As you like, *ma petite*, but it makes it difficult to find truth in her court.'

'Fine, we'll never know if you and Asher were this beautiful before.'

'Asher says his hair was not the color of gold before, so that we do know.'

I was getting distracted. 'Okay, fine, but the point is, when did the beautification take place?'

'You became a vampire, and when you rose the first night you were changed. Due to the vicious nature of some when they experience their first blood lust, it is not always easy to see beauty, but it happens soon after they are brought into their new lives.'

I didn't argue the life part, I'd been too confused too long about what was life and what wasn't. 'So after a thousand years, you are what you are, right?'

There was silence on the other end of the phone. I couldn't even hear him breathing, which didn't mean anything, he didn't always have to breathe. 'Has something happened to Damian? Something more?'

'Yes,' I said.

'I assume the questions about Belle's line were not idle then.'

'Not even close to idle,' I said.

'Tell me,' he said, voice soft.

I told him.

He was calm, asking questions, getting details, in his so matter-of-fact voice. Over the phone without his body posture to go by, or his face, and with him shielding like a son of a bitch, I couldn't tell if he were truly calm, or not.

Finally, he said, 'That is most interesting.'

'Don't go all Mr Spock on me. What do you mean that's interesting?'

'I mean that it is interesting, *ma petite*. Damian is not of Belle's line, and, thus, it should not have happened. Moreover he is a millennium old, and as you so succinctly put it, he should have been what he was, and there would be no changing it, not at this late date.'

'But it happened,' I said.

'May I speak with Damian?'

'I guess so.' I turned and held the phone out. 'Jean-Claude would like to speak to you directly.'

Damian got up slowly, as if he were stiff or the floor wasn't quite even. The floor was even, it was everything else that had gotten a little less steady. He took the phone and said, 'Yes?' And from that moment on, they stopped speaking English. Surprisingly it wasn't

French, it was German. I didn't know either vampire spoke German. If Jean-Claude changed the language because my French was getting better, then he'd outsmarted himself, because I could speak German. Not like speak it, speak it, but I could understand it when I heard it. Grandma Blake had spoken German to me from the cradle up. I'd taken it in high school as my language, because I was lazy and wanted a leg up.

I couldn't catch every word. It had just been too long since I'd used my German, and Damian's accent was different from any I'd ever heard, and I'd grown up around at least two. But I caught enough to know that Jean-Claude was asking him if the changes to his face had happened during sex, or just after, because Damian said something in German about it not happening just after the sex. No, about an hour or so later. I could understand Jean-Claude wanting to save my delicate sensibilities. I did have a tendency to get pissy about sex I didn't choose myself. Then I caught the word for power, and Belle Morte's name. Then Damian saying a lot of, *nein*, or not that I've seen, in German. He hadn't seen me exhibit any of the powers that Jean-Claude was asking about on his end of the phone. I didn't get it all. One, I was privy to just half the conversation, and two, my grandmother hadn't used some of these words a lot. She and I hadn't had a lot of talks about vampires, sex, and metaphysical powers. Funny that.

When the conversation seemed to be winding down, I told Damian that I wanted to talk to Jean-Claude before he hung up. He handed me the phone not long after, and I got to say, 'Hi, *ich kann Deutsch sprechen*.' The silence on the other end of the phone was long. 'If you didn't want me to understand you, you should have stuck to French.'

'Damian does not speak French,' he said in a very careful voice.

'Well then you are shit out of luck, aren't you?'

'*Ma petite* . . .'

'Don't *ma petite* me, just tell me the truth. What other vampire powers can I expect to come on-line?'

'In all honesty, I am not sure.'

'Right.'

'Truly, *ma petite*, I am not. Even Belle has never transformed a vampire from another line the age of Damian. If you had asked me, I would have said it was impossible.'

That sounded like the truth. 'Fine, but what powers were you asking Damian whether I had, or not, and don't lie; if I order him to tell me everything you said, verbatim, he'll do it. He'll have to do it.'

'You might be surprised there, *ma petite*. With your greater commitment to him as your servant, he may not be as much slave to your will. I do not know that this is true, but I know that the more marks you carried of mine, the less pliable to my will you became.'

That was true. I'd always been sort of creeped out by the fact that Damian had to do everything I told him, just because I said so, but it had moments of usefulness, and now it might be gone. Well, hell.

'Fine, then just tell me yourself.'

'You do not understand, *ma petite*. That you could gain my abilities is unusual, but this is an ability that I do not possess, have never possessed. What has happened to Damian is something only Belle could have done, and only if he were a new vampire. So is this a new ability all together, one I have never heard of, and if so, then what could that mean for you, *ma petite*, for us, and all those connected to you? What if you have gained abilities through your necromancy that we cannot begin to guess at?'

I sighed, and was suddenly tired, not scared, just tired. 'You know, I am way tired of this metaphysical shit.'

'You also healed wounds with sex, without calling on Raina's munin, is that so horrible?'

'When I didn't do it on purpose, maybe. Think about that, Jean-Claude, I didn't concentrate and do it on purpose. What else might I do accidentally? You don't even know.'

It was his turn to sigh, 'The only other triumvirate that included a necromancer as their human servant did not exhibit this level of . . . power.'

'You hesitated, what were you going to say before power?'

'You know me too well, *ma petite*.'

'Just answer the question.'

'I was going to say, unpredictableness.'

I wasn't sure that had really been what he'd meant to say, but I let it go. He'd answered the question the only way he was willing to. I knew by now when he'd given me everything he was going to. I'd learned to let it go after that, because anything else was just frustrating, and rarely gained me anything. 'Fine, I believe that you don't know what the hell we're doing either. Is there anyone that would have a clue about what might be happening to us?'

'I will think upon that, *ma petite*. There is no one that I know that has ever managed to form two triumvirates that intersect as ours seem to. But there may be those who could provide some more general information on triumvirates, or necromancy, or . . . in truth, *ma petite*, I don't even know where to begin to ask an intelligent question. I cannot go to most master vampires in the world with these questions. They would see it as weakness. I will think upon it and see if there is anyone we can ask.' He sounded perplexed, which I didn't hear often in his voice.

'Alright, I'll call Marianne and see if she or her coven have any insights. I might even ask Tammy when she and Larry get back from their honeymoon. She is a witch, and her branch of the church has been dealing with supernatural talents for centuries. Who knows, maybe they have archives?'

'That is a good thought,' he said, 'Damian seems most distressed.'

'You could say that.'

'I do not know for certain, but if he were to go to his coffin and you not be near, I think he might sleep as he is meant to during the day.'

'What if he just goes buggers again?'

'Put someone downstairs to watch him. Someone, not you or Nathaniel or Richard, someone that is not part of either triumvirate. If your watcher does not see him sleep, then they can yell for you to come and comfort him.'

It wasn't a bad idea as ideas went, and I had nothing better. Also, I didn't want to spend the day baby-sitting Damian, or anybody for that matter. 'I'll talk it over with him and see if he wants to try it.'

'If he refuses, then you will, what, hold his hand all day?' There was the tiniest edge of jealousy. I hadn't expected that.

I spoke before I had time to think, which I'd tried to stop doing. 'You're not mad at Damian about the sex are you? It wasn't planned.'

'*Non, ma petite*, not the sex, though I do not lightly share you, no matter how reasonable I seem. No, it is that the three of you seem to have shared all four marks, though until I see you all together in the flesh, I will not be able to check that for certain. But if you share four marks and suddenly Damian is able to walk about in the sunlight, I must ask myself, if I had completed our triumvirate, would I now be a daywalker?'

Oh. 'I guess I can see that, but you've been as reluctant as I am to finish the fourth mark. You said you were no longer certain who would be master and who would be slave because of my necromancy.'

'And I am even less certain of it now, but to walk about in daylight as easily as moonlight might be worth the risk. If you have lost the ability to order Damian about, then that might be a telling thing.'

'I'll try to order him around later and let you know.'

'Thank you.'

'But there is also that immortality thing, not aging, neither Richard nor I were sure we wanted to give up being mortal.'

'And if you have bound yourself to Damian with the fourth mark, it might already be a moot point, *ma petite*.'

I stood there in my kitchen and was suddenly scared. 'Shit,' I whispered.

'*Oui*, if you have truly completed all the marks, then your mortality may be a thing of the past. If that were true, then taking the fourth mark with me would lose you nothing.'

'And gain you the ability to walk in the day,' I said, and my voice wasn't friendly when I said it, because I'd heard the tiniest bit of eagerness when he talked about walking in the daylight. I couldn't blame him, but Jean-Claude had been working on his power base for too long not to see the advantages of things. I couldn't blame him, but part of me wanted to. Part of me still wondered if I was more important to him for the power or love. Most of me knew that I would never know for certain, and truthfully, probably neither would Jean-Claude. Love was not the nice, neat, linear thing I'd wanted it to be. It was not just one thing, but many things. I could admit that one of the reasons I loved him was that he was hard to kill. His chances of up and dying on me were smaller than if he'd been human. A large part of me really liked that. I'd seen enough of what death could do, and at too young an age, not to appreciate it.

'Perhaps, or perhaps not, *ma petite*, this is more art than science, or so it would seem.' His voice held a thread of anger in it.

'What are you pissy about? I'm not the one trying to pick a language you can't understand so I can hide things from you.'

'And I am not the one, *ma petite*, that has fucked another vampire, a lesser vampire, one of my own underlings.'

Put that way, it did sound like he had grounds to be pissed. 'Am I supposed to apologize?'

'*Non*, but I do not have to like it. He has come to your body, and now he is free of the tyranny of the dark. One I could forgive, but not both. Both is a bitter thing, *ma petite*.'

'I am sorry,' I said, 'I didn't plan any of this.'

'Of that I am certain. I am even certain that Damian planned none of it. Only you, *ma petite*, could keep having such accidental sex.'

Accidental sex. He made it sound like I fell down, and there just happened to be an erection in the way. I kept that observation to myself. See, I am getting smarter. Out loud I said, 'Accidental sex. That's one way of putting it. Am I ever going to inherit a vampire power that doesn't have sex involved somewhere in it?'

'I would never say for certain with you, *ma petite*, your necromancy makes you too much the wild card, but it is doubtful. So far you have inherited my powers, or Belle's, or some version thereof. To my knowledge Belle's powers revolve around sex, as do mine.'

'Great, can you at least give me a list, so I'll have some idea what to expect?'

'I could, if you truly desire one.'

I sighed. 'No, just tell me in person when we see you tonight.'

'Tonight? I was hoping that you might come earlier.'

'We can't transport Damian in full daylight, his body might be fine, but I don't think his sanity would be. Besides, I've got to work this afternoon.'

'Always the work, no matter what else is happening around you.'

'Look, Jean-Claude, you've never seen what happens around me when I've gone too long between zombie raisings. Let's just say that I don't want a line of roadkill trailing after me, or worse yet, some 'accidental' zombie come shambling into my room.'

'Are you saying that unused, your power raises the dead even if you do not wish to?'

'Yeah, I thought I'd told you that.'

'You have told me of raising the dead by accident when you were a child. I assumed that was merely from lack of training and disipline.'

'No,' I said, 'it took me years to admit it, but no. If I don't raise the dead on purpose, then it happens accidentally, or I start getting followed around by ghosts, or the spirits of the newly dead. I hate that last one, they always want me to take messages to their nearest and dearest, and it's always stupid messages. *I'm fine, I'm happy, don't worry about me.* What kind of message is that to knock on someone's door with? I'm this complete stranger, but your dead son told me to hunt you down and say he's fine. Nothing else, nothing urgent, just, I'm fine, don't worry.' I shook my head. It had been years since I'd thought about that. 'I raise zombies, and the dead leave me alone.'

'Do they? Do they really, *ma petite*?' There was an edge of humor, but it held darker things.

'You aren't dead, Jean-Claude. I've seen dead, and whatever you guys are when you're up and running, dead isn't it.'

'There was a time when you did not believe that. I believe you once called me a handsome corpse.'

'Look, I was young, and I didn't know any better.'

'Are you certain at last, *ma petite*, that I am not just a 'cute dead guy'?' Again he was quoting me.

'Yeah, I'm certain.'

He laughed then, that touchable, raise-goosebumps-all-over-your-body sound. 'I am glad of that. Do you speak Italian, *ma petite*?'

'No, why?'

'Nothing,' he said, 'I will see you tonight then, *ma petite*, you and your new friends.'

I started to say they weren't new friends, but he'd already hung up. I realized as I hung up, I should have lied about speaking Italian, but hell, as good as I'd gotten at lying, my first reaction was still to tell the truth. I guess you can't undo all your upbringing, no matter how hard you try.

24

WE SENT GREGORY in his kitty-cat fur down to watch Damian. Gregory was about the only one in the house not tied to me metaphysically. Well, okay, Fredo and Dr Lillian, but Fredo wouldn't leave her alone, and Dr Lillian said she wasn't finished with Richard's arm. So process of elimination made it Gregory's job.

He informed me as he glided toward the basement, with his spotted tail swishing behind a very human-looking backside, 'I'm supposed to be on stage tonight at Guilty Pleasures. I can't go on like this. Jean-Claude will need to find a sub.' He gave that kitty-cat grin of bared teeth and vanished around the corner.

'What does he mean, he's supposed to be on stage?' Clair asked.

'He's a stripper at Guilty Pleasures,' I said.

She made a little *O* with her mouth. I wasn't sure why, unless her world was so protected that just being in the car with a stripper was a big deal. For her sanity's sake, I hoped her world was bigger than that.

'But, I don't understand, why can't he –' she made a waffling motion with her hands – 'perform tonight?'

Richard saved me the lecture. 'Remember that once in animal form you have to stay that way for six to eight hours.'

'I thought that was just because I was new.'

Richard shook his head, winced as if it hurt, and said, 'No, most shapeshifters spend their lives tied to a cycle of six to eight hours in animal form, then two to four hours of being passed out once they shift back to human form.'

'Sit down,' Dr Lillian said, and her voice indicated she expected to be obeyed.

He eased himself into the same chair he'd vacated. There were lines at his eyes and mouth, those tight pain lines you get sometimes, if something really hurts. How much damage had Damian done to him?

Clair tried to help him into the chair but seemed unsure where to grab him, since he used his good arm on the table to brace himself. She sort of hovered uncertainly by him, as if she wanted to help but wasn't quite sure how. 'But *you* don't have to stay in animal form for eight hours, and *you* don't pass out when you shift back.'

'He is your Ulfric,' Fredo said, 'no one's king is that weak.' His voice was deeper than his chest was wide.

Clair gave him quick eye flicks, as if he made her nervous. Maybe it was the knives. 'Do you pass out when you come back into human form?' she asked in a voice that matched the nervous eyes.

'No,' he said.

'I do,' Nathaniel said. He smiled at her. 'Don't ask the rest of them, they'll all make you feel bad, because they don't pass out either.'

'How long have you been . . .' Her voice trailed off.

'A wereleopard,' he finished for her.

She nodded.

'Three years,' he said.

I did quick math in my head. 'That means that Gabriel brought you over when you were seventeen.'

He nodded. 'Yes.'

'That's illegal,' I said.

'It's illegal in most states to contaminate anyone willingly with a potential fatal disease, regardless of age,' Richard said.

I shook my head. 'I guess I'm starting to treat lycanthropy the way the law treats vampirism. If you're eighteen you can choose.'

'The law doesn't treat it the same,' he said.

I knew that, but I'd spent so much time among the shapeshifters, that I just sort of forgot. Careless of me. 'I guess I forgot.'

'And you a federal marshal,' he said, but the biting comment lacked snap, because he hunched with pain at the same time.

'How hurt are you?' I asked.

'I'll answer that,' Dr Lillian said. She smiled, but her eyes were serious. 'If he were human he'd stand a very good chance of losing the use of that arm. Maybe he'd regain fifty percent, maybe less mobility. Your vampire severed muscles and ligaments all through the shoulder and upper chest region.'

'But he's not human,' I said, 'so he'll heal.' I let the 'your vampire' comment go. I liked the doc, and I didn't want to fight.

'He'll heal, but it will take days, maybe weeks, if he refuses to shift.'

'I promise that I will shift to wolf form when I get home.'

She looked at him like she didn't believe him.

'Just because I can shift back to human form almost immediately doesn't mean that it doesn't come with a price. I'd rather not be exhausted for the rest of the day. If I shift and stay in animal form for a couple of hours, it will be less of a drain when I go back to human form.' I think he was lecturing more for Clair's sake than anyone else's. She really was new. 'So I'll wait until I get home, so Clair won't have to explain why she's driving around with a were-wolf in the car.' That last sounded a tad bitter.

'He won't say it, so I will. I'm new enough that if one of my pack switches form, sometimes it brings on my change, too. And I'm not trustworthy when I first turn animal.' She looked down, not meeting anyone's eyes.

Richard took her hand. 'It's alright, Clair, everyone has problems at first.'

Everyone nodded, some said 'yes.' That seemed to cheer her a little. She looked younger than I'd thought at first, maybe twenty-four, twenty-five, maybe a little younger. If she hadn't been Richard's new girlfriend, I would have asked. But it seemed like prying and none of my business.

'Even if you shift at home, I've never seen you heal this much damage in forty-eight hours,' Dr Lillian said.

'So?' he said, sounding defensive. Had I missed something?

'If you go to school on Monday with your arm useless and then by Friday it's usable, don't you think some of your fellow teachers might wonder about your remarkable recovery?'

'I'll make up a less traumatic injury, something that could heal that fast.'

She shook her head. 'If they find out you're a werewolf, they won't let you teach children.'

'I know that,' he said, voice fierce, and the first thread of his power trickled through the air like a line of heat.

Clair's breath came out in a quiver. She looked dizzy. Micah put a chair under her, and helped Richard ease her into it.

'How long has she been a werewolf?' I asked.

'Three months,' he said.

I looked at him, and he wouldn't meet my eyes. 'Three months, and you took her outside a safe house less than a week before the full moon?'

'Doesn't your house qualify as a safe house?' he asked.

'You can come here to shift form, but I don't have a reinforced room.' Most true safe houses had a room with a steel door and reinforced concrete walls. Most people put the rooms down in their basements and just told those who asked it was storage.

'We were supposed to have a picnic today,' Clair said in her small, uncertain voice.

I had to turn around so Richard wouldn't see my face. You did not take a brand-new shifter out for a picnic, if she was having this kind of trouble.

'She was fine this morning,' he said.

I turned around when I was sure my face would be blank enough.

'She's responding to your anger, and your beast,' Micah said.

'I know that,' Richard said, a hint of a growl in his voice.

She swayed in her chair.

'Richard,' Dr Lillian said, 'you have better control than this.'

He just nodded.

Lillian sighed. 'If there was a way to heal your arm before Monday, your secret would be safe.'

'No,' Richard said.

It took me a moment to get the hint. 'If you're suggesting what I think you're suggesting, not only no, but hell no.'

She put her hands on her hips and actually stamped her foot. 'You are both being childish.'

We said no simultaneously.

'Fine, then I've done all I can for your arm. I will stay until we are certain that the vampire isn't going to rise and cause more havoc.'

'His name is Damian,' I said.

She nodded. 'Damian, then, but if you won't let her help you, then I think you and Clair need to go to your house. I would suggest that you take her to the room in your basement, before you shift. She seems very swayed by your power.' She said the last as if she wanted to say something different, but thought better of it.

'I'll stay until Damian is down for the day.'

'I think you've done your part,' Lillian said.

'They needed my help before,' he said.

I couldn't argue that, but . . 'How did you happen to be Johnny-on-the-spot this morning?'

'Gregory couldn't get anyone here to pick him up. He got worried. On his way over, his car broke down. I was next on the list at the coalition help line.'

I hadn't actually known Richard was helping staff the emergency calls. 'Why didn't he call AAA?'

'He was more worried about why no one was answering your phone than his car.'

'I didn't think Gregory cared that much.'

Fredo said, 'All your leopards are very serious about your and Micah's safety.'

I looked at him. 'I wasn't aware of that.'

He grinned, a brief flash of teeth in his dark face. 'You don't like being babied. They know that.' The smile faded. 'You are their safe harbor; they value that.'

I don't know what I would have said to that, but Lillian interrupted and saved me.

'You need to go home, Richard.

'Micah is here now, and Fredo,' she said, 'I think you can leave it to us.'

He started to shake his head again and stopped in mid-motion. 'I'll stay until we're sure.'

She sighed and shrugged. 'You are a very stubborn man. Fine, stay, stay and be in pain.' Then she turned to me. 'Is there coffee to spare?'

I had to smile. 'I think Nathaniel can fix you up.'

'I'll just bet he can,' she said, and did a polite leer.

Nathaniel took it in stride, with a laugh.

I don't know what the look on my face was, but it caused Lillian to say, 'I'm over fifty, Anita, not dead.'

'No, it wasn't that.' I wasn't sure how to put it into words, but it was more like you didn't say things like that about someone's boyfriend, not in front of them, anyway. There was that word *boyfriend* again in my head, with Nathaniel attached to it.

She was looking at me, sort of narrowly. 'By the look on your face, I stepped in something. Is he more than just a member of your pard?'

I said, 'yes,' and Richard said, 'no.' Which left the two of us looking at each other. 'I don't think you get to answer questions like that for me, Richard.'

'You're right, I'm sorry, but he's not your lover, or your boyfriend.'

'No, he's my *pomme de sang*.'

Richard shook his head and had to stop again. I don't think he knew how often he made that motion until today. 'I thought, we *all* thought, he was your live-in, but now I know he's not.'

'He does live with me,' I said.

Richard started to shake his head, but actually caught himself before he'd begun the movement. 'I know that, but he's not your live-in lover.'

'And that matters, how?'

'Alright, children,' Doc Lillian said, 'I made a careless remark. I didn't understand what a *pomme de sang* means to its, his . . . owner, master.' She sighed. 'I didn't mean to offend anyone, let's just leave it at that.'

'You didn't offend me,' Nathaniel said, and handed her coffee in one of the colored mugs he'd purchased for Furry Coalition meetings. He'd thought it would be nice if we had enough matching mugs to serve our guests. I'd agreed, if I didn't have to shop for them, so he shopped for them. They were all either a deep, rich blue or a dark, forest green. Nice.

He handed me my baby penguin mug with coffee nearly to the brim, just the color I liked it, pale brown. By the color alone, I knew it would be perfect. 'Drink,' he said, 'you'll feel better once you've had some coffee.'

'I feel fine,' I said, but I sipped the coffee. Perfect.

He'd also already plugged in the coffeemaker. I was right about the French press not making enough coffee at a time to satisfy this many people. Hell, it barely made enough for my early morning needs. 'We've got enough for one more cup, who wants it? There'll be more in a few minutes.' He smiled at the room in general, getting more of the blue and green mugs out of the cabinet.

'He acts like it's his kitchen,' Richard said.

'He cooks in it more than I do,' I said.

Richard made a visible effort not to shake his head, though he wanted to. 'No, I mean . . . Jason is Jean-Claude's *pomme de sang*, but he doesn't move around the Circus of the Damned like he owns it. Nathaniel acts like this is his home.'

Nathaniel had his back to the room, but he was close enough to me that I felt his sudden stillness, as he poured coffee and tried to pretend he couldn't hear.

'It is his home,' I said.

I was standing close enough to him to hear the slight sigh of his breath, as if he'd held it waiting to hear what I'd say. He was careful not to look at me, but he was smiling as he puttered with the coffee.

'Jason lives with Jean-Claude, but he isn't . . .' Richard seemed at a loss for words.

Lillian helped him out. 'Jean-Claude wouldn't have minded me remarking how cute Jason was, you minded when I said something about Nathaniel. If they're both *pomme de sang*s, then I think Richard and I are both confused about how we're supposed to act around them. Not boyfriend, not lover, it can get a little confusing.'

Nathaniel was very carefully not looking at me, or anyone, but especially not me. I don't know how I knew that he wasn't just busy getting real cream out of the fridge to pour into an honest-to-God cream pitcher. The little pitcher was blue, and the sugar bowl was green, so the mugs matched everything. I knew his favorite color was purple, and had asked him why blue and green, and not purple? His reply was that blue was my favorite color, and green was Micah's favorite color. The answer seemed to make sense to him. It didn't really make sense to me, but I was beginning to learn that things didn't have to make sense to me if it made the people around me happy, and the new dishes seemed to make Nathaniel very happy.

He set the creamer and pitcher on a little tray, along with little tongs for the sugar cubes. Why sugar cubes? Because Nathaniel seemed to get a kick out of asking how many lumps people wanted. He was like a kid playing house. No, that wasn't fair. He was like a new bride that had never had a house, or a kitchen of her own, and was really enjoying the hostess stuff. But it was like he didn't know what real people did in a house, so he was taking it from movies, books, or magazines. I mean nobody serves cream and sugar anymore on a little tray with little tongs, right?

Nathaniel was wearing one of his favorite pairs of blue jeans, so faded that they were turning white in places. They fit his lower body like they were painted on, and it was a nice paint job. His shoulders had broadened since he moved in with me. He was filling out, developing the body he'd have for the rest of his life, if he took care of it. A 'late bloomer,' my grandmother would have called him. He'd looked younger than he was for years, a delicate body to match the eyes and hair. It had made him popular with a certain kind of clientele that his old Nimir-Raj had pimped him out to. Muscles moved in his arms, shoulders, and back, as he set the tray on the table and began to pass out mugs of coffee. I watched him asking, 'How many lumps?' and 'Do you want cream?' He moved gracefully around the table on his bare feet. He'd thrown his hair over one shoulder like a cape, so that it was out of the way. I'd have never been able to keep that much hair out of the way without help. Nathaniel made it look effortless.

I sipped coffee out of my penguin mug, and watched him play Suzy Homemaker. I waited to be irritated, but I wasn't. In fact, I was somewhere in the middle of amused, proud, and pleased. He was so cute when he did this.

Richard tensed whenever Nathaniel got close to him, as if he'd have moved back if it hadn't hurt. He didn't take coffee, because he didn't drink coffee. Nathaniel offered to fix tea, but Richard said he didn't want any.

Richard looked at me. 'Jason never does this for Jean-Claude.'

'Does what?' I asked.

'Play hostess.'

'Nathaniel isn't playing,' I said. 'He's the closest thing we've got to a hostess. It's not really my gig.'

Richard looked down at the floor as if looking for inspiration, or counting to ten. Since I hadn't done anything to piss him off in the last five minutes, I wasn't sure where all the tension was coming from. He looked at me with those solid brown eyes, and I still missed his hair. The sad remnants of curls were beginning to grace his head, but it wasn't even close to what he'd had before he got mad at himself and butchered his own hair. 'He acts like your wife.'

Nathaniel moved back to the coffeemaker, and since I was still leaning nearly in front of it, that put him beside me. He was very careful not to meet my eyes, almost as if he were afraid where the conversation would go.

'And that seems to bother you, why?'

'You're not sleeping with him.'

'Yeah, I am, almost every damn night.'

'Fine, you want to split hairs, we can do that. You aren't fucking him.'

I shook my head. 'You always were a sweet-talker when you got pissed.'

'I'm not pissed, I'm trying to understand.'

'Understand what?' I asked.

Micah wasn't watching Nathaniel or Richard, he was watching me. His chartreuse eyes were very serious, as if he were afraid of what I was going to do. I tried to give him a reassuring smile, that I wasn't going to blow this, but I'm not really good at reassuring smiles. So his eyes went from serious to a little worried.

'You and Nathaniel and Micah.'

What I wanted to say was, Why do you need to understand it? But I was trying to be nice, or nicer. 'What's to understand, Richard?'

Nathaniel began to pile his hair up into a high, tight ponytail. It was a style women wore more than men, that high, bouncy ponytail that moves when you walk. But his hair was long enough that, to keep it out of the way for cooking, he had to either braid it or do the bouncy ponytail. Once he figured out that I actually thought the bouncy ponytail thing was cute, he'd started doing it more. He washed his hands and went for the fridge.

'How can you watch him like that, when you aren't fucking him?' Richard asked.

By the time I looked fully at him, I knew my face wasn't friendly. 'If you want to play rough, we can, Richard, but you won't like it.'

'What are you talking about?'

'Fine,' I said, 'we'll play it your way. Why don't you watch Clair the way I watch Nathaniel, if you've fucked her?'

His face darkened. 'Don't talk about Clair like that.'

'Then don't talk about Nathaniel,' I said.

Nathaniel seemed to be blissfully unaware of us. He got the big marble board out of the cabinet and put it down beside the sink. The marble was only used for one thing – baking of some sort. He moved to the fridge, getting out the dough that he'd made yesterday before we had to get ready for the wedding. Apparently, we were still going to have homemade biscuits, as planned.

'What is he doing?' Richard asked.

'I think he's making biscuits,' Micah said.

Nathaniel nodded, making the long fall of auburn hair bounce like it was on a string. 'Who's having biscuits, so I'll know how many to make?' He turned peaceful eyes to the kitchen, as if we weren't fighting. Of course, I'd seen what his memory of 'fighting' entailed, so maybe by his childhood standards this wasn't a fight.

'I want some,' Fredo said.

'Homemade biscuits?' Doc Lillian asked.

'From scratch,' Nathaniel said with a smile.

'In that case, yes, please.'

Nathaniel looked at Richard and Clair. 'Do you want some? I know Gregory will.'

'We're only staying until we're sure Damian is safe,' Richard said.

He turned his lavender gaze to Clair. 'Do you want a biscuit?'

She looked at Richard, sort of nervously, then nodded. 'Yes, please.' She patted his shoulder. 'We didn't get breakfast.'

Richard scowled.

I was willing to let the fight go. Nathaniel was right, without saying a word he was right, it hadn't been much of a fight. Of course, just as it takes two people to fight, it takes two sides to call a cease-fire.

'Why do you care what I say about him? He's nothing to you.'

I sipped the last of my coffee, put the mug down carefully on the cabinet, and smiled. I knew without a mirror that it wasn't a good smile. It was the smile I got when I finally got to do something violent, when people had been making me behave. If I'd had any doubts about the smile, Fredo pushing himself upright, hands loose at his sides, clinched it. He knew it was trouble. The look on Micah's face said he knew it was trouble, too. Even Clair looked worried. Nathaniel had gone back to smoothing out biscuit dough. No matter what happened, we'd need breakfast, so he was going to make breakfast. In his own way, Nathaniel could be as practical as I was.

Richard scowled up at me, and I knew in that moment that he wanted to fight. And strangely, I didn't.

'Even if he was only my *pomme de sang* he wouldn't be *nothing* to me, Richard.'

Micah had moved around to stand beside me. I don't think he was sure what I'd do, but, for once, I was okay. I took his hand, partly to reassure him, and partly because he was close enough to touch.

'If he's more than just food to you, why . . .' Again he seemed at a loss for words.

'Why aren't I fucking him?'

Micah moved me in against his body, so that he was spooning me and had his arms around me. Almost as if he thought he'd have to restrain me and give Richard time to get to a door. My temper wasn't that bad, honest. Well, most of the time. Well, some of the time. Oh, hell, I guess I couldn't blame him for being nervous.

I leaned in against Micah, let his body hold me like it was a favorite chair. I could feel tension I hadn't even known I was carrying seep out of my muscles.

'I thought you were screwing them both,' Richard said.

'Such a nice turn of phrase,' I said, and the tension just seeped right back in.

'You won't let me say *sleep*. I'm trying to avoid saying *fuck*.'

'How about sex, or intercourse, those are nice technical terms.'

'Alright,' he said, 'I thought you were having intercourse with both of them.'

'Now you know different,' I said.

'Yes,' he said it, and his voice was softer, less angry.

I felt like I was missing something here. 'What difference does it make whether I was having sex with one, or both?'

He looked down then, and wouldn't meet my eyes. 'Could everybody leave us alone for a few minutes? Please.'

Clair got up a little uncertainly. Dr Lillian got up, and Fredo moved to follow her. Nathaniel had rolled out the dough enough that he was shaping the individual biscuits. The oven dinged, indicating it was preheated. He looked a question at me.

I wrapped my arms around Micah's arms, pulling him around me like a coat. 'You can't kick Nathaniel out of his own kitchen, Richard, and I don't want Micah to go either.'

'It's not his kitchen,' Richard said, and he was angry again.

'Yes,' I said, 'it is.'

Nathaniel turned back to his baking with a small smile on his lips. He'd already greased up the pans, so he began to arrange the thick doughy circles on them, ignoring us again.

Richard stood, and even though he had one arm bandaged up, I was suddenly aware of how tall he was, how broad his shoulders were. He was one of those men that never seemed as big as they are, until they got angry. 'No, it isn't. It isn't even Micah's house. It's yours.'

'They live with me, Richard.'

He shook his head and grimaced, and made a low sound, not a growl, just frustration. 'Micah is your Nimir-Raj, you had the same reaction to each other that Marcus and Raina had. Instantaneous melding, but Marcus didn't move into Raina's house. They couldn't help being attracted to each other, but Raina saw other people. They weren't a couple, not in that way.'

'Raina wouldn't have known what monogamy was if it bit her on the ass,' I said.

Dr Lillian and Fredo were making for the door. Lillian grabbed Clair's arm as she went past, and took her with them. Richard didn't even seem to notice.

'Don't you dare talk about monogamy to me,' Richard said.

'You may have gotten a peek inside my head, Richard, but I saw into yours, too. I'm not having sex with everyone you thought, but you're having sex with almost anyone that will have you.'

'I'm looking for a new lupa,' Richard said.

'Bullshit,' I said.

Micah's arms were tense against my body. He laid his cheek against the side of my face, but he didn't say anything. He knew better.

'You always screw around when we aren't dating,' I said.

'At least I wait until we aren't dating to do it. You always manage to fuck someone else while we're still an item.'

I started to move away from Micah, but his arms tightened just enough. He was right. I didn't trust myself not to get more physical than was wise. Slapping Richard right that moment sounded so good. I stayed where I was, but it wasn't relaxing anymore.

'I can't argue that,' I said.

'I don't mean Jean-Claude,' he said.

'You broke up with me before I was with Micah the first time,' I said.

He shook his head and then screamed, partly pain, and partly anger, I think. 'Once I calmed down, I could have forgiven you about Micah. I'd seen it with Raina and Marcus, but you moved him in here. Even that, I would have let go, or tried to, but I thought you were screwing Nathaniel. I thought you were fucking him before you broke up with me.'

'One, you broke up with me.' I needed not to be held when I was this angry. 'Let me go, Micah.'

'Anita . . .'

'Let me go, I'll try not to do anything stupid.'

He sighed, but he let his arms fall to his sides. I walked out just far enough not to be pressed to his body.

'Like I said, you broke up with me, Richard, not the other way around. You broke up with me, because, quote, you didn't want to love someone who was more comfortable with the monsters than you were, unquote.'

He actually looked embarrassed. 'That was really unfair of me, and I'm sorry.'

He'd finally got me in the mood for a good fight, and he was apologizing, what kind of a fight was that? 'Sorry about what, that you said it, or that you believe it?'

'I'd really rather this was just the two of us, Anita. Please.'

I shook my head. 'You had your chance to be alone with me, and you didn't want it. These are the hands that held me while I cried over you, they've earned the right to stay.'

He nodded. 'I guess fair is fair,' he said, 'but there are some things that you deserve to hear that they don't. If you ever let me be alone with you again, I have things you need to hear, but today in front of them, this is all you get. I thought you were cheating on me with Nathaniel before Micah ever came along. Now I know that wasn't true.'

'What on God's green earth made you think I was doing Nathaniel that far back?'

'The way you looked at him. The way you reacted to him.' He looked at me, and his expression asked, Why wouldn't I think that?

'I'm attracted to a lot of men, it doesn't mean I'm having sex with them.' In my head, I added, *just because you never pass up a piece of tail, doesn't mean I don't,* but I didn't say it out loud. First, it wasn't entirely true, and second, the fight was winding down, I didn't want to wind it back up.

'I know that now, and I'm sorry.' He glanced at Nathaniel, who must have put the biscuits in the oven while we were arguing, because he was starting to get plates down, and the pans of biscuits were nowhere in sight. 'You asked me why if I'm having sex with Clair, I don't look at her the way you look at Nathaniel.'

'I'm sorry, I had no right to say that, especially not in front of her.'

'I started it,' he said, 'but the answer is simple. I don't feel for her what you feel for him.'

I shook my head. 'Why is everyone so determined that we're a couple?'

He smiled, and it was sort of sad, wistful, and bitter all at once. It reminded me of Micah's smile when he'd first come to me. 'Because you're more of a couple right now without the sex than I have been with anyone that I've been sleeping with.'

I didn't say, including Clair, because it was none of my business, and it would have been mean. I didn't want to be mean.

'Sex doesn't make you a couple, Richard, love makes you a couple.' The moment it left my mouth, I would have taken it back. I was just sort of frozen there, afraid to look anywhere but at Richard's face, because I didn't know what my own face looked like, I didn't want to show shock to Nathaniel, but I didn't know what else to show. I hadn't meant to say it.

'You always do that,' Richard said.

'What?' I asked in a small voice, that didn't sound like me at all.

'Fight, rail against it.'

'Against what?'

'Love, Anita, you don't like being in love. I don't know why, but you don't.'

I had no idea what to say to that.

'I'm going to check on Gregory. Either Damian's asleep, or he ate him.' His words tried to make light of it, but his face and eyes couldn't pull it off. But he turned and left, vanishing into the dimness of the living room beyond.

The kitchen was suddenly very, very quiet. If Micah was still standing behind me, no noise betrayed it. I knew he was still there, but he must have been holding his breath, waiting for me to say something, do something. The trouble was I didn't know what to do.

Nathaniel walked past me without a word. He had an armful of plates, green glass, blue glass. He started laying them out on the table in front of the chairs. First a green, then a blue. He went around the table away from me, then laid the last one back at the head of the table within touching distance of me. I'd stayed like some kind of idiot, rooted to the spot, not sure what to say. I couldn't declare undying love, because it's not what I felt. It wasn't.

He moved that small step from the table, and he was suddenly standing right in front of me, close enough that I got a faint whiff of vanilla, and it wasn't the baking. His face was serious, but his eyes held a hint of a smile. He leaned in and laid a kiss on my cheek, while I stood there like an idiot. I was afraid. Afraid that he'd demand that I tell him I loved him, or something equally ridiculous, or equally impossible. But he didn't. He just kissed me, then leaned back with a smile. 'I've had hundreds of people tell me they love me, but they didn't mean it. They just wanted to use me. You may never say the words out loud, but you mean them.'

The timer buzzed on the oven, and he turned with a smile. 'Biscuits are ready.' He used a dish towel for a pot holder and took the biscuits out. They were golden brown, and the smell of them filled the kitchen. He took out the second pan, closed the oven, turned it off, and looked at me. 'I know how you feel about me now, because you'd have died before saying it in front of Richard, unless it was true. If you never say it again, I'll always value that I heard it once.'

He started toward the darkened living room. 'I'll tell everybody that breakfast is ready.' He stopped at the door and turned back, with a grin on his face that I'd never seen before. One accidental confession, and he was suddenly cocky. 'But I still want intercourse.' He vanished around the doorframe, trailing a sound of masculine laughter.

Micah came to stand beside me. 'Anita, are you alright?' When I didn't answer, he gripped my upper arms, and said, 'Look at me.'

I blinked too fast and too often, but I looked at him. Things were moving too fast for me. I grabbed his arms and said the first thing that occurred to me. 'If I faint, Richard will think I did it because of him.'

'You're not going to faint. You never faint.' He started easing me into a chair as he finished saying it. I let him, because I was feeling fuzzy around the edges. I didn't want to sit here and have breakfast with these people. I needed some time to think, and the only way to get it was to hide in my bedroom. I couldn't bear to hide. Damn it, for the first time in my life I wished I was a little less stubborn, a little less brave.

My head was between my knees when everyone trooped back in. I didn't faint, but I don't know how, because sitting across from Richard and watching Clair butter his biscuits made me wish I had.

Nathaniel laid out silverware, fetched more coffee, made sure we had at least six kinds of jam, jelly, and preserves. When had there ever been red currant jelly in my refrigerator? I looked at this man bustling about my kitchen, and knew the answer, since Nathaniel had been doing the grocery shopping.

Part of me wanted to run away, but the other small part of me that usually saves me from being a total pain in the ass was wondering if they made those white frilly aprons wide enough to fit over Nathaniel's shoulders. I mean if he was going to play Suzy Homemaker, didn't he need an apron, and maybe a string of pearls? The thought made me giggle, and I couldn't stop it, and I couldn't share it. I ended up having to excuse myself from the table to let the laughter have its way with me. By the time Micah found me, the laughter had given way to tears again. Nathaniel didn't come looking for us. I was glad, except for a small part of me that kept expecting him to come through the door. I was ready to be angry if he came, and disappointed if he didn't. Some days I don't make sense, not even to me.

25

MICAH TRIED TO lure me out of the bedroom with the promise of breakfast and claiming that I couldn't hide in there all day. I think it was the hiding comment that got me. I accused him of saying it deliberately, and he said, 'Of course, I did. Nathaniel isn't expecting you to fall on your knees and propose. He's happy the way things are.'

'No he's not. He wants sex.'

Micah offered me his hand and looked way too serious. 'I don't understand why you hold that last part back from him.'

I didn't take his hand. In fact I crossed my arms over my stomach and frowned at him. '"That last part," you make it sound like it's nothing.'

He knelt in front of me. 'Anita, I love you, you know that.'

Actually, I didn't know that. People act like they love you, but how do you ever know it's real. I didn't say it out loud, but something about the look I gave him, or my body language must have said it for me, because he moved in close. Close and closer, until he was sitting in my lap with his legs wrapped around my waist. It made me laugh, which was probably why he'd done it.

We ended up with my arms around his waist, and he put his hands on my shoulders. His legs locked behind my back, pressing him up against me, about as close as he could get. 'You do realize that from this position, sex won't work, unless we trade equipment.'

'It's not always about sex, Anita, sometimes it's just about being close.'

'Now isn't that the girl line,' I said.

'Not if you're the girl, and I'm the boy.'

I felt my face going all serious and unhappy. 'I don't know how to do this.'

'What?' he asked.

'Richard's right, I don't know how to be in love. I'm not good at it.'

'You're great at everything but admitting it,' he said. He wiggled himself in even tighter against me, so that I could feel that he was getting happy to be there.

'You're trying to distract me.'

'No, I'm trying to keep you from getting angry.'

'Angry about what?' I asked, and my hands were sliding down his back as I said it. It was hard to be this close to him and not have my hands wander.

'Just angry. You get angry whenever you're uncomfortable, and what happened in the kitchen is going to hit a lot of buttons for you.'

My hands slid past his belt, to touch the top of his jeans. I'd once thought you had to be in love to be able to touch someone like this. It had been a nice thought, I'd liked it, and it had made me feel safe. My hands traveled down the rough fabric of his new jeans, but underneath was the solid swell of his ass. He had a good ass, round and tight, smaller than I liked, but definitely there. I'd told him he needed some ass just to balance out the front of him. Truthfully, Nathaniel had a rounder, fuller ass, more like a woman's, tight and firm, but round. I liked men with booty. My least favorite thing was a man who had severe white-man's ass, where the jeans just bagged over the butt. I wanted something to hold on to, something to sink my teeth into. When I said I liked meat on my men I didn't just mean one thing.

I'd buried my head against his chest, my hands cupping his ass. He rocked himself against me, just a little. Was this love? Was the fact that I could touch every part of him and he could touch every part of me love? Or was it just lust?

I raised my face up enough to touch the skin of his neck, so warm, so sweet. I'd been raised that you only loved one person at a time. If I loved Jean-Claude, I couldn't love Micah. If I loved Micah, I couldn't love anyone else. The only person I was really able to say I love you to without hesitating was, strangely, Asher. I was beginning to suspect that was because Jean-Claude loved him, had loved him for centuries, when they weren't hating each other. In Jean-Claude's arms channeling feelings back and forth for him and Asher, then I could say *love* and mean it. But here and now without Jean-Claude to push me, the word stuck in my throat like it would choke me to death.

Sometimes I thought I loved Micah, but that's not the way a person wants to hear love declared. Sometimes is worse than not.

I put one hand in the middle of his ass, so that one finger could rub back and forth even through the jeans, but my other hand slid up his back, got tangled for a moment in the thick curls of his pony-tail, then touched the warmth of his neck. I knew who was inside my head, even as I put a hand in Micah's hair and pulled his head to one side, so his neck stretched long and clean. Because we were almost the same height, his neck was just in the right position for me to lick along the meat of it. So warm, so incredibly warm. I wrapped my mouth around his neck, felt the pulse of his blood under his skin, and set teeth into that warmth.

Micah cried out, but not in pain. He ground himself against me tighter, giving me more of his neck, like an eager woman would press against a man. I set my teeth into his skin and fought the urge to bite down, to draw blood. Jean-Claude filled my head with images. Images of him and Asher, and Julianna, Asher's long-dead human servant. There was sex, but there was more laughter, more games of chess, and her doing needlework by the fire. There was more holding than fucking. Images of him and me, and Asher, but also of Micah. Micah's neck under his fangs, while I watched them both. Jean-Claude coming to find both of us asleep in his big bed, curled on the silk sheets, Micah's brown curls lying so close to my black curls that he could not tell where one ended and the other began. Jean-Claude let me feel his emotions, as he drew back the sheets and felt the first breath of our warmth. The sensation of him sliding his cold body between us, and how we moved in our sleep, waking slowly to his hands on our bodies. How much he valued that Micah would simply give him blood and not argue, or make less of the gift and the need than it was. Of how much it meant to him, that he could turn from Micah's willing, still bleeding body, to my body, and pierce me in a different way, while Micah watched, or helped. Seeing it from Jean-Claude's point of view was uncomfortable and made me want to slide away, but he whispered through my mind, while my mouth tasted Micah's skin. 'If this is not love, *ma petite*, then I know nothing of it. If this is not love, then no one since time began has ever loved. You ask yourself What is love? Am I in love? when what you should be asking, is What is not love? *ma petite*. What is it that this man does for you that is not done out of love?'

I wanted to argue, but Jean-Claude was too close in my head, and Micah's neck was between my teeth. So many hungers could be fed off this flesh, so many needs, so much . . . so much. The sweet tang of blood trailed across my tongue, and it brought me back into myself, helped me pull back before I hurt him. But he collapsed around my body as if we'd finished sex. He shuddered against me and let his breath out with a sigh.

I held him with my arms at his back, or I think he'd have fallen. He'd given himself completely to me. He hadn't tried to protect himself or worried that I'd eat his throat out, and he should have. But he'd trusted me. Trusted me not to hurt him more than he enjoyed. I'd never bloodied him before, never gone past teeth marks and hickeys. It had felt so good to hold his flesh between my teeth and not to stop, until I tasted that first blood.

He gave a shaky laugh and said in a hoarse voice, 'Nathaniel's going to be jealous.'

'Yeah,' I whispered, 'he's always wanting me to mark him.' The thought that came was, *Would it kill me to give Nathaniel some of what he wanted?* Not kill me, no. The question was, would it break me, and if so, how much? Jean-Claude's echo in my head was, 'Perhaps it will not break you, *ma petite*, perhaps it will heal you, and him.'

'Get out of my head,' I said.

'What?' Micah asked.

'Sorry, nothing, just babbling to myself.' Jean-Claude did what I asked, but his laughter trailed inside my head like an echo for the rest of the morning.

26

I WAS IN the kitchen eating biscuits with butter and honey slathered all over them. The biscuits were good, but the show was Gregory. He was still in leopardman form, but he was eating biscuits. Have you ever watched someone eat bread with teeth that are designed for tearing out the throats of gazelles? It was interesting. If he'd just put the whole biscuit in his mouth at once it would have been okay, but he didn't. He ate the rounds of bread dripping with butter and red currant jelly in pieces, delicately. Except that his jaws weren't made for delicate, so his fur was spotted with jelly, and he kept licking it off with an impossibly long tongue. It was disturbing, distracting, and vaguely fascinating. Like a combination of Animal Planet and Food Network.

It was good that I had something to amuse me, because Nathaniel was being very unamused. I'd known he might be upset about me marking Micah's neck, when he'd practically begged for me to do it to him, and I'd refused, but I had no real clue how upset. He'd been banging things around the kitchen. A cabinet door didn't just close, it slammed. Opening the refrigerator was a chorus of bangs, slaps, and the like . . . I didn't even know that plastic food containers could make that much noise.

In between slamming things around, he was agreeing with everything Gregory said, but his tone of voice sounded like he was fighting. 'We've been advertising a leopard for tonight, if they can't have me, you're it,' Gregory said, then licked that long pink tongue all the way around his 'muzzle.'

'Fine, it's not like I'll be doing anything else tonight.' Somehow I thought that last was directed at me.

Micah was giving me the look, the one that said as clearly as if he'd spoken, fix this. Why was it always me that had to fix it? Because I was usually the one who screwed it up in the first place. Oh, that was why.

My teeth marks were imprinted into Micah's neck. The marks had been smeared with Neosporin, but he hadn't had to bandage them. Good for him, and for me. I'd stopped before I'd hurt him too badly. It was actually less blood than the one and only time I'd let myself mark Nathaniel. It had been when the *ardeur* was new and I was still trying to find ways to feed it that didn't involve intercourse. Silly me.

The last straw was when he took the butter dish off the table, before everybody was finished with it. Gregory grabbed for it, and claws were wrong for grabbing china. The plate fell and broke all over the floor. The butter slid across the floor in a long yellow line, like a really nasty snail trail. I don't know what I would have said – probably something not helpful – but just then the phone rang.

'Someone else get that,' Nathaniel said from the floor where he was wiping up the mess, 'I'm a little busy.'

Micah just kept eating his breakfast, I think because he was upset with me for not saying something to help Nathaniel feel better. Problem was I didn't know what to say. So I got the phone.

'Anita, it's Ronnie.'

'Ronnie, hi,' and I was thinking furiously. Oh, yeah, I wasn't the only one having personal problems. I still couldn't believe that she'd turned down Louie's proposal. Out loud I said, 'How ya doing?'

'Louie left a message on my phone, so I know you know.' She sounded defensive.

'Okay, you want to talk about it?' I didn't take offense. It wasn't me she was mad at.

She blew out a loud breath. 'Yes . . . no . . . I don't know.'

'You can come here, or I'll meet you somewhere.' I was using that careful voice, like the one Micah used so much on me.

'I'll bring bagels,' she said.

'You could have homemade biscuits when you get here, instead.' I said.

'Homemade biscuits? You didn't make them, did you?'

'No, Nathaniel did.'

'Can he cook?'

'Actually, yes.'

I could almost feel her doubt wafting over the phone.

'Honest, he's really good at the baking stuff.'

'If you say so.'

'Well, we'd starve if they waited for me to cook.'

She laughed then. 'That is the God's honest truth. Okay, I'll be there soon, save some biscuits for me.'

'Sure thing.'

We hung up.

I stayed by the phone for a second or two, watching Nathaniel's angry back at the garbage can where he was depositing the broken dish and dead butter. I'd never realized that a ponytail could bob angrily.

Micah looked at me, and the look was eloquent. It said, fix this, fix this, or I'll be mad at you, too. There are a few downsides to having two men living with you. When they both get pissed at you at the same time is one of them.

Nathaniel stayed by the cabinet, hands on the edge of it, and his entire body radiated his anger. I'd never seen him this angry. It should have made me mad, but it didn't. He could be angry if he wanted to be, I guess.

I tried to think of something useful to say. He'd gone from being happy as a domestic lark to being as pissed as I'd ever seen him. The only thing that had changed was the mark on Micah's neck. He'd lived through Micah getting intercourse and orgasm, while he, Nathaniel, got almost nothing. So why was that one over-enthusiastic hickey the breaking point for him? I thought and thought until I could feel a headache beginning just between my eyes. Then I had a good thought – it was almost insightful. I don't usually get too insightful without talking to smarter and wiser friends. But suddenly there it was, the truth, I think.

I walked over to him and touched his shoulder. He jerked away from me. He'd never done that before. It scared me. I didn't want him that angry at me, ever. Micah was right, I had to fix this. But how?

'Nathaniel . . .' It was as if saying his name opened the floodgates.

'I can't live like this. You give me an inch, and then you take it away. Orgasm today, but only because of some metaphysical shit. You'll find an excuse not to do it again. You always do. He gets inter-course and orgasm, and I get nothing. But you marked me, me. Not him, me!' He was still staring at the cabinet, while he ranted louder and louder. 'It was all I had. All I had!' He had to pause to take a breath, and I rushed into that small silence.

'I'm sorry.' I said it fast before he could catch his breath.

'I don't know why I keep hoping . . .' He hesitated, stopped, then turned to me slowly. 'What did you say?'

'I said, I'm sorry.'

His face softened for a second, then hardened, and he narrowed his eyes at me. He looked positively suspicious. 'What exactly are you sorry about?'

'I'm sorry you're upset.'

'Oh.' And he was off again, ranting.

I touched his arm, and he didn't jerk away this time, but he kept listing all the things I wouldn't do for him, or with him. It might have been embarrassing if I hadn't been more worried about stop-ping the fight than almost anything else. 'You have to go to work tonight,' I said.

That stopped him, because I think it made no sense with his train of grievances. 'What? Yes, what about it?'

'If you didn't have to work tonight, I'd take you into the bedroom now and mark you, if that's what you wanted.'

He pulled away again. 'I don't want you to do it just because I'm mad. I want you to do it because you want to, because you'd enjoy it, too.'

God, he could be so demanding. I actually had to stop and count slowly in my head, because this whole dominant-submission thing hit my buttons badly. I'd done enough research to understand that the world of dom and sub was a lot bigger and more varied than I'd believed. That there were people out there that considered my love of nails and teeth during foreplay and sex to be perverted. That they considered even that bondage. I liked teeth and nails during foreplay and sex, I really did. It wasn't pretend, and it wasn't just for Nathaniel's sake. Once I thought it through to that point, I wasn't angry with him. I wasn't mad about what he wanted; I was uncomfortable because I enjoyed it. I knew that now, and I embraced it all the way through my head. Well, I wasn't quite there yet.

I tried for honesty with him and myself. 'I'd love the feel of your neck under my teeth. I'd love to sink my mouth around all the meaty parts of you and bite down until I was afraid I'd hurt you.' I felt heat rush up my face, and I had to close my eyes to finish it. 'I loved the feel of you in my mouth. I loved marking you, but I wasn't ready to admit it. And it still makes me uncomfortable, but it's not because it's you, it's because it just seems so . . . so, I don't know . . .'

'Perverted,' Gregory suggested.

I opened my eyes to glare at him. 'Don't help me, Gregory, okay?'

'Sorry.'

'Do you mean what you just said?' Nathaniel asked, and his voice was oddly empty, as if he were trying very hard not to be angry or hopeful.

I met his face, and even his eyes were being careful. I hated to see him managing me that hard, as if he were afraid if he appeared too eager I'd run. Problem was, he might have been right. I realized I'd been doing my own version of what Richard was doing. I wasn't running from as much of myself as he was, but if I hadn't had the *ardeur* to push me, I might have been. If I could have pretended as cleanly as Richard could, I would have. That I could at least admit to myself. The *ardeur* had made that impossible. But this wasn't about the *ardeur*. This was about Nathaniel and me, and the happy little domestic arrangement that we had.

I'd waited too long to answer. Nathaniel's eyes filled with such sorrow, and he turned away. Oh, hell. I grabbed his face between my hands and went up on tiptoes to make up for that three-inch height difference. I'd startled him so that he stumbled back into the cabinets. I plastered myself against the front of his body and kissed him. I kissed him as if I were eating him. I set my teeth into that lovely lower lip and bit down, not enough to mark, but enough to draw a small sound from his throat. I leaned back from the kiss enough to see his eyes wide and unfocused. His hands gripped the cabinet behind him so tight, they were mottled. It was almost as if he was afraid he'd fall.

I was breathing a little hard myself. My voice was shaky when I said, 'That wasn't metaphysical shit. That was just me, just you.'

His eyes closed, and a shudder ran through him from the top of his head to the bottom of his feet. He swayed, and if I hadn't caught him around the waist, I think he'd have fallen. His arms slid around me, and he laid his head on my shoulder. He hadn't exactly fainted, but he was limp in my arms. I realized, he was totally passive. I knew in that moment I could do anything I wanted to him. The thought didn't excite me, it scared me. I had enough trouble running my own life, I didn't want someone else's. But I kept my doubts to myself. He had enough of his own without me sharing.

'You promise,' he whispered, 'promise you'll mark me tonight.'

He'd said the P word. Shit. 'I promise,' I whispered it into the vanilla warmth of his hair.

He drew a deep breath that moved his bare chest up and down along my clothed one. My body reacted to it, whether I wanted it to or not. Nipples hardening from the brush of him.

He drew back enough to see my face, and the look in his eyes was all male, and brought heat in a rush up my face. It sped my pulse in my throat. He was submissive, but underneath all that was something that could have been very dangerous, and it was there in his eyes now, that promise of disaster.

'Come to the club tonight, see my act, please.'

I shook my head. 'I work tonight.'

'Please.' The please was more than just a word, it filled his eyes. He wanted me to see him on stage, surrounded by screaming fans. Maybe he wanted to impress on me that even if I didn't want him, others did. I guess I'd earned having my face rubbed in it.

'What time do you go on?'

He told me.

'I can catch some of it, but probably not all of it.'

He kissed me, hard and strangely chaste, and bounced toward the door. 'I'll need to see if my costume is ready for tonight.' He turned at the door with that eager look still on his face. 'What if I turn furry, will you still mark me?'

'I don't do furry,' I said.

He poked his lip out at me, like a spoiled child.

'You are so damn pushy, you do know that, right?'

He smiled.

'I don't do furry.'

'But if I'm not furry, you'll do it?' Something about the way he asked it made me suspicious, but I nodded.

'Yes.'

He vanished into the dimness of the living room. 'I'll see you tonight at the club.'

I yelled after him. 'If there's another murder, all bets are off. Murder takes precedence over watching my boyfriend strip.' There was that word again, *boyfriend*.

I heard Nathaniel's laugh trail down the stairs. It reminded me of another man in my life, who'd left me with a laugh this morning. I was just amusing the hell out of everybody today.

27

MICAH'S KISS WAS still warm on my lips when Ronnie rang the doorbell. Having had no sleep last night was finally catching up with Micah, so he'd gone to bed. Besides, Ronnie wouldn't want an audience.

She was eyeing the door as I dragged it open. 'What happened here?'

I tried to think of a short version, couldn't come up with one, and said, 'Let's get coffee first.'

Her eyebrows went up, but it was all I could see of her eyes behind the dark sunglasses. She shrugged. She was wearing the brown leather jacket that had become her latest favorite coat. She had it zipped up more than halfway and a cable-knit sweater peeked out from under it.

I hid my frown. It had to be seventy outside. I eased the door back into its frame. 'Is it cold outside, or am I missing something?'

Her shoulders hunched. 'I've been cold since I left the wedding last night. I just can't seem to get warm.'

I did not remark that most shapeshifters have a slightly higher body temperature than we mere humans, and that maybe the warmth she was missing went by the name of Louie. I didn't say it, because it would have been too obvious, and too cruel.

She walked through the darkened living room, to the opened curtains of the kitchen beyond. When I'd been sure that Damian was down for the day, I'd opened the drapes. She hesitated just inside the kitchen. 'Where is everybody?'

'Micah had to get some sleep. Gregory and Nathaniel are upstairs working on an outfit for work. Something about some straps breaking.'

She sat in the chair that Richard had been in, so she could keep an eye on most of the doors, and still look outside at the view. Or maybe it had been an accident, and I was projecting why. I doubted Richard had thought about safety considerations when he chose the seat. But again, maybe I wasn't being fair. Oh, well.

She kept the dark glasses on, though it wasn't that bright anymore. Her blond hair was straight, but thick, and looked like she'd combed it, but nothing else, so the ends didn't do the curl up that she liked. She almost never went out without more done to it than this. In fact, she sat hunched at the table, over the coffee mug, like a hangover victim.

'You ready for biscuits?' I asked.

'Does he actually cook?'

I almost said, If you were around more, you'd know, but I was good. 'Yeah, he cooks. He does the grocery shopping, most of the menu planning, and most of the housework.'

'My, isn't he a regular domestic goddess.' Her voice was ugly when she said it.

I'd be nice because she was hurting, but that would only cover so much, then she'd piss me off, and I really didn't want to fight with Ronnie this morning. 'I needed a wife,' I said, and managed to keep my voice neutral.

'Don't we all,' she said, and there was no malice now. She took the tiniest sip of coffee. 'I don't think I could eat right now.'

I took a much bigger sip of coffee, and said, 'Okay, do you have a plan for how this talk will go?'

She looked up at me, still wearing the glasses so I couldn't see her eyes. 'What do you mean?'

'You wanted to talk, I assume about Louie and what happened last night, right?'

'Yeah.'

'Then talk,' I said.

'It's not that simple,' she said.

'Okay, then can I ask a question?'

'Depends on the question,' she said.

I took a big breath and plunged into the deep end. 'Why did you say no to Louie's proposal?'

'Oh, not you, too.'

'What?' I asked.

'Don't tell me you expected me to just say yes?'

I wanted her to take off the glasses so I could see her eyes, see what she was thinking. 'Actually, yeah.'

'Why, for God's sake?'

'Because I've never seen you happier for longer with anyone,' I said.

She pushed her coffee away, as if she was angry at it, too. 'Happy the way things *are*, Anita. Why does he have to go and change everything?'

'You spend more nights at each other's places together than alone, right?'

She just nodded.

'He said he offered to move in together first, why not try it?'

'Because I want my stuff. I love Louie, but I hate how he's taken over my closet, my medicine cabinet. He's taken two of the dresser drawers over for his clothes.'

'The bastard,' I said.

'It's not funny,' she said.

'No, I know. Did you tell him you didn't like him moving his stuff in?'

'I tried.'

'Do you want him gone, poof, out of your life?'

She shook her head. 'No, but I want my apartment back, the way it was. I don't like coming home and finding that he's rearranged everything in my cabinets so it's easier to find. If I want to dig through every cabinet to find tomato paste, then it was my choice. He didn't even ask, I just came home one night, and he'd organized everything in the kitchen. I couldn't find anything.' She must have sounded pouty even to herself, because she jerked off the glasses and gave the full force of those pain-filled gray eyes. 'You think I'm being silly, don't you?'

'No, he should have probably asked you before rearranging everything.' The fact that Nathaniel had not only rearranged everything in my kitchen, but also thrown out the non-matching stuff was probably best kept to myself.

'I love dating Louie, but I don't want to marry anybody.'

'Okay.'

'Just okay, you're not going to try talking me into it?'

'Hey, I'm not headed for wedded bliss either, who am I to force you into it?'

She looked at me, as if searching my face for a lie. She was pale and hollow-eyed, as if she hadn't gotten much more sleep than Micah. 'But you've let Micah move in with you.'

I nodded and drank coffee. 'Yes.'

'Why?'

'Why what?'

'Why did you want him to move in with you? I thought you liked your independence as much as I do.'

'I'm still independent, Ronnie. Micah moving in didn't change that.'

'He doesn't try to order you around?'

I just looked at her.

'I'm sorry, Anita, but my dad was such a bastard to my mother. I've seen pictures of her on stage in college. She wanted so much, but he wouldn't have a wife that worked. She had to be the perfect little homemaker. She hated it, and she hated him.'

'You aren't your mother,' I said, 'and Louie isn't your father.' Sometimes in these heart-to-heart talks you have to state the obvious.

'You weren't there, Anita, you didn't see it. She fell into a bottle, and he never noticed, because on the outside she was perfect. She never got roaring drunk, or falling down drunk. It was just like she needed this constant buzz to see her through the day, and the night. A functioning alchoholic is what they call it.'

I didn't know what to say to that. We'd both told each other our sad stories years ago. She knew all about my mother's death, my father marrying the ice princess stepmother, and my perfect stepsister. We'd shared our bitterness toward our familes long ago. I knew all this, so why tell it again? Because something about the proposal had brought it up.

'You told me months ago that Louie is nothing like your dad.'

'Yeah, but he still wants to own me.'

'Own you,' I said, 'what does that mean, own you?'

'We date, we have great sex, we enjoy each other's company, why does he have to move in, or make me marry him?' There was something like real fear in her face.

I touched her hand where it lay clenched on the tabletop. 'Ronnie, he can't make you marry him.'

'But if I don't agree to something, he'll leave. We either move forward, or he's gone. That's him trying to force me to marry him.'

I felt like I wasn't qualified for this talk, because her logic wasn't bad, but it wasn't like that. I knew Louie, and he'd have been horrified that she saw his proposal and his need to finalize things as ownership. I was almost a hundred-percent certain he didn't mean it that way. I squeezed her hand and tried to think of what to say that would help things instead of hurt. Nothing came to mind.

'I don't know what to say, Ronnie, except that I don't believe Louie meant to hurt you like this. He loves you, and thought you loved him, and when people love each other, they tend to want to get married.'

She took her hand back. 'How do I know this is love? I mean *the* love, like till-death-do-you-part love?'

Finally something I could answer. 'You don't.'

'What do you mean, you don't? Isn't there supposed to be a test, or a sign, or something? I thought if I ever fell in love that this panic wouldn't be here. That I would be totally sure and unafraid, but I'm not. I'm terrified. Doesn't that mean that Louie isn't the one? That it would be a terrible mistake? Aren't you supposed to be sure?'

Now I knew I was unqualified for this conversation. I needed like a pinch hitter to offer better advice than I had. 'I don't know.'

'Were you sure when you let Micah move in, sure that it was the right thing to do?'

I thought about it, then shrugged. 'It wasn't like that. He moved in almost before we'd dated, I . . .' How do you put into words things that you only feel, things that have no words attached to them? 'I don't know why I didn't panic when he moved in, it just happened. One day I walk into the bathroom, and there's a razor and a shaving kit. Then, when the clean clothes got put away, his T-shirts got mixed in with mine, and since they're the same size, we left it that way. I've never dated anyone before who can wear the same clothes I can, it's kind of neat to wear his jeans sometimes, or his shirt, especially if it smells like his cologne.'

'God, you love him,' she said in despair, almost a wail.

I shrugged and drank coffee, because talking was making it worse. 'Maybe,' I said.

She shook her head. 'No, no, your face goes all soft when you talk about him. You love him.' She crossed her arms over her chest and looked at me like I'd betrayed her somehow.

'Look, Micah moved in gradually, but I didn't feel crowded the way you did with Louie. I like having his things in the bathroom. I like having a his and her side of the closet. Seeing his stuff with my stuff gives me a full cupboard feeling.'

'A what?' she asked.

'Getting a T-shirt out and realizing that it's one I bought for him because it brings out the green in his eyes gives me that "I've got my favorite foods in the cupboard and it's a winter night, and I don't have to go out in it" feeling. I've got everything I need at home.'

She looked at me in soft horror.

Hearing myself say it out loud was a little frightening, but mostly it was thrilling. Because I'd answered my question, in trying to answer hers, I'd answered my own. I was smiling, even as she looked at me in shock. I couldn't help the smile, I was feeling better than I'd felt in days. But another thought occurred to me. I wasn't smiling when I said, 'Remember how you couldn't understand why I didn't just jump at Richard when he asked me to marry him?'

'I didn't say marry him, I just said dump the vampire and keep the werewolf.'

That made me smile. 'I remember coming home, and Richard had used his key to get in to cook me dinner without asking, and I hated it. I felt all grumpy and like my privacy had been invaded.'

She nodded. 'That's it, it's like putting on a new sweater that's just the right color and fits perfectly, but the next time you wear it, you realize it's scratchy, and unless you wear a shirt under it, it itches you. It's a great sweater, but you need a little distance between it and your skin.'

I thought about it and had to agree. 'That's pretty good, scratchy, yeah.'

'But you didn't feel that way when Micah moved in?' she asked in a voice that had gone soft and small.

I shook my head. 'It was very weird. I knew nothing about him, really, but it just . . . clicked.'

'Love at first sight,' she said, softly.

'"Marry in haste, repent at leisure," they say.'

'But you didn't marry him,' she said, 'why not?'

'One, neither of us has asked, and two, I don't think either of us feels the need.' There was also the matter of Jean-Claude and Asher, and Nathaniel, but I didn't want to muddy the waters, so I didn't bring them up.

'Then why does Louie want to get married?'

'You'd have to ask him, Ronnie. He did say he'd offered to just live together, but you didn't want that either.'

'I like my space,' she said.

'Then tell him that,' I said.

'I'll lose him if I tell him that.'

'Then you've got to decide whether you like your space or him more.'

'Just like that,' she said.

I nodded. 'Just like that.'

'You make it sound simple.'

'I don't mean to,' I said, 'but Louie wants the two of you to go to bed together every night and to wake up beside you every morning. That doesn't sound so bad.'

She laid her head on her arms, so that all I could see was the back of her head. As far as I could tell, she wasn't crying, but . . . 'Ronnie, did I say something wrong?'

She said something I couldn't understand.

'Sorry, I didn't hear that.'

She raised her head enough to say, 'I don't want to go to bed every night and wake up every morning with him.'

'You want separate bedrooms?' I asked before my brain could tell me it was a stupid question.

'No,' she said and sat up, brushing at the tears that had just started. She seemed more angry or impatient than tearful. 'What if I meet a cute guy? What if I meet someone I want to sleep with, and it isn't Louie?' The tears were gone. She was just looking at me with that appeal on her face. That, Don't you understand? look.

'You mean, you don't want to be monogamous,' I said.

'No, I mean I'm not sure I'm ready to be monogamous.'

I wasn't sure what to say to that one, because it wasn't something I'd had to give up. 'Most people want to be monogamous, Ronnie. I mean how would you feel if Louie slept with someone else?'

'Relieved,' she said, 'because then I could be mad and kick his ass out. It'd be over.'

'Do you mean that?' I asked, and I tried to see past the pain and confusion, but there was too much of it.

'Yes,' she said. 'No, oh, hell, Anita, I don't know. I thought we had a good thing going, if I could get him to slow down a little, then he suddenly puts it into high gear.'

'How long have you guys been dating?'

'Almost two years,' she said.

'You never told me about feeling crowded before,' I said.

'How could I? You were drowning in domestic bliss. All the things that I didn't want, you were enjoying.'

I remembered that Louie had said maybe Ronnie hadn't distanced herself because I was dating Jean-Claude, but because she had problems with me not having problems with Micah. I'd thought he was wrong, now I wasn't so sure. 'I'm always willing to listen, Ronnie.'

'I couldn't, Anita. You fuck this guy you've just met, and suddenly he's living with you. I mean, it was everything I hated. Someone moving in, and taking your space, and losing your privacy, and you just lapped it up.' Again, there was that feeling in her voice that I'd betrayed her.

'Am I suppose to apologize for being happy?'

'Are you happy, really happy?'

I sighed. 'Why do I think you'd be happier if I said no?'

She shook her head. 'No, I don't mean it like that, but, Anita,' she took my hand, 'how can you let all these people in your house, all the time? You're never alone anymore. Don't you miss that?'

I thought about it, then said, 'No, I spent my childhood alone in a crowd of family that didn't understand me, or didn't want to understand me. I'm finally with people that don't think I'm the weird one.'

'No, because they're weirder.'

I took my hand back this time. 'That was mean,' I said.

'I didn't mean it that way, but isn't Jean-Claude jealous of Micah the way he was of Richard?'

'No,' I said, and left it at that, because Ronnie wasn't ready to hear the arrangements among the three of us. She thought we were weird already. If she only knew.

'Why isn't he?'

I just shook my head and got up to get more coffee. She thought my lover was weird, she had always hated Jean-Claude, I wasn't about to share intimacies about them with her. She'd just lost her privileges. And that made me sad. I'd thought this crisis with Louie might help Ronnie and me rebuild our friendship, but it wasn't working out that way. Shit.

I poured coffee and tried to think of something useful to say. I finally realized that if I let her last remarks go, then we'd never be friends again. It was truth or nothing.

I leaned against the cabinet and looked at her. Something must have shown on my face, because she said, 'You're mad.'

'Do you realize by saying that my lover is weirder than I am, it says you think I'm weird. You don't think your friends are weird, Ronnie.'

'I didn't mean it that way.'

'Then how did you mean it?'

'I didn't mean it, Anita, I'm sorry, but I am weirded out, I mean, I didn't like Micah coming out of nowhere. And that Nathaniel is living here, cooking and cleaning, what is he, like a maid?'

'He's my *pomme de sang*,' I said, and my voice was as cold as my face.

'Doesn't that mean he's like food?'

'Sometimes,' I said, and I tried to tell her with my eyes that she should be careful.

'I don't take my steak to bed with me, Anita. I don't read bedtime stories to my milkshake.' I'd told Ronnie just enough of my personal arrangements for her to throw them back into my face and belittle them. Great. 'Ronnie, you need to be very careful what you say right now. Very careful.'

'You're insulted, aren't you?' she asked.

'Yes,' I said, 'I came to you with very personal stuff, back when it bothered me that Nathaniel was sharing the bed with Micah and me, and I told you we were reading to each other. That wasn't a complaint.'

'Has something changed between you and Nathaniel? Last I heard, he was food, and one of your leopards, but that was all.'

'Yeah, things have changed.'

'You have two men living with you?'

I nodded. 'Yep.'

'Two men, two lovers?'

I took a deep breath, and just said, 'Yes.'

'Then how can you encourage me to say yes to Louie?'

'I didn't encourage you. I just asked which you value more, Louie, or your privacy. It's him that's made it a choice, not me.'

'But you didn't have to choose.'

'Not yet,' I said.

'What's that mean?' she asked.

'It means that I never underestimate the power of the men in my life to complicate things. So far, so good.'

'So far, so good. How can you let that be enough? Don't you want a guarantee that they aren't going to cut your heart out and stomp on it?'

'I'd love a guarantee, but it doesn't work that way. You've just got to take the plunge and hope for the best.'

'Marry him, you mean.'

'Ronnie, the only one here obsessed with marriage is you. You, and maybe Louie. I've got no plans in that direction.'

'So what, you just keep living with both of them?'

'For now, yes.' I sipped coffee and tried not to let my eyes be as unfriendly as I felt.

'But what about later?'

'Later will take care of itself,' I said.

'That's not enough for me, Anita. I want to know that I'm making the right decision.'

'I don't think you ever know, Ronnie. Most of the people I know that are absolutely certain they're right, are the most wrong people I know.'

'What the hell does that mean?'

'That means, marry him or don't marry him, but don't take your issues out on my relationships.'

'And what does that mean?'

'It means don't ever call my boyfriends weird again.'

'And you don't think that living with two men is a little unusual?'

'It works for us, Ronnie.'

'And how does Jean-Claude feel about you sleeping with Micah and Nathaniel?'

'He's okay with it.'

She frowned. 'So you're, what, sleeping with –' and she started counting fingers – 'three men?'

'Hmm, four, hmm, nope, five.'

'Five? Jean-Claude, Nathaniel, Micah, and who?'

'Asher and Damian,' I said, and my face was nicely empty when I said it.

Her face wasn't. She was left openmouthed, astonished, apparently so shocked, she was speechless. If she hadn't been picking at me, I'd have broken it to her gently, or not at all. Ronnie had started by not being able to handle me dating a vampire, then hadn't been able to handle my being comfortable cohabiting with a man, and less able to handle me living with two men and enjoying it, two extra vampires to hate, well, that was nothing.

'Let me get this straight, you are fucking all of them?'

I knew she meant, was I having intercourse with all of them? Technically, no, but since it was only Nathaniel who was on the 'no' list after today, I said, 'Yes.'

'When did all this happen?'

'Asher happened after you'd made it very clear you hated me dating Jean-Claude, because he's a vampire, so I stopped talking to you about vampires as boyfriends.'

'And Nathaniel moved from food to sex when?'

'Recently.'

'And Damian, I mean, Damian wasn't even on the radar.'

'It's been a busy day.'

She goggled at me again. 'Are you serious, just today?'

I nodded, and almost enjoyed her astonishment.

'All this has been happening, and you didn't tell me.'

'You haven't wanted to hear it. You just get mad about Jean-Claude, and I think you hated hearing how much I enjoyed the very things with Micah that you were hating with Louie. You said yourself that it made it hard to talk to me, because I seemed so happy with the things that were driving you crazy.'

She let out a long, long breath. 'I'm sorry, I've cut you out of so much.'

'I've missed us talking,' I said.

'We talked,' she said, 'but we both started editing ourselves to each other. You can't stay friends like that.' She looked sad.

'No,' I said, 'you can't. You don't have to tell each other everything, but you can't hold back this much.'

'I still don't trust Jean-Claude, and you're the one that taught me that vampires are just dead guys, no matter how cute they are.'

'I've changed my mind.'

'I haven't,' she said.

'So no talking about the vampires in my life.'

'That still leaves you with two men to talk about.'

'Not if you compare one of them to steaks and milkshakes.'

'Look, last time you talked about Nathaniel it was to complain that you were so uncomfortable around him. You talked about Nathaniel the way I felt about Louie, then about the time I thought we had common complaints, you started to change. You started getting all soft when you talked about Nathaniel, too.'

'Did I?'

She nodded. 'Yes, you did.'

'Everyone noticed Nathaniel and me, before I did, even Richard.'

'What?'

I shook my head. 'I do not want to talk about Richard, other than to say I met his new girlfriend, Clair.'

'Jesus, when?'

I shook my head, because there was no way to tell the story without sharing more than Ronnie wanted to know about vampires. The very fact that she got angry when I talked about the vampires in my life made it almost impossible to share my life with her. How did I explain what had happened between Richard and me today without including the *ardeur*, Jean-Claude, Damian, and Damian's old master? And if I did share it all, then she'd give me another lecture about how Jean-Claude was ruining my life, or had ulterior motives. I wouldn't even be able to argue about the ulterior motives. Jean-Claude was what Jean-Claude was; I'd made peace with that a while back.

I finally said some of what I was thinking out loud. I'd learned lately that truth is really the only way for relationships to survive, let alone grow. I wanted to be friends with Ronnie again, really friends, if it was still possible. 'Most of what happened today revolves around vampire stuff, Ronnie. If I can't talk to you about vampires, then I can't even begin to tell you what happened.'

'Jean-Claude fucking up your life some more.'

I shook my head. 'I don't think Jean-Claude could have planned some of this in his wildest imagination. Besides, he's pissed that Damian got to me first.'

She frowned. 'First, you mean he's upset that you and Damian are lovers?'

'I'm not sure we're lovers, so much as we had sex. I haven't decided about the rest.'

'You've always treated intercourse like it's a commitment, Anita. I never understood that. It's just sex, sometimes it's good, sometimes it's not so good, but it's just sex, not a vow of honor.'

I shrugged. 'We agreed to disagree on that topic a long time ago.'

'Yeah, we did. You've been monogamous as long as I've known you. One date and that's it until you either don't want to date him anymore, or you've decided that he didn't deserve the one date he got. Until Jean-Claude came into your life, you were the most strait-laced person I knew. I mean I didn't think I slept around until I had you to compare me to. You made everybody else seem like sluts to your nun.'

That sounded sort of bitter, too. 'I didn't know you felt that way,' I said.

'It never bothered me, in fact you probably saved me from some bad decisions. I'd think, okay, what would Anita say, and I'd wait a while and see if a guy was more than just cute.'

'Gee, I've never been the angel on someone's shoulder before.'

She shrugged. 'I'm not mad about your moral values as opposed to my moral values. I just don't understand how I ended up headed for a life of monotonous monogomy, and you ended up with a harem. It just seems wrong.'

On that we could agree. 'Wait a minute, monogomous maybe, but you told me Louie was the best sex you'd ever had.'

'No, the best sex I ever had was that guy . . .'

I finished the story for her, 'With the really big tonker, who knew how to use it. He was gorgeous, blond curly hair, big blue eyes, shoulders . . .'

She laughed. 'I take it I've told this story too often.'

'It was a one-night stand, and he vanished before you woke up the next day. You tried to find him, and he'd lied about who he was, so you couldn't find him. No sex is good enough to overcome that.'

'Spoken like someone who's never had a one-night stand in her life,' Ronnie said.

My turn to shrug. 'Can't say that I have.'

'If you've never had one, then you don't know what you've been missing.'

I let it go; we'd learned years ago that we had philosophical differences about men, sex, and relationships. 'Fine, have it your way, but Louie is the best repeatable sex that you've ever had.'

She seemed to think about that for a moment, then nodded. 'I'll agree to that. Yes, he is the best steady sex I've ever had.'

'How are you going to feel without it?' I asked.

'Horny,' she said, and laughed, but when I didn't laugh with her, she looked sad. 'Jesus, Anita, don't go all serious on me. I need one friend who just tells me that marriage isn't for me and that it's okay to dump him when he starts giving ultimatums.'

'If you aren't in love with Louie, then dump him, but I wouldn't be your friend if I didn't ask, is it that you don't love *him*, or your fear is too great to allow you to love *anybody*?'

She frowned up at me. 'Great, then I'll die alone and old with a bunch of cats and guns.'

'What I meant was, maybe therapy isn't a bad idea.'

She looked at me in amazement. 'You're giving me the you-need-therapy talk? I thought you hated all those therapists that stand by the graveside and ask people what they're feeling, as their long-dead, abusive parent rises from the grave. God, what a nightmare.'

'There are good therapists out there, Ronnie. I just don't get to meet many on the job.'

'Have you gone to see a therapist behind my back?'

I thought about that, then said, 'I finally realized that what I was going to Marianne for was only partially to learn how to control my psychic abilities. People in New York go to see their witches instead of their therapists. I've just decided to be ahead of the crowd.'

'Who do you know in New York?'

'Another animator, and vampire executioner. She said that going to a therapist who was a witch meant she didn't have to spend time explaining magic or psychic stuff to them, because they already knew it. She'd had some of the same problems I'd had over the years with going to my priest or a regular therapist. I mean, my dad took me to one when I was in my early teens. The therapist tried to help me with my latent issues with my mother's death and my dad's remarriage, but he wouldn't believe that I could raise the dead by accident. He kept trying to tell me that I was doing it on purpose to get back at Judith and my father.'

'You never told me that,' she said.

'It was after the therapist told my dad that I was "evil" that he contacted Grandma Flores and got some help that at least understood what I was going through.'

'So you knew when you started with Marianne it was therapy?'

'No, of course not, I'd never have done it that way.'

She smiled. 'That's the Anita I've come to love and know.'

I smiled back. 'Even now it makes me grumpy to admit it out loud, and you're the only person I've told, though I think Micah suspects. I'm getting easier to live with, something has to be responsible.'

'It's really helped?' she asked.

I nodded.

'You think I should go down to Tennessee?'

'I think you should try something closer to home. You don't have the same issues that I do. A therapist isn't going to tell you that you're wrong, or evil, or simply not believe you.'

'Are you telling me my problems are mundane?'

'Unless you have a problem with Louie being furry once a month, yeah they're mundane.'

She frowned, and dragged her coffee cup back toward her. 'Not really, I mean I've seen the whole show, and I don't do animals. He's okay with that, because most nonshifters draw the line at doing their significant others in animal form. You know it can be transferred via sex in animal form, if the sex is rough and you get some fluid in an abrasion.' She said it like a lecture, or a warning, without thinking about it.

'I did know that.'

'Oh, sorry, you're the preternatural expert, not me.' Again, that trace of bitterness. When had she first gotten mad at me? How far back did it go?

'No, really, Ronnie, it's good to share information when you know someone else is dating the lunarly challenged.'

She looked up then. 'Did you just say "lunarly challenged"?'

I nodded. 'The latest PC phrase.'

'Since when have you been PC?'

'Since I heard the phrase and thought it was funny as hell.' I was still leaning against the cabinet, because there was way more anger in her toward me than I understood. The vampire thing I could sort of understand, but her problems with me letting men into my life, that seemed harder to work around.

'Lunarly challenged, I'll have to tell Louie. He'll get a kick out of it.' The moment she said it, her face fell, and the weight of it all came crashing down on her. 'Oh, shit, Anita, what am I going to do?'

'I don't know.' I came back to sit at the table and patted her hand. If it had been Catherine, she'd probably be clinging to me for support, but Ronnie had my issues on closeness, so we didn't hug as much. Alright, Ronnie had my old issues on closeness, except about sex. I'd never understood why if you don't want someone hugging you for comfort that you'd be okay with fucking them, but that was just me.

'I don't want him just gone from my life, but I'm not ready to get married. I may never be ready to get married.' She looked at me, and there was such anguish in her eyes. 'He wants children. He said, one of the reasons he's happy that I'm not a shapeshifter is so we could have children. Anita, I don't want children.'

I squeezed her hand and didn't know what to say.

'I'm a private detective, and I'm thirty. If we got married we'd have to start thinking about kids right away. I'm not ready.'

'Do you want kids, ever?' I asked.

She shook her head. 'I grew out of wanting two kids and a white picket fence about five years ago. I don't think I ever really wanted it, but it's what you're supposed to want, you know.'

'I know.'

She looked at me with her serious, sad eyes and asked, 'Do you want kids?'

'No,' I said, 'my life doesn't have that kind of room.'

'No, if you had a different job, would you want to be a mother?'

'Once upon a time I thought I'd get married and have a kid or two, but that was before.'

'Before what, Jean-Claude?'

'No, before I became a vampire executioner, and a federal marshal. Before I realized that I'm probably never going to get married. My life works for me right now, but it wouldn't work for a child.'

'Why, because you don't have a husband?'

'No, because people try to kill me on a semiregular basis.'

'Speaking of violence, what happened to your door?' she asked.

'Gregory broke it down because I wasn't answering the phone and he heard screams.'

'Why did he hear screams?'

'Without mentioning vampires, I can't tell you the story.'

She sighed. 'I thought Jean-Claude was a passing thing, your one big fling. You know, he's the bad guy that you have this great sex with, then you wise up and move on.' She looked at me, and she really looked at me, searching my face. 'He's not a fling for you, is he?'

'No,' I said.

She took in a lot of air, then let it out slowly. 'I'm not saying I want or could handle all the details, but tell me enough so I know what happened to your door.'

Even edited down, the story took a while. We were just past the point where Richard dumped me royally, when Nathaniel and Gregory came into the room.

Ronnie had her face all set for massive sympathy, and was actually reaching out to offer a hug, when she saw them. Her face froze, and her arms just stopped moving, as if she was suddenly a statue in that kid's game.

Nathaniel was nearly naked, wearing only a leather thong and a whole bunch of straps across his upper body. So many straps that for a moment it gave the illusion that he was bound in some way. He padded into the room, looking totally comfortable in his nearly nothing bondage gear. That might have been what stopped Ronnie in her tracks, or then again, it might have been Gregory. He was still in leopardman form, and still totally nude. He wasn't happy to be nude anymore, but he was still naked except for his very natural fur coat.

From the look on her face, I wasn't sure Ronnie had really seen that much of Louie in ratman form, or if she had, he'd been more discreet than Gregory was being. He had three straps in his clawed hands and was looking at the rivet on the end of one of them as he glided through the door.

'Hi, Ronnie,' Nathaniel said, as if she wasn't staring at him open-mouthed. 'Anita, have you seen my punch?'

'Your what?' I asked.

'It's a punch for reattaching leather rivets. I forgot that two of the straps came loose last time I wore this.'

'I don't even know what a leather punch looks like,' I said. I sipped coffee and watched both the men, and Ronnie's face. She was trying to recover her cool, but the effort was visible and near painful to watch.

'Sort of like a big stapler, with one of those round things on the top.' He knelt down to open up the tool drawer. This flashed the back of his body to us, and there was a lot of back to flash. The thin black stripe that was all that covered his ass didn't exactly cover anything as much as it emphasized what was there.

If I hadn't had Ronnie's reaction to watch, I'd have been more distracted myself, but I was enjoying her total failure to hide what she was thinking. There'd been a time when Ronnie had been the more sophisticated of the two of us, and I'd been the one who blushed all the time. She wasn't blushing, she'd actually paled, but the shoe was very firmly on the other foot. She hadn't been around much, so she hadn't seen Nathaniel in maybe six months. Her reaction told me that it wasn't just me who'd noticed the shoulders and the extra muscle development. To someone who hadn't seen him in half a year, the changes must have been even more impressive.

'What makes you think a piece of sewing equipment would be in the kitchen?' I asked, and my voice held that first hint of amusement that I was trying to hide from Ronnie. It was kind of nice not to be the one who was embarrassed for a change.

Nathaniel moved from drawer to drawer, talking without turning around, his hair still up in its high, springy ponytail. 'Zane borrowed it to fix his leather jacket and never put it back. You know how Zane is, he doesn't think. He's got to stop borrowing my stuff, if he can't put things back where they belong.'

Zane was one of my wereleopards, and he tried to play dominant, but he really wasn't. And Nathaniel was right, Zane never seemed to put anything back where it was supposed to go. 'I don't think you'll ever teach him to put things back,' I said.

'You could wear it without these three straps,' Gregory said. 'Most people wouldn't notice.' He touched one of the straps on Nathaniel's back, gave it a little flick. 'I mean there must be over a dozen of them.'

'I'll notice,' Nathaniel said, and he kept opening drawers. 'If you were Zane, where would you put a punch?' I think he was asking it of no one in particuliar.

Ronnie had managed to stop gaping. She'd closed her mouth and was trying to look like it was no big deal that two nudish wereleopards were wandering around my kitchen. She watched them covertly out of the corners of her eyes. I don't know if it was because she was embarrassed or because I'd called one of them my boyfriend. Girlfriend rule number one, you don't lust after your best bud's boyfriend.

I got up to help them look. Nathaniel had said it looked like a stapler. Even I could recognize a stapler, so I started opening drawers, too.

Nathaniel found it in the drawer that was supposed to hold only big spoons and oversized cookware. 'Why here?' he asked.

'It does look like a really big stapler, maybe that's why.' I offered it up as the best idea I had.

Nathaniel was shaking his head, making his hair dance around his shoulders, in a way it never did except in that very high, tight pony-tail. 'Whatever the reason, he is not allowed in my stuff anymore.'

'Sounds fair,' I said. I was looking at all the straps. 'You look pretty secured into that outfit, how do you strip out of it?'

He smiled at me. 'Are you trying to get me out of my clothes?' He made it sound like teasing, but underneath was something that wasn't teasing at all. I wished I hadn't said it, because he wanted me to want him so badly. I didn't know how this game worked, and I'd never been good at flirting, not really.

I ended up blushing, which I hated. 'No,' I said, and it sounded whiny even to me.

He could have said a half-dozen things that would have made it worse, but he had mercy on me. 'You get it off the same way you get it on.' He slid his left arm through the front of all those straps, then raised his arm up his chest, along the side of his neck, and did something with his shoulder that I couldn't see from where I was standing. The straps just peeled down, and suddenly he was nude from the waist up, with the straps hanging around him like the petals of a black leather flower. 'The straps come off completely, but it takes time to reattach them, so you'll have to come tonight if you want to see the whole show.' He smiled gently, to take some of the sting out of my embarrassment. I wasn't sure why I was embarrassed, unless it was because Ronnie was there, or I was worried about having to come across soon. Who knew, pick one.

'Your shoulder,' Ronnie said, in a strained voice, 'didn't that hurt what you did to your shoulder?'

He shook his head, sending all that shining auburn hair flying. 'No, I'm double-jointed.'

Ronnie was having trouble with her face, like the expression that was wanting to come there wasn't one she was willing to have. 'How double-jointed are you?'

'Ronnie,' I said.

She shrugged and gave me a look like, Sue me, I couldn't help it. 'Well, you won't tell me. You just told me today that he's moved from food to boyfriend.'

'Ronnie,' I said again, a little more urgently.

She made a face. 'Sorry, sorry, I'm not myself today. I'm babbling more, like you usually do.'

'Oh, thanks a lot,' I said.

'You do babble when you're nervous or horny,' Gregory said.

'Stop helping me, Gregory.'

He shrugged, which looked odd on the leopardman shoulders, not bad, just odd. 'Sorry.'

'Do you want me to answer her question?' Nathaniel asked, in a careful voice.

'Answer the question, don't answer the question, I don't care.'

He cocked his head to one side, the expression on his face clearly said that he knew that wasn't true. He was right, I'd have preferred him to not answer the question. He'd given me the opportunity to be his master and tell him not to answer, but I'd blown it. I'd abdicated the throne he seemed to want me to take, and if you're not in charge, you can't control what happens.

He walked over toward Ronnie, and he made sure he swayed that luscious ass at me as he moved. Sometimes I wondered if Nathaniel knew how beautiful he was, then he'd do something that let me know he knew exactly what he looked like. Like now.

Heat crept up my face just watching him walk, and I finally decided why the embarrassment. I'd promised to mark him, but what he wanted was intercourse, and watching him move across the room like an ad for a wet dream made me all squirmy and uncomfortable, like being a teenager again and having 'those feelings' for the first time, and having no one to talk to about them, because good girls weren't supposed to have feelings like that.

He flicked his head and sent all that hair spilling over Ronnie, and away, like a curtain that she'd walked through, except she was sitting still. It looked as if he'd slapped her instead of teased. He stood up very straight, very tall, beside her chair and clasped his hands behind his back. 'To answer your question, I,' he began to raise his arms backward, 'am,' his arms went to the middle of his back, and kept on moving upward, 'very,' until his straining clasped fingers were even with his shoulder blades, 'very,' his arms rotated all the way up so they pointed at the ceiling, 'double-jointed.' Then he slowly put his arms back down, but it wasn't Ronnie he was looking at when he finished.

I didn't blush, I paled. I felt trapped. Trapped by what? That was the ten-thousand-dollar question. Even to myself, I wasn't sure I had an answer.

They left to repair Nathaniel's costume. The silence in the kitchen after they left was deep, long, and uncomfortable. At least for me. I didn't look at Ronnie, because I was trying to think of something to say. I shouldn't have worried, she found just the right thing to say. 'Damn, Anita, I mean, *damn*.'

I did look at her then. 'What's that supposed to mean?' My voice was a little shaky to come off as indignation, but it was worth the effort.

Ronnie had a look in her eyes that I didn't like. It was way too discerning. We'd been best friends for years, just because we'd drifted apart didn't mean she still couldn't read me. 'You haven't had sex with him yet.' She sounded sure, and amazed.

'What makes you say that?'

'Oh, come, Anita, you're never quite this uncomfortable once that bridge has been crossed. For you, intercourse is permission to have a relationship, until that happens, you never really relax around them.'

I was blushing again, arms crossed over my stomach, leaning against the island, using my hair to try to hide the blush, and failing. 'So you've always known every time I made love to someone?'

'Most of the time, yeah, except with Jean-Claude. He messed up your radar and mine.'

I glanced up then. 'How so?'

'You stayed uncomfortable around him even after the two of you were having sex together. I think it's one of the reasons I didn't like him. I guess I thought if you were that conflicted, then it wouldn't last.'

I shrugged. 'I don't remember being uncomfortable around him afterward.'

She just looked at me.

I had the decency to squirm. 'Okay, maybe I was. But it's not true that I stop being uncomfortable after having sex just once. It takes a few sessions, a little 'montonous monogamy' for me to truly relax.'

She smiled. 'Point taken. The best sex is after you've learned a few things about each other.' She looked at me, very serious again. 'You really haven't had sex with him, have you?'

I shook my head.

'Why not?' she asked.

I looked at her.

'Anita, after the little show he just put on, I'd do him.'

I looked at her harder.

'You say he's been sleeping in your bed, with you and Micah, right?'

I nodded.

'For how long?'

'About four months,' I said.

'Four months of climbing between your sheets, and you haven't fucked him?'

'Pick a different word, okay? If we're going to have this talk, pick a different word.'

'Sorry, okay, you haven't *made love* to him, that better?'

I nodded.

'Why haven't you made love to him? He obviously wants you to.'

I shrugged.

'No, I want an answer on this one. Has Jean-Claude decided to draw the line at sharing you with this many men?'

'No,' I said.

'Micah has a problem with it?'

'No.'

'Then why not?'

I sighed. 'Because when I first let Nathaniel move in, he was like a wounded puppy, something to take care of and help heal. He was so submissive that he wanted someone to run his life and order him around. I've got enough to do to run my own life, so I sort of demanded he change, become more independent. He did it, he's doing really well.'

'He's a lot more confident than the last time I saw him,' Ronnie said. 'I mean he's almost like a different person.'

I shook my head. 'He's a stripper, he has to have a certain level of confidence in himself.'

She shook her head. 'Nope, had a roommate in college that stripped her way through school on the weekends. She had a terrible self-image.'

'Then why did she strip?'

'It made her feel like someone wanted her. Her childhood makes yours and mine read like *Rebecca of Sunnybrook Farm*.'

'Ouch,' I said.

'Yeah, stripping made her feel good and bad all at the same time.'

'What happened to her?' I asked.

'She graduated, found a job, found religion, and is now married with two kids and an attitude so holy that you can't have a conversation with her without her trying to convert you.'

'They say that no one is as holy as a reformed sinner.'

'Stripping isn't a sin, Anita. Being naked isn't a sin, it's the way God sends us into the world, how bad can it be?'

I shrugged.

'Sex isn't a sin either, Anita.'

'Intellectually I know that, Ronnie, but part of me just can't shake my grandmother's voice. Sex was evil, men that wanted to touch you were evil, your body was dirty. It was all bad, and the nuns didn't help change that attitude.'

'I guess once a Catholic always a Catholic,' she said.

I sighed. 'I guess.' Truthfully, I thought a lot of the damage had been my grandmother's doing, and my stepmother, Judith, who made every touch some sort of favor. Physical touch was not a big thing in my family after my mother died.

'You feel guilty about Nathaniel, why?'

'I'm supposed to take care of him, Ronnie, not screw him.'

'Anita, you can take care of someone and still have sex with them, married couples do it every day.'

I sighed again. 'I don't know why he weirds me out, but he does.'

'You want him.'

I covered my face with my hands and almost yelled, 'Yes, yes, I want him.' And just saying it out loud like that made me cringe inside. 'He started life with me on the I'll-take-care-of-him list, not the future boyfriend list.'

'Don't you and your boyfriends take care of each other?'

I thought about that. 'I guess so. I mean, I hadn't thought about it.'

'Why are you so busy trying to find reasons to talk yourself out of Nathaniel?'

I frowned at her. 'Jason told me that it's because Nathaniel won't be aggressive enough. That if a man's just a little commanding, I feel like the choice isn't all mine, and the guilt isn't all mine either. Nathaniel's sort of forcing me to make the move, to be in charge, to be . . .'

'The one to blame,' she offered.

'Maybe.'

'Anita, I am terrified of spending the rest of my life with one man. I mean, what if a body like Nathaniel's comes walking up to me the day after I say yes to Louie? I'm going to turn it down?'

'Yeah,' I said, 'that's what being in love means, doesn't it?'

'Spoken by the girl who's sleeping with more men than I've dated in the last three years.'

'I was raised that marriage would make everything that was dirty okay. Suddenly, all those feelings were legal, holy. Part of me has trouble letting that go.'

'Letting what go?' she asked.

'That I'm never going to get married. That I'm never going to do anything to make how I feel about Jean-Claude, or Micah, or Nathaniel, or Asher, or, hell, Damian, okay. That no matter what happens, I am going to be living in sin.'

'You mean that you'd like to be in love with just one man and do the marriage thing?'

'I used to think so. Now . . .' I sat down at the table. 'Oh, Ronnie, I don't know. I can't see being with just one person anymore. My life wouldn't work with just one of them in it.'

'And that bothers you,' she said.

'Yes, it does.'

'Why?'

'Because this isn't the way it's supposed to be.'

'Anita, "supposed to be" is for children. Grown-ups know that it's what you make of it.'

'My life is working, Ronnie. Nathaniel is like my wife, and Micah is the other husband. He works for the coalition and helps me take care of the leopards and all the other shapeshifters. It's partnership the way I always thought marriage could be, but never seems to be.'

'And where does Jean-Claude fit into this little domestic scene?'

'Wherever he wants, I guess. He runs his business and polices his territory, and we date.'

'You, him, and Asher date?'

'Sometimes.'

She shook her head. 'And Damian?'

'I don't know yet.'

She looked down at her hands on the tabletop. 'I guess we've both been having some interesting personal choices to make.' She looked at me and frowned – a little frown. 'Why is it that your choices seem so much more fun than mine?'

I smiled. 'You have issues with commitment, marriage, and being tied to just one man. I have issues that anything short of that monogamous setup means you're a slut. We're both being set up to deal with our issues.'

'You do sound like you've been to therapy.'

'Glad to hear it shows,' I said.

'So you're saying that we've fallen into the love lives we have so that we can face our demons and slay them?'

'Or realize that what we thought were monsters aren't that much different from us.'

'You really did think that vampires were walking corpses once, didn't you?'

'Down to my toes.'

'That must make it really hard to be in love with one of them.'

I nodded. 'Yes.'

She took my hands in hers. 'I'm sorry I've been pissy about Jean-Claude. I'll try to do better.'

I smiled and squeezed her hands. 'Apology accepted.'

'I'm thirty, and I've never been this happy with anyone. I'll talk to Louie about giving me a little space and maybe finding a premarriage counselor.'

'Can I say I'm happy to hear that, without you accusing me of wanting you to marry him?'

She smiled and had the grace to look embarrassed. 'Yeah, and sorry about that, too.'

'It's alright, Ronnie, we all have our hangups.'

'Trust you to find a witch for a counselor, but if you can do therapy, I guess it's not too late for the rest of us.'

'I was talking to Marianne for months before I realized what it was.'

'You're saying that you went to therapy by accident.'

I shrugged, squeezed her hands, and got up. Please, God, let some of the coffee still be warm.

'So you went to therapy by accident. You became the lover of the Master of the City, kicking and screaming that you wouldn't do it. Now you've fallen into one, or is it two ménage à trois, when your goal in life was monogamous marriage.'

The French press was cold, but the coffeemaker was not. Yeah. 'That about sums it up,' I said.

'And my goal was to never tie myself down to any one person and never to marry. Now here we are, each getting what the other one thought she wanted.'

I couldn't have said it better myself, so I didn't try. I'd never gotten the impression that God had a sadistic sense of irony, but someone sure did. Was there an angel in charge of relationships? If so, that particular winged messenger of deity had a lot to answer for. I got that tiny pulse in my head that I sometimes got when I prayed. It was more feeling than words. Be happy, just be happy. Easy to say, so very hard to do.

28

AT 3:00 THAT afternoon, I was at work, right on time. Neither sex, vampires, shapeshifters, nor metaphysical meltdowns will deter this animator from her appointed rounds. At least not today.

I was sitting in Bert Vaughn's office. He'd been the boss at Animator's Inc. once, but recently we'd had a sort of palace coup. He was still office and business manager, but he was more like our agent than our boss. It hadn't lost him any money, so he was happy, but it had meant that most of the animators here were like partners in a law firm. Once you made partner, you almost had to kill someone to lose your job, well, kill someone and get caught. So Bert wasn't the boss anymore. Which meant he didn't get to treat us like the hired help. He hadn't liked that part, but it was either agree to our terms, or we all walked, and since he can't raise the dead, that would pretty much put him out of business. Especially if we opened another firm in direct competition with him. So we had a new power structure, and we hadn't worked all the kinks out of it yet.

Bert's office was now a warm yellow with orange undertones. It was cozier than the pale blue cubicle it had once been, but not by much. The entire office had gotten a face-lift, along with buying out the offices next door, so that most of the animators at Animator's Inc. no longer had to share their office space. Since most of our time was spent out in the field, or cemetery as it were, I thought the new offices were a waste of money, but I'd been out-voted. Charles, Jamison, and Manny had wanted bigger offices. Larry and I had been fine sharing, but Bert voted with the other three, so they'd taken out a wall and voilà, we were suddenly twice as big. The reason that most of the offices had gone to warmer tones, earth tones, comforting tones of yellows, browns, tans, ecru, was that Bert was dating an interior designer. Her name was Lana, and, though I thought she was far too good for him, she irritated me. She constantly went around talking about the science of color and how with a business like ours we needed to make people feel loved and cared for.

I'd told her that it wasn't my job to love my clients. That I wasn't in that business. She'd taken it wrong and hadn't really liked me since. That was fine, as long as she stayed the hell away from my office.

Mary, our daytime secretary, had asked me to wait in Mr Vaughn's office as soon as I hit the door. Not a good sign. To my knowledge I hadn't done anything wrong at work, so I had no clue what the meeting was about. Once it would have bugged me, but not now; I was used to not knowing things.

Bert came in, and shut the door behind him. Shutting the door was not a good sign either. Bert is 6' 4", and played football in college. He'd started to gain that past-forty, nearing-fifty extra around the middle, but Lana had put him on a diet and an exercise program. He looked better than he had for most of the time I'd known him. She'd even persuaded him that tanning cocoa brown every summer was not healthy for anyone. So he looked pale, but healthy. It also meant that his hair hadn't gone that white-blond that it used to in the summer. His hair was actually a pale yellow, with a little white creeping in, but the white was so close to the way his hair used to look with his tan, that it had taken me days to figure out it was his way of going gray.

I was sitting in one of the two dark brown, nicely upholstered client chairs that had been another of Lana's ideas. They were more comfortable than the straight-backs he'd had before. My legs were politely crossed, my hands folded in my lap. I was the epitome of ladylike.

'That skirt is too short for business hours, Anita,' he said as he rounded his big desk and eased into a chair even bigger and browner and more leathery than the one I was sitting in.

I slumped down in the chair and put my boots up on his desk, with my ankles crossed. The movement raised my skirt up high enough to flash every last inch of the lace tops of my thigh-high hose. I was a little short for the movement to be comfortable, but I doubted Bert could tell I was uncomfortable. I looked at him around the heels of my knee-high black boots.

'The skirt is also black. We all agreed that we don't wear black to work. It's too depressing.'

'No, *you* think it's too depressing. Besides the skirt has flowers embroidered on the side by the slit. Blue, green, and turquoise, which matches exactly the shade of turquoise of the jacket, and the blue of the top, it's like an outfit,' I said. I was also wearing a gold chain with an antique locket on the end of it. It had two tiny paintings, one in either side of it. They were tiny oil paintings of Jean-Claude and Asher. The locket had once belonged to Julianna, and was more than three hundred years old. It was handwrought gold, heavy and solid, and very antique-looking. Tiny sapphires traced its edges, with one larger one in the middle. I'd thought it looked great with the outfit. Apparently not.

The short little turquoise jacket also covered the black shoulder holster and the Browning Hi-Power under my left arm. I'd have put on the wrist sheaths, but with the jacket off, the knives showed under the thin material of the top. I could just take off the gun if it got hot enough in the office, but to remove the wrist sheaths, I'd have to strip off the shirt. It didn't seem worth it. They were in the car, just in case I started to feel insecure.

Bert didn't have any weapons under his rich, chocolate-brown suit, which had been tailored to fit his body. As he'd lost weight, the athletic cut to his suits had emphasized his broad shoulders, which had sort of appeared as his waistline had decreased. His shirt was pale yellow, and his tie was a paler brown, with tiny gold and blue figures on it. All the colors suited him, they even brought a little warmth into his gray eyes.

I slumped down further into the chair, using the padded corner to brace my back and head. The skirt had scooted up far enough that the black silk of my underwear was peeking out, though it probably couldn't be seen from where Bert was sitting.

'If I tell you the skirt is too short, you'll wear something even shorter tomorrow, won't you?'

'Yep.'

'And if I complain about the black . . .'

'I've got black dresses,' I said, 'I've even got short black dresses.'

'Why do I even bother?'

'Arguing with me,' I said.

He nodded.

'I have no idea.'

'At least you're wearing makeup, I appreciate that.'

'I've got a date after work,' I said.

'That brings me to another problem,' he said. He leaned forward and folded his hands on his desk. He was trying for fatherly, but he never quite made it. It came off more as pretentious.

I did straighten up in my chair, because I simply wasn't comfortable. I straightened the skirt as I sat up. There was enough skirt to smooth down the back of my thighs. My rule for skirts was that it was too short if there was no skirt to smooth over your ass. This skirt passed the test, so I was glad Bert had given up. I really wasn't comfortable in skirts much shorter than this one. Wearing them just to spite Bert wouldn't have been as fun as it once would have been.

'And what problem would that be, Bert?'

'Mary tells me that the young man in our waiting room is your boyfriend.'

I nodded. 'He is.' Strangely, the *ardeur* hadn't risen today at all, not a quiver, not a shake. But we'd all been a little concerned about what might happen if it suddenly sprang to life at work. There was nobody at work that I wanted to have sex with, so that meant I needed someone nearby, just in case. Nathaniel was sitting outside in the warm sienna orange waiting room, looking very decorative in one of the brown leather chairs. He was wearing street clothes – black slacks, a violet business shirt that was almost a match to the one he'd worn to the wedding, and black over-the-ankle boots. He'd braided his hair so it looked as professional as ankle-length hair can, and he was reading back issues of some music magazine that he had a subscription to and had fallen behind on reading. He'd brought a messenger bag full of magazines from home and was prepared to wait until I dropped him off at work, or until he was needed, whichever came first.

'Why is your boyfriend out in our waiting room, when you're supposed to be working?'

'I'm dropping him at work later,' I said, and my voice was much more neutral than his had managed to be.

'Doesn't he have a car?'

'We only have two cars at the house, and Micah may need the other one if he gets called into work.'

Bert did the slow blink, and what little warmth he'd managed to get into his gray eyes faded. 'I thought the one in the other room was your boyfriend.'

'He is.'

'Doesn't that mean that you've broken up with Micah?'

'Your assumption is your problem, Bert.'

He gave another long blink and leaned back in his chair, looking puzzled. I'd always puzzled Bert, but just not in the personal depart-ement. 'Does Micah know you're dating . . .'

'Nathaniel,' I said.

'Nathaniel,' Bert said.

'He knows,' I said.

He licked his thin lips and tried a different tact. 'Would you think it was professional if Charles or Manny brought their wives into sit in our waiting room?'

I shrugged. 'Not my business.'

He sighed and started rubbing his temples. 'Anita, your boyfriend cannot sit out there the entire time you're in the office.'

'Why not?' I asked.

'Because if I let you start bringing in people, everybody else will want to, and it would be a mess. It would disrupt business.'

I sighed. 'I don't think anyone else will be bringing their sweeties to work,' I said. 'Charles's wife is a full-time registered nurse, she's a little busy, and Rosita hates Manny's job. She wouldn't darken the door. Jamison might bring a girl around, if he thought it would impress her.'

He sighed again. 'Anita, you're being deliberately difficult about this.'

'Me, deliberately difficult? Why, Bert, you know me better than that.'

He gave a surprised burst of laughter and sat back in his chair and stopped trying to treat me like a client. He looked instantly more comfortable, and less trustworthy. 'Why did you bring your new boyfriend to work?'

'None of your business.'

'It is, if he's sitting in the waiting room that we all share. It is, if you're going to let him sit in on clients.'

'He won't sit in on clients,' I said.

'Then he's going to be in our waiting room for how long?'

'A few hours,' I said.

'Why?' he asked again.

'I told you, none of your business.'

'It is, if you bring him to work, Anita. I may not be the boss anymore, but we're also a democracy. You really think that Jamison won't kick a fuss?'

He had a point. I couldn't think of a lie that came close to explaining it, so I tried for partial truth. 'You know that I'm the human servant to Jean-Claude, Master of the City, right?'

He nodded, eyes uncertain, as if this was not the start of the conversation he'd expected.

'Well, there's been an interesting side effect. Trust me when I say that you'll want Nathaniel here if things go wrong.'

'How wrong are they going to go?' he asked.

'If I take him into my office, just lock the door and make sure we aren't disturbed. No harm, no foul.'

'Why would you need privacy with him? What side effect? Is it dangerous?'

'None of your business. You wouldn't understand even if I told you, and it's only dangerous if I don't have someone with me when it happens.'

'When what happens?'

'See first answer,' I said.

'If it's going to disrupt the office, then as manager I need to know.'

He had a point, but I wasn't sure how to tell him, without telling him. 'It won't disrupt anything, if Mary keeps everyone away from the door until we're finished.'

'Finished?' he said. 'Finished what?'

I looked at him. I tried to make it an eloquent look.

'You don't mean . . .' he said.

'Mean what?' I asked.

He closed his eyes, opened them, and said, 'If I don't want your boyfriend sitting in the waiting room, I sure as hell don't want you fucking him in your office.' He sounded outraged, which was rare for Bert.

'I'm hoping it won't come to that,' I said.

'Why is this a side effect of being a human servant to the Master of St Louis?'

It was a good question, but I was so not willing to share that much with Bert. 'Just lucky, I guess.'

'I would say you're making it up, but if you were going to pull some elaborate joke on me, it wouldn't be this.' That one comment proved Bert knew me better than I thought.

'No,' I said, 'it wouldn't.'

'So you've become like a what, a nympho?'

Trust Bert to find just the right thing to say. 'Yes, Bert, that's it, I've become a nymphomaniac. I need sex so often that I have to take a lover with me wherever I go now.'

His eyes went wide.

'Calm down, boss man, I'm hoping today will be the exception, not the rule.'

'What made today different?' he asked.

'You know, Mary told me to report to your office as soon as I hit the door. Before you could have possibly known that I'd brought my boyfriend with me, or worn a black skirt that is shorter than you would like. So you didn't call me in here to discuss my wardrobe or my love life. Why did you want this little meeting?'

'Did anyone ever tell you that you can be very abrupt?'

'Yes, now what's up?'

He sat up straighter, all professional and client-worthy again. 'I need you to hear me out before you get upset.'

'Wow, Bert, I can hardly wait for the rest of this little talk.'

He frowned at me. 'I turned the job down, because I knew you wouldn't take it.'

'If you turned it down, why are we discussing it?'

'They doubled your consultation fee.'

'Bert,' I said.

'No,' he put a hand up, 'I turned it down.'

I looked at him and knew my face said clearly, I didn't believe him. 'I've never known you to turn down that much, Bert.'

'You gave me a list of cases that you wouldn't handle. Since you gave me the list, have I sent anything your way that was on it?'

I thought about it for a second, then shook my head. 'No, but you're about to.'

'They won't believe me.'

'They won't believe what?' I said.

'They insist that if you'd only see them, you'd do what they want. I told them you wouldn't, but they offered fifteen thousand dollars for an hour of your time. Even if you refuse, the money belongs to Animators, Inc.'

When I said we worked like a law firm, I meant it. That meant that this money went into the kitty for everybody. The more we made, the more everyone made, though some of us got a higher or lower percentage of our fees. We'd based it on seniority. So my turning down money didn't just hurt me or insult Bert anymore, it affected the bottom line for everybody. Most of those everybodys had families, kids. They'd actually come to me en masse and asked for me to be more flexible on my consulting fees, i.e., take more of them. Manny had a daughter about to enter a very expensive college, and Jamison was paying alimony to three ex-wives. Sob stories, but most of them, except for Larry, had more overhead than I did. So I'd started being nicer about at least talking to people when they offered outrageous sums of money. Sometimes.

'What's the job?' I asked. I didn't sound happy, but I asked.

Bert was all smiles. Sometimes I suspected that he'd been behind that en masse meeting, but Manny and Charles swore up and down he hadn't been. Jamison I wouldn't have believed either way, so I didn't ask.

'The Browns' son died about three years ago. They want you to raise him and ask some questions.'

My eyes were unfriendly slits. 'Tell me all of it, Bert, so far I wouldn't have turned it down.'

He cleared his throat and fidgeted. Bert didn't fidget much. 'Well, the son was murdered.'

I threw my hands into the air. 'Damn it, Bert, I can't raise a murder victim. None of us here can. I gave you a list that you were supposed to refuse for all of us, for legal reasons, and that was one of them.'

'You used to do it.'

'Yeah, before I found out what happens when you raise a murder vic as a zombie, and that was before the new laws went into effect. A murdered person rises from the grave and goes after their murderer, no ifs, ands, or buts. They will tear through anyone and anything that tries to stop them. I had it happen twice, Bert. The zombies don't answer questions about who killed them, they just go rampaging off and try to find who did it.'

'Couldn't the police just follow them, sort of like they do bloodhounds?'

'These bloodhounds will tear people's arms off and crash through houses. Zombies do a very straight line to their murderers. And the way the law reads now, the animator that raised the zombie would be liable for all the damage, including the deaths. If one of us raised this boy and he killed anyone, even his own murderer, we'd be charged with murder. Murder with magical malfeasance. That's an automatic death sentence. So no, I can't do it, and neither can anybody else.'

He looked sad, probably about the money. 'I told them you'd explain it to them.'

'You should have explained it to them yourself, Bert. I've told you all this before.'

'They asked me if I was an animator, when I said no, they wouldn't believe me. They said if they could just meet with Ms Blake, they're sure they could change your mind.'

'Jesus, Bert, this is really unfair. It can't be done, and watching their son rise from the grave as a shambling murderous zombie is not going to help them heal.'

He raised eyebrows at that. 'Well, I can't say I put it as well as you just did, but I swear to you that I did tell them no.'

'But I'm meeting with them anyway, because they offered fifteen grand for an hour of my time.'

'I could have gotten them to twenty grand. They're desperate. I could smell it on them. If we turn them down flat, they're going to try to find someone less reputable, less legal.'

I closed my eyes and let the air out in a long slow sigh. I hated that he was right, but he was. When people get to a certain level of desperation, they'll do stupid things. Stupid, foolish, horrible things. We were the only animating firm in the Midwest. There was one in New Orleans and one in California, but they wouldn't take this job for the same reason we wouldn't. The new laws. I could say it was to save the clients pain, but in all honesty the idea that you could raise a murder victim from the grave and just ask them who killed them was so tempting that several of us had tried to do it. We'd thought it hadn't worked because of the trauma of the murder, or that the animators doing it weren't powerful enough, but that wasn't it. If you were murdered, you rose with only one thought in your dead brain: revenge. Until you got that revenge, you wouldn't listen to anyone's orders, not even the animator or voodoo priest or priestess that raised you from the grave.

But just because none of the reputable people would do it, didn't mean that a disreputable person wouldn't do it. There were people here and there across the country that had the talent without the morals. None of them worked for the professional companies because they'd either been fired as a liability, or they'd never been hired. Some because they didn't want to be hired, but most because what they did was secret and rarely something they wanted the authorities to know about. They kept a low profile, and didn't advertise much, but if you started waving twenty grand around, they'd come out of the woodwork. The Browns would find someone willing to do what they asked, if they were willing to pay for it. Someone who would give them a false name, raise the kid, and run with their money, and leave the bereaved parents to clean up the mess and explain things to the police. There was a test case in New England at state supreme court level that was seeking the death penalty for the person who paid a magical practitioner to kill someone by magic. I didn't know how it would go, and it would probably get to the Supreme Court before all was said and done. I'd never forgive myself if the Browns found someone less reputable and ended up on death row for it. I mean, that would just suck, especially if I could prevent it here and now.

I gave Bert the look he deserved. The one that said he was a greedy son of a bitch, and I knew he'd turned down their money for something other than humanitarian reasons. He just sat back and smiled at me, because he knew what that particular look meant. It meant I would do it, even if I hated it.

29

MRS BARBARA BROWN was blonde, and Mr Steve Brown was brunette with gray coming in at the temples. He's was taller than she was by about five inches, but other than that, they matched. You could still see the pretty round-faced cheerleader she'd been in high school. The handsome football player was still there in his shoulders and the edges of his face, but the extra weight and the extra years and the grief had covered over who they'd been. Their eyes were bright, but it was an unnatural brightness, almost shocky. She spoke too fast, and he spoke too slowly, as if he had to think about each word before he said it. She spoke as if talking about her son was something she had to do, or she'd explode, or break down.

'He was a straight-A student, Ms Blake, and here's the last picture he painted. It was a watercolor of his youngest sister. He had such talent.' She held up the picture, which they'd brought in one of those art carriers that looks like a thin briefcase.

I dutifully looked at the painting. It was a very soft picture, all watery blues and delicate yellows, and the child's curls were almost white. The little girl was laughing, and the artist had caught a shine in her eyes that usually required a camera to capture. It was good. For a junior in high school, it was spectacular.

'It's a wonderful painting, Mrs Brown.'

'Steve didn't want me to bring it. He said that you didn't need to see it, but I thought if you saw what kind of person he was, that you'd be willing to do what we want.'

'I don't think that seeing Stevie's paintings will influence Ms Blake, that's all, Barbara.' He patted her hand as he finished, and she didn't react to it at all. It was almost as if he hadn't touched her. I began to understand who was the driving force behind this tragic farce. Because it was a farce. She wasn't talking like she wanted her son brought back as a zombie so he could say who'd murdered him. She was talking like she was trying to persuade me to do a Lazarus on him, to really bring him back. Had Bert heard that in her voice and ignored it, or had she saved it for me?

'He was a track star, and on the football team.' She opened the yearbook to appropriate places, and I looked at Stevie Brown running in shorts with a baton in his hand, head thrown back, a look of utter concentration on his face. His hair was dark and not long. Stevie Brown kneeling on the ground in full football gear, helmet on the ground by his hand. He was grinning out at the camera, his bangs spilling over his eyes. He had his father's hair, and a thinner, younger, brighter version of his mother's face, except for the lips and the eyes, which, again, were his father's.

I saw a picture of him on the yearbook staff, bent over a layout table, face very serious. He looked like someone that would run track, thin, muscled, but not much bulk. I wouldn't have picked him for football, not beefy enough. But who knew if he might have filled out in the summer between junior and senior year. But he never got the chance.

Prom night, he and his senior girlfriend had been crowned king and queen. There was a picture of them in front of a background of fake silver stars and too many sequins. He was beaming into the camera. He'd cut his hair and styled it so it was neat and thick and flattered his face more than the way it had when he ran track. His shoulders were a little broader than in the yearbook or track photos. He looked taller in his white tux. The girl was blonde and looked like a thinner, taller version of his mother. The girl looked confident and lovely, with a smile that was more mysterious than Stevie's had been. Looking at their pictures, it was obvious they didn't know that in less than six hours they'd be dead.

'Cathy and Stevie had been dating for almost two years. High school sweethearts, just like Steve and me.' She leaned forward as she said it, her lips half parted, her tongue moistened them as if she was having trouble keeping her mouth from drying out.

Her husband kept patting her hand and looked at me out of his fine dark eyes, which were so like his dead son's. He told me with those eyes, and his so-tired face, that he was sorry. Sorry I had to see this, hear this, be here now.

I wasn't up to the subtle eye message thing, the best I could do was nod sympathetically and give him more eye contact than I gave her. He gave a small nod where Barbara couldn't see him. There, we'd had our moment, a very guy moment. I see you, I see you, too. I understand what you mean, I understand what you mean, too. If I'd been a better girl, I'd have said something out loud to be sure.

'He sounds like he was a wonderful person,' I said.

She leaned forward a little more, she had a small photo album in her hands, one of those thick ones that grandmothers carry in their purses. She fumbled it open, and I was staring at pictures of a dark-haired baby, toddler, grade-schooler.

I put my hand over hers, stopped her from turning the pages. 'Mrs Brown, Barbara . . .'

She wouldn't look at me. Her eyes were getting shinier.

'Mrs Brown, you don't need to prove to me that your son was a good kid. I believe you.'

Mr Brown stood up and tried to help her put the photo album back in her purse. She didn't want to do it, and he wouldn't fight her. He stood there, sort of helplessly, with his big hands hanging at his sides.

She leaned into the desk again and turned a page. 'Here he is winning the fifth grade science fair.'

I didn't know how to stop this without being cruel. I leaned back in my chair and stopped looking at the pictures. I made eye contact with Steve, and his eyes had grown shinier, too. If they both started crying I was going to leave. If I could have helped them, I would have, but I couldn't. And truthfully, I didn't think Barbara Brown had come to me to produce a zombie.

I looked back down at a picture of Stevie in eighth grade, his first year on the football team. That surprised me, I'd have thought his father would have put him in peewee league. It made me think better of Steve that he'd waited until his son wanted to play.

I covered her hands and the book with my hands. I pressed down enough that she had to finally look up at me. Her eyes were wild, as if tears were the least of our worries. There was something almost violent in that look.

I changed what I'd been going to say, because she wasn't ready to hear me say, Leave, I can't help you. 'You told me that it happened on prom night, but you didn't give me any details.' I didn't really want details, but anything to stop the pictures and the desperate flow of memories. Murder I could handle. The trip down memory lane was getting on my nerves.

Her eyes flicked right, then left, and she leaned back, leaving the album in my hands. I left it open to his thirteenth birthday party. The smiling faces of him and his friends clustered around a cake.

Her breath came out in a long, slow rattle. Not a sound that you hear out of the living much. She swallowed convulsively and reached for her husband's hand. He was still standing. His face relaxed a little just because she'd reached for him.

'They found Stevie's car off the road, as if they'd been run into the ditch. The police think that they were picked up trying to hitch-hike,' he said.

'Stevie wouldn't have gotten into a car with strangers,' Barbara said firmly, 'and neither would Cathy.' Her eyes were a little less wild. 'They were good kids.'

'I'm sure they were, Mrs Brown.' People seemed to want to make saints of the dead, as if their very goodness should have protected them. Purity was not a shield against violence, in fact sometimes ignorance got you killed faster.

'I'm not saying they weren't good kids,' Steve said.

She ignored him, and she'd taken her hand back. Both her hands were clasped around her purse, clutching it in her lap, as if she had to hold on to something, and his hand wasn't enough.

'They wouldn't have gotten in a car with strangers. Stevie was very protective of Cathy. He wouldn't have done it.' She was so certain that there was nothing else to say about that particuliar speculation.

'Then did they know the people that gave them a ride?' I asked.

That seemed to throw her. She frowned, and her eyes darted from side to side, like something trapped. 'No one we know would have harmed Stevie, or Cathy.'

She'd been sure about the stranger thing, but she wasn't really sure about this one. Somewhere in her was enough logic to know that either they got into a car with strangers or they got into a car with people they knew. There were no other choices.

'The police think that they might have been forced into another car, maybe with a weapon,' Steve said.

She was shaking her head over and over. 'I can't bear the thought of someone pointing a gun at them. I just can't think who would have done such a thing.'

He patted her shoulder. 'Barb, maybe you better wait out in the other room, while I finish talking to Ms Blake, here.'

She was still shaking her head. 'No, no, she's going to help us. She's going to bring Stevie back, and he can tell us who did this to him and to Cathy, and it'll be all better. We need to know who could do such a horrible thing.' She looked up at me, and her eyes cleared for a moment. 'Stevie and Cathy would not have gotten into a car with strangers. We'd talked about it. He knew that if someone pointed a gun at him and tried to force him into a car that they wouldn't let him live. We've talked about that since he was a little boy.' Her breath caught, but she didn't cry, not yet. 'I know he would have done what I'd told him to do. He would have grabbed Cathy and run into the woods. The car was parked right next to the woods. They could have hidden in there. It had to be someone he knew, or she knew. It had to be someone we know, Ms Blake,' she said, changing her tune from a minute ago. 'Our beautiful boy was taken away by one of the people that have been over to our house, eating our food, giving us flowers. Someone we know is a monster and we didn't know it.' There, that was the true horror. Not just that her son and his girlfriend had been murdered, but the murderer had to be someone Barbara and Steve Brown knew.

What must it be like to stare into the faces of your friends, your children's friends, and wonder, was it you? Or you? Which one of you did it?

I couldn't even argue with her, because you are more than 80 percent more likely to be killed by someone you know than by a stranger. An ugly statistic, but true.

'You say "monster." Do you mean just that they could kill your son, or something about how it was done?' Maybe it had been something supernatural. Maybe there was more than one reason they'd come to me. I could hope there was something I could do for them.

She put her hands over her face and started to cry, not quietly either.

Steve Brown spoke over her sobs, as if he'd heard them before. 'What was done to them, Ms Blake, what was done to them was monstrous.' He didn't look like a man who'd had to say monstrous a lot in his life. I didn't think it was a word he'd chosen lightly.

Barbara Brown was rocking back and forth, back and forth, while she wept. Her sobs must have been as loud as I thought they were, because the phone on my desk rang.

I jumped, but got it. It was Mary, our very good secretary. 'Is everything alright?'

'No,' I said.

'Do you need me to pretend you have another client?'

'Fifteen minutes,' I said.

'Or sooner if it gets louder?' Mary asked.

'Yes, that would be fine.' I hung up, promising myself to send Mary flowers, or chocolates, or both.

Steve Brown was trying to calm his wife. She'd stopped rocking and was leaning in against him. The sobs had quieted, a little. When her blue eyes turned to me again, they contained that promise of violence again. If she knew who had done it, I wasn't sure what she'd do to them. Looking into her eyes, I wasn't at all certain that she'd wait for a judge and jury.

She spoke very fast, her words almost sliding into one another, 'They raped Cathy, raped her, and they mutilated Stevie, they cut . . .' She just stopped talking, her hands pressed over her mouth, eyes impossibly wide. There wasn't a lot of sanity left in that look.

I kept my eyes on her, while I asked Steve Brown, 'So someone gave them a lift after they had car trouble, and then . . .'

'They found them in a shed in the woods,' he said, 'and they'd raped them both.' He said in such a quiet voice, no change of inflection, as if he felt nothing when he said it, and maybe he didn't, not up where he was aware of it anyway. He'd had to push his pain underground, as far as he could shove it, because Barbara's pain was more important than his, more all-consuming.

'They cut him . . .' He almost broke then, but he rallied, and I watched him fight his face to hold it all together. 'They castrated him.' One of his eyes gave an involuntary flutter. 'While he was still alive.' His voice had gotten softer.

'The police never found it,' she said, and her voice was shrill, 'they can't find it. The monsters took a piece of him away, and the police can't find it. We had to bury him without it. They took it, and we couldn't get it back for him.' Her voice was growing louder and louder, not exactly a scream, but not far from it. The shrill edge of hysteria was in full cry. 'They didn't take anything from Cathy. Why didn't they cut her up? Why just Stevie? Why that? Why did they take that? Why that?'

If I'd had a dart gun full of Valium, I'd have used it. But I didn't. It was awful, horrible, but I couldn't fix this for them, and I really didn't need another nightmare to add to my list. I couldn't help them. It was a human monster, and I wasn't an expert on that kind of monster.

I finally went with that. 'Mrs Brown, Mrs Brown, Barbara!' I yelled it, and it didn't phase her. She was gone, gone into her pain, her sorrow, her loss. I was yelling, but there was no one home to hear me.

Mary opened the door and said something twice before I could hear it over Mrs Brown's voice. 'Your next client is here, Anita. You've gone fifteen minutes over already.' Mary was looking at me, but her eyes were a little wide. She'd been a secretary and law clerk once for a criminal attorney, so she'd seen grieving and hysterical clients before, but either this was a new variety, or Mary didn't like it any better than I did.

'I'll use one of the other offices, Mr Brown. I'll give you and your wife a few minutes to collect yourselves.'

Barbara Brown ran to me. 'Please, Ms Blake, please, please help us.' She grabbed the front of my jacket. Her hand brushed the butt of my gun, and that made her pause, but only for a second. Then she wadded her hands tight in the cloth of my jacket. If she'd been a man, she might have jerked me into her, but she didn't. She just clung to me, and begged, 'Please, Steve, show her the check.'

'Barbara, she's not going to help us.'

She dug her hands tighter into my jacket, making fists of the cloth. It was a girl's jacket, not a man's, and there just wasn't enough material to treat it that roughly. It pulled my shoulders forward and was limiting my mobility, and she'd made it impossible for me to go for my gun. I didn't believe she was going to get so out of hand that I'd need the gun, but it was standard policy for me. No one got to compromise my gun, no one. The trouble was, I couldn't figure a way to get free of her without hurting her physically. And I didn't want to do that.

'Steve, show her the check.' She was so close to me, that it was strangely intimate, close enough to kiss, too close to fight.

'Show me whatever she wants me to see, Mr Brown,' I kept my voice calm, no anger, no hint of what I was thinking, which was get her the fuck off me. I wasn't unsympathetic, but a stranger had breached my personal space, and I never liked that.

His face was all apology as he drew something out of the inner breast pocket of his suit coat. It was one of those oversized checks, a cashier's check. He held it up so I could see it clearly. The check was for a hundred and thirty thousand dollars, payable to cash.

'Take the check, Ms Blake, we'll sign it over to you, now, today. Right now.'

I shook my head and put my hands gently over hers, I was going to have to get her off me. 'I can't take your money, Mrs Brown.' I tried to pry her hands away, but she gripped them tighter. The jacket was going to be permanently wrinkled.

'It's our life savings, but we could refinance the house. We could get you more.' Her eyes were so bright right next to mine. Again that unnatural brightness, and I wondered if she was on something, something prescribed. If it was prescribed, then it was the wrong medication.

I couldn't get her hands off of me without hurting her, and I still wasn't willing to do that. I patted her hands, I'd try to be friendly. 'It isn't a matter of money, Mrs Brown. If I could raise your son and find out who did this, I would. Honest to God, I would, but it doesn't work like that.'

Nathaniel was at the door. He gave me a look, like is there anything I can do? I couldn't think of anything, so I gave a small shake of my head.

Mary must have gone for Bert, because he appeared in the doorway with her behind him. 'Mrs Brown, you need to let Anita go. I told you before you had the meeting how it would go.' His voice was even, almost singsong, as if he'd done this before. He hadn't done it much for me, but not everyone had my charm and ability to scare people. Usually, the gun made most clients nervous, but Barbara Brown didn't give a fuck about my gun.

She glanced at Bert, but then turned immediately back to me, her hands still strangling my jacket. 'You can't say no, Ms Blake, if you say no, then it's over, and it can't be over.' She began to give me a little shake with every other word. 'And it,' shake, 'can't be,' shake, 'over.' Shake.

Mother of God, how do I help her, and how do I get her off me without making it all worse. We had grief counselors on file, but I doubted she'd go to one. She wasn't at that therapy-will-be-helpful stage. She was at that I'm-going-crazy stage.

I stopped trying to pry her off me, but I was tired of being shaken. I decided for truth. 'A murdered zombie kills its killer.'

'I want them dead,' she almost screamed it, and tightened her grip so that she spit in my face, just a little, accidentally.

'The zombie cuts a path of destruction through everything and everyone in its way until it kills its killer. I've seen zombies kill innocent bystanders by accident.'

'Stevie wouldn't do that,' she said, and her face was so close to mine I wanted to draw my face back to focus on her, but she had too much of my jacket in her hands, so that I was effectively trapped. 'Stevie was such a gentle person. He'd never hurt anyone. He'd just tell us who did this awful thing.'

'Mrs Brown, Barbara,' I said, and she looked at me, there was a hint of sanity in there somewhere. 'It won't be Stevie, Barbara. It will be the walking dead. He won't be your son, he'll just be an animated corpse.'

She lowered her face, so that I was looking down at the top of her blond head. Her shoulders slumped, and I thought I'd gotten through to her.

Bert said, 'Mrs Brown, if you'd come into my office for a few minutes, so we can all calm down, so we can all get on with our day.'

I think it was the 'get on with our day.' She stiffened, and I had a second to decide whether I was willing to really hurt her, or not. I hesitated, and that was enough. She had me held too close with the jacket, I couldn't move back, and I couldn't raise a hand until she let me go. She scratched my face. But to do it she let go with one hand. I raised the freed arm up, and blocked her next attempt to scratch my eyes out. She let go with the other arm, but I grabbed her wrist and stepped away, pulling on the wrist at the same time. And used her own momentum to turn her around, and she ended up on her knees with one of her arms behind her back and my other arm across her shoulders. I didn't make it a true choke hold, because I was hoping that someone might drag her off me before it got that far.

My face was burning sharply, from just below my left eye to mid-cheek. Even before I felt the first trickle, I knew it was going to bleed, it just had that feel to it.

She was screaming, loud, ragged screams.

Steve Brown was closest to us, and he said, 'You're hurting her.'

'I'm hurting *her*?' I said. 'She tried to take out my eye.'

I didn't have as good a hold on her as I should have, I was still trying to be nice to the poor bereaved crazy woman. She twisted in my grip and dug her nails across my hand. I tucked my elbow tight across her throat and pulled up sharp on her arm behind her back. She cried out, but it stopped abruptly because I was applying pressure to her neck. I knew how to do a choke hold so that all it did was make you pass out. I knew not to crush the Adam's apple or anything stupid. And I admit I was pissed by this point, but Mr Brown shouldn't have done what he did.

He yelled, 'Let her go!'

I said, calmly, I thought, 'If you can't control her, I will.'

She struggled, and I tucked my head down tight to her. Then two things happened at once: Nathaniel said, 'Anita look out,' and Mary screamed. I looked up, in time to see Steve Brown hit me in the face.

It rocked my head back and made reality shift just a little to the side, like a televison that isn't quite in focus. It didn't really hurt immediately, not like the scratches at all. You can usually judge how bad an injury is by how long it takes for you to feel the pain. Quick pain, small to medium injury; long pain, not good.

It was a good hit, nice and solid. I think he'd expected me to go down, because he had this surprised look on his face. Or maybe he hadn't ever hit a woman that hard before, or maybe at all. We had one of those long seconds that seem to last forever, but are really just the blink of an eye, to look at each other over his wife's head.

I saw his lips move, but couldn't hear what he said. The only sound was a high, white, buzzing, static, and the taste of blood in my mouth. It didn't matter that it was my own blood. It only mattered that it was blood, and I was angry.

I had a moment, a heartbeat, where I smelled Barbara Brown's skin underneath the sweetness of her perfume. A moment where I could smell her skin, salty, sick, almost, sick with her grief like some poison coming out of her skin. She was wounded, she was hurt, I could end that suffering. I tucked myself tight in against her body, tight enough that her husband couldn't hit me without risking her. I still couldn't hear his voice, but I could hear something else. I could hear her heartbeat. So loud, so very loud. It was a thick, meaty sound, not like that fragile tinny sound you get through a stethoscope. This was what a heart would sound like, if you could put your ear inside someone's chest. This was what someone's life sounded like, beating inside their body, beating fast and faster. Barbara Brown had smelled like food before, but now that first flush of adrenaline kicked through her system. Some part of her that she couldn't even name knew something was wrong. Knew that danger was very, very close.

I must have closed my eyes, because I felt him looming over me. I opened my eyes to see Steve Brown about to touch me. I think he was going for my hair to pull me off his wife. But I saw the hand, and I grabbed it, just stopped it with my hand. My hand looked small around his bigger one, but my arm was solid, and when he tried to pull away, he couldn't do it.

I still had his wife on her knees with my other hand around her wrist and her arm up almost to her shoulders. Distantly, I thought, if I kept pulling I'd dislocate her shoulder. But another part of me, which felt much closer, thought, that's alright, we'd have to pull her apart to eat her anyway. True, if we were going to eat her. Were we?

I'd always thought that the beast was a thing of passion, because passionate emotions could bring it on. This wasn't passionate, this was passionless. There was no right or wrong in my head. No sympathy, no sense that these two people were fellow human beings, and it would be wrong to hurt them. That wasn't even in my head. They'd hurt me, and I was hungry, and she smelled so good, and so bad at the same time. She smelled of sickness, and I realized it was drugs. I could smell them in her sweat – acrid, bitter.

I let her go so abruptly she fell forward on the carpet, but I kept my hand on Steve Brown, and I drew him past his wife, because he had bent to see to her, and I'd pulled him off balance. He smelled of fear and anger, but nothing else. He was clean.

He stumbled, and I put a hand in his shirt, while the other used his arm to bring him in closer. I could hear his heart now, thudding, thudding, so thick, so meaty, so . . . so good.

I felt movement behind me, and I whirled, taking Steve Brown with me, tripping him without thinking about it, so that he was on the ground at my feet, with me still gripping his arm. Food should be on the ground.

Nathaniel was there, touching my face. I jerked back, as if he'd hit me, but with that one touch sound roared back into my head. A woman was screaming. Mary was asking, 'Should I call the police?'

'No,' Bert was saying, 'no, we can handle this.'

I doubted that. But the moment I thought that, I looked down at Mr Brown. He was staring up at me, eyes wide, and he was afraid.

I let him go as if his skin burned mine. I backed up, until I bumped into Nathaniel. I grabbed for his hand without looking, and clung to it. Just touching him helped me think. Usually all touching Nathaniel made me think about was sex or food, but today, it helped me remember that I was human and what that meant.

'Help me,' I whispered.

'Everybody out,' he said.

Everyone stared at him.

I screamed it, 'Out, get out, all of you out!' I started to rush at them, but Nathaniel caught me around the waist, and I let him pick me up. I fought not to struggle. But I kept screaming, 'Get them out! Get them out!'

Steve Brown grabbed his wife's arm and started dragging her toward the door. Bert finally moved, taking her other arm, and helping. He was looking at me as if he'd never seen me before, and maybe he hadn't. Bert had a gift for only seeing what he wanted to see.

Mary's pale face was the last thing I saw before the door shut, and the words, *get them out*, changed to a wordless, formless scream. One ragged scream after another, until my throat went raw and I sagged in Nathaniel's arms.

Before I'd only felt the beast like it was some huge pet that rubbed itself against my body and my mind, but today, I knew that that wasn't the most dangerous part of the beast. The most dangerous part was that it was an animal, and true animals have absolutely no sense of right and wrong. I screamed, because to stop and do anything else was to risk that mind coming back up through me, and I wasn't sure I could stop it again.

30

NATHANIEL CALLED MY name, but I couldn't answer. I was afraid to answer. Afraid if I took even a moment to think that that other colder mind would take over again. Nathaniel dropped to his knees with his arms still around my waist. The sudden movement startled me, stopped the screams like a switch had been thrown. That other mind spilled into the silence. But it wasn't cold anymore, it was frightened. Leopards are solitary. There are only three reasons to meet another leopard in the wild. Fighting, fucking, or eating. He was either something that would hurt us, something that would fuck us, or something that would eat us. There were no other choices in the fear that roared through my brain. I thought I'd understood what the fight or flight response was, but I'd been wrong. This made anything I'd ever felt as a human being pale by comparison. The need to strike out, or run away, thrilled all the way down to the tips of my fingers and toes. It was a rush of adrenaline like I'd never known. My entire body was thick with it, stronger, faster, because I was about to fight to the death.

I fought that panic, fought not to struggle, not to fight Nathaniel. I could get away. I knew it, and that other mind knew it. We could get away. We could be safe. But that small part that was still human knew that Nathaniel wouldn't hurt us. We had to let him pin us, had to, because I knew I could escape. What I didn't know was what would happen if I got away. What would happen if Nathaniel couldn't pin me and hold me down until I could think like a person again? I didn't want to find out, because it would be something bad, something I wouldn't want to live with afterward.

I struggled to be still. To let Nathaniel take me down, to be limp in his arms as he pressed me to the floor. That other mind shrieked through me as my body touched the carpet. It shrieked that we would die, and it believed that. It had no friends here. I'd always thought that at least part of my beast was Richard's wolf, but in that moment, I knew it wasn't so. What fought me wasn't anything that recognized the larger social order of the pack. There was only prey, rivals, mates, and young. No part of me saw Nathaniel as a child.

I let him pin me facedown on the carpet. My skirt was too short for being flat on the ground, and it began to ride up. His body molded to my back, his hands on my wrists. I fought that screaming voice in my head, to lay still, to let Nathaniel get as good a hold on me as he could. He had no training in how to pin someone. He did it the only way he knew how, by forcing my legs apart with his hips, so I couldn't just go to my knees and lift him off. The skirt rode up my hips until it was bunched so high that there was nothing between him and me but the silk of my panties and his pants. It was a horribly vulnerable position. Even the part of me that was still me, didn't like it. Because once you're pinned under someone like that, your options vanish. I like options. Options keep you safe.

Nathaniel won't hurt me. Nathaniel won't hurt me. I kept repeating that over and over and over, as he settled his body tighter against mine. The part that was beast knew he could break our spines from this position. The part that was me felt like it was a prelim to rape. I knew that Nathaniel wouldn't do that, and I also knew that truthfully if you're intent on rape you want some clothes off before you get here. Because once you've pinned someone like this, your hands are busy, and men's pants don't unzip themselves. Logically, I was safe, but logic isn't always what wins when you're scared. The beast was scared because it couldn't trust another leopard. I was scared of what would happen if the least dominant person in my life couldn't dominate me enough to keep me from tearing out his throat, or breaking through that thin office door and slaughtering everyone outside. I trusted Nathaniel not to hurt me. I did not trust him to control me and keep everybody else safe. I especially didn't trust him to keep himself safe. Hadn't he begged me just this morning to set my teeth in his throat and draw blood? I didn't trust him to be . . . enough. Enough leopard, enough man, enough person, just enough. And that doubt fed my fear, fed all the fears, and I lost. Lost myself. Lost control. Lost.

The last clear thought I had before panic set in was, *I have to get up off the floor.* I had to get up. I forgot everything I'd ever known about how to use my body, how to fight. Panic was all I felt, and panic does not plan. It reacts.

I went from that limp stillness that I had fought for, to bucking, writhing, throwing my body from side to side. I struggled with my whole body, with every muscle. I literally threw everything I had into simply trying to get up.

Nathaniel's body rocked with me. He fought to keep my wrists pinned to the carpet, my hips pressed down, my legs apart so I couldn't just get to my knees and throw him off. I felt him struggling above me, but he wasn't used to being the one on top.

I threw my body to the left and lifted us both half off the ground. He shoved us back down, and I had a moment to feel the potential strength. So terribly strong as he forced us back to the floor. If he'd been willing to let go of one wrist, and used his other arm for something else, but he kept my wrists, and maybe I couldn't get up, but he couldn't control me either, not enough.

He was saying something, I don't know how long he'd been repeating it, before I understood it. 'Don't make me hurt you, Anita, please, please, please!' He almost screamed the last word.

The panic in his voice told the leopard that we were winning. Make him afraid of us, and he'll let us go. It spurred the cat, and we threw ourselves to the left again. If his back hadn't hit the desk we'd have rolled him. I screamed, but it wasn't fear this time, it was triumph.

We ended sitting with his back propped against the desk. His legs encircled my waist. I scratched at them, and part of me didn't understand why the cloth did not part in bloody strips. One arm went across my chest, and only later would I realize that he'd covered my gun butt with his hand. His other hand balled into my hair, jerking hard enough that it tore a scream from my throat. I had a moment to feel his breath like heat on the back of my neck. The leopard screamed that he would snap our neck, the other part of me was just confused. Nathaniel bit me.

He sank his teeth into my skin, into my flesh. I felt his teeth slide inside me, and I stopped fighting. It was as if he'd hit a switch I didn't know I had. At first I simply stopped fighting. My hands fell limp to my sides. My body relaxed, and what should have been pain, felt warm and comforting.

Nathaniel growled with his mouth still locked against my body, and it drew a moan from my throat. The growl turned to a purr, a deep vibrating sound, and because his mouth was locked over the top of my spine, that deep, pulsing rhythm played down my spine, as if my body were a tuning fork for his voice.

I cried out, but it wasn't fear or triumph now.

He loosened his legs around my waist. I stayed limp and easy against his body. He uncurled his legs, slowly, body tense, as he waited for me to react, but I was past reacting. I was waiting, waiting for him to master me, it was the only word I had for it. It was the most wonderful feeling, so peaceful, so safe.

He kept his teeth around my neck, his hand in my hair, but the other hand, he took slowly away. I sank into him. My body sliding along the front of his, held in place only by teeth and hair. My skirt had bunched like a belt at my waist and rode higher behind from my body sliding against his. Nathaniel slid his arm around my waist, pulling the bunched skirt even higher, I think by accident. He drew us both to our knees with his arm around my waist. He moved his arm away from my waist, slowly. I stayed on my knees, swaying a little, because every muscle was loose and calm. I actually had to concentrate to stay kneeling and not simply fall to the ground, but his hand in my hair, and his mouth at my neck kept me upright, made me want to stay on my knees. But that little bit of effort on my part started to help me climb back into my own head, a little, not a lot, but a little more of me was here. Enough to both worry and enjoy his bite on my neck. Worry, because what would happen when he let go, would I revert back to that cold mind? Enjoy, because part of me that wasn't just cat liked that firm grip, that pull of teeth in flesh.

I knew I was feeling better, because faintly, I could hear what Nathaniel was feeling. Not a sound, but I had no word for sensing another person's feelings. He was scared, excited, frustrated, confused, unsure, scared, unhappy, worried. I felt each emotion like a cobweb blown across my body in the dark. Nothing to see, and when you brush at it, it breaks apart and blows away, as if it wasn't there at all. Animals didn't have this many emotions all at once. Confused and scared, yes, but not the rest. The rest was still too much for my beast.

Nathaniel's free hand fumbled at the waistband of my panties. My skirt was already pushed up around my waist on its own without any help from him. He pulled my panties down to my knees, but since he was working one-handed, they came down in fits and starts, and it was anything but smooth. He growled his frustration against my skin, and it caught my breath in my throat, made me go weak at the knees. He used my hair like a handle, making it clear that if I went down on the floor it would hurt. It helped me stay on my knees. Helped me concentrate, and that helped me slide a little more inside my own skull.

I wanted to say his name. It seemed like that would help. But I couldn't think of his name. Couldn't say it out loud. It was as if *name* were an alien concept. Smell, his smell, that I knew. I tried to say it, and it took me three tries before I whispered, 'vanilla.'

He'd wrestled my panties down almost to my knees. But at that one word, he stopped. He kept his hand on my hair, but he lifted his mouth from my neck, just enough so that his breath caressed like heat on the wound he'd made. 'Anita, can you hear me? Are you in there?'

Was I in there? It seemed like too hard a question for me. Was I in there? I think I took too long to answer, because the next thing I felt was his belt smacking against my bare butt. His pants fluttered against me.

The beast ground my hips against him, but not to slow him down. The thoughts weren't this clear, but it amounted to: He'd bested us in a fight, he'd earned the right to mate. I knew now why the big cats fought before they mated. You had to prove you were strong enough. That old biology imperative to only breed with the best, with the male that can give your offspring the genes they need to survive.

The leopard didn't mind. She was ready. I, on the other hand, had a problem. Of course, I couldn't remember what it was. Couldn't think. Because the human part of me agreed that Nathaniel had earned his right to be here. He'd saved us. Saved all the nice people outside the office door. Office, that was it. I didn't want to fuck at work. That was it. I moved away from Nathaniel's body. I pulled away from him, and his fear skyrocketed. He had no way of knowing that it was the human me that was wanting to pull away. The beast smelled that rush of fear, and let out a sound in my throat that I'd never heard come out of me. It wasn't a human sound.

He pulled on my hair so hard that it brought a gasp from my throat, but strangely, made me relax. It hurt, but it felt good, too, and gave an echo of that wonderful peacefulness that had happened when he bit the back of my neck.

He brushed the head of himself against my body, and the beast writhed for him. He whispered, 'The angle's wrong.' Then he used my hair like a handle and his other hand to put me on all fours on the floor.

The leopard crouched down in front of him, giving him my ass like we were in heat. He pulled my panties the rest of the way down my legs, got them tangled on the boots' heels, then they were gone. Maybe the beast was in heat, but I wasn't. Maybe it was losing my underwear, but the ass-in-air position was a little too undignified for me. I raised back up enough to be on all fours, so I didn't look like I was offering myself to him. I opened my mouth to say something, and he pushed himself inside me, and I forgot that I could talk.

The beast had been willing, but there had been almost no foreplay, and I was tight. So terribly tight. Nathaniel had to work himself inside me. He used his hand and my hair to spill me back to the carpet so that I was back where I started. It was just as undignified, but I didn't seem to care. For the first time the beast and I were in agreement.

I'd slept with Nathaniel, but I'd put very firm rules in place. I'd never touched him between the legs, not on purpose. To go from having deprived myself of even a caress to the sensation of him pushing his way inside my body was overwhelming. It wasn't just that it felt good, though it did, it was that it was Nathaniel. Part of me, though I might never say out loud, had been wanting to cross this barrier, to shove it aside, to bend it, break it, ignore it.

He worked until he was sheathed inside me as far as he could go, then he hesitated, stopped moving, frozen against me. 'Anita, can you hear me?'

Hear him? Hear him? The cat screamed through my head, and that scream spilled out my mouth. I lost some of the ground I'd gained, because the beast wasn't conflicted, not in the least. It, she, began to work our hips, so that Nathaniel stayed still, but we drew him out of our body, out and out, and then when the tip of him seemed about to spill out, we drove ourselves upon him.

His voice came, 'Oh, God.'

We moved over him, against him. Shoving as hard and fast and deep as we could. It was as if nothing would be enough. I wasn't open enough to be this rough. I felt him almost catching on the sides, because I hadn't given myself time to grow wider. But I felt frantic. There was no thought about waiting, just the need. I wanted him to fuck me. *Sex* was too mild a word for it. I couldn't make him do what I wanted. I wanted deeper, I wanted more, and I needed him to help for that.

He let go of my hair, and his hands touched my hips, and he began to ride our rhythm, the cat's and mine. We pushed and he shoved, and just like on the dance floor where I'd followed his body, now he followed mine.

It was a dance of flesh, his into mine, until I was wet and warm, and he moved easily inside me, out and in, out and in. When he could glide inside of me, he shoved himself deeper, harder, as if he understood what my body was asking without words. He used his hands to move me just a little, until he found the spot he wanted, and then he plunged inside me, as if he meant to come out the other side, and I screamed for him.

I looked back over my shoulder, and his eyes weren't lavender, they were blue with hints of gray, and they weren't human anymore. His shirt was open, so I could see his stomach and chest. He did a movement with his stomach like a belly dancer, and his rhythm changed, grew more urgent and somehow smoother, or cyclical, as if he were doing a circle inside me, and out of me. A circle that went lower going in and higher coming out, so that he touched all of me, but not all at the same time.

He'd worked me larger by being rough, making me take all of him and more, and now that he had a hair's breadth of room, he used it. He used it in that circular rhythm, to caress along the walls of me. It was one of the most delicate things I'd ever felt when a man was inside me. So careful, and yet the push of his hips was so strong. The control took more strength than just shoving himself inside me. Strength of so many different kinds.

It was the upper stroke as he was pulling out that found that spot. I'd had the spot manipulated by hand and had it included in intercourse, but never quite like this.

Every time he slid over that one spot, my breathing changed, and he heard it, because he changed his rhythm again. Sliding himself over and over that small spot. Not just the tip of him, but the head, and as much of the shaft as he could manage. He used himself to stroke me in a way that I'd only had done with fingers and hands before. As always when that place inside was touched just right, the sensation of pressure was just this side of unpleasant. My body felt as if when he brought me, all the fluids in my body would fly, and not just the ones we wanted. It was always like that, that pressure, more pressure than any other kind of orgasm, as if you would lose control of your body completely. Jean-Claude had had to ease me through it the first few times. Reassure me that whatever happened it would be fine. It would be wonderful.

The pressure built and built, dancing along that line of too much. A pleasure so large it was almost pain. A pleasure that grew and grew inside me like some warm expanding thing, as if the orgasm were something separate from me, something that grew inside me and would burst out of my body.

I managed to whisper – almost hiss – his name, 'Nathaniel.'

He hesitated a fraction. 'Anita, are you . . .'

'Don't stop, please, don't stop.'

He didn't ask again. He shifted his positon a fraction, then closed his eyes and gave himself to the rhythm of his body. I tried to move my hips, but his hands clamped tight on my hips, keeping me still. Holding me in place.

The pressure built, built, until my body was thick with it, full of it, and then it spilled out. Out in a burst of liquid between my legs, out in shrieks, out in my hands clawing the carpet. I had to claw at something, had to do something with the pleasure. It was as if it were too much pleasure for my skin to hold. If I'd had a beast inside me, it would have spilled out along with that thick liquid between my thighs.

He eased himself out of me, and I lay on the carpet, unable to move. Hell, I was having trouble focusing my eyes, let alone moving anything else.

He crawled to my head, stroking my hair back from my face. 'Are you alright?'

I started to laugh, then blinked and tried to see better. He was still spilling out of his pants, and he was still hard and firm, and though there was liquid on him, it wasn't white enough or heavy enough to be his.

I swallowed the laugh and said in a voice that was still breathy, 'You didn't go.'

'You weren't in a head space where you could give me permission.'

I closed my eyes and willed myself to sober up. When I opened them, I could see again, no bleary edges. Good. 'What do you mean, give you permission?' I asked.

'I don't get to have orgasm unless you tell me I can.'

The look on my face must have been eloquent, because he said, with a smile, 'I knew that would weird you out, but look at the benefits, Anita. I can go for a very long time, because that's the way I was trained.'

'Trained,' I said.

He nodded.

I closed my eyes again. 'You've been begging for orgasm, for intercourse. You had the perfect excuse, and you don't take it.' I opened my eyes and stared at him. 'Why didn't you take it?'

'I want you to want me, Anita. Not just use me for a metaphysical emergency.'

I sat up and was reminded that I had no underwear on. I glanced at the carpet and for the first time was glad it was a dark woodsy brown. The wet spot didn't show as badly. 'Where are my underwear?' I asked.

He started looking around as if he weren't sure either. Great. He was also still perfectly erect, and it was distracting.

'If you're not going to . . .' I started to make a gesture, but stopped, 'then can you put . . . that away.'

He turned with a smile that was perilously close to a grin. 'Why, does it bother you?'

'Yes,' I said, with as much dignity as I could muster, pulling my skirt down over my hips.

He held my underwear out toward me. He was fighting a smile, but it filled his lavender eyes with supressed laughter.

I snatched them from his hand, but couldn't think of a slick way of getting them on. Truthfully, I was wet enough that I needed towels before I got back into my panties.

I walked, a little wobbly, around my desk. I had baby wipes in the desk drawer. They helped with cleanup when I came into work with a spot of blood I'd missed. I was debating whether I could sacrifce my extra T-shirt that I kept in a drawer for blood emergencies, too, when Nathaniel started talking again. And not about anything I was comfortable hearing.

'You know it's rare for a woman to be able to do that.'

I had the drawer open and the moist towelettes in hand. 'What's rare?'

'You're a rainmaker.' He was kneeling on the other side of the desk, with his arms on the desktop and his chin resting on them. It was a strangely childlike gesture, and it did nothing to make me feel better.

'The only definition I know for that term is a lawyer who brings in big bucks for their law firm. I'm assuming that *rainmaker* has a meaning that I don't know.' I made sure my unhappiness about the whole topic showed in my voice. I was uncomfortable enough just cleaning myself up. I was wet down to my knees and beyond. Jesus, what a mess.

'It's a term for a woman who can ejaculate.'

I took in a lot of air and let it out slowly. 'Can we not talk about this?'

'Why are you mad?'

That was a fair question. Why was I mad? I had to think about it to be honest even with myself. I got the spare T-shirt from the bottom drawer and dried off with it. So much for extra clothes. I slipped my underwear back on, and felt better. I always felt better dressed. Why was I mad?

I sat down in my chair, getting out the spare hose that I also kept in a drawer. I went through a lot of hose in my line of work. They just weren't meant to be worn to animal sacrifices, bad guy chases, or vampire slayings. Nope, nylons were just not made for my lifestyle. I started unzipping my boots so I could take off the hose we'd shredded struggling on the carpet.

'Why am I mad?' I said, almost to myself. My fingertips hurt, a sharp immediate pain as the last of the endorphins left. I'd torn off half my nails down to bloody quick. Once I saw the blood it hurt worse. Why did it always hurt worse when you saw the blood?

He stood up and zipped himself back into the dress slacks. There were stains on the legs of the trousers that weren't going to be fixed by baby wipes and a T-shirt. I didn't have extra clothes for Nathaniel. 'Yes,' he said, when he got himself safely inside, still hard, still thick, still ready. 'Why are you mad?'

'You didn't go,' I said, and started peeling off the hose. It gave me something useful to do instead of meet his eyes.

'You're mad because I didn't go?'

'I'm mad because if you'd gone we'd have that barrier crossed, and now we don't.'

'And?' he said.

I sighed. 'And, if we'd crossed it, it would be easier to cross it again. But doing it this way, makes it more . . .'

'Important,' he said.

I nodded. 'Yes.'

He came around the desk and went to his knees at my feet. 'I want it to be important to you, Anita. I don't just want to be someone you take because you have to take someone, anyone. I want you to want me.'

'You said that before.'

He touched my hands where they held the new hose, and he moved them gently out of my hands and laid them on the desk. He took both my hands in his, and there was such a serious look in his eyes that I was afraid. Afraid of what he'd say. 'You loved me before today. You loved me without sex. No one's ever loved me, or even wanted me, without fucking me first. No one since my mother died and . . . Nicholas . . .' He bowed his head for a second, and I squeezed his hands. I'd seen that memory, and I didn't want him thinking about it. So horrible, and he'd been so little. I wanted to protect him from things like that. I wanted to keep him safe.

He smiled up at me. 'Gabriel and Raina taught me that I could be worth something, but that worth was all about my body, the way I looked, and how good I could fuck.' He squeezed my hands tighter. 'You taught me that I was worth more than just fucking. You taught me that I was worth more than just being used.'

I started to say something, but he put his fingertips against my lips. 'I know what you're going to say. You think you use me with the *ardeur*, because I'm your *pomme de sang*. You don't know what using somebody is, Anita. You just don't know.'

There was that look in his eyes that he got sometimes that made his eyes look so much older than he was. A look of murdered hopes and more pain than anyone his age should have had to experience.

I kissed his fingers, then rested my face against his hand. 'Someday I want you to stop getting that look in your eyes. I want there to be enough good in your life to balance that out.'

He smiled, and there was a tenderness in his eyes that made me have to look away. 'See, Anita, you think you're hard, and that you use people, but you aren't, and you don't.'

I pulled away a little. 'I can be hard when I need to be.'

'But not to me, and not to Micah. Not to anyone that will let you be nice to them. If they're shitty, you're shitty back, but you give them the chance first.'

I shook my head. 'I'm not that good a person, Nathaniel.'

He smiled and touched my face where Barbara Brown had scratched me. I winced. 'Yes, you are, you just don't like admitting it.'

'We better get dressed and out there before someone calls the cops.'

'Bert won't call the police, he's too afraid of bad publicity.'

I laughed. 'You haven't met Bert often enough to know him that well.'

'I've known a lot of people like Bert. He's not as bad as they were, but it's the same . . . kind of thinking. He wants his moneymaker to keep on making money more than he wants anyone to be safe or happy.'

I looked into that terribly young face, and there was no one young looking back at me. As much as I'd seen of life, Nathaniel had seen things that would have broken me. Or at least bent me all to hell. I cupped his face in my hands, and said, 'What am I going to do with you?'

'I want you to make love to me,' his voice was soft, but oh, so serious.

I tried to make a joke of it. 'Not right now, I hope.'

He gave me his gentle smile, the one that said he wasn't going to let me get away with it. 'No, not right now, but soon.'

I drew back from him, and I was almost afraid of him, afraid in a way that guns can't help with. 'Why are you making this so hard?'

'Love should be hard, Anita, or what is it worth? You taught me that all these months in your bed, with your body against mine and no release. You taught me how hard love can be.'

'I'm sorry,' I said, 'I didn't understand until yesterday.'

He leaned up on his knees and got close enough to kiss my mouth. 'Don't be sorry, make love to me.'

My voice was shaky as I said, 'Not right now.'

'No,' and he breathed against my lips, 'but soon.' He kissed me, one chaste touch of lips, then he stood and moved away to give me some room.

I watched him move across the room toward the door. 'I'll tell them we're alright.'

I nodded, because I didn't trust my voice. He'd given me room, physically, but emotionally, emotionally, he was giving me no room at all. I waited for the panic to set in, but it didn't. What came was the memory of him inside my body and the thought of what it might be like to have him spill himself inside me.

31

I'D BEEN LOUD enough, and it had taken long enough, that part of me wished there was a back door to my office. But there wasn't, so I couldn't slink off even if I'd been willing to do it. Besides, if Bert ever suspected that I was that bothered by it, he'd use it against me. Try for some kind of leverage in the ongoing game of one-upmanship that Bert and I had played for years. The only cure for it was a bold face. Sigh.

I ran my fingers through my hair, which is all you're supposed to do when your hair is as curly as mine. Brushing just makes it frizz. I checked my makeup in the little mirror that I'd started having to keep in the desk. The problem with dressing more like a girl was that it forced you to have to care. Once you put on the lipstick, you had to look at it periodically to make sure it hadn't smeared like clown makeup. I liked the way lipstick looked on me, but I hated having to think about it.

The eye shadow had surived pretty well, but the lipstick was pretty much smeared all over my mouth. Again, I was grateful that the carpet was dark. Red lipstick on a pale carpet would have looked awkward. On the deep brown, you couldn't see it.

I used some makeup remover that was supposed to be used to take off eye makeup, but I'd found it worked dandy on lipstick. I used a moist wipe to get everything off and then had to reapply the lipstick. See, so much trouble. I was just happy that I almost never wore base makeup. That would have been a bitch to get off the carpet.

When my mouth was as red as when I started, I put everything back into the desk drawer, got up, straightened my skirt, took a deep breath, and went for the door. With everything that had happened to me in the last twenty-four hours, having to face Bert down still took more courage than was pretty. You do not fuck at work. You just don't. It's déclassé to say the least. Shit.

When I stepped out into the reception area, I got a surprise. No one assumed we'd been having sex. The screams had been violent enough that everyone assumed it had been a bloody battle, a near thing. The fact that both Nathaniel and I came out bloodier than when we started helped. Mary had sat him down in her very own office chair. She was laying out bandages, while Nathaniel cleaned the wounds on his hand. They were deep, bloody nail marks. Once I would have said that it looked like a leopard ripped him up, but I'd seen the damage that real leopards could do, and I knew better now. I was sort of amazed that I'd done that much damage, though.

I went to stand near him. 'I'm sorry,' I said.

'I'm not mad.'

This close I could see that the front of his knuckles on both hands were raw as well. I frowned. 'I didn't do your knuckles.'

'Carpet burn,' he said.

I looked at the bloody scrapes and made a face. 'Ow,' I said.

'I don't mind,' he said.

Mary looked up at me. 'That woman and man are in with Bert. They wouldn't leave without their son's things.' She looked pissed. 'I cannot believe that they abused you like that.'

I licked the edge of my lip where Steve Brown had belted me and realized that it was healed. I'd put on lipstick and it hadn't hurt. Shit, and wow. A very positive side effect. It's nice that there were positive ones.

I touched my cheek where Barbara Brown had sliced me, and it still hurt. I hadn't seen it in a mirror, but it had probably looked worse an hour ago.

'I'll help you clean that up, when I'm finished with your friend,' Mary said without a trace of sarcasm. *Friend,* without any double meanings. It wasn't just her typing skills that had kept Mary on as our daytime secretary. She had a real gift for taking things in stride. She had Nathaniel hold a gauze pad over his hand while she taped it. She hadn't put plastic gloves on. I couldn't remember if I'd told her what Nathaniel was, or not.

In human form he wasn't contagious, but she probably had the right to know. Almost as if Nathaniel read my mind, he said, 'I tried to get her to let me clean it up myself.'

Mary glanced back at me. 'He told me' – she seemed to search for a word – 'he told me, and I told him, that you can't catch lycanthropy from a human being.'

Nathaniel looked up at me with those big eyes. The look said, I tried.

'You're right, Mary, in human form there's no contagion.'

She smiled at Nathaniel in a very motherly way. 'See?'

'Most people don't want to take the chance,' he said, softly.

Mary finished bandaging his hand and patted him on the shoulder. 'Most people are just silly.'

He smiled at her, but it left his eyes wounded. Most people are just silly. She had no idea. I guess I didn't either, not really. I'd just begun to get the reactions from people who thought I was a lycanthrope. I hadn't lived with it for years the way Nathaniel had.

Mary turned to me, touching my cheek gently. She was shaking her head. 'I wanted to call the police on them. It's enough to file assault charges.' She started dabbing at the scratches. There must have been some alcohol in the stuff, because it stung.

I took a deep breath so I wouldn't wince. 'I don't want to press charges.'

'You feel sorry for them?' she asked.

'Yes.'

'You're a better woman than I am, Anita.'

I smiled, and the cheek was a little tight for it. 'I've been hurt a lot worse than this, Mary.'

'Never by a client,' she said.

I let that go. There were stories that Mary didn't know, and we all stayed out of jail that way.

She was frowning at me. 'If I didn't know better, I'd say you're healing.'

'It's clean enough, Mary, thanks.' I went around her to the desk and the bandages. I'd need a gauze pad bigger than the one on Nathaniel's hand. Of course, my scratches would probably be healed by dawn, and his hand wouldn't be. Damage that I caused seemed to heal as if another lycanthrope or vamp had cut them up. We'd noticed that just lately.

Mary turned me around with a hand on my shoulder. 'You hold the gauze in place, and I'll put the tape on, just like I did for your friend.' The look in her eyes said plainly that I was being silly, too.

I let her tape up almost the entire left side of my face just short of the eye. Barbara Brown had done this before, I'd have bet money on it. Women will try to scratch in a fight sometimes, but most of them aren't good at it. Barbara was good at it, like she'd had practice.

Mary looked at my torn nails. 'Does that hurt as much as it looks like it does?'

I never know how to answer questions like that. Hell, yes, or how should I know? 'It hurts,' I said.

She handed me a small bottle of alcohol. 'Take this and soak your hands in the bathroom until they stop bleeding.'

I looked at her. 'Hell, no.'

She gave me the parental look. 'You've ripped off most of the nails on both hands. Do you want to get infected?'

I thought about telling her that I couldn't get an infection, but we didn't know that for sure. I wasn't truly a lycanthrope, and while I'd gained their ability to heal, I had no way of knowing if I'd gained all their abilities to keep healthy. It would be a bitch to ignore Mary's advice, and then lose a finger to gangrene or something. But damn, it was going to hurt.

The door to Bert's office opened before I could run off to the bathroom. His face was very solemn, though there was something in his eyes, some flicker, that I didn't trust. Not supressed laughter, but something.

'Anita, do you want to press assault charges on the Browns?' He said it straight-faced, in a serious voice. He spent a great deal of effort making me take all kinds of shit from clients and never before suggested we press charges.

I studied his face, trying to read where this was going. 'No, I don't think that will be necessary.'

Steve Brown showed at the door first, with his arm around his wife. 'We are so sorry, Ms Blake. Really, I don't know what came over us. It was . . . inexcusable.'

'Thank you for not pressing charges, Ms Blake,' Barbara Brown said. She'd been crying, and the last of her makeup had worn away. She looked older than when she'd entered my office, and it wasn't just the lack of makeup. It was as if what had happened had sucked a little more of her life away.

'We just need our son's things, and then we'll go,' he said. He looked horrible, too. Not that they shouldn't have looked horrible, but something else was going on. I didn't know what, but something wasn't right. Something beyond just grief and embarrassment, and fear of the cops.

'Mary will escort you into the other office for your things,' Bert said.

Mary couldn't keep her opinion completely off her face, but she led them into my office. When they were out of earshot, I stepped up to Bert and said quietly, 'What are you up to?'

He gave me innocent eyes, which meant he was lying.

'What did you do, Bert? You know I'll find out eventually, so just tell me.'

He kept giving me that innocent blank face of his, with that false sincerity that was still in place for when the Browns came back out.

I had an idea. But the act was so low I didn't think even Bert would have tried it.

'You pretended to call the cops, didn't you?'

He gave me a 'who-me' look, which meant I was right.

'You took their check. The house check.'

'Anita, even I wouldn't do that.'

'Yeah, you would, if you thought you could get away with it.'

His eyes thawed to their usually level of insincerity. 'They're coming back, just smile and agree with me.'

'Bert, either you tell me what you did, or I'll blow it all to hell.'

He took hold of my arm, which he never does, and smiled over my head. 'Ms Blake needs a little more persuasion to agree to our deal.'

'Oh, please, Ms Blake, please, don't press charges. I don't want it in the papers that I'm crazy. Our daughters have seen enough bad publicity about us.'

I turned and would have said something, but Bert whisked me into his office and closed the door. Unless I was going to put up a fight, I had no choice but to let him manhandle me a little.

He stayed by the door, with his back against it, as if he were afraid I'd bolt. 'Anita, this is fair.'

'What is fair?' I said, and my voice was already warming up, ready to be pissed.

'We could press charges against them,' he said.

'But we're not going to,' I said.

'But we could.'

'Bert, either tell me the truth, or get away from the door.'

'A bonus, Anita, for them beating the hell out of you. What's wrong with that?'

'How much?' I said.

He looked uncomfortable.

'How . . . much?'

'Ten grand,' he said, and then went on hastily, 'he owns his own construction firm. He can afford it, and they did go way over the line.'

I shook my head. 'Bert, you bastard.'

'The wife offered me the check for the refinancing of the house when I started to talk about pressing charges. I didn't take it. So I'm not quite as much of a bastard as you think I am.'

'You can't take money not to press charges. That's illegal.'

'I didn't say outright that that was what the money was for. Hinted at it, maybe, but I know better than to say something specifically. Give me a little credit.'

I stared up at him. 'You get as much credit from me as you deserve, Bert. If they calm down and tell the cops what you did, what will you say the money is for?'

'A retainer,' he said.

'I can't raise their son, Bert, or his girlfriend.'

'Can you at least talk to the detective in charge of their case?'

'So you can keep the money?'

'I was thinking more that you might offer your expertise to the police.'

'I am not a specialist in murder, Bert, not unless there are monsters involved.'

'Does a serial killer count as a monster?' he asked.

'What are you talking about?'

'Their son and his date were the first, but not the last. He killed a couple the year after.'

'Are they sure it was the same person?' I asked.

He shrugged. 'You'd need to talk to the police on the case, and for that you'll need the permission of the parents, since as you pointed out it's not a crime that you have jurisdiction over.' He almost smiled.

'I'll make you a deal, boss man. I'll talk to the cop in charge. If they think they know who it is, but don't have proof, then I can't help, but if they're lost, then I have one idea.'

Bert smiled full out. 'I knew you would.'

'But if my idea tanks, and they get nothing out of it, you will write them a personal check for ten grand.'

'Anita, I'll just give back the money.'

I shook my head. 'No, your personal check for ten grand.'

'You can't make me,' he said.

'But I can start a vote to kick your ass out of here. You don't know shit about raising the dead, or crime, or vampires. You're the money man. But you're not the only money man in the world, are you?'

'Anita . . . you really mean it,' he said, and he sounded surprised.

'You just cheated these people out of ten thousand dollars, Bert. It makes me wonder what else you've done. Makes me wonder if we need an audit of the books.'

He was getting angry, it showed in his eyes and the tight line of his mouth. 'That is out of bounds. I have never cheated anyone in this company.'

'Maybe, but if a man will cheat in one way, he'll cheat in another.'

'I cannot believe you would accuse me of that.'

'I can't believe I haven't wondered about it before,' I said.

His face was darkening with his effort not to explode. You could watch his blood pressure rise. 'Audit and be damned.'

'I'll make you a deal, Bert. I'll settle for you giving them back their check, instead of a personal check from you, but you have to stop this shit. We make enough money, Bert, you don't have to cheat people.'

'They offered the money. I didn't ask for it.'

'No, but I bet you made it so they'd think of it. Nothing said outright, like you said, but you put it out there, somehow, you made them think of it.'

He opened his mouth, closed it, then leaned back against the door. 'Maybe I did, but, Anita, they made it so easy.'

'You just couldn't resist, could you?'

He let out his breath in a long shoulder-moving sigh. 'I lost my head, a little.'

I shook my head and almost laughed. 'No more losing your head, Bert, okay?'

'I'll try, but I can't promise. You wouldn't believe me.'

I did laugh. 'I can't argue that.'

'Do you want me to tear up the check now?'

I watched his face for the signs of pain that parting with money usually cost him, but all I saw was a resignedness, as if he'd already given the money up for lost.

'Not yet.'

He looked up, hope showing momentarily in his pale eyes.

'Don't get excited. It's a slender little hope, but if it helps lead to something that can help the police then we'll have earned some money. If it doesn't, then we can return the money.'

'Do I want to know what your plan is?' What he was asking was, was it illegal, and did he not want to know so he'd be able to deny it later. Bert knew that I stepped over lines that wouldn't just get jail time, but an execution notice. I knew that he was just this side of a con-man, a swindler, but he knew, or suspected, that I was just this side of a cold-blooded killer. There were bosses that couldn't have handled that doubt, or that almost knowledge. We stood and met each other's eyes, and we had an understanding, Bert and I.

'I'm going to see if the cops will bring down some of the boy's clothes for Evans to look at.'

'The touch clairvoyant that tried to cut his own hands off?' He made a face when he said it.

'He's out of the hosptial,' I said.

He frowned. 'But didn't the paper say that he tried to cut off his hands so he wouldn't see murders and violence every time he touched something?'

I nodded.

'Anita, I never thought I'd say this, but leave the poor guy alone. I'll give back the money.'

I narrowed my eyes at him. Was he being nice to fool me? Did he mean it? Out loud, I said, 'Evans is feeling better than he has in years. He's taking active clients again.'

Bert looked at me, and it wasn't an entirely friendly look. 'This man has tried to kill himself to keep from seeing these things, and you want to take items from a serial killer case where he cut up a nice teenage couple. That's cold, Anita, that's truly cold.'

'Evans put himself back on the market, Bert, I didn't. He's married now, and he's a lot more relaxed than he ever was before.'

'Love may be grand, Anita, but it doesn't cure everything.'

'Nope,' I said, 'it doesn't.' What I didn't try to explain to Bert was that Evans's new wife was a projective psychic null. She negated most psychic abilities within yards of her. Evans was a lot calmer around her. She truly had saved him.

His small pale eyes narrowed at me. 'That man out there, the boy, he's your boyfriend.'

I nodded.

'Just your boyfriend?' he made it a question.

'What else could he be, Bert?' And it was my turn to have the innocent face.

He shook his head. 'I don't know, but the noises from your office were a hell of a show, and that was without any visuals.'

I didn't blush, because I was working too hard at keeping control of my face and eyes. 'Do you really want to know, Bert, or do you want deniability later?'

He stood there for a moment, thinking, then shook his head. 'I don't need to know.'

'No,' I said, 'you don't.'

'But you'd tell me the truth, if I wanted to know?' he asked.

I nodded.

'Why, why would you tell me?'

'To watch your face,' I said, and my voice was soft, and not altogether pleasant.

He swallowed hard and looked just a little paler than his untanned face had a moment before. 'It would be something bad, wouldn't it?'

I shrugged. 'Ask and find out.'

He shook his head again. 'No,' he said, 'no.'

'Then don't ask questions you don't want the answers to,' I said.

'Don't ask, don't tell,' he said.

I nodded, again. 'Exactly.'

He gave that roguish, I-know-something-you-don't smile. 'But we get to keep the ten grand.'

'For now. If Evans agrees to see the evidence, we'll need a bankroll.'

'Is he that expensive?'

'He risks his sanity and his life every time he touches another clue. I'd make people pay for that, wouldn't you?'

A light came into Bert's eyes. 'Does he have a business agent?'

'Bert,' I said.

'Just asking, just asking.'

I had to shake my head and give up. Bert had a real genius for making money from psychic gifts that other people thought of as curses. Would it be so bad if he could help Evans make more money? No. But I wondered if Bert understood that Evans was one of the most powerful touch clairvoyants in the world. That to brush against another person with his fingertip told him more about that person than most people would ever know. Bert would probably offer to shake hands, and the deal would be off. I only suspected what Bert was. One touch, and Evans would know for sure. In a way, if Evans didn't run screaming it would be reassuring for me. I would never offer to shake hands with Evans. One, you never offer your hand to a touch clairvoyant, just bad form. Two, Evans had brushed up against me before, by accident, and he hadn't liked what he saw. Who was I to throw stones at Bert, when he might pass Evans's radar unscathed, and I knew that I would go down in bloody flames?

32

THE REST OF the afternoon appointments were damned boring compared to the Browns. Thank God. Nathaniel sat, quietly, in a corner of my office through all of them, just in case. Bert didn't argue now. I'd had two appointments with lawyers to discuss wills and other privileged material. They'd objected to Nathaniel, but I'd told them that legally the conversation with me wasn't privileged, so why did they care. Legally, I was right, and lawyers hate for a nonlawyer to be right. Or at least the ones I meet get cranky about it. So then, they'd wanted to know who he was and why he got to sit in on their meetings.

I told the first one, do you want this meeting, or don't you, and he let it go. The second one didn't let it go. My fingers hurt where I'd torn off the nails. My face hurt even if it was healing. My pride was hurt from having sex in the office. I was not happy, so I told the truth.

'He's here in case I have to have sex.' I smiled when I said it, and knew that it didn't reach my eyes, but I didn't care.

Nathaniel had laughed and done his best to turn it into a cough.

The lawyer, of course, didn't believe me. 'It was a perfectly legitimate question, Ms Blake. I have every right to protect my client and his interests. You don't have to insult us with ridiculous lies.'

So I stopped insulting him with lies, and we got down to business.

Every client, or group of clients, had to ask about Nathaniel. I told them he was everything from domestic help, to lover, to office boy, to personal assistant. Nobody liked any of my answers. I stopped caring long before I stopped seeing clients. I actually started telling the truth again, and the two new groups that I told it to got insulted. Insulting lies, they called it. Try to tell the truth, and no one believes you.

What I'd wanted to talk about all afternoon had been my beast. I had a lycanthrope right there, and we didn't get five minutes of peace to even begin the discussion. I had so many questions, and no time to ask them. Maybe that was why I was so grumpy to the clients. Maybe, or maybe I'm just grumpy. Even I wasn't sure sometimes.

It was seven o'clock by the time we climbed into the Jeep. Bert had passed my 7:30 cemetery appointment on to Manny without me having to ask. He even apologized for overbooking me. He always overbooked me, and he'd never apologized before. I think the realization that I could call a vote and get his ass kicked out had made him a better boy. Or maybe it was just the realization that I knew that any one of us could call a vote and kick him out. If Bert had any weakness in business it was assuming that those of us without a business degree didn't understand business. A little fear isn't always a bad thing. In fact, it can be downright therapeutic for some people. I didn't expect for the nicer version of Bert to last, but I'd enjoy it while I had it.

I'd actually turned off onto Olive in the direction of the city. I had just enough time to drop Nathaniel off at Guilty Pleasures and be only about fifteen minutes late for what was now my first outside appointment of the evening.

'Where are you going?' Nathaniel asked.

'Guilty Pleasures,' I said.

'You need to eat first.'

I glanced at him as I slowed for a stoplight. 'I don't have time to eat.'

'You know how when you don't feed one hunger the other hungers get worse?' His voice was so gentle when he asked, but I'd begun to mistrust that particular gentle tone. It usually meant he had a point to make, and he was right, and if I'd only accept it, I'd see that he was right, too. It usually meant that the argument was lost before it had begun. But I never considered defeat a reason not to put up a fight.

'Yeah, I know. If I deny the *ardeur* the beast wants meat more, or the vampire wants blood. I know all that.'

'So what happens if you don't feed your human stomach, you get hungry, right?'

The light changed, and I eased forward. Saturday night traffic on Olive was always fun. 'Yeah,' I said. I was looking for the trick, and didn't see it.

'So if your body gets hungry for normal feeding, then doesn't that make all the other hungers worse?'

I almost hit the car in front of me, because I was staring at him. I had to slam on my brakes and endure much horn blowing, and, if it hadn't been so dark, I'm sure I'd have seen some hand gestures. 'What did you say?'

'You heard me, Anita.'

I sighed and started paying better attention to the traffic. But inside I was kicking myself, because it was so simple. So terribly simple. 'I don't eat regularly when I'm working, and that usually means that I'm running home with the *ardeur* riding me every night.'

'Sometimes twice a night,' he said. 'How much do you eat on those nights? Real food, I mean.'

I tried to think, and finally had to say, 'Sometimes nothing.'

'It would be interesting if you kept a food diary to see if there was a correlation between starving your human body and the other hungers rising.'

'You talk like you know this already,' I said.

'Haven't you noticed that lycanthropes cook and eat?'

I shrugged. 'I don't know.' I thought about it. Richard cooked, and had always been either taking me out to dinner or wanting to cook for me. Micah cooked, though Nathaniel did more of it. We usually had a house full of wereleopards for at least one meal a day.

'You mean there's a reason that all the lycanthrope men I've dated have been domestically talented?'

He nodded. 'We need to eat a nice balanced diet, heavy on protein. It helps keep the beast at bay.'

I glanced at him, and in the near dark of the streetlights, he was mostly in shadow. His lavender shirt was the palest thing about him. 'Why didn't someone mention this to me before?'

'We've been treating you like you're mostly human, Anita. But what I saw today . . .' He seemed to be searching for words. Finally he said, 'If I didn't know that you were human and couldn't slip your skin and be a leopard for real, I'd think you were one of us. The way you felt, the way you fought, the way you smelled, everything was shapeshifter. You did not come off like a human. Turn into the parking lot here,' he said.

'Why?' I asked.

'Because we need to talk.'

I did not like the sound of that, but I turned in to the strip mall that had Culpeppers at one end. I parked in the first space I found, which was far away from any restaurant. Most of the stores were dark and closed. When I turned off the engine, the world was suddenly very quiet. The traffic on Olive was still snarling by, and in the distance was music from one of the restaurants, but inside the Jeep it was quiet. That silence that you get inside cars after dark. With one switch of a key, the space inside a car becomes private, intimate.

I turned to face him, having to work against the seat belt, but I wasn't comfortable taking if off until I was ready to get out of a car. 'So, talk,' I said, and my voice sounded almost normal.

He turned in his seat as far as his seat belt would allow. He knew my thing about seat belts. He faced me, putting one knee up to prop himself against the center panel. 'We've been treating you like you're human, and now I'm wondering if we were right.'

'You mean I'm going to shift because I'm in a new triumvir-ate?'

He shook his head, and his long braid slid across his lap like a heavy pet. 'Maybe what happened with that has made it worse, but I think one of the reasons you haven't been able to get a handle on the *ardeur* is because you've been taking almost all your advice from a vampire. He doesn't need to eat, Anita. There is only blood lust and the *ardeur* for Jean-Claude, that's it. A lycanthrope doesn't stop being human. You still have to eat like a person, you just add the hunger of the beast, but you don't lose a hunger, you just add on to it.'

I thought about it. 'So you mean that since I'm already fighting off normal hunger pangs, that it makes it harder to fight the *ardeur*?'

He nodded, and his hair slid across his lap again, as if the braid were moving closer to me. 'Yes.'

I thought about it, and it seemed utterly logical. 'Okay, say you're right, what do I do? I'm still running late tonight. I'm usually running late.'

'Tonight we go through a drive-up. You get something easy to eat behind the wheel, and I get a salad.'

I frowned at him. 'A salad, why? Most drive-up salads suck.'

'I have to eat before I go on tonight.'

'So you'll be able to control your beast better,' I said.

'Yes.'

'But why a salad? I thought you needed protein.'

'If you were going to take off all your clothes in front of strangers, you'd get a salad, too.'

'One burger a few hours before you go on won't make you gain weight.'

'No, but it might make me bloat.'

'I thought only girls did that.'

'Nope.'

'So you're eating a salad so you'll look good tonight,' I said.

He nodded, and his hair slithered over the edge of his leg and across the gear shift. I had this horrible urge to touch that heavy band of hair. A little voice in my head said, Why not? After what we'd done this afternoon, what's a little hair touching. Logical, but logic didn't have much to do with how I acted around Nathaniel.

I clasped my hands together in my lap to keep from touching him, then felt silly. What the hell was I doing anymore? I reached out to that heavy curl of hair and pet it, like it was more intimate to him than it was. The hair was soft and warm. I petted his hair while I talked. 'The beast isn't conflicted about anything, is it?'

'No,' he said, and his voice was both loud and soft in the quiet dark.

I began to pull his braid, gently up from around his body where the end had slid. 'It's not just the hunger for flesh and blood that you fight, is it?'

'No,' he said.

I got to the end of his braid and spilled it into my hands. 'I thought that the hunger was the beast. That desire to chase and feed; I thought that was all of it.'

'And now?' he asked.

I stroked the tip of his braid across my palm, and just that made me shiver. My voice was shaky when I said, 'Richard always talked about his beast like it was all his baser impulses, you know, lust, sloth, the traditional sins, but to sin implies a knowledge of good and evil. There was no good or evil, there was nothing like normal thought. I hadn't really understood how all my thoughts are based on things. I'm always thinking about how one thing affects another. The consequences of your actions.' I lifted more of his braid in my arms, and it was like holding a snake, a soft, thick serpent. I gathered his hair into my arms and let myself cuddle it against my body. I was about at the limit for the seat belt, and I wanted to be closer to him. The seat belt stayed.

I hugged an armful of his braid to my chest as I said, 'I stopped thinking about the Browns' grief, their dead son. It wasn't that I chose to ignore it. I wasn't being callous, it just never entered my mind. It was just that they hurt me, and I got mad, but mad translated directly to food. If I killed them and ate them, then they couldn't hurt me anymore, and I was hungry.' I met his eyes on that last word.

Some trick of reflected light made his eyes shine for a moment, like the eyes of a cat in a flashlight's beam. He turned his head, and it was gone, his eyes lost in shadow again. The turn of his head tugged on his hair, and I had a second to decide whether I would let it go, or keep it. I kept it, and it put a strain down the line of his hair, a strain like pulling on a rope, and knowing it was tied tight.

His voice was a little breathy when he said, 'You're always hungry when you first change shape, especially if you're new at it.'

'How do you keep from tearing into the crowd at the club?' I asked, and my voice was a little shaky, too.

He leaned back away from me, and it made the pull on his hair tighter, harder. 'By channeling the hunger into sex instead of food. You don't eat your mate. If you can fuck it, it's not food.' His voice was lower, not deeper exactly, but lower.

'So how did I not eat anybody? I wasn't thinking about sex with the Browns.'

'At first you are just the hunger, but after a few full moons, you can think, but you don't think like a person. You think like your animal. A few more full moons after that and you can choose to think like yourself in animal form.'

'Choose?' I said, and began to pull him toward me, using his braid like a rope, but this rope was attached to his skull, and he didn't come easily. He began to pull against me, and I knew that it had to hurt just a little.

His voice was low and soft. 'Some people enjoy the purity of the animal. Like you said, no conflicts, no inner struggles. Just decide what you want and do it.'

'Undo your seat belt,' I said.

He undid his seat belt.

I pulled him to me with his hair tangled around my arms, like you'd coil a rope or a strings of lights. 'Does anyone use the animal for a patsy, you know, crime? A lot of what keeps some people good is their conscience. The beast doesn't have one of those.'

He was close enough to kiss, his face lower than mine, because of his braid holding him just a little to one side. 'The animal is very practical,' he whispered. 'It's why so few people use their animal form when they commit murder. I don't mean accidental kills, because they don't have the control, but deliberate murder.'

I leaned over him. 'Example.'

'Say, your uncle will leave you a fortune but he needs to be dead so you can inherit it. Unless your beast is hungry, it won't kill your uncle for money, because the beast doesn't understand money.'

I leaned close enough to almost kiss him. 'What does the beast understand?'

He spoke with his lips almost against mine. 'It will kill someone you truly fear, or someone who's hurt you, especially physically. The beast understands being hit, being injured.'

I almost asked if he'd hunted down the man who beat him and his brother, but I didn't. I'd seen his memories. If someone had done that to me, what would I have done? Bad things, most likely. And I didn't want to fill the car with hurt and bad memories. I'd had enough of those.

I laid a kiss on his mouth, and he pressed me back against my seat. I found that still being seat-belted, I couldn't move well. My arms were tangled in his braid so that it felt like I was being bound. I had a moment of panic, then I relaxed into it. Nathaniel would not hurt me, and it was my own fault about the hair being where it was. He hadn't wrapped me up, I'd done that.

He drew back just enough to talk, his lips brushing mine. 'What about your clients?'

I drew my head back as far as I could, which wasn't far, and said, 'I'm not offering to fuck you here and now.'

'You're not?'

That made me mad, though I wasn't exactly sure why. 'No, I'm not.' I started trying to untangle myself from his hair.

He drew back with a smile that showed for an instant in the lights. 'I want to encourage you to touch me. God knows I do, but if you do too much with the *ardeur* not fed, and neither of us fed, then the night is over. You'll be pissed with yourself, and me, and I don't want that.'

I got most of me free from his braid, except for the part that was caught on the back of the Browning. If it hadn't been a gun, I'd have jerked, but even with the safety on, I didn't trust it enough. Stupider accidents have gotten people shot. Neither Zerbrowski nor Edward would ever let me live it down. So I took a deep breath and forced myself to carefully untwine Nathaniel's hair from my gun.

Nathaniel had buckled himself back into his seat. 'I would love to repeat this some time and place where we didn't have to stop.'

I was still trying to get his hair off my gun. The fact that he was in his seat but his hair wasn't told you just how long his braid was. 'You had your chance,' I said, and I sounded mad.

'Don't be grumpy at me,' he said, 'I wasn't the one who pulled you into my lap.'

I had the last of his hair free of my gun. I started to fling the end of his braid back at him, but stopped myself. He was right. Right about who started it. Right about how mad I would have been if the *ardeur* had risen before I got my work done. He was right. When people are right, you shouldn't get pissed at them. Or that was the new theory.

'Fine, I'll go through a drive-up. I'll eat a burger, you can have your salad. Will that make you happy?' I turned on the engine and started pulling out of the parking space.

'No, but it'll get us both to work tonight.' He sounded sad.

I glanced at him as I maneuvered may way through the parked cars. 'Don't be sad.'

'I'm not sad,' he said, but he sounded it.

'What's wrong?'

'It's just that you reached for me. There wasn't a metaphysical emergency. The *ardeur* hadn't risen, yet. The beast was nowhere in sight. Blood lust wasn't anywhere, and I had to say, stop. But the *ardeur* will rise tonight, Anita, and having sex with it not being fed yet is just inviting trouble.' He leaned his head against the window. His shoulders were rounded, as if he'd hunched in upon himself.

'You're right about the schedule and the *ardeur* and needing to eat, Nathaniel. I don't know what came over me just now.'

He turned to look at me, and we were in the bright halogen lights of the street, so I could see his face clearly. He looked almost in pain. 'Couldn't it just have been that you wanted to touch me, is that so wrong?'

I sighed and concentrated on the road, because I had to. But also, it gave me time to think. I turned us back the way we'd started, but this time I knew we'd go through the drive-up at McDonald's. Honest.

I finally did the only thing I could think of to take that miserable look off his face. I touched his thigh, because it was the only part of him I could reach easily. He'd pulled so far away in his seat that I couldn't reach anything else without straining. I was driving, and that had to take priority over offering comfort, even when it was my fault for saying stupid things. I touched his leg, gently, tentatively. I wasn't always good at touching when sex wasn't involved. I was trying to get better at it, but the learning curve seemed to rise and fall depending on my mood, or someone else's.

He touched my hand with his fingers. I held my hand up to him, eyes still on the road. He laid his hand in mine.

'I'm sorry, Nathaniel. I'm sorry that I'm such an ass sometimes.'

He squeezed my hand, and when I glanced at him, he was smiling at me. That one smile was worth a lot more than hand-holding to me. 'It's alright,' he said.

'I notice you don't disagree that I'm being an ass.'

He laughed. 'You don't like it when I lie.'

I stared at him for a second, mouth open, then I went back to staring at traffic. 'I can't believe you said that.'

He was laughing so hard that our hands jiggled up and down on his leg. 'Neither can I,' he said.

But I didn't get mad. When you've been an ass to someone you care about, you should just admit it, move on, and try not to do it again.

33

THERE IS ALMOST no parking on The Landing. The streets are narrow, and most of them are cobblestoned. It's very quaint, but the streets were originally planned for horses, not cars, and it shows. There is no employee parking at Guilty Pleasures, because there isn't room. So I had to park the Jeep down a ways, and we got to walk, but Nathaniel touched my arm before I got too close to the blood-red neon sign and the front entrance. He took me down an alley that I hadn't even known was there. I mean, I knew it was there, but not where it went. I'd never really thought that there must be a performers' entrance just like for Circus of the Damned.

The alley was an alley, which meant it was narrow, cramped, not as clean as you'd like, not as well lit as you'd prefer, and made my claustrophobia complain. Not badly, but enough to let me know that any alley that I could touch both sides of was too damn narrow for comfort.

I'd meant to simply drop Nathaniel at the club and run to my next appointment, but a call on my cell phone had taken a lot of the angst out of my schedule. My second appointment for the night, now my first, had to cancel. Mary said that the lawyer had told her that he had to tend to the needs of another client unexpectedly. Translation: He needed to bail someone out. It didn't have to be that, but it probably was. I'd gotten better at translating lawyer over the years, though no better at legal jargon. Jargon is meant to be as unclear as possible, and it's good at its job.

So suddenly my first appointment of the night was at nine o'clock, and I had time to escort Nathaniel inside and talk to Jean-Claude.

God knows there was enough to talk about. So that's how I came to be threading my way down an alley, following Nathaniel's broad shoulders. His shoulders almost brushed the walls. I don't think Dolph would have fit at all.

Nathaniel hesitated, and I couldn't see around him, but just his posture let me know something was wrong. Women's voices, high and excited, called, 'Brandon, Brandon!'

He waved, then turned sideways so I could see past his chest. There was a handful of women near the steps leading up to a door with a bright light over it.

I leaned in to him and whispered, sort of, 'Why do I think you're Brandon, and are they supposed to be here?'

He whispered back, smiling and waving at the women, who were beginning to come down the steps, as if trying to decide whether to come meet him. 'My stage name, and no. Security is supposed to keep this area clear.' He started to walk toward them.

I grabbed his arm. 'Shouldn't we go back the way we came?'

'They probably just want an autograph or to touch me. It'll probably be okay.'

'Probably,' I said.

He patted my hand. 'If I tell you I'm sure that they won't get bad weird, then I'd be lying, but probably they don't mean any harm.'

'I'd feel better if we went back,' I said.

'No,' he said, and he sounded very firm. 'These are my fans, Anita, and this is my job. I'm going to smile and talk to them, and you can pretend to be my bodyguard, or pretend to be security, but it's bad business for you to be my girlfriend. It hurts the illusion.'

'The illusion?' I made it a question.

He smiled. 'That they can have me.'

I gave him the long blink, the one that means I've just received more information than I wanted and don't know what to do with it. 'Okay,' I said, 'I'll be security.' There, I was cool. I could handle this. Sure, I could.

He let me go in front, because that's what I'd do if I were security. He didn't try to argue, since he could wave and smile and call to them over my head. I fought to keep my face blank and not cranky, but I think I failed.

There were four of them: two blondes, one brunette, and one with hair as black as mine. Though I could tell hers came out of a bottle, because it was too solid, all-over black, no highlights. Black hair isn't supposed to look like you've poured ink on your head. But again, maybe that was just me being cranky.

Nathaniel, alias Brandon, chatted the women up like a pro. The two blondes were regulars, apparently, on a first-name basis. 'We were so excited when we got the E-mail that you were going to be here tonight,' one gushed. She kept touching his arm while she talked. They'd brought a friend, the one with black hair, who was new, but had seen his pictures on the club's Web site. I hadn't known that Guilty Pleasures had a Web site. Of course, I didn't own a computer, so what did it matter to me?

Raven-hair said in a voice that was breathy with nervousness, 'Your pictures were amazing.' She looked at him with little covert glances, as if she was afraid to stare at him head-on. One of the blondes got an honest-to-God autograph book out for Raven-hair, who was quote, too shy to do it herself, unquote.

The brunette wasn't joining in the squeal fest. She was looking at me, and it wasn't a friendly look. 'Who's she?' she asked.

I was standing beside the door at the top of the steps, hands loose at my sides, trying to look bodyguardish, and probably failing. My little blue and black skirt outfit, complete with high-heeled boots, didn't look much like security detail.

'Security,' he said smiling, and signing Raven-hair's book.

'She doesn't look like security,' the brunette said.

'I'm new,' I said.

Brunette didn't look like she believed me. She crossed her arms underneath her small, tight breasts and glared at me.

I smiled back sweetly.

That deepened her scowl and gave her little lines between her eyebrows. I felt better.

Nathaniel gave me a little flicker of a look that said as clearly as if he'd spoken, 'Be nice.' I was nice. I smiled and stood and let the blondes touch his arms, his back, but when one of them patted his ass, that was it.

I pushed away from the wall, and said, 'Ladies, Brandon here needs to get inside and prepare for his performance.' I managed to keep smiling even when one of the blondes threw her arms around his neck and kissed him on the cheek. Then the other blonde grabbed him and kissed him on the other cheek.

I grabbed his arm and moved him back far enough so I could open the door. The two women were still clinging to him. Raven-hair was blushing, and the brunette was still scowling at me. I kept my smile in place, though it felt more like a grimace.

Nathaniel said, 'Beth Ann, Patty, if you don't let me go, I can't get on stage.'

'Stay out here with us, and we wouldn't care,' one of them said.

I glanced behind me and saw a black-shirted man. It was Buzz, the vamp that usually worked the door here. He had the same black crew cut that he had always had, small pale eyes, and more muscles than you should need as a dead man. His black shirt said GUILTY PLEASURES SECURITY in red letters. I didn't usually like Buzz much, but tonight I was glad to see him. Help had arrived.

I could have cleared the steps if I was allowed to be mean, but having to be nice at the same time I was trying to be firm was beyond me. My skill set simply did not include it.

He forced his face into a smile before the women behind me could see him clearly. He was the newly dead, around twenty years, which meant he looked very alive for a dead man. Most humans wouldn't have spotted him in a crowd. Most people think that vamps gain the ability to pass for human, but that's never been my experience.

Older is less human, just better at the mind games so humans don't notice.

'Ladies, you're not supposed to be back here,' Buzz cajoled. He moved past me, and his chest was so muscle-bound that it looked like there wasn't room for all of us and his upper body to stand on that small landing.

The brunette said, 'Is she really security?'

'If that's what she said,' he said in the same good-fellow-well-met voice. He was cheerfully extracting Nathaniel from the blondes. He managed to make a game of it, and they spilled around Buzz's muscular body, as if to say, if they couldn't cling to Nathaniel, any male would do. Of course, from the sound of the joking conversation, the blondes knew Buzz, too.

Raven-hair had backed down the steps, eyes a little wide. She didn't want to play. It made me think better of her.

I drew Nathaniel in through the open door, with the brunette giving me a murderous glare. She was taking this way too personally. It was sort of unnerving. Nathaniel and I were safely through the door, but I didn't like closing it and leaving Buzz out there alone. I mean, he'd helped us. What were the rules about security guards? Did they get protected, too, or just the dancers and customers? If you cut a security guard did he not bleed? So I stood there uncertainly with Nathaniel. It was Nathaniel who gently closed the door.

'Buzz will be fine, he knows how to talk to them.'

'What, you read my mind?'

He smiled. 'No, I just know you. He helped us, and now you feel obligated.'

I fought the urge to squirm or shuffle my feet. I hated when anyone figured me out that clearly. Was I that transparent? Apparently so.

I decided to change the subject. 'How did they know that "Brandon" would be here tonight?'

'When we change headliners, we have an E-mail list that we notify. There's even a list just for Brandon.'

I looked at him. 'You mean that some of these women dropped everything, changed all their plans, because they found out that Brandon was going to be here tonight?'

He shrugged and managed to look a little embarrassed. 'Some of them, yes.'

I shook my head. I changed the subject again, because I was losing again. 'Who was supposed to be keeping the fans away from this door?'

The door in question opened. Buzz laughed and joked, until the door closed behind him, then he leaned against it and looked tired. 'Primo was.'

It took me a second to realize that he'd answered the question I'd asked with the door closed. 'You heard me ask the question?'

He nodded. Then he grinned flashing fangs, the sign of a new vamp. 'You didn't know I could hear you through the door?'

'Hear, yes, but I thought you were too busy concentrating on the women outside.'

He looked past me at Nathaniel. 'Are you alright?'

'I'm fine.'

Buzz pushed himself away from the door and stood, settling his big, overdeveloped shoulders like a bird settles its feathers. 'I better go talk to Primo, for what good it will do.'

'What do you mean, good it will do?' I asked.

He looked at me. 'Primo is old, really old. He wants to be one of Jean-Claude's vamps, but he had his eye on like the number two, or at least the number three slot. He's pissed that he's having to be security at a strip club. He's more pissed that a baby like me is his direct boss.' Buzz looked worried. 'He's old school, and he thinks if he keeps pushing me, that I'll call him out. But I am not going to challenge that thing. He'd kill me.'

'Have you told Jean-Claude what's going on?'

He nodded. 'He told Primo that if he couldn't stomach this job and obey me, then he could get out of town.'

'Did that help for awhile?' I asked.

Buzz smiled. 'Have you heard this story before?'

'No, but I know how the really old vamps can be. They are proud bastards.'

Nathaniel touched my arm. 'I need to talk to Jean-Claude about tonight's performance.'

'I'll join you in the office in a minute.'

Nathaniel started to say something, then seemed to think better of it and just went down the white hallway. I watched him go into the office that was just a few doors down. Then I turned back to Buzz. 'Is it just not doing what he's told, or is there more?'

'He's started taking money to let in people we don't let in.'

'Like who?'

'Men.'

I raised eyebrows. 'You don't let in any men?'

'Not a lot. It makes the women uncomfortable, and some of the dancers don't like it either. You're either comfortable shakin' your thing in front of other men, or you're not.'

'I guess that makes sense, but you let some in.'

'Couples, just like they do at most female strip clubs across the river.'

'But Primo is letting in single men,' I said.

He nodded.

'What did Jean-Claude tell you to do about it?'

'He told me to deal with it. That if I wasn't vampire enough to control Primo that maybe I didn't deserve my job. Jean-Claude is old, too, Anita. I think they're both setting me up for some kind of showdown, and Primo will hurt me, or kill me.'

'You look like you can take care of yourself.'

'If it's just strong-arm stuff, yeah, but Primo isn't a brute, Anita, he's dripping with power. I even agree with him that Jean-Claude isn't using him well. He's too powerful to be down here doing this, and he doesn't have the temperament for it.'

'What do you mean?'

'He's more likely to start fights than stop them. He'll take money from men to get in, then he'll throw their asses out.'

I shook my head. 'You know, Buzz, this doesn't sound like a problem that Jean-Claude would let go this far.'

'Not normally,' he said, 'but it's like Jean-Claude is waiting to see what we'll do before he steps in. I'd just as soon not be dead before he does it.'

'Is it really that bad?'

'The women out there were okay, but we've had one dancer that was stalked. Another one had an irate husband go after him with a knife, because he was jealous that his wife was a member of the dancer's fan club.'

'The dancers have fan clubs?'

'The headliners do.'

'Nathaniel has a fan club?' I made it a question, because it seemed like it should be.

'Brandon has a fan club, yeah.' He looked at me and laughed. 'You didn't know.'

'I don't really pay attention to the day-to-day business here.'

He nodded. He was back to looking worried.

I'd never liked Buzz. I didn't exactly dislike him, but he wasn't my friend. But, if his version of what was going on with Primo was accurate, he was in a bad spot. A spot that I didn't understand. Jean-Claude was a good business vampire, and this didn't sound like good business.

'I'll talk to Jean-Claude, Buzz. I'll find out what his thinking is about Primo.'

Buzz sighed. 'Well, I can't ask for more.' He grinned, suddenly flashing those fangs again. 'In fact, until now I thought you didn't like me.'

It made me smile. 'If you thought I didn't like you, then why pour your problems in my ear?'

'Who else do I have to go to?'

'Asher is Jean-Claude's second in command.'

He shook his head. 'I work here, problems stay here, all the businesses are run that way.'

'I didn't know that,' I said. It was probably a holdover from the days when each business was run by a different vamp. 'So, because I visit all the businesses, I'm what, an ambassador?'

He gave that fang-flashing grin again. 'Kind of.'

'I'll try to find out what's going on, that's the best I can do. If Jean-Claude is really setting you up for a power struggle with Primo, I'll tell you.'

He looked relieved. 'I just need to know where I stand, ya know.'

I nodded. 'I know.'

A black-shirted man came running through the door at the end of the hallway, accompanied by a sudden blast of music and noise. He was blond and looked like a college student, but he ran down the hallway like he was on springs. Lycanthrope of some kind.

He was talking before he got to us. 'We got a problem out there. Primo let a bunch of guys in, they started heckling Byron. You said come get you the next time it got ugly. It's ugly.'

Buzz was already moving down the hall, not exactly running. I hesitated for a second, then started trotting with them.

Buzz glanced at me. 'You coming along?'

I sort of shrugged. 'I'd feel funny just walking away.'

'Our job is to tone things down a notch,' he said. 'Not make it worse.'

'Are you saying you don't want me?'

'Hell no,' the blond said. 'The Executioner on our side. I'll take that.'

'Who are you?' I asked, running to keep up with their fast walk.

'Clay,' he said, offering his hand over the front of Buzz's body.

'Be sociable later,' Buzz said. He hesitated at the door, as if he were gathering himself. There was suddenly a faint hum of energy coming off of Buzz. I'd never felt anything from him before. His gray eyes glowed – if gray could glow. 'I am so tired of this shit,' he said, and opened the door.

34

THE MUSIC WAS still playing, a pulsing beat, but the man on stage wasn't dancing, because *he* wasn't the show anymore. The show was a small ocean of college students surrounding a man that towered above them. He was like a pale tower caught in the middle of their jeans and letter jackets. The tallest of them only came to his shoulder, but there were a lot of them, and almost all of them were wearing a jacket that indicated they did some kind of sport. Some of them looked almost as muscle-bound as the club security. Primo had picked a good bunch if he wanted to start trouble, and he so wanted to start trouble.

The other black-shirted security guards didn't seem to know what to do. Their divided loyalties showed in the fact that they hadn't waded in to help Primo. They were on the fringe of the gang of college guys, keeping them contained as best they could, but they weren't pulling them off the big vampire. If I hadn't known anything about Primo and what had gone on before, I'd have learned something just by watching the other men refuse to help him.

It wasn't Primo's size that was the problem. It was the waves of power that radiated off of him. Most vamp power, and even lycanthrope power, filled a room like water rising, until you drowned in it. Primo's power literally pulsed and flowed. Every time he smacked someone with his big open hand, the power spiked and tightened along my skin. His power seemed to feed off his own violence. But he was keeping his big hands open, just slapping them around, which was, of course, insulting the college students' manhood.

One of the biggest of the group jumped onto Primo, hanging on to his shoulder and arm. Primo grabbed him by the shoulder and peeled him off like he was nothing. He tossed him into the coat check booth and earned a scream from the holy item—check girl that worked there.

Primo's power was thick enough to walk on, but only for a second, then down it went. He couldn't sustain it.

'Enough,' Buzz said, and he sounded unhappy to have to say it. He motioned, and that one motion ended the security guards' hesitation. The other black-shirts moved in and started helping the college guys move toward the door. They made some progress, but the guys didn't want to leave their buddies ass-deep in giant vampire. I couldn't really blame them.

Again, this was outside my skill set. I could have drawn badge and gun and stopped it, if I was willing to arrest, or kill Primo, but I didn't know how to tone it down. As Buzz had said, their job was not to make it worse, but to make it better. I didn't know how to do that. Not really.

Buzz was yelling, 'Primo, Primo, stop fighting back. We need to get this out of the club.'

Primo's answer to that was to pick up two college students by the throat, one in each hand, as if he meant to bang their heads together. But while his hands were busy, another enterprising young man, with short brown hair and shoulders nearly as wide as Buzz's, hit him in the face. He knew how to throw a punch. It rocked the vampire's head back, and blood blossomed at his mouth, like a crimson flower on all that white skin.

The music from the stage died abruptly, and into that sudden silence Primo screamed. A huge rage-filled battle cry. He dropped the two men in his hands like they were nothing and went for the man who'd hit him. I expected him to throw him around like he had the others, but he didn't. He picked him up by the front of his jacket until his feet dangled off the ground, and he was probably choking on his own collar. But instead of those big pale shoulders bunching to throw the man, Primo's hand went back, and this time he closed his fist. From that close up, with that kind of strength, he was going to snap the man's neck.

I drew the Browning, but truthfully without a court order of execution, I was in the same boat as a police officer. I couldn't shoot him if I thought he was only going to hurt someone. How did I argue in court that I knew how strong a vampire was and how fragile the human body could be? And call it a hunch, but I figured once I shot Primo, I had to kill him. I did not want that level of muscle and magic touching me. I was harder to kill, not immortal.

I aimed down my arm, because court and explanations would come later, and that kid was about to die. I was about to take a shoulder shot, because it was my best bet with this many people around, when everyone else got brave, too.

Clay was closest, and he jumped him. Primo tossed the shapeshifter into the first row of tables. Women screamed and scattered. Clay was getting to his feet, but that big fist was pulling back again.

Buzz was screaming, 'No, Primo, no!'

I had the gun pointed at the floor, because when you're tense, your fingers are tense, too. If I shot someone, I wanted it to be on purpose. I started to move closer and to one side for a better shot, when the black-shirts swarmed him, and I had no shot at all.

If I'd been ready to kill his ass, I'd have yelled for them to get away, but I was still hoping to avoid it. I moved closer, and to one side, farther away from the tables, where I thought I had a better chance at getting a clear shot. I'd never tried to shoot anyone in the middle of a bar fight. Just the tumble of bodies was intimidating. It was like trying to hit a target with civilians flying around it.

Primo tossed them around like they were dolls, while still holding the man straight-arm. The more they fought him, the stronger his power spiked and billowed, as if every blow, whether his or theirs, powered him up. He was lost behind a mound of black-shirts, then I felt his power draw in like an atom bomb breathing, and I had time to yell, 'Everybody down!' I wasn't sure what was coming, but it was going to be bad.

I hit the floor like I'd told everybody else to do, though I put myself flat to the ground. I glanced at most of the women and waiters behind me and saw them crouching on the floor. Jesus, didn't anyone know how to take cover?

Primo didn't use his body to throw them off in a burst of black shirts, he used his magic. It blew them airborne in a spray of black shirts and falling bodies. If I'd been crouched like the people I'd complained about, I could have moved faster. But flat on the ground, I had a split-second to decide whether I was going to cover my head and hold my ground, try to roll farther away, or get to my knees and scramble for it. Flat to the ground doesn't help when things as heavy as bodies are falling. I got up to scramble away, and a body smashed into me. I had a moment to be quietly stunned, and then another one landed on top of me.

I'd been hit, I'd been thrown, I'd been a lot of things, but I'd never had two adult men land on me from the air. All the breath was crushed out of my body, and if I'd been as human as I looked, things would have broken. I laid there for a second, stunned, and the two men on top of me weren't moving at all.

The first thing I moved was my head, back to look over my shoulder to where Primo had been. He was still there. Still standing. He'd picked up a different college student and was dangling him in his hand. His big fist was cocked back again. Fuck.

I realized two things at once. One, I could move my hands, two, my gun wasn't in either of them. My body was pinned underneath several hundred pounds. I was strong, and I could get out, but it wouldn't be quick, and I had no idea where my gun was. No one that he'd thrown off was moving. Primo's fist started forward, and there was one of those moments where the world slows down. I had all the time in the world to watch him land that blow, all the time in the world to watch him snap that man's neck and know I couldn't stop him.

35

I REACHED OUT toward him and screamed, 'No!' I didn't expect it to help, but I had to do something.

Blood spurted from Primo's arm, and he hesitated, staring around the room as if he didn't know where the scream had come from.

I wasn't sure either, but I'd spent months learning how to control what power I had, and I'd felt something. This was the second time I'd done something like this, both times when I was desperate. The question was, could I do it on purpose?

Primo raised the man upward again, as if he'd set his goal and nothing would turn him from it. I reached out with my hands, and I thought about it. I thought about what it had felt like. Like my thoughts hit something around him, formed it into glass to hurt him.

Primo raised the man higher and seemed to be saluting someone behind me, but I didn't glance back, there wasn't time.

I reached out not just with my hands but with that power I had over the dead, that link I had with two vampires, and I slashed at him. Blood flared along his arm again, more red to join the first. It wasn't as much blood, and I didn't know why, because I really didn't understand what I was doing. A few bloody cuts were not going to distract him for long.

'You are not doing this,' he said. His voice was a deep rumbling growl that matched the big body and held an accent that I couldn't place.

Jean-Claude's voice floated up from behind us. 'No, but I am doing this.'

I wanted to look backward and see him, but I didn't dare take my eyes off the vampire in front of me to look at the vampire behind me. But I didn't need eyes to feel his power. It flowed through the room like a comforting hand. It caressed the bodies that pinned me to the floor. I got a whiff of musk and wolf fur and knew that both men were pack. That scent of fur and home filled me, too. I knew that it was partly his tie to Richard, but it was more than that. His magic was seeping down through them to me. He hadn't meant for it to, but I had my own ties to Richard and his wolves. It was hard for him to reach out to them and not touch me.

They both drew long shuddering breaths, as if they'd come back to life, though I knew that wasn't it. The blond, Clay, blinked at me from inches away. He looked surprised, and I couldn't blame him. The one on top had hair the color of mine, though it was straight as straight could be. He blinked dark eyes at me as if he didn't remember seeing me before, or know how he came to be lying on top of me.

He muttered, 'Sorry, miss,' even as he started moving slowly, stiffly off the top of the pile.

Clay made small protesting noises as the first man began to get off him.

'How do you think I feel? I'm on the bottom,' I said.

Clay wasted a smile on me.

Buzz was getting stiffly to his knees from a few feet away. He caught my eye and gave me a look. I didn't know him that well, but it seemed to say, well that solves that.

Jean-Claude was here, and his power filled the room like a warm blanket. It felt so good, and so unlike his power in some ways. I knew what was wrong, it felt too alive. But he was the Master of the City, and none of his vampires would defy him to his face. I believed that was the only excuse I have for letting my guard down and looking away from Primo. You'd think I'd learn that crazy is crazy, dead or alive.

'All of them could not stop me before, Jean-Claude. Three will not do.'

The way he said it, made me look back at Primo. He didn't sound like he was giving up. That wasn't right. Challenging Buzz was one thing. Challenging Jean-Claude was another thing entirely.

'They are not here to stop you, Primo, for you are stopped. I am the Master of this City, and I say you are stopped.'

'These humans bloodied me!' There was such rage in his words that they scalded along my skin. He fed on his own anger, as well as violence. I realized in that moment that he was a master vampire of sorts. At least some of his powers were master-level powers. That was bad.

Clay was on all fours, which meant I was finally able to get out from under him. I'd been looking around for my gun, but I couldn't see it. It had to be here somewhere. Fuck, the shit was about to hit the fan, and I didn't have a gun.

'How did a vampire of your power allow a mere human to bloody you?' Jean-Claude's voice was easy, conversational, but in my head, his voice whispered something else, 'I fear I have underestimated him.'

'No, shit,' I said.

Clay asked, 'What did you say?'

I shook my head, my eyes still scanning the floor for my gun, but I couldn't find it. Then I thought, *Fuck it, I'd cut him twice without a gun. I could do it again.* Part of me didn't believe it. I told that part to shut the fuck up, too. I had enough problems without self-doubt creeping in.

Primo still had the man he'd picked as his scapegoat, but he was holding him sort of nonchalantly down at his side like a forgotten bag of laundry. I realized that the man had passed out, and got to my feet, trying to see if he was breathing. I didn't like the way Primo had the man's jacket collar twisted around his neck. Had I been so worried about the fist that I'd let Primo choke the man to death?

Jean-Claude's voice breathed through my head. 'He is not breathing, but his heart still beats.'

I said out loud, 'We're out of time.'

'Yes,' he said, and I think that was out loud. He reached out to me, not with his hand but with his power, and this wasn't the warm living power of the lycanthrope. The cool grace of the grave touched me, and it flared that part of me that raised the dead. I suddenly knew how I'd cut him. I suddenly knew how it worked. It was like a puzzle box in my head, and suddenly I knew just where to press and just what it meant. Slashing from a distance used the beings' own magical aura against them. It turned their magical shielding into a slender invisible blade that could be turned against them. Jean-Claude had known what it was and how it worked for centuries, but he'd never been able to do it himself. He knew the how, but could not do it. I could do it, but didn't know the how. Together we suddenly had it covered.

My goal was not to kill Primo, but to make him let go of the man. I held my hand out toward him, and he still didn't look scared.

'Do you think your little cuts will stop me?' he demanded.

'No,' I said, and I threw power at him, almost like throwing a ball, and that ball caught against his aura, his shielding, like a burr on a piece of cloth. But the ball didn't stay a ball, and it didn't exactly pierce Primo's shielding. It was as if the ball melted onto it, and where it melted, it invaded the shielding, became one with it, and turned that protective coating into something long and slender and sharp. I visualized that sharpness cutting across his belly, and his shirt split like a skin to show white flesh and blood.

It was a bigger wound than the other two, and his hand went to it, as if it hurt, or as if he wasn't sure how hurt he was.

'How do you like that one?' I asked. 'Big enough for you?'

He snarled at me, flashing fangs that looked too big for his mouth.

It had done exactly what I wanted it to. Thanks to Jean-Claude's centuries of frustrated study, I had a new weapon. I'd been afraid before to hit too close to the victim. All it would have taken was the vic to have a little psychic gift, and I could have done more damage to him than to Primo. But now I had it, I knew it, I felt it.

I flicked a hand at the arm that held the man, and that arm split open from elbow to wrist. Blood spilled down his arm in a crimson wash, if his heart had been beating enough, the blood would have jumped out of his open arteries, but he didn't have the blood pressure for it. Not anymore.

'Do you seek to save this?' he lifted the man by his twisted collar. 'It is dead and only meat for the animals now.'

'His heart still beats,' Jean-Claude said.

But we had only moments before mouth-to-mouth wasn't going to save him from brain damage. I threw both hands up, and I cut him. I tried slicing his arm like you'd bone a fish, but I could not break the deeper tissue. I could cut his skin and meat away but the ligaments held, and that was all Primo needed to hold the vic until he died. Stubborn bastard.

'If you do not drop the man now, Primo, I will see this as a direct challenge to my authority.'

'See it any way you like, but I will not be a whipping boy for this,' and he pointed not at me, but at the men that lay unconscious around him, at Buzz who stood near, but not too near. We were out of his league, and he knew it.

'So be it,' Jean-Claude said. In my head he said, '*Ma petite*, it is not a knife, it is not a single blade, it is magic. If you can turn one small piece of his power against him, then why not all of it?'

I started to ask, what did he mean, then he showed me. It was like my mind was a wall, and he'd just plugged that bit of answer directly into my brain. I understood, and I didn't hesitate. It wasn't in me to hesitate when lives were at stake.

I didn't point or throw up a hand. It wasn't a game of ball. I could affect his shielding, and that shielding covered his entire body. I thought at that skin of magic, I threw power into all of it, and when I felt all of his shielding, as if I was caressing that invisible skin with my hands, I turned it all against him. I turned it all into inward-pointing blades. It was as if Primo were suddenly standing in the center of a reverse porcupine, a porcupine with spines the size of daggers.

Every inch of his skin I could see was just suddenly covered in blood. He screamed, screamed with a mouth that poured blood, screamed with a throat that was pierced in a half-dozen places. He screamed, and he let go of the man.

Clay and the dark-haired werewolf grabbed the man and dragged him over the bodies of his friends, and away, just away. I wanted to watch, to make sure they got him breathing, but I had other problems.

Primo started to charge us, but he stumbled and fell to his hands and knees. I realized in that moment that I'd blinded him. It wasn't permanent, but it was permanent enough. For tonight he was blind.

He roared at us and yelled in a voice that sounded like he was trying to swallow broken glass. 'Damn you, Jean-Claude, damn you. You are not vampire enough to do this. You were never vampire enough for this.'

'Did you come to St Louis to destroy me and take my place?'

Primo raised his bloodied face toward the sound of Jean-Claude's voice. 'Why not? Why not be Master of the City?'

'You cannot even be master of your own self, Primo, that is why. Power alone is not enough to rule this city.'

I wanted to look behind me and watch him speak, but I didn't need to. In that moment I felt closer to him than if I'd stood holding his hand. I knew then what I'd known before, but only in the back of my mind. He'd used the vampire marks between us more openly, more intimately than ever before. I should have been angry, but I wasn't.

One of the waiters was bending over the man Primo had tried to kill. The waiter had bent back the man's head and was breathing into his mouth. The man gave a sudden jolt, and his first gasp of breath was loud.

The dark-haired werewolf that I could give no name to raised a thumbs-up. The man would live. He would be alright. No amount of muscle that we had here would have freed him in time. Nothing else would have freed him without killing Primo, though I wasn't sure that was a good thing. I thought we should kill Primo, and do it now, before he recovered.

Jean-Claude's voice whispered in my ear, 'If someone dies, I will have much more difficulty convincing them all that nothing bad happened here.'

I shook my head and thought, there aren't enough vampire mind tricks in the world to blank the mind of an audience this big. Not about something this traumatic.

'Do you doubt me, *ma petite*?' He was suddenly standing just behind me. His slender white hand appeared on my shoulder, a spill of white lace around it, and a flare of black velvet sleeve framing that lace.

I raised my hand up to touch his and found his skin cold, as if he had not fed or had used a great deal of energy up. There was more warmth to the velvet as it brushed my fingers than to his skin. He was drained. How much energy had it taken for him to talk mind to mind with me, or had things been happening that I didn't know about yet?

The rest of the black-shirted security began to move, slowly, stiffly, as if things hurt. Primo seemed to sense their movement, because he said, 'Even blind, I am their match.'

He moved into a crouch on the balls of his feet. The movement must have hurt like hell, but he never winced. He put one big bloody hand on the floor and the other in the air, as if he were sensing movement. It was too close to a martial arts move for comfort. He was huge, a vampire, nearly impervious to pain, crazy, and trained in the martial arts. It didn't seem fair.

Nathaniel came to my side, and he had my gun. He held it out to me wordlessly, exactly the way I'd taught him, butt first, fingers well away from the trigger.

I gave him half the smile he deserved, because I was still keeping an eye on the bloody giant on the floor. I clicked the safety off before I holstered it. Call it a hunch, but when Primo rushed us, I wouldn't want to waste that second. I'd need it.

But he didn't rush us. No, Primo had a much more interesting idea in mind. There was something about being this hooked up to Jean-Claude that made me feel safer, and that sense of safety was a type of arrogance. Arrogance made me forget that a really old vampire can do more than just hurt you physically. Jean-Claude's arrogance made me forget.

Primo didn't move a muscle, but he thrust power at us, poured his rage like flinging a red hot bucket of boiling anger on us. There was no time to shield against it. No time to do anything but take it. Jean-Claude tried to let it wash over him, but I felt that awful rage trying to find a place to grow inside him. The Master of the City consumed by rage would be a very bad thing. But I understood anger, and I wasn't Master of the City.

I took that anger, not to wash over me, but to drink, to swallow, to bathe in it. I drew his rage around me like a coat of fire, and I opened up a part of me that I kept hidden from everyone. I let Primo's rage meet the great seething mass of my own rage. The rage I'd carried inside me since my mother's death. The deep endless seas of my anger welcomed his anger, embraced it, fed on it. I ate his rage and let him feel me do it.

I laughed, laughed while I stood there and burned with our twin furies. Laughed while I felt his anger falter and begin to pull back. Laughed while I let his anger mingle with mine. I already carried a bottomless pit of it, what was a few more buckets?

He stared up at me with sightless eyes, and then he did half of what I'd expected. He moved forward, but not in a mindless rush. He moved forward with a speed that was breathtaking, and I'd seen speed. He was blind, so he grabbed in the dark, and it was Nathaniel he grabbed. Nathaniel who was standing near us. I don't know if that was who Primo was aiming at, or if he missed. He grabbed Nathaniel's wrist and tried to yank him in against his body, but Nathaniel braced and would not go.

We were suddenly all moving. I was aware that the security guards were moving, but they'd be too late. My gun was almost free of its holster, but Primo had started forward as soon as he felt Nathaniel's resistance. I was closest, and I moved faster than I planned. I wasn't used to being more than human quick. I was reaching out for Nathaniel's arm, but I got too close to the vampire's face.

Primo sank fangs into my wrist, and I knew better than to try and jerk free. It would have torn my wrist open. I had my gun out as I screamed. Screamed as his mouth fed on me. Screamed as I put the gun to his head.

My finger had started that pull on the trigger, when Primo's mind slammed into mine. It wasn't his rage. It was his memories. Roman army, the murder that got him condemned, the arena where he could murder to his heart's content, where he could slack that rage, or feed it. Death after death after death. And each one fed him in a way that nothing else did.

Then one dark night a noblewoman requested he come to her bed with the blood and sweat of his victory painted on his body. He went, and found so much more than he'd ever dreamt of. She offered him freedom and a new way to feed his rage. A new way to kill. He did not know her real name. She had simply said, 'I am the Dragon, and you will serve me,' and he had.

Abruptly, the memories stopped. It staggered me, and I had a moment to fight not squeezing the trigger. A moment to point the gun skyward and try to relearn how to breathe and use my body at the same time.

Primo still had his mouth pressed to my wrist, but now there was healed flesh, and sight in his eyes. I knew with Jean-Claude's knowledge that Primo could heal almost anything with a little special blood. He'd been aiming for a lycanthrope. But my blood had done the trick. I understood why Jean-Claude had wanted him. Such a powerful soldier, if you could control him. The calmness in my head wasn't me.

Primo released my wrist, and his eyes rolled white with terror. 'What are you?' he whispered.

'Not what, Primo, who,' I said, and I reached the hand he'd wounded out to him. I meant to touch his face, but he cringed back from me as if I'd offered him harm. 'Who am I, Primo?'

That great body cowered before me. He abased himself before me, and I remembered him doing it long ago for the one who had made him. 'Master,' he whispered, and the word seemed to be forced from his lips. He hated it, that he would never be his own master. When he took that bloody kiss, he had always assumed that someday he would rule, and now he knew different. 'You are my master.'

The moment he'd tasted my blood he had been bound in a way that had nothing to do with sex, or love, or friendship. It was a belonging that was possessive in a way that none of the others were. Primo simply was mine, no, ours.

The marks between Jean-Claude and I were wide open and had been when Primo attacked me. When he bit me, he wasn't just tasting me. *Blood of my blood*, wasn't just a pretty phrase. It was real. I understood in that moment that with the marks cranked open, to take blood oath to one was blood oath to both. I could control the dead, and Jean-Claude had power over any vampire that took blood oath, or that he'd made. Primo had been overwhelmed with a double whammy. Because in that instant, my blood had been Jean-Claude's, and his mine. I had a moment to wonder what all this might be doing to our reluctant Richard, but the thought didn't last. I had enough problems of my own without borrowing his.

I looked down at the big man at our feet and knew that Jean-Claude was utterly sure of him. Utterly certain that Primo's oath to us would hold him. It wasn't like reading minds. I just knew that Jean-Claude was no longer worried about Primo. He was confident of him. I wasn't.

I turned to look at Jean-Claude, to try to persuade him of just how dangerous Primo could still be, but of course, my being willing to turn away from Primo said that in my way I was certain of him, too. And that was wrong. He was like walking rage with a big muscular body to back it up. That wasn't safe. That could never be safe.

I think I would have turned back to Primo, but I was suddenly looking at Jean-Claude, and the world vanished. There was nothing but Jean-Claude. Black velvet had been made into a waist-length military jacket with silver buttons down the front and a high stiff collar to frame a white mound of cravat. A silver tie tack with a sapphire in its head pierced the white at his throat. The jacket fit the spread of his shoulders, emphasized his slender waist, and took the eye to the black leather pants that looked as if they'd been braided together on the sides, as if he hadn't so much slipped them on as been bound into them. The boots were only knee high, made of the same rich dark velvet as the coat. I was bespelled and I knew it, and I couldn't help but stare, but I left his face for last, because I knew in what was left of my self-control that if I looked into his face, I would truly be lost.

One slender hand came up to my lowered face. That hand surrounded by a spill of white lace. He touched my chin, the barest of touches, and began to raise my face upward. It was a delicate touch, I could have fought or stopped him, but I didn't want to. It had taken all of my willpower simply to avoid his face at first glance.

His black curls mingled with the velvet until it was hard to tell where one began and the other ended. His eyes were huge and beautiful, a color darker than the sapphire at his throat. His eyes were as dark as blue could be and did not hold a single shade of black. His face was a pale perfection like a painting almost finished. He was pale, and the fingers against my face were like ice. He was like some pale sculpture waiting for someone to breathe it to life, except for the dark glitter of those eyes. Those eyes held all the life in the world.

His voice was low and soft, like fur sliding across my skull. '*Ma petite*, let me in. Let me in. Do not leave me to the cold.'

I actually opened my mouth to say, of course, but closed it. Once before when we'd been less bound than this, he'd taken energy from me without drawing blood. That had been because big bad vamps were in town and he needed to not look weak in front of them. And if they were to find out that his human servant didn't allow him to take blood, he would have looked weak indeed.

He needed to feed, desperately so. 'Why?' I found my voice, hoarse and not at all like the smooth pull of his. 'Why is your energy so low?'

'I have done what I could from a distance to make your day easier.'

I reached up and laid my fingers against his cheek. 'You've drained yourself for me.'

'For your peace of mind,' he whispered, and his voice trailed down my spine like a tiny drop of water trickling low and lower.

'You want to feed,' I said.

He gave a small nod, moving his cold skin against the warmth of my fingers. In my head, he whispered, 'If I am to maintain our control of Primo, I need to feed.'

'You don't mean blood,' I said.

'No,' he raised his other hand to my bandaged cheek. 'Are you hurt?'

'Not much,' I said, and my voice was sounding almost like my own. I realized that he'd pulled back. He was letting me think. He didn't have to, but he knew me too well. If he didn't let me think now, I'd be mad later.

'You don't mean like you did when the council was in town, do you? You're asking something else.'

His voice in my mind, 'Something has happened with your binding of Damian and Nathaniel. More power is everywhere, but also more need. I have denied myself for a very long time, *ma petite*.' His hands slid along the edge of my jawline, until they cradled my face, and his fingers were buried in the warmth of my hair. I heard him think that he was warming his hands against my hair. So cold, so empty, so needy. I'd never seen him like this, never.

This wasn't his need. I turned enough so that I could see Nathaniel, who had gone to lean against the wall. He wasn't close enough to project like this. He gave me innocent lavender eyes. I couldn't feel him in my head. It was just Jean-Claude and me, but even with only two of us connected, it still felt like Nathaniel's need, or Damian's skin hunger.

I looked back into those dark, dark blue eyes and whispered, 'You've inherited their neediness.'

Aloud, he said, 'I fear so.'

'What can we do?' I asked.

'Let me in, *ma petite*, let me through those wonderful shields. Let me in,' and his voice spilled over my skin as if he'd covered me naked in satin and drawn it along my body.

I shivered, and only the cool touch of his hands kept my knees from buckling. I stared into those eyes, that face, and I whispered, 'Yes.'

His face filled my vision, then his lips brushed mine. I expected him to take me in his arms and kiss me with the desperation I felt in his need, but he didn't. He touched me only with his mouth, and even that was the barest pressure of his lips against mine. I actually pushed against him, raised a hand to touch him, and he put a hand on my shoulder and held us apart. A second after he'd done it, I understood why, because it was as if my soul spilled up into my lips, as if the very essence of me was a taste upon my lips. My power, my magic, my heart, my soul, everything was there for the taking in one soft brush of lips. I'd thought we'd fed the *ardeur* upon each other before, but I'd been wrong. He sipped from my lips, delicate, so much more he wanted. I could feel it. Feel his need. But he held me back with his hands on my shoulders, while I struggled to close that distance. But I knew with his knowledge that bare skin was bare skin, and all of it could drink me down.

It was the most careful kiss I'd ever been given, and one of the most frustrating. I was making small noises deep in my throat, because I wanted more. I wanted so much more.

When he drew back, he held a spot of my lipstick like a crimson stain in the center of his lips. There was the tiniest bit of color to his cheeks. He was like the cold of winter touched by the barest breath of spring, so that warmth was only a promise, not real, not now, but a distant hope. But hope is better than the alternative.

He swallowed convulsively, his eyes fluttering closed for a moment, before he straightened and his hands on my shoulders were firm. 'That is but a taste of what I need, *ma petite*.'

'Don't stop,' I said.

He smiled, but it was sad. 'Let the effects wear awhile, then give me an answer about more.'

I shook my head. What was he talking about? Of course, of course he could have more.

'It is my fault, *ma petite*. I asked you to let me in your shields. I did not mean for you to drop all the defenses in your considerable repertoire. It was nearly overwhelming for both of us.' He looked at me as if he saw something new there, or someone new. 'I must attend to our fair audience.' He almost came to me again for a good-bye kiss, but he pushed away, and he called to someone, 'Attend her until she recovers. No, not you, not until she is herself again. I fear what she would do if you touched her now.'

His voice when it came again, filled the club, echoed into the shadows of it, and yet, seemed intimate, as if he whispered it against your skin, and only your skin. 'Primo has walked through fire and blood to be reborn for you tonight. Transformed before your eyes from the warrior of nightmares to the lover of dreams.'

'They're too scared, they won't believe it.' It was Nathaniel's voice.

I turned toward that voice, but met a different face. Nathaniel was standing just beyond, out of reach, but Byron was standing so close that it startled me. He wasn't quite three hundred years old, and I normally heard him move as if he were human. He wasn't powerful, and never would be, but tonight, I hadn't even known he was standing nearly touching me. That helped sober me up more than anything else. I hadn't heard one of the weakest of the new vamps that Jean-Claude had welcomed to town. Bad necromancer, no cookie.

'You've never seen him after he's fed like this,' Byron said in that nicely accented British voice, 'watch.'

I fought not to look at Jean-Claude. I looked at the audience instead. Their eyes were wide, their faces pale, or flushed. Some of them were still hiding under the tables. If the fight hadn't taken place between them and the most obvious door, they'd have probably fled. All they needed was a sign above them that said 'scared shitless.' It was probably the most spilled blood that any of them had ever seen. Scary stuff.

As long as I looked at the audience I agreed with Nathaniel, but when my eyes drifted to Jean-Claude's back as he spoke with them, well . . . I had to look away. I had to not look, because the craving was still there. I'd been told that my desire to touch him had been part of the same craving that any servant felt for their master, but I hadn't really believed it. This, this was craving.

I found myself staring at Primo, who was still on his knees, looking confused, a half-circle of black-shirted security guards standing around him. He looked up at me, and his eyes held something like pain. He spoke, and no one at the tables heard him, just me and security, and the vampire and wereleopard at my back. 'You have trapped me.'

I opened my mouth to say, 'I didn't mean to,' but someone touched my left wrist, and it hurt. A sharp immediate pain. I whirled and found Byron touching me. 'Let go of me.'

He opened his hand and just let my arm fall back. He whispered, 'You're bleeding. Jean-Claude told me to attend to you. Let me tend your wound.' Here was a face younger and more innocent-seeming than Nathaniel's. He'd been in his late teens when his master had brought him over. His hair was a soft brown that fell in loose curls just past his ears, leaving his slender neck bare and showing the V of white skin at the neck of the robe he wore. I remembered that someone had said the college students were heckling Byron. He must have been the one on stage.

He was shorter than I was, and slender, not preadolescent, but young, unfinished, and he'd be unfinished forever. Whether his shoulders would have broadened, or he'd have gotten taller, we'd never know. He could lift weights and add definition, in fact, he had, at Jean-Claude's insistence, but he'd never have the body he might have had if the vampire that killed him had waited a year or two.

His eyes were gray and seemed to take up most of his face, huge, soft gray. The color that fog can have when it's at its thickest, that close suffocating wall of mist.

I had to shake my head and draw back. Shit. Byron had almost rolled me with his eyes. That shouldn't have been possible. Jean-Claude had said that I'd let down all my defenses. I hadn't meant to. It was more as if Jean-Claude had taken down all my defenses. But Byron was no Jean-Claude. Him I could keep out.

I actually closed my eyes and did the deep-breathing exercises that I'd learned. Draw yourself to the center of your body. Draw yourself in and center yourself down a line that goes into the earth itself. Marianne called it grounding, and it was. Grounding, as in being grounded, solid on your feet, secure.

But it was hard to stay focused, because Jean-Claude's voice was still there, and closing my eyes didn't get rid of it. 'Who among you has not wished to tame a savage heart, to take a man and change him beyond reckoning? To make him into what you wish him to be? Primo kneels before your beauty, and he is what you will make of him. He will rise and fall to your desires.'

I felt Jean-Claude walk between me and Primo. Even with my eyes closed, even with me trying to anchor myself, I felt him like a hand sweeping all my concentration away. I looked up and saw him touch Primo's face, the lightest of touches. 'Show them that magnificent body.'

Primo shook his head. He did not want to play.

I felt Jean-Claude's will flex, like a muscle squeezing around Primo. I felt that flare of warmth spill out from him to the bigger man. I had actually stepped closer to them, when Byron pulled me back.

'I wouldn't advise that,' he said, and again I felt the pull of those soft gray eyes, like being wrapped in the warmest of blankets.

Primo stood, and that turned me back to them. The big man balled his hands into his black, blood-soaked shirt, and tore it like it was paper. Naked from the waist up, he was magnificent, if you were into giants. It wasn't the hugeness that came from weight lifting. It was just how big he was.

'Who will be his first kiss?' Jean-Claude asked.

I felt the movement before I turned and saw the audience. There was no fear now, Jean-Claude's voice had taken their fear. All I saw now was eagerness, at worst, uncertainty, as if they just weren't sure. The first few hands went up with money in them, and once that happened, more followed. No one wants to be first, but no one wants to be left out, either.

Byron pulled gently on my shoulder. 'We need to bind that wound, Anita. Let's go backstage.'

'He's right,' Nathaniel said, and he was closer now. Close enough that I could see that there was some blood spattered on his lavender shirt. He must have been closer to Primo than I remembered. But I wasn't thinking well. It was as if I hadn't been quite myself since I got out here. What was wrong with me?

I nodded. 'Okay, okay, yeah.'

I let Byron and Nathaniel lead me away, but my glance stayed turned to the room. The brunette from the alleyway was running her hand up Primo's skin, and that skin was clean and smooth, no blood, no signs of the struggle. She ran her hands over his skin, but his glance was for me. His eyes held a mute appeal for help, and I didn't understand why.

Jean-Claude touched the big man's bare back, and Primo's face turned back to the woman. There was no confusion on his face now. There was nothing but lust, and in that moment I understood. Jean-Claude was controlling Primo. He was manipulating the vampire more than he had ever manipulated the audience. They'd come for a little bit of lascivious fun. Primo had come to be Master of the City, but instead, he was just another act at Guilty Pleasures. He kissed the brunette like he'd breathe her in, as if to kiss her were life itself. When he let her go and one of the security guards eased her shaking body into her seat, money sprang up in hands throughout the room. *Welcome to show business, Primo*, I thought.

36

THE DOOR CLOSED, and like magic it was quiet. The backstage area was soundproofed, but it was more than that today. It was as if with the closing of that door I could think again, really think. I knew that proximity to Jean-Claude could make things worse, usually proximity meant touching. Tonight, in the same room was too close.

I shook my head. 'What the hell is happening?'

'We have a first aid kit in the dressing rooms,' Byron said. He tried to lead me toward one of the doors on the right.

I took my arm out of his grip and looked at Nathaniel. 'Did I hear Jean-Claude tell you not to touch me?'

He nodded. 'He's not sure what will happen right now.' His face was very solemn, serious, closed. He was being careful around me again, and I didn't know why.

'Have I missed something tonight?'

'You're dripping blood,' Byron said, and he motioned at my arm.

Blood was trickling down my hand to drop, drop onto the white floor. The hallway was so white and so empty that the spot of crimson seemed loud, as if color were sound. I shook my head again. 'Something's wrong.'

'You've lost more blood than you realize,' Byron said.

'Anita,' Nathaniel said, and it seemed like it took longer than it should have for me to turn and look at him. 'Anita, come into the dressing rooms. We'll take care of you.'

I nodded and raised my arm up to about chest high. It would help slow the blood loss. The sleeve of my jacket was a bloody mess, and I hadn't noticed until now. Something was terribly wrong, and I didn't know what it was. I knew that making a new triumvirate with Damian and Nathaniel was probably the cause, but that only told me why it was happening, not what was happening. Why didn't matter very much to me right that moment; what was happening, that mattered a great deal.

Byron touched my arm, only enough to guide me through the door that Nathaniel opened for us. As I walked past Nathaniel, I felt something open between us, as if there were a door in the middle of our bodies. A door that wanted to close around us, to press us tight together.

Byron literally put his body in front of mine and kept me from touching Nathaniel. I growled at him, and Nathaniel echoed me at his back. 'Ease down, kitty-cats, I am only doing what the Master of the City ordered me to do.' His eyes were a little wide, and I got a whiff not of fear but something close to it. 'Do you remember what Jean-Claude's kiss felt like out there?' He grabbed my hurt wrist and ground his fingers into it.

'That hurts,' I said, and I turned on him, angry, ready to be angry.

'But you can think now, can't you?'

That made me take a step back into the dressing rooms beyond. Byron followed, a hand still on my wrist, but loosely now, not to hurt, but more to guide.

'What's happening to us?' I asked.

'It looks like you've all hit a new power plateau,' Byron said, as he led me between the little lighted tables scattered with makeup and bits of costume.

'Which means what?' I asked.

He stopped in front of a big gray metal cabinet that was at the far end of the room. 'Which means, answer my question. Do you remember what the kiss felt like in the other room?' He opened the cabinet, and it seemed to be full of cleaning supplies and extra bits of things that people might need. On the top shelf, so he had to stand on tiptoe, was a first aid kit, a big one.

'It was like he drank my soul,' and saying it out loud was too poetic for me. I blushed and tried again. 'I thought he'd fed the *ardeur* during sex with me, but if that kiss was feeding the same thing, he's been holding back.'

Byron tried to find enough clean space on the nearby tables to open the medicine chest, but gave up and asked Nathaniel to hold it, while he rummaged through it. 'He's been holding back, luv, trust me on that.'

'How do you know?' I asked.

He gave me a very flat stare out of his big gray eyes. 'Jean-Claude liked London once, he liked it a very great deal, and I liked that he liked it.' There was something almost unfriendly in the way he finished that sentence.

'Why do I feel like apologizing?' I asked.

'Just hold your arm up higher,' he said. He had his hands full of things, but still wasn't satisfied. 'Nothing to apologize for, duckie. Except for Asher, Jean-Claude prefers his meat of the gentler persuasion, always did. Ah, here it is.' He held up an unopened package of gauze pads. He smiled at me, and the smile was so harmless, so not matching the situation. 'Now, let Uncle Byron see to the big, bad boo-boo.'

I gave him a look that wasn't entirely friendly. 'I'm bleeding, not brain damaged, can the baby talk.'

He shrugged. 'Whatever you say, lover.'

I started to correct him, but Byron used pet names, mostly the same pet names, for everybody. If I took it too personally, it would be impossible to have a conversation with him. I was tired tonight. I let it go.

'Why doesn't he want me to touch Nathaniel?'

Byron looked at me like I was being slow. 'Because, luv, if Jean-Claude's kiss is suddenly more, then maybe yours will be, too. The servant rises in power with his master.' He looked at everything in his hands, then shook his head, looked impatient and dumped it all back into the box. 'Hand me things when I ask for them,' he said to Nathaniel.

Nathaniel nodded, but he was looking at me. I found myself staring into those lavender eyes.

Byron snapped his fingers in the air between our faces. It made us both jump. 'The two of you are so not touching right now. Dangerous is what it would be. Now take off your jacket.'

I did what he asked, and it hurt to get the sleeve off, but it wasn't until I saw my wrist that I gasped, and Nathaniel said, 'Oh, shit.'

Most vampire bites are neat, almost dainty things. This wasn't. It was as if, even once his fangs sank home he'd used his other teeth to bite down, so that it looked more like an animal bite. A big, angry animal bite. Blood was seeping out of the two deepest fang marks, seeping in a nice steady line. The moment I saw it, I was dizzy, and it hurt like hell. Why does it always hurt so much more when you see the blood?

'You are lucky you're still standing,' Byron said. He hooked a chair with one naked foot, and said, 'Sit.'

I sat. Because truthfully, I was a little shaken. It was a bad enough wound that I should have noticed it sooner. Really noticed it. A fraction of an inch better, or worse, or just deeper, and I could have bled nearly to death before I noticed it.

'Why didn't I notice sooner?'

'I've seen bespelled humans bleed to death from tiny wounds, a smile on their face all the way to the end, duckie.' He ripped open the sterile gauze pads. 'Put this on it, and press hard. You've lost enough blood for one night, let's see if we can save the rest.' When he was serious, the nicknames vanished. He'd only been in town a few weeks, and already I knew that when the duckies, luvs, and crumpets disappeared, things were bad.

'What can I do to help?' Nathaniel asked.

'Find more gauze pads. That's the only pack in here, and she's going to need more.'

Nathaniel put the first aid kit on a chair that he moved close to Byron, then he went for the door. Apparently he knew where they kept the extra gauze. 'How bad do you guys get cut up here?'

'Usually scratches,' he said, 'though you'd be surprised the number of women that try to bite.'

I looked at him.

He grinned. 'Now, duckie, why would I lie?'

One second I was looking at Byron and thinking nothing really. My wrist hurt, and I wondered why I hadn't noticed it sooner, and then suddenly I was wondering if he was naked under the robe, and I was hoping he was.

I closed my eyes and tried to shield. Tried to nail anything and everything I had between me and Jean-Claude, but his voice came through. 'I am sorry, *ma petite*, so sorry, but Primo is still fighting me, and I have not fed enough. I cannot feed and control him, but you can feed for me. You can give me what I need, *ma petite*. Please, please, do not deny me. If I lose control of Primo now, he will slaughter these women. He will see himself humiliated by them. Please, *ma petite*, hear me, and know that I speak only truth. Help me!' He cut contact abruptly, and I got a glimpse of Primo's rage stabbing at the lust that Jean-Claude had fed him. It was as if Primo were a human besotted, but still fighting, fighting to break free.

'Damn you, Jean-Claude,' I whispered.

Byron touched my arm. 'Don't faint on me.'

I opened my eyes, and his gray ones were so close to mine. He was so close. I don't know what showed in my eyes, but he let go of me like I'd burned him. His eyes were a little wide, and his voice was breathy when he said, 'I don't like the look in your eyes. It doesn't look much like you.'

I leaned into him, and he leaned back. I kept moving forward, and he kept moving back, so that I slipped out of the chair, and he ended up on the floor for a second, before he rolled to his feet. I was left kneeling on the floor, but I had a handful of his robe.

The cloth stretched away from his body, and I saw that he was wearing something under it, but not much. It was lust, but it was more than that. It was lust, as if sex were food. I'd thought the *ardeur* was the worst of it, but this felt . . . less, worse. Except for that first time I'd had some control over the *ardeur*. Not liking someone, or knowing someone helped me fight it off. This was different. It wouldn't have mattered. This was need so raw that it just wouldn't have mattered.

Jean-Claude screamed through my head, 'Anita, help me!' He'd used my real name, and his desperation cut through me like a knife.

Some of that desperation fell into my voice. 'I'm sorry, Byron, but Jean-Claude is about to lose control of Primo. He needs more food.'

'And who gets to be the food?' he asked, and there was that edge of fear to him.

I had to close my eyes and take a deep breath. 'There's no time.'

'I won't let you tear my throat out, just because the master has bitten off more than he can tame.'

I shook my head, eyes still closed. 'Don't be afraid, Byron, please, that fuels the beast. I'm offering the *ardeur*.' I opened my eyes and stared up at him. He still stood as far away as the stretched fabric of the black robe could take him. My voice had found an edge of growl when I said, 'But it's a limited time offer. Either come across, or food won't be a euphemism.'

A funny look crossed his face. 'Do you mean sex? Real sex? Not a euphemism for anything?'

If I'd had time, it would have been funny. 'Yes.'

'Oh, duckie, why didn't you say so?' He came to me, undoing the sash of his robe and letting it fall away. He was wearing only the tiniest of black thongs, with his pale, pale body exposed everywhere else. The muscles that he'd managed to acquire in less than a month worked under his skin as he dropped to his knees in front of me. 'Who gets to be on top?' he asked with a smile.

I put my hands on his bare shoulders, and the moment I touched his skin, the smile faded. 'I do,' I said, and pushed him to the floor.

37

BYRON LAY BACK against the floor with my body riding him, my hands on his wrists, pinning him to the floor. The only thing I'd ripped off my own body had been underwear. There was no fore-play, there was no time for it, no need for it. Everywhere I touched him, I could feed a little. Bare skin was all I needed now, but it was an incomplete feeding. It wasn't enough. I pressed our mouths together, slid my tongue into his mouth, and again I could feed, but it wasn't enough. I ground myself against him, but he was still trapped in the thong. I let go with one wrist, and his hand found the side of the thong first.

'Snap away,' he said, in a voice that was deeper, more real than his usual.

I tore the cloth away, and he was suddenly naked against me, not inside me, but pressed against me, and he was warm. Warm with the blood he'd taken from someone else. The feel of him pressed against me made me cry out.

Nathaniel said, 'Anita?' He came pressed as far from us as he could get and stayed where I could see him. 'It's like the *ardeur*, but worse, more.' He looked almost panic-stricken. He had an armful of gauze packets.

I wanted to say I'm sorry, or something civilized, but Byron moved his hips underneath me, and that one small movement brought my attention back to the man underneath me. His eyes had dark-ened like sky before a storm. And staring down into them, I wondered how I'd ever thought they were soft. He spent so much time being the charming youth, playing to the body he'd been given, but now suddenly out of his eyes I saw just how much grown-up I was dealing with.

'Fuck me,' he said, and it came out softer the second time, 'fuck me, fuck me.' He whispered it over and over, softer and softer, until his breath itself whispered, 'Fuck me.'

I leaned over him, pressed my mouth to his, and it was as if I could feel his soul down the long tunnel of his body, as if I knew how to reach in and snatch it away. I knew in that instant that I could feed on everything that Byron was. I could feed on that divine or infernal spark that made him vampire. I could eat him up, completely and utterly, and leave only the lovely corpse behind.

I came off his mouth screaming, because the urge to do it was almost overwhelming. The hunger wanted it all. All of him. It couldn't have all of him. It couldn't. I wouldn't do that to him. I wouldn't do that to anyone. For the first time I understood just what they meant by a fate worse than death, or rather that sex wasn't it.

If I could feed the *ardeur*, then maybe this darker thing would go away, but even willing, I had trouble. I didn't know Byron's body. I tried to simply rock back onto him, slide him inside me, but twice we slid across each other but didn't go in. I finally yelled my frustration, and he said, 'Let me have my hand, lover, and I'll help.'

A hand appeared between us, and it actually took me a moment to realize it was Nathaniel. He had a condom in his hand. 'We don't know where he's been.'

I growled at him, but he growled back. 'The only way you can catch something from a vampire or lycanthrope is if one of us has fucked someone who's got something, then fucks you after. You want to take that chance?'

'Let me have my hands, lover, and I'll put on anything you want.'

I let go of his wrists, and he moved himself just enough so he could open the foil packet and slip it on. Then he slid himself back where we'd started, with him pressed against me, but not inside. He put his hands on either side of my thighs and lifted me at the same time that he shifted his own hips. He slid inside me, in one smooth movement that threw my head back and made him yell, 'Oh, yes!'

When I looked back at him, his gray eyes had lost focus, his lips were half-parted. I wanted to cover his mouth with mine, I wanted that brief sweet taste of his soul again. I finally realized it wasn't the *ardeur* we were fighting, not entirely. Something else was happening, something darker, something worse. I'd thought the worst would be sex with strangers, but I was wrong. Byron wasn't my friend yet, I didn't make friends that quickly, but he wasn't a bad man. I liked him, with his 'duckie' and 'luvs.' I liked that he had told me the first time we'd met, that no, he wasn't that Byron, and that actually Lord Byron wasn't one of us, that had just been a rumor spread by people that wanted an excuse to burn him at the stake in some backwater country. Though if he'd known the great poet was going to get himself drowned before the age of thirty, he'd have offered.

I liked Byron. He didn't deserve to die. There was an angry echo in my head. I thought it was Primo, and then knew it wasn't. He didn't have the kind of power it took to interfere from a room away, not through my shielding and Jean-Claude's. I asked myself the question, Where would the power go if I sucked Byron's life away? I threw the question out to Jean-Claude. I let him see that darkest of desires in my head.

'That is not our hunger,' he said.

'Who is it?'

'She is the Dragon.' He spoke in my head, and there was urgency there.

'She made Primo,' I said, and it was only then that I realized I wasn't talking out loud.

'She's using him as a conduit for her own power.'

'How do we stop it?'

Byron suddenly drew back and thrust himself inside me again, and did something with his hips and legs at the same time. It blew my concentration all to hell, and all I could do was stare down at him. 'A man likes to know he's not boring a girl,' he said, but there was no smile to go with the lighthearted comment.

Jean-Claude echoed through my head. 'We stop her as we did Moroven, by sending her something she does not understand.'

'Let me guess,' I said, and again it wasn't aloud.

'Sex, or love, *ma petite*, what else is there for us?'

I don't know what I would have said, because Byron rolled me. He rolled us over in a sudden amazingly fast, fluid movement, and never fell out of me, which is harder to do than it sounds. I was suddenly on the floor staring up at him, my hands on his shoulders as if I'd grabbed the nearest thing to prevent me from falling. He grinned at the surprised look on my face and said, 'You're not moving enough, luv, let me show you how it's done.'

He did two quick thrusts that left me breathless, then he raised up on his hands like he was trying to do a bad push-up with his groin pressed tight against mine. His smile faded, and he frowned. 'You're bleeding, luv.'

I'd forgotten about my wrist again. I followed his glance and found that blood was seeping out from it. There was blood spattered across my blue top.

'Some gauze, please,' he said.

I think it took both Nathaniel and me a second to realize who he was talking about, and why. Nathaniel fumbled a package open and handed it to him. It was acutely uncomfortable to be trapped under the body of a strange man while Nathaniel knelt beside us. It was more embarrassing than having Richard watch with Damian. It just felt worse, as if I should apologize.

I think I would have done just that, but Byron pressed the gauze to my wounded wrist, pinning it to the floor. It hurt, sharp and immediate, and I was left gasping and staring up at his face. He pinned my other wrist, so that he was pressed above me, and I was very, very pinned.

I might have complained, but Jean-Claude roared through my head. '*Ma petite*, I need to feed. You are not moving fast enough with Byron.'

'You're a big vampire, feed yourself,' I said, and that was out loud.

'Do you understand what you're giving permission for, *ma petite*?'

'Tonight, yes, help me, Jean-Claude. Feed, for God's sake, feed.'

Byron hesitated, poised above me. 'Something wrong?'

'We're not moving fast enough for him, apparently.'

A nearly evil grin crossed Byron's face. 'Oh, we can fix that, luver, we can fix that.' And he fixed it. He moved himself in and out of me in long writhing waves of his body. It was as if the thrust started at his shoulders and danced its way down his body until he thrust himself inside me. Once inside me, he did something with his hips that seemed almost to make him roll inside me. It was as if that writhing dancelike movement went all the way down his body and inside mine. It wasn't fast, as in speed, but it was fast in other ways.

My breathing had sped up, and my body had figured out at what point in his writhing that he plunged inside me, so that my hips thrust upward to meet him. It began to be like a dance, except we were both flat on the floor, but when he realized that I wanted to move, he changed how his lower body pinned me, so that mostly only him sliding in and out of me pinned my lower body, and the rest of me was left to rise and fall against his body.

He kept my wrists pinned, and I kept thinking I should say something about that, but I kept forgetting, and I finally realized I didn't want to say anything.

Another British voice came from behind us. 'Jean-Claude said I was needed in here, but it looks like you've got a queue.'

I said his name, 'Requiem,' just that and nothing more, but he came to me. He knelt in a fall of black-hooded cloak. He pushed the hood back to reveal hair as straight and black as the cloak itself. His eyes were a deep, rich blue like startled cornflowers in the white skin and black hair of his face. The thin mustache and Vandyke beard were as raven dark as his hair and the eyebrows that framed those startling blue eyes. He'd once told me that Belle had wanted to buy him from his old master. She'd wanted a third blue-eyed lover. Asher had the palest blue, Jean-Claude the darkest, and Requiem had the brightest. His master had refused, and they had fled France.

He knelt by my head, kneeling over us on his knees like some dark angel in the cloak he would not give up for any modern coat. 'What would you have of me, my lady?'

My voice came breathy, but clear. Good for me. 'If you take blood at the same time I feed on him, then I'll feed on both of you.'

He didn't argue. He simply laid down behind us, so that his face was close to mine. 'As my lady wills it, so shall it be done.'

'Well if it's to be done, do it fast,' Byron said, and his voice sounded more strained than mine.

Requiem looked up at him, propped on his elbows by my head. 'Are you implying that you won't last much longer?'

'Yes,' and his voice sounded half-strangled.

'You're out of training,' Requiem said.

'You haven't fucked her. Don't criticize until you've tried.'

'Are you implying that she's such a good shag that she's going to bring you early?'

'Stop bickering,' I said, and my body still rose and fell with Byron's. He was still fighting to keep the rhythm even and pretty, but he was beginning to lose that smooth glide, and I knew when he stopped dancing above me, that that would be it. 'Hurry, or you'll miss us.'

'As my lady bids.' Requiem dropped to his chest, his stomach, and ran his hands through my hair. 'Bad angle,' he whispered, 'may I improve the angle, m'lady?'

'Yes,' and it was a strangled sound.

He dug his fingers through my curls and pulled my head sharply to one side, exposing a long line of my neck. He balled his fist in my hair and pulled it sharp. I gasped, and it wasn't a pain sound.

I found myself staring not into Byron's gray eyes, but at Nathaniel. He was still there huddled near, but not too near. He looked both afraid and eager, and I didn't understand the look. I wanted to, and I had an instant to feel how he saw this. One lover pinned my wrists to the floor, grinding his hand into a fresh bite, plunging himself into me over and over, while I writhed underneath him. Now another man had jerked my hair tight and painful, exposed my neck, and when I orgasmed, he would plunge his fangs into my neck. Both vampires would plunge inside me at the same time, and there was nothing I could do to stop it. It didn't matter to Nathaniel that I'd given permission. It mattered that I was trapped and helpless and at their mercy, and the entire scene did it for him. It just flat did it for him. He was enjoying watching, because this was the closest he'd come to what he'd wanted in months.

I felt his need like a weight in my mind, and I knew that he would have given almost anything to be the one on the bottom.

Byron's body began to lose its smooth gliding rhythm, and he seemed to be fighting not to simply plunge in and out as fast as he could. 'Close, very close,' he whispered.

I started to turn my head back so I could see his face, but Requiem's hand tightened, and I couldn't move. His breath was hot on my throat, and I knew that he'd borrowed that warmth from someone else. 'Are you close, m'lady, are you close?' His voice spread like heat down my skin.

Byron leaned heavier on my wrists, grinding them into the floor, and his body took on a more urgent rhythm. I felt that weight in my groin, that grew and grew and would spill out, would spill out. I whispered, 'Close, almost.'

Requiem's lips touched my neck, just his lips, as if he kissed me. Byron fought for something smoother, more controlled, but his voice was hoarse, breathless, 'Almost, almost, almost.'

That heavy warmth inside me burst outward, and I screamed. Fangs plunged into my throat, and Byron's body bucked over me, convulsed against me, inside me. Requiem's mouth sealed over the kiss of his fangs, and he began to feed. And it was as if every suck of his mouth brought a new orgasm.

Byron cried out above me, and his body rocked with mine. Requiem's hand convulsed in my hair, and his hand gripped my shoulder, dug nails into me, and I felt his body jerking, rocking with us.

I screamed until my voice went hoarse, and still he fed, and still Byron stayed pinned inside me, thrusting into me. It was like being caught in an endless loop of pleasure, one movement feeding the others, until we finally collapsed into a quivering heap. Requiem's mouth fell away from my neck. 'I can drink no more.' His perfect voice was breathless, barely a whisper.

Byron collapsed on top of me like a puppet whose strings had been sliced. He lay on top of me, and I could feel his heart thudding inside his chest like a trapped thing. His breathing was ragged and sounded painful, and mine wasn't much better.

He found his voice, hoarse, and shaking. 'If I wasn't dead already, I'd say I was having a heart attack.'

I tried to laugh and ended up coughing.

'Oh, don't do that,' Byron said, 'oh, please.' The coughing fit had tightened me around him again, and it jerked him up on his arms, pushed him one last time against me, which made me writhe under him.

He collapsed again, and begged, 'No, more, please, Anita, no more. I never thought I'd say that from just one time, but give me a moment to catch my . . . breath.'

'Breath,' Requiem said with his face collapsed next to mine, 'not breath, pulse. I knew you had the *ardeur*, but you should warn a vampire if you can do things like that.'

I found my voice, 'Like what?'

He moved his head just enough so that he could look me in the eye with his face on my shoulder. 'I knew you would feed from me, but I didn't know you would bring me.'

'Bring us,' Byron said, 'bring us again and again.' He was collaped across my chest and body so all I could see was his brown curls. 'I usually try and keep track of things like that, but I gave up when we passed five. Or was it six?'

'Eight,' Requiem said, 'or maybe more. I think if I could have kept feeding, we wouldn't have stopped.' He closed his eyes, and a faint shiver ran through him. 'I'd forgotten how many different ways the *ardeur* could be fed. I'd forgotten how good it could feel.'

'I don't have anything to compare this to,' Byron said in a hoarse voice.

'You never met Belle Morte, did you?' Requiem asked.

Byron seemed to want to look at the other man when he spoke, but he gave up when raising his head was too much effort. 'No, never had the pleasure.'

'It was a pleasure,' he said.

If I could have moved, and been sure I wouldn't fall over, I'd have told everyone to get off of me, but I couldn't move, and if I couldn't, I knew at least Byron couldn't, either. He'd been using more muscles than I had. But it felt odd to lay there with them draped around me and talk as if I wasn't there. I asked him, 'Why didn't you let Belle keep you, then?'

'Have you met her?'

'In a manner of speaking, yeah.'

His blue, blue eyes, looked sad, the excited exhaustion fading in the light of memories. 'Then you should know the answer. No pleasure is worth her price, and besides, I don't like men, not even a little, and if you aren't at least bisexual, you can't survive at her court.'

'Why?' I asked.

'When she's not fucking the men, she likes to watch the men fucking each other. I don't think there was ever a waking moment at her court when someone wasn't having sex either with her, or for her entertainment, or the entertainment of her guests.'

Byron managed to lever himself around so he could give gray eyes to the other vampire. 'I like men, but you make it sound like I wouldn't have liked it, either.'

'There is no pleasure without payment. No pleasure without some pain attached, and not the kind of pain you'll enjoy. First she finds what you most desire, she learns your body as no other lover can, then she begins to deny you that love. She begins to make you beg for it. She addicts you to her, if she can. Then when she has you, truly has you, she begins to pull away, so that you spend the rest of eternity gazing into the face of paradise, but you are locked outside the shining gates and can only touch glimpses of heaven.'

I found that I could move my arm again. I reached around Byron's curls, and touched Requiem's face. 'You didn't end up with Belle,' I said.

His eyes lost their remembering look, but they didn't regain the shine of pleasure. 'If Jean-Claude had not offered me a home when our old master got himself executed, Belle Morte would have had me. If any other master had offered for me, anyone less than a *le sourdre de sang*, then I could not have refused her. You have no idea how rare it is that Jean-Claude has gained enough power to be his own fountainhead of blood. Not more than three vampires in nearly eight hundred years have gained that kind of power. It protected all of us when our old master lost his mind and went against the council's orders. An entire court of nearly all Belle's line, when it fell apart, she tried to pick up all the pieces.'

Britain was the only other country in the world where vampires were legal. They had rights, and you couldn't just kill one of them simply because they were a vampire. It was murder. But in America we'd been doing it almost four years, and the Brits were newer at it. There'd been some hitches. Hitches that the human media and powers that be didn't know about. The Master of the City of London had been very old. He'd been one of the first master vamps that Belle Morte made, oh, so long ago. Sometimes the really ancient vampires don't take well to newfangled ideas. You know, electricity, modern medicine, and the fact that they were supposed to expose themselves to public view in a very modern, rock star sort of way. London had had more of Belle's lovely vampires than any but three other groups, and that included Belle's own court. So when the vamps got legal, the vampire council wanted the Master of the City to play to the human media. He called himself Dracula, because once the real vampire Dracula was assassinated, the name was up for grabs. Only one person at a time can hold a name per country, and only one person per time can hold some of the more well-known names. Dracula wasn't really Dracula, but the news media didn't seem to understand that, and they'd enjoyed talking about how they had the real Dracula as their Master of the City. They'd only wanted him to be as politically correctly visible as Jean-Claude and a lot of the masters in this country, but the new Drac didn't take well to it. In fact, he went buggers and started slaughtering humans.

The council managed to hush most of it up. To assassinate Dracula again, and just to prove that vampires can be as superstitious as the next bunch, they declared *Dracula* a dead name. No other vampire was allowed to choose it, or hold it. There had been two of them, and both had broken council law and had to be assassinated. Two was enough.

Jean-Claude had offered the London vamps a home. Not all of them, but many of them. All of them that could trace their lineage to Belle Morte. Who better to be strippers and dancers than the most beautiful and seductive vampires in the world? I couldn't argue with his logic. But lying there trapped under the weight of two of those vampires, I had to wonder if part of what was happening was just too damn many of them in one place. Was there such a thing as vampire pheromones? Probably.

'You're safe now,' I said, 'so everybody off the animator. I need to get up.'

'That I did not offer means I am no gentleman,' Requiem said, and he came to his knees with more grace than I was going to manage.

Byron got to all fours, head hanging down like a tired horse. I could see down the line of his body, and he looked tired, spent. 'I can't feel my legs below my knees, so I'm as far up as I'm getting for awhile. Sorry, luv.'

His getting up even that far left me suddenly naked from the waist down, or as naked as mattered to me. I never felt dressed in just thigh-highs and boots, and still wearing the shirt complete with gun didn't matter either. My skirt was up so high that the front of me was totally exposed, and for me, that was naked. I know, I know, how middle-America, how small town. But truth is truth. If you gave me a choice of covering anything, that would be it.

I tried to pull the skirt down, but I was lying on too much of it. Requiem stood and offered me a hand, but Nathaniel was on the other side, with his hand out. There was a look I couldn't quite read on his face, and this time I fought not to read his mind. I'd had enough surprises for one evening. But I took Nathaniel's hand and not Requiem's.

Nathaniel had to take both my hands to pull me out from under Byron. When he got me standing, my knees wouldn't hold, and he had to catch me around the waist. I looked at Requiem, who had spilled his black cloak around himself. I thought he was insulted, so I said, 'Nothing personal, Requiem.'

He gave me a brief and rare grin. He smiled, but grinning was rare. 'I am not insulted, my lady.' He spread the cloak wide suddenly, so that the front of his body showed. The cloak was black, but his slacks were not. The pale gray slacks were stained on the front as if he'd not quite made it to a bathroom, but that wasn't really what the stain was. It wasn't the stain that got me, it was the fact that the stain ran from his groin down one leg of his pants nearly to his knees.

I gave him raised eyebrows.

I expected embarrassment, but didn't get it. 'A task well done, m'lady, a task well done.'

That made me blush, which made him laugh, that deep rolling chuckle that was all masculine. Byron joined it, and his was not as deep a sound, but had just as much maleness to it. He was finally on his knees, instead of all fours.

Nathaniel didn't join in the laughter. He was helping me pull my skirt into place. Something about his face, his silence, reached the vampires.

Requiem made a low sweeping bow that flared the cloak around him, like wings. He used the cloak, or one similar to it, on stage. 'My apologies, Nathaniel, it did not occur to me to ask your favor when I entered. Jean-Claude is our master and hers, but not yours.' He looked up at Nathaniel, giving him the full force of those startling blue eyes.

'Anita doesn't need my permission for anything,' Nathaniel said, but his voice made the words not ring true.

I sighed. I guess I couldn't blame him. He'd spent a lot of time lately watching everybody else but him get so much more than just sleeping privileges. But I couldn't apologize in front of the vampires without explaining way too much. So I didn't try.

'You get to sleep with her every night, mate, don't begrudge us a few crumbs from your table.'

He took a breath like he'd say something, but I stopped him with a hand against his lips. 'It was a metaphysical emergency. Nathaniel wants to opt out of those for awhile.'

He looked at me, and I felt his smile against my hand. A smile just for me, because no one else could see it. He kissed the palm of my hand and moved it away from his mouth, but some piece of unhappiness had faded from his eyes. It made me smile.

'Let's bandage that wrist.'

I glanced at the wrist in question. The gauze had glued itself to the wound, and it had begun to close. Byron had put a lot of pressure on it. 'And find my underwear,' I said.

Byron lifted what was left of my black undies from under the tables. 'I think they've had it, luver.'

I sighed. Bert had been right, the skirt was too short, and it was certainly too short to wear without underwear.

'I might have something that fits you,' Byron said.

'What?' I asked.

'A thong, but at least the front bits will be covered.' He smiled when he said it.

I shook my head, but I took his offer. A little underwear was better than no underwear at all.

38

THE CLUB WAS dark except for a single soft spotlight in the middle of the stage. In that soft, white light Jean-Claude stood. The light hit only his shoulders and face, the rest of him was lost to darkness. It gave the illusion that his body formed from the darkness itself, to rise to the shining paleness of his face, the gleaming white of his cravat, the tiny colored spark of the sapphire winking only when he moved. His hair looked as if the darkness had been drawn out into some dark thread and formed into curls. The only color was the drowning blue of his eyes and the crimson smear of lipstick across his face. It wasn't my lipstick, or at least not most of it.

His voice floated through the darkened room. 'Who will taste my kiss?' Taste, left a sweetness on my tongue, as if I'd licked a piece of candy. Kiss, gave a ghost of lips brushing my cheek. 'Who will embrace me?' Embrace made me feel faintly warm, as if I'd been given a really good hug by someone I cared about.

Jean-Claude's voice had always been good, but not this good. Not this good. With my partial immunity, I probably wasn't getting all of it. I had no idea how much more the audience was getting. It took a force of will to look away from him in that shining circle of light. I made myself look out at the audience. It took a moment for my eyes to adjust to the dark, but when I could see, nearly every face was turned to him. They gazed up at him in the dark as if he were the rising sun and they had never seen anything so bright before. Only a handful of faces weren't turned toward the stage. A few women were shaking their heads and looking confused. A little psychic talent of the right kind or with the right practice helped.

Marianne had proven to me that you didn't have to be a necromancer to have some immunity to vampire mind tricks.

One of the few men was standing up, and the woman with him was tugging on his arm, trying to get him to sit back down. He was shaking his head, adamantly. No, no, he wouldn't sit in the dark and let that voice wash over him. He didn't understand that it wasn't a matter of sexual orientation. It was Jean-Claude. His power was seduction, and it had nothing and everything to do with sex.

Two of the waiters were escorting a woman up on stage. She was tall and almost anorexically thin. She'd apparently been waving more money than anybody else, because Jean-Claude preferred more curves on his women. As he'd pointed out to me, the beauties of his day in the French courts were today's size twenty. Most of the old vamps liked short women with curves. Most of us were living in so the wrong century.

The lights around the stage had been growing brighter so gradually that if you'd been gazing at the stage the entire time, you might not have noticed. The light was just barely bright enough so the audience could see more of their bodies. From the waist up, you could see his pale hands sliding over her body. Nothing déclassé, but he got more out of simply touching a woman's back, shoulder, or waist, than some men got out of touching breasts and groin. Sometimes it's not what you touch but how you touch it.

He pressed her against the front of his body so there was no space between them, so that her thin frame seemed almost to mold itself to his body. He lifted her face up to meet his, using one pale hand to cradle her face so that he would control the kiss. His arm slid around her waist, and tightened. Tightened enough to bow her neck and make her mouth open in a surprised little *O*. One of the women before this one had groped him, so he'd made sure there wasn't enough space between the front of their bodies for anyone's hands to wander too far. The women seemed to take the closer frontal contact as a sign of favor. I knew it wasn't. It was a sign of control and damn near displeasure.

But when he bowed his head to her mouth and locked their lips together in a kiss, there was no displeasure. He kissed her as if he were trying to breathe her down through his mouth. He fed from her lips almost as if he were feeding from her neck. And in a way, he was, feeding at least.

He fed from their mouths in a way that the Dragon's presence in my head had told me about. Except she knew how to eat the essence of the dead and make the undead, really, truly dead. This was not that, but it was eerily similar. He was feeding the *ardeur*, from a kiss.

'Nikolaos would never let him feed like that,' a quiet voice said from behind me.

I turned to find Buzz just behind me. I hadn't heard him, or sensed him, which meant that I'd been more caught up in the show than I'd realized.

'What do you mean?' I asked.

'Nikolaos knew that he was feeding off the audience without ever touching them, so she forbade him to touch any of the customers.' His gaze went past me to the stage. 'I think she had some clue what he could have been, and she did everything she could to make sure he didn't come into that power.'

'She's been dead almost three years. You make it sound like tonight is the first time you've seen this show.'

He looked at me. 'It is.'

I gave him wide eyes. 'Nikolaos was dead, she couldn't stop him.'

'But you could,' he said.

'What do you mean?'

'Do you really think three years ago you would have dated him after you saw this?'

I glanced back at the stage. I watched him kissing a strange woman as if she were his deepest love, or at least deepest lust. Would I have tolerated it three years ago? No. Would I have used it as an excuse to dump his ass? Oh, yeah.

The woman swooned in his arms. Her mouth falling away from

his as she seemed to half-faint, as if the kiss alone were so intense that she couldn't stay conscious. I would have thought she was play-acting, or exaggerating, but I had to believe it, when the waiters carried her off stage and gave her back to her friends at their table.

Jean-Claude gazed out at the audience with fresh crimson lipstick smeared across his entire lower jaw. It looked eerily like blood, and I knew him well enough to know that the resemblance was not acci-dental. His blue eyes had bled to solid blue light, as if a summer's dusk could burn in his eyes. 'Who will be next?' And it was as if he whis-pered along my skin, as if he were standing just behind me. The illu-sion was so strong that I had to fight not to turn around and look. I was supposed to be immune to this crap, if this was how I was feeling, what must the women connected to all those eager faces be feeling?

I lowered my shields just enough to see Jean-Claude shining with power. This was what he was meant to be. This wasn't just feeding the *ardeur*. This wasn't a substitute for a blood feed. This was an end in itself. This was something I'd never seen, not in Jean-Claude, not in anyone. It was akin to all his other abilities, but more, somehow this was more.

I turned back to Buzz. 'Him feeding like this is what saved me.'

He looked puzzled, vampires under twenty years dead have so many more human facial expressions. 'Saved you from what?'

'If he hadn't fed, then I'd have had to feed for him. That's one of the things a human servant is for. We feed when the vamps can't. I would still be trapped backstage fucking my metaphysical brains out.' I shook my head. 'No, thank you.'

'So you're not disappointed that's he's doing strangers?'

I felt my face go sort of unfriendly. 'You sound disappointed that I'm not upset about this, why?'

He raised his hands, making his big arms flex. I think by accident. He meant it to be a harmless gesture, but he was too muscle-bound for it to look anything but impressive, or scary, depending on how you looked at it.

'It just seems like a fast turnaround, that's all.'

I sighed. 'The last time Jean-Claude asked me if he could feed off the audience, I didn't really understand what he was asking.' I smiled, but not like I was happy. 'Besides, I wasn't fucking strangers to feed the vampiric powers then. Strangely, that's changed my mind about a lot of things.'

He looked way too serious for my tastes.

I didn't know what was up with Buzz, so I decided to change topics. 'Primo all tucked away in the spare coffin?'

'We put him in while you were cleaning up.'

I nodded. I'd been told about it, but I'd also laid my hands on the coffin and felt Primo trapped inside, behind silver chains and a holy item. It wasn't that I didn't trust everybody, it was just good business to be cautious. Buzz's odd behavior hadn't changed my mind about that, not one little bit.

'Lisandro told me that you ordered him to baby-sit the coffin.'

I nodded. 'Yes, I did.'

'Primo is in a cross-wrapped coffin, Anita. He's not getting out.'

I shrugged. Lisandro was tall, dark, handsome, with the longest hair that any of the new security had. He was also the only one with a gun tucked into the small of his back under the black T-shirt. Once I spotted the gun, I pegged him for a wererat, and I'd been right. I told him if Primo started to tear out of the coffin, to kill him. Jean-Claude would probably have agreed with me, but he'd been busy on stage, so I'd made the call. I was happy with the call, and I didn't like that Buzz wasn't.

'Let's just say that I feel better going off to raise the dead, knowing that Lisandro is sitting by that coffin with silver ammo, and a willingness to shoot.'

'I'm head of security here, Anita. You should have cleared it with me.'

I sighed. 'You're right. You're right, I should have. I'm sorry.'

He just blinked at me like a deer caught in headlights. I think he'd expected an argument. But I was tired, and late, and feeling squidgie about having had sex with Byron and Requiem.

'I've got to go, Buzz.'

'Your security detail is waiting at the door,' he said, and nodded toward the door in question.

Requiem was by the door in his black cloak, wearing a fresh pair of pants that he'd borrowed from someone. The new pants were leather, so he'd probably borrowed them from another dancer. But we had a new addition, and that was the dark-haired werewolf that had fallen on top of Clay and me when Primo was fighting everyone. His name was Graham, and his body had that width of shoulder and impressive swell of arm that only semiserious weight lifting can get you. His black hair was cut in a longish layer on top so that it fell like a silken fringe over his ears, but underneath the hair was shaved close to his head and upper neck. It seemed an odd haircut to me, but it wasn't my hair.

His face was exotic, in the way that people can be when some ancestor didn't come from Northern or Southern Europe. The straight black hair, the ever-so-slight uptilt to the edge of his eyes made me bet he'd come from somewhere much farther east.

I'd argued that I didn't need or want guards, but just as I'd made the call about Primo and Lisandro, so Jean-Claude had given his orders about this before he got carried away on stage. I was to go nowhere without someone with me. He wasn't sure the Dragon was done with us for the night, and it would be a shame if something went horribly wrong. What he hadn't told the security detail, vampire or otherwise, was about what had happened earlier in my office. That had had nothing to do with the Dragon and everything to do with my own metaphysical shit. Well, mine, and Jean-Claude's.

Jean-Claude had even left a list of people he thought were appropriate to the job. Byron had not been on the list, nor had Clay. It had been a damn short list, actually, basically Requiem and Graham. The last thing I wanted to do was be trapped in a car with Requiem, but I didn't have time to argue. I'd gone from having plenty of time, to having to call my clients and tell them to hold fast in the cemetery, I really was on my way.

I was wearing Byron's leather jacket to take the place of my bloodied suit jacket. His was the only one that came close to fitting me and not making me look like I was wearing the upper half of a gorilla. It smelled faintly of his cologne.

Buzz's eyes left me and went to the audience. The man who had been arguing with his date was still standing, but now so was the woman, and she was starting to make a scene. 'Sorry, gotta catch that.'

'Be my guest,' I said.

Nathaniel seemed to appear from nowhere. He escorted me toward the outer door. He was smiling and seemed terribly at ease, more so than I'd seen him in a long time, maybe ever. It seemed an odd night for him to be happy. 'You promised to get back in time to see some of my act,' he said, smiling.

'I've got two clients stuck in cemeteries,' I said.

He gave me the look that was half-pout and half-he-knew-he'd-already-won-the-argument. 'You promised.'

'Can't we just fuck at home later?' I asked.

He gave me a frown. 'I'll be furry, you don't do furry.'

I had an idea, an awful idea. 'I promised to mark your neck tonight. Oh, no, you so are not planning on me doing it in front of an audience?'

He smiled, and there was something in that smile that I hadn't seen before. Some hint of confidence, of security that hadn't been there before. He'd watched me have sex with two near strangers, and suddenly he felt more secure. Go figure.

'You little exhibitionist, you,' I said, 'you like the idea of me marking you for the first time in front of all these people.'

He gave an aw-gee-shucks shrug, which was all act, because his eyes were bright with the answer. 'I like a lot of things, Anita.'

I tried to frown at him, but couldn't keep it up. 'You got me to promise I'd mark you, and now you're taking advantage of it.'

'You're running late,' he said, 'clients waiting in the cemetery.' He looked solemn except for the glint of humor in his eyes, which spoiled the effect.

I shook my head, smiling. 'I've got to go.'

'I know,' he said.

'Would it ruin the illusion if I kissed you goodbye?'

'I'll risk it,' he said.

I kissed him. It was chaste, a touch of lips, a little pressure, barely any body language. I drew back with a suspicious look on my face. It made him laugh and push me toward the door. 'You're late, remember.'

I went, but I went out into the October dark even more certain that I knew absolutely nothing about men. Alright, to be fair, that I knew absolutely nothing about the men in my life. I glanced back to see Jean-Claude on stage with another woman, kissing her as if he were trying to find her tonsils without his hands. Most people looked disturbing or awkward when they kissed that deep. He didn't. He made it all seem suave, erotic, and perfect. I realized I'd kissed Nathaniel goodbye, but not Jean-Claude. Didn't want to interrupt, but didn't want him to feel left out, either. I blew him a kiss as his arms emptied of the woman. He returned the gesture with one pale hand. The lower half of his face was smeared bright crimson with lipstick. It didn't really look like blood, not if you'd seen enough of the real deal, but it was still a less than comforting image to take away into the night. One of the other men in my life was smiling at the door, looking forward to having me do foreplay on him in front of an audience. Sometimes the parts of my life that are weirdest to me aren't the parts dealing with vampires and werewolves and zombies. Even vampire politics didn't confuse me as much as my own love life.

39

WE WERE ON Gravois, trapped between an endless line of store-fronts that had seen better days. The entire area was doing that slow slide into not being a good area to be in after dark. It wasn't quite a danger zone, but if nothing saved it, in a couple of years it would be. The Bevo Mill restaurant, an honest-to-God windmill, loomed like a ship in a sea of lesser buildings and harder times. The Bevo Mill still served great German food. The slowly turning windmill was just ahead, and suddenly we were driving under the stone over-pass blocks past the mill. I didn't remember passing any of it. That wasn't good. I was missing things, like my attention was going in and out. Not good at all, since I was driving. Graham squeaked a second time, you know, that sharp intake of breath that comes out when you're trying to swallow the sound.

I glanced at him. 'What? What is your problem?'

'You've almost hit two cars,' he said in a strangled voice.

'No I haven't.'

'Yes,' Requiem said from the back, 'yes you have.'

There was a white car in front of me, like magic, it just appeared. I slammed on the brakes, and Graham squeaked again. My pulse was thudding in my throat. I hadn't seen that car. I signaled that I was turning right. Right meant I didn't have to cross any lanes of traffic. The suddenly appearing white car had scared me.

I eased us into Grasso Plaza, which held the Affton Post Office, a Save-A-Lot, and a lot of empty storefronts. This whole area along Gravois seemed tired, as if it had given its best and its best hadn't been good enough. Or maybe it was projecting. I cut the engine, and we sat in silence for a minute.

'Are you well?' Requiem asked, his voice was very quiet and deep like he was talking from inside a well.

I actually turned around and looked at him, and even turning around seemed to be slower, as if I wasn't moving at the same speed as the rest of the world.

Requiem was just sitting in the backseat, with his hands clasped in his lap. He wasn't far away, or doing anything odd. He was sitting, very still, as if he didn't want to attract attention to himself.

'What did you say?' My voice seemed hollow, too, as if I had an echo in my head.

'Are you well?' he said, slowly, distinctly, and as I stared at his lips, watching them move; the sound and the movement seemed just a little out of sync.

I had to think about it as if it were a much harder question than it should have been. 'No,' I said, finally. 'No, I don't think I am.'

'What's wrong?' Graham asked.

What was wrong? Good question. Trouble is, I wasn't sure I had a good answer. What was wrong? I was having something close to a shock reaction, why? Had I lost more blood than I knew? Maybe. Maybe not.

I was cold, and I huddled in the borrowed jacket, burying my face in the collar. Byron's cologne, the scent of him, was there, and I jerked back from it, because the smell of his skin in the leather brought it all back. Scent brings memory stronger than any other sense, and I was suddenly drowning in the feel of Byron's body, the look of his face as he gazed down at me, the weight of him, the sight of him going in and out of my body.

I fell back against the seat, my head thrown back, and it was as if all the pleasure of it was suddenly there again, rolling over me, through me. It wasn't the exact experience, but like a strong, strong, echo. Strong enough to shake my body against the seat and leave my hands clawing at the air, as if I needed something to hold on to, anything to hold on to.

I heard Requiem's voice: 'No, don't touch . . .' And I found something to hold on to.

Graham had tried to grab me, hold me down, keep me from hurting myself. I think he'd thought I was having a fit. His hand touched mine, and my hand convulsed around his, and it was as if from the moment our palms locked together that all that memory, all that pleasure, poured down my hand and into him.

Graham shuddered against me. I felt the shiver of it go down his arm, and it threw him against the seat so hard the Jeep shook from the impact. I let him have the memory, the pleasure, the sights and smells of it, I let it all pour away from me and into him. It wasn't a conscious thought, because I hadn't known until I did it that I could put it into someone else and not have to be pulled along for the ride. I didn't mean to do it, but I wasn't unhappy about it. I was glad, for once, to be the calm one on the other side of the seat, while I watched Graham writhing in just the echo of what we'd done. I was glad it wasn't me. Because I knew now why I'd had the shocky reaction earlier, before the metaphysics had gotten out of hand.

I killed without thinking much about it. Not in cold blood, but if it came time to kill, I had no real problem with it. I'd mourned the fact that killing had stopped bothering me. Then on my first trip to Tennessee to help Richard back when we were still a couple, I'd tortured someone. The bad guys had sent us Richard's mother's finger in a little box, along with a lock of his brother Daniel's hair. We had a time limit to find them, and we already knew that they'd been tortured. The man who'd delivered the box had bragged that they'd both been raped. I'd tortured him, made him tell us where they were, and when we were done with him, I'd shot him in the head, and made the screaming stop. I'd done it to save Richard's family, and because I couldn't see another way to do it. I'd done it because I never ask anyone to do anything that I'm not willing to do myself. It's a rule. Of course, before that, my rule had been I did not do torture. That was a line I did not cross, and I'd crossed it. The terrible part was that I hadn't regretted doing it, only having to do it. He'd raped Richard's mother, if I could have I'd have killed him slower, but that wasn't in me, not even for what he'd done. We'd saved them, but before all of it, the Zeemans had been like the Waltons, and now they weren't. They weren't broken completely, but they weren't as fixed as when they started, either. I'd killed the men that did it, or helped them get killed, but all the revenge in the world wouldn't really fix what was broken.

How do you give someone back their innocence? That wonderful sense of perfect safety that only exists for people that have never really had anything bad happen to them. How do you give that back? I wish I knew.

I'd crossed a lot of lines over the years, but one line I'd never crossed until tonight had been I didn't have sex just to feed. I didn't have sex with strangers. Byron and Requiem were strangers. I'd known them for two weeks, give or take. I had fucked them because Jean-Claude needed me to feed.

Requiem had moved to one side of the backseat, so he was close enough to see my face and to watch Graham still twitching on the front seat, but not close enough so I could touch him easily. 'You had a flashback, didn't you?'

I nodded, still staring at the werewolf in my front seat.

'Has that ever happened before?'

'Only after Asher rolled me completely with his mind, and we all had sex.' I didn't look at him as I spoke, I watched Graham's body begin to grow quiet.

'But Asher was not involved tonight.'

'No,' I said, 'he wasn't.' My voice sounded very even, very neutral, empty. Empty, just like I felt.

'Did you know that you could send that memory into someone else?'

'No,' I said.

Graham's eyes were fluttering, like butterflies trying to open, but not able to do it. He looked boneless, as if he could have slid into the floorboard, if his body had been a little less solid.

'You spilled it into him, then watched him writhe. How did it make you feel?'

I shook my head. 'Nothing, just glad for once that it wasn't me twisting in the seat.'

He moved to lean against the back of Graham's seat, a little closer to me. 'Is that true? Is that really how you feel about it?'

I moved my whole head to meet his eyes, as if a glance wasn't enough. I let him see how dead my eyes felt, how empty I was inside. 'You're a master vamp, can't you smell it if I'm lying?'

He licked his lips like he was nervous. 'The last vampire I knew that could do what you just did, did it on purpose. She would recall a memory of pleasure, and she would pick someone to give it to. It could be a reward, and it was, but it could also be punishment. Sometimes she would choose someone who did not wish to feel such pleasures, and she would force them to experience it.'

'A kind of rape,' I said.

He nodded.

'You're talking about Belle Morte, aren't you?'

He nodded, again.

'She enjoyed watching them writhe, especially if they didn't want to do it,' I said.

'You say that as a statement, not a question.'

'I've met her, remember?'

'You are exactly right. She loved watching prim, proper women and men, forced to spill themselves upon the floor and flop about, experiencing a pleasure greater than any they had ever felt before. It pleased her to watch the righteous brought low.'

'Yeah, that sounds like her.'

'But you truly felt nothing. It did not excite you to watch Graham writhe.'

'Why should it?'

He smiled then, and there was relief in his eyes. 'That you would ask the question makes me worry less about you.'

'Worry how?' I asked.

'It has been speculation for centuries whether Belle was formed into the type of,' he seemed to search for a word, 'creature she was by the *ardeur* and her powers running to flesh and pleasure, or whether she was always as she is, and the power simply made her more.'

'It's been my experience, Requiem, that people become more of who they are in extremes, both good and bad. Give a truly good person power, and they're still a good person. Give a bad person power, and they're still a bad person. The question is always about the person in between. The one that isn't evil, or good, but just ordinary. You don't always know what an ordinary person is like on the inside.'

He looked at me, with an odd expression on his face. 'That was a very wise thing to say.'

I had to smile. 'You sound surprised.'

He gave an almost bow from the neck, as much as he could sitting in the seat. 'My apologies, but in truth I've always thought of you as more muscle than brain. Not stupid,' he added hastily, 'but not wise. Intelligent perhaps, but no, not wise.'

'I guess I'll just take the compliment, and leave the insult alone.'

'It was not meant as an insult, Anita, far from it.' There was a look on his face, a feel to him, that was anxious.

'Don't worry, I won't hold it against you. A lot of people under-estimate me.'

'They see the delicate beauty, but not the killer,' he said.

'I'm not a delicate beauty,' I said.

He gave a small frown. 'You are most assuredly delicate in appearance, and you are beautiful.'

I shook my head. 'No, I'm not. Not beautiful, pretty, maybe, but not beautiful.'

His eyes widened a little. 'If you do not think yourself beautiful, then you are using a different mirror from the one in front of my eyes.'

'Pretty words, but I'm surrounded by some of the most beautiful men living or dead. I may clean up well, but when comparing beauty, I don't rank that high, not in this company.'

'It is true, perhaps, that your beauty is not a flashy beauty, as is Asher's, or Jean-Claude's, or even your Nathaniel's, but it is beauty nonetheless. Perhaps the more precious, for it grows not at the first sight of the eye, but a little more each time one speaks with you or watches you move so commandingly into a situation, or watches the truth in your eyes when you say that you are not beautiful, and I realize that you mean it. That you are not being humble, or playing silly games, you simply do not see yourself.'

'See, that's not beauty, that's pretty with a personality that you like.'

'But do you not see, Anita, that there is beauty that hits the eye like a bolt of lighting, that burns and sears and blinds. It is more disaster than pleasure. But yours, yours is a beauty that lulls one into comfort, into not protecting one's eyes from the light, then one night you realize that the moon, too, has its beauty.'

I shook my head. 'I have no idea who you're talking about, but it's not me.'

He sighed. 'You are a very hard woman to compliment.'

'You know, you're not the first person to say that.'

He smiled. 'That does not surprise me at all.'

Graham let out a long, long sigh, and sort of spilled himself back up onto the seat. It was like watching liquid fall upward. He had that same liquid grace that all the wereanimals seemed to have. He leaned his head against the headrest, but at least he was upright again. He gave me a slow, lazy blink, and his eyes were a dark, wolf amber, almost brown, but I knew the difference. I'd seen it often enough.

He smiled, and even that was lazy. 'That was amazing.'

'I didn't do it on purpose,' I said.

'I don't care.'

I frowned at him.

'Can you do it again, is all I want to know.'

I frowned harder.

Some of the laziness began to seep away from his face. 'Look, you give me one of the most amazing orgasmic experiences of my life, and now you're acting like the injured party. You're the one that spilled all over me.'

'Not on purpose,' I said.

'You keep saying that, like you're apologizing, why? Why are you apologizing?'

I looked at Requiem for help, though I didn't hold much hope. But he did help. 'I believe that Anita sees it as unasked-for sexual contact. A sort of rape, if you will.'

'Can't rape the willing,' Graham said, and he stretched himself taller in the seat, settling more into it, and his eyes were bleeding back to human.

'I didn't know you were willing, when it happened.'

He nodded. 'Okay, but I'm okay with it.' He looked at me. 'But you don't seem okay with it at all. What's wrong now?'

'What's wrong?' I asked. 'I just had a flashback so strong that if I'd still been driving, we'd have wrecked. I fed it into you by accident. I didn't mean to do it. What else am I not going to mean to do?'

'She and Jean-Claude have hit a new power plateau,' Requiem said.

'Oh,' Graham said, as if that made perfect sense to him, 'so you don't know what all the new power can do, yet.'

'No,' I said.

He nodded. 'Yeah, that can get scary. I'm sorry, I didn't know this was the first time you'd done something like this. I enjoyed it, you don't owe me an apology.'

'But what if I grab a client next time?' I said.

'You had warning,' Requiem said, 'or you wouldn't have pulled off the road.'

'I don't think that had anything to do with new powers.'

'Then why did you nearly run us up the back of three different cars?' Graham asked.

I opened my mouth, closed it, and didn't know what to say. 'I think I crossed my last few lines tonight.'

'What does that mean?' Graham asked.

'I broke some personal rules tonight, that's all.'

'Rules that you thought would never be broken,' Requiem said softly.

I looked at him, surprised. 'You say that like you know.'

'A person likes to think of himself in a certain way, and when something happens that makes that no longer possible, you mourn the old self. The person you thought you were.'

I shook my head. 'I am still the person I thought I was, damn it.'

He gave a shrug that reminded me of that graceful lift of shoulders that Jean-Claude always did. 'As you like, m'lady.'

I turned around in my seat and put my forehead against the steering wheel. I just wanted this night over with. I didn't want to have to explain myself to anyone, let alone one of the men that I'd had sex with by accident tonight. The trouble was, I wasn't sure that I believed what I'd just said. It wasn't just the sex with Byron and Requiem, it was that tonight, for the first time, I'd let Jean-Claude into my head as far as he could go. For the first time we'd touched what might be possible if only I'd get out of our way. Until tonight, I hadn't realized how much I'd crippled us. As much in my own way as Richard. I'd thought that sleeping with Jean-Claude and doing small things with him was being his human servant. I'd learned differently less than an hour ago, and that knowledge was eating me up. It wasn't that I had crippled us as a triumvirate of power. No, I'd guessed that before, just not the amount of crippling. I thought my limits and boundaries had hobbled us, not cut both our legs off at the knees. What I hadn't expected, what I hadn't wanted to know, was how good it felt to let Jean-Claude roll me. It had been a-fucking-mazing. Peaceful and intoxicating all at the same time. I'd never really known what I was doing without, because I had been so careful not to let him show me. And he had respected my wishes.

I knew now that it had cost him dear. Cost him in power he might have had, safety he might have built for his vampires, and in the sheer pleasure he might have experienced. He'd cut himself off from so much, just because I couldn't handle it. That made me feel guilty, but part of the real problem was that after I'd let Jean-Claude in that deep, I'd then turned around and had sex with Byron, and let Requiem bite me. Two things I didn't do lightly. Yeah, it had been imporant, maybe urgent, maybe it had saved the lives of most of those women in that club. Maybe it had even saved Jean-Claude's life. I'd felt Primo's power and the whisper of the Dragon. But that wasn't what bothered me the most.

Jean-Claude had gained Nathaniel and Damian's neediness. What had I gained? I'd had sex with Byron and Requiem, and I didn't feel bad about it. Even now, I felt bad only because I didn't feel bad. It hadn't bothered me. That's what made me almost run into three cars, and pull into the parking lot so I could have my little moment of shock reaction.

I didn't feel guilty about Byron. I only felt guilty about not feeling guilty about it. And even now, I wanted to turn the car around and go back to Jean-Claude. I wanted him to hold me, to kiss me, to feed from me. I wanted the whole ride, now that I'd had a taste. I wanted it the way junkies want their fix. That's not love. That's control. I wouldn't let anyone control me like that. I couldn't, not and still be me.

I didn't explain any of this to Graham or Requiem. They weren't close enough to me for a heart-to-heart. I just said, 'Whoever feels better to drive, drive.'

'I do not know how to drive,' Requiem said.

'I'll drive,' Graham said, 'just don't touch me while I'm behind the wheel.'

'I'll do my best to resist,' I said, and made it plain by my tone that it wouldn't be hard.

He laughed and got out his door to walk around. In the moments it took him to walk around the car, Requiem said, 'You feel very serious tonight, Anita.'

'I'm always serious,' I said.

'Perhaps,' he said, and he might have said more, but Graham opened the door and I got out. I walked around the car and got into the passenger seat, as Graham started the engine. 'Where to?'

'Sunset Cemetery. It's less than five minutes from here.'

'Do you feel well enough to raise the dead tonight?' Requiem asked.

'Just get me there, and don't let me touch any of the clients. I'll do the rest. Just don't let me fuck anybody or tear anybody's throat out.'

'What if you order us to allow you to fuck someone?' Requiem asked.

'Or kill someone?' Graham said.

'I'm not planning on it tonight, okay?'

'You weren't planning on it earlier,' Requiem said quietly.

Graham pulled carefully into the traffic on Gravois, as if he were trying to make up for my bad driving earlier. 'What do we do if some new vampire power kicks in?' he asked, as he eased us to the first stoplight.

'Just keep me from hurting anybody,' I said.

'And if the need arises for you to feed again, what then?' Requiem asked.

I turned in my seat as far as the seat belt would allow, so I could see his face in the streetlights. He was revealed in startling white light for an instant. It made his eyes glow, then shadow swept over the backseat, and his eyes faded to a dim blue glow. 'What are you getting at?' I asked.

'Did you wonder why Jean-Claude chose us, and only us, to guard you tonight?'

'I had some ideas, but enlighten me.'

'He wanted people with you that were strong enough and dominant enough that if they had to, they could override you. That they would use their best judgment and not blindly follow.'

'Bully for you both,' I said.

'But it wasn't that alone.'

'Just spill it, Requiem, the foreplay is getting tiresome.'

'I heard that about you,' Graham said.

I turned and looked at him. 'What?'

'That you don't like a lot of foreplay.'

I gave him a very cold look. 'One, no one that would actually know would tell you shit, and two, don't let a little metaphysical sex go to your head. Remember, I watched you writhe all over the seat, and it didn't appeal to me. It wasn't foreplay, or a preview, it was just an accident.'

'Sorry.'

I turned back to Requiem. 'Now, you, just tell me what you need to tell me. No preface, no long explanation, just say it.'

'You won't like it,' he said.

'I already don't like it. Just tell me, Requiem, just tell me.' I was getting a headache. I didn't know if it was loss of blood, or tension, but whatever, it was beginning to pound right behind my eye.

'He thought that if things went as badly as they could go . . .'

'Games, word games, just say it.'

He sighed, and the sigh seemed to fill the Jeep with echoes. 'If you had to feed the *ardeur*, or if your beast rose, we were the two most likely to survive an attack without having to resort to hurting you.'

'You left something out,' I said.

'I've said enough,' he said.

'All of it, Requiem, I want to hear all of it.'

'No,' Graham said, 'you don't. That tone in your voice, no you don't.'

'Just drive,' I said, and turned back to the vampire. 'Tell me the rest.'

He sighed again, and it flittered through the interior of the Jeep like it had a life of its own.

'And can the voice tricks, or you're really going to piss me off.'

'My apologies, it is automatic for me, when faced with an angry woman, to try and pacify her, by whatever means.'

'Talk to me, Requiem, we're almost at the cemetery. I want that last bit before we get out of the car.'

He drew himself up even straighter in his seat, very formal. 'We were also the two at the club most likely to be able to turn violence to seduction, if the need arose.'

'He must have a high opinion of you both, or a low opinion of me.'

'That last is not true, and you know it,' Requiem said.

I sighed. 'Just the way I'm feeling tonight.'

Graham said it. 'You're feeling slutty because you did Byron.'

I looked at him. 'Well, that's one way of putting it.'

'It's exactly how you're feeling,' he said, sounding sure.

'And you're sure of that?'

'The way you're acting, yeah. Besides, I know your reputation. If anyone can resist temptation it's you.'

'Everyone keeps telling me that, but I don't seem to be resisting much anymore.'

'I have lived with others more powerful than I in Belle Morte's line for centuries, Anita. I, more than most, know just how much you must fight every night of your exisitence not to be consumed by their power.' He paused and then whispered so that it filled the darkened car, 'If you are not careful, their beauty will become both heaven and hell, you will betray every oath, abandon every loyalty, give up your heart, your mind, your body, and your immortal soul to have them near you but one more night. Then one cold night, a hundred years after the passion is spent, and nothing but ashes remain, you look up and see someone gazing at you, and you know that look, you've seen it before. A hundred years later and someone gazes upon you as if you were heaven itself, but you know in your heart of hearts that it's not heaven you're offering them, it's hell.'

I didn't know what to say to that, but Graham did.

'Now I know why they call you Requiem. You're poetic, but fucking depressing.'

Tonight, I just thought he was accurate.

40

SUNSET CEMETERY WAS a nice combination of old and new. Big monuments of angels and weeping virgins combined with flat, modern stones – so much less interesting. It was still a place for the rich and famous to be interred, like our local famous brewery family, the Busches.

In his day, Edwin Alonzo Herman had been a very important man, and his monument showed that he thought so, too. It loomed up into the darkness like some winged giant. There was enough light to see that the huge angel had a sword and shield, and it gave you a sense that it was waiting to pass judgment, and you wouldn't like what it decided. Of course, maybe that was just the way I was feeling tonight.

There were more than a dozen people waiting at the paved road, most of them lawyers, though with enough family members to have nearly caused a fistfight when I introduced myself and briefly explained what I'd be doing. I'd started telling people up front that I'd be using a machete and beheading chickens, for two different reasons. I'd had an overzealous bodyguard of a very wealthy man nearly shoot me when I drew the big blade. At a different graveside for a historical society, the secretary of said society had jumped me and tried to save the chicken. She'd turned out to be a vegan. That's like a rabid fundamentalist vegetarian. I'd been glad later that it hadn't been cold enough to wear a coat, because leather is the only kind of coat I own.

Tonight was cold enough for coats. October isn't usually that chilly in St Louis, but tonight had decided to be cold. Or maybe it just felt colder because I was wearing a thong. I'd been surprised by two things about the skimpy underwear: One, once I got over the sensation of having something in the crack of my butt, the thong wasn't uncomfortable; two, a thong under a short skirt on a cold night was damn cold. I'd never fully appreciated how much warmth a little extra bit of satin or silk could hold in against my ass. I certainly appreciated it as I walked over the grass in my little boots and skirt. I huddled in the borrowed leather jacket, but kept my face away from the collar. I did not want a repeat of what had happened in the car. I willed the warmth in my upper body to travel downward. I was suddenly wishing I'd taken one of the taller men's jackets. It wouldn't have looked as good, but it would have covered my ass.

I stood in front of the grave, though, since it had been nearly two hundred years in a cemetery that was as well-maintained as Sunset, there was no way for me to truly be sure of where the grave had been, not really. A lot of the graves had been moved here from smaller cemeteries over the years, as increased population had needed the land. But I had dropped just enough of my shields to know exactly where Edwin Alonzo Herman's grave lay. His bones were under there, I could feel them.

To the watchers from the road who had paid for this show, it must have looked like I was standing a little far away from the impressive angel. But it had been my experience that once the zombie crawls out of the grave, the crowd always thinks they've had a good show. They'll forgive almost any lack of showmanship on my part, once they've seen me raise the dead. Funny, that.

The crate with softly clucking chickens was near my feet. Graham had carried it and put it where I said to put it. No arguments. Once we left the Jeep, he went back into serious security guard mode. He was the unsmiling, business only person he'd been when I first saw him at the club. He was wearing a plain white T-shirt with his black jeans, jogging shoes, and his own short, leather jacket. He'd changed out of the Guilty Pleasures shirt without being asked. The joking, half-flirting man of a few minutes ago had vanished behind a very serious face and a pair of dark eyes that kept searching the cemetery, the people near us, and farther away, so he was very obviously aware of the perimeter. He seemed to vibrate bodyguard. I'd let the lawyers think he was and showed them the many bandages on my face, wrist, and fingers, to prove the necessity. No one had argued that this was private business and they didn't like anyone but me here with them, once Graham put his dark gaze on their faces. He had a really good stare, a hardness to his face and eyes that did not match what he'd been like in the car. Interesting.

Requiem had carried my gym bag with all the rest of the zombie-raising equipment, except the chickens. I could have carried the bag, but it would have taken me two trips to get the chickens. They tended to squawk if you didn't carry them upright and carefully. Since I was planning on killing them tonight, I tried not to scare them. I had to kill them to raise the dead, but I could make it as painless as possible. And fear definitely goes under the heading of pain in the wrong situation. Being a blood sacrifice probably qualifies as a wrong situation, even if you're a chicken.

I'd persuaded Requiem to leave his long, black cloak in the Jeep, because in it, he looked like a cute version of the Grim Reaper. Out of it, he looked like he should have been going clubbing. Maybe it was the leather pants? Or the boots? Or the long-sleeved silk shirt in a deep green jewel tone that made his white skin almost shine in contrast. The shirt had made his eyes turquoise in the light, as if there was green in that bright blue somewhere. He'd been harder to explain than Graham, because even without the cloak, he didn't really look like a bodyguard. He looked like what he was, and that was nothing that any of Herman's descendants thought should be here tonight. The only walking dead they wanted to see tonight was Herman himself. I'd told them the vampire stayed, they could like it, or lump it. I also reminded them that I was not obligated to return their down payment if they changed their minds about raising Edwin

Herman from the grave. I was here, ready to fulfill my part of the bargain.

When you start needing more than a hundred years worth of zombie raised, it's sort of a seller's market, and I was the seller. There were two other animators in the United States that could do it. One in California, and one in New Orleans, but they weren't here, and I was. Besides, they were nearly as expensive as I was, and they also came with the cost of plane fare and hotels. More money.

So the lawyers got them to shut up. Though there was an elderly woman on the side of the family that had inherited the money that wanted to leave if the 'demon' stayed. Demon? If she thought Requiem was a demon, she'd never seen one for real. I had, and I knew the difference.

But the lawyers had settled them down, and one of the grand-daughters had settled the grandmother down, and now they were waiting in the dark for me to do my job.

I had the chickens in their crate, and my gym bag with the machete and other paraphernalia. But before anything else, I had to drop my shields enough to do this. I'd learned how to shield, really shield, so that I could fight off the urge to use my gift. I'd learned long ago to control it enough so I didn't raise the dead by accident. There'd been a professor in college that committed suicide. He'd come to my dorm room one night. He wanted to tell his wife he was sorry. That was back when I wasn't raising anything, just shut it down, ignored it. I'm too damn gifted to ignore it. Psychic ability will come out one way or another, if the power is big enough, it'll find a way. And you probably won't like what it will find.

I dropped my shields, not all of them, but enough. Enough so I could open that part of me that raised the dead. It was like a fist that stayed clenched and tight, and only when I relaxed, spread wide those metaphysical fingers, could I be free. I knew people that had studied with animators or voodoo practitioners to acquire the skills needed to raise the dead. I'd studied to learn how *not* to raise the dead. But it took a little effort, all the time, to keep that fist closed, that power shut down. It was like a piece of me never completely relaxed, not even when I slept, unless I was here, with the true dead. Here to call one of them from the grave. It was the only moment that all of me could be free.

I stood there for a minute with my power spilling, cool and seeking, like a wind, except that this wind didn't move your hair, it only crept along your skin. It was like I'd been holding my breath, tight, so tight, and finally I could let it out, let it all out, and relax. Once I'd stopped being afraid of it, it felt so good to be with the dead. Peaceful, so peaceful, because whatever was left in the grave had nothing to do with souls or pain. *Quiet as the grave* wasn't just a saying. But I'd forgotten that there were dead near at hand that weren't underground.

My power touched Requiem. It should have ignored him, but it didn't. That cool not-wind curled around him like the arms of some long-lost lover. I'd never felt anything quite like it. For the first time I truly understood that my power was over the dead, all the dead, and that undead is still dead. I'd always thought, and been told, that vampires killed necromancers for fear that they would be controlled by them, but in that second, I knew that wasn't the whole truth. It was as if a door opened inside me, to a room that I hadn't known existed. Inside that metaphysical room stood something. It had no shape that my eye could see, no weight, nothing to touch, nothing to hold, but it was there, and it was real, and it was me, mine, sort of. A 'power plateau' Byron and Requiem had called it, but that wasn't it. Plateau is static, not growing, not changing. This wasn't static.

It blew out toward me, and if it had been a real room in a real house, the house would have exploded outward with the force of its coming. It would have roared outward in a blizzard of wood and glass and metal, and there would have been nothing standing in that metaphysical yard, except ground zero of some mysterious blast.

It was inside me, so it couldn't slam into me, that was silly, but that's still what it did. It slammed into me, and for a second I was blind, deaf, weightless, nothingness. There was nothing but the rawness of that power.

I came to, with Graham's voice. 'Anita, Anita, can you hear me? Anita!' I felt him holding me, knew we were on top of the grave. I could feel the grave, could feel Edwin Alonzo Herman lying underneath me. All I had to do was call his name.

'Something's wrong, Requiem.'

'No,' he said, and that one word was enough. I opened my eyes and saw the vampire standing over me.

'She's awake,' Graham said, and he tried to cradle me into a sitting position, but I lifted my hand up toward Requiem.

The vampire reached down for me, and I reached for him. Graham helped, by pushing me upright, but he wasn't there for me in that moment. My business was with the dead, and Graham was too warm for me. The blood I wanted was slow and thick, and holding its hand out to me.

Requiem's fingers brushed mine, and the power inside me steadied, as if the world had been trembling, and now it was still. I touched his hand in that sudden stillness, and there was no pulse in his palm. No beat of blood to distract the senses. He blinked at me, his lips moved, but he did not breathe. He was still. He was dead. He was mine.

He pulled me to my feet, and we stood on the foot of the grave, hand in hand. I looked up into that face, met the turquoise flame of his eyes, but it wasn't me that was pulled into his gaze. It was he that fell into mine, and I knew, because I had a glimpse from his mind to mine, that my eyes were solid pools of black with stars glittering in them. It was the way my eyes had looked when Obsidian Butterfly, a vampire that thought she was an Aztec goddess, had shown me some of her power. She was powerful enough that no one argued with her about whether or not she was deity. Some things aren't worth the fight. I'd used the power I'd learned from her only twice, and both times my eyes had filled with stars.

The night was suddenly less dark. I could see details, colors, things that my own eyes could never have seen. Requiem's shirt was so green it seemed to burn like his eyes. It was a kind of hyperfocus, and it wasn't just sight. His hand in mine felt heavier than it should have, more important than it should have, as if I could feel each whorl of his fingertip like tiny silken lines against my hand. To make love like this would either be the most wondrous experience of your life, or drive you mad.

I remembered this power, but it wasn't what I needed. I had another flash from Requiem's mind, a tiny flash of fear, quieted almost immediately, because I was touching him and I didn't want him to be afraid. The stars in my eyes drowned in a rush of flame, black flame with a center of brown, as if wood were the flame, and fire what it ate.

My eyes were, for a moment, what they'd be if I'd been a vampire. They filled with dark, dark brown light, so dark it was almost black. I turned those glowing eyes toward the grave, and Graham saw them.

'Oh, God,' he whispered.

'Get off the grave, Graham,' I said, and my voice was mine, almost. He just knelt on the ground and stared up at me.

'Move, Graham,' I said, 'you won't want to be there when I'm finished.'

He scrambled to his feet and moved, until I told him, 'Good enough.' He stayed close, eyes wide, fear like a scent off of his skin, but he didn't run, and he didn't try to distance himself. Brave boy.

I knelt on the hard ground and drew Requiem down with me, so that he knelt behind me with his hands on my shoulders. He was like some huge solid wall of quiet strength behind me. I'd known that I amplified Jean-Claude's powers when I was near him, but I'd never felt anything like what was happening now. It wasn't a triumvirate of power between Requiem and me, it was that he was one of Jean-Claude's vampires, and that made him mine in a way. Mine to call on, mine to use, mine to reward.

I bent until my hands touched the ground, until I could feel the dead just below me. It was as if the ground were water, and I knew there was someone drowning just below me, and all I had to do was reach down and save them.

I whispered, 'Edwin Alonzo Herman, hear me.' I felt him stir, like a sleeper disturbed by a dream. 'Edwin Alonzo Herman, I call you from your grave.' I felt his bones grow long and straight, felt his flesh coalesce around him. It was like restuffing a broken doll. He remade himself, and it was so easy, too easy. The power began to spread outward, began to seek another grave, but some small part of me that was still me, knew better. It wouldn't be just one more grave. I knew in that instant that I could raise this cemetery. That I could raise them all. No blood sacrifice. No chickens. No goats. Nothing, but the power blowing through me, and the vampire at my back. Because the power wanted to be used. It wanted to help me, help me caress them all from their graves, pull them to the light of stars, and fill them with . . . life. It would feel so good to lift them all up, so good.

I shook my head and fought that helpful power. Fought not to spread like a sweet sickness through the graves. Fought to hold on to what was left of who I'd thought I was. I needed help. I thought about Jean-Claude, but that wasn't it. I needed to remember that I wasn't just the dead. I was alive.

I reached out to the other third of our triumvirate. I reached out to Richard. He looked up at me as if I hovered in the air above his family's dining-room table. I saw his father like an older clone of Richard himself, and most of his brothers, sitting at the table, passing a blue bowl. Charlotte, his mother, came in from the kitchen's swinging door just behind that chair. She was still about my size, with honey-blond hair and a figure that was both petite and full-figured. Except for the hair color and skin tone, Charlotte even reminded me of me. There was a reason that most of the Zeeman brothers had chosen small, tough women. I watched her bring in a big platter, smiling, chatting with her family. I couldn't hear what she was saying, or any noise from the crowded, smiling family scene. They all seemed so happy, so perfect. I didn't want to bring this here.

I started to pull away, and Richard's voice was in my head. 'Wait, wait, Anita, please.' He excused himself from the table and walked through the big living room, out onto the sweep of porch, and down the handful of steps until he could gaze up into the same sky that rode above me. By the time he gazed up into the air, gazed at me, he seemed to have sensed some of what was happening, because he said, 'Dear God, Anita, what's happened? I've felt your power before, but not like this.'

I didn't have enough control to talk in my head, so Requiem was going to get the out loud version, but I was past caring. 'The vampires keep saying that we've hit a new power level.'

He hugged his bare arms in the T-shirt. He hadn't stopped for a jacket. 'It's like the night is breathing your power. What can I do?'

'Remind me that I'm not dead. Remind me that my ties are with things that have a heartbeat.'

'How will that help?'

I wanted to scream my frustration at him. 'God, Richard, just help me, please help. If you don't, I'm afraid of what I'll raise in this cemetery tonight.'

He nodded. 'I'm sorry, I'm sorry for so much, Anita.' He looked down, and I knew the gesture, he was thinking, or gathering his will for something. Usually something he didn't want to do. But I didn't have time to worry about Richard's hangups tonight. I was too scared of the power that pulsed in the ground underneath me. A cold pulsing, but it promised to spread to all the graves. I knew that tonight I could raise one of those shambling zombie armies that the movies are so fond of portraying, and usually has nothing to do with real necromancy.

He looked back at the house and said, 'I'm fine, Mom. I just need a little privacy. Keep everybody close to the house, okay.' He shook his head. 'No, Mom, it's not that close to the full moon.'

He walked out into the openness of the yard away from the lights of the house and he let down his shields – the metaphysical walls that kept his beast caged and helped him pass for human. The night was suddenly alive in a way that it hadn't been. The still air held a thousand scents: the ripeness of apples from the orchard behind the house; grass like a thick green blanket against our face; trees, the spicy tang of sweet gum, the softer scent of birch, the sweet pungent wood of poplar, and over it all, the dry richness of fallen leaves all around us. Sounds, then. The last crickets of the year chirping their plaintive song. Other insects from the woods, singing their last songs before the cold came. The wind raised, and the trees creaked and groaned around the house. The big oak by the driveway threw its branches against the stars, and Richard raised his head to watch that wild wind. There was barely a breeze on the ground, but up high in the highest trees, the wind ran fast and pulled at the bare limbs at the very top of the trees. Most people don't look up, animals look up, because they know that there is no true safety. They don't worry about it the way we do, but they're aware of it in a way that we aren't.

Richard walked into the edge of trees that began the woods that bordered the western edge of the family land. He touched a trunk, laid his hands on it, and it was rough and hard, with deep grooves in the bark like tiny tunnels. He laid his face against that roughness, and it was spicy and pungent, and I knew it was sweet gum. He gazed up into the bare branches where the tiny rough balls still hung on to the edges of the tree. He hugged the tree, hugged it so tight that the bark dug into his skin, he rubbed his cheek against the roughness of it, like he was scent marking, then he was off. He was running at an easy lope through the trees, into the woods. He wasn't hunting. He was running for the joy of it.

He twisted through the underbrush like it wasn't there. And as I'd felt only once before, it was as if the trees and bushes welcomed him, or turned aside for him, or as if green growth could be water, and he dived through it, running, dodging, twisting, giving himself to the brush of twigs and branches and the feel of the living ground underfoot. There was life that didn't run or hide, it was all alive, alive in a way that most humans never understand.

Richard ran, and he took me with him, as he had one night long ago. Then he'd held my hand, and I'd struggled to keep up, to understand. Now it was effortless, because I was inside his head, inside him. The night was alive for him in a way that it wasn't for Jean-Claude, or for me. I was too human, and Jean-Claude's interest in life was too shallow. Neither of us could feel what Richard's beast could give him.

Something touched my hand, and I was jerked back to the grave. Requiem was still at my back, dead still, but Graham was on the grave. He looked uncertain, but he was sniffing the air near my skin. 'You smell like trees and pack,' he said softly.

Richard looked up at us. 'Why is Graham there?'

'Bodyguard. Jean-Claude was afraid of what would happen if I didn't have someone with me.'

'Tell him he's supposed to guard you, and he can't do that on the grave.'

'You're supposed to guard me, Graham, you can't do that from here.' The sharp scent of wolf thickened around me as I said it.

Graham reacted to it like he'd been struck. He cringed to the ground, doing the wolf grovel. 'I'm sorry, you just smelled so good. I forgot myself.'

'Stop groveling and get back to work.' Richard said it first, and I echoed it for him.

Graham did what he was told. He went back to very serious bodyguard mode, looking out into the dark for whatever might come.

Richard took in a deep breath, and I smelled that thick, sweet scent of deep woods. He'd run miles, effortlessly, not for the same reason that a human will run well, but because the land itself helped him run, gave him strength, welcomed him.

He stood there in the middle of the woods, his feet anchored into the ground. I realized that Richard was my ground, my center, his joy, his heart pumping in his chest from that joyous run. I kept my tie to him open and full of scents and sounds and things faraway from here. I put my hands on the grave, and even with Requiem at my back, touching me, it wasn't as real as the pounding of Richard's heart miles away.

'Edwin Alonzo Herman, with will, word, and flesh, I call you from your grave. Come, come now!' It was all wrong, all different from usual, but it was right just the same.

I felt the corpse shift, solidify, piece itself together like a puzzle, and begin to rise up through the earth as if it were water. I'd watched this happen countless times, but I'd never been kneeling on the ground when it happened. The earth buckled and rolled like an earthquake that was trapped in a few feet of ground. The ground flowed under my hands like it was something else, not water, not mud, but something both less and more solid. I don't know what Requiem thought was happening, but he didn't try to pull away, he stayed solid at my back. He rode it with me and never made a noise. Brave vampire.

Hands met mine through the shifting earth, cool fingers wrapped around my warmth. Edwin Alonzo Herman's hands wrapped around mine like a swimmer who's given up hope and finally touches a rope. The grave threw him upward like a flower springing free of the earth, but the push of it forced me to pull him upward, to find my feet with Requiem steadying me. If the vampire hadn't been there to hold me standing on the writhing, twisting ground, I would have fallen. But Requiem kept me standing, and I pulled the dead man from his grave, pulled him perfect and whole, until he stood taller than me, with the grave dirt falling away from a perfect black suit that looked as if it had been freshly pressed. His hair was balding with a thick fringe just above the ears and down the collar, and thick sideburns that curved to a walrus thick mustache. He was portly, nearly fat, which had been in style among the rich. When Edwin Alonzo died, only the poor were skinny, only the poor looked starved.

I felt Richard still standing by the edge of that small stream. The air was cooler by that musical run, and his pulse was beginning to slow from the run, the light sweat starting to cool on his skin. He wasn't afraid, or horrified. He simply stood rooted to the ground, steadying me with the pulse and beat of his body, the thick musk of wolf faint in the autumn air.

I stared up at the zombie, and even to me, it looked like damn good work. With a big enough blood sacrifice I could raise a zombie that looked alive, close at least, but this, this was perfect. His skin looked full and healthy in the starlight. He had a faint smile on his face, and his clothes looked as if he'd just put them on. Even his shoes were near spotless and gleaming with polish. Polish so shiny I noticed by moonlight. The hands that were pressed to mine were cool, but they didn't feel dead. He wasn't breathing, but he looked, felt, more alive than dead. It was unnerving. I'd known there was a lot of power tonight, and I'd had to force all of it into this one grave, so I guess it was alright that he looked this good, but for a moment when I looked into that plump, smiling face, I was afraid. Afraid that I'd done more than I'd been paid for, but when I reached his eyes, I let out a sigh of relief. The eyes were thick and full and looked, again, perfect, grayish in the starlight, probably would be blue in the brighter light, but there was no one home in those eyes. They were empty and waiting. I knew what they were waiting for, those empty eyes.

I lifted my left hand away from the zombie's, and he didn't cling to me, his fingers just opened as I moved. I held my hand at shoulder level, toward the vampire at my back. 'Undo my bandage.'

Requiem kept one hand on my shoulder, but used the other hand to peel back the tape on my wrist.

'Take it off,' I said.

He finally ripped the bandage away. I couldn't stop a small jerk of pain.

Richard called inside my head, 'What are you going to do?'

'He needs blood, so he can speak. I didn't kill an animal. This is all the blood I've got.'

He didn't say anything, but I felt his pulse begin to pick up speed.

I offered my wrist upward to the slightly taller body in front of me. Something slid through those pale eyes, something I'd seen before in the better preserved zombies. It was as if something went through them, something that paused in their eyes, as if there were darker things waiting, waiting for a chance for a body to inhabit. Something, not so much evil, as just very, very not good. But that whiskered face turned toward my wrist, sniffed the air, and the moment it scented the blood, that otherness in its eyes vanished. Driven out by the promise of something that all the dead value, a bit of the living.

The zombie grabbed my arm with both of its hands and smacked its mouth against my wrist like you'd grab a kiss from your dearest lover. Just the impact hurt the wound, made me gasp. But I knew what was coming, because I'd fed zombies off my own blood before. Not often, but often enough. The mouth locked around the wound, and his mouth was wide enough to take it all in, to set his teeth against the torn edges, and grind. I made a small sound, because I couldn't make no sound. Usually the zombie's mouth felt less real than this one. Except for how cool the flesh was, I couldn't tell the difference between the zombie and a person. It was a very good job, solid all the way through, even in places that only I would feel.

Richard bounded across the stream, hitting the edge of it with one foot, as if he wasn't quite steady. He began to run up the other bank, began to run with the night and the trees and the smells.

Edwin Alonzo Herman's mouth locked around my wrist and began to suck. The wound had begun to heal more than I'd realized, because to get to the blood, he had to pull hard and tight on my wrist. It hurt, really hurt. Yeah, I liked teeth in the right situation, but this wasn't it, and what might feel good during sex just fucking hurts during violence.

Richard was running full out now. I'd thought he was fast before, but he'd just been playing. Now, he ran. He ran so fast that branches slashed at him, that the earth didn't give to him, and part like water. He was running, running . . . running from himself. I had a bright glimpse inside his head. The sensation of teeth in my wrist, of that forceful mouth on my wound excited him. Excited him as both man and beast. He could have accepted if it was just about food, but it wasn't. The mixture of human and animal blurred the differences between food and sex. Blurred so many lines. Lines that Richard had never known existed, let alone wanted to cross.

He ran, and slipped in the leaves, and fell and was on his feet and running before his body had time to realize it was down. It was only in that moment that I remembered his injured shoulder, and the thought got me the memory, he'd shapeshifted, briefly, and healed himself. So much more powerful than he wanted to be.

The zombie had fallen to his knees, as if sucking at my wrist was the most exquisite thing it had ever tasted. It cradled my wrist against its mouth, and its tongue explored the wound.

My breath came out in a harsh word, 'Shit!'

'Are you hurt?' Requiem asked softly.

I shook my head. It hurt, but I wasn't hurt. There was a difference, but usually a zombie starts to slow down about now. This one was still sucking hard and fast, as if he were a baby that had been starved. Of course, I'd never raised anyone this long dead without an animal sacrifice. Maybe that was the difference? I hoped so, because anything else would mean that something had gone wrong, really wrong.

He shook his mouth like a dog with a bone, and I swallowed a scream. It wasn't just that it hurt. That was way too much enthusiasm for a zombie. 'Edwin, stop feeding.' My voice was clear, and he ignored me. Shit. I licked suddenly dry lips. 'He's had enough.

Help me pry him loose,' I said, voice low. Mustn't scare the clients. Mustn't let them know that everything had gone wrong tonight.

Richard fell again, slid in the damp autumn leaves, slid until a tree stopped him, sudden, and abrupt and bruising. He looked up, and I saw those wide brown eyes, saw what he was running from. He wanted to be there on his knees, he wanted to lick my wound, taste my blood, maybe widen that wound with sharp teeth. The thought didn't just excite him. The thought did it for him, just flat did it for him. What he wanted to do in the deepest, darkest, places in his soul gave a whole new meaning to oral sex.

He waited for me to be horrified, but I wasn't. If there was anyone who could resist doing the great bad thing, it was Richard. I trusted his control, not always his temper, but his control — that I trusted without doubt or reservation. I whispered, 'Just because you want to do something, doesn't mean you will do it, or even that you have to do it. You're human, Richard, you have a mind and willpower. You aren't just your beast.'

'You don't understand,' he said, and the moment he said it, I knew what he'd done, by accident.

'You can feel what the zombie is doing?' I said.

He hid his face from me and scrambled to his feet, and ran. He ran out of the trees, and hit a paved road, and was across it before the headlights could be sure what they'd seen. Fast, faster, run, run. Run, but what he was running from, he couldn't outrun, because no matter how fast, or how far, he would still be there. How do you outrun the monster, when you are the monster?

'Richard, make the zombie stop feeding on me.'

'I don't know how,' and he was gone, crashing through the trees, but it wasn't friendly now, or joyous.

The zombie bit me, hard, and damn it, it hurt. 'Requiem, get him off of me.'

The vampire moved around so he could touch the zombie's face and hands, but nothing holds on like a zombie. I'd had to help clean up other people's zombies that had gone wrong, and sometimes you had to cut them apart a finger at a time to get them to let go of someone. Human teeth could still bite deep enough to sever a vein or artery. I wanted him off of me.

Requiem tried to pry him off, but he finally looked up at me. 'I can pull him apart in pieces, but I cannot pull him off of you.'

I looked at the very bodyguarding werewolf and called him over. He came, face serious, hands behind his back, as if he didn't exactly trust himself not to touch me again. Did I smell of wolf and forest, or was it the fresh blood? Don't ask unless you want to know. I didn't want to know.

The zombie plunged his tongue into the wound, as if he were trying to get the blood to flow faster. It hurt, and it surprised me, and I screamed, a little scream, but enough that one of the lawyers called, 'Are you alright, Ms Blake?'

'Fine,' I called back, 'fine.' Mustn't let the clients know that the zombie you raised for them is beginning to eat you. Fuck!

Using every ounce of strength he had, Graham was able to pry one finger off of my wrist, but he had to hold on to that finger, or it curled right back into place. 'He shouldn't be this strong.'

'You've never tried to fight zombies, have you?' I said.

He gave me wide eyes. 'If they're this strong, I don't want to.'

'They're not just strong, they don't feel pain.'

'Anita, I can tear his fingers off,' Requiem said, 'or break his jaw, but other than those extremities, I have no other suggestions.'

The bad part was, neither did I. The zombie bit me harder, and I knew it was only a matter of time before he hit something major. He was digging his teeth in deeper by the tiniest of increments, but eventually it was going to get bad, and I was no longer sure what would happen if a gush of fresh blood hit its mouth. I'd seen what flesh-eating zombies could do to people. I wasn't exactly human, but I wouldn't grow back a hand if you ripped it off.

We could burn him up, but he wouldn't let go, and I'd burn with him. Shit.

Richard was sitting in a clearing under a tangle of naked limbs. 'I have to shut the link between us, Anita. I have to. I can't separate myself from the zombie. I keep feeling what he's doing. Keep wanting him to find more blood.' He cradled his face in his hands, and he'd lost his shirt somewhere, so that his back was bowed and naked as the trees overhead. 'I'm sorry, Anita, I tried, I really tried.'

'It's okay, Richard, we'll do what we can from here. Go take care of yourself.'

He looked up, and there were tears shining in the starlight. 'I'm supposed to take care of you.'

'It's a partnership, Richard, we're supposed to take turns helping each other.'

He shook his head. 'I fucked this up, Anita, I'm sorry.' I wasn't sure I'd ever heard him say fuck when he wasn't referring to sex.

'Go, Richard, go back to your folks' house. They'll be worried.'

The zombie bit hard enough that I screamed, and Richard was suddenly gone. He cut the tie so abruptly that it staggered me, and only Requiem's and Graham's hands kept me from falling.

'Anita!' Graham said, and he lost his grip on the zombie, trying to keep me standing. But the hands on my wrists eased.

I looked down at the kneeling zombie, and the eyes were filling up. There was personality there, someone home. I'd been stupid. Richard had accidentally tied the zombie to him, and when he broke the link to me, the zombie was mine again. Good news, but I felt stupid that I hadn't thought of it sooner. The dead are supposed to be my specialty. I wasn't feeling very special tonight.

The zombie blinked up at me, drawing its mouth back from my wrist. His big mustache was stained with my blood. He frowned up at me. 'I'm sorry, I don't know what I'm doing here.' He let me go and stumbled to his feet, staring at his hands and my bloody wrist, horror showing on his face. 'I beg your pardon, miss, I don't know what I was doing to you. I do apologize most sincerely, it's monstrous, monstrous.' He was staring at the blood on his hands and wiping at his mouth.

Shit, he didn't know he was dead. I hated when they didn't know they were dead. And as if on cue he backed up enough to bump into his own monument. He gazed up at that uncompromising stone angel, and then he had the Ebenezer Scrooge moment. He saw his own name on the tomb, complete with a date. Even by starlight, all the color drained from his face.

'Hear me, Edwin, by right of the blood you have tasted, hear me.'

He turned huge, stricken eyes to me. 'Where am I? What's happened to me?'

'Don't be afraid, Edwin, be calm.'

The panic began to slide away from his face, his eyes began to fill with that artificial calm, because I willed it, and because I'd been the one to call him from the grave, and it was my blood on his lips. I'd earned the right to order him around.

I told him to be calm. I told him to be clear and concise and answer the questions from the nice lawyers. He informed me that he was always clear and concise thank you very much, and I knew he'd do what the lawyers and his descendants wanted him to do. This group of lawyers and clients had decided ahead of time that they didn't want me asking the questions. Something about not trusting that I couldn't control the zombie enough to get the answers that certain people wanted. The implication had been that some of the clients feared that other clients would bribe me. At the time they'd set the guidelines down, I'd been a little offended, tonight I was glad. It meant that I could go back to the Jeep while they questioned the zombie. I had a first aid kit in the Jeep, and I needed it.

The zombie hadn't exactly reopened the wound, he'd made the old wound bloodier, and put new teeth marks into my wrist. So it was like a new wound around the old one. Some nights it feels like

I have a target on my left arm. If I take a major hit, that's usually where it lands.

'You've lost more blood,' Requiem said.

'No shit,' I said.

He gave a small frown. 'What I am saying is, could you not allow them to take the zombie home for the night and put him back tomorrow?'

I shook my head and winced as Graham raised the gauze to see if the bleeding had stopped. 'He bit me, he actually injured me, zombies aren't supposed to do that. They take blood from an open wound or animal that's already dead, but they don't make a wound. They don't feed that actively.'

'This one sure as hell did,' Graham said, frowing at my wrist and putting pressure and a fresh gauze pad back on it.

'Exactly, so much is going wrong tonight, or not working exactly like it's supposed to, that I can't risk letting it have that much time. I have to put it back tonight, as soon as possible.'

'Why?' Requiem asked.

'Just in case,' I said.

'In case what?' Graham asked, this time.

'In case it becomes a flesh eater.'

They both looked at me, like you've got to be kidding. 'I thought that was like legend,' Graham said.

'I have seen such things,' Requiem said. 'Long, long ago. I thought that the power to do such,' he seemed to think what word to use and settled for, 'things, was lost.'

'*Evil*, you were going to say, power to do such *evil*, was lost.'

He gave me a faint smile. 'My apologies,' he said.

'That's alright, nobody likes necromancers. Christian, Wiccan, vampires, whatever, nobody likes us.'

'It is not that we do not like you,' Requiem said.

'No,' I said, 'it's that everybody's afraid of us.'

'Yes,' the vampire said, softly.

I sighed. 'Tonight for the first time I felt that I could have raised this entire cemetery without a sacrfice of any kind. I could have raised them, and they would have been mine, totally mine. I contacted Richard, because I was fighting the urge to raise my own personal army of the dead.'

'Contacting your Ulfric went very wrong, from what I understood from your side of the conversation,' Requiem said.

Graham said, 'He tried to help.'

'Yeah, he did, but just as Jean-Claude and I are gaining powers, so is Richard. Neither of us expected him to be able to link up with the zombie.'

'I have never heard of such a thing,' Requiem said.

'We're a u-fucking-nique bunch here in St Louis,' I said.

'Unique,' Requiem said, as he and Graham began to bandage my arm. 'Well, that is one way of putting it.'

'How about scary?' I said.

He looked at me with those blue, blue eyes with their hint of green from the shirt near his face. 'Oh, yes,' he said, 'oh, yes, scary will do.'

Yeah, scary would do.

41

I CANCELED THE rest of the clients for the night. It had been too close for comfort. I would put this zombie back, but that was it until I figured out what the hell was going on. Bert would be pissed. The clients would be pissed. But not half so pissed as they'd be if I raised a shambling army of the dead and terrorized the city. No, that would be more bad press than even Bert could figure out how to cure.

Besides, I'd finally lost enough blood that I wasn't feeling well. It wasn't metaphysics, it was just physical. I was light-headed, vaguely nauseous, cold even with the leather jacket and a blanket from the back of my Jeep. I'd lost enough blood over the years to know the signs. I didn't need like a transfusion or anything, but I didn't need to lose anymore blood tonight, either. In fact, I'd have Graham drive us back to the club, pick up Nathaniel, and beg off on any big sexy scene tonight. Sex called on account of blood loss. Surely he'd accept that as a good enough excuse.

We were all huddled in the backseat of the Jeep. Me, because I felt like shit. Graham and Requiem because I couldn't get warm on my own. A blanket, the leather jacket, and I was still shivering.

'My lady, may I make a bold suggestion?' Requiem asked.

It took me two tries to stop my teeth from chattering long enough to say, 'Sure.'

'If we do not get you warm, you will be fit for nothing tonight.'

'Just say it, stop –' I shook so hard it almost hurt, when the shuddering passed – 'stop talking me to death, Requiem.'

'Graham under the blanket would double your body heat.' He said it very crisp, no wasted words, it was nice to know he could be concise when he needed to be.

If I could have stopped my teeth from chattering I might have argued, but I couldn't, so I didn't. Besides, a little fully clothed cuddling under a blanket seemed pretty tame after what had happened earlier tonight. What could it hurt? Oh, hell, don't answer that.

Graham was still in his serious bodyguard mode, so he eased under the blanket, as if I'd bite. 'I can't really be security while trapped under a blanket in the backseat,' he said.

It took me three tries to say, 'You carrying?'

'You mean a gun?'

'Yeah.'

'No.'

'If I'm the only one armed, then you ain't my security.'

He looked like he'd argue, and Requiem said, 'There are many ways to guard someone's body, Graham. If we do not help her warm herself, then I fear we will be going to the emergency room with her. Would you like to explain to Jean-Claude how you let that happen, when you could have prevented it with such a small action on your part?'

'No,' Graham said, and eased himself in around my right side. It was as if he were a totally different person from the one that got that taste of orgasm from me earlier. He seemed stiff and uncomfortable. He slid his arm across my shoulders tentatively, awkwardly.

'She will not break, Graham,' Requiem said.

'I've forgotten my job twice tonight. I don't want to do it a third time.'

I snuggled in against the warmth of his body, burrowing under his leather jacket to find where the heat was trapped between his own body and the leather. He was so warm, so incredibly warm.

'God, she fits under my arm.' That arm curled around me, almost reflexively, as if he just couldn't help himself. 'She seems so much bigger when she's moving around, or talking, or doing anything.'

His voice sounded puzzled, and soft. His arm wrapped around me, tucking me close in against the line of his body, and he was right, I did fit. He was around six feet, and I so wasn't. He could have cradled me like a child, and I hated that, but he was so warm, so warm. His body felt almost hot. We were about a week away from full moon, and some lycanthrope's body temperature went up before the change, almost like a fever. Either I was colder than I thought, or Graham was one of the wereanimals that ran hot.

My teeth stopped chattering, and it was as if my muscles began to unclench. I still had small involuntary spasms, but it was better.

'Can I pick you up?' Graham asked, and he sounded like he expected me to say no.

I said, 'Why?'

'You'll be warmer,' he said.

I thought about it. He was probably right, but it would reinforce that I was tiny enough to sit in his lap and cuddle against his chest like a child. I really hated doing shit like that. But he was probably right, it would be warmer. Damn it.

'Yes,' I said, and even to me it didn't sound happy.

'Are you sure?'

'The lady has spoken, Graham, do not make her repeat herself,' Requiem said.

Graham hesitated for a second, then he scooped me up in his arms, like I weighed nothing. He sat me on his lap, and I found another downside to the thong. He must have been wearing new jeans because they weren't soft. I was so not wearing enough underwear, or enough skirt. But I'd dressed mostly for meeting Jean-Claude and Asher later in the evening. I'd been thinking date, not medical emergencies. Silly me.

He was able to curl most of me underneath his jacket against his chest, the rest of me curled into a small ball in his lap, with just a little leg off to one side. He put one of his arms across that spill of leg, and the other arm held the jacket tight around me. Requiem

helped us get the blanket draped around us, and the only thing uncov-
ered was the top of my head. It was dark and warm, and I laid my
head against his chest, and the T-shirt was a thin barrier between
me and the heat of his skin. I let my body ease into the warmth of
his skin, and the scent of leather, and just him. I realized why his
scent seemed so comfortable to me. He smelled like pack, that faint
scent that all of Richard's wolves had. I was too friendly with too
many of them not to equate that faint ruffling musk with safety. I
let myself sink into a warm nest of leather, and blanket, and body,
and shared warmth, and the distant smell of wolf, and I slept.

The next thing I was aware of was Graham's voice, very soft, as
if he didn't really want to wake me. 'Anita, Anita, they're done with
the zombie.'

For a second I couldn't remember where I was, or who was talking
to me. Fresh from sleep, to me his body felt more like Richard's than
anyone else's. The size and the musculature and the faint scent of
musk was all Richard, but the voice didn't match.

'Anita, you are wanted by the graveside.' Requiem's British accent.

The last of sleep and whatever wolf-scented dreams I'd had slipped
away, and I knew where I was and whose lap I'd fallen asleep in.

Graham stroked my hair, and said softly, 'Anita, are you awake?'

I sat up, pushing his arm, his jacket off of me, but we were tangled
in the blanket. I pushed at the soft gray material, but it was caught
at the edges, wedged under his body. I could punch at it, but I couldn't
get free of it. I had one of those moments of claustrophobia that
make no sense. I wasn't actually trapped, but there was something
about being close to trapped with two people that I knew so little
about. If it had been anyone on my list of people that I trusted impli-
citly, it wouldn't have happened. But I didn't know Graham, not
really, and I'd fallen asleep in his arms. I'd fallen asleep with only
him and Requiem to watch over me. Careless, terribly careless.

Maybe it was some remnant of an unremembered dream, or maybe
there is no excuse, but whatever, I lost it. I panicked. If I'd been

thinking clearly, I could have gotten out of a stupid blanket, but I wasn't thinking anymore. My head was screaming, *Trapped, trapped, we're trapped!*

Graham grabbed my arms, and I shoved an elbow back into him as hard as I could.

He let go and made a satisifying *hummph* sound. 'Shit, you'll crack a rib doing that.'

'Don't grab me, okay, just don't grab me.' My voice was breathy, but I was a touch calmer. Calm enough not to fight the stupid blanket. Calm enough not to struggle so that Graham thought something was wrong with me. My pulse was still wild in my throat, like I'd choke on it, but I could think again.

Requiem was there on his knees, looming over both of us. The panic flared through me in a cold wash that left my fingertips tingling with static, but I fought it off this time. I tried to relax as he pulled at the edge of the blanket and started to ease us free.

'I'm sorry,' I said, 'I think I had a bad dream.'

'No shit,' Graham said, and he sounded slightly offended.

I'd apologized once, he wasn't getting it twice. Truth was I'd gotten claustrophobic from two things, a diving accident years ago, and waking up in a vampire's coffin. Waking up in the tight darkness with a dead body wrapped around you. The stuff of nightmares.

There was a look on Requiem's face that was eloquent. He knew I was lying, and I didn't care. I made it policy not to parade my phobias in front of people. Never let people see what really scares you, they may use it against you later.

When he pulled enough blanket, I scrambled out, and was damn rude getting out of the Jeep. But I felt better as soon as I hit the open air. I took in deep breaths of the cool night air. About the time I got myself calmer, my lower body started to be cold. Shit.

'You're shivering again,' Requiem said, from right behind me.

I jumped, because I hadn't heard him slide out of the car. 'I'm alright.'

'No, you are not.'

I frowned at him.

Graham slid out of the backseat. 'He's right.'

I frowned at them both. 'It doesn't matter how I feel. I've got a job to do.'

'Yes, you have a job to do, but how you feel still matters,' Requiem said.

I opened the front door and got my gym bag out of the seat. I didn't leave it graveside because of the machete. The machete might only be magical in my hand, or in another animator's hand, but it was still a damn long blade, and I didn't trust civilians around it.

I shut the door, hit the beeper to lock it, and started walking back to the grave with the bag in hand. I'd gone about four feet into the grass, when I tripped and nearly fell.

Requiem's hand was at my elbow. 'You are not well.'

I stood there and let him steady me. 'I don't know what's wrong with me. Usually raising the dead makes me feel good, better.'

'Tonight did not go as planned.'

I shook my head. 'No, it didn't. Part of that was my fault.'

'No,' he said.

'Yes,' I said, 'I got distracted by all that new power and forgot to put up a protective circle. It keeps the zombie in, but it also keeps other things out. A lot of metaphysical shit likes to mess with bodies, if they get the chance. I knew better.'

'You were distracted.'

'Yeah.'

'Can I carry the bag for you?' Graham asked, though I noticed he was staying just out of reach. I wondered how hard I'd hit him in the ribs. I hadn't hurt him, but I was more than human strong now, and I could have hurt him.

'Yeah, thanks,' I said.

He took the bag and then stood to one side and let Requiem and me go first. The vampire kept his hand on my elbow, and I let him.

I was getting cold again.

'I've lost more blood than this before and not felt this bad,' I said, softly. One group of cars had left the cemetery, the group that had brought the suit. The lawyers from the winning side were at graveside, and there was a cheerful murmur of voices, as the descendants got to talk to their patriarch. He had a big booming laugh.

'Have you fed tonight?' Requiem asked. His voice brought me back to the dark and how far we still had to walk. It seemed like a long way, but it wasn't that far, it just wasn't.

'Yeah, I had dinner.'

He shook his head. 'That is not what I meant.'

I thought about it for a second, or two, then said, 'You mean like the *ardeur*?'

'Yes.'

'Yeah, I fed off of you and Byron.'

'No,' he said, 'you were feeding for Jean-Claude. He got that energy.'

'I guess so. But if the *ardeur* needs feeding it just flares up, and I have to feed.' I put my hand on his arm, because my legs were feeling wobbly.

'Perhaps you have gained more control over it?'

'What does that mean?'

'It means you can go without feeding it, until you choose to feed it.'

I stopped walking and looked up at him. 'What?'

'You have many of the symptoms of a vampire that has not fed enough. The blood lust rules us at first, but once we are masters, then we can go without feeding if we must. We can choose to feed.'

'But I feel like shit.'

'The choice comes with a price,' he said.

'I'm confused,' I said.

'I think it took a great deal more energy from you than it should have to raise this zombie and fight what the Ulfric did by accident.

I think it took energy to defeat Primo. To feed on Byron and myself. I think that took not just physical energy, but mental, as well. You are not a creature of casual lusts, and I think it cost you more than you will admit to feed your master tonight.'

I would have argued the master part, but it was becoming a case of the lady protesting too much. 'So what do I do?'

'You need to feed,' he said simply.

I gave him a look.

He smiled and raised a hand as if to prove he was innocent. 'It does not have to be me, or even Graham. It does not have to be this moment, but it must be soon, Anita. Surely, you feel that.'

I just stood there and stared at him. I'd wished for control of the *ardeur* for so long, and now I had it, sort of. I didn't have to feed unless I wanted to, but if I waited too long, I'd get sick. I shook my head. 'I thought control of the *ardeur* meant you could just skip it and not feed it at all.'

'Who told you that?'

I started to say, Jean-Claude, then stopped. What had he said about the *ardeur*? That I'd gain control of it. That I'd learn how to feed from a distance. Had he ever promised that it would go away? No, he hadn't. I'd just wanted *control* to mean it would be gone. No one had promised that. No one. Shit.

'No one,' I said, 'I just heard it that way. I wanted the *ardeur* to be gone. I wanted it to go away, so I just kept thinking that's what it would mean.'

'I am sorry to be the one to tell you that it is not so.'

I looked at his face, studied it. 'You sound like you know what you're talking about.'

'I do not carry the *ardeur*. To hold the complete *ardeur* as our dark mistress does is very rare, even among her own bloodline.'

'Then how do you know that that's what's happening to me?'

'Logic,' he said, 'and just because I do not carry it, does not mean I have not seen one who did.'

'Who?'

'Ligeia.' He turned away as he said the name so I couldn't see his face.

'I don't know the name, at least not as a vamp.'

'It does not matter, for she is dead.'

I touched his face. 'What happened?' I asked.

He looked at me, but his face held that distance that the old ones have when they don't want you to know what they're thinking. 'Belle Morte killed her.'

'Why do I feel like I should say I'm sorry for asking?'

He gave me the smallest of smiles. 'Because you are not insensitive.'

That one comment let me know that Ligeia's death meant a lot more to him than just another cruel death. She'd meant something to him, and it was none of my business.

'The customers are getting restless,' Graham called back to us. He was standing a little ahead of us with my bag in his hands. He'd given us privacy like a good bodyguard.

I looked past him and saw one of the lawyers waving at us. Restless indeed.

'Even if I was willing, I don't think they'd wait while we went back to the car to feed the *ardeur*.'

He gave me a real smile this time, with enough humor to drive out the blankness in his eyes. 'I fear you are right.'

'Then we muscle through this, and you guys can drive me back to the club.'

'Where your *pomme de sang* waits,' he said.

'Yeah.' I wondered if I was going to get back in time to see any of Nathaniel's dance. I suddenly saw Nathaniel in front of a mirror. He was putting eyeliner around his lavender eyes. He stopped in the middle of it and said, 'Anita?' – a question like he wasn't sure.

Requiem had both my arms now. I'd have gone to my knees, if he hadn't caught me. 'Anita, what happened?'

'I thought about my *pomme de sang*, and I could see him. He's getting ready to go on.' I was dizzy, and when Requiem cradled me against him, I didn't complain. 'I've had mind-to-mind communication with Richard and Jean-Claude. It's never been this draining.'

Requiem picked me up, and again I was wishing I'd worn a longer skirt. God knew what he was flashing the graveside with. But I couldn't stand, the world was swimming. 'Jean-Claude is the master of your triumvirate with the Ulfric, but you are the master of Nathaniel and Damian. It is your power that makes this partnership move, and that, too, uses energy.'

'Does everyone know what happened between the three of us?'

'No, he told only Asher and myself, among his vampires. Perhaps his own *pomme de sang*, Jason. He keeps little from him.'

I frowned at him, as the world stopped spinning. 'Why you?'

'I am his third, after Asher.'

News to me, though of the vamps I'd met, I couldn't think of anyone I'd have preferred for the job. The night was solid again. 'I think I can walk.'

He looked doubtful.

'Let me try,' I said.

He lowered me to the ground, but kept an arm around me like he expected me to collapse at any minute. I guess I couldn't blame him, but it bugged me anyway. I didn't collapse. Great. In fact, I felt pretty good, considering. I kept a hand through his arm, so it looked like he was escorting me the last little bit of the way. Only he and I, and maybe Graham, knew just how shaky I was feeling.

Edwin Alonzo Herman was regaling his audience with a story of how he'd tricked someone into signing away a small fortune. In these modern times it would have been considered swindling, but not back in the late 1800s or even early 1900s. Many of the laws on the books about money and how you can legally acquire it stem from the old robber baron days when almost anything was fair game. Most of the ways that the first millionaires in this country won their fortunes would be illegal today. But Herman had them laughing. He looked positively rosy-cheeked, and very much the center of attention of the group of lawyers and descendants. Everyone was willing to be happy, they'd won, and the man telling the story had helped them win. If someone had saved me millions of dollars, I'd like them, too, I guess.

He finished his story to laughter, and shining faces. 'I'm ready to complete the contract, gentleman, and ladies,' I said.

Some of them had to shake my hand.

'Splendid job, Ms Blake, splendid job.'

'Wow, I mean, like wow.'

'Honestly, I wouldn't have believed it if I hadn't seen you do it.'

Apparently, I was included in the good feelings. Most people get a little uncomfortable when it's time to put the zombie back, if he looks alive enough.

Requiem stopped the compliments. 'Ms Blake has had a difficult night, gentlemen, if you could allow her to finish her work, then she can rest.'

'Oh, terribly sorry . . . We didn't know. Thank you . . . worth every penny.' And they began to drift away.

Edwin Alonzo Herman looked down at me, and it wasn't a friendly look. 'I understand that I am supposed to be dead and only your magic gave me life again.'

I shrugged and asked Graham to please get the machete and the salt from the bag.

'I've also been told that vampires have rights and are considered citizens. Am I not merely another kind of vampire? If I were declared alive, I would be a very, very wealthy man. I would be willing to share that wealth, Miss Blake.'

I clung to Requiem's arm and looked up at the zombie, so self-assured. 'You know, Mr Herman, you're one of the few old ones that I've ever raised that have grasped the possibilities so quickly. You must have been something special in your day.'

'Thank you for the compliment, and may I return one? This must be a unique gift that you have. Together we could turn it into an empire.'

I smiled. 'I have a business manager, but thanks anyway.' I let go of Requiem and found I could stand without falling. Good to know. I was actually feeling a little better just standing on the grave by the zombie, because no matter how good he looked, that's what he was. I took the jar of salt from Graham's hand.

'Miss Blake, if I am only another type of walking dead, then is it fair to deny me the same chance that this vampire has gotten?'

'You're not a vampire,' I said.

'And how great could the difference be between what I am, and what he is?'

I did something that Marianne had tried to teach me, and I just had been too stubborn to try before. I wasn't sure I had enough energy left to walk the circle, so I just pictured it in my mind, like a glowing circle around the grave, around the great stone angel, around all of us. It closed with the same neck-ruffling power rush that it did when I walked it with steel and blood. Good, very good.

'You want a difference, try and walk away from the grave.'

He frowned at me. 'I don't understand.'

'Just walk to the road, where you answered their questions.'

'I don't see what it will prove.'

'It will prove the difference between what you are and what he is.'

Herman frowned at me, then took a deep settling breath and strode off of his grave, toward the road. He hesitated, then slowed, then stopped. 'I seem unable to move forward. I don't know why. I just simply don't seem able to go farther.' He turned back to me. 'Why? Why can I not go where I just stood?'

'Requiem, walk outside the circle.'

He looked at me, then he walked past the man. He hesitated for a moment, and I worried that I'd done too good a job on the circle, but it should have only kept in the zombie, and out other things. The vampire shouldn't have been affected by it. Requiem pushed through, and the circle flared. It did recognize him as a type of undead, but not the one tied to this grave. I realized that with a little tweaking I might be able to throw up a circle that bound a vampire to its grave, or coffin, or a room. It couldn't be kept up forever, but for awhile. I filed it away. It would be a sort of desperation measure, but I'd been desperate before.

Herman pushed against the circle, or rather pushed against his own unwilliness to cross it. Requiem glided back through it, and out again, and in again.

'Enough,' I said, 'I think we've made the point.'

'Why can I not cross this point, and he can?'

'Because this is your grave, Mr Herman, your body knows this ground, and it knows you. It holds you to it, now that I've made it do so. Now come back and stand on the grave like a nice zombie.'

'I am not a zombie.'

'I said, stand on the grave.'

He took a step toward me, before he stopped, and fought me. He fought his body, as he'd fought to cross the circle, now he fought not to come to me. I'd never had one that could fight me when I gave it a direct order, especially not one that had tasted my blood. I watched that well-made body, that so-alive person, struggle not to move closer.

I threw power into the next command, 'Edwin Alonzo Herman come and stand on your grave, now.'

He walked toward me, slowly, jerkily, like a badly made robot. He had to come now, but he was still fighting me. He should not have been able to do that. Even when he stood on the grave, facing us, his body jerked and spasmed, because still he fought my control.

I had the jar of salt open. I handed it to Requiem. 'Just hold it.'

Graham handed me the machete, and suddenly the zombie's eyes went wide. 'What are you going to do with that great knife?' He sounded uncertain, not afraid, he was made of tougher stuff than that.

'It's not for you,' I said. I'd already pushed the sleeves of the leather jacket up above my wrists. Now, I started to lay the machete tip against my arm, but Requiem's hand was suddenly wrapped around the hand holding the machete.

'What are you doing?' he asked.

'I need blood to bind him to his grave. I'd rather do a smaller fresh wound than reopen my left wrist.'

His hand stayed around my wrist. 'You do not need to lose more blood tonight, Anita.'

'I need blood to finish this,' I said.

'Does it have to be yours?' he asked.

'Normally, it's animal blood, but I'm not going to slaughter a chicken just to lay a zombie. The chickens have survived this far. If I spill a little more blood, they can make it through the night.'

'Would my blood do?' he asked.

I frowned at him. 'You're seriously not going to let me do this without an argument, are you?'

'No,' he said.

I sighed, and relaxed my arm just a little to save muscle cramp. He kept his grip on the arm with the machete. 'I've used vampire blood by accident, but it went a little . . . odd. I don't need more odd tonight, Requiem.'

'Will his do?' He pointed at Graham.

'Will my what do?' Graham asked.

'Your blood,' Requiem said, as if it was an everyday request.

'How much blood?' Graham asked, as if it wasn't the first time he'd been asked.

'Just enough to touch the face, sprinkle or smear.'

'Okay,' Graham said, 'I agree that you don't need to lose more blood tonight. If mine will do, then okay. Where will you make the cut?'

'Lower arm, but above the wrist, less risk of hitting something that'll bleed too freely. Also a wound in the wrist hurts more, because of all the movement that goes through it.'

He stripped out of his jacket and tossed it on the ground behind him.

I looked up into his face, searched it for some sign that he felt used, or abused. I didn't see that. He looked like he said he was, okay with it.

'The look on your face,' he said. 'Really, it's okay. It's not like I don't donate blood on a regular basis.'

'Your neck and arms are clean,' I said, 'no bite marks.'

'There are other places to donate from, Anita, you should know that.'

I blushed, which was bad, since I didn't have enough blood to spare. There were other places to donate from, most of them intimate. 'You someone's *pomme de sang*?' I asked.

'No, not yet.'

'What does not yet mean?'

'It means that some of my brethren are hesitant to commit themselves to a single wolf, when your Ulfric has suddenly decided to share such bounty,' Requiem said.

'He asked for volunteers,' I said.

'Oh, I'm willing,' Graham said, 'I just don't like going around advertising the fact. Besides,' he said, and he put his hands on his hips, palms flat, 'it is a wild,' he smoothed his hands down his jeans, 'ride,' until his hands touched either side of his groin, 'when they feed,' and his hands formed a frame of fingers and thumbs around the bulge in his pants, 'down low.'

My gaze had followed his hands the whole way, like I was mesmerized. I think I was just tired. I blinked and tried to concentrate on what we needed to do. I was not going to feel well until I'd fed, but I also wasn't feeding on anyone standing here. Nathaniel was waiting back at the club, and so was Jean-Claude. I had people who were willing, now that I could say no to the *ardeur* until I chose, I didn't have to depend on the kindness of strangers.

'Fine, hold out an arm. I'd recommend it be your nondominant arm.' I had the machete in my hand. I'd made small cuts in the arms of other animators when we shared power so we could raise a bigger or older zombie. I choked up my hold on the hilt and held out my other hand for his arm. He tried to give me his hand, and I had to say, 'No, I'll hold your wrist to help steady us both.'

'Have it your way,' he said, and he let me grip his wrist in my left hand. Normally this was quick, but my hands were shaking tonight. It's not good to be cutting on people when your hands are shaking. I blew out all the breath in my body, as if I were aiming down the barrel of a gun, and pressed the edge of the tip against his arm. I had to take a breath and did the downstroke as I breathed out. I was slower than I would have been if I'd felt steadier. I was working on not going too deep, rather than not causing pain.

He hissed, 'Shit,' under his breath.

Blood welled out, almost black in the starlight. Not a lot of blood, just a trickle along the edge of the cut. The blood began to glide out of the wound, and I rubbed my fingers through it. I turned with my fingers stained with Graham's blood, turned to the zombie still waiting on the grave.

'Don't touch me with that,' he said, and he recoiled away from me.

'Stand still, very still,' I said, and he froze in place, unable to move, or back away. Only his eyes showed, wide and frightened.

I had to stand on tiptoe to touch his face, and Requiem was at my arm, as I wobbled. 'With blood I bind you to your grave,' I said.

Herman's eyes didn't get one bit less frightened.

I raised the machete up, and he made small protesting sounds, because I'd told him not to move and he couldn't scream. I tapped him with the flat of the machete. 'With steel I bind you to your grave.'

I spoke to Requiem, 'The salt now.'

He turned and got the open jar that he'd laid down by the foot of the grave. He held it out toward me. I took a handful of salt, and I'd used the wrong hand and gotten blood in the white crystals. All the salt would have to be dumped. Damn it.

I turned to the frightened zombie and threw the salt on him. 'With salt I bind you to your grave.' I waited for what should happen next, and prayed that this part, at least, would go like normal.

The fear, and fierce personality in those pale eyes began to fade, to leak away, until he stood open-eyed, but empty. His eyes were the eyes of the dead.

Relief poured through me, because if his eyes hadn't gone dead, then we'd have had more problems on our hands than I wanted for tonight. But he was just a zombie, a really good, well-made zombie, but just a zombie. Yeah, he'd fought me, but he was just dead clay, like all the others.

'With blood, steel, and salt, I bind you to your grave, Edwin Alonzo Herman, go, rest, and walk no more.'

He lay down on the ground like it was a bed, and then he simply sank into the ground. I moved us off the grave, so that that heaving, shifting earth settled around him, without us having to go along for the ride. When it was over, the ground was undisturbed. It looked as it had when we'd first walked up, like an old grave in an old cemetery.

'Wow,' Graham said into the silence, 'wow.'

'Wow, indeed,' Requiem said, 'you are very good at this.'

'Thanks. There are aloe baby wipes in the Jeep for cleaning up. First aid kit for Graham, then get me back to the club.'

'As my lady commands, so shall it be done.'

I looked at the tall vampire and frowned at him. 'There's going to come a time between us when I'm going to ask you to do something and you won't say that.'

'How can you be certain of that?' he asked, and offered me his arm for the walk back to the Jeep. Graham was already packing everything up, except the machete, which I had cleaned with a rag for that purpose, and was oiling down with a cloth that I'd bought for the occasion. The two rags lived in the same bag, until one got bloody. Then it went in the trash. Organization is the key.

'Because, eventually, everyone says no.'

'You are terribly young to be so cynical,' he said.

'It's a gift,' I said and put the machete back in its sheath, and that went on top of the bag that Graham had waiting. He was awfully efficient for a werewolf.

'No,' Requiem said, 'it is not. It is something learned through harsh experience.'

Speaking of harsh experience, I had to check something. I knelt on the now pristine grave. I laid a hand on the hard ground.

'What are you doing, Anita?' Requiem asked.

'This zombie fought me more than most. It seemed more . . . real. I'm just checking to make sure that it is back to being bones and rags.'

'Why, what happens if he isn't?' Graham asked.

I closed my eyes and opened just a little of that metaphysical hand that I'd had to squeeze back into a fist. 'Then the zombie would be trapped down there, thinking, aware, but imprisoned. He won't rot. He can't die.' I thrust my power into that cold ground. It was quiet down there, peaceful again. Bones and rags were all that lay underneath. Good.

'Could you really trap someone like that?' Graham asked.

'I don't know for sure, but I don't want to take the chance. I wouldn't want to leave anyone down there like that.' I dusted my hands off.

'Is it okay?' Graham asked.

'Yeah, just bones.'

'Vampires do not die when buried, either,' Requiem said. 'There have been accidents where new vampires were buried too deep, or those that were appointed to retrieve them failed.'

Graham shuddered. 'That's just creepy.'

I stood and I almost fell. Requiem caught me, steadied me. 'Is that buried alive stuff what they tell bad little vampires?'

He looked at me, and there were suddenly centuries of pain in those eyes. 'I, too, have learned from harsh experience.'

'Just get me to Guilty Pleasures, and we'll try to avoid adding tonight to the harsh list.'

'As my lady commands,' he said, smiling, and offering his arm. I took his arm and let him walk me to the Jeep, because I wasn't sure I could have walked that far without falling over. I didn't feel well enough to mark Nathaniel in public. I felt weak and ill, and didn't want to be part of the show, but I also needed to feed, and he'd be furry after the show. Choices, choices, too many damn choices, and not enough options.

42

I WAS COLD by the time we got to the Jeep. Graham had to drive, and I wouldn't ride without a seat belt, so we worked out a compromise. I rode in the backseat with the blanket, and Requiem did his best to cuddle with me while I was strapped into the seat. Which was a lot harder than it sounded.

He started with his arm around my shoulders, his body pressed as close to my side as he could get. The blanket spread over us. He was warm, warm with the blood he'd taken from me, but his wasn't the heat of the werewolf, and sitting side-by-side wasn't as warm as sitting in someone's lap. By the time we'd pulled out of the cemetery I was shivering. A mile or so down Gravois and my body started to do those little involuntary spasms.

Requiem gripped my hand under the blanket. 'Your hand is cool to the touch.'

'Yeah,' I said.

He wrapped his arms tighter around me, and the blanket slid off. He grabbed it, tried to spread it back over us both. 'Allow me to unbelt you. Allow me to hold you as Graham did.'

'If –' and I had to fight past chattering teeth – 'we get in an accident, I could die.'

'It is true you are no vampire and couldn't survive a car crash, but it is also true that a vampire that goes too long without a feeding, cannot die. They may whither, as a grape upon the vine, but they will spring back to plump, ripe, life with the first taste of blood. I fear that you will not.'

My teeth began to chatter as if I was sitting on snow instead of in a car with the heater on high and a warm man wrapped around me. I was so cold that my muscles were beginning to ache from it.

'Allow me at least to cover more of your body with my own. I know you felt that the position lacked a certain dignity, but allow me this liberty, I beg of you.'

I would have said, no, but my teeth were shaking so hard I was afraid I was going to chip one of them. He took the silence for a yes, and slid to the floorboard. He burrowed under the blanket and laid his head against my stomach, his arms wrapped around me.

I fought to tell him, move, but the involuntary muscle movement eased, and my teeth stopped sounding like castanets. He'd been right, with more of his body against mine, it was warmer. Not a lot, but maybe just enough. I was still cold, so cold, as if I were ass-deep in the snow and more was falling all around me. I'd thought freezing to death was an easier way to die. You just fell asleep. This wasn't easy, and I didn't feel the least bit sleepy. A little scared, but not sleepy.

I wanted to be warm. I wanted heat. I needed something warmer.

Requiem's voice came from under the blanket, his upper body completely hidden under the gray folds. 'The shivering has slowed.'

'I noticed,' I said, and it was nice to just be able to talk without risking a tongue injury.

He snuggled his face against me, an oddly catlike gesture. I'd had enough of the wereleopards rubbing over me to know what I was talking about. 'I would do anything that my lady required.'

'What's that supposed to mean?' I asked, and I was feeling better enough to sound suspicious.

He laughed and pressed his body against my legs hard enough that my knees moved just a little apart. His body was covering my legs, but that one little movement was like the beginning of something. It's hard for most men to keep their thoughts above the waist when they're touching below the waist, no matter how innocently. He was a vampire, but he was still male. I guess I couldn't fault him for thinking about it, as long as thinking was all he did.

'I'm feeling better than I was. I don't think we need any heroic measures.'

'The tone of your voice, the stiffening of your body,' he said from under the blanket, 'such disapproval, as if you think I will try to ravish you.'

'Let's just say that I'm not the trusting sort.' Though it felt a little silly talking to a lump under a blanket, when the lump was wrapped around my body. It did lack a certain dignity.

He laid his head against the side of my body, because he was too tall to lay his head in my lap with so much of him covering my legs. His hands wrapped around the back of my body, sliding between me and the seat. It was way too intimate for my tastes, and not long ago, when the *ardeur* was hungry this much up-close-and-personal would have raised it, but there was nothing. Nothing but the warmth and movement of him, and the awkwardness of having a near stranger that close to me. But I could think. I felt like crap, but him this close didn't bring it on. I'd fed on him earlier tonight, and even that thought didn't raise anything through the chill. If I'd felt better, I would have been happy. The *ardeur* wasn't my master anymore. It couldn't make me do impossibly embarrassing things anymore. Yeah, maybe I had to feed it, but it could be on my own terms. Or close to my own terms.

I sat there with a gorgeous male curled around my body, and smiled. Even cold and aching with emptiness, I was still happy. Still willing to trade that overwhelming heat for this cold waiting. Because it was a waiting that I could feel now. The *ardeur* wasn't gone. It was like a fire that had burned down to cold ashes, but there was still life in the heart of that dying wood. It just needed a good poke and stir, and there would be flames, oh, yeah.

Just thinking that hard made it curl to life, a tiny flare. I squashed it. Pressed it down. Not yet, not yet.

Requiem raised his head against my body, so that the top of his head brushed my breasts, but through the leather jacket it wasn't much of a touch. The jacket was bulky enough that it could have been accidental on his part, though I doubted it. If Requiem was anything like Jean-Claude and Asher, then he was very aware of where his body was, and what it was doing. But I let it go. I wasn't that cheap a date for the *ardeur* anymore. Yeah!

I felt Damian. I would like to say, I heard him, or saw him, but that wouldn't be true. I felt him. He was sitting against a wall, and he was cold, so cold. Colder than I'd ever been. I called to him, 'Damian, Damian what's wrong?'

I didn't hear him answer, but I felt his body, felt that aching cold at the center of it. Why, what was happening to him? What was wrong? 'Damian, what's wrong?'

'Did you say Damian?' Requiem asked.

'Yes, he's hurt. He's so cold, so cold, that he's collapsed against a wall. There are people around him, but I can't see who. He's so cold, so cold.'

Requiem knelt upward, pushing his head out of the blanket and meeting my eyes. 'You are his master now, Anita, you make him live. Your energy makes him live.'

'Oh, shit.'

'Yes, you can refuse the *ardeur*'s call, but you are cold to the touch, and it is your warmth that gives warmth to Damian, in a way that goes far beyond sharing blood.'

I closed my eyes and leaned my head back against the seat. 'Shit, shit, shit.'

'Will you let him die for embarrassment's sake?'

I opened my eyes. 'That question would have a lot more merit if you weren't the one kneeling by my knees.'

He put his head to one side, and a curious look came over his face. He looked as if he'd say something, then shook his head as if he'd decided better of it, and I was almost certain that what came out of his mouth wasn't what he'd thought of first. 'Are you able to feed the *ardeur* without intercourse, or donating blood?'

'Yes,' I said.

'Then allow me to offer myself as a tiding over snack until you reach the club and your *pomme de sang*.'

'Define *snack*,' I said.

Damian screamed through my head, and I got a confused glimpse through his eyes of a blonde woman bending over him. It was Elinore, one of the new vampires. She was speaking, but he couldn't hear her anymore, only watch her lipsticked mouth move, noiseless.

I grabbed the front of Requiem's shirt. 'Out of time. Damian needs . . . needs to be warm.'

'Then let me share my warmth with you,' Requiem whispered it as his face bent toward mine. As happened so often, tonight I didn't have to explain, or give detailed instructions. He just grasped what was needed, and acted.

His lips touched mine, and the kiss was gentle, and no liberites were taken, his tongue stayed nicely in his own mouth. Of course, that did nothing to raise the *ardeur*.

He drew back and searched my face with his gaze. 'You are still cold in every way.'

I nodded, and down that long metaphysical line, Damian called out for help. He was dying, not like a human dies, but like you watch a flame fade from lack of oxygen. It was as if some invisible spark were being blown out inside him. I was his spark now, and I didn't know how to fix this.

I looked up at the man in front of me. He was handsome enough, but without the *ardeur*'s heat, he was still a stranger, and I didn't lust after strangers. I had to be seduced not by the color of someone's eyes, or the flawlessness of their face, but by a smile that had become dear to me, a conversation so familiar that it had become like music to me. Familiarity never bred contempt with me, it made me feel safe, and until I felt safe, I did not lust after people, at least not in the front of my head, and it was the front of my head that I needed. I'd finally found the lock for my subconscious, which meant I had to bring the *ardeur* out on purpose, not just get out of its way, or stop fighting it, but truly had to coax it to life. Again, I hadn't thought what it would mean to control the power to this degree. I seemed to spend my life not understanding the mess I was making until it was too late.

I grabbed Requiem's arms, dug my fingers into his flesh. 'Damian is dying, and I don't know how to save him.'

'Simply raise the *ardeur* and feed.'

'I don't know how to do it, without the *ardeur* pushing on me. Shit.'

'Do you mean you do not know how to raise lust for me?'

'Nothing personal, but I don't know you.'

'There is no shame in not being a creature of casual lusts,' he said.

'Damian is dying,' I whispered it, because I could feel it. I could feel him beginning to pull away from me. He was trying not to drag me to the grave with him, so he was shielding as best he could.

'I can raise lust in you, Anita, it is not the *ardeur*, but it is one of my gifts.'

If we'd had time I would have asked him what the difference was, but we were out of time. 'Do it, help me feed. Don't let me kill Damian, not like this.'

'Drop your shields, or I am helpless to bespell you.' He cupped the side of my face in his warm hand.

Damian felt like a cold wind in my head. I dropped my shields, and two things happened at once. Requiem's power crashed into me. It was as if that power had been pushing at me all night, and I simply hadn't felt it. He couldn't have gotten past my shields, he was right, but without them . . . without them, I was suddenly wet, soaking through what panties I had. It left me breathless, helpless, staring up at him, my body already moist and ready for him. It wasn't lust, it was like hours of really good foreplay packed into seconds. The second thing that happened was my own special little power went, wow. It was as if his power complemented the *ardeur*, as if it were a key to the lock, or maybe all of Belle's line were like this, that we could bring each other.

Whatever the reason, whatever the cause, the *ardeur* roared back to life. And I felt it smash into him the way his power had hit me. His eyes drowned in bright, blue flame, like gas lights sparkling in his skull. Our mouths met, and this kiss wasn't gentle. This kiss was like feeding. Like we were trying to suck each other's souls from between our lips. The thought brought the memory of what the Dragon had shown me, had tried to get me to do, but it was distant and gone. It wasn't souls we were after.

I fed on him and shoved it down that cold line to Damian. I heard him in my head, 'Anita,' but still he was cold, still he lay in someone's arms.

The Jeep skittered around a turn and stopped. Graham yelled from the front seat. 'What the fuck are you two doing back there? My skin is crawling with it.'

My hand was on the seat belt a second before Requiem's. The seat belt unsnapped, and he spilled me to the seat with him on top. He was suddenly grinding me against the seat, and I was suddenly very aware that the front of the leather pants were laced up tight. Those lacings began to rub against me. I tore the side of the thong panties and pressed naked against the front of his leather pants.

He hesitated, as if afraid he'd hurt me, but I pulled at him, made him collapse on top of me. He looked down at me with eyes like drowned flames, and whatever he saw on my face seemed to decide him, because he slid hands on my naked hips, cupped my ass, and angled me up against the front of his pants, so the leather bindings rubbed directly onto the most delicate of places.

The sensation bowed my spine, threw my head back. I wrapped my legs around his waist, pressed myself tighter against the front of him, dug that strangely smooth roughness in against me.

That distant spark was growing brighter. I shoved the energy into Damian, shoved the feel of it, the heat of it, and knew he was awake.

Knew he gazed up at the world through eyes that had swum to green flames.

His voice sounded soft in my head. 'Anita, what are you doing?'

'Feeding.'

Requiem did something with his hips that brought me back into my head, my skin. I knew I was still giving energy to Damian, small bits of the pleasure, but I was back to gazing up at Requiem. His hands, his arms were around my waist, his groin pressing into me, the leather braiding rubbing up and down the front of my body. He rotated his hips and rubbed back and forth between my legs. I could feel him swollen and thick behind the leather.

I let my head fall back, so that my upper body draped backward, my hair trailing along the seat, and was staring upside down when the door opened. Graham stood looking down at me. He went to his knees, as if he meant to kiss me, but Requiem picked me up, moved me out of reach. He put one hand under my shoulders and lifted, so that my back was pressed against the back of the seat. I was suddenly trapped between his body and the seat in a way that I hadn't been before. The push of his body was firmer, harder, rougher. It was as if he'd spread me wider with the push of his body, peeled back the layers of my most intimate places, until the leather braiding rubbed directly on those spots, that spot.

It was as if he knew exactly what he'd done, because he looked down at me with those burning eyes, and said, 'Does it hurt?'

'No, not yet.' I put my hands on his shoulders, and would have drawn him down to a kiss, but he drew back, and stroked himself against me, so hard, so rough, so smooth. The leather was wet from my body, from how wet he'd made me. If I'd been a little less wet, he'd have hurt me, but it didn't hurt. He began to pivot his hips, rubbing his groin against mine, beginning to rub across me, not just back and forth, but around, rolling himself over me, around and around, over and over. That bright spark of pleasure began to build inside me. It all felt good, but it was at the height of his stroke, as his groin brushed over that one small point, that the spark grew. It grew as if he were feeding some tiny flame. Every stroke, every rub of the leather, soaking wet from my body, every time he touched me there, the spark flared bright, and brighter. It was as if fire had weight to it, and that bright light grew heavy inside my body, until I could feel the brush of that heat every time he moved over me. Until it was as if my lower body became heat and weight, nothing but the building pleasure, and then finally at the height of one of those rough strokes, all that heat and weight spilled over me, through me, washing like heat across my body. Spilling in screams from my mouth, dancing down my hands, so that I ripped his shirt until I found skin to drive my nails into.

It was only then that he drove himself against me hard enough that it was almost pain. Hard enough that I felt his body convulse against me through the leather of his pants. His hands were on the back of the seat, holding us in place, but his neck was bowed, his eyes closed, and his body pinning me to the seat as if he would press himself through the leather and find himself inside me. His body convulsed a second time, and he crushed me against the seat, and the cry I gave him was part pleasure and part pain.

It was only then that the *ardeur* truly fed. It had gotten small bits, but not what it needed, not what I needed. Requiem had been controlling himself with an iron will, and that iron will had kept me out of something that I needed. Only with his release had all his walls come tumbling down, and the *ardeur* had roared into that breach, and fed.

His body collapsed down the seat, so that he was resting on his legs, still on his knees, still with my legs wrapped around him, but no longer pushing us against the seat. His shoulders slumped, and he pressed his face against the top of my head, one hand on the back of the seat, and the other around my waist.

I could hear his heart racing, feel his pulse against the side of my face, where his neck lay, warm and close above me. If I'd taken blood from him it would have left him colder, but the *ardeur* wasn't blood, and it didn't mind sharing its warmth with those who fed it well.

I felt Damian like a warm wind inside my head. He blew me a kiss. 'Thank you, Anita, thank you.' Then he pulled away, and there was someone touching his arm, taking his hand. He let them lead him onto the dance floor, and I was alone inside my head with Requiem still holding me.

'Oh, God,' it was Graham, still kneeling in the open door of the Jeep. 'Why wouldn't you share, Requiem, why wouldn't you share?'

Requiem turned his head, slowly, as if even that small movement were an effort. 'She is not mine to share.'

Graham laid his head on his arms on the seat, almost as if he would weep.

I spoke staring at Requiem's chest, where the lovely green shirt had been ripped away, and there was a glint of scarlet from my nails. The sleeve on his right arm was ripped away too, and there were more marks there. I said the only thing I could think of, 'Did I hurt you?'

That made him laugh, and then wince as if the laughter hurt. 'I think, m'lady, I should be asking that of you.' He eased me off his body, and himself to the floorboard, so that I was sitting on the seat, and he was kneeling in front of me. It was almost exactly how we started.

He moved down, until he was sitting flat in the floor, with his back against the opposite door from where Graham was still kneeling. 'Did I hurt you?' he asked.

'Not yet,' I said, but even as I said it the endorphins began to fade, and the first ache began. It was suddenly harder to find a comfortable place to sit on the seats.

'I have hurt you,' he said, 'and I am a clumsy fool.'

I eased until I was sitting more on one hip. 'Fool, I don't know you well enough to answer, but clumsy, that I know is a lie. You may be a lot of things, but clumsy isn't one of them.'

'You compliment me, even as I see your discomfort.'

'Why didn't you just take off the pants and fuck her?' Graham asked. His face looked more in pain than either of ours.

'I told her to let down her shields, and she did it. She trusted me, but she did not understand what my power can do.'

'You told me that it was lust,' I said, and my voice still sounded lazier than normal, almost sleepy.

'Yes, but it is not seduction as Jean-Claude and Asher can do. It is simply lust.'

'It was like hours of really good foreplay all at once. It felt wonderful.'

'But it is purely physiological, purely of the body. My gift does not touch the mind, only the flesh.'

'What's wrong with that?' Graham asked.

'If a woman's body reacts to my power, but her mind does not, I see it as little better than rape, and I have never been interested in such things.' He sighed. 'Anita did not want to have intercourse with me, she made that clear. She'd offered me blood once tonight, but she needed to keep the rest for herself. I was hoping to be able to stop sooner, but you kept demanding more. The *ardeur* did not quiet as I had hoped.'

'I could feel it,' Graham said, 'it was amazing, like what you did to me earlier, but more. It felt like if I could have just touched you, it would have been more.'

Requiem said, 'More, yes, it would be more.'

'What could be more than orgasm?'

He looked at me, and I looked at him, and neither of us looked at Graham.

'I knew it,' Graham said, 'I fucking knew it.'

'I obeyed Anita's wishes. We did not have intercourse, we saved her vampire servant, and the *ardeur* has been fed.'

I looked at him as he sat on the floorboard. He still looked elegant, but sort of dissipated, like an elegant rake. If he'd unfastened those leather pants and made it intercourse, I wouldn't have said no, because truthfully, I'd thought that was all that would save Damian. Or maybe I was just too American, and only intercourse meant sex. Maybe. But whatever the reasoning, Requiem had behaved himself in circumstances where most men wouldn't have. He got a lot of brownie points for that. If I'd had a gold star, I would have pinned it on him.

I did the next best thing. I kissed him on the cheek and said, 'Thank you.'

43

GRAHAM DOUBLE-PARKED IN front of Guilty Pleasures and said he'd valet the car for me. I let him do it, which said just how well I was feeling. I was better, but I'd shoved a lot of the last feeding into Damian, and apparently, not kept enough for myself. The learning curve on the new version of the *ardeur* was going to take some getting used to.

Requiem offered me his hand to help me out of the Jeep, and I took it. I was stiff and more than a little sore, and since he'd helped get me that way, it seemed fair he help me out of the Jeep. Besides, I couldn't just flounce out of the Jeep like normal. I had no under-wear on, and one of my great goals in life was not to flash anyone tonight by accident.

Clay, the new blond werewolf, was at the door. A trio of women were chatting him up. A man in coat and hat slipped past his back and into the club. Clay didn't seem to notice. He was far too busy staring at the redhead's chest.

He noticed us in time to suddenly usher the women into the club, before we got there. He stood, one hand on the opposite wrist, as if he'd been doing it all night. But everything about him screamed *kid caught with his hand in the cookie jar*.

Requiem had a little trouble with the steps leading up to the door, too, which let me know that vampire or not, he might have a few rubby spots of his own. When we were at the top, even with Clay, I stopped long enough to say, 'All those women better be of age, Clay.'

He looked surprised, either at the thought of it, or that I'd seen him. 'They're over twenty-one.'

'You see ID?'

He looked perplexed. 'Well, Marla said that her friend had left her ID at home. I know Marla.'

I shook my head. 'You better hope someone catches her friend inside.' I let Requiem lead me past the puzzled werewolf.

It was 1:00 in the morning, but when Requiem opened the door, the sound of many people in a small space, having a very good time, spilled out around us. It was hot inside the doors, and it wasn't caused by the heating system, it was just that many bodies in a small space. I couldn't see if Nathaniel was on stage yet, because my view was blocked by a curtain of black-shirted security.

Buzz was talking to the three women. 'If she doesn't have ID, she doesn't get in.'

'But Clay told us it would be alright,' the redhead said, and I assumed it was Marla.

'Marla,' Buzz said, 'you know the rules. No exceptions, not even for regulars.'

The man who'd come in just ahead of us was facing two of the largest security guards I'd seen. One was as blond as Clay, and the other was very, very brunette, as in African American brunette. They were both over six feet, with a shoulder spread that was nearly as wide as I was tall. They made Buzz look small, and I wondered where they'd been when Primo was beating everyone's ass.

The brunette said, 'You are not allowed in here.'

'I have a right to see my own son,' the man said.

'I told you, Marlowe is not dancing tonight. He called in sick.'

Marlowe was Gregory's stage name, and he only had one biological unit that called itself his father. The man who'd sexually abused them as children, pimped them out to other pedophiles, and even put them in films. I knew he was in town, but we had a restraining order against him. Alright, Gregory and Stephen did.

I patted Requiem's hand and said, 'Excuse me a minute.' I went to the big security guards. Buzz saw me moving, and he gave the three women over to someone else to usher outside. He followed me. You'd think he didn't trust me not to start trouble.

'Excuse me,' I said, 'are you Anthony Dietrich?'

He turned, then had to look down, as if he'd expected me to be taller. 'Who's asking?'

The creepy thing was that he had their eyes. Those beautiful corn-flower blue eyes stared out of a lined and aged face. He was close to six feet tall, and the face was flat and harsh, not the delicate bone structure of the boys. Only the eyes staring out of a stranger's face.

The eyes shook me, so that I stood there staring for a second, and it was Buzz who said, 'The boys have a restraining order against you. You can't enter this club without violating it. Charon, Cerebus, get his ass out of here. Don't hurt him, but get him out.'

The two big men took an arm apiece, lifted, and carried him, without his feet touching the ground, out the door.

I turned to Buzz. 'Does he try to get in here often?'

'A couple of times, whenever Harlow or Marlowe are scheduled.'

I shook my head. 'That is just so . . . wrong.'

Buzz nodded, then took a deep breath and shook his shoulders, like a bird settling its feathers. 'I'm going to have to talk to Clay.'

'You talk to him, then send him to me, because I want to talk to him, too.'

He looked at me. 'Okay, but Brandon saved a chair by the stage for you, and I think he'll be very disappointed if you don't at least catch the end of his act.'

It took me a second to remember that Brandon was Nathaniel's stage name. 'Oh, yeah, sorry, got distracted.'

'The fact that that piece of shit keeps trying to get in and watch his sons strip distracts me, too.'

I nodded. 'Yeah.'

'Requiem will take you to your seat. Enjoy the show.'

The vampire was just suddenly at my elbow, and I let him lead me through the crowd, but my eyes were back toward the door. What did Anthony Dietrich want with Gregory and Stephen? What could he possibly want from them after all these years? They were too old for a pedophile to be interested in them, weren't they?

I bumped into a chair and had to apologize to the woman who sat in it, and pay more attention to what was in front of me than what was behind. It was worth paying attention to.

Nathaniel was on stage. I don't know what I'd expected. I knew he stripped. I knew he performed. But I'd never seen him do it.

It wasn't that Nathaniel was shy, but he was quiet, gentle. The person on stage was neither of those things. He stalked, he strutted, and he danced. It was similar to what he'd taught me, moving to the beat of the music, but this was the real deal. Him throwing himself around the stage, springing up in the air, and spilling himself back down, every movement fluid and graceful, and amazing.

He was down to a cream-colored G-string. It left his ass bare and held him tight in front, so that he filled the cloth, and I knew him well enough to know that he was already excited. That he liked what he was doing. His eyes sparkled with it, his face shone with a fierce joy. He threw himself into the air again and landed in a push-up position. The audience screamed.

Requiem lowered me to the chair by the stage and lifted the reserved sign off the seat before I sat on it. I forgot to smooth my skirt down in back until I touched the cold chair. I had to sit up enough to smooth it down and not put my bare cookies on a chair that someone else would have to sit on later. Just politeness. But my eyes never left the stage.

Nathaniel did push-ups, then his hips dropped lower, and his body came up, and he did a movement that managed to look like he was fucking the stage, and at the same time, was a bigger movement than that, like a wave that went from his head to his feet. Over and over again, until the women in the audience were almost hysterical. A woman two chairs to my right was pulling down her blouse, flashing her breasts at him.

He crawled across the stage in that way that the wereanimals had, as if they had muscles in places that humans didn't. It was graceful and dangerous, and utterly sensual, as he slinked on all fours toward the end of the stage.

From the back, with his legs tight together, he looked nude. He laid his head on the floor, and the ponytail of his auburn hair spilled out around him like a cloak. He stayed that way for a moment, in a tight ball that looked so terribly nude. Then the music changed and his head flew up, his hair spilling in an arc through the air like a shining spray of colored water, until it fell around his back, and I realized that he had it up in a high, tight ponytail. So that the hair bounced and moved with him. He used it like it was a piece of costume, to hide his body, to peek pale flesh through it, then to swirl it around him so that the hair itself was the show for a moment, then he began to do that sensuous crawl around the stage, and people began to put money in the thin strap of his G-string. There was already a pile of money at the far end of the stage, as if he'd been getting it all along, but only now was he letting them slip the bills in so close to his body.

One woman pulled on the G-string, pulling it away from his body, and he cupped his hand over the front of him, to hide, and I almost got up. Almost rode to his rescue, but he didn't need to be rescued. He kissed her, and she let him move her hand away from his clothes and sat back like he'd stunned her. He joked and chastized and flowed through their hands like muscled water. He was always almost close enough, but never quite where they reached, if they were reaching where they shouldn't have.

I watched the other women, and the one or two men, and I felt something. Lust, I think, it was lust, but it was as if their lust was solid enough to grab, to pull out of the air itself and wrap around my body like a coat. Jean-Claude's voice whispered through my head, '*Ma petite*, do you want to know how to feed on their lust, to feed without touching?'

'You know I do,' I whispered.

And it was like before with Primo, it was as if he stepped inside my skin almost, so that I suddenly knew what he knew. I knew how to open myself up and pull in the thick air. It wasn't like breathing, and it wasn't like feeding when I touched someone, it was closer to literally pulling at the air with metaphysical hands and dragging the lust hand over hand and pulling it inside me. It was the oddest sensation, as if the lust were silk or satin and I pulled it inside my body, as if silk scarves could pass through a hole in my skin. The sensation felt like I'd made a wound in my body and was pulling things through that wound. It was a sensation just this side of pain.

Jean-Claude's voice in my head, 'It will not be so uncomfortable when you have practiced it.'

'It feels awful.'

'But are you feeding?' he asked.

I had to think about it, because all my attention was on how disturbing it felt to draw the lusts of strangers inside me. But once I thought about it, I realized I was feeding. I felt less cold than I had, but . . . 'Do you ever fill up this way?'

'It keeps one from starving, but it is not a meal, no.'

I don't know what I would have said to that, because suddenly Nathaniel was in front of me. I think he was repeating himself, but I hadn't heard him the first time. 'I said, do you want to come play with the kitty?'

Jean-Claude was gone from my head, and I'd stopped feeding from the audience. Everything just shut down, everything but the lavender eyes staring at me from the edge of the stage. His hand was held out. Women's voices were calling, 'I'm not shy . . . pick me, if she doesn't want to go. Brandon, Brandon, she doesn't want you, but I do . . .'

I put my hand in his, but I made a face to show just how uneasy this whole thing made me. I didn't like to dance where strangers, or even friends, could see me. Being dragged on stage at a strip club was so far beyond my comfort level. Until that moment, I hadn't really thought about what it would mean to mark him tonight. On stage, in front of people. Eek!

I stumbled going up on the stage, because I remembered the short skirt and the lack of anything under it, so I was very lady-like getting up on stage. Trouble was the stage was too high from the floor to be that ladylike, so I stumbled, and he caught me and gave me a look. That look gave me a last refuge. That look said, If you can't do this, I'll let it go. He would have, too, but I also knew that if it wasn't me, it was going to be someone else. Truthfully, I wasn't sure how I felt about watching him get pawed, or paw another woman. The fact that I thought flaunting myself up on stage would be a lesser evil than watching someone else flaunt themselves at Nathaniel, said clearly that my priorities had become skewed.

They'd brought a chair up on stage, and I hadn't seen it. The money was missing from his G-string, I think he'd put it with the pile at the end of the stage. I hadn't seen that either, which meant that I'd missed some of the act while I was feeding off the audience.

He led me to the chair and sat me down in it with a flourish of his arm. I looked up at him and knew that the look on my face was suspicious. It said clearly, What are you going to do to me?

He laughed, and it was that full-throated laugh that turned his face from handsome to something younger, more *innocent*, for lack of a better word. I valued that laugh, because I didn't get to hear it often. If me sitting here like this made him feel that good, then it just couldn't be that bad.

He put a hand on the back of the chair on either side of my shoulders, leaning his face very close into mine. I could see the eyeliner around his lavender eyes now and realized that there was mascara there, too, not a lot, but his eyes didn't need a lot to go from beautiful to freaking amazing. 'You're not allowed to touch me, and I'm only allowed limited contact with you, but your hands need to stay on the chair most of the time.' His lips showed the shadow of the smile that gleamed in his eyes.

I don't know what I would have said to that, because the music came up, or maybe it just began, and he started to dance. It had been spectacular enough from the edge of the stage, up this close, it passed from spectacular to embarrassing. It didn't matter that I slept with him almost every night, or that I'd seen him more nude than this more than once. It mattered only that it was in public, and I didn't know what to do.

He started by writhing over me with his hands still on the back of the chair. His chest was so close to my face that it was harder not to have my lips touch him, than to touch him. I'd seen him use his body before, but not like this. It was as if every muscle from shoulder to groin was capable of moving independently, and he was using every one of them. It was amazing, and in private I would have told him so, but here and now, I blushed.

He sat in my lap with his legs wide around the chair, his hands still on the back of it. If he'd just sat, I could have handled it, but of course he didn't. He moved his hips around my lap, like he was stirring something, but the movement didn't stop at the hips, it danced up his body, so that it was a bigger movement and more of the crowd could see it, as if there was any doubt what he was pantomiming.

My face was hot, as if my skin would burn if you touched it.

He leaned in against my hair, where I'd hidden my face, and whispered, 'I'll stop and pick someone else if it's too much.'

I raised up enough to meet his eyes. 'Pick someone else?' I said.

'The act doesn't change,' he whispered, 'just who's on stage.' The smile was gone from his eyes. He was serious again. I'd killed the smile in his face, or my embarrassment had. God.

I touched his face, cupped the edge of his cheek against my hand. I looked into those suddenly serious eyes, while the music beat and pulsed around us. In that moment there was no crowd. There was nothing but his face and my decision. I forgot the people, forgot that

I was supposed to be embarrassed, forgot everything but that I wanted him to smile again.

'No, don't pick anyone else. I'll try. I'll really try.'

He gave me that flash of smile that I'd only recently known he had in him, and he dropped to his knees in front of me. His hands played lightly on my knees, and he began to spread my legs apart, but he was still dancing to the music, even on his knees, and he saw the problem before the rest of the audience did.

He put his body between my knees and leaned in enough to say, 'You're not wearing anything.'

I had to smile at the almost surprised embarrassment on his face. It was nice to know that he could be embarrassed. 'Nope,' I said.

He laughed again, and raised up high on his knees, his hands on the back of the chair again. He thrust against me, not touching, but it must have looked worse to the audience, because they yelled and screamed and began to throw money onto the stage.

He didn't so much fall down my body, as spill down it, again that sense of liquid grace that the wereanimals had when they wanted to. He ended with his face in my lap, across the stretched fabric of the skirt, his upper body actually hiding the rest of me from the audience. The skirt had ridden up enough that everyone knew I was wearing black lace thigh-highs. His hands traced up my hose, above the boots, across my knees, and up my thighs, until his fingers came to the edge of the lace.

His fingers traced just above the lace, played along the bare skin of my thighs. He turned his head in my lap, just enough so that his lips were close to my bare thigh, and he kissed the inside of my thigh. That one small touch made me shudder, and close my eyes in a sigh.

He was up while my eyes were closed, hands putting my knees together so when his body moved, I wasn't flashing anyone. He danced behind me, and suddenly his hair fell over my face and body like an auburn waterfall. I was suddenly drowning in the vanilla scent of his hair.

He whirled around me, touching me only with his hair, then he had my hand in his and pulled me hard and fast out of the chair, so that I was forced against his body. It was like a move in a dance but more forceful, if you wanted your partner to stay on her feet. If he hadn't caught me, I might have fallen, but his body was there, and my hands were on that body, I couldn't help it. I just caught myself with his arm and chest, but the sight of me touching him like that sent more money onto the stage, and raised the frenzy of the women grouped around the stage.

His other hand had gone to the back of my skirt and tugged it down. He made it look like he was taking liberties when it was the exact opposite. Whatever they thought he was doing, they liked it.

The music had slowed, changed, and he was suddenly dancing with me. It was almost a waltz, and he did three quick turns across the stage, and we were back at the chair. He used my hand to whip me out from his body and have me facing the back of the chair. He put my hands on the curved back of the chair, then put his body as close to mine as he could. He was close enough that I could feel the tightness of him pressing against the back of my skirt.

He whispered against my hair, 'This would be easier if you were wearing underwear.'

I started to turn and ask what would be easier, but his hands covered mine, trapping them against the curve of the chair, and he suddenly started pressing that tight part of him against my ass.

I'd said he pantomimed sex before, but I'd been wrong, because he was doing it now.

He thrust against the back of my body, with his hands trapping mine against the chair, and his body curved over me. With my legs together he wasn't brushing up against anything that Requiem had hurt. With my legs together, the angle would have been wrong if we were actually trying to have sex, but that wasn't what the show was about. As he'd said hours ago, it was an illusion, the illusion that they could have him. The illusion that he could bring someone up on stage and have them in front of everyone else.

The cloth of the G-string was satiny, but what lay inside that satin was hard and firm, and all I could think of was earlier in my office. Of the feel of him inside of me for real. Of him pushed inside me as far as he could go, of him sliding in and out of my body, of him stroking over that spot inside me, of the feel of him so careful, so delicate, so very strong, as he moved inside me. My imagination was suddenly not my friend. Because between one breath and another, the memory overwhelmed me, and suddenly that heavy warmth spread from low in my body to spill over my skin in a dance of goosebumps. I spasmed against the chair, against Nathaniel's body. His body was still bent over mine, and the weight of him rode me as I spasmed, as I orgasmed. It was a small one, no screaming, no clawing, just that helpless spasming, and not much of that by my standards.

He whispered against the side of my face, his breath almost hot. 'Anita . . .'

But the next moment there was movement behind us, I felt it like a disturbance of air, and there was a sound I didn't know, and a sharp sound of something heavy hitting flesh. Nathaniel's body reacted to the blow, spasmed, almost like mine had. A second blow came, and this time words, Jean-Claude's voice, 'Bad cat, very bad cat. Away from her bad cat, away from her.'

Nathaniel's body responded to every blow, almost like it was a miniature orgasm. His body tightened around me, as if the feel of my body next to him while Jean-Claude whipped him was something he didn't want to lose. But Jean-Claude drove him off, with a joking voice, and Nathaniel made sure my skirt was in place before he let Jean-Claude drive him across the stage.

I was left holding the chair, so weak-kneed I didn't trust myself to move yet. Jean-Claude had a small many-tailed whip in his hand. Nathaniel crouched and crawled across the stage, and Jean-Claude beat him. It was like an odd version of an old-time lion tamer act, except the chair served an entirely different purpose.

'You are a very bad kitty-cat, very bad. How do we punish our bad kitty?' For a second I thought he was asking me, but he wasn't. The women around the stage started to chant, 'Tie him up, tie him up, tie him up.'

Jean-Claude smiled, as if that had never occurred to him, but what a good idea it was. At a gesture from him, chains descended from the ceiling. I hadn't noticed them in the welter of lights and cables. Oh, hell, I hadn't even looked up.

Two bare-chested waiters, wearing only leather pants, came up on stage and dragged Nathaniel to his feet. They chained his arms spread wide, wrists above his head.

Jean-Claude came to me, walking so that his hips rolled more than they should have. He touched my arm and whispered, with a smile that did not match the words, 'Are you alright, *ma petite*?'

I nodded and whispered, because I knew he'd hear me. 'Flashback.'

'Not as strong as those that our Asher can give.'

I shook my head.

'Interesting,' he said, 'are you well enough to finish this show?'

'I promised,' I said.

His smile widened, and his voice was suddenly that room-filling, jolly sound, 'Now, you may help us punish our bad kitty. You may make him pay for taking liberties.' I got a shadow of what he was doing to the audience. When he said 'punish,' it was a sharp pull on the body; 'bad kitty' made you think of very naughty things; 'pay,' and more money hit the stage; 'liberties' had a lascivious lilt to it that made the audience do that nervous giggle, like what they were thinking was worse than anything they'd seen tonight.

I just nodded and let him take my hand. That one touch was both a mistake and a help. It made me feel less shaky, but it also opened me to him more. Touching just his hand was more distracting than touching so much more on most men. He led me a little dazed across the stage, until we were standing behind Nathaniel, facing the bareness of the back of his body.

Jean-Claude let go of my hand and went to him. He touched the bare back. 'You may hit him here –' his hand slid down Nathaniel's back to his buttocks – 'or here. He has been a bad kitty, but we don't want to damage him. He is far too pretty for that.'

The audience agreed with him, most of them.

Jean-Claude handed the whip toward me. 'I don't know how to use a whip.'

'First, it is a what, my sweets?'

Most of the women yelled, 'Flogger!'

'And second, it would be my *pleasure*,' and that one word slithered over my skin, and apparently over the other women as well, for they squealed, 'to show you just how it works.' And every word seemed darker, more suggestive than it should have.

He tried to show me first by simply using it on Nathaniel. He made the heavy leather tails blur and blossom against Nathaniel's skin. Nathaniel reacted to every blow with a spasm that went from his fingers to his toes and everything in between. I could see enough of his face to know that those closed eyes and parted lips weren't from pain. Jean-Claude whipped Nathaniel, or I guess *flogged* him, until his skin was pink in places and the stage was littered with money at their feet.

He leaned close to Nathaniel's face, said something, and Nathaniel said something back, then Jean-Claude turned to me. He held the flogger out again. 'He's such a bad kitty.'

I shook my head.

'Shall I show her how it's done?' he asked the audience, and they yelled louder, and I wished I'd just taken the damn thing and tried, but too late now.

He put the flogger in my hand and pressed his body against the back of mine, with one arm around my waist and the other hand on the hand that held the flogger. It was the way lecherous men stand when they try to teach you how to golf or swing a bat. He swung my arm back and tried to make me give that sharp crack against Nathaniel's body, but it wasn't sharp, it was sort of flabby.

'You must relax and let me do the work, *ma petite.*' Loud enough for the audience he said, 'Relax, my sweet, relax, and we will show him pain, and perhaps more.' The 'perhaps more' was like a whisper in the dark against your skin.

I let out the breath I was holding and tried to relax, never my best thing. But I also knew that if I didn't relax, this part of the show would last longer, and I wanted this part over. It was sort of demeaning, like I was a girl who couldn't swing at the ball without help. Okay, maybe I didn't know how to use a flogger, but I really didn't need this much help.

We got a couple of good blows in, enough to make Nathaniel shiver in his chains. Then Jean-Claude stepped away from me, leaving the flogger in my hand. 'Give the bad kitty what he wants.' And what he said was not what it felt like in my head, or on my skin, or deeper in my body. The women around the stage and farther into the room made small noises. Shit.

I threw the flogger at Jean-Claude the way you'd throw a base-ball bat when you want someone to catch it. He caught it by the handle like I'd known he would. 'I know what the bad kitty wants, and I am going to give it to him.'

The women made 'ooh' and 'aah' sounds, and several said, 'you go girl!' One yelled, 'lucky bitch!' I walked to Nathaniel and stood in front of him. His eyes were only partly focused. He'd liked the flogger. I'd known sort of academically that he would, but seeing it in his face was different. It bothered me, and I wasn't sure if the entire thing bothered me, or if what bothered me was that this was something he liked this much, and I wasn't sure I was willing to do it for him. I let the doubts go, because what I was about to do was something I could do, and wanted to do, and had promised to do.

I looked up at the chains and just wasn't familiar enough with the concept to know, so I asked Jean-Claude, 'Does this swivel?'

'It can,' he said, 'why?'

'Because they'll want to see his face.'

The audience liked that, and they shouted more encouragement, but I didn't need it. I don't know why, but suddenly I was calm. I wasn't bothered that we were in public, or that we were on stage. It was very peaceful inside my head, very calm.

The waiters turned Nathaniel around so that he faced the audience. His eyes had gone back to almost normal. I could see his face reflected in the distant glass of the far wall. I'd never really noticed how much shiny surface there was all around until that moment, when I could watch Nathaniel's face and mine.

I grabbed his ponytail, grabbed it and wound it around my hand, tight, tight enough that he gasped. I think the audience screamed, but the sound of them was receding, pulling away, and leaving me in a well of silence, where the only noises were Nathaniel's breath and mine.

I pressed my body along his back, tucked him tight against me, so that his ass pushed against my stomach and my breasts pressed into his back. I kept my hold on his hair, and used it like a handle to keep him from moving, pulling harder if he shifted his weight, until he hung suspended, afraid to move, eager not to. I had to go on tiptoe to get the angle I wanted for the smooth expanse of his neck. I put my free hand around his upper chest, holding us tight together. I used his hair to stretch his neck to one side, to give me as much of that smooth, delicate flesh as possible. His breathing had already changed, already sped in anticipation.

I licked his neck, a quick flick of tongue, and he gasped for me. I licked harder, and he shuddered. I kissed his neck, and he made a small noise, not of protest, but of eagerness. I opened my mouth wide, and let my breath touch hot upon his skin, and then I bit him. No more foreplay, no more games. I bit him.

He struggled against me, he couldn't help it, and I used his hair and my arm around his body, and the press of my body against his back, to hold him in place. I felt his skin under my teeth, felt the meat of him in my mouth, and underneath that was that frantic beating pulse. I could taste his life underneath his skin, taste it, and know that it was mine, mine if I wanted it. Mine because part of him wanted to give it up to me.

The sensation of that much meat in my mouth was almost overwhelming, and I fought not to bite down and take away all that flesh. I fought not to take everything that he offered in that moment. I bit down, held him as he struggled, held him as his wrists jerked on the chains, as his body began to spasm, and still I sank my teeth into his flesh. The first sweet taste of blood like salt and metal and something so much sweeter filled my mouth, and I felt him convulse against me, heard him cry out. And I fed, I fed the *ardeur*, and hadn't even known it was coming. I fed on his blood, fed on the meat of his body, fed on his sex, fed on all of him. I fed, and when I looked up from his body, I saw my eyes reflected in the mirror. Black light, with that flash of brown light, my eyes drowned with power.

I let go with my mouth, abruptly, and saw blood on my mouth, on my chin, shining in the lights. I let go of his hair, his body, and stepped back, and I knew that my eyes were still full of that dark light. I was afraid for a second what I'd done, but found that other than a perfect set of my own teeth marks, set like a bloody necklace on his skin, I hadn't bitten through to his pulse. I hadn't hurt him, not more than he wanted to be hurt.

Jean-Claude was standing there, in front of me. '*Ma petite*,' he whispered, '*ma petite*.' But I knew what he was thinking, I knew what he wanted. Bound closer than we'd ever been, it cut both ways. He mouthed something about how did I feel, was I alright, but that wasn't what he was thinking. Not really.

'Say what you want,' I said, 'say what you want.'

He stopped trying to be careful, and said, simply, 'Kiss me.'

I went to him, and he kissed me. He kissed me as if he were tasting me, as if with tongue and teeth and lips he could drain from me every last drop of Nathaniel's blood and the taste of me along with it. He licked the roof of my mouth and drew a sound from low in my throat. His eyes had bled to midnight blue light, as if the darkest of water held starlight in it.

I caught the glint of my own eyes, and they were still full of light, blind with the darkness of it, except it wasn't blind, it was anything but. It was like being hyperaware of everything, anything. I knew suddenly that as long as the light lasted, that every sense would be heightened. I remembered thinking in the cemetery that to make love like this would either be the most wondrous thing ever, or drive you mad. Staring up into Jean-Claude's drowning blue eyes, I was willing to bet on wondrous.

'We must see to Nathaniel first,' he said, but his voice was hoarse and thick with need.

I nodded. 'Yes, Nathaniel first.'

'And then?' he asked.

'Say what you mean,' I said, and my voice wasn't as hoarse as his, but it didn't sound exactly like me either.

'And then there is a couch in my office,' he said.

'I was thinking the desk,' I said.

He looked at me, and even with those drowning eyes, the look was very male. 'Either will do for me, but it is you who will be on bottom, so it is your choice.'

'I'll be on bottom?' I made it a question.

He nodded. 'Yes.'

'Why?' I asked.

'Because that is what I want.'

'Okay,' I said.

44

NATHANIEL WAS DONE for the night, there would be no shapeshifting. He was barely conscious in that after great sex kind of way. A few of the customers complained, but not many. Most of them felt that they'd had a show worth the price of admission. We got Nathaniel settled in what the strippers called the quiet room. It had an oversized couch, blankets, low lights, and was just what the name implied, a quiet room, where you could either sleep or get your shit together when things went odd. There were smaller rooms where you could pay to have a private dance, but this wasn't one of them. This was more a room for crashing when you were tired or had to pull a surprise double shift.

I stroked Nathaniel's hair, and asked him, 'Are you alright?'

He'd opened his eyes just barely and smiled up at me. I'd never seen his face so content. 'Yes, very, yes.'

I told him to enjoy the afterglow, and I put Requiem on the door, because Nathaniel was mine to take care of, and I planned on being busy for awhile.

My eyes had bled back to normal by the time I walked down the hallway toward Jean-Claude's office. He stopped in the hallway and called after me, 'Where are you going, *ma petite*?'

I paused at the door and looked at him. 'To your office.'

'Your mood is cooler now, and the power has left you.' He was trying to be utterly neutral, and failing just a bit.

I opened the door still looking at him. 'Come into the office, Jean-Claude, and lock the door.' I didn't wait to see what he'd do, I went through the door, leaving it open behind me. I went to the desk and hopped up on it. I could have tried for subtle, but it was late, and I didn't feel the least bit subtle. I put my boots up on the desk, my legs apart, and let the skirt ride up as far as it wanted to go. It was outrageously slutty, but the look on his face as he came through the door made me glad I'd done it.

He leaned against the door and locked it, and was unbuttoning his jacket as he walked across the floor. I pulled off the leather jacket and threw it to the floor. His jacket was on the floor, the fluffy white cravat undone so that his upper neck showed pale. I slipped the shoulder holster off my arms but only had the belt partly undone, when he pulled the shirt over his head, and was naked from the waist up. I finished the belt, but he was at the desk before I got it off, slipping the shoulder holster free and setting gun and all beside me on the big black lacquer desk.

I went to my knees on his desk and fell upon the silken muscle and lines of his chest with hands and fingers and mouth. I licked the cross-shaped burn scar. I drew first one nipple and then the other into my mouth. Rolled them with my tongue, sucked them. Used my hands to mound the flesh of his chest, so I could take more of his nipple into my mouth, more of his breast. Until I could lock my mouth around as much as would fill it, and bit down until he cried out and his hands found my face, drew me away from his body, and to his mouth.

We kissed as we had on stage, as if we were exploring every inch with tongue, lips, teeth. He drew back from the kiss, and his eyes had bled to blue. Mine were still my own, but I didn't care. His hands found my shirt, and he pulled it over my head and bent over me, kissing down the line of my neck, my shoulder, and mounds of my breasts where they spilled up from the black lace bra. He stuck his hands inside my bra and lifted my breasts out so they rested on the underwire, like it was a black frame for the pale mounds of my breasts.

He went to his knees and pulled me to the edge of the desk so he could run his tongue over my breasts. Flicking against my nipples, quick, and light, and wet, until I made small noises. He locked his mouth around my breast and drew as much of my breast as he could between his fangs without nicking me. He sucked, hard and harder, rolling his tongue along my nipple and drawing harder on my breast until he stretched me out in a line that felt so good, but I could feel how careful he was being. It wasn't the first time he'd played with me like this, but it was the first time that I'd known that this was only the beginning of what he wanted. It wasn't like telepathy, or a picture in my head, I just knew. I knew what he wanted to do. What he was fighting not to do.

'Bleed me,' I said.

He rolled his eyes up to me, so he could see my face.

'Bleed me, I know how long you've wanted to do that now. How careful you've been.'

He stopped and released my breast slowly, carefully. He said, '*Ma petite*, you are drunk with the new powers, but tomorrow night, you will not be.'

I shook my head. 'Let me feel what it's like to have you stretch me tight in your mouth and draw just a little blood. I'm not saying that the whole ride will appeal to me, but I am saying that I'm willing to try a little, to see if I'll like a lot, or not.'

He looked strangely suspicious, and I realized that it was my expression in his eyes, more than his, as if I'd taught him that look, and this caution.

'I give you my word that I won't punish you for anything I agree to try tonight. A little blood tonight, only a little, barely a nick, just a taste.' I leaned in toward his face. 'I know that you want to feed there now. You never told me.'

'Nor would I have, *ma petite*, you let me take blood so infrequently, that I would never have dreamt to ask such a liberty. When you will not share your neck, why would I think to ask for more delicate parts?'

'I'm offering now. I'd take me up on it, if I were you. Who knows if I'll ever offer again, if you say no now.' I stared into his face from inches away and let him see that there was no conflict here, no doubts, just eagerness. Eagerness to try.

'What has gotten into you, *ma petite*?'

'You, you've gotten into me, or I want you to. I want you inside me, Jean-Claude, I want you inside me. I want you to lie me back across this desk, with my breasts bare and your mark on them. I want you to push yourself inside me and watch the blood flow from the wound that you made. I want you to watch the blood flow fast and faster, while you fuck me.'

'You are echoing my fantasy, *ma petite*, have I taken you over?'

'I don't think so,' I said, but even the thought of it didn't panic me. 'Just a little tonight, Jean-Claude, just a little nick.'

He reached around my body, and it took me a second to realize he was undoing the back of my bra. He slipped it off my shoulders, down my arms, and let it fall to the floor. He gazed up at me, and his eyes never got higher than my breasts. I didn't mind in the least.

He cupped my breasts in his hands, gently, reverently, and laid the gentlest of kisses upon each of them. He raised eyes to me that were back to their normal midnight blue, as human as his eyes ever became. 'Are you sure, *ma petite*, are you sure?'

I nodded. 'Yes, oh, yes.'

He cupped my right breast in his hand, then took just the tip of it in his mouth, a quick drawing of his mouth over my flesh. He sucked and pulled until my nipple was tight and thick under his touch. It brought my breath faster, made my pulse race. He rolled his eyes upward to watch my face, and whatever he saw there reassured him, because he drew hard and fast, made me gasp. Then he drew, slowly, so slowly, more and more of my breast into his mouth. He'd never taken so much in at once, because to do even this much was to risk drawing blood. His mouth was so warm, so wide, the hard press of his teeth was as distant as he could make it and still hold me in his mouth.

He used his hands to help his mouth, pour so carefully over me, his breath like heat against my skin. He moved carefully off of me, his mouth sliding back until there was much less between his lips. He went back out to the safe distance that he'd been before. He drew just the tip of my breast in his mouth, and he sucked. He sucked and pulled and stretched it out and out, until I made small sounds low in my throat.

He squeezed my breast between his hand, squeezed it, and rolled his eyes up to watch my face. When I didn't tell him to stop, he squeezed tighter, tighter until it felt like he was trying to garrote my breast with his fingers. It hurt, it did, but it was all mixed up with the sucking and the pulling on my nipple, and that didn't hurt, not really. In fact it felt good, so good.

It fell out of my mouth in a voice that was almost a moan, 'Yes, please, please, yes.'

He rolled his eyes up again to watch my face, and there was something in those eyes, some knowledge, or warning, and suddenly he bit down, not as hard as I'd seen in his head, but a little. He let the barest tips of those sharp fangs graze my breast as he sucked it, as he squeezed it with his hand. It was sharp, but it didn't hurt. It was lost in the other sensations. His hand squeezing so tight, his mouth sucking so hard, the tiny bite of the fangs was nothing compared to the rest.

He let his mouth slide down my breast until only the nipple was caught between his teeth. But there on the mound of my breast were two tiny dots of crimson. As I watched those two tiny dots began to glide down my skin. He drew my nipple out and out, and we both watched those two tiny trails of red slide down my skin. He pulled on my nipple so hard and so long, that I cried out, 'Enough, enough.'

He drew back, gently, and knelt for a moment watching the colors flow on my skin, not just of the blood, but of the marks of his fingers. They faded, but the two lines of blood didn't fade. They glided down my skin, and as the sensation returned to my breast, they tickled down my skin. The feel of that tiny gliding touch, the sight of it easing down my skin, made me shiver.

He smoothed his hands up the insides of my thighs, and it was only as his fingers brushed certain parts that I made real pain sounds. 'No manual manipulation tonight.'

He frowned. 'Are you hurt?'

I explained as briefly as possible. 'Let's just say that the *ardeur* needed feeding and Requiem was a gentleman. I think we'd both be less sore if he'd been a little less of a gentleman.'

He looked puzzled.

'I'll explain everything in detail, but later, please, Jean-Claude. Take off the pants, I've had all the leather pants up close and personal that I can handle tonight. Let me see you nude.'

He peeled off boots and the leather pants with the practiced ease of someone who wears a lot of them. I'd seen him nude more times than I could count now, but he never stopped amazing me with his beauty. Flawless was the only word I had for him. White and pale, and perfect, as if someone could carve cold white marble and breathe life into it, and plant a blush of color at his groin, where he sat straight and thick and ready. The hair that trailed from the delicate thimble of his belly button down to his groin was as black as the curls that fell around his shoulders. That black, black hair stark and unreal against the whiteness of him.

There should have been gentler words for what I wanted, but all I could think of was how much I wanted him inside me. How much I wanted him to sink that shining color inside my body. 'Fuck me,' I said, because *make love* was not what I meant. I wanted the sex that went with what he'd done to my breast. I wanted the sex that matched the blood trailing down my skin.

'Fuck me.'

He bent over me and licked the blood off my chest, not a quick lick, but thick, long movements of his tongue, as if he'd never tasted anything so good and didn't want to lose a single drop. I was making small wordless noises and writhing on the desk by the time he raised his face up and showed me eyes that had drowned in blue flame.

I whispered, 'Please, Jean-Claude, please.'

He did what I'd seen in his head, he did what I'd offered. He laid me back against the desk and pulled my hips to the very edge of the wood. My skirt was completely bunched around my waist like a belt. I was still wearing the thigh-highs and the boots, and nothing else. He used his hands to spread my legs apart, then came to me, the tip of him sliding against my opening.

'You are wet, but you are still tight.'

'Fuck me,' I said, 'please, just do it, please, please, please, please . . .'

Somewhere in the last *please*, he began to force himself inside me. I was tight, so tight, and so wet. On another night, I would have asked for more foreplay to make that horrible tightness loose, but tonight I wanted to feel him push his way in. I wanted to feel him shove himself inside me.

He pushed himself between my legs, using his hips and legs to drive himself into me. It was just this side of too tight, and I started to struggle underneath the push of it. Not struggle to get away, but struggle because I couldn't help it. My hands and arms swept over his desk and knocked everything within reach off, including my gun. I wanted something softer to touch, something to scratch and hold on to, but there was nothing but the cool wood of the desk, and that wasn't what I wanted to touch.

When he was as far inside me as he could go, he began to pull himself out, slowly, as if my body were trying to hold on to him, and maybe it was. He drew himself out slowly, and then began to work himself in, just as slowly. If he didn't hurry, I wasn't going to be tight anymore. I wanted that feeling of him forcing himself into my body, and we were going to lose that if he kept being gentle.

'Fuck me, Jean-Claude, fuck me while I'm tight, please.'

'That will hurt,' he said.

'I want it to hurt.'

He gave me a look, then gripped my hips in his hands, let me feel some of that otherworldly strength, and he did what I asked. He drove himself into me, and pulled himself out of me, as fast and hard as he could. It did hurt, and I wasn't ready for it, and it was exactly what I wanted.

He drove himself in as deep and hard as he could, so that the impact of our bodies tore a grunt from my body and a sound in his that I'd never heard before. He trapped my hips under the strength of his hands, and he forced himself inside me, fought the tightness of my body, as if he were piercing my body, making a new hole, because this one wasn't wide enough.

The blood was flowing across my chest in widening lines, as my heart beat faster, and my blood pumped itself out of those two little holes. The blood looked so red, so red, on the white of my skin.

He lifted my legs so that my feet were by his face, he grabbed my hips and pulled me further down the desk, closer to his body, and used his weight to push my legs back over my body, so that he changed the angle inside me, made it deeper, sharper.

I cried out.

He moved his hands to my waist and pulled me farther into his body, and he rode my legs down so that I was almost bent in two. We'd done gentler versions of this, and he knew I was limber enough for it, but it was suddenly a much different position. Because he rode my body into a tight knot, fucking me as hard and as fast as he could, but he pushed my body together so that he could lick my chest while he fucked me.

He raised his face up from my chest, and his mouth and jaw were crimson with my blood. He spilled my legs to either side, and jerked me up, off the desk, so that I was suddenly pressed to the front of his body, my legs wrapped around his waist. He kissed me, kissed me with the taste of my own blood like metalic candy in his mouth.

He was making low sounds in his throat, and he drove us into the wall hard enough that my back slapped against it, hard enough that if he hadn't cradled my head, it would have hit the wall. He drove himself into me again and again and again, as hard and as fast as he could. I wasn't tight anymore, I was wet and loose, and it didn't matter.

His chest and stomach were decorated with my blood. Startling crimson splashes against the white of his body. He pressed his entire body against me as tight and close as he could, so that the slickness of blood began to flow between us, as he pinned me against the wall. I held him with my legs locked around his body, my arms locked around his shoulders, I held him, and he fucked me. It was like he was trying to put a hole in the wall behind me, so that every thrust felt like it was pounding me into the wall, crushing me against his body. I almost said, enough, almost said stop, but as I drew breath for it, the orgasm came like a huge overwhelming wave. It engulfed me, and I clawed at him, and screamed, and bucked against the weight and strength of him so that the orgasm became another kind of struggle, another kind of fight. My teeth dug into his shoulder, my nails tried to find a way through his back, and my body rode his, while he pounded me into the wall, and somewhere in all of that I felt his body convulse, felt his hips drive in one powerful effort up and inside me.

He screamed as he came, and I felt him pour himself inside me, felt it as he put his hand against the wall and tried to steady us as his knees collapsed, and we ended on the floor with my legs still wrapped around his waist, him still inside my body.

His breathing was ragged, and his eyes unfocused, as he stared into my face. '*Mon Dieu.*'

'"Wow" seems too junior high, but "amazing" doesn't cover it,' I said. I tried to touch his face, but found that my arms weren't working that well yet. 'Just promise me we can do it again some night.'

He smiled, and it was a tired smile, but it held an absolute delight in it. 'That is one promise, *ma petite*, that I will happily make.'

'I'll hold you to it,' I said.

'Oh, no,' he said, and found that he had enough strength left to lean in against me, 'I will most certainly hold it against you.'

45

WE'D MADE OUR plan for the rest of the night. When we'd recovered enough to walk, we'd throw on our clothes. Pick up Nathaniel and drive to the Circus of the Damned. We'd tuck Nathaniel in somewhere, and Jean-Claude and I planned on a nice, hot bath. But before we'd even gotten to the throwing the clothes on part, my cell phone rang.

I almost didn't answer it, because no one calls at three in the morning with good news. The number blinking in the little window was Detective Sergeant Zerbrowki. 'Shit,' I said.

'What is it, *ma petite*?'

'Police.' I flipped the phone open and said, 'Hey, Zerbrowski, what's up?'

'Hey back at you. I'm across the river in Illinois, guess what I'm looking at?'

'Another dead stripper,' I said.

'How'd you guess?'

'I'm psychic. I assume you want me to come down and look at the body.'

'Never assume anything, but in this case, yeah.'

I looked down at my blood-covered chest and the wound that was still seeping. 'I'll be there as soon as I get cleaned up.'

'You covered in chicken blood?'

'Something like that.'

'Well, the body isn't going anywhere, but the witnesses are getting restless.'

'Witnesses,' I said, 'we have witnesses?'

'Witnesses or suspects,' he said.

'What's that supposed to mean?'

'Come down to the Sapphire Club and find out.'

'The Sapphire, isn't that the high end club, the one that calls itself a gentlemen's club?'

'Anita, I'm shocked, I didn't know you frequented the titty bars.'

'They wanted to use vampire strippers, and I got to go talk to them about it.'

'I didn't know that was part of your official job description,' he said.

If it had been Dolph, I would have let it go, but it was Zerbrowski, and he was okay. 'The Church of Eternal Life doesn't allow its members to strip, or do anything else the Church considers morally questionable. So the club needed Jean-Claude's permission to import vamps from the next territory over.'

'He give it?'

'No.'

'And you went with him to help decide?'

'No.'

'You went alone?' he asked.

'No.'

He sighed. 'Oh, hell, just get down here. If you said vampires were supposed to stay away from this place, your boyfriend isn't going to be happy.'

'Just no vamps on stage,' I said, 'other than that, not our business.'

'Not on stage, at least not paid,' Zerbrowski said.

'You said witnesses or suspects, and now you say no vamps paid on stage. Shit, are you sitting on some vamps that were in the audience?'

'Come and see, but I'd hurry, dawn's coming.' He hung up.

I cursed softly.

'I take it a languorous bath is not going to be happening tonight,' Jean-Claude said.

'No, unfortunately.'

'If not a bath for you, then may I offer a quick shower here.'

I sighed. 'Yeah, I can't go see the police like this.'

He looked down at his own blood-spattered body and smiled. 'Perhaps for me, as well, tonight.'

'We could conserve water, and share,' I said.

He raised an eyebrow at me and smiled again. The smile said worlds.

'Okay, okay, I guess we'd get distracted.'

'I am not sure I have the strength to be, as you put it, distracted quite so soon.'

'Sorry, I keep forgetting boys don't recover as quick as girls.'

'I am not human, *ma petite*, with another blood donation I could indeed recover.'

'Really?' I said. My pulse sped just a little bit at the thought. Shit, I was too tired and too sore to be thinking of it again.

'Truly,' he said.

'I think if I donate any more blood to anything tonight, it would be bad.'

'It does not have to be your blood,' he said.

I stared at him, and he stared at me. I said what I was thinking, which I'd almost broken myself of. 'So what, you take blood from me, then we fuck, and you have a blood donor standing by, and we fuck. We could like, what, have a room full of donors and just screw until we were so sore, or so tired, we couldn't move?' I was sort of kidding. The look on his face wasn't. The look on his face, the expression in his eyes, made me blush.

I had a sudden image so strong, if I hadn't already been on the floor, it would have put me there. I saw Belle Morte stretched in the big bed, surrounded by candlelight. Asher and Jean-Claude were on the bed, too. There were men tied to the big posts of the bed, nude and pale, they were. Blood glittered in thin lines on their bodies, from neck, chest, the inside of their arms, down their legs. Not one bite apiece, or even two, but more than I could count. One man's head had slumped forward onto his chest, and he sagged against his bonds. If he breathed, I could not see it.

Jean-Claude pushed me out of his memory, it was almost a physical shove. I came back to myself, on the floor of his office, covered in my blood, the phone still in my hand.

'I would not have had you see that.'

'I'll bet.'

He closed his eyes and shook his head. 'We were young and knew no better. Belle Morte was our God.'

'You bled them to death so you guys could have some marathon sex session,' I said it, and my voice wasn't horrified, in fact, it sounded empty. Because I could still see the memory, not in livid detail like it had been, but now it was in my head, too. God, I did not need someone else's nightmares.

'There are many things I have done, *ma petite*, that I would not have you know. Things I am ashamed of. Things that burn inside of me like bile.'

'It was your memory, remember. I felt what you were feeling. There was no regret.'

'Then I pushed you out too soon.' He didn't pull me in, he simply stopped pushing me out, and I was back in that room. Back in that bed. I was inside Jean-Claude's head when he noticed the man on the bed that wasn't moving. He crawled across the bed and touched the cooling flesh. I felt his sorrow, felt his shame. Had his knowledge that these were humans that trusted us. Humans that we had promised to protect. Give us your blood and your bodies, and we will keep you safe. I looked back at Belle Morte stretched nude and luscious, under Asher's body. Asher's body before the human church had scarred him. I watched Asher's face lift up, meet our eyes, and in the middle of what Belle thought was the most sensuous of nights, the seed was sown that we must escape. That there were things that you did not do, and lines you did not cross, and she was not a god.

And I was back in his office, with my blood drying on my body, and my breast beginning to ache, and I was crying.

He stared at me, dry eyed, and he expected me to run. To turn away, and run. Like I had so many times in the past. Nothing was pretty enough for me, nice enough, clean enough. I didn't like messy people in my life, and once that had been true, until I woke up one day and realized that I was one of the messy people.

My voice was steady, and didn't sound like I could have tears drying on my face. 'I used to think I knew what was right and what was wrong, and who the good guys are, and who the bad guys are. Then the world got very gray, and I didn't know anything for a long time.'

He just looked at me, his face closing down, hiding from me, because he was certain where I was going, what I would say.

'There are days, hell weeks, when I still don't know anything. I've been pushed so far outside what I thought was right and wrong, that somedays I don't know my way back. I've done things in the name of justice, in the name of my version of justice, that I wouldn't want anyone to know. I can look a man in the eyes and kill him, and I feel nothing. Nothing, Jean-Claude, nothing. You didn't mean to kill, and you felt bad about it.'

'You take life to protect life, *ma petite*. I have taken lives for pleasure, for the pleasure of she whom I served.' He shook his head and slowly drew his knees into his chest, hugging himself tight. 'Did you ever wonder why I did not replace the vampires that you and Edward, and even I later, killed, when we destroyed Nikolaos?'

'I hadn't really thought about it,' I said. 'I know we're suddenly lousy with vamps when we seemed a little empty before.'

'I called vampires home to me, because I had taken them long ago. But I have not made a new vampire since I became Master of the City. It had kept us dangerously low. If we had truly had another territory's master declare full war, we would have lost. We simply lacked the manpower.'

'So why not make more?' I asked, because he seemed to want me to ask.

He looked at me, and there was something in his eyes that reminded me of someone else. It was a look of pain and confusion, and centuries of hurt. I'd never seen his eyes so raw, so human. 'Because, to make them vampire, I must first take away their mortality, their humanity. Who am I to do that, *ma petite*? Who am I to decide who will live on, and who will die in their appointed time?'

'Who are you to play, God?' I asked.

'Yes,' he said, 'yes, who am I to know what it will change. Belle used to use our power to change countries, wars, who ruled, who was assassinated. There was a time when she ruled more of Europe secretly than anyone knew, even among the vampire council itself. She killed millions through war, and famine. Not by her hand, but by her choices.'

'What stopped her?'

'The French Revolution, and two world wars. Even death itself must bow before such wanton destruction. Now the council rides tighter rein on its members. The time when any in Europe could build such a secret power structure is finished.'

'Glad to hear it,' I said.

'What if I take someone and make them as I am, and that person would have cured cancer, or invented some great thing. Vampires invent nothing, *ma petite*, we are consumed by death and pleasure, and senseless power struggles. We seek money, comfort, safety.'

'So do most people.'

He shook his head. 'But not all, and my kind are attracted to those who hold power, or wealth, or are unusual in some way. A beautiful voice, a gift of artistry, of mind, or charm. We do not take the weak, as most predators do, we take the best. The brightest, the loveliest, the strongest. How many lives have we destroyed over the centuries that could have made some wonderful, or terrible, difference to humanity, to the world at large.'

I looked at him, and not that long ago I would have distrusted this sharing. But I could feel him in my head. I worried about whether I was a monster. Jean-Claude knew for certain. He did not regret what he was, for he could not imagine another life, but he worried about others. He worried about making the choice for others. He worried about playing some dark god. He worried that one day he would become that which he ran from. One day, he would become a version of Belle Morte.

What do you do when you are suddenly able to see that far into someone's darkest fears? What do you say to that much truth about someone else? I said the only thing I could think of, the only thing that would give him any comfort. 'You'll never become like Belle Morte. You'll never become as evil as that.'

'How can you be certain of that?' he asked.

'Because I'll kill you before I let that happen,' and my voice was soft when I said it, because it wasn't a lie.

'Kill me to save me from myself,' he said, and he tried to make light of it, and failed.

'No, kill you to save everybody else you'd destroy.' My voice wasn't soft anymore.

'Even if it destroys you at the same time?'

'Yes.'

'Even if it drags our tortured Richard down with us?'

'Yes,' I said.

'Even if it cost Damian his life?'

I nodded. 'Yes.'

'Even if Nathaniel died with us?'

I stopped breathing for a second, and time seemed to do one of those stretches where you have all the time in the world, and none of it. My breath came out shaky, and I had to lick my lips, before I said, 'Yes, on one condition.'

'And that would be?' he asked.

'That I could guarantee that I wouldn't survive it either.'

He looked at me, and it was a long, long look. A look that weighed me down to my soul, and I realized that in a way, that's exactly what he'd done years ago.

'You told me once that I'm your conscience, but that's not all I am, is it?'

'What do you mean, *ma petite*?'

'I'm your fail-safe. I'm your judge, your jury, and your executioner if things go wrong.'

'Not things, *ma petite*, me. If I go wrong.' There was a peaceful-ness in his eyes, as if some weight had gone from his shoulders. I knew exactly where that weight had gone.

'You bastard. I'd have been happy to kill you once, but not now. Not now.'

'If it is too much to ask, then consider it unasked, unsaid.'

'No, you bastard, don't you understand? If you do go mad and start slaughtering the innocent, I am exactly who they will send. I am the Executioner.' I stared at him.

'But, *ma petite*, you were always the one they would send. You have always been the Executioner.'

I got to my feet. My knees weren't weak anymore. 'But I've never been in love with someone I had to kill before.'

'But you have told me that your love for me would not stop you from doing your duty.'

My eyes burned. 'No, it won't. If you go bad, I'll do my duty.' I closed my eyes, and shook my head. 'You Machiavellian bastard, I would have killed your ass without being in love with you.'

'I did not want you to love me because you would be my fail-safe, as you put it. I wanted you to love me, because I was in love with you.' His voice was close, and when I opened my eyes he was standing in front of me. 'It is only lately that I have worried that you were so besotted with me that you might forgive me crimes in this lifetime, now.'

I shook my head. 'No, no.'

'I had to know, *ma petite*.'

'Don't call me that, not right now.'

He took a deep breath and let it out. 'Anita, I am sorry. I would not cause you pain, not deliberately.'

'Then couldn't this conversation have waited until the afterglow faded?'

'No,' he said, 'I had to know if you loved me more than your sense of justice.'

I swallowed hard. I would not cry, I would not fucking cry. 'I could not love thee, dear, so much, Loved I not honor more.'

He took my hands, and I almost jerked away, but I made myself stand there and let him touch me. I was so angry, so pissed, so . . .

'Tell me not, sweet, I am unkind,' he said, 'That from the nunnery, Of thy chaste breast and quiet mind.'

I looked up at him, and said the next line, 'To war and arms I fly.'

'True, a new mistress now I chase,' he said.

'The first foe in the field,' I said, and let him draw me closer.

'And with a stronger faith embrace,' he said.

'A sword, a horse, a shield.' And the last word was whispered against his chest, still looking up into those eyes, searching his face.

'Yet this inconstancy is such, As thou too shalt adore,' he whispered against my hair.

I finished the poem with my face pressed against his chest, listening to the beat of his heart, that truly beat with my blood. 'I could not love thee, dear, so much, Loved I not honor more.'

'To Lucasta, on going to the Wars,' Jean-Claude said. His arms were around me, holding me close.

I eased my arms around him, slowly. 'Richard Lovelace,' I said, 'always liked his stuff in college.' I kept moving my arms until they were around his waist, and we just stood there holding each other. 'I don't think I would have remembered the whole poem if you hadn't helped.'

'Together we are more than we are apart, Anita, that is what love is.'

I held him, and the tears started down my face, hard and hot, and choking. 'Not Anita.'

I didn't have to see his face, to know the smile was there, I could hear in his voice, '*ma petite, ma petite, ma petite.*'

There comes a point where you just love someone. Not because they're good, or bad, or anything really. You just love them. It doesn't mean you'll be together forever. It doesn't mean you won't hurt each other. It just means you love them. Sometimes in spite of who they are, and sometimes because of who they are. And you know that they love you, sometimes because of who you are, and sometimes in spite of it.

46

THE SAPPHIRE CLUB is a low, wide building and doesn't look that nice from the outside. It doesn't look that different from many of the rest of the bars and clubs in the area, so why is it a gentlemen's club and the others are just titty bars? Security, decor, and a dress code for the dancers, for starters. Tonight the VIP parking area was so full of official and semiofficial vehicles that you could barely see the front of the club through the flashing lights and milling people. There was even a big fire truck and a rescue truck alongside the regular ambulance. I had no idea why we needed the big truck, but murder scenes always attract more people than you really need, more cops, and more civies, more everything.

There was a crowd pressed against the police tape and sawhorse barriers. Some of the women looked barely dressed for the October cold, so it had to be people from the nearby clubs. Most of the dancers arrived at work in street clothes then changed there. So at least some of the women shivering in the cold had left work elsewhere to join the gawkers.

I actually had to park in the lot of the nearest club, the Jazz Baby, live music, and live entertainment. What could be better? Sleep, maybe. It was nearly four in the morning. My shower had beaten the record for speed, but it was still quite a drive from the Riverfront. We'd managed to get blood on the front of my shirt, so I was wearing a T-shirt that Jean-Claude had found for me somewhere. It was white, so the black bra showed through, or would have if I hadn't been wearing Byron's leather jacket again. Maybe I could just keep the jacket on. No, it'd be warm inside. Oh, well. If the worst thing that happened tonight was that someone noticed I was wearing a black bra under a white shirt, we'd count ourselves lucky.

Jean-Claude had also found underwear, again it was thong, but it was actually comfortable, because it was made of soft T-shirt material, even the bit that went between your cheeks. Most of the girl thongs I'd looked at had had elastic or lace running up your ass, and that just didn't look comfy at all.

I had to flash the badge just to get through the crowd. When I got up to the line, the officer closest to me didn't really look at me. He saw a woman in boots and a short skirt and a leather jacket and said, 'Club's closed for the night, you won't be working.'

I shoved my badge into his face, and he had to back up to focus on it. 'Actually, Officer,' and I read his name tag in the bright lights, 'Douglas, I think I will be working tonight.'

He looked down at me, because he was taller than me. I watched his face try to wrap around the look of me and the badge in one package. He wasn't the first police officer to have a problem putting it all together, and he wouldn't be the last. I might think like a cop, but I don't really look like one. Especially not tonight.

'I'm Marshal Anita Blake, Sergeant Zerbrowski called me.' Always good to remind people that I hadn't invited myself into their party. I had the authority to do it, but I tried to do as little uninvited butting in as I could. No cop, no matter what the flavor, likes someone horning in on their case. Especially not a big one.

Officer Douglas stared at my badge like he didn't believe it was real. 'No one told me that the feds were coming.'

'Ya know, it's four in the morning. I asked your permission to cross this line as a courtesy, but this badge is a federal badge and it gives me the right to cross this line, enter this crime scene, and do my fucking job. If you stop me, Officer Douglas, I will charge you with obstructing a federal officer in the performance of her duty.'

He looked like he'd swallowed something sour, but he waved

another officer over. He had him take his place at the barrier and held the tape for me. 'I'll walk you through, ma'am.'

I guess I couldn't blame him. I mean what if the badge wasn't real, or wasn't mine? Of course, if I'd been a big, strapping guy, he wouldn't have had a problem with it. You can always tell a new cop from a veteran. New ones still judge a lot on appearance, once you've been on the cop for a few years, you stop doing that. Because by then you've learned that what's on the outside doesn't tell you that much about what's on the inside. A cute little old lady can pull a trigger just as well as a big scary-looking guy. Rookies don't know that yet. They haven't learned the lesson that you can't tell by looking.

Officer Douglas didn't shorten his stride for me, and he didn't need to. I was used to walking scenes with Dolph, who made Douglas look petite. I kept up with him even in the high-heeled boots. He looked like he wanted to say something, but he didn't. Probably just as well.

Some of the police on this side of the river don't know me on sight. They thought what Douglas had thought, that I worked here, because they catcalled after us, 'Hey, Dougie, going to get a piece. No lap dances on company time, Douglas.' And worse. I ignored it all. It was four in the morning, and I hadn't been to bed yet, I didn't care. Besides, I'd learned the hard way that the more attention you pay to shit like that, the more you have to shovel. Ignore it, and it usually goes away, because it just isn't any fun if they don't get a rise out of you. Besides, they were teasing Douglas more than me. I was just the nameless girl who gave them an excuse.

He ignored it, but his face was blazing by the time we got to the main doors. He actually held the door for me, and I let him. There'd been a point in my life when I would have not let him hold the door. But with his face already burning with embarrassment, I wasn't going to arm wrestle him for the door. I might have to work with him again, so screw it, he could hold the door. Besides, if I put him on the spot about the door, it would have given his coworkers more to tease him about, and I didn't want that.

We went through the glass doors into a little entry area that reminded me of the front of a nice resturant, complete with a little desk and a maître d'. Though that probably wasn't the tall guy's official title. But hey, he was wearing a white suit jacket with a tie, he did look like a maître d'. When I'd seen him last, he was tall and self-assured and had taken my name and Asher's and called on a phone to have a 'hostess' escort us in. Now he leaned on his counter, head in his hands, looking ill.

There were bathrooms off to the left, and a short hallway that led into the club. From the door you really couldn't see into the club. It gave them a last chance to keep out the undesirables, or the under-agers, before someone saw breasts. The color scheme was muted blues and purples, and if they hadn't had silhouettes of naked women on the walls, it would have looked like a restaurant, oh, and the poster advertising that Wednesday was amateur night.

I couldn't remember the big guy's name, just couldn't remember it. But it didn't matter, because Douglas took me past him without a word. Up the little ramp, and the club spilled out around us. There was a good solid bar area to the left that would have done any club proud, but the rest of the room was all strip club. I mean, what else do you use little round stages for? The room was mostly blues and purples, and maybe other colors. I couldn't tell for sure, because most of the big room was lit by black light, or other odd lighting, so that the room was lit, but it was still terribly dark. I'd been surprised the first time I was here, it was as if light could be dark, so that though there was no actual shadowed area, the whole room seemed like it was in a shadow.

It was a weekend night, the place was packed, but quiet. They'd had to turn off the music, and the DJ's endless prattle was merci-fully absent. In fact, the room seemed wrong this quiet, as if the noise was part of the decor. There were men, and more women than you'd think in the audience, huddled now all together like mourners at an unexpected funeral. The dancers were all in one corner with a plainclothes detective that I didn't recognize. A big man in a uniform that matched Officer Douglas's strode toward us, with a notebook in one hand and a pen in the other. He still had his hat on, as if his round face would have been incomplete without it.

'Douglas, what the fuck are you bringing me another stripper for? We got all the girls that were in the club tonight over there.' He motioned with his thumb over his shoulder. He had small, beady eyes, or maybe I was just tired of being called a stripper, and discounted like I didn't matter, just because I happened to be a girl and not in uniform. 'Unless, you saw somethin' outside. Did you, girlie, see anything?'

I raised my badge so he could see it, and stepped around Douglas so I was facing what had to be his boss. 'Federal Marshal Anita Blake, and you are?'

I could see his face darken even in the odd lighting. 'Sheriff Christopher, Melvin Christopher.' He looked me up and down, not the way a man will if he thinks a woman is pretty, but like he was sizing me up, and wasn't impressed. 'You know, if you don't want people thinking you're a stripper, you should dress better, miss.'

'That's Marshal Blake to you, Sheriff, and in the big city, this is called date clothes. Dresses down to your knees went out of style a few decades back.'

His face got a little darker, his eyes went from unfriendly to hostile. 'You think you're funny?'

'No,' I said, and I took a deep breath in and let it out slow. 'Look, you stop calling me a stripper, and I'll stop making cute remarks at you. Let's both pretend we're here to solve a crime, and just do our jobs.'

'We don't need federal help here.'

I sighed. I looked around the room and didn't see anyone I knew. 'Fine, you want to do it this way, we can do it this way. If you prevent me from questioning all the vampires before dawn comes, I will charge you with obstructing a federal officer in the performance of her duties.'

'Some of them your friends, that it? I heard you were coffin bait.'

I shook my head and walked wide around Douglas, which put me out of reach for the sheriff.

'Where the hell are you going?'

'To question the witnesses,' I said, and I kept a little bit of an eye on the sheriff, because I wasn't sure what he would do.

'How do you know where they are?'

'They aren't out here, or out in the parking lot, so they've got to be in the Sapphire Room.' I was almost to the little raised platform in front of a pair of nice wooden doors. There was another uniformed officer in front of the doors. I had been in there before, so I knew the sound was muffled inside the room. That's why I hadn't yelled for Zerbrowski already.

I unzipped the leather jacket as I went up the steps. I had my badge in my left hand, held where the uniform on the door could see it clearly. I wasn't really sure what I was going to do if the sheriff told his man not to let me in. I'd learned that just because I had the legal right to be somewhere, didn't mean the local police would make it easy. They wouldn't actually lay hands on me, or boot my ass out, but if they wanted to be uncooperative, they could be.

'Please move aside, Officer.'

He actually started to step to the side, but the sheriff said, 'You don't work for her. You move when I say you move.'

I sighed and thought, *Well, shit.* Then I had an idea. I reached into the pocket of the leather coat.

'Be careful what you reach for,' the sheriff said from far too close behind me.

I turned so I could see him and the other officer. I held up my cell phone. 'No need to get excited, Sheriff. Just going to make a phone call.'

He had his hands on his hips above his Sam Brown belt. He hadn't unsnapped his gun, so he wasn't serious. He was just trying to see if I'd spook. If he thought this kind of shit could intimidate me, he'd been playing in the shallow end of the pool for too fucking long.

I hit the buttons, keeping an eye on the officers in the room. A lot of them had stopped questioning or guarding or whatever they were doing, to watch our little show. Zerbrowski answered on the second ring. 'I'm in the club, just outside the doors.'

'And why aren't you inside the doors?' he asked, sounding puzzled.

'The sheriff has ordered his man not to move away from the doors.'

'Not true,' the sheriff yelled, 'but you sure as hell can't order my man to do shit.'

I sighed loud enough so Zerbrowski could hear it. 'A little help here.'

Zerbrowski opened the door with the phone still in his hand. 'Thanks, Sheriff Christopher, I think Marshal Blake and I have it from here.' He clicked the phone shut, smiled at everybody, and moved aside enough for me to pass through, but not enough for the sheriff, who stood at the bottom of the steps glaring at him. I finally realized that the pissing contest had started before I got there, and I'd just gotten caught in it.

Zerbrowski shut the door behind us, and leaned against it shaking his head. He's 5' 9", with short black hair going more and more gray every year. When his wife makes him get it cut, the hair is short and neat. When he forgets, or she's busy, it's curly and wavy, and as untidy as the rest of him. His suit was brown, his tie was pale yellow, and so was his shirt. I think it was the first time I'd seen all his clothes match in all the years I'd known him. Okay, match and not have food stains on them.

His glasses were silver and helped hide that his eyes were tired, but not that he was pissed. He took me off to one side by the fountain with a once-real-live stuffed lion crouching beside it. The

Sapphire Room is a cross between a hunting lodge, a safari room, and other things people think men think is masculine. Most of the room was carpeted in leopard print, so that my first thought was, always, *Oh, no, a leopard blew up and plastered itself all over everything, but hey, animal prints are in this year*. People pay hundreds of dollars a night to be back here, so they must like it.

Zerbrowski turned his back on the room and motioned for me to move in front of him so that no one would see us talking. 'Welcome to the party.'

'Why are you keeping out all of the sheriff's men?'

'When we pulled up, they had the vampires in here and were using crosses on them. They didn't touch them, just made the crosses glow like hell, and basically said, you talk, or we keep crosses out.'

'Shit, use of a holy item on a vampire for questioning was ruled assault, what, three months ago in federal court?'

'Yeah,' he said, and he raised his glasses up and rubbed at his eyes with his thumb and forefinger.

'Every vamp here could press charges,' I whispered.

He nodded and readjusted his glasses. 'Like I said, welcome to the party.'

Before the ruling, a lot of police departments had holy items as part of their uniform, like lapel pins or tietacks, but now they were back to carrying them undercover somewhere on their bodies. Holy items were now considered weapons when dealing with vampires. Which meant what the sheriff had done constituted assault with a deadly weapon.

'Was it just him, or his men, too?'

'Some of his men. Before we got here, they were all wearing little cross-shaped lapel pins. I got them to remove them, but only after I threatened to call the closest FBI office.'

I looked at him, because no cop likes to call in what they so affectionately call the Feebies.

'I'd rather let the FBI take this entire case away from us than let crap like this go down. The vampires are scared shitless now. If there are any guilty ones here, I can't tell it, because they're all either royally pissed, or scared. Most of them won't even talk to us, and legally they don't have to.' It didn't really show in his voice, but he was as angry as I'd seen him. I could see it in the tightness around his eyes, the way his hands kept stiffening up. Zerbrowski was usually one laid back guy, but everybody has their limits. 'We got a hit from New Orleans and Pittsburgh. Very similar crimes. Two in Pittsburgh, five in New Orleans, then they moved here.'

'Lucky us,' I said.

'Yeah,' he said, 'but that means we have at least three more bodies to look forward to. We need these nice citizen vamps to talk to us.'

'I'll see what I can do. Do you have anyone you want me to start with? I mean it's 4:30, we've got about three hours or less until dawn. They've got to be allowed to go home before dawn, unless you can charge them with something.'

'We've got a woman dead in the side lot here, multiple vampire bites, and they're vampires. I could probably get a judge to agree to holding them as material witnesses. I know a judge that hates vampires enough to give me a court order.'

I shook my head. 'We're trying to smooth this over, not make it worse. Right now they can only sue this city, let's not give them a reason to sue us, too.'

He nodded then stepped aside and made a sweeping gesture with his hand. 'They are all yours, good luck.'

There was a group of vampires around the big fireplace in the center of the main room. None of them belonged to Jean-Claude. Some of them were clustered around a table set in front of the fireplace, in huge thronelike chairs, some on a cushioned seat near the fireplace. One of the vampires was clutching an animal print cushion while he sat in front of the fire. His eyes were wide, and he looked shell-shocked. The other five were scared, or angry, or a mixture of both, but they were holding it together better than the cushion-hugger.

I showed them my badge and explained who I was. But it wasn't the badge that made the cushion-hugger whimper, 'Oh, God, they're going to kill us.'

'Shut up, Roger,' a tall vampire with sleek black hair and angry hazel eyes said. 'Why are you here, Ms Blake? We are being held against our wills, and we are guilty of nothing except being vampires.'

'And you are?' I asked.

He stood and straightened a rather nice, conservative suit. 'I am Charles Moffat.'

'I know that name,' I said.

He looked nervous, just for a moment, then he tried to swallow it. He wasn't twenty-years dead, a baby.

'You're one of Malcolm's deacons for the Church of Eternal Life,' I said.

He opened his mouth, then closed it, and stood very tall, and said, 'Yes, I am, and I'm not ashamed of it.'

'No, but Malcolm has forbidden any of his church members to frequent this side of the river for nefarious purposes.'

'How do you know what our master dictates?' He was trying to bluff, and it wasn't going to work.

'Because Malcolm talked to the Master of the City and got him to agree to tell Malcolm if any of the church's members frequented his clubs. You guys aren't allowed to be anywhere this naughty. You must, and I quote, be absolutely above reproach.'

One of the vamps who was balding and wore glasses, started rocking in his chair. 'I knew we shouldn't have come. If Malcolm finds out . . .'

'She is Jean-Claude's servant, and she must tell him, and he will tell Malcolm.'

'Actually, the agreement was just to tattle about you coming to our clubs. Malcolm didn't ask us to keep an eye this side of the river.'

The bald vampire looked up at me as if I'd offered him salvation. 'You won't tell?'

'If you guys tell me everything you know about this, I don't see a reason to.'

The bald vampire touched Charles Moffat's arm. Charles jerked away from him. 'How can we trust you?'

'Look, I'm not the one who signed a morals clause with my master and has just been caught in a titty bar – you guys have. So if anyone is questioning someone's word, shouldn't it be me? I mean a vampire that goes against the express orders of his master, what good is he either to his master or his kiss?'

'We of the church do not use the word *kiss* for a group of vampires. Malcolm feels that it is too sensuous a word.'

'Fine, but my point stands. You've betrayed your master, your church, and your oath, or don't you in the church take blood oath, either?'

'A barbaric practice,' Charles said, 'we of the church are held by our own moral standards, not some magical oath.'

I smiled and motioned around the room. 'Hmm, nice standards.'

Charles blushed, which isn't easy for a vamp, but it let me know he'd fed tonight, fed a lot. 'Who was your feed for tonight?'

He just glared at me. 'Look, guys, it's 4:30 in the morning. We have less than three hours to get your asses back to your homes. We want you all out of here before dawn, alright?'

They all nodded. 'Then answer my questions. I can tell which one of you has fed and which hasn't. I need to know what dancers, or donors, you fed on. If they're in the other room, I need to talk to them. If they aren't, I need names, and a way to contact them tonight.'

'The relationship between a vampire and their partner is sacred.'

'Look, Charles, you've got enough blood in you to blush. You want me to start speculating where you got that much blood to waste?'

'We have already been threatened and abused. You can do no more to us.'

I turned to the rest. 'Who wants to answer my questions and get an I-won't-tell-Malcolm card?'

The bald vamp stood up. Charles yelled at him. But Baldie shook his head. 'No, you aren't my master, Charles. We are all free beings in the church, it's one of the reasons we joined. I'm going to answer her questions, because it's within my rights to do so.'

'Let's find a private room,' I said, and motioned for him to follow me. There was a truly beautiful saltwater aquarium in a little area that was probably meant to be a smoking room, but there were smaller rooms off of it, where normally you could take one of the dancers and get a private dance.

I took Baldie into the first room. It was actually nice, not tacky in the least, with a small couch, a chair, a coffee table, and area lighting. The room still pulled off that leather and manly den theme, without being obnoxious about it. 'Have a seat,' I said.

He sat, rubbing his hands over his knees, nervous. He was a little plump, and soft. He looked like an accountant, except that when he licked his lips, he flashed a little fang. The new ones do that. 'How long have you been in the church?'

'Two years.' He was shaking his head. 'I thought it would be sexy, you know, vampires, the clothes, the romance.' He clasped his plump hands together. 'But it's not like that at all. I'm still a law clerk, just at a different office where they let me work nights. I can't drink, can't eat a steak, and dying didn't make me sexier.' He spread his hands wide. 'Look at me, I'm just paler.'

'I thought the church required six months minimum of study before they let you take the last step?'

He nodded. 'They do, but they made all the moral stuff seem high-minded, you know, we're better than those other vampires. We aren't perverts like Jean-Claude and his vamps.' He looked up and was scared, and it showed. 'I'm sorry, I didn't mean . . .'

'I know what the church says about normal vampire society.'

'It sounded so noble.'

'Let me guess, there was this woman that happened to be a vampire.' He looked up, startled. 'How did you know?'

'Lucky guess, and after you made the change, what happened?'

'She was my partner for the first few months, but after that, she had other duties.'

That was interesting, and I filed it away for later. If the church deacons were seducing members, that might be called illegal, at the very least questionably moral. 'Who'd you feed off of tonight?'

The question threw him, and he blinked at me like a rabbit in headlights. 'Sasha, her name was Sasha.'

'And you brought her back here?'

He nodded.

'You're a club member?'

He nodded again.

'Charles is, too?'

Nod.

'Most of the people at the table are members?'

Nod, then, 'It was Clarke's first time here.'

'And Clarke is the one with the pillow?'

'How did you know?'

I shook my head, smiled, and said, 'Do you remember any other girls that people fed off of, names or descriptions?' He remembered a lot. I ended up with four names, two descriptions, and only poor Clarke had not fed. Of course, I'd known that last part, but it's always nice to have things confirmed.

With Zerbrowski as my guard, we ventured out into the club and fetched the women in question. We matched up every vamp with at least one girl. Charles had fed on three, and he was a big tipper. Two of the girls were his regulars. Pretty naughty for a church deacon.

It took me a little more than two hours to match up those who had fed with whom they'd fed on. It didn't mean they hadn't snuck out and fed again, but it made it less likely. I suggested that we could compare bite radiuses on the dead girl with the vamps later, if we needed to. We knew their names, and knew how to find them.

The most interesting bit of information I found out was given up only by the first vamp I talked to and by Clarke, who was so scared he'd have given up his mother. There had been three other church members here earlier in the evening, and they were also part of the crowd that liked to frequent the stripper bars. But none of them were members of the Sapphire Room VIP club. I had their names and an address for the most newly dead of them. Maybe they'd had something to do with the murder, or maybe they just gotten bored and went home early. It wasn't a crime to leave a place.

Zerbrowski had actually called in state troopers to back us up, as we escorted the vampires to their cars. None of them was powerful enough, or old enough to be able to fly home. When we'd gotten the last of the undead safely off in their minivans and compact cars, Zerbrowski took me to one side and said, 'Did I hear you right? The vamp church makes their members sign a morals clause?'

I nodded. 'Other vamps call them nightshift Mormons.'

He grinned. 'Nightshift Mormons, really.'

'Honest.'

'Oh, I will have to remember that one, that's good.' He looked behind us at the waiting ambulance, fire truck, and all the personnel. 'Now that you've helped save the vamps, how about looking at the acutal crime scene?'

'Thought you'd never ask.'

He grinned, and it almost pushed the tiredness out of his eyes. 'I get to go first down the ladder,' he said.

I frowned at him. 'What ladder?'

'Our murder scene and body dump are in a hole left by some overzealous construction workers. According to the club manager, they broke ground, but didn't have all their permits in line, so it's just a big hole. That's why we need the firemen to help us get the body up out of the hole when you're done with it.'

'You are not going ahead of me down the ladder, Zerbrowski.'

'What are you wearing under that little bitty skirt?'

'None of your damn business, and if you don't let me go first down the ladder, I'll tell your wife on you.'

He laughed, and a few people looked our way. They were colder than we were, and just as tired. I don't think they saw anything to laugh about. 'Katie knows I'm a lech.'

I shook my head. 'How messy is it down in the hole?'

'Let's see, it's rained, it's frozen, it's thawed, and it's rained some more.'

'Shit,' I said.

'Where are those overalls you used to wear to all the crime scenes?'

'It's against company policy to wear crime scene gear to a zombie raising now.' What I didn't say out loud was that I'd forgotten and worn overalls that had blood on them to a zombie raising. The client's wife had fainted. Was it my fault that she had a fragile constitution? It wasn't Bert who said no more, it was a majority vote at Animator's Inc. So I actually had to pay attention to the rule. 'I didn't plan on climbing into holes and looking at bodies tonight.'

The grin faded from his face. 'Me neither, let's get this done. I want to go home and hug my wife and kids before they go off to school and work.'

I didn't point out that it was 6:30 in the morning, and his chances of making it home in time to see Katie and his kids before they rushed off to their days was slim to none. Everybody needs a little hope, who am I to take it away?

47

THE WOMAN IN the hole was beyond hope, or fear, or whatever had happened to her. Her face looked empty, the way the dead always do. You get an occasional one that looks scared, but it's just happenstance. The way their face muscles worked at the moment of death. But mostly, the dead look empty, like something essential is missing, something beyond just no breath, no heartbeat. I'd seen enough eyes do that last glaze, to say that something more precious than breath goes with death. Or maybe I was just tired and didn't want to be standing ankle-deep in mud, staring down at a woman that was probably younger than I was, and now always would be. I get more morbid the closer to dawn it gets, if I haven't been to bed.

There were a lot of similarities to the first body. This one was lying on her back, just like the last one. They'd both been strippers. They were both killed just outside the clubs that they worked in. This one was a blonde, and white, which was the same as the first one. There were a set of bite marks on either side of the neck, and one in the bend of her left arm, right wrist, and chest. To see if she had thigh bites I was going to have to kneel in the mud, and I didn't want to. Simple as that, I didn't want to. I promised myself I would never again be caught out, anywhere, without a pair of coveralls, and mud boots. I'd had to borrow gloves from Zerbrowski. I'd been thinking about my date, not about my job when I packed the Jeep earlier. Stupid me.

I stood up and debated on whether I could get away without crawling around in the mud and looking at all the bites. 'She's taller, by almost a foot than the last one. Blond hair but very short, the last one had long hair. Other than that, it looks damn similar.'

'The bite radiuses are the same.'

'Who took the measurements?' I asked.

He told me, and the name meant nothing to me. I was across the river, and I didn't actually do a lot of crime scenes here. I killed vamps for Illinois, but I didn't do much actual investigative work. I couldn't let someone else do it, not if I didn't know them. If even one bite radius was off, it would mean a change of players in our vampire group. We needed to know if we were looking for five, or six, or more.

I sighed and fetched my little tape measure out of the jacket pocket. That I'd started keeping in the glove compartment with the baby wipes. I measured the easy-to-get-to bites first and had Zerbrowski take notes. Then I planted my knee carefully in the mud, between her knees. The mud was cold. I spread her legs and found the inner thigh bites. I measured everything I could find. The bite radiuses matched, or ballparked. I was using a different instrument to do the measuring, which I shouldn't have done. I shouldn't have let the CSU technician let me use something I wouldn't have with me next time. What you measured with could make a difference in the field. The field was not a laboratory.

I got up from the ground carefully, my goal was still not to slide on my ass in the mud. High-heeled boots were not the best thing to wear to guarantee that. So I was careful. 'The Sapphire has security people walking their lot. At least one security guy at any given time. It's the weekend, there should have been two. Did they see or hear anything?'

'One of them saw the girl come out with her coat on. She was headed home, done for the night. He saw her go toward her car –' he riffled back through his notebook – 'then, she wasn't there.'

I looked at him. 'What did you say?'

'He said, she was walking toward her car, he waved at her, then something attracted his attention to the other side of the lot. He's a little vague on what attracted his attention, but he swears he only glanced away, then when he looked back, she was gone.'

'Gone.'

'Yeah, why do you have that look on your face, like that means something?'

'Did he check her car right away?'

He nodded. 'Yes, and when he didn't find her at the car, he went back into the club to see if she'd gone back inside. When he couldn't find her inside, he got the other security guy, and they started searching the area. They found her.'

'How long does he think he looked away for?'

'He says a few seconds.'

'Has anyone checked with anyone else inside, who might have seen her leave? I'd like to know what time she left the building, and how long he was really staring off in the other direction.'

'Let's just get out of the hole and find someone who saw her leave and actually looked at a clock.'

He was riffling through his notebook again. The lights that they had directed down into the pit illuminated everything, in fact made it all a little stark, and pitiless, as if she needed to be covered up and not stared at anymore. Maudlin, I was getting positively maudlin.

'Actually, one of the ladies inside, a customer, had liked the blonde a lot, she and her husband. So she noticed the time when she left.'

'And how does it tally with the security guy's statement?'

He checked the times back and forth. 'Ten minutes.'

'Ten minutes is an awfully long time to stare at something he isn't even sure he saw.'

'You think he lied?'

I shook my head. 'No, I think he told what he thinks is the truth.'

'I'm lost. What are you getting at?' Zerbrowski asked.

I smiled at him, but not like I was happy. 'One of the vamps has to be a master, we figured that, but they also have to be able to cloud men's minds enough to pull something like this off.'

'I thought all vamps could cloud men's minds.'

I shook my head. 'They can mesmerize one person with their gaze, and if they bite them, then they can blank their memory. If they're powerful enough, they can mesmerize with the eyes and blank most of the memory. But the vic will usually have this vague memory of eyes, or sometimes an animal with blazing eyes, or car headlights that were very bright. The mind tries to make mundane sense of what's happened.'

'Okay, so one of the vamps zapped him with its gaze.'

'No, Zerbrowksi, I'm betting it wasn't eyes. I'm betting it was from a distance with no direct gaze. I'll talk to him, see what he remembers, but if he's bite-free and doesn't have some weird memory, then it was done from a nice safe distance, with no direct contact.'

'So what?' he asked, and he sounded irritated and tired.

I didn't take it personally. 'It means that one of the vamps is old, Zerbrowski. Old, and a master vampire. We're talking fairly major talent here. It's a limited list.'

'Names?'

I shook my head. 'Let's talk to the security guy and get him to strip down for us.'

He looked at me over the rims of his glasses, before he pushed them back up his nose. 'Did you just say what I think you just said?'

'We've got to check him for vamp bites. If he's clean, then we're looking for a major player, vampirically speaking. If he's got a bite, then not so major. Trust me, it'll make a difference in who we talk to.'

'Is this Jean-Claude's people?' Zerbrowski asked.

'No,' I said.

'How can you be sure?' he asked.

How could I be sure? I was tired enough that I let that be a question in my head, let me wonder what Jean-Claude would say. Would he guarantee that this couldn't have been his people? The thought was enough, he was suddenly in my head. Shit.

He was seeing what I was seeing, not good at a murder investigation when the vic had been done in by vamps. I started to shield, to kick him out, but I suddenly knew the answer to my question. 'My blood oath will hold them from this, because it is against my express orders to bring us to the negative attention of the human police.'

I thought, *Liv broke your oath once,* and he heard me. 'I was not *le sourdre de sang* then. My oath is not so lightly shaken off now, *ma petite.*'

I'd been quiet too long. Zerbrowski said, 'You okay?'

'Just thinking,' I said. I'd known about blood oaths, but I hadn't actually understood how important they were, or what they were supposed to mean. 'Because all of Jean-Claude's people have to take a blood oath. It binds them mystically to the Master of the City. He's forbidden his vampires to do shit like this.'

'You're saying the blood oath makes this impossible?'

'Not impossible, but harder. It depends on how strong the master is that they make the oath to.'

'How strong is Jean-Claude?'

I thought about a way to explain it and finally settled for, 'Strong enough that I'd bet good money this wasn't his people.'

'But you wouldn't guarantee it.'

'Guarantees are for major appliances, not for murder.'

He grinned. 'That's cute, I may just have to use that one sometime.'

'Knock yourself out.'

The grin faded round the edges. 'I still don't really understand this whole blood oath thing. Maybe I'm just too tired for metaphysics, explain it to me again later.'

'Let me simplify it.'

'That'd be nice,' he said.

'I just learned tonight from the vamps I questioned that Malcolm has abolished the blood oath for the Church. It's too barbaric.'

Jean-Claude was still in my head and heard what I said. I got a rush of fear from him, fear bordering on panic.

'Okay, and that means what exactly?' Zerbrowski asked.

I had to take a deep breath to talk around Jean-Claude's fear. His voice in my head said, 'Are you certain of this, *ma petite*?'

I let my out loud voice for Zerbrowski answer Jean-Claude's question, too. 'It means, Zerbrowski, that you have hundreds of vampires in this area that have nothing to keep them from doing shit like this, except their own consciences, and a morals clause they all sign.'

Jean-Claude was cursing in my head in French, and though I caught a word here and there, most of it was too fast for me.

Zerbrowski smiled, and the smile broadened until it was a grin. 'You're saying that the Church trusts its members to be good little citizens, and your boyfriend isn't that trusting.'

'I'll look at the new masters that have come to town at Jean-Claude's invitation, but my money is on the Church of Eternal Life.'

'Dolph would say it's because you don't want it to be Jean-Claude's people.'

'Yeah, he would, but I'll tell you this, Zerbrowski, the thought that all these new little vampires have only their human morals to make them be good, makes me almost agree with Dolph.'

'Agree on what?'

'Kill them all.'

Jean-Claude said, 'Do not say this out loud to the police, *ma petite*. It may come to that, and you do not wish your friend to remember this conversation.' He was right.

'Shit, Anita, some of your best friends are bloodsuckers.'

'Yeah, but there are rules to being a vampire, and Malcolm is trying to treat them like they're just people with fangs. They aren't, Zerbrowski, they really aren't. Even if this turns out to be a bunch of rogues that somehow slipped through everyone's radar, mine, Jean-Claude's, and Malcolm's, we are so going to have to talk to him about his new policy.'

'Why do I think when you said, *we*, just now, you weren't including me, or any of the cops?' He was looking at me, and the joking, lecherous comments were gone. I was seeing a very intelligent pair of cop eyes.

I sighed and took a step toward the ladder. I'd said too much, way too much. Jean-Claude's voice in my head, 'You must say something to take the sting out of your words, *ma petite*.'

Out loud, to Zerbrowski, I thought of something to say. 'I'm tired Zerbrowski, please don't tell Dolph that I think all the vamps in the Church should be done in. I don't mean it, not really.'

'I won't tell anyone, especially not Dolph. He'd probably start with his new daughter-in-law, and wouldn't that be a shit.'

I nodded. 'But if we had hundreds of vamps go bad, all at once, I'm still who gets the call. I so don't want to ever have to try to take on that many of them. I'm good, but not that good.'

'For a few hundred, even you'd need help,' he said. He let out a long breath. 'I can see where the thought would piss you off, and make you tired. Hell, it makes me tired, and nervous.'

'I'll try to find out how long this no-blood-oath policy has been in effect,' I said.

'And then what?'

I had my hands on the ladder. 'I'll deal with it.'

'*Ma petite*, you are being uncautious again.'

I whispered, 'Get out of my head.'

'What does that mean, Anita? You're a federal marshal, you can't do the Lone Ranger shit anymore. You got a badge.'

I leaned my forehead on the ladder, got mud on my face, and jerked back. I told him as much of the truth as I could. 'We'll give Malcolm a choice, either he blood oaths everybody, or Jean-Claude does.' Jean-Claude was suddenly louder than ever in my head. 'Stop there, *ma petite*, I beg you, do not say it out loud.'

What I didn't say out loud was that any vampire that didn't want to take the ceremony was probably dead. I had Jean-Claude's memory of it now, and I knew the blood oath was one of their most strenuously observed laws. I'd seen what could happen if the oath wasn't strong enough, what would happen if it wasn't there at all.

I was actually on the ladder, when Zerbrowski said, 'And what if the vamps don't want to take the oath?'

I stayed frozen on the ladder for a second, then lied, 'I'm not sure. I'm hoping that it's just Malcolm and not every church of their's across the country that's doing this. You're talking about something that's never been done before, Zerbrowski. As far as I know, no master vamp has ever just allowed vamps to breed like this without securing himself as their leader in more than just name. It's never been done before. Vamps aren't big on new ideas.'

'Are you talking about killing the ones that won't take the oath? Anita, they've got rights.'

'I know that, Zerbrowski, better than most.' I was cursing Malcolm, cursing him for the mess he'd started. Even if the murderers weren't his people, it was only a matter of time. Vampires are not people, they don't think like people. I realized that Malcolm was trying to do with the Church of Eternal Life what Richard had tried to do with the Thronnos Rokke Clan. Both of them were trying to treat the monsters like they were just people. They weren't. God help us, but they weren't.

Jean-Claude whispered, 'We will need to send envoys to the church and see how bad it truly is.'

I didn't answer, because I was pretty sure who one of the envoys would be. Me.

I started up the ladder, and only when Zerbrowski whistled did I remember what I was wearing under the skirt. 'Blake, you have a very nice . . .'

'Don't say it, Zerbrowski.'

'Why not?'

'Because if you say it, I'll put you on the ground.'

'Ass,' he said.

'I warned you,' I said.

He laughed.

When we were both on solid ground, I footswept him into a convenient patch of mud. He cursed me, everyone laughed. He said, 'I'll tell Katie you were mean to me.'

'She'll be on my side.' And she would be. In fact, I knew Katie Zerbrowski well enough to know that her husband wouldn't tell her he'd told me I had a nice ass. She'd consider it rude.

Jean-Claude's echo in my head was, *but you do*. I told him to shut up, too, and this time he listened. 'Dawn is near, and I must rest. We will speak again when I wake.'

'Pleasant dreams,' I whispered.

'The dead do not dream, *ma petite*.' And he was gone.

48

THE SECURITY GUY hadn't liked stripping. I told him he could do it in privacy with just me and the nice officers watching, or he could do it on one of the stages. His choice. He'd looked like he didn't believe me, but wasn't willing to risk it. He was clean, no vamp bites. On the one hand, shit, because a master vamp is harder to catch, harder to keep, and harder to kill. On the other hand, great, because the list of vamps that could do this was pretty small. Or it was if I understood the deal between Malcolm and Jean-Claude. Okay, technically it had been a deal struck between Malcolm and Nikolaos, the old Master of the City. Having met her, hell, having killed her, I'd sympathized with vamps flocking to the church and not wanting to owe her a damn thing. But Jean-Claude had honored her treaty with the church, on a few conditions. One, no master-level vamps allowed in town without running it by Jean-Claude. So either Malcolm had reneged on the deal, or he didn't know that he had someone that powerful in his community. Or neither Malcolm nor Jean-Claude had felt someone that powerful enter their territory. If that last were true, we were in deep, deep trouble, because that would raise the power level to something none of us would want to deal with.

Or had Jean-Claude approved a master for Malcolm without understanding that there would be no blood oath to keep control of it? I had so many questions that my head hurt, and no way of getting them answered until Jean-Claude woke for the day. I drove back to St Louis in dawn's early light, happy I had sunglasses with me. Happy that I wasn't driving directly east. The indirect brightness was bad enough.

The Circus was closer than my own house, so that's where I went. I bunked there sometimes to have a date with Jean-Claude, but often just because it was closer to crash. My eyes were so tired they burned, and my body had that achiness that feels almost like you're sick, but is just your body using up all its reserves to keep you awake and moving.

I pulled into the employee parking lot of Circus of the Damned at nearly 8:30 in the morning. There were three other cars in the lot. One was Jason's, and I didn't know the others on sight. But it had to be people who didn't just work here, but also lived here, and knew how to drive. That narrowed it down. I thought Meng Die drove, and maybe Faust, but I just wasn't sure, and was too tired to care.

I walked across the parking lot in the fast growing light, and fought off an urge to hunch my shoulders. I used my key on the back door, and I pushed my way into the blessed dimness of a storage room.

I locked the door behind me, leaning against it for a second or two. Not long ago there hadn't been a lock on the back door at all, you had to have someone let you in, but I'd had them put in a better door, reinforced steel, with a lock. Without the lock they'd had to keep someone in a little lookout up near the roof. The lookout would send someone down if the person at the door needed in. I said it seemed silly, since there was a lock on the outer doors in front. It just made it harder for the employees to get in, and besides there was a small window just before dawn when sometimes the lookout was empty, and that was often when I was trying to get inside. Banging on the door at dawn just got discouraging.

I made sure the door was secure behind me, then I wound my way through the boxes that were always there, to the big door that led to the stairs. The stairs went down, a long way down. I was tired enough that if there'd been an elevator I would have taken it. But there wasn't. The stairs were actually part of the defenses of the Circus. One, it was a lot of stairs, so you had to be fairly serious to go down them. Two, there were places along the way that we could set up ambushes if we needed to. Three, the stairs were oddly made, as if whatever they'd originally been made for hadn't walked on two legs, or at least hadn't been the size of a human being. If you didn't know what awaited you down below, you might start wondering what used these stairs. Actually, just vamps and wereanimals, but our enemies didn't know that. Jean-Claude encouraged the rumors that there were other things down here, bigger, less human things. Fine with me, keep your enemies scared and guessing.

By the time I got to the big iron door at the bottom, my vision was blurry from lack of sleep. I dragged my keys back out. The key to this door wasn't hard to find. It was the only huge, old-fashioned key on the ring. It looked like a giant among dwarves compared to the modern keys.

I put the key in, and the lock moved, smooth and well-oiled. The hinges were just as quiet, though probably if I had only been human strong I might have had to struggle with the weight of the door. It was meant to withstand battering by bigger things than hands.

I closed it behind me, and locked it, and set the big bar in place. If anyone else was dragging their ass in this late, they were out of luck. But you were usually safe this far after dawn to set the bigger lock in place. The fact that it hadn't been set probably meant Jean-Claude had figured I'd come here for the day.

I passed through the long, silky curtains that formed the walls of the living room. I actually didn't give much attention to the gold and white and silver furniture, or the painting above the faux fireplace. Sleep was the only thing on my mind, now that the outer door was locked.

I went to Jean-Claude's room, but I should have known better. I found him and Asher curled under the sheets. Both of them beautiful in death as in life. Asher's golden waves lay like metallic foam upon a white pillow. His eyes were closed, so I couldn't see his pale blue eyes, like the eyes of a Siberian husky. As pale a blue as Jean-Claude's were a dark blue. Asher lay on his side, so that the unscarred side of his face was up to the light. They'd left a light on for me, probably. Without a light, the room was dark as a cave. No windows. Jean-Claude lay spooning against Asher's back, one arm over the other man's waist, his hand trailing along the scars on the right side of Asher's body. Asher had been the blond beauty to Jean-Claude's brunette once, then some well-meaning Church officials had captured him and used holy water to drive the devil out of him. Holy water acts on vampire flesh like acid on ours. Those same officials had burned Asher's human servant and love, Julianna, at the stake. Christianity is a fine religion, but some of the things done in the name of it, aren't so nice.

I touched Jean-Claude's face, moved a stray lock of his hair behind one pale shoulder. His skin was cool to the touch, and would just get colder. I kissed Asher's forehead, and it was like kissing the dead. Vampires didn't sleep at dawn, they died. They truly were animated corpses. I just wasn't sure what exactly animated them.

I couldn't sleep in the bed with two corpses. The cooling flesh just creeped me out. I wasn't sure I'd ever be able to sleep with a vampire, I mean really sleep. Which left me wondering what bed to use. If there'd been a couch in the room, I would have used it, but there wasn't. Until I'd asked, there hadn't even been chairs. When you've got a bed this big, I guess who wants to sit in a chair?

I walked back out and closed the door softly behind me, not that it would wake them, but just out of habit. I went to Jason's room. I'd bunked with him before. I didn't knock, because I expected everybody to be asleep, and I was right. Jason was curled up tight on the far edge of the bed, his blond hair showing just above the covers. Someone else was curled against his back, and for just a second I thought I'd goofed, and it was a woman, but I knew that spill of auburn hair. Nathaniel was bunking here for the night. Again, not the first time.

They'd left the bathroom light on, with the door opened a crack.

I wasn't sure if it was for my benefit, or so Nathaniel would know where he was if he woke in the middle of the night. The first few times I'd woken in absolute darkness in one of these windowless rooms, it had been claustrophobic. I liked a little light.

I'd cleaned the mud off my face in the car with the baby wipes, and once I got my boots and hose off, I was going to be mud-free. It was nearly a miracle that I hadn't fallen down, wearing the heels in the mud. I took off the leather jacket and folded it nicely. There was no chair, so I sat flat on the floor and unzipped the boots and stripped off the hose, putting them against a wall, so no one would stumble over them. The skirt was stiff with dried blood. The fact that none of the vamps in the club had said anything about it said either that they couldn't smell it, or they thought remarking on it would have been too barbaric.

I left the skirt in a pile by itself. I wasn't even sure dry cleaning could save it.

I took off the white T-shirt and made a third pile for clothes that were actually clean. The bra went in that pile. I put the T-shirt back on and kept the thong underwear, too. I'd have slept better without the thong, but the T-shirt wasn't enough clothes. I'd never slept nude with Nathaniel, and I had with Jason only once, when I'd passed out that way. I needed jammies. What I wanted more than anything in that moment was to wrap as much of my tired body around Nathaniel's body as I could, and sleep.

I crawled under the sheets on the far side of the bed and moved until I touched Nathaniel's bare back. The moment I touched him, he stirred in his sleep. I slid my body along his, until I spooned him from behind, which was how we slept most nights at home. He wasn't wearing anything. It wasn't a comment on sexual orientation for Nathaniel and Jason. It was a comment about them both being were-animals. Wereanimals just didn't see the point in clothes, not if they could go without them.

I settled in against Nathaniel's body, and he snuggled himself between my body and Jason. Who never so much as stirred. I put my face against Nathaniel's hair, and the vanilla scent of it was enough. I was home, and I slept.

49

SOMETHING WOKE ME. I wasn't sure what. I was just suddenly awake in the dimness of Jason's bedroom. I was still curled against Nathaniel, and Jason was a dim blond shape on the other side of him. Nothing had changed, so what had woken me?

I lay there, straining to listen. There was nothing to hear. It was just the boys' quiet breathing, the rustle of a sheet when Jason moved in his sleep. The room was utterly quiet. Had I heard something? Then I did hear something – water. Water running in the bathroom.

I slid my hand under my pillow, and the Browning was there in its holster. If I wasn't at home with the gun in its bedframe holster, then I kept the gun holstered and snapped, just in case. It'd be a shame if someone's hand accidentally offed the safety, and another hand hit a trigger, and well, you get the idea. I unsnapped the holster, drew out the gun, and put a hand over Nathaniel's mouth.

He jerked awake, eyes wide. I motioned with the gun toward the crack of the bathroom door. He nodded and touched Jason's shoulder, as I slipped out of the bed and moved toward the bathroom.

I had the safety off, the gun held two-handed, pointed at the ceiling. It could have been one of the other shapeshifters come to borrow a shower. It would be like them, not to wake anyone and just assume it would be alright. It'd be a hell of a thing to kill someone because they used the wrong shower.

I crossed wide around the door, so my shadow wouldn't cross the light, though probably with the dark room behind me, that wouldn't happen. But better careful than not. I had to ball the black silk robe up over one arm to keep from tripping over it. I didn't remember putting on a robe.

I was at the hinge side of the door, and I went to one knee, because if someone was on the other side with a weapon, most people aimed higher than where my head was when I knelt. I kept as much of myself against the doorjamb as I could and began to ease the door open with my hands, which were still cupped around the gun. I was hoping to give my eyes time to adjust to the light, before whoever it was noticed the door moving. I knew better than to simply jump into the room from almost dark to bright light. I'd be blind for a second or two. If I'd been sure it was a bad guy, I'd have fired blind, but I wasn't sure.

There was water seeping out from under the door, the robe under my knees was wet with it. What I thought had been the shower running was the bathtub. I could hear the difference now. Someone had flooded the bathtub. What the hell was going on?

I had the door flat against the wall now, and there was no one to be seen. There was just the bathtub with water spilling over its sides and the water still rushing out of the faucet at full blast. The lower part of my legs were soaked. It was cold, so cold. Like they'd turned on only the cold. Who took a bath in only cold water?

There was just the sink area, a partial wall, the stool, and the bathtub/shower. The room was small enough that I could see it all in one glance. There was no place to hide. Was this joke? Had someone crept in while we slept, plugged the bathtub, and turned on the water? Did they think we'd notice before it flooded? Did they care? Stupid joke.

I got to my feet and started wading through the water. It was ankle deep, and that seemed wrong. I mean, it shouldn't be that deep. The hem of the robe caught in the water, pulled in the current, like I was wading through a stream. It was like ice, so cold, so very cold.

I was standing over the bathtub now, and the water was cloudy. I couldn't see to the bottom of the tub, and that was wrong. It wasn't that deep. It was a white tub, and this was clear water. Why couldn't I see through it?

I kept the gun up, but reached to turn off the water. I half-expected something to grab my hand, but it didn't. The faucet just turned off, and the silence that followed was deafening. Small noises now, water sloshing, sliding around the room. The water cleared like a glass of water from a tap when there's too many minerals in the water. That milky stuff settling to the bottom, and there was something in the water. Something swimming out of the murk, coming into focus.

A pale hand, a spill of red hair, and I was staring down into Damian's face. His eyes were wide and dead, but it was daylight. He was dead. He didn't need to breathe. He could be under water. It wouldn't hurt him. But logic didn't help. Seeing him floating there, I did what I would have done if he'd been human – I reached for him.

I dropped the gun to the floor and plunged my hands into the tub. I touched him, grabbed handfuls of his shirt, and I started to pull him up, up through the water, but it was as if the water was heavier than it should have been. So heavy and so cold. He was almost at the top, almost when I realized it wasn't water, it was ice. He was frozen in a huge block of ice, and my arms were frozen with him, trapped with him.

'Anita, Anita,' Nathaniel's voice, his hand on my shoulder, and I woke to Jason's bedroom. My pulse was choking me. I sat up and stared around. The bathroom door was open a crack but there was no sound of water. Dream, just a dream.

I started to shiver. Except that I was still freezing. So cold, so very cold. 'I dreamed, dreamed of Damian. He was so cold, in ice.'

'Your skin is like ice,' Nathaniel said.

Jason was sitting up, his short blond hair tossled and his eyes heavy with sleep. 'What's wrong?'

Nathaniel wrapped his arms around me, rubbing his hands against my cold arms. 'When did you eat last, Anita?'

'With you, the drive-up.'

'That was over twelve hours ago.' He looked at Jason. 'She needs food now.'

Jason didn't ask questions, just crawled over the bed and dropped to his knees beside the mini fridge that acted as one of his bedside tables. He pulled out a bowl of fruit – apples, bananas.

'I don't like cold fruit,' I said.

'Anita, you dreamed about Damian because you're eating his energy. Eat a banana,' Nathaniel said.

I suddenly knew he was right. The cold was making me stupid. Jason handed me the fruit. But Nathaniel helped me peel it, because the shivering had gotten worse, and I couldn't peel it. Shit.

Nathaniel fed it to me in pieces, while my teeth started to chatter. When I'd managed to get it down, the shivering was a little less, but not a lot. 'Meat, protein,' Nathaniel said.

Jason lifted out a carton of Chinese takeout, but shook his head without offering it. 'Too old.' He got out a flat foam container and handed it up. 'Fajita fixings from El Maguey, from yesterday.'

Nathaniel opened it, lifted out a piece of the beef with his fingers, and held it close to my mouth. 'Eat.'

I ate, and the meat was unbelievably good, even cold. The meat seemed to fill up more than just my stomach. I picked through the grilled onions and peppers, and ate the beef. When my skin wasn't cold to the touch, and I'd stopped shivering, I slowed down, then shook my head. 'I can't eat any more.'

'You've eaten most of the meat,' Jason said. He was kneeling beside the bed, his arms propped on it, his chin resting on his arms. 'Did I hear Nathaniel say that you were eating Damian's energy?'

I nodded.

'Jean-Claude said that you'd formed a second triumvirate with Nathaniel and Damian.'

'Apparently,' I said.

'I take it there's a learning curve,' he said.

'You could say that. This is the second time in less than twenty-four hours that I've almost killed Damian.'

Jason's eyes went wide. 'How?'

'She's trying to do what she always does,' Nathaniel said, handing the now closed box to Jason. 'Barely eat, barely sleep, not do anything to take care of herself except exercise.'

'I can't tell the cops, oh, sorry, I need a nap,' I said.

'No, but I told you that you needed to eat more. I told you that you were acting more like a lycanthrope than a vampire. All you had to do was go through another drive-up. There are all-night drive-ups.'

I didn't like his tone. 'I didn't think of it. I just wanted to get to sleep. I was so tired I was nauseous.'

'Or maybe you were nauseous because your energy was bottoming,' Nathaniel said, and he was angry, 'but you didn't think of that did you?'

'No, I didn't. Happy?'

'No,' he said, 'because once Damian's dead, who do you think you'll start draining next?' He was so angry that his eyes had darkened, so they were almost purple.

I started to be angry back, because the nightmare had scared me, and endangering Damian again had scared me. I felt stupid that I hadn't thought to eat, when Nathaniel had explained it to me. I'd just been so tired. Come to think of it, I'd been more tired than I should have been, hadn't I? I wanted to be angry at him, because it was my fault. I hate it when it's my fault. I hate being wrong, especially this wrong.

'You're right, you're right. I'm sorry. I am.'

'You're not going to argue?' Jason asked.

'Why argue when I'll lose? I was careless. It's not just the triumvirate, or the new one, it's the *ardeur*. I've finally got it conquered, sort of.'

'What does "sort of" mean?' he asked, and came up to sit on the edge of the bed. He was nude. He'd been nude the whole time. I just really hadn't noticed. I noticed now, and gave him very good eye contact.

'It means that the *ardeur* doesn't rise on its own anymore.'

'That's a good thing, right?' Jason said, he was studying my face like he was puzzled by my expression.

'That's the good news,' I said, 'the bad news is that the *ardeur* doesn't rise, but it still needs to be fed. It won't remind me, it's time to be fed. That's what happened with Damian earlier. I hadn't fed the *ardeur* in over twelve hours, a lot over, but it hadn't raised either.'

'So you didn't feed it,' Nathaniel said, softly.

'Exactly,' I said.

'And you started sucking energy off of Damian,' he said.

I nodded. 'He called inside my head, sort of.'

'Then you fed the *ardeur*,' Jason said.

I nodded.

'Before you got to the club,' Nathaniel said, and his voice was soft.

'Yes.' I turned and looked at him, and what I saw in his eyes both made me feel bad and pissed me off. He looked hurt, and it wasn't my fault. But saying it wasn't my fault that I had to have sex with other men sounded wrong somehow, so I didn't say it. He had every right to be tired of me fucking everyone but him.

'I did the minimum for a snack, just to tide me over,' I said.

'With who?' he asked, and his eyes were wide and careful.

'Requiem.'

'If you were already feeding off of Damian's energy, then you needed to have fed the *ardeur* earlier, right?' Jason said. I think he actually wanted to know, but I think he was also trying to stop a fight before it started. I wasn't sure we were going to fight, but I wasn't sure we weren't, either.

I thought about Jason's question and finally said, 'Yeah, I guess so.'

'You gain energy through the *ardeur*, right?'

'Yeah.'

'And now you're the power source for a new triumvirate. Your energy powers Damian especially, and to a lesser extent, Nathaniel?'

'Why a lesser extent for me?' Nathaniel asked.

'You're alive. You make your own heart beat; Damian doesn't.'

Nathaniel nodded. 'Okay.'

'What's your point, Jason? I know you have one.'

'Would I have a point?' he said with a grin.

I shook my head. 'There's a very fine mind hiding beind those baby blues. You just don't let everyone see it, so yeah, you have a point. What is it?'

'Anita is having to eat more often, right?'

We both nodded.

'What if she needs to feed other things more often?'

I think we both took breath to ask what he meant, then we both got it at the same moment. 'Oh, shit,' I said.

Nathaniel said, 'Oh, God.'

'Before tonight it was every twelve hours, fourteen if I stretched it,' I said. 'How much more often could I need to feed?'

Jason spread his hands wide. 'How should I know? I'm just pointing it out.'

'It makes sense,' Nathaniel said. 'You fed off of Requiem about how long before we fed?'

I thought about it, tried to do the math in my head, and it was harder than normal, because that little flutter of panic was so loud. 'Two hours, maybe less.' I shook my head. 'No, absolutely, not. I cannot feed the *ardeur* every two hours.'

'No, but you could keep like snacks in the Jeep and eat every two hours,' Nathaniel said. 'Like I said, if you meet one hunger, the other hunger lessens.'

The panic pulled back a little, not much, but a little. 'Are you sure that peanuts in the car are going to do it?'

He shrugged. 'I don't know, but I think so.' He suddenly looked young, and not sure at all.

I hugged him, and he hugged me back. 'God, Nathaniel, God, we were already low on daytime feeds. What am I going to do?' I let some of that panic out in my voice.

He squeezed me tighter. 'We'll work something out. I'm sorry, I got mad about Requiem. It's just . . .'

'That everyone gets me, and you don't,' I said.

He nodded. Then drew back enough to smile at me, that wonderful smile. He took my hand and placed it on the side of his neck. I felt the marks of my teeth under my fingertips. 'This was good, Anita. This was exactly what I wanted in that moment, exactly.'

I had to smile back at him, but the smile didn't last. 'What time is it?'

Jason answered, 'Ten o'clock.'

Great. Less than two hours of sleep. Out loud I said, 'I fed on you at about two in the morning, which means it's only been eight hours. Eight hours is too soon, Nathaniel.'

He looked at me, and there was a fierceness there, a determination. 'Make love to me, Anita. Make love to me, and then you can feed on someone else. But you're right, I am tired of watching everyone get there before me.' He was on his knees, and he touched my arms, not quite clutching at me, not quite holding me. 'Make love to me, and I won't have a reason to be jealous.'

'I'll still be having to have sex with other men,' I said. 'Why won't you be jealous?'

'Because I'll know that you want to make love to me, and you have to have sex with them.'

My head was beginning to hurt. Nathaniel often made me feel out of my depth. I loved him, and wanted him, but, hell, I didn't know what to say to him. 'If it was you in other women's beds, I'd be jealous, no matter the why.'

He blushed. 'Would you really be jealous of me?'

'I wasn't entirely happy watching you get pawed at the club, so yeah, I think it would bother me.'

'I think that's the nicest thing you've ever said to me.'

'That I'm jealous of other women around you?'

He nodded.

'You've had girlfriends be jealous of you before,' I said.

He shook his head. 'I've never had a girlfriend.'

I stared at him. I didn't know what to say. I knew he wouldn't lie about it, but I just found it hard to believe. 'You've been in pornographic movies. You've—'

'Been a prostitute,' he finished for me, and his eyes never flinched.

'Yeah, I'm sorry, but . . .'

'Fucking isn't dating, Anita. Fucking for money really isn't dating.'

'But . . .' I said.

He touched my lips with his fingers. 'Hush,' he said, 'you are the first girlfriend I've ever had.'

I stared at him with a sort of soft horror growing in my mind. I was his first girlfriend? I couldn't wrap my mind around it. How can you do porn and be a prostitute and not date? Some of the confusion must have shown on my face, because he smiled and touched the side of my face. The bandage had come off and he traced the healing scratches that Barbara Brown had given me.

'I told you, you're the first person who ever wanted me, for me. Not because of the way I looked and what I could do with my body. You love me without sex. You let me take care of you. You let me organize your kitchen.'

'You cook in it more than I do,' I said.

He smiled, and his eyes were gentle, as if I were the child and he was so much older than I was. 'That's it, Anita. You let me buy the tea set, even though I know you think it's sort of silly.'

'You like the tea set,' I said.

He nodded. 'You do things not because you want them or enjoy them, but because it makes me happy. I've had people buy me jewelry, clothes, weekends in great hotels and spas, but no one ever let me buy what I wanted with their money, only what they thought I wanted. Let me remake their schedule. Let me make a place for me in their life.' He cupped my face between his hands. 'Maybe *girl-friend* isn't the right word, but I think any other word I could think of will make you run away, and I don't want that.'

My lips were suddenly dry.

'Make love to me,' he whispered and started to lean in for a kiss.

I felt the bed move on the other side. I had to fight the urge not to grab Jason's arm or something, anything to keep him with us. Anything not to be alone with Nathaniel. Ronnie was right, it wasn't rational, but I felt like if I consumated our relationship, I had to keep him. She was wrong. It wasn't sex that was a commitment for me anymore. The *ardeur* had taken that away from me. But sex with the right person was still a commitment, and the person bending in to kiss me, oh, so gently, was the right one.

I turned out of that kiss, to see Jason going for the bathroom. 'I'll turn the shower on, enjoy.'

'Sorry to kick you out of your own bed,' I said. And I was, for more than one reason.

He grinned, and tried not to, as if he were pretty sure it would get him into trouble. 'It's not like I won't be back in it.'

I stopped Nathaniel from pressing closer with a hand on his shoulder, and stared at Jason. 'What's that supposed to mean?'

He fought to control his face, and failed, and finally looked pleased with himself. 'You can't feed on Nathaniel, it's too soon. Jean-Claude won't wake for awhile yet. And if Jean-Claude won't wake, then Asher is out, too.'

I narrowed my eyes at him. 'So?'

'If there's another shapeshifter here that you'd rather feed on than me, I'll get them for you. Graham is just down the hall.' The look on his face said, plainly, he didn't expect me to take him up on it.

'You arrogant little—'

'Uh-uh-uh,' he said, 'now is that anyway to talk to someone who's going to let you feed on the very essence of his body?'

I scowled at him, then looked at Nathaniel. His face was utterly peaceful. 'And you're okay with this?'

'Honestly?'

'Yeah, honestly?'

'As long as I'm first, yes.'

'I could stay and help with the foreplay,' Jason said.

Before I could answer, Nathaniel answered, 'Not the first time, Jason. I want this to be just the two of us.'

Jason grinned more for me than Nathaniel, because he could see the expression on my face caused by Nathaniel's casual attitude toward making it a threesome later. 'I'm going to go hide in the bathroom now.' He shut the door behind him, and we were left with the bedside lamp.

I looked at him, sort of outraged. 'Thanks for volunteering me for a threesome.'

He looked puzzled. 'I sleep with you and Micah almost every night.'

'But we're not having sex all at the same time.'

He looked at me, and the look said that I was protesting too much.

'We don't,' I said.

'Anita, you wake up, you need to feed, and whoever you didn't feed on the day before you touch, but the other man doesn't always crawl out of bed. I've watched you have sex with Micah more than once, and he's watched you feed off of me.'

The headache was begining to pulse behind my eye. I was having trouble swallowing, and it had the familiar taste of panic.

'I know that you and Jean-Claude are with Asher together. I know that that's a true threesome.'

'Not all the time,' I said, and even to me it sounded weak.

He frowned at me. 'There's nothing wrong with enjoying being with two men at the same time, Anita.'

My pulse was threatening to choke me. 'Yes, there is,' and my voice was breathy.

'Why, why is it wrong?' He leaned into me as if he'd kiss me, but I leaned away, and it was one of those stupid moments, because leaning away put me on the bed, so that I was looking up at him. There was no logic to pulling away from a kiss and putting myself flat on the bed. Of course, there was no logic to the screaming panic inside my head either.

He propped himself up on his arms and looked down at me with that smile that said I was being silly. I understood in that moment that I'd been wrong to think of him as a child. That one look let me know that in his own way, he'd been as careful of me as I'd been of him. That he thought of me as sheltered, innocent. That in many ways, I was a child in the face of his experience. It was one of those moments when a relationship changes, when the way you look at the world suddenly expands or explodes, and the world that was, isn't the one that is there a heartbeat later.

We stared at each other, and I don't know if it showed on my face, or if it just occurred to him, too, or what, but he hesitated and smiled down at me. 'What's wrong?' he asked.

The question seemed so ridiculous that I laughed. 'Oh, I don't know, I've almost killed Damian twice. I thought controlling the *ardeur* would make things easier, and it hasn't. I had intercourse with Byron, *Byron*, of all people. I almost raised the entire cemetery tonight. I could feel it, like some army of the dead just waiting for me to wake it. I could feel it, Nathaniel, feel the power of it.' I was crying and hadn't meant to be. 'So much went wrong today.'

He kissed my tears as they slipped from my eyes, gently, so gently. 'Let's make something go right.' He kissed me, and the salt of my tears lay on his lips.

'But . . .'

He kissed me again, a little more forcibly. 'Anita, please stop talking.'

I frowned up at him. 'Why?'

'So we can fuck,' he said.

I opened my mouth, and don't know what I would have said, because he spoke first, 'Make love to me,' and he leaned over me, 'consummate me,' I thought he was going to kiss me, but his lips moved lower, and he kissed the front of my neck, then moved a little lower, 'screw me,' and he kissed the mound of my breast through the T-shirt, 'suck me.' He raised the short shirt up, spilling my breasts free. I started to protest, but the look in his eyes, on his face, stopped me. He put his lips over my nipple, just below the bandage that covered Jean-Claude's bite. He licked a long solid line over my breast and rolled his eyes to meet mine. 'Fuck me.'

I'd like to say that I had something equally salacious to say, or something suave, but for the life of me, the only thing I could think to say, was, 'Okay.' It wasn't suave and debonair, but when you love someone, you don't always have to be suave and debonair, sometimes you can just be yourself, and okay said at the right moment is sweeter than any poetry and can mean more to someone than all the pillow talk in the world.

50

THE T-SHIRT AND undies went in the first rush of hands, but I'd never tried to touch him when it wasn't a metaphysical necessity. I'd never just turned to Nathaniel because I wanted him. It wasn't that I didn't find him attractive. God knows I did, but I hadn't realized until those first few moments how much I'd come to rely on the *ardeur*. I'd thought of it as only a curse, but I appreciated for the first time that it greased the wheels for me. It got me over the embarrassment, the awkwardness, the good-girls-don't-do-this attitude. Without the *ardeur*, it was just me, and the inside of my head was ugly.

Nathaniel noticed, because he notices everything. He propped himself up on one elbow and looked down at me. 'What's wrong?'

I wasn't sure how to say it, and that must have shown on my face, because he said, 'Just say it, Anita, whatever it is.'

I looked up at him and fought the urge to gaze down the length of his body. I had to close my eyes, and finally said, 'Without the *ardeur*, it's just me. It's just me, and I'm . . .' I sat up. 'I'm not comfortable.'

'With me?'

I started to nod, then stopped, and said the real truth. 'With myself.'

He moved forward on the bed so that he rested his face against the small of my back. He was so warm. 'What does that mean, exactly?'

How did I explain something to someone else, that I didn't really understand myself? 'I don't know if I can explain it,' I said.

The bathroom door opened, and we both looked up. Jason was there with a towel around his waist. He wasn't wet, but he was wearing a towel. I'd been around the shapeshifters long enough to think that was odd.

'I can't stand it,' he said, 'I just can't stand it.'

'What?' I said.

'You're going to fuck this up.'

I looked at him, and it wasn't a friendly look.

'Don't glare at me.' He came to stand at the end of the bed, hands on hips. 'I've told you that I'd give almost anything to have someone look at me the way Nathaniel looks at you.'

'Yeah, but . . .'

'But nothing,' he said, 'I thought you were growing, changing, but what you just said blames it all on the *ardeur*. You didn't do any of it. Not your fault. If you fuck everything that moves while under the sway of the *ardeur*, you're still blameless.'

I started to argue with him, but couldn't think how to do it. I finally said, 'I sort of agree with what you said, what of it?'

'God, Anita, it's not about blame. You act like it's a sin.'

Something must have shown on my face, because he made a sound in his throat that was part growl, and part exasperation. I had to look away from the expression in his eyes, the anger in them. 'I was taught that it was a sin.'

'They also taught you that Santa Claus was real, and you don't believe that anymore, do you?'

I crossed my arms across my body, which lost some of its intended sullenness, because I was naked, and it's never easy to be sullen when you're nude. 'What's that supposed to mean?'

He went down on his knees by the bed. 'It means, look at him.'

I looked stubbornly at Jason, and not at Nathaniel.

'Turn around and look at him, or I'll turn you around.'

'You'll try,' I said.

'Fine, you want to wrestle, we can wrestle, but wouldn't it be less embarrassing, and less childish, if you just turned around?'

I took a deep breath, let it out slow, and turned around.

Nathaniel was lying there on his stomach, propped up on his elbows. His face was what you noticed first. Those amazing lavender eyes with the remants of the eye makeup still there, making them look darker, larger, as if they needed any help to be amazing. His eyes held such patience, a calm surety that I'd fix this. That it would be alright. I didn't like anyone looking at me like that, because life had taught me that it usually wasn't alright. That I couldn't save everyone. That I couldn't fix anything. His lips held a slight smile. There was no anxiety in him. No fear that I'd run. He looked at me with the calm face of a saint staring into the face of God. Secure in his faith, safe in his knowledge, trusting in a way that I had lost so long ago. How could he look at me like that? Didn't he know better? He'd lived with me for four months. Didn't he know by now that I was screwed six ways to Sunday, and he shouldn't depend on me?

He ducked his head, almost a bashful movement, but it drew my gaze across the sweep of his shoulder, down the curve of his back. I'd only allowed myself to touch him below the waist once. When the *ardeur* was very new. I'd covered his back and buttocks with bites, and he'd loved it, and I had fed, and I'd never let myself touch him that much again, until the last two days. That first time had been about feeding, and I hadn't taken time to really see him, really enjoy him, because I'd looked at it as an evil necessity. Looking at him now, I felt guilty for ever thinking of him like that. He deserved better.

I'd made him put clothes on for months, at least shorts, even in bed. But he was entirely too comfortable nude for me not to have caught glimpses of him. Even last night, at the club, I hadn't really let myself look at him, not really. Because if I'd allowed myself to linger on his body, I'd have lingered on the part that seemed to fasci-nate me most, and, no, it wasn't what you think. His back had a slight sway to it, a curve that spilled to a lovely ass, but at the farthest line of his back, before it became not his back, were dimples. Maybe *dimple* wasn't the right word for them, but I had no other word to use. I stared at him now, let my eyes linger, rather than glance and look hurriedly away. I let myself see not that he was nude, but see his body.

I reached out to him and let myself do something that I'd wanted to do for months. I traced my hand down the curve of his back and came to rest just there, just at the end of his back, before the swell of his ass.

He shivered just a little under the touch of my hand, even though all I had done was lay my hand flat against his skin. Let the weight of my hand rest between those two dimples so low on his body. It was as if when the clay had been wet, God had placed his thumbs just above the swell of Nathaniel's rump, as an extra sweetness, like the idea that a dimple near the mouth is the kiss of an angel before the baby is born, so those dimples on his body were like some extra grace.

I kissed, ever so gently, each of those smooth hollows, like tiny shallow cups in his skin. Each mark was the size of my lips, as if they were meant for me to kiss them. I laid my head in the curve of his back, rested my cheek on those marks of grace, so that my face was slightly uptilted with the swell of his body, leading my eyes down the curve of his rump and his distant legs and feet, but for the moment I was content where I was.

I used his body as my pillow, and just as my mouth fit to those kissable dimples, so my head fit neatly in the curve of his body, as if I were meant to rest there. Nathaniel's breath went out in a long sigh, and his body seemed to settle into the bed, as if some tension that I hadn't even seen had run out of him and left him able to rest.

I trailed my hand across the curve of his ass, and he made a small sound for me. I trailed my fingers lower, tracing the line of his thigh. It wasn't that his legs were off-limits in the way that other areas had been, but I realized that I'd divided his body along a line at his waist, like some boundary in a war. Above the line was us, below the line was forbidden. His thigh was lush and smooth-skinned, and firm with muscle.

I brought my hand back up his leg and allowed my fingers to trace circles on his derriere. Those small movements drew small, quick, sounds from him, almost sounds of protest.

I asked, and my voice was as lazy and soft as my touch, 'You're almost making pain noises, does it hurt?'

'No,' he said, and his voice showed a strain that his body didn't even hint at. 'It's just that I've wanted you to touch me for so long. It feels . . . amazing to have your head resting on me, your hands on me. God, it feels so good.'

I let my hand trace, very delicately, along the crack of his ass, so that if there had been any little hairs I could have played with them, but he was smooth, utterly smooth. It made me wonder if other things were as smooth.

I brushed my fingers down the line of his ass again, tracing the separation between the cheeks, until I found that first line of warm flesh that was neither ass nor more, but a line of soft, silken skin.

I put a finger on either side of that skin, the softest of pinches, and slid my fingers up and down. Nathaniel writhed under the touch. His hands struggling against the sheets as if he wasn't sure what to do with them.

I raised my head from his back and kissed my way up his cheeks until I could lay my head one side of him, like a pillow. I caressed my hand down his thigh again, and this time I made circles behind his knees, and kept going, until my fingertips could play with his ankles.

He laughed and struggled against the bed again, like he had when I touched much more traditionally intimate places. There are so many more erotic areas on the body than the small list that most people make. I raised up from the pillow of his body, so that I could pay more attention to his ankles, drawing my nails lightly across that apparently sensitive skin. He writhed for me, his upper body coming off the bed, and his breath shaking out in something between a sigh and a laugh. I sat up so I could run my fingers across the bottoms of his feet, and he sighed, 'Oh, God.' I touched the front of his feet, very lightly, and he kicked his feet, as if it were almost too much. Not everyone's feet are that sensitive for foreplay, but when someone's feet are, they really are.

I gazed up the line of his body, while he lay gasping against the sheets. I'd barely started. So many choices. I bent over his ankles and licked along the round bone, tracing the skin with my tongue, in thick, wet, circles.

He made protesting noises and started to kick his feet, but I grabbed his foot with both my hands and held him against my mouth. He made a sound that was almost a scream and gazed down at me, along the length of his body. There was something in his eyes that was wild, and tender, and amazed.

I bit down on that shallow flesh, not hard, just a graze of teeth, but it rolled his eyes into his head and folded his shoulders onto the bed, as if he'd swooned.

I moved back up the bed, so that I could lay my head, not on one cheek, but across that part of his body, so that it was indeed my pillow. The feel of his cheeks spreading under the side of my face made me close my eyes, and have to relearn how to breathe for a moment. I spilled my hand down the line of his body, until I found that silken skin again. But this time I used it like a line to trace to something else. I found what I wanted, and the skin was so soft, softer than anything else I'd touched on his body. His testicles were trapped underneath his body, thick, and round, and delicate. Only part of them were trapped where I could touch them, and the combination of his body weight and the excitement had made them swell, so that the skin wasn't as loose as it would have been otherwise. I'd wanted to play with all that fragile loose skin, but it was already pressed tight around him. To pull on it now might be more pain than pleasure. No matter what Nathaniel liked in that area, I wasn't ready for it.

I slipped my body over his legs and pushed them farther apart, so that I lay between them. I laid my mouth against the inside of his thigh, but stopped before I could decide whether I was going to kiss him, lick him, or bite him. I stopped because I could see Jason over the slope of Nathaniel's thigh.

Truth was, I'd forgotten he was there. Was that a bad thing to say, or a good thing? Did it mean I was getting more comfortable with myself, or that I was falling into the pit of whoredom? Whatever, but I was suddenly frozen, gazing over Nathaniel's body into those pale, blue eyes. It was what I saw in them, that made me freeze. Lust would have been embarrassing, but logical. But that wasn't what I saw. Jason watched us with something in his face that was close to sorrow, and his eyes held a longing, a sense of loss. I didn't know what to do with that look, so I stopped, and raised my face up from Nathaniel's body.

Jason realized I saw him, and he ducked his head. When he looked back, he had his face under control. He almost pulled the joke off, when he said, 'Don't stop on my account. I'm enjoying the show.' His voice was fine, but his eyes, the lightness never quite reached his eyes.

'Liar,' I said.

He gave me an unhappy smile. 'I thought you were too busy to notice me. I should know that without the *ardeur* you pay better attention.'

'What's wrong?' Nathaniel asked.

'I'm not sure,' I said.

'Don't worry,' Jason said, 'I'm not pining for you, Anita, or Nathaniel for that matter. But I am pining for someone to take that much time and attention with me.'

I frowned at him.

'You can have sex, and it can be good, but I'd give almost anything to have someone touch me the way you touch Nathaniel. We'll prob-ably have sex later, and it will be great, but you won't look at me like that.'

I sighed. 'I think I remember us having this conversation before. You want to be consumed by love, and my goal in life is never to be consumed at all.'

'Ironic, isn't it,' he said, 'I want just once for someone to look at me the way you look at Nathaniel, and you've been scared to death of it. You keep saying that the *ardeur* is a curse, but if the *ardeur* had never come along, you wouldn't have Nathaniel, or Micah. I'm not even a hundred percent sure you'd be double dating with Asher and Jean-Claude.'

I laid my arms across Nathaniel's cheeks and rested my face on my arms and looked at Jason. I looked at him and tried to hear what he was saying. 'Maybe, about Asher, I mean. Once you've crossed enough lines, one more doesn't seem that big a deal.'

'Exactly,' Jason said.

'So the *ardeur* is what, a blessing?'

'Look at what you're propped up on, and tell me it isn't? I heard you earlier, Anita. If the *ardeur* hadn't come to you, you'd still be stuck where you had been. You'd still be fighting what you want, and what you think you're supposed to want.'

I looked at him, while I rested against Nathaniel's body. Nathaniel had propped himself up on his elbows and was looking at Jason. We both seemed utterly comfortable with him there. Was that wrong? It didn't feel wrong.

I wanted to argue, but I couldn't, well, I could, but I would have sounded silly. If the *ardeur* hadn't come, where would I be? I thought, I'd still be with Richard, but as soon as I thought, I knew better. Richard had used the *ardeur* as another excuse to run from me, but he hadn't liked any of my life. He hadn't liked the police work, the zombie raising, my comfort with the vampires and shapeshifters. Strangely, the thing he'd liked less was that I seemed willing to accept him and his beast. I'd seen too far into his head in that one moment in my own bathroom. Damian had said it best; Richard loved his shame more than he loved anything else.

So, where would I be without the *ardeur*? No Micah, no Nathaniel, no Asher. My life still nothing but murder cases, zombie raisings, and vampire slayings. Hell, without the *ardeur* would I have stayed with Jean-Claude, or would I have found another reason to run from him, too? Maybe. It sounded like something I'd do.

I looked at Jason and settled more solidly against Nathaniel's body. He sighed, and laid his head down on the bed.

'So what, the *ardeur* is the universe's way of getting me where I needed to go?'

'Maybe,' he said, then grinned, 'I can't speak for whole universe. All I know is that I envy you, and I don't envy many people.'

I frowned.

'Are you jealous?' Nathaniel asked.

Jason looked surprised, either at the question, or at who had asked it. He finally shook his head. 'Not jealous of you or Anita, like in love with you jealous, no. Jealous of what you have together, hell yes. Jealous of not having that many people in love with me, hell, yes, again.' He smiled, and then grinned, and it reached his eyes this time. 'Besides, I'm not Anita's type for a relationship.'

'What's that supposed to mean?' I asked.

'I'm not submissive enough, or dominant enough for you. I'm certainly not domestic enough. I'm also not willing to take on all the responsibilities that Micah seems to embrace so easily. You've found another person who thrives on his job and taking care of other people's crises. Not my idea of fun.' He spread his hands wide. 'You and Jean-Claude, well, that's something else. I know I can't compete with it.'

'It's not a competition,' Nathaniel said.

'You don't see it that way,' Jason said, 'but I'm just dominant enough, and guy enough, to see it that way.'

'If anyone of them saw it as a competition, it wouldn't work,' I said.

'I know,' Jason said. He shook his head. 'I'm going into the bathroom again, and this time I'm staying there until I'm called, or until I feel the *ardeur* rise. You guys have fun. Sorry, if I flattened the mood.'

'My mood's fine,' I said.

'Mine, too,' Nathaniel said.

Jason stared at us both. 'No *ardeur*, and I've made you talk and think too hard, and you're still okay with this?'

'Yes,' I said.

'Why?'

'Because a very wise and dear friend told me I was going to fuck this up, and I don't want to do that.'

He smiled and his face softened. 'If you do ever pick one of them to actually marry, and it's Nathaniel, I get dibs on being best man.'

'I don't think that's going to come up,' I said, 'but if it does, you'd be our first pick.'

'You didn't ask Nathaniel,' he said.

'She didn't have to,' Nathaniel said.

Jason walked toward the bathroom, shaking his head. 'Too dominant by half.'

I called after him. 'You know I have to be the better man in any relationship, Jason.' I meant it to be a joke.

He turned at the bathroom door, and said, 'Fuck, Anita, you are the better man. Just because you don't have the right equipment, doesn't change what you are.' He closed the door behind him, firmly, until it clicked.

We were left alone in the bedroom. Nathaniel raised up and looked down at me. 'You don't have to finish tonight, Anita. Jason's right, the way you touched me. I know if not this time, then next. The sooner you feed the *ardeur* the better you'll feel.'

I smiled at him, then unfolded my arms and slid my face down, until I was as far between his legs as I could get. He wasn't as excited now, and the skin was loose. I licked that most delicate of skin and heard his breath go out in a long sigh. I drew the loose skin into my mouth, pulling it gently out and away from his body. The skin didn't stay loose for long, and when it was tight and I could lick the balls inside that skin, I told him, 'On all fours.'

He did it without being asked twice.

I drew his balls into my mouth, one at a time, carefully, so carefully. I rolled them in my mouth with tongue and lips, until they were wet and slick. I caught glimpses of the rest of him, just in front, but not all, and not well. I'd only seen him nude from the front three times. Once when I first met him, once when I made the triumvirate between him and Damian, and earlier in my office.

'Roll over,' I said, and he spilled himself over onto his back. He lay thick and quivering against his stomach, pointing like an exclamation mark against his own body. 'I don't remember you being this big the first time I saw you nude.'

'I was in a hospital. Someone had almost killed me. I wasn't at my best.'

I gazed down at him, and said, 'I can see that.' I reached for him, slowly, and laid my hand against the warmth of him. But I was losing my patience. Another time I'd be slower, but now I wrapped my hand around him, let the thick round hardness of him fill my hand. His upper body spasmed, raising a little off the bed. I slid one hand to his balls and massaged them, while I stroked the thick velvet warmth of him. 'So soft, and so hard, all at the same time.'

I stroked him, until his eyes lost focus and his neck spasmed, so that he was closed eyed, and didn't see me bend down. I slid my mouth over the tip of him while he wasn't looking, and he cried out, as I worked my mouth down the length of him. I knew what I wanted. I wanted all of him inside my mouth, down to his balls, at least once. Next time I'd start with him smaller, now I had to fight for it. I'd gotten better at deep-throating, because sharing a bed with Micah, it was either get better at taking more, or stop doing one of my favorite things. Practice paid off, I sealed Nathaniel inside my mouth in one hard, clean line, until my lips touched the top of his testicles. I could only stay for a moment, then I had to come up. Up to breathe, up to let the wetness from my mouth trail down the shaft of his body.

I raised up on my knees, between his thighs, and the look on his face was worth all the effort. In fact, worth so much, that I had to do it one more time. Then I came up more shallow on him, so I could move better, thrusting him in and out of my mouth. Licking him, rolling him, sucking him, and when he was making enough noise, very lightly, I used teeth.

'Oh, God, yes, yes, please.'

I moved off him enough to ask, 'Please, what?'

'More teeth, please.'

I frowned at him. 'Most men think that hurts.'

'I'm not most men,' he said, and there was something about the way he said it that made me press my mouth back over him. I sucked him, pulling hard and firm, then forced my mouth down on the shaft, not as far as before, and bit him, not too hard, but harder than I'd bitten any other man I'd done this with. I kept my eyes on his face, so I could see if it hurt him. The look on his face had nothing to do with pain. His eyes were wild, and he said, 'Harder.'

I looked at him.

'Please, Anita, please, you don't know how long I've wanted this.'

It wasn't my bits being bitten, but I was reminded that Nathaniel had once had no stopping point, no danger-do-not-cross sign. I could do what he wanted, but it was up to me to make sure it didn't go too far. I was finally doing what he'd always wanted. I was topping him.

I went down on him fast and hard, and this time I bit him hard enough that my teeth closed around that thick, meaty flesh. I had a momentary flash of not the *ardeur*, but of the beast, and its craving for flesh between teeth. I pushed it away, but I also came off of him and didn't do it again. But I'd done enough, because his eyes were rolled to whites, and he was writhing on the bed. His hands had grabbed mounds of the sheet, and his body strained, and bucked against the bed.

I waited for him to lie still, though his eyes stayed like butterflies, eyelashes fluttering against his cheeks. When I caught a glimpse of lavender eyes between the fluttering, I stroked him gently. I stroked him with my hands, until I had his eyes looking at me instead of the inside of his own eyelids.

He looked up at me, his lavender eyes lazy, and his smile was like the cat who got the cream. I wrapped my hand around that warm, thick, length. Wrapped my hand and squeezed. 'I want this inside me.'

When his eyes opened, he said, 'You haven't had any foreplay.'

I squeezed him again, watched his spine bow, and his head throw back, sliding the long braid of his hair off the bed, like something escaping off the edge. 'Trust me, Nathaniel, I've had foreplay.'

When he recovered enough, he said, 'You're not the only one who hasn't gotten to touch someone below the waist.'

I closed my eyes. 'Please, Nathaniel, please, just make love to me. I want you to finish what you started in the office, please.'

He looked at me, and there was something in that look that was very male and very grown-up. 'You liked that, did you?'

I gave him a look, then said, 'You were there, what do you think?'

He sat up, and I was suddenly surrounded by his legs, his arms. He kissed me, and the kiss was gentle, but not chaste. He explored my mouth the way I'd explored his legs, and ass, lightly, delicately, savoring it. But one hand was sliding down the front of my body, until his fingers slid over me. My body reacted to that light touch, but his hand didn't stop. He traced a finger around the opening to my body. 'You are wet.'

'I told you so.'

He slid the finger inside of me and stole my breath. Then he pushed two fingers inside of me, and with the tips of his fingers found that spot. He flicked the tips of his fingers, just the tips, flexing them fast, and firm against that spot. And it was as if that part of my body had been waiting for him, as if all the work he'd done earlier, was still there, because those quick, firm touches, brought me. Brought me screaming, nails digging into his shoulders, and back.

He caught me with his other arm around my waist, or I would have fallen back to the bed. He slid his fingers out from inside me, and said, 'Now, you're ready.'

Since all I was seeing was the inside of my eyeballs, and speech was not an option, I tried to nod, but I really don't think I needed to. As they say, actions speak louder than words.

51

I WATCHED HIS face above me, as his body worked in and out of mine. He stayed propped on his arms, his legs were bent toward me, so that he acted as a frame for his own body. Seeing him sliding inside me threw my head back, spasmed my body, but I fought for control. Fought to see him. To watch him, this first time. This first time after so many false starts. I fought my body, fought the amazing sensations that were filling me, fought, because I wanted to see his face.

Propped up like he was, it was shallow, and usually I liked it deep, but something about the angle, or the depth, or lack of it, or the rhythm, which was quick, so quick, began to bring me. I could feel it starting. I remembered in time to gasp, 'When I go, you go.'

His voice was strangely controlled, as if he were concentrating very hard on what he was doing. 'You can go more than once, I may not be able to.'

I touched his face, held it light between my hands. 'When I go, you go, no more near misses.'

His eyes smiled down at me. 'Agreed.'

And suddenly there was no time for words, no time for debate. The orgasm tightened my body, then spread outward, blowing through my body, my skin. I rode that wave after wave of pleasure. His eyes went wide, as if they were surprised, and his breathing quickened, his body hesitated, paused almost, then he thrust himself deep inside me, and if I hadn't held his face he'd have thrown his head back, but I wanted to watch his eyes. They were almost frantic. His body spasmed again, and this time the orgasm caught me unprepared and my hands lost his face, my eyes rolled back into my head, and I screamed.

He collapsed on top of me and thrust as hard and sudden as he could. I shrieked under him and clawed at his back. His skin gave under my nails. He writhed on top of me. Writhing with his body still thrust deep inside mine, caused my nails to dig deeper, and I set my teeth in his shoulder, screaming into his skin. Making a gag of his flesh between my teeth.

Nathaniel's body liked the pain. It was as if, as long as I hurt him he wasn't done. The more that my nails and teeth dug into him, the more his hips pumped into me. It was like we were caught in an endless loop of pain and pleasure, and the line from one to the other blurred.

His breathing changed again, and when his body threw itself backward, in orgasm, I still had my teeth in his shoulder. He tore himself out of my mouth. I released him in time to not take a bite out of him or lose a tooth, but not in time to keep from drawing blood. I was suddenly drowning in the taste of his blood. Sweet and salty and metalic, and underneath that, something else, something more. I'd bitten his neck only hours before, and I had not been as aware then of the taste of his blood. It was like the difference between gulping water because you were thirsty and sipping wine to enjoy the bouquet. I let Nathaniel's blood rest on my tongue, licked it against the roof of my mouth, played with the taste, the texture, the warmth of it.

I let it slide down my throat. I made it last, as if it were the last sip of liquid I would ever have. I'd craved blood before, but as with the beast, I'd thought that one part was all of it. In that one sweet taste I knew better. I'd tasted blood before, but I'd never enjoyed it or known that it could taste like this.

Power trailed over Nathaniel's skin, and trapped under his body, that power marched over me in a skin-tingling, breath-stealing rush. It made me shiver, and my beast stirred, like something furred and half-asleep, disturbed from its nap.

Nathaniel bowed down toward me again, his eyes were pale gray with a hint of almost blue. I stared into his leopard's eyes and felt his beast stretch inside his body, like it was rubbing against the bones of its cage.

My beast stretched inside my body, I'd had the sensation before, but I'd never been able to feel it as if my body were somehow hollow and this long shape stretched the length of me. It made me shiver, and it was hard to breathe for a moment, as if something truly was inside me and had reached up high enough to compromise my lungs. The pressure lasted for a moment, then it was gone, but I hadn't liked the sensation of it.

'You smell of blood,' Nathaniel said, and there was an edge of growl to his voice.

'It's your blood,' I whispered, and my heart was already beating faster.

'But it's in your mouth,' he growled, just above my lips. His mouth was suddenly on mine, his tongue pushing between my lips. He kissed me, hard and long and deep, pushing his tongue so far into my mouth that it was almost like deep-throating. But his tongue was neither as long or wide as he was. But this had teeth that almost cut at my lips, a bruising force, that no amount of oral sex could equal. His tongue licked along the roof of my mouth, the inside of my cheeks. He was licking the taste of his own blood from my mouth.

The leopard screamed through my brain, he's eating us! I knew better, but something moved inside me, in places that nothing was supposed to move. I felt it, not like some liquid amorphous shape, but as if something very solid and very real was sitting in the center of my body and moving around. It stirred, and this time I felt something like a hand stretch upward, and something else stretch down. It hurt, and I was suddenly choking on Nathaniel's kiss.

He drew back, and the smile on his face was fierce and joyous, a savage beauty, as if the thoughts behind his face weren't very human anymore. 'You taste good,' he said, and his voice was painfully low. It didn't sound like Nathaniel's voice at all.

The leopard didn't react to that growl, it was gone from my head. But that thing in the center of my body stretched, stretched legs and arms inside my body. I could feel it touching things that should never have been touched. I screamed and stared up into his eyes and wondered if there was enough of Nathaniel in there to help me.

'Anita, what's wrong?' With leopard eyes and a voice of a stranger, but his face was all Nathaniel, all concern and worry.

'It hurts.'

'What? Did I hurt you?'

I shook my head, and claws tickled along my ribs, and made me struggle underneath his body. 'Help me!'

He rolled off of me and yelled, 'Jason!' He had to yell twice, before Jason came out, dripping from the shower, a towel in his hand. He looked at us, and the smile was gone instantly.

'What's wrong?'

'I don't know,' Nathaniel said, still in that low voice, 'she says something hurts.'

The thing stretched again, stretched and stretched and my body stretched with it, as if it fit inside my arms and legs. It didn't hurt, exactly. It was as if my body were a glove and it was seeing how much room it had.

'Did you feel that?' Jason asked. His body had broken out in goosebumps.

Nathaniel nodded. 'It's her beast.'

Jason knelt by the end of the bed. 'Yeah, but it's never felt like this before.'

My beast stretched to the limits of my body, then found that there was nowhere else to go. I'd gotten a tiny piece of Richard's beast years ago, and somehow Belle's line had given me an animal to call – the leopards. Through that I was Nimir-Ra to Micah's Nimir-Raj. Nathaniel had been my *pomme de sang*, but now he was my animal to call, as Richard was to Jean-Claude. Now that part of me that was beast, cat, stretched inside my human body. I'd felt it as power before, more metaphor than physical, but this was very, very physical. I could feel it. Feel it struggling inside me, looking for a way out. It was as if I was a lycanthrope, except I lacked that last bit of the puzzle, that one last bit that would allow the beast to slip out of my skin and be real.

It shrank back into that small center of my body, where it stayed most of the time. But now it was like one of those leopards at the zoo in a small metal cage. It paced, paced, paced, and finally rushed the bars, slashing and clawing. But these bars were my body, and I screamed. I reached out, trying to grab something, anything that would help me. How do you fight something that's inside your body? How do you destroy something that is in the very meat of you?

Jason grabbed my hand, and I was suddenly breathing in the sweet musk of wolf. But it was as if touching Jason's hand acted like a conduit, and suddenly I could see Richard. He was in the bright sunlight of his kitchen, cooking something in a pan. He wore nothing but jeans, with a dish towel stuck into the waistband of his pants. His back was covered in claw marks, or really serious nail marks. It looked more like the result of good sex than an attack. His head came up, and he sniffed the air, and only then did he turn and stare behind him, as if he could see me. He said, 'Anita, is that you?'

'Help me.'

'What's wrong now?'

I squeezed Jason's hand, and it was like that extra bit of contact took me closer to Richard. It was like I hovered just in front of him. He reached out, and his hand brushed through me.

My beast reacted to it, screaming and clawing, going wild. It didn't want the wolf inside us, there wasn't room for it. There certainly wasn't room for both.

Richard drew his hand back, and said, 'Anita, Anita can you hear me?'

I screamed his name, because screaming was all I could do. It felt like the leopard was cutting me up, trying to dig its way out, and it couldn't get out.

'Give your beast to someone else, Anita. Someone who's body can let it out.'

I didn't understand what he meant. I started to tell him so, but he seemed to feel my puzzlement. Because he shared a memory with me. They say a picture is worth a thousand words; a memory with complete sensory surround sound is worth so much more. Saves so much time, shares the pain faster.

We were in the center ring of the Circus of the Damned. I reached out to Richard's beast, his rage, because if we couldn't control it, the council would kill him. I reached out to that rage. That power that he called his beast came at my touch. I smelled like home to it, somehow, and it poured into me, over me, through me, like a blinding storm of heat and power. It was similar to the times I'd raised power with Richard and Jean-Claude, but this time there was no spell to use the power on. Nowhere for the beast to run. It tried to crawl out of my skin, tried to expand inside my body, but there was no beast to call. I was empty for it, and it raged inside me. I felt it growing until I thought I would burst apart in bloody fragments. The pressure built and built and had nowhere to go.

Richard had crawled to me on hands and knees, bleeding. He'd laid his lips against mine in a trembling kiss. A sound came from low in his throat, and he was suddenly pressing his mouth against mine, until it either bruised or I opened my mouth to him. I opened, and his tongue plunged inside me, his lips feeding on mine. The cut inside his mouth filled my mouth with the taste of him, salty, sweet. I held his face in my hands, my mouth searching his, and it wasn't enough.

We moved to our knees, mouths still pressed together. My hands slid over his chest, his back, and something deep inside me clicked and relaxed. His power tried to spill outward, but I held it back . . .

Richard's hands slid up my legs, finding the lace top of the black panties. His fingers traced my naked spine, and I was undone.

The power spilled upward, outward, filling us both. It flared over us in a rushing wave of heat and light, until my vision swam in pieces, and we both cried out with one voice. His beast slid inside of him. I felt it crawl out of me, pulled like a large, thick string, spilling inside of Richard, coiling into his body. I expected to feel the last bit of it spill between us, like draining the last drop of wine from a cup, but that drop remained.

The memory rolled back and left me gasping on the bed. Nathaniel was leaning over me. 'Anita, Anita, are you alright?' His eyes had bled back to lavender.

Jason was nuzzling my hair. 'You smell like pack.'

Richard was standing in his kitchen, one hand on the edge of the cabinets as if he were steadying himself. 'Now, do you remember?'

'I remember,' I whispered.

'What do you remember?' Nathaniel asked.

'Can't you smell it?' Jason asked. He was rubbing his lips against the side of my face.

Nathaniel leaned over me, his face very close to mine. 'Wolf,' he sniffed my skin, 'Richard,' he whispered the name against my skin.

The feel of their lips against me made me close my eyes for a moment. But once sight was gone, the scent of them covered me like a blanket. The sweet musk of wolf and the acrid sweetness of leopard were everywhere, like invisible water, and I was drowning in it. I expected my cat to complain, but it didn't. It was strangely calmed by both scents.

'You're still pack, Anita, as much as you're pard. Give your beast to them.' Richard stared up at me, and I noticed for the first time that he had scratches low on his right cheek. Not usually a place you mark in the heat of passion.

I stopped seeing Richard's scratched face in his sunny kitchen. I opened my eyes to a wisp of auburn hair across my eyes. Nathaniel was pressed against the side of my face, his mouth just under the line of my jaw. His body was back on top of mine, laying his weight along me. He was so warm.

Jason still had my hand, and his mouth was rubbing along the side of my neck on the side opposite from Nathaniel.

I was warm and safe, and I realized that Richard had given me some of his control. He'd given me breathing space. I needed to use it before my beast shook free of this warm, comfortable lassitude.

I thought back over the memory of giving Richard's beast back to him. How had it worked? A kiss, why did everything take a kiss, or a touch? Jean-Claude had answered that question last night. Because we could only use the tools we had available. Most of our tools came from Belle Morte's line, and that meant that our tools, our skills, were going to have a certain theme. I waited to be tired of that theme, and part of me was, part of me thought we really needed some new skill sets, but most of me was warm and safe, and covered in the scent of pard and pack.

Their lips worked gently at each side of my neck, soft kisses. Nathaniel's body was so warm pressed the length of mine, warmer than any blanket, better than simply being held in someone's arms. Jason's hand smoothed along the edge of my hip, and I couldn't help but cuddle into the feel of his touch. That one small writhing movement seemed to affect Nathaniel's body. He was suddenly heavier than he had been, heavy in the way Richard's kiss had been in the memory. Nathaniel's hips pressed in against me, and as with the remembered kiss, he pushed against me, and I had a choice of opening to him, or keeping him outside my body.

Richard's beast had left through a kiss. I could only kiss one of them at a time. The thought came that I could do other things, and still kiss. But I'd had enough of threesomes and more. My battered morals had had about all the multiples they could handle for awhile. That little voice whispered, *but it feels so good*. And the voice that I'd learned at my grandmother's hand yelled, *Slut!* You work so long and so hard to listen to your inner voice, but sometimes guilt or habit makes you listen to those other voices – the ones that beat you down. Sometimes you just can't shake them.

'I need to give my beast to my cat,' I said, and my voice was thick, slow. I tried to draw my hand out of Jason's, but he held on. He whispered into the bend of my neck, 'I'll be your cat.'

Nathaniel whispered against my other cheek, 'I'm her cat.'

Jason's voice against my skin, 'I'll be your doggy then.' He licked along my neck, and it made me writhe, but I shook my head, just a little, turning my head so I could see the side of his face.

'Not tonight, Jason.' This time when I pulled my hand, he let me go.

His blue eyes came into my vision, and he kissed me, long and deep, and my beast lay quiet. 'You taste like blood and other men's kisses,' he whispered, as he pulled away.

My beast woke inside me, as if it had only been napping. It woke and tried to spill upward. It filled my body like someone trying on a coat that was far too small. I could feel it stretching out inside me, feel it filling me, like hot water spilling up and up inside me until it filled every inch of me, and still there was more to come. It poured and poured, if water could have bones and muscle and anger. Because when it found that there were limits, that my skin did not burst, my bones did not bend, my body did not give, the beast began to rage inside me. It slashed with claws and fought with muscles that should have been metaphoric but felt all too real. It was trying to tear its way free of the cage, and the cage was my body.

I screamed, screamed and struggled, but you can't fight something that you can't touch. Nathaniel was still on top of me, eyes wide and frightened. He started to slide off of me, but I grabbed his arms, and managed to say, 'Kiss me.'

If it had been almost anyone else, they would have argued, but he didn't. He put his mouth against mine, and the next scream was muffled into his mouth. I willed the thing inside me into him. I tried to force it, but it was panicked, and could not hear me. It was like a wild animal, cornered, it heard nothing, but its own fear.

I tore my mouth from Nathaniel's and simply screamed. Jason was there, a hand on either side of my face, and the moment he touched me, the beast hesitated. The cat paused long enough to sniff the air, as if wondering what he was.

I looked up at Nathaniel with Jason's hands still holding my head. 'Try again, kiss me.'

He kissed me, and this time I was able to kiss him back, but the beast didn't rise. It sat inside me, sniffing, puzzling, but it did not rise. I broke the kiss and screamed not from pain, but frustration. 'Richard said to share my beast with someone who can give it release, but it won't go. It won't leave.'

'Are you still fighting for control of the *ardeur*?' Nathaniel asked.

I blinked at him and thought about it. Was I? Not consciously, but controlling it had become automatic. Now that I didn't have to control it, but had to, instead, call it into being, was I still quashing it? Was I still shielding? The answer was, yes.

'Yeah.'

'Stop fighting,' Nathaniel said, 'just let everything go.'

'No,' I started, but he touched my lips with his fingers.

'Hush, Anita, you can feed off of both of us, and it won't drain me that badly. It's not a good idea, but it's not a disaster. Stop fighting, and maybe the beast will stop fighting, too.'

I opened my mouth with his fingers still touching me. He slid his fingertips just inside my mouth, playing along the edge of my lips. The movement stopped me from talking more effectively than anything else could have done. I just lay there and let his fingers play around the edge of my mouth, delicate, sensual. 'Let go, Anita, just let go. We'll catch you.'

Jason leaned in against my face. 'I'm here, Anita. I won't let anything bad happen to Nathaniel. I promise.' He laid his face against my forehead. 'We can do this, Anita, but you have to let go. You have to let us catch you.'

Let go. It sounded so simple. But letting go of anything was so not my best thing. I wasn't even sure I knew how to do it. How do you let go? How do you open your hand and let yourself fall, and trust that other people will catch you? That they'll catch you and not let you hurt them, or yourself. Did I trust Nathaniel and Jason that much? Sort of.

Did I trust anyone that much? Maybe. Okay, not really. I took a deep breath, let it out slow, and I let go. I let go, and trusted. Trusted, even as a small voice inside me whispered, *stupid, stupid, stupid*.

52

HELL IS CLAWS and teeth, and bodies fighting. I sank my teeth into someone's chest, took in as much meat as my mouth would hold, and began to bite down. I wanted meat. I wanted to feed, and the leopard was screaming that if we didn't kill them, they'd kill us. Let go, they'd said, I'd let go, and now instead of the beast being something struggling to get out, it was me that was small and trapped and couldn't get out.

That part that wanted meat and blood and found struggling somewhere between sex and food was in the front of my head. I'd always thought being an animal must be peaceful, but it wasn't peaceful. It was simpler, but it wasn't peaceful.

I remembered only pieces. The taste of blood in my mouth. The feel of my teeth sinking into flesh. My nails cutting through someone's body. I was on my stomach, and I couldn't move. Couldn't move. Someone was on my back, and someone had my hands, and I couldn't move. Teeth on the back of my neck. A moment of mind-numbing panic, then it was peaceful. Like what had happened earlier in my office, when Nathaniel bit me there. Peaceful.

Jason was kneeling in front of me, off the edge of the bed, holding my wrists. The left side of his face was a bloody mess, and distantly, I knew that my nails had done that. His eye blinked out painfully from the bloody furrows. His arms were traced with bites and scratches, so it looked like he was wearing red gloves all the way up to his shoulders. His chest and stomach were bloody, too.

Nathaniel's teeth on my neck bit down a little harder, and my eyes fluttered up, and when he growled against my skin, my body writhed under him, not struggling, but offering. Jason spoke, and a trickle of blood trailed from his mouth, as he did it. 'Next time we do this, you get tied up.'

Nathaniel growled, but I didn't think it was meant for me.

Jason looked past me, to meet the other man's eyes, and said, 'Okay, okay. Give me your beast, Anita. Let me swallow it down.' He leaned into me, and the blood that trembled on the edge of his mouth fascinated me. I tried to strain toward that trembling drop of red, and Nathaniel's teeth made me stop, forced me to wait for Jason's mouth to come to me.

His mouth stopped just out of reach. I tried to raise my hands and touch him, but his hands forced my wrists down tighter on the side of the bed. He laid his mouth against mine, and I didn't kiss him, I licked the blood from the edge of his lip.

He drew back, laughing. 'You'd rather eat me right now, than kiss me.' But he leaned in toward me, his mouth half-parted, and I could smell the blood inside his mouth. I'd bitten him. I remembered the feel of his lip between my teeth. I made a sound low in my throat, and he laughed again, a purely masculine sound with his lips so close to mine that my tongue could touch them. His voice held that masculine laughter, and an edge of growl, 'God, she's eager.'

Nathaniel growled again, with his teeth still tight on the back of my neck. The growl was low and deep and vibrated down my spine like my body was a tuning fork. It made me push my body against his. My mouth reached for Jason, but my body was offering itself to the hard weight against the back of my body.

'Alright, but if she bites my tongue off, I'm going to be pissed.' And he pressed his lips against mine, but I didn't try to bite him, because his mouth was full of blood and tasted of meat. I'd already started this meal, all I wanted to do was finish it.

My beast was right there, under my skin, only Nathaniel's hold kept it peaceful. The taste of fresh blood, of meat, and the feel of Jason's mouth on mine, brought the beast like heat against my skin.

I could feel my body cooking with the heat of it, as if my skin was a container for something so much hotter than human flesh. Something that was almost there, almost ready, almost . . .

Nathaniel raised his mouth, and only his weight and Jason's hands held me down. He whispered something against the wound in my neck, I think he said, 'Now.' But I would never be sure, because in that moment my beast rose.

It rose up the line of my spine like heat. It spilled out my mouth and into Jason's, in a scalding, burning wave of power. It tore his mouth off of mine, forced his head back in a scream, and Nathaniel's body bowed on top of mine, and he screamed, too. My beast was like a sword thrust through both of them. I poured my energy into their bodies, until their bodies burst with it.

I saw Jason's skin split, and I felt Nathaniel tremble above me. One moment they were there, and the next I was drenched in liquid, warm, so warm, like being dipped in fresh blood, but it wasn't blood. It was clear and viscous — that fluid that the shapeshifters leave behind when they pull their bodies from one shape to another.

I was covered in it, dripping with it, and because Jason's claws were still pinning my wrists, I couldn't wipe it away from my face. I blinked at the wolfman kneeling in front of me. His fur was dry, like it always is, like magic. I stared into wolf eyes the color of early spring grass. His fur was thick and shades of pale gray. He opened a jaw that was longer than a human's, and full of teeth that any wolf would envy. He ran an impossibly long tongue over those teeth and stared at me with eyes that held things that I'd only begun to guess at.

A claw curled into the wet sheets on one side, and that claw was a black-furred hand. I turned back and did that slow, horror-movie take, where you know what's behind you, but you just can't keep from looking. You have to look, even with the feel and press of fur against your naked body. I knew what I'd see, and still I turned and looked.

Nathaniel's face was a strangely graceful mix of human and leopard. The face shape was closer to human than the werewolf's, but when I met those gray-blue eyes, there was no one home to talk to.

I'd gotten rid of my beast by bringing theirs, and now I was suddenly covered in warm liquid that mimicked blood, with two freshly turned lycanthropes holding me down. Nathaniel put his furred hands against the bed on either side of me, and he flexed those hands, and claws like white knives sprang out from his fingertips. Just seeing them, lying there, unused, made my pulse speed just a little.

I knew they wouldn't hurt me. I trusted them. But part of me trusted Jason and Nathaniel more than I trusted their beasts. I tried not to be afraid, because fear is like spice for their meat. Fear excites a lycanthrope, it just does. So I lay very still and tried to calm my heartbeat, tried to think how to ask them to let me go, without sounding like a victim.

Nathaniel moved his hands so that they lay on either side of my body, with the fur of his thumbs caressing my skin. My heartbeat didn't like it. Neither did I. He flexed his hands again, and the claws vanished into the fur. He caressed that fur down the sides of my body, and that brush of warm, warm fur brought my breath in a shuddering line.

His voice was more growl than anything else, when he said, 'I've never had hands before when I shifted.' He put those 'hands' back on either side of my body, so close that the edge of the fur touched the sides of my breasts. He pointed the claws downward, and I felt his muscles flex against the side of my body. His hands were right next to my breasts, and I felt his claws grip into the bed. He began to pull those claws downward. The sheet ripped, but it was the sound of the mattress tearing that brought a sound like a whimper from my throat. The mattress made a meaty sound, as his claws tore through it, easily. He moved his body so that he could trace the outline of my body against the mattress and sheets. He carved the outline of me with his claws. And I couldn't not be afraid.

Jason laughed, and strangely that masculine chuckle translated just fine through the wolf's throat. The sound made me look at him. He flashed fangs as he said, 'Don't be afraid, Anita.'

'Then let me go,' I said, and my voice was nicely calm, barely a tremor. If they'd been human they wouldn't have been able to taste my speeding pulse, or smell my fear. But they weren't human.

Nathaniel collapsed his body on top of mine, and he was taller, broader, more muscled, or muscled in places he hadn't been before. It was like a different body pressed against mine, one I'd never touched. The fur was thinner on his chest, stomach, groin, but the skin was warmer, almost hot against my naked body, as if in this form his blood ran hotter.

He licked my shoulder, and a sound very like a small squeal came out of my mouth. I closed my eyes and concentrated on my breathing, just my breathing. Not on the feel of his body, or of Jason's hands with their not-so-retractable claws tickling my wrists. I breathed, breathed while a tongue that was rougher than Nathaniel's licked in long, thick sweeps across my shoulders and upper back.

When I opened my eyes again, my pulse was normal, and I realized that Nathaniel was cleaning off the clear goop that he and Jason had gotten on me. He growled next to my ear, 'We got you messy.'

'Yeah,' I said, and my voice was a whisper.

He settled his hips against my thighs and did a small, powerful movement, somewhere between a wiggle and a push. He was suddenly resting against my ass, and I could feel that he was different there, too. Bigger, it felt like, but I might just have been scared. Everything seems bigger when you feel threatened.

He made a sound by my face, sort of a snuff, not like he was sniffing me, but like it was a noise that I should have understood. 'You're hungry. Hungry like we are. I can feel it.'

I fought to keep my pulse nice and normal, my breathing even. I wasn't going to do anything to escalate this, not if I had a choice. 'I'm not hungry,' I said.

He leaned harder against me, sliding lower between my legs, not inside, but moving that way. The thought sped my pulse, I couldn't help it. He rubbed his furred cheek against the side of my face. 'You need a shower.'

'Okay,' I said. At that point I'd have agreed to anything that would get me on my feet and out from under the two of them.

'We're not going to eat you, Anita,' Jason said. 'If that was really an option Jean-Claude wouldn't have trusted me with you, you should know that.'

I raised my face and met those wolfish eyes. 'Sorry, but you guys going all tooth and claw on me, makes me wonder.'

'We won't hurt you,' Jason said.

'Then let me go,' I said, and my voice was even, normal, my pulse slowing down.

'Not yet,' Nathaniel said, with his face still pressed against my face.

Jason looked at him. 'Why not?' he asked, before I could.

'Because she still needs to feed the *ardeur*.'

I wouldn't have thought that a wolf face could show that much incredulity, but Jason's did. 'Anita doesn't do furry.'

The leopardman on my back moved his hips another fraction of an inch down. He pushed against me, not inside, but knocking at that most intimate of doors. 'You are empty inside, I can feel it. I couldn't feel it before.'

Saying it once, was wishful thinking, twice, and I tried to look inside myself. Tried to see the *ardeur* without raising it. I needed some kind of metaphysical gas gauge, but all I could find was an emptiness in the center of me. A place where something should have been, and there was nothing.

'I feel it,' I said.

'I don't feel tired, now, Anita. I feel new.' He moved gently against me. 'Say yes.'

'Let me go, and maybe,' I said.

'I like holding you down. I like us both holding you down,' he growled against my skin.

'I thought you didn't like to be in charge,' I said.

'I don't usually, but today I do. Today I love the feel of your body under mine. I love feeling you fight not to struggle, not to panic. I can taste your self-control on my tongue. I want to lick it away.'

'Nathaniel,' I said.

'Say yes, Anita, just say yes. Feed the *ardeur*, then you can shower, while we go looking for other things to eat.'

'What other things?' I asked.

'There are supplies deeper in the underground,' Jason said, 'we've got too many wereanimals in here now not to be stocked up.'

'Stocked up on what?' I asked.

He leaned in, hands still on my wrists. 'Nothing human, nothing illegal, promise.' He licked my face, a quick flick of the tongue, and then he laughed, and it wasn't masculine, it was just Jason making a joke. Jason who would make a joke on the way to hell, even if it meant extra time and a worse punishment. No matter what form he was in, he was still Jason.

That thought made a tension go out of my shoulders, out of my body, that I hadn't even realized was there. It was still Jason under all that fur and claws. It was still Nathaniel rubbing his cheek against me.

Once upon a time I'd begged Richard to show me his beast. But when he did it, I hadn't been able to deal. It took me a long time to realize that Richard had shown me his beast in the worst light possible, because part of him didn't want me to be able to accept the beast, because he couldn't. I'd run from him after seeing him eat Marcus. I'd run from him to Jean-Claude, because the vampire had seemed less the monster that night.

Was I still the same person who hadn't been able to deal? Was I still the person who could deal with the handsome prince, but not the beast? Was it beauty, more than love, that moved me?

Nathaniel pushed gently against me. 'If you don't feed now, who will you feed from?'

'Graham really is just down the hall,' Jason said. 'He'll be in human form because Meng Die won't do him furry. She won't even sleep with him furry.'

I didn't want Graham. Was it just the human form I was in love with? Was it some anthropomorphic idea that I loved? Shit. These were just not the kind of relationship questions that the magazines gave you answers to. Did Miss Manners have an answer for being freaked by your boyfriend's animal form? I doubted it.

Jason drew his claws delicately away from my wrists. 'I'll get Graham and send him down.'

'No,' I said, and reached for his furred forearm. The fur was so soft, and his arm was so real. 'No, I don't want Graham.'

Jason gave me another of those looks, that said, you're joking. 'You don't do furry, Anita.'

'But I do Nathaniel, and I do you, on occasion.'

He grinned, though it wasn't exactly the same coming from the wolf muzzle. 'On occasion.' He sank back down in front of me. 'You want me to be your puppy tonight?'

'I was thinking more that we'd just fuck,' I said.

His face was either more expressive than any wolfman I'd met, or it was still enough Jason that I could read his face. He was still under there, somewhere. I'd surprised him, not in a bad way, but I'd truly surprised him.

Nathaniel pushed against me, and he whispered against my cheek. 'Is that a yes?'

'Yes,' I said.

He made a sound that was half-growl, and half pure eagerness. He raised up just a little, and then plunged himself between my legs. I was screaming before he'd finished, and not in pain. He was bigger, thicker, more, and all those extra bits were plunging inside me.

53

HE BROUGHT ME with the size of his body, the rhythm of his hips, and the flash of white claws like small knives against the tenderest parts of my body. The thought of what those claws could do to me if they wanted to, brought me struggling under him. Everything that I'd fought not to do, I now let myself do. I struggled, I screamed, I fought, and he held me carefully, delicately, but with no doubt that he could have torn me to pieces if he'd wanted to. It was both the most delicate of lovemaking, and the most dangerous. Not because of what he did, but because of what he could have done.

He raised me to my knees, cradling me against his body with his arms, and I caressed my hands over those arms, those muscles, that fur, so soft, and so different from the wolf. I pet him, not like you'd pet a dog, but like you'd pet a lover. I felt his rhythm change, knew he was close, felt his body strain not to claw me to pieces. Felt the dainty press of the tip of each of those claws, as he held them against my flesh. I came watching the pinpoints of those blades begin to crease my skin, almost, almost cutting, almost, almost piercing, almost, almost killing. At the last moment, he retracted the claws and held me hard and fast against his body, with the fur and padding of those hands lost somewhere between leopard and man.

The *ardeur* fed. Fed on the strength of his body, the heat of his skin, and the spill of his seed, which spilled hotter inside me than anything I'd ever felt from a man.

A thought cut through my mind, *He isn't a man*. The words weren't angry, but the emotion that came with them felt like it would burn a hole through my skin. Rage, such rage, and I knew who it was before the door opened.

54

RICHARD STRODE THROUGH the door, and his energy flung across the room like hot sparks from a fire. It hurt where it touched my skin, like small biting insects. What do you say when you find your ex-fiancée fucking a leopardman? Richard knew just what to say. 'The last time I saw anything this sick was in one of Raina's porno movies.'

Jason rolled off the bed and faced him. I think he was trying to give Nathaniel time to stand up without me attached to him. Or maybe he was trying to give me time. Whatever his motive, he stood between me and his Ulfric, and that wasn't the wisest thing he'd ever done. Brave, even gallant, but not wise.

Richard's power filled the room like scalding water. Nathaniel rolled off the bed, and I wondered if the air was as heavy and hard for him to breathe as it was for me. The thought was enough. I knew that he felt Richard's power like something you had to fight to walk through, like Richard's power was some sort of storm, a blizzard, or a sandstorm. Something that would blind you and take your life, unless you found shelter.

My shelter was crouching between the bed and the door. The wolfman was tall and broad and dangerous. Richard in his human form should have looked frail, but he didn't. He could have been a foot shorter, and with that much power rolling off of him, he would have seemed huge.

'Get out of my way, Jason. I won't ask again.'

'Tell me you're not going to hurt her, or Nathaniel, and I'll move,' he said it in a deep growling voice that would have given any red-blooded human pause, but Richard wasn't human.

Nathaniel was off the bed and moving toward them. Richard would hurt Jason enough to get him out of the way, but he'd hurt Nathaniel for other reasons. Reasons he might never admit out loud, but I didn't want to see it. I called Nathaniel back to me.

I had a gun under my pillow, but I didn't want to shoot Richard, and unless you're willing to shoot, a gun is just a rock made of metal. I was still trying to think of something to do that would make this less awful, when Richard backhanded Jason.

Blood flew in a little arc, sparkling in the lights, but Jason stood his ground. He didn't offer to fight back, but he didn't get out of the way, either.

I yelled, 'Richard, no!'

He picked Jason up like he was a dumbbell. Clean, jerk, Richard's arms bulged with effort as he lifted the werewolf over his head and held him there for a heartbeat.

We had one of those frozen moments, where everything slows down and you know bad stuff is about to happen, and you can't stop it. You can make choices and change what gets damaged, but you can't save it all. I was drowning in Richard's rage, his power boiling like a sea. I'd touched his rage before, his beast, and this wasn't it, not exactly. I had a second to realize that his rage tasted like an old friend. It was my rage, or tasted more like mine. I only had time for my aha moment, then he threw Jason, not across the room, but at the bed. Maybe he meant to hit me, but I rolled off the bed, and when Jason landed hard enough in the middle of it to collapse the frame, no one was on the bed but him.

I was on the far side of the broken bed, and Nathaniel was with me. He'd put himself a little in front of me. He hadn't pushed me behind him like I was a damsel in distress, but it was close. I was his Nimir-Ra, and supposedly his dominant. Shouldn't I be in front?

Jason lay on the collapsed bed, stunned. He'd been thrown from less than eight feet onto a bed, and he was breathless, frozen while he recovered. I didn't have the recovery power that Jason and Nathaniel had. Maybe me being in front wasn't bright, but shit. I didn't know what to do. Like so often with Richard, I didn't know what to do.

'Why don't you all get back on the bed? I'm sure it's a hell of a show. Raina and Gabriel would have loved it.' Since I'd had to kill both of them so they wouldn't star me in a rape/snuff film, it was a truly vicious cut. But the time when that kind of shit from Richard could make me angry was passed. I was afraid to add my anger to his.

His power was everywhere, as if the very air stung and burned. But it wasn't just his rage I could feel. Disgust, horror, and under that the thing that fueled the rage . . . envy. Why envy? And he was too wide open, he was hardly shielding at all. I got my answer.

It was as if someone threw a puzzle into the air, and I saw pieces. Clair and Richard in bed. Richard doing his usual vigorous job of it. Clair shifting in the middle of it. Her claws cutting up his back and shoulders. Clair in human form, screaming.

Richard shoved his anger at me, and I stumbled as if he'd actually pushed me. 'Stay out of my head.'

'Then stop projecting so hard that I can't help but hear it.'

He screamed, a full-throated cry of rage. It echoed in the big room, and I heard running out in the hallway. I knew who this was, too, or at least what.

Three people spilled into the room. One woman, two men, all with guns. They pointed them at Richard. Claudia, who was almost as tall as Dolph, and had broader, more muscular shoulders than most of the men in my life, did quick eye flicks around the room, taking in everything. Her tight ponytail flicked as she moved, because it was high on her head. A girl ponytail to offset the lack of makeup and those amazing arms. I didn't recognize the men with her, except that they held guns like they knew how, but I'd come to expect nothing less than professionalism from Raphael's people. The wererats didn't recruit amateurs.

'What is happening here, Anita?' Claudia asked. Her voice was even, just a little tight, as if she were gearing up to do her job, and she'd have less qualms than I would about that job.

'A difference of opinion,' I said.

She laughed, not like it was funny. 'A difference of opinion, well, hell.'

'This is not Rodere business,' Richard said, 'it concerns the pack and the pard, not the rats.'

Claudia's gaze went around the room again, took in the bleeding werewolf and the collapsed bed, my hand on Nathaniel's arm to keep him with me and away from Richard. She came back to Richard and smiled, again not like it made her happy. 'This doesn't smell like pack or pard business, it smells personal.'

'That's not your call,' he said, and his voice was lower, not growling, but lower.

She smiled again, and this time it was just a baring of teeth. 'It is when we we're being paid to guard the Circus and everyone in it. You've already bloodied one of the people in our care, Ulfric, we really can't let you harm anyone else.'

'He defied me. No one gets to defy the king. Raphael would agree with that.' He'd turned to face her, and I realized that he was one of the men in my life that didn't look frail next to Claudia.

'What our king would agree with and what he wouldn't is not in question.' She sighed and lowered the gun to point at the floor. The two men followed her lead.

Richard turned back to stare at the bed and the rest of us. He even took a step toward the bed.

'No, Ulfric, you don't just go back to abusing them. We may not be able to shoot you without political problems, but we also will not stand by and let you abuse those we have contracted to protect.'

He looked at her, and all that burning power seemed to draw away from the rest of the room, to concentrate like some great weapon. I wasn't close enough to feel it, but I was betting that all that power was now focused on Claudia.

She shook her head, like she'd been slapped. The two men with her moved back from Richard, as if they wanted more room to maneuver if things went wrong.

Claudia answered him, her voice warm with the beginnings of her own anger. 'No one disputes your power, Ulfric, it is great. It is your self-control that I question.'

Richard was mad, so mad, and he was looking for a fight. I'd rather it not be me, but I didn't think things would escalate as far with us as it would with the wererats. Someone could get seriously injured, or worse. Richard being in a pissy mood wasn't worth someone dying over. I know, I know, it probably wouldn't go that far, but the wererats were usually ex-mercenaries, or ex-military. They fought for keeps when they fought. Richard wasn't either of those things. He got mad, but he didn't really like going for the kill. It could all go so badly, so fast.

'Everybody ease down,' I said. 'It's not worth dying over.'

Richard looked at me. 'No one's talked about killing anyone, except you.'

'Richard, all three of the guards that are looking at you wondered about killing you the moment they hit the door. Ask them, go ahead, ask them.'

He glanced at the wererats, still with their guns pointed at the floor. 'Is she right?'

The three of them exchanged glances, then Claudia answered, 'Yes.'

'You thought about killing me, just like that?'

'We didn't know it was you doing the damage, Ulfric. But we are allowed to use any means necessary to do our jobs. We cannot allow you to harm anyone under our care.'

'You're not allowed to interfere with me disciplining one of my wolves, either.'

She nodded. 'You are right. It is not allowed for one animal to interfere in the internal disputes of another. If you can prove that this is pack business, and not personal, we can leave, and you can finish this, but you must prove it is business.'

One of the other men, who was small and dark, and looked like he'd spent a little too much time in rat form, said, 'Smells like jealousy to me.'

'Roberto, you are not helping,' Claudia said, her eyes still on Richard.

Jason rolled over and started to sit up. He moved like it hurt.

'He defied me,' Richard said, pointing at Jason.

'How?' Claudia asked.

'He refused to get out of my way.'

'What would you have done if I'd moved?' Jason said, and his voice held something thicker than normal, as if he was still bleeding inside his mouth. 'If you didn't throw me around, who would it have been? Nathaniel, Anita? She doesn't heal like we do, Richard.'

'I wouldn't . . .'

'When you hit the door, you were going to hurt someone,' Jason said, and let blood trickle from his mouth, because he couldn't spit in wolfish form. 'I thought it was better it was me.'

Some of that burning power began to fade. Richard's shoulders slumped, and he screamed again. A full-throated, all-out scream, as long and as loud as he had breath for. He dropped to his knees and smashed his hands into the floor. Apparently, he liked doing it, because he kept smashing his hands into the carpeted floor, over and over. Only when the stone floor underneath began to buckle visibly, did he stop.

The sides of his hands were bloody where he'd scrapped them on the carpet, like really bad rug burns. He raised those bloody hands up and just knelt there staring at his hands. He didn't cry, didn't swear, didn't do anything.

We all froze, waiting for him to do or say something. At least a full minute passed, and he hadn't moved. Claudia looked across the room at me. I shrugged. I'd been engaged to him once, and I'd been his lover, but I had no clue what to do. That was one of the problems with Richard and me, we so often didn't know what to do with each other.

I started to walk around the bed, but Jason grabbed my wrist. 'Close enough.'

I didn't argue. I just stopped and looked down at him. He was still staring at his scraped-up hands. 'Richard, Richard, are you in there?'

He laughed then, but it wasn't a good laugh. It was one of those laughs that held more bitterness than humor. Everyone in the room, except me, jumped when he laughed, as if they'd expected anything but that. I'd learned not to try to guess what he'd do.

'I want to lick the blood off my hands,' he said in a strangled voice.

'Then do it,' I said.

He looked up at me. 'What?'

'It's your blood. It's your hands. If you want to lick your own wounds, then do it.'

'Won't you be disgusted?'

I sighed. 'Richard, it doesn't matter what I think. It matters what you think.'

'You'd think it was disgusting,' he said.

I sighed, again. 'No, Richard, actually, no. The licking will make the scrapes feel better, and you'll enjoy the taste of blood.'

He frowned up at me. 'You wouldn't have said that a year ago.' It was almost a whisper.

'I might not have said it six months ago, but I'm saying it now. Lick your wounds, Richard, just don't live in them.'

'What's that supposed to mean?' he asked, and his anger flared, like a small hot whip against my skin.

'Don't get pissy, Richard. I'm trying to live the life I've got, not some dream of a life that I'm never going to have.'

'And you think I am.'

'You're Ulfric of the Thronnos Rokke Clan, and you're afraid to lick your bloody hands because someone else might think it's not very human. So, yeah, I think you're still pretending that you're going get another shot at a life. This is it, Richard. This is who and what we are. This is it. You need to embrace that.'

He shook his head, and his eyes glittered in the lights, as if there might be tears in those perfectly brown eyes. His voice when it came was even, no hint of those glittering eyes. 'I tried.'

I was shielding as hard as I could. I didn't want anymore peeks into his and Clair's love life, but I could guess. 'With Clair?'

He looked up, and the anger was winning over the tears. I'd never seen him this out of control of his emotions. I'd seen him angry, bitter, sad, but never this see-saw. It was like angry and sad were the only emotions he had left. 'You saw it, then.'

'I'm shielding like a son of a bitch right now. I saw that you had a fight, a bad one. But that's about all I saw.'

He opened his mouth, then glanced behind him. 'I won't hurt anyone, but this isn't a conversation for a crowd.'

The wererats looked at me. I sighed and wondered if I was being stupid. Maybe, but I was going to do it anyway. 'You guys can go.'

Claudia gave me a look. 'I don't think it's a good idea, Anita.'

'Neither do I,' I said, 'but do it anyway.'

She shook her head but motioned the two men through the door. She turned with the door halfway closed. She looked at me, and said, 'We'll be right outside. You yell, if you need us.'

I nodded. 'I will, I promise.'

She gave me a look that said she didn't believe me, but she went and closed the door behind her.

'Get out, Jason,' Richard said.

'It's his room, Richard,' I said.

'He doesn't get to hear this,' Richard said.

Jason got off the bed, slowly, like he still hurt. 'If I leave and you hurt her, neither you nor I will ever forgive you.'

Richard stared up at the tall wolfman. They had a moment of simply staring at each other, and whatever they saw in each other's faces seemed to satisfy them both. Richard said, 'You're right. I won't hurt her.'

'What about Nathaniel?'

Richard looked past him to the tall, dark form of Nathaniel. 'He needs to leave, too.'

'Only Anita can order me to leave,' Nathaniel said.

Richard looked at me, then down. 'Two requests, clothes for you, and everyone leaves. Please.'

The clothes were hard, because I was still covered in goop. What few clothes I had, I didn't want to get messy. What I needed was a robe, but I didn't have one in this room. I hesitated too long for Richard's mood, because he said, 'Don't make me have this talk with you naked, Anita. Please.' He said the *please* like he had the first time, like it was its own sentence, not an afterthought, but as if the please was more important than normal, and needed to be set apart.

'I'd love to get dressed, Richard, but I'm still covered in that clear goop. I'd rather not get it all over my clothes.'

'I've got a robe hanging on the back of the bathroom door,' Jason said, 'it should fit.'

'Since when do you wear a robe?' I asked.

'It was a present.'

I looked at him.

'Jean-Claude thought I looked cold.' I think he tried to grin at me, but the wolf muzzle just wasn't made for it.

'Let me guess, black silk?'

'Blue, to match my eyes.' He started toward the bathroom, not exactly limping, but close.

'I'll get it. Everybody stay put, and be nice, until I get back.' I went for the bathroom, though search me if I could remember a robe on the back of the bathroom door. But it was there, hanging exactly where Jason had said. It was a lovely blue, sort of soft and bright all at the same time. I'd been more tired than I'd known to miss it last night.

I put the robe on and caught sight of myself in the mirror. The remnants of yesterday's makeup still outlined my eyes, though it had smeared a little so it looked a little more Goth than my usual. The lipstick was gone. The clear goop had dried one side of my hair into a case of bed head that only a shower would cure. My body was covered in more of the drying goop, so that it was beginning to flake as I moved. If you have sex with condoms, you forget that what goes in eventually comes out, and I took the time to clean up just a little, because it was too embarrassing not to.

The blue was too pale for my coloring, and too big through the shoulders. It was one of those moments that I wondered why anyone wanted me. I just didn't see it. Of course, feeling this bad about myself might have had something to do with dreading Richard's little talk. Maybe.

I took in a lot of air, let it out slowly, and opened the door. It was one of the braver things I'd done in awhile. I'd much rather have dealt with bad guys than with Richard. Bad guys were simple, kill them before they kill you. Richard was a lot of things, but simple was so not one of them.

55

JASON LEFT WITHOUT a word, but Nathaniel said he'd wait outside with the wererats. No one liked leaving us alone, not even me. Hell, I wasn't sure Richard liked being left alone with me, but he'd asked for it, and I hadn't.

Richard stayed on the floor, as if he'd never move again. Since there was no chair, I stripped the stained sheets from the bed and sat on the edge of it. I sat sort of half-cross-legged, with one leg dangling off the bed, but I made sure the robe covered as much of me as it could.

We sat that way in total silence for at least a minute, though it felt like longer. I broke first, because just watching him kneel there, head bowed, made me want to comfort him, and that would go badly. Richard didn't take comfort from me anymore, or at least he didn't without making me pay for it later. That was a game I was no longer willing to play.

'What's up, Richard? You wanted privacy for a talk. We've got the privacy, now talk.'

He moved just his eyes up at me, and that one look was enough. Angry. It didn't spill out into his power, or fill the room, but I think that was because he was shielding, probably as hard as I was. 'You make it sound easy.'

'I didn't say it was easy. I just said, you wanted to talk, so talk.'

'Just like that.'

'Hell, Richard, you're the one who asked for this talk. I didn't invite you into a private conversation.'

'You asked about the fight with Clair. I don't want to share that with everyone.'

'You don't have to share it with me.'

'I think I need to.'

'What's that supposed to mean?'

He swallowed hard enough for me to hear it, then shook his head. 'Let's start over. I'll try not to be mad, if you try not to pick at me.'

'I'm not picking at you, Richard. I'm trying to get you to talk to me.'

He looked up at me, full face, not so much angry anymore, but not happy. 'If a friend had something hard to tell you, would you say, "so talk"?'

I took a deep breath and let it out. 'No, no I wouldn't. Okay, how's this. I'm sorry, you feel like you have to tell me something that is so obviously painful for you. But what I said before is still true, you don't owe me an explanation about a fight you had with your girl-friend, Richard. You really don't.'

'I know that, but it's the quickest way I can think to explain every-thing.'

I wanted to say, 'explain what?' but fought the urge. He was obvi-ously hurting, and I tried not to rub salt into anyone's wounds. But the call for privacy, and the big buildup was making me nervous. As far as I knew, Richard and I didn't have anything this important to say to each other. The fact that he thought differently made me down-right uneasy.

I sat on the corner of the bed, one hand going to the top of the robe, because even with it belted tight it was gaping. Too big through the shoulders, so it just didn't fit quite right. I kept one hand on the top and the other hand in my lap, so I didn't accidentally flash him. I'd been buck naked in front of him for minutes, but suddenly I was all worried about him catching a glimpse. I think it was his comment, that he couldn't have this talk with me naked. Would I find it hard to talk seriously if he was naked in front of me? I wanted to answer no, but truthfully in my own head, the answer was yes. Shit, I did not need this.

He was back to staring at the floor. I couldn't stand it. I had to prompt him, but I tried to prompt him more kindly than before. I tried to think of him as my friend and not as the ex who always seemed to rain all over my parade.

'What do you want to tell me about the fight with Clair?' I even managed to keep my voice neutral. Points for me.

He took in a lot of air and let it out, then raised a pair of sad brown eyes to me. 'Maybe that's not where to start.'

'Okay,' I said, voice careful, 'start somewhere else then.'

He shook his head. 'I don't know how to do this.'

I wanted to yell, 'do what?' but I resisted. But my patience had never been limitless, and I knew that if he continued to be obtuse, I'd blow it. Or my temper would. That gave me an idea: Maybe if I started talking, he'd just jump in.

'It's been a while since I felt your rage,' I said.

'I'm sorry about that. I lost control, I don't . . .'

'It's not a complaint, Richard. What I meant to say was that it felt different than the first time I touched it.'

He looked at me. 'What do you mean?'

'It felt, no, it tasted like my anger, like me, almost more than you.'

I had his attention now. 'I don't understand.'

'I'm not sure I do either, but follow my thought. Asher once told me that Jean-Claude had become more ruthless because I was his human servant. But with Damian being my vampire servant, I gained some of his emotional control. You can only gain what your partner has to share.'

He was looking at me, and the sadness was fading under him thinking. There was a good mind in there somewhere, he just didn't always seem to use it. 'Alright, I understand that.'

'If Jean-Claude gained some of my practicality, making him more ruthless, then what did you gain? I mean I got some of your beast and your hunger for flesh. I got Jean-Claude's blood lust and the *ardeur*. What did you gain from us?'

He seemed to think about that. 'I gained some of Jean-Claude's blood lust. Blood is as attractive as flesh to me, almost. It wasn't before.' He moved so he was sitting Indian fashion on the floor. 'It's easier to talk mind-to-mind with you lately, and last night, I interfered with you controlling that zombie.' He shivered just a little, like something about that scared him. Guess I couldn't blame him.

'But the mind-to-mind thing being this easy and the zombie stuff is recent, Richard. What did you gain the first time?'

He frowned at the floor. 'I don't see . . .'

'What if you gained some of my anger?'

He looked up then. 'Your anger can't be worse than the rage of the beast.'

I laughed, and it was closer to humor than his earlier laugh had been, but not by much. 'Oh, Richard, you haven't spent enough time in my head if you believe that.'

He shook his head, stubbornly. 'A human isn't capable of the kind of mindless rage that the beast is.'

'You haven't researched many human serial killers, have you?'

'You know I haven't,' he said, and he sounded grumpy.

'Don't go all grumpy on me, Richard, I'm trying to make a point here.'

'Then make it,' he said.

'See, that's exactly what I'm talking about. That sounds more like me, than you. You've been quicker to anger for the last bit, and I've been less quick to anger, why? What if you got some of my anger, and I got some of your calmness?'

He shook his head again. 'You're saying that your human anger is worse than my beast's rage. That's not possible.'

It was my turn to shake my head. 'Richard, you seem to think that human is better than lycanthrope. I don't know where you get that idea.'

'Humans don't eat each other.'

'Shit, Richard, yes, they do.'

'I don't mean cultures that have ritual cannibalism.'

'Neither do I.'

'Comparing lycanthropes to serial killers isn't going to make me feel better about being a lycanthrope.'

'My point is that humans can be just as rage filled, just as destructive. The difference is that a werewolf is better equipped for mayhem than a mere human. If human beings had the fangs and the claws that you guys do, then we'd, they'd, be just as destructive. It isn't lack of wanting to do it, it's lack of the right tools that make humans less scary.'

'If this is your rage, Anita, it's awful. It's worse than almost anything I've ever felt. It's like being crazy. So angry, almost all the time. I can't believe it's something that was in you.'

'Not past tense, Richard, trust me. I had to embrace what I operate on a long time ago.'

'What you operate on, what does that mean?'

'It means that at the heart of me, is this deep, seething, bottomless, pit of pure rage. Maybe I came with it. I know my mother's death helped fill it up. But as far back as I can remember, it's been there.'

He shook his head. 'You're just saying this to make me feel better.'

'Why would I say something that wasn't true just to make you feel better?'

Anger filled his eyes, like magic. One moment trustworthy brown, the next moment serial killer dark. 'Thank you, thank you very much, for reminding me that I don't mean shit to you anymore.'

I shook my head, and let my hands fall into my lap. 'If you meant nothing to me, Richard, nothing at all, we wouldn't be in this room alone.'

'You're right, you're right. I'm sorry. I just get so angry, so angry.' He tried to rub his arms, but the bloody scrapes hurt.

'You said you wanted to lick the wounds, go ahead. It won't bother me.'

'It will bother me,' he said.

'No, Richard, licking your wounds would make you feel better. You'd enjoy it, and that's what bothers you. Not the wanting to do it, but how good it feels when you give in to it.'

He nodded, staring at his hands. 'I tried to embrace my beast, Anita. I really tried.'

'I felt you feeding on a deer. I felt how happy you were in wolf form. It felt like you had embraced it.'

'When I'm in animal form, yes. But it's being human on the outside, and not human on the inside that gets me confused.'

'Does it get *you* confused, or Clair?'

He gave me a look that wasn't exactly angry. 'I thought you didn't hear the fight.'

'I got one word when she was screaming at you – *animal*. Am I wrong? Was she complaining about herself and her beast?'

'No, you got it exactly right.' He laid his hands in his own lap, and his eyes were back to being sad, like someone had hit a switch. Angry, sad, angry, sad. It was like some sort of demonic baby hormones. 'She accused me of raping her.' His voice was soft when he said it.

I gave him very wide eyes and let just how impossible I thought the idea was to show in my face.

He gave a very small smile. 'Just the look on your face now is worth something. You don't believe it, just like that, you don't believe I could do that to her.'

'I don't believe you would do that to any woman, but that's beside the point.'

'No,' he said, and his voice sounded more relaxed than it had since he entered the room, 'that's not beside the point, not for me. After what a bastard I've been to you, that you still believe in me, that means a lot.'

I wasn't sure what to say to that. If I agreed that he'd been a bastard would that start a fight? If he thought I believed in him, was that going to give him the wrong idea? I mean, not believing that Richard would rape someone didn't mean that much to me. He was a decent person, that's all.

'I'm glad it makes you feel better, but remember, I saw the beginning of the lovemaking session. You can't rape the willing, Richard.'

His eyes looked haunted, as if there was something I'd missed. 'She said that I always make love like it's rape.'

That made my eyebrows go up again. 'Excuse me? Tell that to me slowly, because it made no sense fast.'

He looked up at me, and there was something in his eyes, some demand, something he wanted me to say, or do, but I didn't know what. 'Do you mean that?'

'I mean, explain what she meant by it.'

'She said, I'm always so rough, that it's like rape. That I don't know how to make love, that I only know how to fuck.' His eyes looked raw, as if the pain in them had been skinned naked to shine out of his face. It hurt me to see it, but I didn't look away. I gave him my eyes and let him see what I thought of what Clair had said.

'Is she still your girlfriend?'

'I don't think so.'

'Good, because I'd hate to say she's crazy if you were still going to date her.'

'Why is she crazy?' he asked.

'What kind of head job has she done on you, Richard? *Rape* isn't a word that anyone should use lightly.'

'She didn't use it lightly,' Richard said, and the small smile was bitter. 'She meant it.'

'How?'

He looked at me, and the pain was still raw. 'Did I ever hurt you when we were together?'

I started to ask, 'emotionally, or physically?' then decided to just ask, 'You mean physically?'

'I mean did I hurt you when we made love?' He shook his head. 'I'm sorry to ask you this. I don't have a right to ask, but I didn't know who else to ask. I knew you wouldn't lie, because I was your Ulfric, or because you didn't want to hurt my feelings. I knew that if I asked, you would give me a real answer.'

I looked at him and hoped I didn't look as amazed as I was feeling. After everything we'd done to each other, all the fights, the hurts, and he still trusted me. He trusted me not to lie, not to make it worse than it was, or better than it was, but to tell the truth. I wasn't sure if I was flattered or insulted. I decided to be flattered, because anything else would have pissed me off. But the amount of trust he was putting in me scared me, not for me personally, because he was right, I'd give him the truth. But a lot of people wouldn't. A lot of people would have used it as an excuse to twist the knife a little deeper. He was damned lucky I wasn't one of those people.

I opened my mouth, closed it, stroked my hands down the silk of the robe, and finally had to look away from those pain-filled eyes while I tried to think how to answer. Not truth or lie, but how to say it.

He stood up, suddenly, abruptly. 'That's alright, I shouldn't have asked.'

'Sit back down, Richard. I'm just trying to think how to say it, so it doesn't sound stupid.'

He stood there, his face all set to be angry, as if he didn't believe me.

'Fine, stay standing, but you asked if you'd ever hurt me when we made love, right?'

He nodded.

'Yes, and no.'

The scowl turned into a frown. 'What does that mean, "yes and no"?'

'It means that Mother Nature has made it almost impossible for you to be anything but rough, unless you're very careful.'

He frowned harder. 'I don't understand.'

Of course he didn't, of course he would make this as embarrassing as possible. 'Richard, you are aware that you're well-endowed, right?' I felt the blush start creeping up my neck, and there wasn't a damn thing I could do about it. I'd always blushed fairly easily, but I'd seldom hated it as much as I did in that moment.

'Raina said I was. It was one of the reasons she wanted me for the movies.'

'You didn't know you were large before Raina?'

It was his turn to blush. 'I was a virgin before Raina.'

I shivered, and the look on his face was so raw, that I said out loud, 'The thought of a virgin with Raina is just frightening. She was one very sick puppy.'

He nodded. 'I know that, now.'

'Did you know it at the beginning with her?' I asked.

'I didn't have anything to compare it to,' he said.

I had an idea. Raina had been his first lover, and Raina had been into sadomasochism on a scale that made a joke out of safe, sane, and consensual. She'd done porn, hell, snuff films. She'd been one of the scariest and most twisted people I'd ever met, and I'd met a lot. Richard had nothing to compare it to, what exactly did that mean?

I tried to lead up to it, obliquely, my version of subtle. I went back to my orignial point. 'You're big, Richard, which means when you're making love, unless you're careful it can hurt.'

'I did hurt you,' he said, and he sounded desolate.

'I didn't say that.'

'Yes, you did.'

'Richard, listen to what I'm actually saying, don't editorialize in your own head, okay?' I stood, so I could pace. This was not a conversation for sitting still.

'I'll try,' he said.

'Good enough.' I came to stand in front of him and tried again. 'A lot of women don't like their cervix bumped during sex.'

He gave me that puzzled frown again. How did I end up giving my ex-fiancé sex education? How does anyone end up in these kinds of conversations? Just unlucky, I guess.

'If you go too deep, you reach the end of most women. You bump into the end of the vagina, you hit their cervix.'

He nodded, then said, 'I always come to the end.'

I made a voilà gesture. 'That's my point.'

'What's your point?'

I put hands on hips because either he was being deliberately obtuse, or he really wasn't getting it. 'You're big enough that you always bump someone's cervix if you're in a position that allows all of your . . . penis to go inside her. I can't be any plainer, Richard, so please make the connection here.'

'You mean it hurts them,' he said.

'Yes.'

'It hurt you,' he said.

'No. I like having my cervix bumped. I have a whole different kind of orgasm from it, so I don't mind.'

He was frowning again, but more like he was thinking. 'You're saying that if you didn't like it, that it would hurt.'

'It would just hurt,' I said, 'because in some positions, with someone as well-endowed as you are, it is a sort of pain. But for me, and I'm betting for Raina, it was more pleasure than pain.' I hated putting myself in any category that contained Raina, but I would have bet good money that I was right.

'I hurt you, but I didn't?'

I sighed. 'Look, this is an area that I've only recently embraced myself. Sometimes my pain and pleasure centers get confused. What would hurt most people feels good to me, at least during sex.' It was my confession, so I didn't have to meet his eyes, since it was my pain and not his.

'Me, too,' he said.

I looked at him. 'Well, that would explain a lot.'

'What do you mean by that?'

'The sex was always great, Richard. Even when everything else was going to hell, the sex never stopped being great.'

'You mean that?'

I nodded. 'Yes.'

He smiled, and it was almost a real smile, except for that flinching in his eyes. 'So you think I was too rough for Clair, because of my size?'

'And your technique is vigorous.'

He gave that frown again.

'Richard, haven't you ever been with anyone where you weren't as . . . vigorous?'

He gave me a look that said more clearly than any words that the answer was no.

'Okay, a friend of mine told me that men are ducklings, they tend to imprint on their first lovers. Which means they tend to make love the way they are first trained to make love. You were trained by a woman who was a sexual sadist and made porn movies, violent porn movies.'

He looked shocked, then horrified. 'You're saying Clair is right. I was too rough. I did hurt her.'

I shook my head. 'Did she ask you not to be so vigorous during the lovemaking?'

'She never asked about my . . . technique at all. She just blew up and said I was too rough. That I enjoyed making her beast come. That I enjoyed her clawing me up. That I enjoyed making her a monster. That I always made love like an animal no matter what shape I was in.'

Eeeah. I said what I was thinking, 'Did Clair mean to hurt you as much as possible, or was it just an accidental hit?'

'What do you mean?'

'I mean, that if I were trying to hurt you as much as possible, I couldn't do better than that.'

'I think she just meant it. I mean if I'm having sex rough enough for Raina, then how can it be anything but rape to anyone else?'

I shook my head and waved a hand in front of his face, so he'd look up and at me. 'Don't ever use the word *rape* to me again, Richard, because you don't do that. If you're with someone who likes sex the same way you do, then it's just good sex.'

'But rough,' he said.

I shrugged. 'You don't start out rough, but yeah, you usually end up there, but it was never anything I didn't want to do. All Clair had to do was ask for what she wanted, but she treated you like so many women treat men, like you should be able to read her mind. You aren't a mind reader, Richard, just a man, and men are usually less able to read a woman's mind than another woman is.'

'I'm not a man, Anita, I'm a werewolf. I'm an animal.'

I grabbed his upper arms. 'Don't let me hear you say that, ever again. You say *animal* like it's a dirty word, Richard, it's not. But until you own that it's not, don't let anyone make you feel that bad about yourself.'

He smiled then, a little sad around the edges, but it was a real smile. He touched my arms with his hands, and I pulled away. I was so not going to hug and make up. I would help him through this, if I could, but we were not a couple anymore.

'If I didn't hurt you, then why did you pull away just now?'

I hugged my arms tight and paced a little farther away from him. 'You came here for truth, fine, here's truth. We're not a couple anymore, Richard, but that doesn't mean I don't feel . . . oh, hell, I don't want you to get the wrong idea.'

'And what would that be?' His voice was back to being guarded.

'You were very clear at my house yesterday. I was in your head, Richard. I know what you were thinking, what you were feeling. I was there inside your head.'

'Then you saw what I wanted to do to you.' He turned away, so that all I could see was the back of him in jeans, and the jean jacket that was a few shades bluer than the jeans. His hair was beginning to have waves, but it still looked shorn to me. 'It was sick, Anita. I wanted you afraid of me. Having you afraid while I fucked you, would have been . . . would have—'

'Just flat done it for you,' I finished for him.

He turned and looked at me. His eyes were desolate, as if something in them had died. 'Yes, yes, exactly.'

'Richard, every lycanthrope I know is a little confused about the fear response, food, and sex.'

He shook his head, and it must have been too vigorous, because he winced. 'But no lycanthrope I've met, except for Raina and Gabriel, thought fear was an aphrodisiac.'

'Since I've met some of the same lycanthropes that you've met, I know that's not true. What is true, is that Gabriel and Raina were the only ones willing to admit it to anyone and everyone.'

'No, no,' he said and stalked toward me, his anger starting to rise in a warm prickling wash. 'No one else wanted what they wanted, not like that. Not the real thing.'

'Aha,' I said, then apologized for saying aha, 'but the point is, you said *not the real thing*. I've met a lot of shapeshifters who are into the bondage and submission scene, but it's a game with rules. Safe, sane, consensual. There are safe words, and once that agreed-upon word is uttered, then it stops, it's over.'

'There was no word that would keep you safe from Raina and Gabriel.'

'Exactly, Richard, exactly. But you can enjoy the game without doing what they did.'

He grabbed for me, and I tried to be out of reach, but in the end, I had only a shadow of his speed, not the real thing. He got one wrist instead of two, but he still got one. He jerked me a little toward him, not hard, but enough that I planted my feet and set up for not being pulled any closer. Just principle, instinct, nothing personal.

'What if it's the reality I want, Anita? What if the reason Raina liked me so much was that I'm just like her?' He didn't hurt me, didn't do anything but keep holding my wrist, keep me, so that I knew I couldn't get away, easily, if at all. I was stronger than a normal human, but I wasn't as strong as a real lycanthrope.

I let out a breath that was even, and my voice sounded normal, but I couldn't help it. I started with, 'Let go of me, Richard.'

'You're afraid of me,' he said.

'No, but you aren't my boyfriend anymore. You don't have the right to touch me without permission.'

'The fact that you're trying to pull away, and I know you can't, excites me.'

There was a time in my life that I would have argued, but we'd argue about it later, if we needed to. I didn't repeat my request, because I wasn't sure what would happen if I upped the physical stuff. I knew I didn't want to find out, so I talked. 'All you need is a submissive of your very own who likes to play these games, and you're all set, but I am not your anything, so let go of my wrist.' Okay, I couldn't not ask again.

He let go of me, so abruptly I stumbled a little. I guess I'd been pulling harder away from him than I thought. Fancy that. I resisted the urge to rub my wrist. Never let them see that they've hurt you. It's a rule. 'You're nothing like Raina, Richard.'

'Yes,' he said, 'I am.'

'I carry her munin, remember, I've had her in full technicolor glory in my head, and I've been in your head, too. Trust me, you don't think like she did.'

'Sometimes I fantasize about horrible things, Anita.'

What I wanted to say was, I wasn't his mother confessor, but I didn't, because I didn't know who else to send him to for this talk. Who else would I trust? No one. Damn it.

'So don't we all, Richard, the difference isn't what you think, it's what you do about it. Most of us know the difference between fantasy and reality. We know that what works as pretend doesn't work in the real world.'

'What if I want things that would hurt other people?'

I so didn't want to be having this talk, but looking into his face, I knew that this was part of the demon that had driven him to nearly destroy himself, and us. 'If it's going to permanently maim, scar, or kill someone, you don't do it. Outside of those parameters you talk to your lover and see what they want to do. What they're willing to do.'

He was frowning at me. 'No maiming, scarring, or killing, and everything else is okay? Just like that.'

I shook my head, 'No, everything else that your partner says "yes" to, is okay. If you're on top, dominant, then you have to hold it together and make sure it's all safe and not too scary.'

'I want it to be scary,' he said.

I shrugged. 'I said, "not too scary." Through ... friends, I'm beginning to understand that a little fear goes a long way as foreplay.'

'You don't mean friends, you mean Nathaniel.'

'If I'd meant just Nathaniel, I'd have said just Nathaniel. He can't teach me how to be a good top. To learn to be dominant you've got to talk to a dominant, not a submissive.'

'You sound like you've researched it.'

'Most of the wereleopards in my pard are into bondage and submission. I can't be a good Nimir-Ra for them if I don't understand them.'

He looked at me, considering something. I wasn't sure exactly what he was thinking, but at least it wasn't sad or angry. At this point I'd take almost any emotion that wasn't one of them. 'I know that before today you weren't fucking Nathaniel. I was in your mind, and I know. You really did research to try to understand your leopards, not just for your lover.'

'You sound surprised,' I said.

'Because Raina was our lupa for so long a lot of the werewolves are into BDSM, too, but I learned everything I ever wanted to know about it from Raina and Gabriel, and their accomplices.'

I almost didn't say it, but he said he'd come to me for the truth. I'd see if he really wanted truth, or just some of it. 'Richard, you say you like fear with your sex. You like the game of fear, and you like your sex rough.'

He was looking at me, the look was a warning. Those dark brown eyes were willing me not to finish, but if I didn't tell him, who would?

'You enjoy the scene, too, Richard.'

'I don't—'

I held up a hand. 'You don't do what Raina and Gabriel and some others did, but you can be a little in without being a sexual sadist. Some people think just enjoying teeth and nails during sex is sadistic.'

He was shaking his head over and over. If it hurt the scratches on his face, he didn't show it this time. 'Just because I like teeth and nails doesn't mean I'm like that. I'm not like them.'

'If you mean Raina and Gabriel, no, you're not. But you didn't run from me just because you thought I was bloodthirsty. You ran because with me you couldn't keep pretending.'

'Pretending what? I'm not pretending anything.'

'It's not just you that's been pretending, Richard.'

'Pretending what?' His anger started to fill the room, hot and close, like a storm that hadn't broken yet.

'I like teeth and nails during sex. Hell, I like biting alone without much sex. I like the feel of flesh between my teeth.'

He looked away. 'That's my fault, and Jean-Claude's. It's our hungers in you.'

'Maybe, but they're still in me, and it's still something I enjoy. I may never be as comfortable around the scene as Nathaniel is, and that worries me, because if he's mine, then I want him to be happy. But I've had to stop pretending that I don't like rough sex. Jason said that I like dominant men, because they sort of take charge, and I don't have a choice. The reason I was able to avoid Nathaniel for so long was he tried to get me to do all the moves. I need a little dominance play, or I don't play. I thought he was crazy, but it's been a busy twenty-four hours, and I'm tired of running.'

He looked back at me. 'Running, running from what?'

'Same thing you are, myself.'

'You're not—'

I stopped him with a hand again. 'Yeah, I was. Maybe I still am. There are parts of my life that I don't want to look at. Someone told me that it's okay that I like two men in bed with me. I argued with them, Richard. I argued that, no I didn't.' I took two steps closer to him. 'But arguing is pretty silly, don't you think?'

'I don't know what you mean.'

'I'm dating Jean-Claude and Asher. I was dating you and Jean-Claude.'

'Not at the same time in the same date,' he said.

I waved it away. 'Fine, I'll leave you out of it. But I'm still dating Jean-Claude and Asher. I'm living and sharing a bed with Micah and Nathaniel. Yes, it was sort of accidental. I didn't try to get into either situation on purpose, but I'm there. And now with Damian and Nathaniel, I've got another threesome where I'm the only girl. Not on purpose, but after awhile, Richard, arguing that I don't enjoy two men together with me just sounds silly.'

'Do you?' he asked.

I didn't owe him the answer, but maybe I owed myself one. I'd only admitted it to myself seconds ago. 'Yes, being in the middle of two men just flat does it for me. Just the feel of them on either side just flat does it for me.' I waited for the blush to start, or at least the embarrassment, but it didn't. It was true, and it was okay. I was okay. I had men in my life that thought it was okay.

Richard looked at the floor, as if whatever he saw in my face he didn't want to see. Or maybe there was something in his face he didn't want me to see. 'I could never do that.'

'No one's asked you to.'

He looked up then, and his anger lashed out, almost like he'd laid a hot whip across my skin. I jumped from the feel of it. 'Ow,' I said.

'Sorry, I didn't mean to hurt you, but the hell you say, no one's asked me.'

'Alright, to my knowledge no one's asked you.'

'Everyone, everyone in the preternatural community, whatever animal, or thing they are, thinks that I was doing Jean-Claude and you. That we were some happy little ménage à trois.'

'I've run into that rumor,' I said. 'You know what you were doing, and who, so what does it matter?'

He let out a shadow of that inarticulate scream he'd done before. 'Anita, how do you think I feel when almost every leader in this town that I have to do business with thinks I'm shagging the Master of the City?'

'Are you saying that people thinking you're bisexual hurts your standing as a leader?'

'Yes.'

'It doesn't seem to hurt Jean-Claude's,' I said.

'That's different.'

'I don't think so.'

He made fists, and that hurt, and he made that sound again. 'You don't understand, Anita. You're a girl, and you don't understand.'

'I'm a girl, and I don't understand. What does that mean?'

'It means it's still more socially acceptable for a girl to be bisexual than it is for a man.'

'Who says?' I asked.

'Everyone!' His anger flared outward like hot water, and it was about waist high, and rising.

'You're homophobic,' I said.

'I am not.'

'Yeah, you are. If it didn't bother you so much that people thought you were bisexual, then you wouldn't care what they said. You'd know the truth, and it would be enough.' I moved closer to him, pushing through the heat of his power, his anger, his frustration. 'Besides, what's wrong with being bisexual, or homosexual, or whatever? What does it matter, Richard, as long as you're happy and no one is getting hurt?'

'You don't understand,' he said.

I was standing close enough to touch. Standing so close that his power bit and sizzled almost against my skin, as if the robe wasn't there. God, he was so powerful, more than the last time I'd touched his power. He'd gained from Jean-Claude and me, just like Jean-Claude had, like I had. If we could get our triumvirate to truly work the way it was meant to, no one would touch us, no one would dare.

That one thought wasn't my thought, not exactly. Jean-Claude wasn't awake yet, I'd have felt it, but the thought was more his than mine. I remembered last night at the club, and how we'd been joined tighter, closer, than ever before. I'd done things last night that hadn't been possible before. I'd reached new levels of power both with Jean-Claude and with my own abilities. I'd also had sex with a vampire I'd known less than two weeks, and only Requiem's gentlemanly ways had kept it to once. That wasn't like me, and standing this close to Richard's pain, I was thinking about the power and not the cost to him. That wasn't like me either. But they were both very like Jean-Claude.

'What's wrong?' Richard asked. 'You've thought of something.'

'Just wondering what other parts of Jean-Claude I'm carrying around inside myself.'

'You told me, the *ardeur*, the blood lust.'

I shook my head. 'I've never been very practical with relationships, or sex, and lately, like the last twenty-four hours, or so, I have been. At least a lot more practical than I've ever been before.'

'Is it true that you had sex with two of the new British vampires at Guilty Pleasures last night?'

'My, my, the rumor mill does grind fast.'

He relaxed, some tension going out of him. 'Then it was just a rumor.'

I sighed, and was getting tired of doing that, but it seemed like Richard just brought it out in me. 'Half true.'

'Which half?' he asked.

I didn't like the look on his face. It wasn't angry exactly, which should have been an improvement, but it wasn't neutral either. 'One vampire, not two.' I shook my head. 'But you know what? I don't think I owe you an explanation, Richard. I don't keep track of the swath you're cutting through your own pack, and Verne's pack when you're in Tennessee.'

He was looking at me, studying my face, as if he was trying to figure out what I was hiding. 'If you weren't ashamed of it, then you'd just tell me.'

'Richard, you aren't my dad, or my boyfriend. I don't owe you an explanation about who I do, or don't, sleep with.'

'You slept with Nathaniel for four months before you had sex with him. What changed? Why these two vampires, why now? I heard it was a hell of a show last night, what the hell happened?'

'Are you asking from some macho possessiveness?'

'No, as the third of your triumvirate. Or should I say, one of your triumvirates?'

As the third of our triumvirate he had a right to know how close we'd come to losing control of Primo and some other choice bits. He had helped me last night, even if it had gone wrong, he'd tried. He'd really tried.

I sat down on the edge of the bed, and he sat on the floor with his knees drawn up to his chest, while I gave him a thumbnail sketch of the near disaster and an edited version of what I'd done to help Jean-Claude feed. I didn't leave much out, I just didn't elaborate.

'I can't believe you fucked Byron. I didn't even think he liked girls.'

'He took one for the team,' I said, and tried to keep the irony in my voice to a minimum.

He actually blushed. 'I didn't mean it that way. I meant, if I was shopping for men for you among the new vampires, he wouldn't have been high on my list.'

'Truthfully, he's not high on mine. I mean he's a nice enough guy, but as a friend, not as more.'

'Then, why?'

'He was the person that was there, Richard. If I accidentally sucked someone's soul out through their mouth, Jean-Claude thought I'd be less cut up if it was Byron and not Nathaniel.'

'Is Primo like some kind of Trojan horse?' he asked, and him asking that made me think better of him, lots better. It was a very good question.

'You mean did the Dragon let Jean-Claude have Primo so she could try and take over here?'

'Or just cause enough destruction that Jean-Claude got up on charges. Or his business was ruined, something. From what Jean-Claude's been hearing from Europe, the council isn't too happy with him.'

It must have shown on my face, because Richard said, out loud, 'I have been paying attention Anita.'

'I'm sorry, I'm really sorry, I didn't think you had.'

'I admit I wasn't before, maybe like a month before, but I am now. I told you, I've decided to live and not die by inches. That means I've got to pay attention to business, and I may not like it. I may hate it, but being part of this triumvirate is business.'

'I don't know about Primo. He might be, as you so aptly put it, a Trojan horse. I left one of the wererats on guard outside his coffin. I gave orders that if Primo breaks out, he's to be killed. No third chances, because he's already on his second.'

'Why would Jean-Claude bring in something that dangerous?'

'I saw Primo fight, and I saw him heal more damage than any vampire I've ever seen heal. It was impressive. We've got a lot of powerful vamps, but most of them are Belle's line, and that runs high to beauty, seduction, which is great for the clubs. I mean we have some really choice people to strip and to dance with the tourists at Danse Macabre, but if we had a war, a real war, then we have almost no soldiers.'

'You have the wolves,' he said, 'and through two treaties, the wererats.'

'Yeah, but it's unusual to have such close ties with other groups. Vamps scouting us for takeover won't count beyond the wolves. It won't occur to most of them that a treaty with an animal that isn't the master's to call will come through when the going gets tough.'

'So you approve of Primo being here?'

'No, definitely not, not after last night. I think we should shoot his ass, but I understand why Jean-Claude took the chance. We need some vamps that can fight, not just look pretty.' As if on cue, the door opened, and it was my favorite pretty vampire.

56

WE BOTH TURNED to look at the door, though my turn was less turny than Richard's. Jean-Claude was in the doorway wearing the black robe I was so fond of. The one that was edged with real black fur at the lapels, and framed his pale chest so nicely. His long black curls had been combed out, so that he looked fresh and lovely. I still needed a shower. Oh, well.

'I didn't feel you wake. I always feel you wake.'

'You are both shielding very, very hard,' he said, as he strode into the room. His bare feet were very pale against the dark carpet. 'I heard your last comment, *ma petite*, should I take it as an insult?'

'Sorry, but we need soldiers not seducers. We've got plenty of those.'

He gave that wonderful Gallic shrug that meant everything and nothing. It was a graceful movement. Sometimes I wondered if *shrug* was the right word. If what Americans do is a shrug, whatever Jean-Claude did wasn't the same.

'I told your Nathaniel to go and feed his new and surprising form. He will be even more popular when the ladies see this new shape of his.' He was being very pleasant, very casual. His face held a smile, and his movements were graceful and a little flamboyant. He was hiding something. I'd learned long ago that this wasn't the real Jean-Claude. This was one of his many faces that he used when reality would be too harsh, or too shocking, or too something.

'What's up, Jean-Claude?'

'Whatever do you mean, *ma petite*?' he asked, and came to sit down on part of the bed near me. The part that I'd removed the sheets from, so we were sitting on the relatively clean mattress. The bed bobbed unevenly as he settled on it. He looked at Richard, as the bed moved oddly. 'I think you are going to owe my *pomme de sang* a bed frame, Richard.'

Richard actually had the grace to look embarrassed. 'I lost my temper, I am sorry for that. I'll replace the frame.'

'Good,' he crossed his legs, one a little higher than it needed to be, so he could lace his hands around the knee, and expose a line of pale leg. Was he flirting? No, that wasn't it.

It wasn't me who said the next part, but it was like my thoughts came out Richard's mouth – scary. 'Cut the act, Jean-Claude, just tell us what's happened now?'

The face he gave us was way too innocent. 'Whatever do you mean, *mon ami*?'

Richard and I exchanged glances that said worlds. Richard spoke for us. 'No games, Jean-Claude, remember.'

'You are beginning to sound painfully like *ma petite*.'

'Thank you, I'll take that as a compliment.'

That earned him a smile and a nod from me.

Richard smiled at me, and it was the first real smile I'd seen on him since he stepped into the room. It was good to see it, and I found that I had one of my own to give back. There, we were all being friendly.

'You're doing your flamboyant, happy, casual act,' I said. 'Cut the act, and tell us what's up.'

'You do realize, *ma petite*, that Richard has become almost as blunt at times as you are.'

'And I'm starting to have moments when I sound like you, Jean-Claude. Let me guess, the closer binding last night has had some interesting side effects.'

'Not just us being closer, *ma petite*, but you're binding of a new triumvirate to you. That has upped the side effects, I believe.' His face was still lovely, but the nearly pretentious movements were fading, changing to a seriousness that I didn't like seeing. He wasn't happy about something. I didn't know what it was, but it had to be something that he either thought both, or at least one, of us really wouldn't like.

He started by confessing that my being willing to do Byron and feed Requiem was probably his less-finicky tastes coming out through me. I stopped him before he got through it. 'If I hadn't fed on Byron and Requiem, you wouldn't have had enough energy to control Primo. He would have slaughtered the audience. My virtue versus the lives of dozens of people, hmm, let me think.' I shrugged. 'It's okay, though I'd rather not make a habit of it.'

'You surprise me, *ma petite*.' But he relaxed against the bed. His posture was still perfect, a lot of the old vamps had good posture, but it was more relaxed all the same.

'I've learned that a little sex isn't a fate worse than death, Jean-Claude.'

'Is that all?' Richard said. 'Or is there more that you'd rather we don't know, but feel that we need to know?'

'See, see, he is like you now. Two of you, I do not know if I can—'

'Just tell us,' I said.

He gave me a small frown. 'You seem to have figured out that we are mixing and mingling our abilities in more than just a metaphysical way. I do not know all we will gain, or lose, depending on how one looks at it, only that it is happening.'

'I think that Nathaniel and I traded a little dominance and submission.' I saw the look on Richard's face, and added, 'I mean that ever since we became a triumvirate, Nathaniel seems a little more dominant, and I seem to enjoy being a little more submissive. Admittedly, Nathaniel was trying to be more dominant before, but he really seems to be taking to it.' Saying it made me want to squirm with discomfort, but I fought it off. I'd be damned if I'd apologize even by a gesture. I'm nothing if not defiant, especially if I'm uncomfortable.

'Then, apparently, we can expect a mingling of our basic person-alities, as well,' Jean-Claude said, and he tried for casual and failed.

'This could get really strange,' I said, and it was my turn to draw my knees up to my chest, though for Richard, I think it had been comfortable, for me it was comforting myself.

'Is that all the bad news?' Richard asked, and looked directly at him.

'I do not see it as bad news, *mon ami*, but the two of you might.'

'Spill it,' I said, knees hugged to my chest.

'You have turned my *pomme de sang* into his animal form, one of them anyway. I, like you until recently, prefer my food without fur.'

I did my best not to look at Richard. 'Who did you have in mind?'

'Requiem told me of the amount of blood you lost last night, *ma petite*. I think it is wiser if you do not donate more quite so soon.'

I heard Richard's sigh from where I was sitting, and he wasn't sitting that close to me. 'I would say it's always me, but it's usually not. I know that Anita isn't your regular feed, but I know she lets you feed.' He put his face against his knees and sighed again. 'Fine, but only if Anita is here, too. No just you and me.'

'Define Anita being *with* us?'

'That's not what I said,' Richard said.

'Is that not what you meant?' Jean-Claude asked.

Richard seemed to think about it for a second, then gave a small nod. 'I guess it is, but hearing you say it, it seems—'

'I'll second Jean-Claude's question, define me being *with* you guys.'

Richard blushed. He didn't blush often, and this was two in one conversation. 'I don't mean it the way you make it sound.'

'Then tell us how you do mean it, *mon ami*.'

'I don't want. I mean . . .' he made that sound again, wordless, frustrated. 'Why is it that every time I do anything that includes both of you, I always end up feeling like I'm wrong?'

I made one of those mental leaps, because I was remembering Richard's problem with everyone thinking he was, or had been, doing

Jean-Claude. I decided to rescue him. He was, after all, going to open a vein for Jean-Claude. That deserved some consideration, considering that his rules about feeding vamps used to be the same as mine. Richard was still trying to explain, and failing.

'Look, I understand what Richard is trying to say.'

They both looked at me. Richard doubtful, and Jean-Claude amused, as if he, too, understood Richard's discomfort, but couldn't afford to let the other man see that he saw it. Or maybe something else amused him, you never can tell with Jean-Claude.

'You don't want it to be just the two of you when Jean-Claude feeds,' I said.

Richard looked relieved, and nodded.

I did not say out loud, no you're not homophobic, because if Richard wasn't as comfortable with having another man touch him, then he was entitled. I'd never fed a female vamp voluntarily, so who was I to bitch?

Jean-Claude's smile deepened just a touch. 'And why is it such a problem for it to be just the two of us?'

I gave Jean-Claude a dirty look, and Richard was back to not knowing how to explain. 'Jean-Claude, you know the old American saying, about not looking a gift horse in the mouth?'

'*Oui.*'

'You're checking this one's teeth.'

He laughed, that touchable laugh, which, even through the hardest shielding I had, made me shiver, and not from fear. I caught Richard's movement out of the corner of my eye. He'd shivered, too. For the first time, I wondered how much of Jean-Claude's abilities worked on Richard. I was terribly heterosexual, and sometimes I just didn't think outside that box. Richard didn't like boys, so Jean-Claude didn't affect him the way he did me. That's what I'd believed, now I wondered if Richard had more problems with Jean-Claude than I'd thought. If you were terribly hetero, but Jean-Claude's powers could affect you, you had a problem if you were a man. The fact that it had never occurred to me before, proved beyond a doubt that sometimes I just wasn't bright about the men around me.

'But before we get up close, I've got to get this stuff off of me. It's flaking, and I just don't feel clean.'

'That would give us time to have the sheets changed, perhaps,' Jean-Claude said. He touched the drying, caked sheets. 'I have never seen a bed where more than one lycanthrope has shifted. It is, how do you say, a mess.'

His English was better than that, even for slang. He was back to being pleased with himself, and I didn't know why. If I dropped shields enough for him to talk inside my head, I'd also have more of Richard in my head. I didn't want that, so I'd have to ask him later, or I'd figure it out. Whatever.

'I'll make the shower quick,' I said, and started for the far door.

'If it was him going into the shower,' Richard jerked a thumb at Jean-Claude, 'I wouldn't believe quick, but you I'll believe.'

That one comment made me wonder how much time Richard had spent with Jean-Claude when I wasn't around. I didn't say it out loud, though, I am getting smarter. Richard was uncomfortable enough with Jean-Claude. I didn't need to add to it.

'We will be here when you are finished, *ma petite*. Hopefully with the bed in better order.' He was standing looking down at it, as if he wasn't sure it could really be fixed.

'Why not use your room?' Richard asked.

'Asher is in my bed. Now he is dead, and *ma petite* finds that disturbing. If he woke in the middle of the feeding, I think you, Richard, would find it disturbing.'

Richard stood and just huddled in his jean jacket. '*Disturbing*. You could call it that.' He didn't sound happy, and I wondered if there was some incident between him and Asher I should know about. Probably not. None of my business.

I had to walk back to the bed and hunt for my holstered gun underneath the pillows. I sort of waved it at them both. 'I wouldn't want this thrown down the laundry chute.'

Jean-Claude waved me toward the bathroom. 'Go, shower, *ma petite*, we will be ready if you are not too quick.'

'*We*' will be ready, he'd said. Didn't I have enough 'wes' in my life? I went for the shower and left them debating on whether the bed would hold, or whether it would be safer to simply remove the frame entirely. It wasn't until I closed the door behind me that I thought to wonder why we needed the bed. Jean-Claude could feed on Richard kneeling on the floor, couldn't he? If this was my first chance to touch both men at the same time in months, then I preferred not to be covered in drying goop. But once I was clean, we could still all do it on the floor. We didn't need the bed.

I thought about going back out and telling them that, but didn't. No matter what else, they were both still men, and men feel better when they have something to do. They could straighten the bed and sheets and get everything all neat and tidy. It would keep them from having any more of those awkward silences. Or, that was the hope.

57

WHEN I STEPPED out of the shower, my black robe was hanging on the back of the door. How had I not seen that, or heard it? If Jean-Claude could do that while I was in the shower, and me have no hint, then I was shielding too tight. In shielding this hard, I was losing some of my awareness of my surroundings. Not good.

I dried off, wrapped a towel around my hair, and put the robe on. I'd have given a great deal for clean underwear, but hell, if I tied the sash tight and the little string tighter, the robe didn't gap. I checked that nothing showed in the mirror but a little upper chest, very proper. I'd washed away all the makeup. I looked pale and clean, and, with my hair up in a pale blue towel, I looked sort of too pale, almost sickly. I started to take the towel down, because I knew I looked good in the robe with my hair down, wet, or not. But I resisted the urge. First, my hair was too wet, and silk doesn't like being wet. Second, I had only one boyfriend in the other room, not two. I wasn't trying to look my best, just help Richard not have a fit about letting Jean-Claude touch him.

I looked at my face, my eyes so dark, and wondered if I could admit, even to myself, that I still cared that Richard thought I was attractive. Yeah, to myself, I could say it, but I left the towel on.

They were arguing about candles when I came out. Jean-Claude had had some brought in for the bedside tables, and Richard was saying, 'We don't need candles, Jean-Claude. You're just feeding. That's it.'

'I vote with Richard. We don't need candles.'

'The two of you are not romantics.'

'This isn't about romance, it's about food,' I said.

Richard motioned to me. 'See, Anita agrees with me.'

'Of course, she does, *mon ami*.' Jean-Claude didn't sound too put out, he still had that cat-who-ate-the-cream sound to his voice.

The mattress and box springs sat on the floor, covered in new, bloodred sheets. Even the pillowcases had been changed, so that the bed shimmered scarlet in the subdued light. The bed frame being gone probably explained why Richard had removed his jean jacket and was just in an olive green T-shirt.

'I had not realized how dark Jason's room is,' Jean-Claude was saying. 'I have no extra places to put lamps, but we could have more light with candles. I would prefer a romantic reason, but in truth, it is simple practicality. I would like more light.'

'You're a vampire,' Richard said, 'you see in the dark better than I do.'

'True, but if you were allowed to touch someone who rarely allows you to touch them in any intimate fashion, would you not wish light to see what you are doing?' He gave Richard a look, then his eyes slid past him to me. It was a quick look, but Richard followed it, and suddenly he didn't seem to know what to do with his face, so he turned it back toward the other man.

'Have I missed something here?' I asked, 'or am I about to miss something?'

'You miss very little, *ma petite*.'

'Candles are fine,' Richard said, still not looking at me.

I was shaking my head, but I felt a small touch against my skin. I knew that touch. I dropped the tiniest edge of my shields. Jean-Claude's voice blew through me like a caressing wind. 'Does it mean nothing to you, *ma petite*, that the mere sight of you in your robe has changed Richard's mind?'

I shook my head and tried to answer back as silently as he did. I still wasn't great at it. What I tried to think back was, 'Me in this robe with this towel, is not worth him changing his mind.'

'You still do not value yourself, as we value you, *ma petite*.'

There was that 'we' again. I started to open my mouth, to add something out loud, when a warm rush of energy danced through my body. It stopped me in midstep. 'Talking in someone's head, when the other person isn't allowed into the conversation is rude,' Richard said. 'It's like whispering and pointing.'

I couldn't argue it, but wanted to. 'Trust me, Richard, it's not worth repeating.'

'I'd like a chance to be the judge of that,' he said.

I sighed, for what felt like the thousandth time today. What had I been thinking? I should have told Jean-Claude that we didn't need the bed, that Richard could kneel down and he could just feed. Voilà, and we'd be done with it.

Richard took off his T-shirt. 'It's too pale, if you get blood on it, it looks like blood.' He explained it out loud, and it made sense, but I was glad he wasn't looking at me when he pulled the shirt off, because seeing him shirtless had its usual effect. I'd said before that the day I could walk into a room and not have my body react to Richard, I knew it was over between us. But hormones are traitorous little bastards. They don't care how broken your heart is, only that there's an attractive man in the room. Shit.

Jean-Claude was moving from candle to candle with one of those long battery-operated lighters. I could never get them to light. He moved effortlessly, from candle to candle, the other hand holding the draping sleeve of his robe back out of reach of the flame.

Richard sat down on the corner of the bed. His blue jeans and the solid line of his black belt looked fine against the red sheets. His tanned upper body looked better, and as if he'd heard me think it, he lay back against the sheets, not flat, but propped on his elbows, so that the shimmering scarlet framed his muscular upper body. There were tiny folds in his stomach, like there are on real people, unless they have washboard abs, and Richard had better things to do with his time than do that many sit-ups. His stomach was flat and perfect, but perfect doesn't mean perfectly flat. Lines are flat, people had curves and bumps and places to explore.

Richard turned his head and looked at me. His face wasn't neutral anymore. His dark eyes held heat, and it wasn't his beast, or at least not just that. It was a look I'd seen before, a look that said he knew exactly the effect he had on me, and enjoyed it. Of late, that look had been to tell me, I know you think I'm gorgeous, and you don't get to touch this anymore. Now, I wasn't sure what the look meant, but I didn't like it.

Jean-Claude moved to the other side of the bed, his tall, black-robed figure breaking Richard's and my stare. When Jean-Claude cleared the way, though, Richard had pulled himself farther onto the bed, so that his legs were no longer touching the floor. So that all six feet one of him was on the bed, framed by sheets the color of fresh blood, and the flickering light of candles.

My mouth was dry. Not good. 'I've changed my mind,' I said. 'You guys don't need me, not really.' My voice sounded breathy.

Jean-Claude turned from lighting the last candle. He smoothed the sleeves of his robe down around his long-fingered hands, and stood looking at me. His eyes glittered like dark sapphires, catching the flickering light in a way that human eyes just didn't. 'Ah, but we do, *ma petite*. We most certainly do. You are the bridge between us. You are the third of our power. Does that sound like someone we do not really need?'

'I don't mean like forever, just not now, not here. I mean, you can feed without me here. You can . . .' I was having trouble concentrating.

Richard rolled over onto his stomach, and he did a little head movement that showed me that his hair had grown out just enough to fall a little forward around his face. Not long, but thicker than I'd thought. The candlelight didn't dance on his jeans, but Richard's body in tight jeans didn't need anything else, it was sort of self-explanatory.

'I'm going now. I'm leaving now. Yep, that's what I'm doing.' I was babbling, and I couldn't stop it. But I did start for the door, so many points for me that I can't count that high.

Jean-Claude called, '*Ma petite*, do not go, please.'

I turned back, and I don't know what I would have said, because he'd sat down on the bed, but he'd done something to the top of his robe, so that it gapped, and I could see almost his entire chest framed by the black fur of the lapels. The burn scar looked very black against the white of his skin and the shimmering black of the fur. His nipples were palest pink, and from that alone, I'd have known he hadn't fed. His hand touched his chest, as if he knew where I was looking. The hand moved down, and so did my gaze, so that I looked at the flat line of his stomach, the line of dark hair that started just below his navel, and swept down to vanish into the shadow of the robe. I had an almost irresistible urge to go over there and rip open the sash and see his body pale and perfect against the dark of the robe and the crimson sheets. I knew just how he'd look against it all, because I'd seen it before. That thought moved my gaze to Richard, because I'd never seen him against red silk. I'd never seen him by candlelight.

He rolled onto his side as I watched, propped up on one elbow, one arm slung low across his hips, as if to bring my attention to his jeans and what I knew was in them. But no, Richard wasn't that aware of his body, at least not for seduction. It was something Jean-Claude would have done, not Richard. Then I had one of those horrible thoughts. What if one of the things that Richard had gained with the tighter binding of the marks was some of Jean-Claude's skill at seduction. Oh, that just wouldn't be fair.

I closed my eyes and started for the door again. It was better if I couldn't see either of them. Jean-Claude called, '*Ma petite*, you are going to hit the wall.'

I stopped abruptly and opened my eyes, and was inches away from the wall. The door was about two feet to my left. Great, just great.

'*Ma petite*, do not leave us.' His voice crawled through the tiny hole I'd made in my shields for him. It crawled inside and played along my skin, made me shiver, and God help me, I turned back and looked. Stupid me.

Jean-Claude had crawled up on the bed, near the pillows. He was lying full length across the red silk, with the robe gaping open, barely covering anything. His white, white shoulder was framed at the top with scarlet silk. His long legs spilled half in the black robe and half on the scarlet of the sheets. Only the barest fringe of fur covered his hips.

Richard was still on his side. They were lying in almost identical positions, except that Richard's head was pointing away from the door, and Jean-Claude was angled toward it.

'This isn't fair,' I said. 'Not both of you, not at the same time.'

'Whatever do you mean, *ma petite*?' But he looked entirely too pleased with himself to really need to ask.

'You bastard, you knew.'

'I knew nothing, but one lives in hope.'

I was having trouble breathing, or rather breathing nice even breaths. I was shaking my head, and the towel started coming unwound. I caught it, and stood there with it in my hands. The cloth was wet and cold. I was shivering, but it was only partly from the wet hair sliding down my neck.

'Richard, you are getting your shoes on the silk sheets. Has no one taught you that you do not wear hiking boots on silk?' He didn't even try to make it sound real, it was teasing, but it wasn't Richard he was teasing.

Richard just sat up, bunching his stomach muscles nicely, and put one foot on his jeans and began to unlace the short boots. He didn't look at me while he did it, but he knew I was watching.

I needed to leave now. I really did. I knew that, but somehow I was still standing there when Richard threw his first boot onto the floor. The sound made me jump.

He watched me while he took off the other boot, or watched me, watch him. I felt like one of those little birds that they say are fascinated with the snake's movements. So pretty, so sinuous, so dangerous. He was just taking off his shoes, damn it. It shouldn't have meant this much to me, hell, to anyone.

When both boots had been thrown to the floor, he took off his thick socks without any prompting from anyone. He lay back on the bed on his stomach with his feet naked against the sheets. He watched me over his shoulder with that wave of hair barely curling around his eye. The look managed to be both coy and knowledgeable. Like a fallen angel, innocence and the promise of sin, all in one look. It was a very good look.

It was not a look I'd ever thought to see on Richard's face. It didn't seem very much like him. 'How much of this is you, Richard, and how much of it is him?'

He lay flat on the silk and rolled over onto his back in a movement that was doglike and catlike at the same time. Or maybe I'm just prejudiced that dogs don't move with that same liquid grace when they writhe on their backs. He stretched his arms over his head, stretched his whole, long body out from toes to fingertips, stretched until his body shook with the effort, then he relaxed against the bed. He laid his hands across his stomach and smiled at me with that same mix of innocent sin.

'I'm not sure,' he said in a voice that was thicker than it should have been this early in.

'Doesn't that scare you?' I asked, and my voice was breathy for a different reason now.

Richard frowned, just a little between those dark, dark brown eyes. Then he shook his head. 'I'm not scared, in fact I feel calmer than I've felt in days.'

I looked past him to Jean-Claude, who had laid back against the mound of pillows so that the crimson of the sheets framed his black curls perfectly.

'Oh, stop being so damned picturesque. You're messing with his mind.'

'Not really.'

'What does "not really" mean?'

'I mean that I did not mean to do it. I am still adapting to this new power level, too, *ma petite*. I was worried for you earlier today. I was afraid what would happen with Nathaniel and Damian. I thought, I wish she was not so afraid of Nathaniel and what he wants from her. I swear to you that is all I thought, nothing more, but today I find that you have crossed several lines with him that you swore never to cross.'

'Are you saying you made me do it?'

'*Non, ma petite*. I am saying I wished you to be less afraid of what you wanted, and you were. I did not realize that it could possibly have had an effect upon you, until just moments ago, when I simply thought, I wish Richard was not so afraid of what he wants, and now he is not.'

'Did you hear all that, Richard? He's using vamp powers on you.'

Richard gave me a lazy smile. 'I feel calmer, less afraid, less conflicted. I hadn't realized how bad I was still feeling until now.'

'Fine, I'm afraid enough for both of us, if you really did mess with me earlier today, then why am I about to walk out of this room?'

'I thought merely that I wished you would be less afraid of what you wanted from Nathaniel, and what Nathaniel wanted from you. I was not so specific with our Richard.'

'You wondered if it worked the first time, so you tried it again, and voilà, you have your empirical evidence, because it worked twice.'

'Perhaps, or perhaps it is merely coincidence. It will take us weeks, or months, to decipher what is true power and what is simply all of us coming to terms with ourselves.'

I didn't like the sound of that, at all. 'I can't do this.'

'Why ever not?' Jean-Claude asked.

'Because, once I would have given nearly anything to have you both like this. I need to know what this means.'

Richard sat up enough to prop himself on his elbows. 'You said it yourself, Anita, you're already dating Jean-Claude and Asher, and living with Micah and Nathaniel. You said that the thought of a man on either side of you "just flat does it" for you. What's one more pair?'

I glared at Jean-Claude. 'Do you have like some metaphysical fist up his ass, like he's some kind of ventriloquist dummy, because that doesn't sound like him. That sounds like you.'

'Don't talk to him, when you want to talk to me,' Richard said. He sat up, and the sleepy smile was gone. 'Does it bother me that you're with Micah and Nathaniel and Jean-Claude and Asher? Hell, yes. Does it bother you that I'm with Clair and half a dozen women in my pack?' He looked at me when he said it. I looked back. He finally said, 'That was a question, Anita, can I have an answer?'

'Yeah, it bothered me to see Clair, and to meet your girlfriend for the first time, while I was nude. Yes, that was a special treat. I try to know as little about your personal life with the ladies of your pack as possible, so the rest, I didn't know about.'

'I felt how much you wanted me earlier at your house, and you know how I felt about you. So let's not pretend anymore about that.'

I hadn't known we were pretending, but I didn't say it out loud. 'I don't know what you mean by that, Richard.'

'It means we both want to be able to touch each other again. You fucked Byron for God's sake. Why are you okay with doing him, and not about this – us?' He motioned as if taking in the whole bed. I didn't think the 'us' meant him and me. For the first time from Richard, I was pretty sure that he was talking about him and Jean-Claude.

I clutched the cold towel and tried to say out loud something that made sense. 'I'm not –' change that – 'Byron was emergency food. Once upon a time, I thought you and I were going to be it for each other. When you dumped me, it broke me up. Touching you is still not like touching other people for me.'

'I feel the same way. You know I do,' he said.

'I know you want me, but I also know that you'll be ashamed later. When Jean-Claude isn't there to calm your fears, you'll start to drown in them again.' I laughed. 'God, for the first time I understand what Asher was saying about me and the *ardeur*. I don't want this to be a good time now, then we go back to cutting each other up. I couldn't bear it.' There, that was the truth. I had a glimmer for the first time why some people do casual sex with people they don't care about. If you don't care, and it goes horribly wrong, it's not that important.

'I don't want us to keep cutting each other up, either, Anita. I really don't.' He rolled to the edge of the bed and stood up. The dozen or more candles painted his upper body in shadow and light. I missed the thick fall of his hair around his shoulders, but it was still Richard. Still the man who had come closest to making me try for the picket fence, and the two-point-five kids. 'You still need at least one more daytime feed.'

The topic change was too quick for me. I pressed myself against the door, so that the doorknob was in reach. If I had to run for it, I wanted to hit the door, not the wall. 'Yes, though I found out that I can feed on human form, then feed again on the animal form, and it's like two different feeds.'

Jean-Claude crawled closer to the end of the bed, the robe more framing his body like lingerie than hiding anything. 'So in effect, you now have four daytime feeds, yes?'

'Sort of, right now Nathaniel and I are estimating I need to feed the *ardeur* about every six hours, or I start draining Damian's life energy. Since I can't feed on the same person everyday, that still leaves me short.'

'It may leave us, as you say, short, at night even. You'd fought to push your feedings to every twelve hours.'

'I don't know, Jean-Claude, but I seem to need to feed more often.'

'You are the energy for your new trimuvirate. It takes energy to maintain it.'

Richard turned and looked at the other man. 'Are you saying that Anita and I drain energy from you?' He turned back to me before he got his answer, and the look on his face said he wasn't happy with the show Jean-Claude was putting on.

'Not precisely, but in a way, *oui*. All power comes with a price, Richard, and that price can be high.'

'I think until I understand how to distribute the power among the three of us, that it's every six hours. I hadn't thought about the fact that only you and Asher feed me at night. Shit.' I said the last with feeling.

'You have Damian now,' Richard said. 'Won't three be enough?'

I looked at him, tried to see jealousy, or anger, but he seemed to have offered it as simply a fact. 'I don't know, maybe.'

'I trust *ma petite* to control what she can,' Jean-Claude said, nearly from the end of the bed, the robe sliding over his upper body until almost everything above the still-tied sash was naked to light. There was something about the way his body caught the flames, shining and pale, almost unreal, as if he were some kind of living work of art, that you would touch and he would fade, too beautiful to be real.

Richard snapped his fingers, and the sharp noise brought my attention back to him. He was frowning. 'Are you actually turning me down?'

This was too hard a question for me. I closed my eyes so I couldn't see either of them. 'Not exactly, but I need to know what to expect, Richard. I need to know what this changes.'

'Every third day or so, I come to your house, and you feed the *ardeur*.'

I opened my eyes then. 'Just a little sex, and that's it.'

'What do you want from me, Anita?'

I pushed away from the door, because now I was getting angry. 'Not dating, just fuck-buddies, is that it?'

'You're living with two men now, I don't think there's room for me in your life.'

What I wanted to say was, if you can just fuck me and nothing else, then we were never really in love. What I said out loud was, 'It's not just the sex I miss, Richard. I miss weekend movie marathons. I miss going places with you. I miss you, not just your body, Richard.' I almost kept the next part to myself, but I had to know. It was time. 'Do you miss me, Richard, or just my body?'

I managed to make it neutral, very neutral. Brownie points for me.

He looked down, and emotions fought across his face. His power flared like a warm wind, then died down. When he looked at me, there was pain and anger in his eyes. 'You're the one who said it first, Anita. We don't work as each other's one and only. I'm working hard to accept my life as it is, but I can't live like you do. I still want one woman to be my forever person. I still want marriage, and maybe kids. I want a life, Anita. I know now that I can't have what I want with you.' He reached out toward me, then his hands curled into fists. 'But I miss you. Not just the sex. I miss the smell of you on my pillow, on my skin. I owe you an apology. When everything happened in Tennessee, I blamed my beast first, then I blamed you. It took six weeks of therapy to get me to see that I was pissed at you for saving my mother and brother when I couldn't do it.'

'You would have given your life to save them,' I said.

'Yes, but then we'd all be dead.' It wasn't just pain in his eyes, it was anguish. The kind of emotion that eats you up and spits you back out. 'You did horrible things, Anita, horrible things to find out where they were in time. You tortured a man, cut him up to get the information. I couldn't have done that. I wouldn't have let anyone do it in front of me. It wasn't just that you saved them and I didn't, it was when I heard all that happened, I realized that even if I'd been there with you, they would have died. My mother and Daniel would have died because I wouldn't have let you do what was necessary to save them.'

I just looked at him, because I couldn't think of anything good to say. I wasn't proud of what I'd done in Tennessee, not all of it anyway, but I didn't regret any of it, because to save Charlotte and Daniel, I would have done worse. My only true regret had been that I didn't get there before they were raped and tortured. I would go to my grave regretting that part, because I'd seen Charlotte break into tears in her kitchen. She would say, 'I don't know why I'm crying. So silly.' It wasn't silly, and I'd recommended a good therapist I knew. The one I usually recommended to people wanting to join the Church of Eternal life, as a forever member.

'You're the Bolverk for my pack. The evildoer, the one who does what the Ulfric won't, or can't do. Raina was Bolverk for Marcus.'

'Yeah,' I said. See, I could still talk, but I still didn't have anything good to say.

'I want the white picket fence, Anita, and I know you don't.'

'It's not that I don't want it, Richard, it's that it's too late for me. My life won't fit in that picture.'

He nodded. 'I know, and maybe mine won't either, but I still want to try. There are Ulfrics that have a wife and family separate from the pack. I've been trying to find a new lupa for the pack, and no one measures up. No one is you.'

I was back to not knowing what to say, so I said nothing. I rarely got in trouble keeping my mouth shut.

'I think the reason your beast got out of control today is that you've been spending too much time with just one animal. I think if you have personal contact with something besides leopards that your beast will go back to being just amorphous, more metaphysics than physical. I want your permission to send some of the wolves over to bunk with you.'

'Richard—'

'I don't mean fuck them, but sleep with them. Or take some wererats home, pick an animal, but if your power only touches leopards, it's going to think it's a leopard.'

'And you're one of the wolves that will be stopping by?' I couldn't keep the irony and the unhappiness out of my voice.

'I don't mean it to be casual, Anita. I mean, be our lupa. Bring the leopards with you, and they can hunt with us on the full moon.'

'I'll be your lupa, which means, what? What changes?'

'We're a couple within the lycanthrope community. You'll have more contact with my wolves outside of just crisis situations. Micah has really been working his tail off helping everybody out. We need at least one other person full time on the hotline. He's running himself ragged.'

'I didn't know you were keeping track.'

'I'm trying to pay attention, Anita. I'm trying to see what's there, not what I want to be there. I couldn't share you the way Micah shares you with Nathaniel, not everyday, every night. I don't think I could tolerate you dating Jean-Claude and Asher. I certainly wouldn't be able to play blood donor on as regular a basis as Micah and Nathaniel do.'

I just blinked at him, because this was a talk I never thought I'd have with Richard. It was way too logical. 'I agree with everything you said in that last bit. But it doesn't change anything, does it?'

'I felt the power of your triumvirate with Damian and Nathaniel. Damian's not a master, and Nathaniel is no Nimir-Raj, but the three of you together are an amazing amount of power. What would we be, the three of us, if we did this right? If we did this the way it was meant to be done?'

'That so doesn't sound like you,' I said.

'Tell me you haven't thought about it since you did the other triumvirate?'

I couldn't in all honesty, so I didn't try. 'I felt what Jean-Claude and I could do at his club when Primo got out of control. I felt what

Jean-Claude could do when I let him feed the *ardeur* in a way that was closer to a full feeding with other women. So, yeah, I thought about it, sort of.'

'You said it yourself, Anita, we don't have enough soldiers. We need to look strong and not just for the vampires that might want this territory. Our pack has a bad rep, thanks to me, and Raina and Marcus before me. My reputation is shit among the other Ulfrics. They think I'm weak, and I've had some scouts from other territories that have too many dominants and not enough land. So far our pack is so screwed up that they leave without a challenge. No one wants the mess I've made of it. But as I get a better handle on my wolves, that may change. If we all joined together the way you and Jean-Claude did last night, if we were really a triumvirate of power, no one would touch us, Anita, no one would dare.'

It was almost a direct quote from something I'd thought earlier. I looked past him to Jean-Claude. 'We're parroting what you've been thinking for months, aren't we?'

He shrugged those lovely bare shoulders. '*Oui*, but I did not put the thoughts there, *ma petite*. I believe that both of you have come to the same conclusion at the same time. Is that so hard to believe?'

'I don't know,' I said, and I was tired. Tired of the games, tired of hurting, tired of being scared.

Richard lay back on the bed, one knee up, the other down, so that he looked winsome as hell against the red sheets. 'I'm scared again, Anita. I don't want everything we're building to go down in flames, because we're mad at each other. Let Jean-Claude take the edge off my fear. It felt great.'

I looked past him to the vampire who was still draped against the pillows. 'Did you pull back from his mind?'

'*Non, ma petite*, he simply fought, a little, and I was cast out. Both of you have the power to thwart me if you wish to.'

'I don't wish to,' Richard said, and that smile came back. It was lazy, and sleepy, and filled his eyes with that knowledgeable innocence again. I realized in that moment that it wasn't Jean-Claude's look, it was Richard if he wasn't afraid, or angry, or conflicted. It was what he might be if he didn't get in his own way all the time.

'*Ma petite.*' Jean-Claude raised his hand toward me. 'Join us.'

I was shaking my head.

Richard reached out toward me, too. 'You want to, you know you want to.'

'My life is as close to working as it ever has been, I don't want that to go to wrack and ruin, either.'

'I'm not offering to go back to what we had, Anita. I understand that that won't work for us. You are harder and more ruthless than I will ever be, and I can let you be that, but not if you're my only sweetie. I need a little distance from the worst of it, so I can pretend a little. Not much, but just enough so I don't lose my mind.' He snuggled back until his head was resting against Jean-Claude's side. Jean-Claude was all black fur and velvet against white skin. His hair spilled around his naked upper body like a dark dream. He turned his head so he could look at Richard lying there. Richard was all tan and jeans, and seemed to burn with how very alive he was. They looked like they'd stepped out of two very different porno movies.

Jean-Claude looked up at me, and there was a pleading in his eyes. Without a word, he asked, 'Please, *ma petite*, please do not spoil this.'

'No fourth mark,' I said.

'Agreed,' Jean-Claude said.

'For now,' Richard said.

I looked at him.

'Right now a lot of things seem like a good idea. No, don't frown, Anita, if a little vampire magic can take the edge off my anxiety, I'm all for it. It works better than the pills the doctor gave me.'

'Lycanthropes' bodies work too fast for most medicines to stay in the body long enough to help,' I said.

'I know,' Richard said, and he raised his head up just enough that he was resting directly on Jean-Claude's bare back. It was probably just as well that he couldn't see Jean-Claude's face when that thick hair touched his skin. He probably wouldn't have liked any man looking like that because of him.

'Come, *ma petite*, let us be a true triumvirate at last. Be lupa in more than just name for Richard and his pack. Keep your living arrangements as they are, but allow Richard to visit.'

'While he keeps searching for Ms Right among the human population.'

'You will have your men, and he will have his woman. It is fair, *ma petite*.'

I wasn't sure how I felt about the fairness of it. 'I don't know how I feel about all of this, some great, but others, I don't know if I'll be able to live like that.'

'We can but try,' Jean-Claude said.

Richard held his hand out to me. 'Anita, please, please, if you leave, you know I won't stay. You were able to let Jean-Claude get closer without me being there to buffer it, but I need you to help me.' He pushed up to his knees and held out his hand. 'Please, Anita, I promise not to run, no matter how dark my fantasies get.'

'Just feeding for Jean-Claude and some slap and tickle?' I asked, and couldn't help but sound suspicious.

Richard glanced back, and he and Jean-Claude had one of those rare guy moments. The looks they exchanged said plainly that that hadn't been what they had in mind. Jean-Claude said, voice mild, 'If that is all you wish from us, we can restrain ourselves.'

I closed my eyes. Was that all I wished from them? No. Was that all I could stand right now? Maybe. It was a wonderful offer. It seemed to fix most of the problems that we'd raised with the new power, so why was I still hesitant? 'You know, finding a wife that would be okay with you sleeping with another woman isn't going to be easy.'

'Nothing worth doing is easy,' Richard said, 'and maybe I'll find that the white picket fence isn't for me, after all. All I know is that right now, right this moment, I know what I want, and what I want is you.'

A lot of women would have run to him, thrown their arms around him, and said something like, 'Oh, Richard.' But that just wasn't me. What I was thinking was that if Clair had been his little fuck-buddy, he wouldn't be here now. He wouldn't want me, now. I dropped the towel on the floor and was shaking my head. 'I'm not sure this is a good idea.'

Richard was still holding his hand out to me. 'Neither am I.'

'Then why are we doing it again?'

'Because we want to.'

'Doesn't seem like a good enough reason.' But I moved, slowly, toward the bed.

'Because when I'm near you, all I can think about is the smell of your skin, and the way your hair spreads like black foam on my pillows. Because when I'm near you, all I can remember is how your body feels against mine. I have to be a bastard to you, so that I don't fall down at your feet and beg you to take me back. Tell you that it wasn't you I hated. It was me, and I'm sorry that I took that out on you. Sorrier than I can say. That you had the courage to make a life that worked for you, regardless of how far that life was from where you wanted it to be. Help me have the courage to do the same, Anita. Help me be who I am.' He moved his hands just a little closer to mine. His fingers brushed mine. I think I would have jerked away like you do when your skin brushes something so hot it will burn. But he grabbed my hands, wrapped them in the warmth of his hands. His hands that were so much bigger than mine, so that he could hide my hands in his, as if I were a child. I'd never really liked that about Richard. He was so much bigger than me, that sometimes I felt overwhelmed. Like now.

I'd learned a long time ago that if something sounds too good to be true, it is. If someone promises you everything your heart desires, they lie.

He drew me into the circle of his arms, so that the front of my body was pressed against his. He buried his face against my chest, still covered by silk, but the weight of his face against me made me close my eyes, and when I opened them, I was looking at Jean-Claude. He looked not at Richard's bare back, but at me, at my face. I watched him be afraid. Be afraid that I'd say, no.

Richard rubbed his face against the silk, and his breath came through the cloth like something that should have burned, but it didn't. It made me shiver as if I were cold, but held in the circle of his arms with his breath hot on my skin, I felt as if I would never be cold again. I couldn't stop my hands from stroking his hair. Still woefully short, but thick and heavy, and just . . . Richard's.

Jean-Claude was on his knees. He didn't raise his hands, but he put the word *please* into his face, those eyes. His voice whispered through my head, '*Ma petite*, we endanger everyone that depends on us by this hesitation. Everything we have worked so hard to build hangs upon the next challenge to my power, or to Richard's. If we do not embrace our power as a triumvirate, there will come a night when someone sweeps over us and we will not prevail. The worst that could happen is not that Richard may come to your bed, then come no more, or that you may grow discontent with Micah and Nathaniel. The worst is that we are dead, and our people will be at the mercy of others that do not love them.' He held his hand out to me. 'Come to us, *ma petite*, come to us, and let us build a fortress behind which our people, all of our people, may be safe.' That last he said out loud.

Richard raised his face enough to gaze up the line of my body. 'Please, Anita, don't punish everyone because I've been a bastard.'

Jean-Claude was close enough that I could have taken his hand, while Richard still held me in his arms. 'Please, *ma petite*, if there is word or deed that would move you, I would say it, or do it. Tell me only what to say, or what to do, and it is yours.'

I took in a lot of air, and let it out slow. I reached out and let his fingers brush mine. He came that fraction closer so he could take my hand, and that was the deed. He took my hand, and I knew that nothing he'd whispered in my head had been a lie. What would I do to keep my leopards safe? Anything. What would I do to undo the damage that Richard had done to his wolves? Almost anything. What would I do to keep Jean-Claude's vampires from being at the mercy of masters like Belle Morte? Anything.

A night of metaphysical, or not so metaphysical, sex, with one man that I loved and another man that kept breaking my heart, so I must love him, too, or he couldn't keep doing that, seemed a small enough price. Or maybe I just wanted to be with them both in a bed for the first time. Yes, the first time, contrary to all the rumors. Maybe I feared the chance would never come again, and I simply didn't want to be the one who said no. Maybe.

58

WE STAYED ON the corner of the bed, as if there was no more bed to use. I was still not sure it was a good idea. I think Richard was uncomfortable with Jean-Claude being in the bed. Jean-Claude was just being patient, biding his time, because he knew if he pushed, one of us would bolt. When Richard's mouth first found mine, and I drank in the taste of him like some almost forgotten addiction, I thought I'd be the one to run screaming for the hills. But the third time Richard winced when Jean-Claude brushed his bare back, I began to think it wouldn't be me that screwed this up.

He cursed in French, then said in English, 'I put my hand on your shoulder to steady myself, nothing more. You are acting as if I am after your virtue. I assure you that I am after *ma petite*'s virtue, not yours.'

Richard sighed and looked down so that even sitting in his lap I couldn't see his face. 'You keep touching me.'

Jean-Claude made a sound low in his throat. 'How am I to touch her, if she is in your lap, your arms, kissing you, without at the very least brushing your body with mine? I am not such a magician that I can share a woman with another man and never once touch the other man's body.'

'Trust me, he hasn't been doing much more than holding me,' I said. I touched Richard's chin, and he let me raise his face up to me. I looked into those solid brown eyes, and all I saw was pain, confusion. 'What's wrong? You were the one who was all hot for this. You talked me into it, remember?'

'I'm sorry,' he said. He pressed his forehead to my shoulder. 'I'm sorry,' he said again.

Jean-Claude and I stared at each other over his bent head. I asked the question with my expression, what the hell is going on? 'Tell us what is wrong, *mon ami*, and we will try to help.'

'The last time I was in a bed with another man and a woman, it was Raina and Gabriel.'

I'd known that Raina had been his first lover, but that he'd ever let Gabriel touch him, that I had not known. I was so astounded that I was glad he couldn't see my face. Raina had been bad enough, but both of them, at the same time. Uckies, uckies, uckies.

Raina's munin was usually quiet behind its metaphysical cage bars, but my reaction gave her a tiny opening. Raina had behaved herself for so long, that it caught me off guard. Made me a little less quick to squash her back down, and protect us all. Or maybe it was the fact that I was touching one of her pack, one that she knew in every way.

I saw Gabriel like a technicolor ghost, with his black curls just long enough to touch his pale gray leopard eyes. The silver ring through his nipple glinted in the lamplight. I was lying back in the middle of a big bed, and Gabriel crawled from one side, and Richard crawled from the other, both moving in that graceful stalk as if they had muscles in places that humans did not. It was a younger Richard, less muscled, face a little less sure of itself, his hair cut neat and clean. Richard when he was twenty, before I ever met him. His face so open, eager, laughing. We'd told him it was a game. Raina wanted to have two men ravage her. A little rape fantasy among friends.

He pinned my wrists, her wrists, and as requested, there was no foreplay. It was supposed to be rough. I could see through her eyes, as she watched Gabriel come in behind Richard's back. It was a rape fantasy, alright, but Raina wasn't the victim.

Richard screamed, and stood up, dumping me to the floor. He took two shaking steps, and collapsed to his knees. Something about what Raina's munin had done, had torn down his shields. I wasn't getting the memory, just his reaction to it. Shame, anger, rage. I got glimpses of Gabriel and him fighting. Not struggling, but beating the hell out of each other. Both of them nude, slick with each other's blood. Raina watching from the bed, her mouth wet, her tongue playing along her lips, enjoying the show.

Richard tried to shield, but he couldn't. It was as if the emotions had stripped him of his shields. It was Jean-Claude's cool touch in my head that shut it down. He shielded Richard from me, and I think from himself. He gave him back his metaphysical clothes, so that he wasn't raw before us.

'I, too, have my memory of Gabriel,' Jean-Claude said, his voice soft.

We both looked at him. Richard said, 'You, and Gabriel?' The look on his face showed his disgust.

'Not by choice. It was her price for convincing Marcus that he should continue to ally with me.'

'A night with both of them?' I asked.

Jean-Claude nodded.

'Did you know?' Richard asked, 'before, did you know what they wanted you for?'

He nodded again. 'I negotiated that night as completely as any night I have ever bargained for.'

Richard was still on his knees on the floor. He looked back at Jean-Claude. 'And you knew, you knew that she wanted to watch Gabriel . . . have you?'

'She wanted many things, but that was one she was most adamant about.'

'How could you let him do that to you?' A strange look came over Richard's face. 'Oh, but you don't mind. You like men.'

Jean-Claude's face went blank, him hiding away. 'Actually, yes, I did mind. I minded very much, but it was one of the points that Raina would not give up. She wanted certain things, and that was one of them.' He raised his robe around his shoulders as if he was cold, and would not look at either of us. 'I talked her out of a great many things that would have hurt a great deal more.'

'You didn't enjoy it,' Richard said.

Jean-Claude gave him a look, such a look. It sent the vampire's power like cool water through the room. 'Rape is rape, Richard. Is a woman less raped because she likes men? That's a question, Richard.'

'No, of course not,' he said.

'Then why is it less rape for a man who likes men to be raped by another man?'

Richard looked away at that.

I was left sitting on the floor not knowing what to say, or who to comfort, or even how to start comforting. 'I didn't know any of this.'

'My bargain with Raina was based on it not being known. It would have undermined my authority, which would have defeated the purpose of the bargain.'

I got up off the ground and went to Jean-Claude. I reached out to him, half-afraid he'd move away. No one's good with this kind of pain, but men seem especially bad at it. I think it's because they have a hard time thinking of themselves as potential victims. Women are raised with the possibility. Most of us understand from an early age that we are not the biggest or strongest. It's why when women fight, they fight dirty; something's got to make up for the lack of upper body strength.

I touched his face, and he gave me that blank beautiful look. As if he were a painting that held color and line, and beauty, but not life, as if telling the secret sucked something precious away from him. 'I'm sorry,' I said, softly.

He smiled, and some tension left him, and something of him began to seep back into his eyes. 'I thought you might be upset, find me sullied goods.'

I raised eyebrows at that. 'You never blame the victim, Jean-Claude. Don't you know that by now?'

He smiled a little wider and laid his face against my hand. 'I have never thanked you for killing them both.'

'They were trying to kill me at the time, and film it for a snuff flick. Trust me, it was my pleasure to whack them both.'

Richard got to his feet and came to stand near us, just out of comfortable reach. 'That night was why I broke up with Raina.' He laughed, and it sounded bitter, as if he would choke on it. 'Broke up, God, that sounds so high school. Gabriel and I nearly beat each other to death, while she watched.' He was shaking his head, and even with his hair barely grown out, it was already longer than it had been in the memory. I wondered if that was one of the reasons that he grew it long, so it would help him feel different.

'I can find other food,' Jean-Claude said. 'You do not have to do anything you are not comfortable with.'

Richard looked at us, my hand still on Jean-Claude's face. 'What I said earlier is still true. We need the three of us to be as close as the two of you are.'

'I do not believe you are ready to do what is necessary for such a binding,' Jean-Claude said.

'What is necessary, exactly?' he asked.

Jean-Claude licked his lips. 'This is magic, not science. In truth I am not sure. We could do the fourth mark, that I know how to do, but what happened at the club last night was not the fourth mark. It was as if *ma petite* slipped into me. We were joined as never before, and it made us unbelievably powerful.'

'How did it work?'

'We touched.'

'We were in the middle of a crisis of police proportions,' I said.

'*Oui*, but I think it will work with touching. We are of Belle's line, and most of her magic can be reached through physical closeness.'

'Physical closeness,' Richard said, and he shook his head. 'Define physical closeness.'

Jean-Claude smiled. 'Tell me what you would have of me, Richard. What rules and restrictions would make you feel safe?'

'If I said, don't touch me?'

'Then I say we are wasting our time. *Ma petite* and I were touching when it happened, not intimately, but the contact was important. Physical contact makes most of my powers easier.'

'Define not intimate.'

'I think he was holding my hand,' I said.

Richard smiled, a quick flash in his tanned face, 'Hand-holding I can manage.'

Jean-Claude smiled, and it was nice to see them smiling at each other for once. 'I would ask that if I need to touch you for balance that that be allowed.'

Richard narrowed his eyes a little. 'Depends on where you're touching me, but okay.'

Jean-Claude shook his head. 'That is not Richard's look, that is your look, *ma petite*. Your look from our Richard's face.'

'Well, you know what they say, couples start looking like each other after awhile.'

Richard looked at me. 'Couple?'

I shrugged. 'If I'm going to be lupa to your Ulfric, then yeah. That's how your pack will see it.'

He nodded, then smiled again. 'Just like that, you agree to it all.'

I reached out my hand, and after a moment's hesitation, he took it. There was no flash of munin or Raina, it was just his hand so warm in mine. 'We'll try it, see if it works, depends on what I have to do as your lupa. I just want you to know that you can walk out the door right now, and I'll still try to play lupanar with you.'

He squeezed my hand. 'You won't force me?'

'Not my kick.'

'Nor mine,' Jean-Claude said. 'I have been victim too many times over the centuries. It has given me no taste for it.'

Richard took in a big breath, which moved his chest and shoulders, and raised his stomach up and down, as if he'd drawn air all the way down to his toes. He let it out slowly, then nodded. 'Let's try. If I can't do it, then I can't do it, but I'll try.'

I kept my hand in Jean-Claude's, but stepped away from him, until I was standing in front of Richard. I went up on tiptoes, and he bent down so I could kiss him, gently, on the mouth. 'Have I told you recently that I think you are very brave?'

His eyes filled with something warm and good. 'Never.'

'Then I'm saying it now.'

'Thank you,' he said, and his arm slid around my waist, the warmth of his skin pulsing even through the silk. No, not his warmth, his power.

Jean-Claude stood up, and I drew him into the back of my body. Richard tensed when Jean-Claude's body pinned his arm, but he fought it. Fought to relax. He wasn't entirely successful, but he tried. *A* for effort.

'Now, let's get naked,' I said.

I actually made them both choke and laugh at the same time. '*Ma petite*, what has made you so bold?'

'It takes the three of us forever to do anything. We discuss it, we argue it, we fight, we make up, we fight. I don't want to discuss anymore. If we're going to do this, let's do it.'

'Just like that,' Richard said, 'off with the clothes, no sweet talk first.'

I leaned into the circle of his arm, and the weight of Jean-Claude behind my back. I looked up Richard's face, and said, 'I want to see if I can deep throat you.'

He blinked at me, then started to laugh, then stopped, and finally said in a strained voice, 'You couldn't before. It was great, but you never quite—'

'I've been practicing,' I said. I smiled up at him.

'That smile,' he said.

'What smile?' I said.

Jean-Claude answered, 'The knowing smile.'

'The one that says you're thinking dirty thoughts, and you want to do them all with me. You're the only woman I know that can put innocence and evil into the same look.'

'Evil,' I said. 'Am I supposed to be offended?'

'I just never expected to see that smile directed at me again.' He kissed me on the forehead. 'For that smile, I'd do a lot.'

'I still don't get the idea of innocence and evil in the same smile.'

'You have the look of a fallen angel, *ma petite*. An angel does not stop being an angel merely because they fall from grace; their wings are not so easily taken.'

I remembered thinking almost the same thing about Richard earlier. Like a fallen angel. Should it have bothered me that Jean-Claude and I were using the same analogy? Yeah, but out loud all I said was, 'I thought you were the dark angel here?' I turned so I could see his face.

He smiled and whispered, 'Nothing I could have offered would have gotten him out of his pants.'

'I heard that,' Richard said.

Jean-Claude laughed. 'And will you refuse her offer?'

He looked from Jean-Claude to me, then back to Jean-Claude. Richard laughed, a very masculine laugh. 'No.'

I was suddenly very aware of the two of them pressed on either side of me. Enough foreplay, off with the clothes.

59

THE CLOTHES CAME off, then Richard argued with me on what position I'd be better able to deep throat him. Like I said, the three of us together have to argue about everything. Jean-Claude settled the argument by simply saying, 'Let *ma petite* try her way, and if it does not work, we can try yours.' I began to realize that Richard and I as a couple was truly impossible, but as a threesome, if the third was our diplomat, it might work. What does it say when you need another adult in the bed to referee? Nothing I wanted to think about too deeply, not at that moment. At that moment, I let all the doubts go, all of them. I knew Richard and I too well not to suspect that we would wreck this later. But for now, right now, we had this moment. I tried to get out of my way and enjoy it, and had to trust the men to do the same.

I'd seen Richard nude, and recently, but it had been a long time since I'd seen him stretched nude on a bed, on his back, with the long length of his body spilled out in front of me. I made him spread his legs so I could lie down between them, rest my head against the muscled swell of his thigh, and gaze up the length of him. It was a form of teasing myself, almost. So close to his groin, but not touching. But it wasn't that I just wanted to look, it was the whole package. And it wasn't just that he was lovely to look at, it was that I'd looked at the groin, only partially erect, and still impressive, the flat plain of his stomach with its perfect dimple of belly button, the swell of his chest with his nipples like dark brown punctuation to all that permanently tanned muscle; the swell of his shoulders, and finally his face. His face gazing down at me. The pure brown of his eyes like chocolate, the look in them already a little unfocused, when all I'd done was lay my cheek against his thigh and breathed out along his testicles. A feather of a touch, and already his face was showing the effect, as were other parts of his body.

It wasn't just the body, it was Richard looking down at me. The weight of him in his eyes. Him staring down the line of his own body, while I lay between his thighs. I used to think that only death would take someone away from me. But I had learned that so many lesser things can steal someone away, just as completely, just as forever. They live, they breathe, but you never get to touch them, you never see them nude, you never wake to their smile, the smell of their skin on your sheets. There are things so much less dramatic than death that are just as permanent. If I never got to be here like this with Richard again, I wanted it to last. I wanted to take my time.

Where was Jean-Claude? Sitting in the far corner of the bed opposite us. He was nude, but sitting with his back against the wall, one knee drawn up so that he was covered, for the most part, even if you looked directly at him. He looked like a great pale cat curled on the pillows. Once I would have said he looked utterly relaxed, but I knew him too well now. I saw the way he held his shoulders, the tension in one leg. He was holding himself in check, being oh, so careful.

I settled my cheek against Richard's thigh, the way a cat will scent mark you, rubbing back and forth. Just that, nothing more, but it made him writhe. His legs tensing around me, so that his legs flexed on either side of my body. The feel of even that much made me close my eyes and rest my cheek between his legs, so that my face was cradled, oh, so gently against the soft warmth of his testicles. I nestled my mouth against that silky skin. The tiny stiff hairs tickled along my face as I licked that soft, moveable skin. More hair to tickle along my lips. I preferred smoother skin, a little less fuzzy. But of course, I could have that by simply moving up.

I went up on my knees and licked along the front of his shaft, licked it like it was a big piece of candy, and I didn't want it to melt. Licked it back and forth, up and down, just on the front of the shaft, until he cried out, and his hands convulsed on the red sheets.

'Anita, please, no more teasing.'

I raised up so I was kneeling between his legs. 'Teasing, that's not teasing, that's foreplay.'

He swallowed, and it looked like it was an effort, or maybe his throat was dry. 'Then less foreplay, at least for me. I don't need it.'

I looked down at him, the eagerness in his eyes, his face, his whole body. I could feel what he wanted, feel it almost like he was yelling it in my head. I looked at Jean-Claude. 'Some men like a lot of foreplay.'

Jean-Claude gave that Gallic shrug. 'But it is not me that you are pleasing now.'

'I thought you said we had to all three be touching for this to work?'

'I thought I would give you and Richard a chance to reacquaint yourselves before I joined you.'

I climbed over Richard's thigh, so I could kneel beside his hip. 'Sometime during all this sex, the boundaries between us will come crashing down. If we aren't all three touching when it happens, we may miss our window to bind ourselves closer.'

'Perhaps,' Jean-Claude said, 'what do you propose?'

'Come hold Richard's hand.'

'Anita,' Richard began.

I wrapped my hand around the base of him, and found that he wasn't quite as hard as he had been a moment before. The thought of Jean-Claude joining us did not do it for him. I was sorry that it bothered him, but I hadn't crawled into this bed for just sex. It was an all-or-nothing deal. Sex and more metaphysical muscle, not just sex.

I squeezed him, one quick pulse, and it stole his words, made his breath shudder from between his lips. 'Richard's going to need something to hold on to soon, and there's no headboard.'

Richard found his voice. 'That was oversharing,' and he sounded a little angry.

'You know you like to hold on to something solid while I do this.'

He gave me sullen eyes. It was not a look I wanted to see today, not from him. 'Hold his hand, Richard, that's all I'm asking right now. Just hold his hand, or let him hold yours. Is that so much to ask?'

I turned so that I was facing away from him, but facing directly another part of his anatomy, which also had a head. I kept my hand on the base of him and slid my mouth over him. He wasn't completely hard yet, and I fought to take as much of him in as I could before he stiffened. It was easier a little softer, less hard to swallow past a certain point. Even soft, there came that moment where my body said, no, we're choking, that nothing this big should be coming down this far in one piece. It was as if I was swallowing him down, but because he was still attached and so big, it was more like I walked my throat over him, up him. I'd found that if I didn't struggle, that I could breathe with this much down my throat. I could breathe, if I didn't struggle. I could fight my way down the long, thick shaft of him, if I relaxed while I fought for it. It was a struggle to get all the way down, but at the same time, the trick was not to fight. Only I could make oral sex into a zen moment.

When my lip felt the solid touch of the front of his body, then, and only then, did I let myself begin to slide back up. It was always so much easier going up than coming down. I came up off of him, breathless, but pleased. I'd only recently been able to do that with Micah, after some very embarrassing failed attempts. Like in throwing up embarrassing. It's one of the reasons you should never try this stuff with people unless you love them. People who love you don't point and laugh.

I didn't give him time to catch his breath, only for me to catch mine. I slid my mouth back over him, swallowed him down, until the back of my throat convulsed around the end of him, and I could feel my throat close around the end of him, so deep, so terribly deep. I slid back up the long, thick, shaft of him, then forced myself down, down, until I met his body with my lips, and there was nowhere else to go, no more of him to take inside me. Then it wasn't that I tried to squeeze him in my mouth, but that my throat convulsed on its own, tightening down around him, my body trying to get rid of something so big, so impossible to swallow. I swallowed my own saliva, so I didn't choke on it. Only when I knew I couldn't take anymore, that one more time shoving him so deep in my throat would hurt, did I let myself stop swallowing. I let the wetness of my own mouth trail behind my lips, slide down the thickness of him, trail in thick, wet, lines down the shaft of him, until he was as wet from my mouth as he would have been between my legs.

Richard's voice, 'God, Anita, God.'

I raised my mouth off of him, my own saliva trailing in thick lines from my mouth to his body. I raised up and turned carefully, slowly, so he'd get the full visual.

He was staring down his body at me, his eyes too wide, face almost frantic. 'Anita,' and then, he saw me, and the visual threw his head back, spasmed his hands out, searching for something to hold on to. He'd already thrown off every pillow near him. Richard's hands searching for a headboard that wasn't there, searching for something to hold on to. His hand hit Jean-Claude's hand with a sharp smack of flesh on flesh.

Richard stopped his frantic flailing, looked at the other man, who had been so quiet, so still, pressed against the wall and the top of the bed. They had a moment when they were meeting each other's eyes. I don't know what Richard would have said, or done, because I rolled my hands up and over his groin, used the thick liquid to smooth over him, to glide over the head of him. It closed his eyes, and bowed his spine.

I turned, so that I was facing them. I wanted to watch their faces. I wrapped my hand around him, about halfway down, then bent my face back over him and slid him into my mouth, until I came to my hand. It was easier to take him in, faster, harder. With all of him it had been a fight, and no matter how good it felt having him in my mouth, down my throat, I was still fighting my body to keep him down, to breathe, to swallow, so that saliva didn't build up and make me choke. There was so much to concentrate on that I didn't have time to enjoy it as much as I wanted to. With only about half of him to work with, it was just fun. It wasn't just the feel of him, so ripe and hard in my mouth, but the skin was so soft, softer than any other skin on the body. It was like rolling muscled silk on my tongue, pounding it inside my mouth.

I watched Richard's body while I did it. His whole body writhed, his frantic breathing making everything from his stomach to his shoulders move. Both his hands were clasped in Jean-Claude's hands now. Richard's hands convulsed, until the muscles in his arms bulged, and he came up off the bed, crying a sound that was both a moan and scream that ended with my name. He settled back to the bed, his eyes closed, and I had a moment to look into Jean-Claude's face without Richard watching. For an instant Jean-Claude let me see how much this meant to him. The feel of all that strength in his hands, that Richard's struggles had pressed more of his body up against Jean-Claude's legs, that he was able to be here while Richard gave himself over to such abandon. For an instant it shone in his eyes, and I knew in that moment that as patient and careful as he'd been with me, it was nothing to how careful he had been with Richard.

'Stop,' Richard said, 'stop, or I'll go. Oh, God, stop.' He raised his head up, laughing, breathless, and the look on his face was joyous, free in a way that he seldom looked these days.

I slid him out of my mouth, while I watched his face. He let his head fall back to the bed, his arms, shoulders beginning to relax, beginning to slide away from Jean-Claude's hands. I licked the head of him, and he convulsed again, muscles cording in his arms and chest, his hands crushing around Jean-Claude's. If there'd been a headboard, it might not have survived. But vampires are made of sterner stuff than wood, or metal.

'Please, Anita, please, stop. Let me catch my breath, or I won't last.'

I stroked my hand up the wet, thickness of him.

He shuddered, and said, 'Hand, too, God, just stop, please!'

The last please did it, an element of franticness. I took my hand away and knelt beside his body, my hands in my lap. It's hard to be demure when you're naked in a bed with two men, but I did my best.

Richard let himself relax into the bed, let the tension of pleasure slide away. His head rested against Jean-Claude's thigh, his hands still loose in the other man's hands. Either he was too high on sex to think about it, or he didn't mind. As a shapeshifter he shouldn't have minded mere physical contact with someone. Hell, the shapeshifters slept in big naked puppy piles, but Richard had always made a very clear line between vampires and shapeshifters. Vampires didn't get the up-close and personal stuff, period.

He turned his head, found that he needed a better angle, and used Jean-Claude's thigh like a pillow, to raise his face up enough to look at me comfortably. He moved his hands out of the other man's, but he kept his head propped there, and the two of them were framed against the dark of the wall and the crimson of the sheets, both nude, both so terribly right. It was as if I'd waited a long time to see them like this. If we hadn't been shielding so tight, I'd have wondered if it was my thought, or someone else's.

'Give me a few minutes, or the next thing we do will be the last thing we do, and it won't last long. God, you were good before, but not like that.' He rolled his head back so he could look up the line of Jean-Claude's body to his face. 'Did you teach her that?'

'Why is it that all men assume that only men can teach a woman how to have good sex?' I said.

Richard turned back to me and smiled – a smile more relaxed than any I'd seen in so long from him. 'Are you saying you learned this from another woman?' He was teasing and let it show in his voice.

The teasing tone made me smile. 'No, I figured it out on my own, thank you very much. Like I said, I've been practicing.'

He rolled his head back to look at Jean-Claude, who obliged him by looking down to meet Richard's gaze. 'On you?'

Jean-Claude smiled, '*Non, mon ami*, I am well-endowed, but not so blessed as to help *ma petite* learn such technique.'

Richard looked back down toward me. There was a look on his face that I'd seen all too often lately, a not-happy look. 'Who?'

'I'll make you a deal, Richard. You don't ask me about my lovers, and I won't ask you about yours.'

'What's that supposed to mean?'

'It means if you weren't a lycanthrope, I would never have gone down on you like this until you proved you were disease free. You can get AIDS, gonorrhea, hepatitis, all just from oral sex. But lucky for you, you can't get anything. The lycanthropy destroys everything but itself, so you're disease free. Do you even know how many of the women in your pack and Verne's you've slept with?'

'Yes,' he said, and the anger was still there.

'Do I want to know the number?'

'No,' he said.

'But I'll bet I've never even come close to a number that large in my bed.'

'I thought you said you hadn't kept track of what I was doing.'

'I've heard a little, enough to know you've cleared three digits, or close to it. So let's agree not to get too possessive, or too self-righteous. Neither of us has the room for it.'

He covered his face with his hands and made a sound, almost a growl.

Jean-Claude looked at me, his face was fighting for neutral, but not quite making it. We were closer than we'd ever been to being a true triumvirate, and Richard and I were blowing it.

'Fine, you're right, you're right. If this is going to work, you're right,' Richard said.

I was the only one who saw the relief and surprise on Jean-Claude's face. By the time Richard lowered his hands and sat up, Jean-Claude's face was back to pleasant and unreadable.

I guess my face was surprised enough for both of us.

Richard smiled at me, though his eyes were still not happy.

'I wanted you in this bed. I'm not going to throw it away being stupid.' His smile brightened and finally filled his eyes. 'Alright, I'll try not to be too pigheaded, but lately I can't seem to help it,'

'Welcome to my world,' I said.

The smile got warmer. 'Trade me places,' he said.

I frowned. 'What?'

'Trade me places.' He scooted away from Jean-Claude and patted the bed next to the other man.

'You here.'

I was still frowning, but not unhappy. I was more puzzled than anything. 'Why?'

'I want to return the favor.'

'The favor?'

'Lay down,' he said, and patted the bed again. 'Let Jean-Claude hold your hands.'

I couldn't help frowning harder. 'I'm not a headboard rider. He doesn't need to hold my hands.'

'I felt how strong he is. Stong enough that when he holds your hands down you won't be able to get free.'

I looked at his face.

'I am to be your ropes,' Jean-Claude said.

Richard nodded, but kept looking at me.

'And what will you be doing while Jean-Claude holds me down?'

'Whatever I want to do.'

I frowned harder. 'Uh-unh, I need more of a clue than that.'

'Don't you trust me?' And just the way he said it, the look in his face made me want to say no. If we'd been alone I don't think I'd have let him tie me up without a detailed list of planned activities. But Jean-Claude I trusted to referee. This new, more reasonable, more seductive Richard, I wasn't sure of yet.

'Anyone who's said "trust me" or "don't you trust me" to me couldn't be trusted.'

'So you don't trust me,' he said, and the smile faded at the corners.

'I didn't say that.'

'What did you say, *ma petite*?' Jean-Claude asked.

'Yes.'

Richard frowned at me. Jean-Claude made a small line in his forehead, for him a frown, when he was trying not to show anything.

'Yes,' I said.

Jean-Claude smiled. It took Richard a moment longer to get it. 'Yes,' he said.

I nodded.

'Yes,' he said again.

I nodded, again.

He smiled, and the smile was that wonderful smile. The one that made him look younger, more relaxed, more . . . himself, somehow.

I felt a smile spread across my face, a smile that I couldn't stop and didn't want to.

'Yes,' he said, still smiling.

'Yes,' I said.

'At last,' Jean-Claude said, and he was smiling, too.

60

JEAN-CLAUDE'S HANDS ON mine, his body spilled out along the head of the bed. The pillows had all been thrown to the floor, so there was nothing but the silk sheets and the three of us. 'Trade places,' Richard had said. It had seemed so simple. I should have known nothing about Richard was ever simple.

He put his hands on my arms, just under where Jean-Claude held me. He wrapped those big hands around my arms, then began to slide his hands down my arms. He was only touching my arms, such an innocent place to touch, but he made the movement slow, and sensuous, trailing an edge of fingernail like the tiny press of something harder, and so much more dangerous against my skin. His hands reached under my arm, the trail of nails tickled, and made me writhe and giggle. Half because it tickled, and half because of the slow, sure movements of his hands. I'd forgotten what it was like to have all of Richard's attention in a bed. When you think you'll never be able to touch someone again, you try to forget.

I waited for him to curve his hands over my breasts, but he didn't. He moved his hands just a little lower on my sides, so that his hands barely brushed the edges of my breasts and kept moving down my body. That one small brush against the edges of my breasts caught my breath in my throat, and closed my eyes, to shudder under his hands.

His hands, so large they cupped my ribs, and nearly met at my waist, his thumbs pressing over my belly button, my lower stomach. I waited for his hands to go lower, and just as he had above, he moved his hands to the sides of my hips. Swept that sure, heavy, glide of skin and nails away from even the beginning of my pubic bone, so that he was only touching my hips, my thighs, but nothing more. His hands kept sliding downward, but he'd skipped the parts I most wanted him to touch. It left me making small noises, low in my throat, not from what he was doing, but from what he hadn't done. From what I wanted him to do.

It made me raise my arms, or try to, but Jean-Claude's hands were there. He kept my hands pressed to the bed. I put more effort into it, and found that I could raise my hands off the bed an inch or so, but Jean-Claude pressed me back to the bed, going up on his knees to get the leverage he needed. I'd made him change positions, made him work a little harder, but that was all. I put more effort into raising my wrists, freeing my arms. I don't know why, maybe because I hadn't really thought about not being able to get away. Being trapped in theory is one thing, knowing it for a fact, is different. Or different for me.

'Why struggle?' Richard asked, in a voice that held a tone I'd never heard from him. 'You know that Jean-Claude won't let anything bad happen.' His big hands finished their glide down my body, to end with his fingers wrapping around my ankles. He didn't press them to the bed, just held them, held my ankles in his hands.

I tried to get away from him. I couldn't help it. It was just one of those things. Tell me I can't, or show me I can't, and I have to try. I wasn't trying as hard as I could, but I was trying. Trying enough to feel the strength in his hands, a strength that could bend steel. I couldn't get away.

He spread my legs, using his hands on my ankles. He spread my legs, wide and wider, while I tried to stop him. It was a game, because we'd all agreed to this. I wanted him to make love to me, but game or not, there was something about the way he spread my legs with the strength in his hands, while Jean-Claude pinned my arms, that sped my pulse, and made the struggles go from halfhearted to not so halfhearted. It was stupid, but I couldn't help myself. I had to try to stop him from spreading my legs, from exposing me, and the fact that I couldn't both scared me and excited me. The two feelings should have been mutually exclusive, but they weren't.

'Tell me to stop,' Richard said, and his voice had grown deeper.

I shook my head. 'No.'

'Then why are you struggling?' he asked, and there was a look in his face, eager, dark, happy, all at once. He pushed my legs farther apart, until it was just this side of hurting. Until the muscles in my thighs began to ache with the stretch. 'Why are you struggling, if you don't want me to stop?'

I said the only thing I could think of, 'I don't know.' My voice was breathier than I thought it would be, as if my pulse was interfering. I realized then, that he'd spread my legs so far apart that I really couldn't struggle, not unless I wanted it to hurt. It made me push harder against Jean-Claude's hands. I raised up a few inches, so that he actually had to come to his knees, and press down, to hold me secure. Him coming to his knees meant that suddenly his body was exposed just above my head. He hung loose and soft just above me, and until he fed he would stay soft. I loved the sensation of him in my mouth when he was like this, because it didn't last, except when he had not fed. Now, I could explore the softness of him as long as I wanted, and it wouldn't change. I strained back for him, neck bowing, mouth reaching, and he was out of reach. Dangling just above me, but his hands held me down, and I couldn't get to him. Jean-Claude had to know what I was trying to do, but he kept his weight on my wrists, and his body arched above me, out of reach.

My voice came out strained, breathless, 'Please.'

'Please, what?' Richard's voice from the other end of the bed.

'*Ma petite* has a penchant for men when they are soft. Until I feed, she could indulge this . . . desire.'

'And you're keeping it just out of her reach,' Richard said, his voice dropped an octave lower so that it was almost painfully low, his voice just before it began to growl.

'*Oui.*'

'Why?' he asked.

'Is that not the game that you wish to play?'

A thin line of growl trickled from Richard's throat. 'Yes, yes, it is.' He was up on all fours, too, but unlike Jean-Claude he was thick and heavy against the front of his body. 'But I don't want it to be you she's begging for, I want it to be me.'

'Why can it not be both of us?' Jean-Claude asked.

The two men stared at each other, and I had a moment to feel their, not power, but almost as if their wills were suddenly power. I could feel the strength of their wills aimed at each other. 'You chose not to let me feed,' Jean-Claude said, 'deliberately. You thought she would not have a use for me until I could be erect.' He smiled. 'You underestimate *ma petite*'s love of the male body. She loves us in all our many forms.' That last held some note, some jab, that I didn't understand. I should have, but the feel of their hands on my body, and the view of both of them nude had me distracted. I never seemed to think as clearly around them when they were naked, embarrassing, but true.

Richard's face darkened with anger, and the first trickle of his power slipped past his so tight shielding. It danced along my legs like a breeze off the plains of hell. Hot, so hot. It raised goosebumps in a shivering line down my body. Me, shivering brought their attention back to me. Jean-Claude's face was pleasantly neutral, hiding. Richard looked down at me, and the anger was still there, but underneath that was something else. It held sex, but it also held something darker. Something that promised things beyond sex, beyond anything safe and sane. A moment to glimpse in his eyes things he probably didn't want to see in any mirror, before he turned away, so I couldn't see his face. As if he knew what I'd seen.

'If you're going to fight, get off of me,' I said. It was a little tough to put much authority in my voice when I was naked and they were holding me down, but I managed. My voice was suddenly mine again, not breathy, not sexy, just mine.

'That is not up to me, *ma petite*,' Jean-Claude said. 'Are we going to fight, Richard?'

That hot, hot wind eased out from his body again. A line of heat to trail like something solid and reaching across my skin. It was like fingers, fingers made of heat climbing up my skin, touching places Richard had very deliberately avoided. When that seeking heat caressed between my legs, I gasped, and managed to say, 'Stop it, whatever it is, stop it.' The heat climbed higher, using my body like a fleshy ladder.

'Does it hurt?' Richard asked, but he was looking at Jean-Claude, not me.

'No,' and the power caressed my breasts as if some great monster had breathed their breath hot across them. I shuddered under that touch, eyes closing, neck bowing.

I opened my eyes staring up into Jean-Claude's face. His face was still pleasant, unreadable, hidden. 'Are you well, *ma petite*?'

I nodded. I might have said something else, but Richard's power caressed my throat, flowed over my lips, so that my mouth felt hot, as if some hot, thick liquid lay on my tongue. I looked up into Jean-Claude's midnight-blue eyes, and whispered, 'Richard.'

Jean-Claude lowered his face over mine, more of his weight pressing in his hands, against my wrists, so even as he came closer, I was held more tightly. I opened my mouth for him, but he paused just short of a kiss. He licked the air above my mouth. I thought at first he'd missed, but he raised up enough to look down my body to Richard. 'What game is this?'

'You and she aren't the only ones who gained power when she bound herself to Damian and Nathaniel.' His voice wasn't happy when he said it, in fact the anger was back. The anger fed directly into his power so that a line of scalding heat flashed up my body and tore a scream from my throat.

Jean-Claude put his mouth to mine, and his power was in his kiss. A blessed coolness to glide over my tongue, down my throat, to spill in a chilling line through my body and quiet all that heat. And as if Richard's power had been waiting for that very thing, it surged forward, and I was suddenly covered in their power. It was as if my body was the wick for Richard's candle and the spout for Jean-Claude's cool water to flow down. But you can't be both flame and water. You can't burn and drown, not at the same time. My body tried, it tried to be cold and hot, flame and water, life and death. But wait, that last, that last we understood, my power and me. Life and death, especially death.

My power didn't simply rise, it burst my shields, like a dam smashed, and the power of that torrent, so long contained, poured over us all. It swept us not away, but together. We were on our knees on the bed with Richard pressed to the front of me, and Jean-Claude against my back. They say there is no light without dark, no good without evil, no male without female, no right without wrong. That nothing can exist if its direct opposite does not also exist. I don't know if that's true, but in that moment I understood that though each opposite needs the other, they also can't exist simultaneously. They are two sides to a coin, but what of the coin? What is the coin that separates good from evil, light from dark, what is it that binds them together, yet keeps them eternally apart? Good and evil, light and dark, I don't know, but with Richard and Jean-Claude, it was me.

I was the metal that both separated them and bound them together. I was their coin, and they were my different sides. Always apart, always together, different, but all of one piece. Richard pressed to the front of my body, and it was as if he burned, as if his body was so hot, it should have burst into flames, as if the sun itself lay within his skin. Jean-Claude pressed at my back like water, cool, cold water, that had risen from the very depths of the sea, where it runs cold and black, and slow, and strange things glide there. If you look at the sun too long you go blind; if you swim too deep into the sea you drown.

I screamed, screamed because I didn't know what to do with the power. I was their coin, but I didn't know how to forge us into one piece. It was like trying to fit three people into one body. How do you start? Who gets shoved in where?

But I wasn't master here, it wasn't my job to find a way to fit three such huge pieces into one. Jean-Claude's cool power flowed over me, soothed the burning, touched the edge of Richard's power, and brought us all back up to the surface of our metaphysical sea. He said almost exactly what I was thinking, 'I can only hold it back for a moment, when next we drown, we must not fight it. We must embrace it, and each other.'

'Define embrace,' Richard said, and his voice was thick with effort, as if he were holding back his side of some huge weight, and maybe he was.

'You into Anita's body, and I will feed upon yours.'

We didn't have time to say yes or no or anything. The power was just suddenly back, as if we'd opened a door and found the building falling down around us. We were out of time. We either rode the power, or it would bury us. Bury us along with everyone we loved, everyone we'd vowed to protect. Distantly, I had the thought, if we would but take the fourth mark, it would be easier to ride, but the thought vanished under the press of Richard's body. His body was ripe and thick and ready, and he'd made certain that Jean-Claude's wouldn't be. There might have been other ways to bind us, but Richard had taken some of Jean-Claude's choices, and mine, by simply not allowing the other man to feed. Funny how you try to avoid one evil, and fall headlong into another.

Richard pushed himself inside me. I was tight, and he was thick, but the moment he began to push inside me, the terrible weight of power eased. It was as if Richard's body broke the plane of some barrier, as if my body were a door, and we'd pushed inside.

Richard's voice came strained, 'Tight, so tight. I don't want to hurt you.' He was above me in a sort of push-up, and the view between our bodies was perfect. Perfect for watching him push his way inside me.

I grabbed his arms, and said, 'Don't stop, God, don't stop.'

'You're too tight.'

'Not for long,' I said.

'Is she wet?' Jean-Claude asked.

Richard gave him a look, and it wasn't friendly. 'Yes.'

'Then you will not hurt her.'

'You said it yourself, Jean-Claude, you aren't this well-endowed, you don't know how you can hurt a woman without meaning to.'

I slapped Richard's shoulder, because I couldn't reach his face. He looked down at me, anger so ready in his eyes. 'I am not Clair. I want you, Richard. I want you inside me, please, Richard, please. Don't stop, please, don't stop.'

He looked down at me, and the look on his face was very male, and very Richard all at the same time. I watched him, felt how much he wanted to shove himself inside me, but that part of him that was still Richard, still thinking so hard, was afraid. Not afraid that he'd hurt me, but afraid to see the same look on my face he'd seen on Clair's. I tasted the fear of that on my own tongue. Felt the pulse in my neck speed, not with lust, but fear. Fear that Clair was right. That he was an animal. If I could have slapped her around in that moment, I might have. The last thing Richard needed was more emotional shit to shovel.

'If you will not do it, *mon ami*, then let me feed, so that we may finish this.'

'I am not your friend,' Richard said, and his anger spread like hot oil on my skin. It didn't hurt like earlier, and I knew that was Jean-Claude's doing. He was dulling the edge of Richard's power, or rather turning it from burning pain, to something more fun. Heated oil rolling down my skin instead of biting bits of fire; how could I argue?

'Be my enemy then,' Jean-Claude said, 'but one of us must do this. If you will not, then you must help me do it.'

I sat up, and he wasn't far enough in for it, so that he slipped back out. That pressure came crashing back. Jean-Claude grabbed a handful of my hair, pulled my head back, and kissed me. Hard, deep, tongue searching my mouth. I melted into that kiss, gave my mouth to his, my face to his hand, my head to the hand still wrapped in my hair. His other hand slid from my face down my neck, my shoulder, to caress the front of my breast. He bent me back against his body, and I understood. As we'd discussed, his power lay in seduction. He was literally building a deeper binding on the foundation of sex. Each touch, each caress, each penetration, another stone to keep us safe. I'd have argued with his choice of building materials, but I wasn't master here. This was his ball game, not mine. Of course, there was more than one way to play ball.

Jean-Claude's hands slid over the front of my body, until he held my breasts. He squeezed them between his hands, squeezed them hard and sharp. I came away from his mouth with a gasp, and a sound low in my throat. 'You will not hurt her, Richard.'

Richard hadn't moved back. He was still sitting where my body had left him, his body between my knees, close enough that he could have joined Jean-Claude in the foreplay, but he just knelt there.

I stroked my hand over him, found him not as hard as he had been. I wrapped my hand around him, tight and hard. Brought a small sound from him. 'I want this,' and I squeezed him again, watched his eyes lose focus, 'this inside me.'

I could feel that he wanted to, but his fears held him closer than any lover's arms ever would. I let go of him and turned with a cry to Jean-Claude. I felt suddenly half-crazed with need. A need to have someone inside me. Jean-Claude hadn't fed yet, but there was still something I could do for my own pleasure. I turned my back on Richard, and laid a light kiss on Jean-Claude's mouth, but that wasn't what I wanted. He rose up on his knees as if he knew where I was headed.

I licked my way down his body, and his hand on the back of mine, guided me to him. I drew him into my mouth, and the texture of him so small, so loose, was wonderful. I sucked him, rolled him with my tongue. Small, I could have my way with him, and not have to fight for it. I sucked him as hard and fast as I could, in and out, in and out, until he cried out above me. I used my hand to lift the loose tenderness of his balls up, so I could draw them gently into my mouth. It was hard having all of him in my mouth at once, even this small, there was barely room. I had to be so careful of him, so careful, not to hurt him, not to crush such delicate pieces. Like rolling some precious priceless work of art between your teeth. When I didn't trust myself not to bite down on those tender bits, I spilled them out of my mouth. But I kept that soft, flexible, givable, forgiveable bit to roll and coax, until he cried out above me, and his body thrust forward, but he couldn't complete it. I could have teased him all night, and he couldn't have finished it. I was ready to offer to open a vein myself, when I felt hands on my hips.

I felt Richard push himself against my body. He wasn't soft now, he was oh, so hard. He kept one hand on my hip, and used the other to guide himself in. He pushed against the opening in my body.

I started to raise up, but Jean-Claude's hand pushed on my head, kept me where I was, kept my mouth wrapped around his body, sucking him deep into my mouth, as Richard pushed his way into my body. I was wetter now, more open, but Richard still had to work his way in, push, and shove, for each tight, wet, inch. The feel of him inside me forced small sounds from my throat, made me whimper and moan, all of it with Jean-Claude still in my mouth.

Richard pushed his way in, until there was no more. Until he hit the end of me, and had nowhere to go but to draw himself back out of me, slowly, so slowly. I didn't want slowly. I wanted fast. I wanted hard. I wanted Richard at his best, not this careful dance.

I raised my head up off of Jean-Claude, and this time he let me, but he kept his hand against my hair. I raised up enough to gaze back over my body and see Richard there on his knees. Seeing him with his body inside of me, rolled my eyes shut for a moment, but the feel of all that thick potential being so carefully used, made me want to scream at him.

'Fuck me, Richard.'

He looked at me, and the control on his face in his body, stopped for a moment. He looked at me, and said, 'Anita.'

'Fuck me,' I said, 'fuck me, God, fuck me, just fuck me. Fuck me, fuck me, fuck me, fuck me, please, please, please just fuck me.'

'I am.'

I shook my head, hard enough to send my hair flying around my face. Jean-Claude moved his hand enough for me to do it. 'No, no, no, no!' Freed of Jean-Claude's hands I could move. I shoved myself onto him. I shoved myself down hard and fast until the sound of our bodies hitting slapped together. Having him shoved that hard, fast, deep, inside me, made me cry out, but not in pain.

I leaned my upper body forward, and angled my hips, and I fucked him, as hard and as fast, as I could. It wasn't quite as good as he could have done on his own, but it was still good. Still so good.

Richard caught the rhythm of my hips and started shoving himself inside me, as hard and fast as he could. Harder and faster than I'd been able to manage on my own. So hard, so fast, so deep, hitting that spot deep, deep inside my body, until I cried out around him.

Jean-Claude's hand pushed me back down, and helped my mouth find him again. Helped me feed on his soft, soft flesh while Richard pounded himself inside me. Jean-Claude moved up high on his knees, and his hand helped me stay where he wanted me.

It wasn't until I heard Richard's voice, 'Jean-Claude,' and felt Richard's rhythm falter, that I suspected what Jean-Claude was doing up there, behind my back.

Jean-Claude was suddenly not soft, or limp. He grew in my mouth like ripened fruit, like something sweet and tender that had waited a very long time to spread and grow thick and heavy. He filled my mouth. I drew back to breathe, and he forced my head farther down, forced himself deeper into my throat.

I suddenly had both of them as deep inside me as my body could hold. Richard pounded himself between my legs, and Jean-Claude thrust himself between my lips. They found a rhythm together, so that they mirrored each other. I fought to open my mouth wide enough, to keep teeth out of the way, while Jean-Claude mouth-fucked me. I'd never let anyone do that before, not like this, not so that what was happening at my mouth was almost exactly what was happening between my legs.

Richard had taken me at my word. He pounded into me so fast and so hard, until the sound of it was like a continuous thud of flesh on flesh, and though it felt wonderful, if Jean-Claude hadn't been in my mouth I might have begged him to go. It was almost too much, almost pain. Jean-Claude was more careful up front, because he had to be, but he still forced me to hold the same rhythm, fast, hard, thudding, swallowing almost continuously, barely time to breathe between one thrust and the next. One minute I was fighting to breathe, fighting not to start begging, the next, orgasm hit me, and I was screaming, but it wouldn't stop. I screamed my orgasm around Jean-Claude's body still shoved deep in my mouth. I screamed, and my body spasmed around them both. I sucked hard and harder, I drove my hips into Richard. A moment before I'd been ready to stop, and now I helped them fuck me. I drove my body into them both, as hard and fast as I could, while my body danced between them. The orgasm grew, grew until it wasn't enough to just scream, and I raked my nails down Jean-Claude's thighs.

I felt their bodies tighten at the same time. Richard spasmed at my back, driving himself so deep inside me that I screamed for real this time, but Jean-Claude drove himself down at the same moment, and my scream was lost to the sensation of him spasming inside my throat. He wasn't as long as Richard, but he was far enough down, that it wasn't a matter of swallowing. It was simply a matter of not choking it back up. Of letting that hot thickness go down my throat, and not struggling against it. I let them have my body in that instant. I let their pleasure fill me and pour down me, through me.

It was at that moment when our bodies were joined, sharing things as intimate as blood, that it clicked into place. That we'd done enough to bind us without bleeding Jean-Claude. Maybe it was what it needed to work, or maybe we just all three had to let down our guard enough to stop fighting.

We collapsed in a breathless, panting heap. Jean-Claude drew himself out of me, gently, and lay on his back with me on top of him, pinning his legs. Richard was still on top of me, still inside me, but now he was almost dead weight, and I was short enough, and he was tall enough, that he was lying partially on Jean-Claude. I was just pinned between them.

Richard got to his knees, just enough to pull himself out of me, then collapsed onto his side, half-spooning me, but not quite touching Jean-Claude. In a voice that was still breathless, he asked, 'Did I hurt you?'

I couldn't help it, I laughed. I laughed, even though my jaw was beginning to ache as the endorphins faded. I laughed, as I began to feel the ache of him between my legs. I laughed, not because it hurt, but because it felt so good.

Jean-Claude started to laugh, too.

'What?' Richard said.

Jean-Claude and I lay on top of each other, too tired to move, and laughed. It took Richard a few minutes, but finally, a deep chuckle escaped him. He moved his body enough to throw an arm across mine, and laughed. The three of us lay unable or unwilling to move, and we laughed. We laughed until we could move, then we moved up on the bed and lay quiet, in a big, warm, naked, puppy pile. Me in the middle, but when Jean-Claude's head touched Richard's arm, neither of them moved away. It wasn't perfect, but damn, it was close.

61

I'D TRIED TO call my friendly neighborhood vampire hunter in New Orleans to see what I could learn about the vamps we were after, but Denis-Luc St John, vamp hunter and federal marshal, was in the hospital, still in intensive care. They'd damn near killed him before they left town. Worse and worse.

The sun was a bloody strip of red against the western sky when Zerbrowski and I got out of his car to question the first witness. I always felt like I should have to wash my jeans when I got out of his car. The backseat was so full of paper and old fast food bags that it looked like a landfill. The front seat wasn't actually dirty, but the rest of the car was so messy that it just felt like the entire car was icky.

'Do Katie and the kids ever ride in this thing?' I asked as we started up the steps to the first apartment on the list.

'Naw, she and the kids take the minivan.'

I shook my head. 'Has she seen the inside of it recently?'

'You've seen our house, it's perfect, everything in its place. Even our bedroom is immaculate. The car is the one place that's mine. It gets to be as messy as I want it to be.'

Strangely, it made more sense to me now than it would have a few months ago. I understood the fine art of compromise between a couple in a way that I never had before. I'm not saying I was good at it, just that I understood it more.

Zerbrowski read off the number of the apartment, and it was on the second floor, in a line of concrete walkway and metal railing. The doors were all identical. I wondered if the neighbors knew that they had a vamp living next door. You'd be amazed at the number of people that don't figure it out. Vampires hit my radar hard, so they don't pass unnoticed for me. More humans than I'm comfortable with get fooled. I don't know if it's because they want to be fooled, or if it really is harder for them to spot a vamp. I don't know which would bother me more, that normal humans can't spot them, thus implying that I am even more outside the norm, or that people want to be fooled that badly.

Since we were looking for vampires that had killed at least two people, I stretched out that part of me that sensed the dead. It wasn't the same part that raised zombies. Though explaining the difference was like explaining the difference between sky blue and turquoise. They were both blue, but they weren't the same color.

Zerbrowski reached for the doorbell, and I touched his hand. 'Not yet.'

'Why not?' he asked. His hand swept back his wrinkled trench coat and suit jacket, to touch the butt of his gun on his hip. 'You hear something?'

'Ease down, it's okay. He's just not awake yet.'

Zerbrowski looked puzzled at me. 'What does that mean?'

'I can feel vampires, Zerbrowksi, if I concentrate, or they're doing something powerful. He's not awake yet. I was hoping he would be, he's supposed to be the oldest one of the three, longest dead. Longest dead usually wakes up first, unless one of them is a master. Masters wake up first.'

'I knew the part about longest dead,' he said. 'So a master vampire that is two years dead can wake up before a vampire that is five years dead, but not a master?'

'Yeah, though some vamps don't accumulate enough power in five hundred years to rival masters I've met that were under five years.'

'That'd be a bummer. A flunkie for all eternity.'

I nodded. 'Yeah.' I felt that instant spark inside the room. It hit me almost like a punch to the stomach, or lower. Once I could only sense vamps that I had a connection to, to this degree, and once it was just a small quiver of recognition. Apparently, I'd gone up a power level or two.

'You okay?' Zerbrowski asked.

'Yeah, just, yeah. Now you can use the doorbell.'

He gave me a look.

'I was concentrating too hard when he woke up, okay? My bad.'

I don't know if he really understood the comment, or was just used to me being weird, but whatever, he pushed the button. We heard the strident sound inside the room beyond. So many people think that being a vampire automatically gets you the big house on the hill, or a coffin in a dungeon somewhere, but most of the vamps I knew had apartments, houses, and lived pretty much like everyone else. Vampires living in a central location surrounding their master, the way Jean-Claude had it, was becoming a thing of the past.

I missed it. Not nostalgia. If I had to kill a bunch of vamps, having them spread miles apart made my job harder. But we weren't here to kill anybody, not yet. Of course, that could change. All we needed was proof, or, depending on the judge, strong suspicion. Once I'd been okay with that. Now, it bothered me. To my knowledge, I'd never killed vamps that hadn't done the crime, but I had to admit that at the beginning of my career, I hadn't checked as carefully as I did now. They were just walking corpses to me once, and making them lie down and be still hadn't felt like murder to me. My job had been easier then, fewer conflicts. Nothing helps you sleep at night so much as being absolutely certain that you're right, and everyone else is evil.

The door opened, and the vampire stood blinking at us. His blond hair was tousled from sleep, and he'd thrown jeans over his boxers, or maybe slept in both. They were wrinkled enough. He squinted at us, and it took me a second to realize the squint was permanent, like someone who'd worked outdoors all their life, and not worn sunglasses. His eyes were pale and washed almost colorless. He looked tanned, but he was five years dead, and it couldn't be a tan. Artificial tan was starting to be big business among the recently dead. The ones who hadn't gotten accustomed to that paler than pale look. His looked better than most, a professional job, not homegrown.

'Jack Benchely?' Zerbrowski made it a question.

'Who wants to know?'

He flashed his badge, and I flashed mine. 'Sergeant Zerbrowski of the Regional Preternatural Investigation Team.'

'Federal Marshal Anita Blake.'

Jack Benchely blinked harder, like he was really trying to wake up. 'Shit, what did I do to get the Spook Squad and the executioner at my door just after sundown?'

'Let's go inside and talk about that,' Zerbrowski said with a smile.

The vampire seemed to think about that for a second. 'You got a warrant?'

'We don't want to search your place, Mr Benchely. We want to ask you some questions, that's all.' Zerbrowski was still smiling. The smile didn't even look strained.

I wasn't trying to smile, I didn't feel like it.

'What kind of questions?' he asked.

I said, 'The kind about you being across the river at a strip club, when I know for a damned fact that Malcolm has ordered you all to stay away from shit like that.' Now I was smiling, but it was a smile the way a flash of teeth is a smile. Sometimes it's a smile and sometimes it's not. Put your hand close to the dog's mouth and find out.

Benchely didn't look like he wanted to find out. He looked awake now, awake and almost scared. He licked his thin lips and said, 'Are you going to tell Malcolm?'

'That depends on how cooperative you are,' I said.

'What Marshal Blake means, is if we get enough information from you, there won't be a need to trouble the head of the Church of

Eternal Life.' Zerbrowski was still smiling and pleasant. I guess I was bad cop for the day. That worked for me.

'I know what she meant,' the vampire said. He moved to one side of the open door and was careful to keep his hands where we could see them. Jack Benchely, human, had a record. Minor stuff. A few drunk and disorderlies, an assault charge that started out as a domestic disturbance call. Nothing too serious, and all of it involving too many drinks and not enough common sense.

When we were inside, he shut the door and went to the couch. From a coffee table that had almost as much crap on it as the back-seat of Zerbrowski's car, he fished out a cigarette and a lighter. He lit up without asking if we minded. How rude.

There were no other chairs in the room, so we stayed standing. Again, rude. Though the place was so messy that I wasn't sure I'd have taken a seat if it had been offered. There was so much clutter that you expected it to smell stale, but it didn't. It did smell like the inside of an ashtray, but that's not the same thing as dirty. I've been in houses that looked spotless, but still reeked of cigarettes. Being a nonsmoker, my nose isn't dulled to it.

He took in a big drag on the cig and made the tip glow bright. He let the smoke trickle out through his nose and the corners of his mouth. 'What do you want to know?'

'Why'd you leave the Sapphire early last night?' I asked.

He shrugged. 'It was after eleven. I don't call that early.'

'Okay, why'd you leave when you did?'

He looked up at me, eyes narrowed as smoke oozed past them. 'It was boring. The same girls, same acts.' He shrugged. 'I swear that strippers were more fun when I could drink.'

'I bet,' I said.

Zerbrowski said, 'What time did you leave exactly?'

Benchely answered. We asked the usual questions. What time? Why? With whom? Was there anyone in the parking lot that could verify that he got in his truck and didn't linger in the parking lot?

'Linger,' Benchely said, and he laughed. Laughed hard enough to flash fangs. The fangs were as yellowed from nicotine as the rest of his teeth. 'I didn't linger, officer. I just left.'

I debated on whether I could tell him to put out his cigarette in his own house, and if he'd do it if I asked. If I ordered him and he didn't, we'd look weak. If I grabbed the cig and smushed it out, I'd be a bully. I tried to hold my breath and hoped he'd finish it soon.

He took another healthy pull on the cig and spoke with the smoke coming out of his mouth. 'What did I miss? One of the other vamps get out of hand with a dancer? One of the other upstanding church members trying to frame me for it?'

'Something like that,' I said softly.

He fished an ashtray out of the mess. It was an older one, pale green ceramic, with upturned sides and a tray of cig holders in the middle, like dull teeth. He stubbed out his cig and didn't try to hide that he was angry. Or maybe five years dead wasn't enough time to learn to hide that well. Maybe.

'Hell, it was Charles, wasn't it?'

I shrugged. Zerbrowski smiled. We hadn't said yes, we hadn't said no. Noncomittal, that was us.

'He's a member of their damn club, did he tell you that?'

'He didn't volunteer it,' I said.

'I'll bet he didn't. Damned hypocrites, all of them.' He ran his hands through his hair, made the thickness of it stand up even more. 'Did he tell you that he's the one that recruited me for the damn church?'

I fought the urge to share a glance with Zerbrowski. 'He didn't mention that,' Zerbrowski said.

'I'd tried to quit drinking. I tried just quitting, twelve steps, you name it, I tried it. Nothing worked. I'd lost two wives, more jobs than I could count. I've got a son who's nearly twelve. There's a court order against me seeing him. Isn't that a hell of a thing, my own son?'

Zerbrowski agreed it was a hell of a thing.

'Moffat was at the club one night. He made it sound so easy. I would have to stop drinking, because I couldn't drink anymore. Simple.' He reached for another cigarette.

'Can you wait until we're gone for that?' I asked.

'It's the last vice I got,' he said. But he stuffed the cig back in its pack. He kept the lighter in his hands, playing with it, as if even that was a comfort. 'I'm what my counselor calls an addictive personality. Do you know what that means, officers?'

'It means that if you can't drink, you've got to be addicted to something,' I said.

He smiled, and really looked at me for the first time. Not just like I was a cop come to hassle him, but like I was a person. 'Yeah, yeah, my counselor wouldn't like that definition, no siree she would not. But yeah, that's the truth. Some people are lucky, and it's just they're addicted to drinking, or smoking, or whatever, but for those of us who are just addicted to being addicted, anything'll do.'

'The blood lust,' I said.

He laughed again, and nodded. 'Yeah, yeah, I can't drink liquor but I can still drink. I still like to drink.' He slapped the lighter down on the table, and both Zerbrowski and I jumped. Benchely didn't seem to notice. 'Everyone thinks you get to be pretty when you're made over. That you get to be suave and good with the ladies just because you got a pair of fangs.'

'You get the gaze with the fangs,' I said.

'Yeah, I can trick 'em with my eyes, but legally that's not a willing feed.' He looked at Zerbrowski as if he represented all the laws that had held him down all his life. 'If I use vampire tricks, and she comes out of it yelling force, I'm dead.' He looked at me, and it wasn't exactly an unfriendly look. 'It's considered sexual assault, as if I slipped her a date rape drug. But I'm a vampire, and I won't see trial. They'll give me to you, and you'll kill me.'

I wasn't sure what to say to that. It was true, though they'd amended the law so that you had to have more than one count of gaze-induced blood taking to execute someone. That's what they called it, gaze-induced blood taking. The far right was crying that it was letting sexual predators loose on our communities. The far left just didn't want to agree with the far right, so they'd help push for the change in the laws. Those of us in the middle just didn't like the idea of a death warrant being issued on the say-so of one date who woke up the next morning with a bad case of buyer's remorse.

'I don't have the money to throw around that the church deacons do,' Benchely was saying, 'I've got to get a woman to donate her blood through *charm*.' He said the last word like it was curse. 'I know drink ruined my life, but I am a hell of a lot more charming when I've had just a few drinks.'

'That's not usually true,' I said.

He looked at me. 'What isn't true?'

'A lot of drunks think they're charming drunk, but they aren't. Trust me, I've been the only teetotaler at a lot of parties. There is nothing charming about a drunk, except maybe to another drunk.'

He was shaking his head. 'Maybe, but all I know is that I'm reduced to feeding off the church. The church makes taking blood as tame as it can. Something that should be better than sex, and they make you feel like you're at one of those places where you only get your food after you've listened to the sermon. It makes the food taste bad.' He picked up his lighter again turning it over and over in his hands, until the gold of it swirled in the dim light, shining. 'Nothing tastes good when you have to swallow your pride with it.'

'Are you saying that Moffat, a deacon of the church, misrepresented what life would be like after you became a vampire?' I tried for as casual a question as I could make it.

'Misrepresented, not exactly. More like he let me come in believing all the stuff in the books and movies, and when I talked about it like it would be that way, he didn't tell me different. But it is different, real different.'

If you were Belle Morte's line you spent eternity with people lining up to donate. If you were from some of the bloodlines that gave power, but not beauty or sex appeal, then in a country where using vampire tricks was illegal, you were screwed. The only vamp I knew well that was descended from a line like that was Willie McCoy. I had never wondered what Willie, with his ugly suits and uglier ties and slicked back hair, did for food. Maybe I should have.

The Church of Eternal Life didn't promise much more than most churches promised, but you could join the Lutherans, and if you didn't like it, you could quit. Joining the Church of Eternal Life as a full member meant never being able to do anything about regrets you might have.

Zerbrowski got us back on track. 'You didn't see anyone in the parking lot who could confirm when you left the Sapphire?'

He shook his head.

'Did you smell anything?'

Those washed out eyes flicked up to me. He frowned. 'What?'

'You didn't see anything, or anyone, but sight isn't the only sensory input you've got.'

He frowned harder.

I bent down so I could meet him eye-to-eye. I would have knelt, but I didn't want to touch the carpet with anything but my shoes. 'You're a vampire, Benchely, a bloodsucker, a predator. If you were human I'd just say what did you see, or hear, but you're not human. If you didn't see or hear anything, what did you smell? What did you sense?'

He was looking positively perplexed. 'What do you mean?'

I shook my head. 'What did they do, make you a vampire, then not teach you anything about what you are?'

'We're the eternal children of God,' he said.

'Bullshit, bull-fucking-shit! You don't know what you are, or what you could be.' I wanted to grab him by the shoulders and shake him. He was five years dead. I didn't think he was involved, but he'd walked through that parking lot damn close to the time of the killing. If he hadn't been such a pitiful excuse for the undead, he might have been able to help us catch the bad guys.

'I don't understand,' he said, and I believed him.

I shook my head. 'I need air.' I went for the door, leaving Zerbrowski to mutter, 'Thanks for your help, Mr Benchely, and if you think of anything, call us.' I was on the cement walkway, breathing in all the night air I could, when Zerbrowski came to find me.

'What the hell was that?' he asked. 'You just decide we stop questioning a suspect?'

'He didn't do it, Zerbrowski. He's too damn pitiful to have done it.'

'Anita, listen to yourself. That doesn't even make sense. You know as well I do that murderers can make you feel sorry for them. Some of them specialize in pity.'

'I don't mean I felt pity for him, I mean he's too damn pitiful a vampire to have pulled it off.'

Zerbrowski frowned at me. 'You've lost me.'

I wasn't sure how to explain it, but I tried. 'It's bad enough that they let him believe that becoming a vampire would fix everything that was wrong with his miserable life, but then they killed him. They took his mortal life, but they've done everything they can to cripple him as a vampire.'

'Cripple him, how?'

'Any vampire that I know would have noticed things, Zerbrowski. They're like this hyperfocus predator. Predators notice things. Benchely may have fangs, but he still thinks like he's a sheep, not a wolf.'

'Would you really want every member of the church to be a good predator?'

I leaned my back against the railing. 'It's not that. It's that they took his life and didn't give him another one. He's not better off than he was before.'

'He's not getting arrested for drunk and disorderlies anymore.'

'And how long will it be before he can't take it anymore and he uses his gaze on somebody, drinks their blood, and blows it? They wake up and decide they were abused. He's not a good enough vampire for them not to wake up and regret it.'

'What do you mean he's not a good enough vampire? Anita, you're not making sense.'

'I don't know if it'll make sense to you, Zerbrowski, but I've seen the real deal. They're terrible, or can be, but they're like watching a tiger at the zoo. They're dangerous, but they have a beauty to them, even the ones that aren't from a bloodline that makes them prettier after death, even those have a sort of power to them. A certain mystique, or an aura of confidence, or something. They have something that every member of the church that we've talked to since last night lacks.'

'I say, again, would we want them to be powerful and mysterious? Wouldn't that be bad?'

'For stopping crime and keeping the peace, yes, but Zerbrowski, the church talked these people into letting themselves be killed. Killed for what? I've tried to talk people out of joining the church for years, but I've not really talked to many of the members once I can't save them.'

He was looking at me funny. I guess I couldn't blame him. 'You still think that vamps are dead. You're dating one, and you still think they're dead.'

'Jean-Claude hasn't made a new vampire since he became Master of the City, Zerbrowski.'

'Why not? I mean, it's considered legal now, not murder.'

'I think he agrees with me, Zerbrowski.'

He frowned harder at me, took off his glasses, rubbed the bridge of his nose, put them back on, and shook his head. 'I am just a simple cop, and you are making my head hurt.'

'Simple my ass. Katie told me you double majored in law enforcement and philosophy. What kind of cop has a degree in philosophy?'

He looked at me kind of sideways. 'If you tell anyone else I'll deny it, say sleeping with the undead has made you hallucinate.'

'Trust me, Zerbrowski, if I hallucinated, it wouldn't be about you.'

'That is a low blow, Blake, I wasn't even picking on you.' His cell phone rang. He flipped it open, still smiling about my low blow. 'Zerbrow—' He never even got to finish his name, before his smile vanished. 'Say again, Arnet, slower. Shit. We're on our way. Holy items out. They'll glow if the vamp is close.' He started to run, as he flipped the phone closed. I ran with him.

'What happened?' I asked.

We clattered onto the stairs before he answered. 'Woman dead at the scene. Vamp missing. Apartment appears empty.'

'Appears?' I said.

'Vampires are tricky bastards,' he said.

I would have argued, if I could have. But since I couldn't, I saved my breath for running and beat Zerbrowski to his car. If we hadn't both been afraid of what we'd find when we got to the scene, I would have teased him about it.

62

THE APARTMENT WAS so much nicer than the one we'd just come from. It was clean and neat enough to have pleased even my stepmother, Judith. Well, except for the dead woman on the carpet and the blood trail leading back to the bedroom. Other than that, the apartment looked freshly scrubbed.

I know by now that murder happens in the best of neighborhoods. I know for a fact that economics, or neatness, or niceness are not barriers to violence. I know that, because I've seen dead bodies in some of the nicest houses. Everyone wants to believe that violence only happens in horrible places, where even the rats fear to go, but it isn't true. I didn't think I had any illusions left about murder and murderers, but I was wrong. Because the first thing I thought when I saw that neat-as-a-pin, well-decorated apartment with the dead woman on the carpet was, the body would have fit in Jack Benchely's apartment better. Hell, you could have hidden her body in the coffee table debris.

The body lay so close to the door that they'd had to move her arm just to open the door enough to let Arnet and Abrahams inside. Abrahams had transferred over from sex crimes. I glanced at him across the room, standing near the neat, sparkly kitchen. He was tall and thin with dark hair and an olive complexion. Brown seemed to be his favorite color, because I'd never seen him when he wasn't wearing it. He was talking to Zerbrowski, who was taking notes.

So far I hadn't learned enough to need to take notes. Maybe it was because the body was right at our feet. Arnet's and mine. Dead bodies can be a real conversation stopper. The body was on its stomach, legs slightly spread, one hand reaching out toward the door, the other arm folded back where Arnet had moved it when she opened the door.

Arnet was standing beside me, looking down at the body. She looked a little pale around the edges. Maybe it was only the lack of makeup, but I didn't think so. She was actually wearing a little eye makeup and pale lipstick. But her eyes were a little big, and her skin pale against her short dark hair. Not like pale with contrast, but pale like I was ready to grab her elbow in case she started to faint on the body.

I wanted to ask her if she was alright, but you don't ask cops that, so I tried to get her talking. 'How did you know she was in here?' I asked.

She jumped and turned startled eyes to me. She was seriously spooked.

'Why don't we step outside and get some air?' I said.

She shook her head, and I knew stubborn when I saw it, so I didn't argue. 'I saw blood under the door, or what I was almost certain was blood.'

'Then what?'

'I called for backup, and we kicked the door open.'

'You and Abrahams,' I said.

She nodded.

'The door bounced into her arm, but we didn't know it was her until we shoved the door again. I took low, and I was kneeling on the ground, so I saw her first. Saw that we were trying to shove the door through her.' Her voice shook a little at the end.

'Let's move over there by the kitchen, okay?'

'I'm alright,' she said, and was angry suddenly. 'Why is it that you think you're the only woman that can handle this kind of shit?'

I lifted eyebrows, but didn't say anything for a count of five. I wasn't mad, I just wasn't sure what to say. I finally tried the truth. 'I'm not the one that's pale and looks ready to faint.'

'I'm not going to faint,' she hissed at me. Angry whispers always sound so evil.

'Fine, then we'll stay right here.'

'Fine,' she said, still angry.

I shrugged, strangely not angry. 'Fine. You checked the woman, found she was dead, and then . . .'

'You know, I don't have to report to you. You're not my boss.'

That was it. 'Look, Arnet, if you've got a personal beef with me, fine, have a personal beef with me, but not on her time.' I pointed down to the body.

'What do you mean, her time? She's dead. She doesn't have anymore time.'

'Bullshit. We're on her dime right now. This is her murder, and catching the son of a bitch that did this to her is more important than anything else right now. You stonewalling me and acting like some damn rookie is just giving him more time to run. We don't want him to run. We want him to be caught, right?'

She nodded. 'I am not acting like a rookie.'

I sighed. 'I apologize for that, and if you want to fight, we can fight, but later, when we're not wasting valuable time, when we're not wasting her time.'

Arnet looked down at the body again, mostly because I pointed again. Maybe it was overly dramatic, but I already spent time fighting with Dolph at crime scenes, I didn't need another prima donna on my hands. Murder first, personal stuff later, that had to be the order of things, or you lost your way.

Zerbrowski was behind her. I noticed him walking up, but I don't think Arnet did. 'Go outside, Arnet, get some air,' he said, smiling, trying to take some of the sting out of it.

'I'm a detective on this team, she isn't.' She pointed at me with her thumb.

'Outside, now,' Zerbrowski said, and his voice had lost all of its hail-fellow-well-met cheer.

Arnet stood there glaring at him.

'If I have to tell you to go outside again, Arnet, it won't just be for air.'

'What's that mean?' she asked, and her hands were starting to tremble. She was so angry she was shaking. What the hell had I done to make her this pissed about me? Was it about Nathaniel? Hell, she'd never dated him. She'd never met him before he was already living with me.

'Do you want to be off this case?' Zerbrowski asked, voice low and suddenly not at all like Zerbrowski's voice.

'No,' she said, and she looked sullen, but surprised, as if she hadn't known that he had a voice like that in him. Me, neither.

He looked at her, it was a look to match that new voice. 'Then what should you be doing?'

She opened her mouth then closed it until her lips were a thin pink line. She turned on her sensible, two-inch heels and marched out.

Zerbrowski sighed loudly and frowned at me. 'What did you do to Arnet?'

'Me? Nothing.'

He gave me a look.

'I swear, I didn't do a damn thing to her.'

'Katie says Arnet was pretty pissed at something you said at the wedding.'

'How does Katie know she was pissed?'

His look got really narrow. 'You did say something, didn't you?'

I opened my mouth, closed it, and glanced down at the body. 'We're wasting time with all this personal shit,' I said. Okay, I also hadn't wanted to discuss my boyfriend situation with Zerbrowski, but we really did have a murderer to catch.

'True, but when this slows down, you fix this between you and Arnet.'

'Me? Why me?'

'Because you're not wicked pissed at her,' he said, and his face was as matter-of-fact as his words.

I wanted to argue with the logic, but as far as it went, it made sense. 'I'll do what I can. What did Abrahams tell you?'

'Arnet saw the blood under the door. They called backup and entered. Searched the place and didn't find one Avery Seabrook. The bed was unmade, and the blood trail seems to start in the bed.'

'Not in the bedroom, but the bed,' I said.

He nodded.

'Do we have an ident on her?'

Funny, he didn't ask who 'her' referred to. 'Purse is beside the bed with her neatly folded clothes. Sally Cook, age twenty-four, 5'3", and I never believe the weight on a woman's driver's license.'

'Yeah, women fudge the weight, but men will add an inch to their height.'

He grinned at me. 'Most of us just aren't smart enough to remember how tall we are.'

I smiled at him and resisted the urge to punch him on the shoulder. He can have that effect on me, even at murder scenes.

'I noticed you were doing fingertip push-ups looking at the body. You messed up our blood pattern.'

'I wasn't doing push-ups, and I touched as little as I could. But I know why she bled out, at least partly why.'

'Talk,' he said, he was starting to sound like Dolph. Not a bad a thing, just a little unnerving.

'She's got a partial bite mark on her very inner thigh. Looks like it punctured her femoral.'

'Why did you say "partial" bite mark? Either he bit her, or he didn't.'

I shrugged. 'He bit her, but it looks almost like he started, then either she jerked away, or he wasn't able to finish. For lack of a better analogy, it's like being bitten by a snake. If it's not poisonous, you're better off not jerking away. Vampire fangs are recurved, not as much as most snake teeth, but still, if you pull away abruptly, you're going to tear yourself up worse than if you just let it chew on you and try to pry it off, sort of gently.'

'It's instinct to pull away from something that's biting you, Anita.'

'I'm not arguing that, Zerbrowski, I'm only saying that it's not a good idea. You will tear yourself up.'

'So he bit her, and she pulled away, and that tore her femoral open. Are you saying he didn't mean to kill her?'

I shrugged. 'I'm saying that you can bleed out from your femoral in about twenty minutes, maybe less. Most people don't understand that.'

'Anita, don't do this to me.'

'Do what?' I asked.

'I saved the best for last. She's got a little case in there with what sure as hell looks like a stripper outfit to me. All fringes and not much else. If she's a stripper, then we've got one of our vampires. But you're standing here telling me that he didn't mean to kill her. If that's true, then he isn't one of our guys. I'm in the process of getting you a warrant of execution for his ass. I'd hate to have you killing the wrong guy.'

I shook my head. 'He was responsible for her death, Zerbrowski. The way the law is written, he's dead either way. If he's part of our serial killer team, he's dead. If he accidentally nicked her femoral and either didn't know enough to call 911, or panicked, or maybe dawn caught him before he could finish. It doesn't matter which it was, by accident or by design. The law says it's murder when a vampire kills a human being using its bite. There is no charge of manslaughter, if you're a vampire.'

Zerbrowski looked at me, and his eyes were very serious behind his wire rimmed glasses. 'You think it was an accident, don't you?'

I shrugged again. 'If he meant to rip her femoral open, I think the bite would be different, more vicious. I've seen a lot of vamp kills, Zerbrowski, a lot. This looks like a new vamp, a really new one, that doesn't know how to use its fangs yet. Someone who's two years dead shouldn't make mistakes like this.'

'So he did it on purpose.'

I sighed. 'I'm beginning to wonder what kind of education the little vampires at the Church of Eternal Life are getting.'

'What do you mean?'

'I mean, that I thought their mentoring system was like most of the wereanimals that I know. You teach the rookies how to hunt, how to kill, clean, and efficiently.'

'You confessing to something for your furry friends?' he asked, and he wasn't smiling enough for the comment, not for my peace of mind.

'Animals, Zerbrowski, animals. Jean-Claude hasn't brought over any new vamps since I've been hanging with him, but I've seen other vamps that were around two years dead, and they aren't rookies. They aren't experts, but this is a rookie mistake. Remember when Jack Benchely said that they'll give the vamps victims, but they make it clean and neat, and not fun?'

'Yeah.'

'What if feeding on the femoral, the inner thigh, is considered too taboo, too sexual for the Church to teach its members?'

'What do you mean?'

'You know the theory that if we don't tell teenagers about sex that they won't think of it on their own.'

'Yeah,' he said and smiled and shook his head, 'speaking as someone who was once a teenage boy, and who will one day have two teenagers on my hands, it's a nice theory, but it doesn't work that way.'

'Yeah, I know that, but what if the Church is like the right-wingers? If you don't talk about it, or tell the new little vamps about the dirty stuff, they won't do it, or think of it on their own.'

'Feeding from the inner thigh is too much like oral sex for the Church,' he said, and there was no teasing in his voice when he said it. He was working, thinking.

I nodded. 'Exactly.'

'But Avery, our newish vampire, did think of it, and did try it, but didn't know what he was doing.'

'Yes, and because he'd had no information, he didn't know how dangerous it could be. It's like the kids who came up pregnant in junior high, because they used candy bar wrappers for condoms.'

Zerbrowski looked at me. 'You're joking.'

'My hand to God, I am not making that up. The point is that if you don't educate the newly emerging vampire, just like the newly emerging teenager, you end up with them doing stupid shit. Dangerous things that get them or others, killed, or hurt. Ignorance is not bliss when it comes to basic sex ed, or beginning blood donations for vampires. Ignorance will get you killed in both.'

He looked down at the body. 'She fits the physical profile of the first vic. If you ignore the difference in height, she's even blond, which fits all three vics.'

'But this one's not a natural blond.'

Zerbrowski frowned at me.

'I don't mean that, I mean her roots are showing. I didn't really check that closely, but it looks like she either shaved everything, or had very little body hair to begin with. A lot of strippers shave.'

'Like your new boyfriend,' he said, his voice was mild, but his eyes weren't.

I shook my head. 'None of your damn business, Zerbrowski.'

'You guys were getting pretty cozy on the dance floor, but then he's living with you now, isn't he?'

'Somebody talks too much.'

'Hey, I'm a trained detective, I detected that you're shacking up with a stripper who's what, seven years younger than you?'

'As the detective in charge at the scene, shouldn't you be solving this murder?'

'I'm thinking. Teasing you always helps me think.'

'Glad to hear I inspire you. What are you thinking about?'

'I'm thinking that I want to talk to Avery Seabrook before he gets executed. If he's part of the other murders, then I want the names of his friends. If he did this by accident, then I think we need to know that, too. If you're right, and the Church isn't teaching basic vampire 101 safety to its members, then we've got hundreds of potential accidental deaths walking around out there tonight. That ain't good.'

'Legally, we can't do anything to force the church to change its teaching methods. Separation of Church and state, and all that.'

He nodded. 'I can't, and Federal Marshal Blake can't, but Anita Blake, sweetie to the Master of the City, might.'

'Are you encouraging me to encourage someone else to put undue pressure on an upstanding member of the community?'

'Would I do that?'

I nodded. 'Yep.'

'My head's sore,' he said, 'I give up. How the hell do we catch a vampire and hold him for questioning without getting anyone else killed?'

'He's only two years dead, Zerbrowski. He's not that big and bad.'

He glanced down at the body. 'Tell that to her.'

He had a point.

'If this was an accident, then he might, just might, run to the church for sanctuary or absolution, or whatever.'

'What if it wasn't an accident?'

'Then he's off joining up with his killer friends, and I have no idea where to start looking for him. We know his hunting ground is across the river in the clubs.'

Zerbrowski nodded. 'Sheriff Christopher, who you met, is putting all his men on alert. The Staties are helping out, trying to keep it low profile.'

'You're not going to keep it out of the media much longer.'

He shrugged. 'I know.'

'So if extra people are patrolling the clubs, then we can check out the other theory.'

'The church,' he said.

I nodded.

'I'll talk to Abrahams, let him know what's up. You go outside and make nice with Arnet.'

'Zerbrowski . . .'

'Do it, Anita, I don't have time to baby-sit any more feuds. You've got less than five minutes to fix this. I'd go outside and get started if I were you.' He had that strange un-Zerbrowski-like tone to his voice again. Not hostile, but no room to debate. It was a voice that expected to be obeyed, and strangely, I did. At least I went outside. I had no idea how to fix things with Arnet. You can't fix something until you know what's broke. I couldn't believe she was that pissed about not being able to date Nathaniel, and if it wasn't that, I was clueless. Yet another interpersonal relationship that I had no clue about. Was it just me, or are people really this confusing?

63

A GLANCE OUT the partially open door didn't show Arnet. There was a forest of uniformed officers, plain clothes, and the coroner's wagon complete with coroner waiting to take the body away. We were still waiting for the crime lab, CSU. It was rare for me to arrive on the scene this soon. I peeled off my bloody gloves at the door, but no one had set up a trash bag for debris. I ended up holding the gloves between two fingertips by a clean edge. Awkward, but I couldn't just drop them.

The newest dectective on the RPIT payroll came around the door frame with an open, but empty trash bag in his gloved hands. His name was Smith and I'd met him once at a crime scene long ago when he was in uniform. It had actually been one of the very first times I'd met Nathaniel. Smith had been comfortable enough around the lycanthropes that I'd remembered it. Remembered it enough to tell Dolph. Apparently, Dolph had remembered it, too. Seeing Smith in plain clothes had been a reminder that Dolph didn't really think I was evil, and might even still value my opinion.

He smiled at me. 'Looks like I'm just in time.' He held the bag open so I could drop the gloves in.

I smiled back. 'The nick of time.'

Zerbrowski yelled, 'Smith!'

Smith moved toward Zerbrowski with the bag still in his hands. He was the newest detective on the squad, and that meant he was their version of a grunt. It wasn't as bad as being a uniformed rookie, but it was still low man on the totem pole. I walked outside without waiting to see what Zerbrowski wanted Smith for. Not my problem. No, my problem was waiting outside.

I actually expected Arnet to be somewhere in the hallway with all the extra personel, but she wasn't. I went down the stairs and out the glass doors of the little entryway. She had taken Zerbrowski literally, or maybe she really needed the air. The October night was soft, warmer than last night, but still cool enough to feel like autumn. The air tasted like it was time to go somewhere and pick apples.

Arnet was sitting on the curb. The halogen light was bright enough that her pantsuit still looked the same shade of brownish burgundy that it had in the apartment. I would have looked sickly in the color, but it brought out highlights in her short hair that you didn't see when she wore black or navy. She had her arms around her knees, not exactly clutching them, but obviously not happy even from a distance.

I took a deep breath, let it out, and kept walking toward her. I so didn't want to do this. I stopped short of her, and said, 'Is this seat taken?'

She jumped and glanced back at me. She scrubbed at her face, trying to hide tears. 'Oh, great,' she said, 'just great. You catch me crying. Now you must think I really am a loser.'

She hadn't said I could sit down, but she hadn't said I couldn't either. I decided to take it, and sat down. Close enough to talk privately without being overheard, but not so close that I invaded her personal space more than I could help it. Sitting down on the curb, I was happy that I was wearing jeans, jogging shoes, and a T-shirt. They were perfect curb-sitting clothes.

'What's wrong, Arnet?' I asked.

'Nothing.'

'Okay, why are you mad at me?'

She glanced sort of sideways at me. 'Why do you care?'

'Because we have to work together.'

'You know, almost any other woman would have led into this conversation. Chatted a little.'

'Zerbrowski said I had less than five minutes. I don't have time to chat.'

'Why less than five minutes?'

'We're going on a road trip.'

'Do you know where Avery Seabrook is?'

'No, but I thought of people to ask.'

She looked away from me and shook her head. 'And how did you come up with people to ask? Not through police work.'

I frowned, but she couldn't see it. 'What's that supposed to mean?'

She licked her lips, hesitated, then said, 'I could work for years as a cop on this kind of crime, and I wouldn't have your insight into the monsters.' She looked at me sideways again, but this time she held the look. 'Do I have to fuck the monsters to be as good at this as you are?'

I gave her wide eyes. 'Please tell me that you are not this pissed just because I'm dating Nathaniel and you don't get to.'

'I saw you at the club last night.'

There was a time in my life where I would have said, Guilty Pleasures, but the time when I would volunteer information was past. 'What club?' I asked.

Her eyes were suddenly cop eyes, maybe a little more hostile than they needed to be, but cold and looking at me as if she could see into my head. It was part lie and part truth. She didn't know as much as that look seemed to say, but she probably knew more than I wanted her to.

'Don't play games, Anita.'

Oh, goody we were going to have a fight on a first-name basis. 'I'm not very good at games, Jessica, so I don't play them much.'

Her hands gripped her knees tighter. I think to keep from gripping me. 'Fine, Guilty Pleasures. I saw you at Guilty Pleasures last night.'

My face showed nothing, because she'd given me plenty of time to brace for it. I just blinked at her and had a slight smile on my face.

Pleasant, empty, on the outside. Inside I was thinking hard. How much had she seen at the club? How much did she remember? Had she been there for Primo's part of the show?

I almost said, I didn't see you, but stopped myself. I wasn't going to help her fill in any blanks. 'So, you saw me at Guilty Pleasures. I'm dating the owner.'

She looked away then, off toward the parked cars and beyond that a news van. The uniform that was still putting up yellow crime scene tape to help block off the parking area paused and looked at the van. Would someone warn Zerbrowski?

Arnet turned and yelled, 'Marconi, go tell Zerbrowski we've got a news van.'

Marconi said, 'Shiiit,' with real feeling to it, and went for the entryway.

Great, it was like all I had to do was think and someone else did it for me. Cool. I would try to use this power only for good.

She looked back at me. 'How can you be dating him and Nathaniel at the same time?'

'Just lucky, I guess.'

If looks could have hurt me, that one would have. 'That's not an answer, that's an evasion.'

I sighed. 'Look, Jessica, I don't owe you an answer to that particular question. Who I date, and why, or how, is none of your business.'

Her hazel eyes got dark, almost solid brown. I realized it was her eyes' version of going black with rage. 'I thought I'd go down and see Nathaniel without you there. I thought maybe if you weren't there to interfere . . .' She looked away then, stared out at the parked cars and the gawkers being kept back by the uniforms. Stared at them as if she were really seeing them, which I doubted. It was just somewhere for her eyes to go, while she talked.

'But you were there. Oh, my God, were you there.' Her voice broke, not with tears, but with emotion. I didn't understand this depth of emotion from her.

'You're acting like I stole Nathaniel from you. You never dated him. Hell, when you met him, he was already living with me.'

She looked at me then, and it was unnerving to see the anger, because I didn't understand it. 'But I didn't know that. You let me believe that he was just your friend. He let me believe it.'

'Nathaniel likes to be nice to people.'

'Is that what you call it?'

'Look, Arnet, sometimes Nathaniel flirts without really meaning to. I think it's like an occupational hazard.'

'You mean because he's a stripper.'

I nodded. 'Yeah.'

'I didn't know what he did for a living until the wedding reception. I should have known he was some kind of hustler.'

That pissed me off. 'He isn't a hustler.'

'The hell he's not. I've got a friend in juvie. He was picked up for prostitution twice before he hit fifteen. Male prostitution,' she said the last like it made it all somehow worse.

I hadn't actually known he'd been picked up for it, but I didn't give her that. 'I know what Nathaniel was doing before he got off the streets.' Which was sort of true and sort of not true, but not completely a lie.

'Did you save him? Did you see him and take him home? Are you his sugar mama?'

'Sugar mama. You made that up. That's not really a word.'

She had the grace to look embarrassed. I almost got a smile out of her, but she fought it off. 'Whatever you want to call it. Are you? Is he your . . .'

I didn't help her. If she was going to say it, I wanted her to say it. 'My what?' I asked, and my voice was a few octaves lower, cold, clear. It was a voice that, if you knew me, you might worry when you heard it.

If Arnet was worried, it didn't show. 'Gigolo,' she said. She threw the word in my face like it was something solid and hurtful, as if she'd thrown a fist at me.

I laughed, and she didn't like it.

'What's so damned funny? I saw you on stage with him, Blake. I saw what you did to him. You and that vampire of yours.'

I gave her wide eyes then, because I finally thought I had a glimmer of why she was so pissed at me. 'Are you under the impression that I whisked Nathaniel off the streets as a child and made him my boy-whore?'

She looked away then. 'When you say it like that, it sounds stupid.'

'Yeah,' I said.

She turned back to me, still angry. 'I saw what you did to him last night. You chained him up. You hurt him. You humiliated him in front of all those people.'

It was my turn to look off into the distance, because I was trying to think how to explain without explaining too much. I was also wondering if I even owed Jessica Arnet an explanation. If we didn't need to work together, and I hadn't been afraid she'd share what she'd seen with the rest of RPIT, I might not have explained anything, but we did work together, and I didn't want her version getting around the squad room. Not that my version was going to be that much better if it got spread around. At their core, most policemen are closet, or not so closet, conservatives.

How do you explain color to the blind? How to explain that pain can be pleasure to someone who isn't wired that way? You can't, not really, but I tried anyway.

'It took me a long time to understand what Nathaniel wanted from me.'

She looked at me, horrified. 'You're going to blame him? You're going to blame the victim?'

This was not going to go well. 'Have you ever met someone who's been blind from birth?'

She frowned at me. 'What?'

'Someone who's never seen color, ever.'

'No,' she said, 'but what does that have to do with Nathaniel?'

'You're blind, Jessica, how do I explain to you what blue looks like?'

'What are you babbling about?' she asked.

'How do I explain to you that Nathaniel enjoyed being on stage, that he sort of forced the situation on me?'

'*You're* the victim, please, you weren't chained up.'

I shrugged. 'I'm saying there was no victim on stage last night, just a bunch of consenting adults.'

She was shaking her head. 'No, I know what I saw.'

'You know what you would have felt if it had been you chained on stage and treated like that, and you're assuming that because that's how you would feel, that that's how everyone would feel. Not everyone feels the same way about things.'

'I know that. I'm not a child.'

'Then stop acting like one.'

She stood up then and stared down at me, her hands in fists at her sides. 'I am not acting like a child.'

'You're right, you're being way too judgmental to be a child.'

Zerbrowski called, 'Anita, we need to roll.'

I stood up, brushed off the back of my jeans, and yelled, 'I'm coming.' I looked at Arnet and tried to think of anything that would make this better. Nothing came to mind. 'Nathaniel is my sweetie, Jessica, I would never hurt him.'

'I saw you hurt him,' she said, and she sort of threw the words at me like she had the word *gigolo*.

'He doesn't see it that way.'

'He doesn't know any better,' she said.

I smiled and fought the urge to give one of those laughs that is half nerves and half exasperation. 'You want to save him. You want to ride in and save him from a life of degradation.'

She didn't say anything, just glared at me.

'Anita, we need to go, now,' Zerbrowski yelled. He was standing in the open door of his car.

I glanced back at Arnet. 'I thought Nathaniel needed saving once, too, needed me to fix him. What I didn't understand is that he isn't broken, well, not more broken than the rest of us.' And that was probably more truth than I owed Detective Jessica Arnet. I left it at that, and jogged for Zerbrowski's car. He asked me how it had gone with Arnet. I told him it could have gone better.

'How better?' He asked as we eased past the news van and a crowd of gawkers.

'Oh, like the Valentine's Day Massacre could have been a better party.'

He gave me a look. 'Jesus, Anita, it isn't enough that you and Dolph are pissed at each other, you've got pick a fight with Arnet?'

'I didn't pick a fight with either of them. You know I didn't pick one with Dolph.' We were easing past the tape and barriers that the uniforms had moved for us. The television crew had the camera pointed straight at us. Great. I resisted the urge to give them the finger, or something else equally childish.

'I shouldn't have said that about Dolph. I know you didn't start that.'

'Thanks.'

'What's eating Arnet?'

'If she wants you to know, she'll tell you.'

'You're not going to tell your version first?'

'No one ever believes my version, Zerbrowski. I'm fucking coffin bait. If you'll fuck vampires, you'll do anything, right?' And just like that, I started to cry. Not loud, but tears, real tears. I turned away and stared out the window. I had no idea why I was crying. Stupid, so stupid.

Did I really care what Arnet thought of me? No. Did I care if she trashed my reputation to the rest of the squad? Yeah, I guess I did. Shit.

Zerbrowski was either so astounded that I was crying that he didn't know what to say, or he was treating me like he'd treat any other cop. If they don't want you to see them cry, you don't see it. Zerbrowski drove to the Church of Eternal Life, concentrating on the road like a son of a bitch. I stared out the window the entire time, and cried.

64

THE PARKING LOT was full, and I mean full. So full that Zerbrowski parked in front of the church in the fire only zone. We had Marconi and Smith in a car behind us, along with two marked cars. Apparently, Zerbrowski had been planning our strategy while I was trying to fix things with Arnet. Apparently, Abrahams or Arnet had been left in charge of the murder scene. I was betting on Abrahams. I wouldn't have left Arnet in charge of a little league team tonight. Of course, I might have been a little prejudiced right that moment.

He had two uniforms station themselves at the doors, and he told them to get their holy items out. 'Nobody leaves, unless you clear it with me, is that clear?' It was clear. I suggested that there was another door at the parish hall entrance, and since we had enough manpower to cover it, Zerbrowski just nodded and said, 'Do it.' It was like he was channeling Dolph, but it worked. Everyone just did what he said.

Marconi shook his head and said what I'd been thinking. 'Commanding presence tonight, Zerbrowski.'

'You're just jealous that he's better at channeling Dolph than you are,' I said.

Marconi smiled at me and gave a nod. But his hand was at his belt, and he was moving his gun a little more forward. Sometimes the more jokes you do, the more nervous you are.

Smith was new enough that his eyes were all sparkly, and he was almost vibrating with eagerness, like a dog straining at a leash. He hadn't been a detective for a month yet, and that can make you eager to prove yourself. I hoped not too eager, since I'd recommended him.

Zerbrowski noticed and gave me a nod, like he'd keep an eye on him. He asked my advice about only one thing. 'Do we go in bold, or quiet?'

I thought about it for a second, then shrugged. 'They know we're here, Zerbrowski, at least the ones near the back.'

'They can hear us?'

I nodded. 'But let's ask an usher near the back to get Malcolm's attention. Being polite doesn't cost a thing.'

He nodded, then went to the big, polished, wood doors. Before he could push them open, a man opened them from inside. He was young with short brown hair and glasses. I'd seen him before on another case. His name began with a *B*, like Brandon, or Brian, or Bruce, or something. *Bruce*, I thought. He eased the door shut behind him, before we had more than a glimpse of people turning to stare. His brown eyes were still lovely behind his glasses, and there was still healing bite marks on his neck. It was as if no time had passed, but it was nice to know that he was still among the living.

'You are interrupting our worship service.' His voice was soft, measured.

'You're Bruce, right?'

His eyes widened just a little. 'I'm surprised you remembered me, Ms Blake.'

'Marshal Blake, actually,' I smiled when I said it.

His eyes did that little widening act again. 'Do I say congratulations?'

'Is he stalling?' Zerbrowski asked.

'Not in the way you mean,' I said. 'He doesn't want us to interrupt the services, but I don't think he'd deliberately hide a murderer.'

That got me another eye widening. 'Murderer? What are you

talking about, Ms Marshal Blake? We of the church do not advocate violence in any aspect of our lives.'

'There's a dead woman in the home of one of your members who would argue that, if she could,' Zerbrowski said.

A pained expression crossed Bruce's face. 'Are you certain that it is the home of one of our members?'

We both nodded.

Bruce looked down at the ground, then nodded, as if he'd decided something. 'If you will remain near the back of the church, I will tell Malcolm what has happened.'

Zerbrowski looked at me as if to ask if that was okay. I shrugged and nodded. 'Sure.'

Bruce smiled, obviously relieved. 'Good, good, please keep your voices low. This is a church, and we are having services.' He led the way through those highly polished doors. The uniforms stayed outside, but Marconi and Smith followed us in.

There was no vestibule inside the doors. The doors led directly into the nave, so we were just suddenly facing pews packed full of congregation members. The vamps close to the doors were already glancing our way.

Bruce motioned for us to stay where we were, then walked wide around the pews up the side underneath the red and blue abstract stained glass windows. Where there should have been saints or the stations of the cross, or at least a cross or two, there was nothing but the bare white walls. I think that was why the church always looked unfinished to me, naked like the walls needed clothes.

It's never comfortable for me to be standing in front of a group of people unexpectedly. To be on display, especially when it's a potentially hostile group. Zerbrowski had his smile in place, the good-to-meet-you smile. The one that I'd finally realized was his version of a blank face. Marconi looked bored. A lot of cops perfect that I've-seen-worse boredom after a few years on the force. Smith's face was all shiny with excitement like a kid on Christmas morning. He was looking around at everything and totally not bothered by the staring crowd. I guess most cops don't get to see inside the Church of Eternal Life much, or see hundreds of vampires in one place at one time. Hell, even I didn't usually see that many at one time in one place.

The first few pews had had their look-see at us, but the glances spread upward from there. Quick glances with whispers, so it was like a wind moved through the room. A wind that turned faces toward us, widened eyes, sent more furious whispers spreading through the room, until it crashed against the pulpit and the strangely empty altar area at the front of the church.

Malcolm was standing at the white altar, but had already stepped out from behind it and moved to one side so he could meet Bruce, as the young man came up to one side of the raised area. Even the steps leading up to it were white. The only color was a strip of blue cloth that hung in the back of the sanctuary. A brilliant royal blue that moved slightly in the central air, as if the cloth didn't sit flat to the wall. I wondered what was behind the cloth. It was the only thing that was different since I'd last been inside the building, some three years ago. About two years ago, the building had been fire-bombed by right-wing extremists. The attack hadn't stopped the church. The attack had gotten the Church of Eternal Life some of its best national and international coverage ever, and donations had flooded in from people that were not so much for vampires as against violence. I'd seen what had been left when the fire department had gotten through with the building. Standing here now, I would never have known there had ever been even a small fire in this white, white space, let alone a bomb.

Malcolm spoke with Bruce at the side of the altar area. I wasn't at all surprised when he came down the wide main aisle between the pews. Bruce trailed after him. The first thing you notice about Malcolm is that his short blond curls are the bright yellow of goldfinch feathers. Three hundred plus years in the dark will do that to bright blond hair. The next thing is, he's tall, and almost painfully thin, so that he looks even taller than he truly is. He was wearing a black suit tonight, modest cut, but thanks to Jean-Claude's fashion sense, I knew that that simple-seeming suit was tailored to that lean body, and probably cost more than most people make in a month. The shirt was a blue that helped point out that his eyes were the blue of a robin's eggs. His tie was narrow and black with a silver tie bar, unadorned. Up close once you can look past the hair and the eyes, Malcolm has a very angular face, almost a homely face, as if the angles needed smoothing out to make them work together.

The first time I'd ever set eyes on Malcolm I'd thought him beautiful, but with even one vampire mark on me, I'd known differently. He prided himself on not using his vampire powers on us mere mortals, but he wasted enough to make himself seem handsome. That bit of mind-fucking he allowed himself. Vanity, all is vanity.

I'd also thought him one of the most powerful vampires in St Louis once; now as he moved toward me, he seemed somehow diminished. Or maybe I was just shielding too well now for his power to creep over me. Maybe.

He held out one of his big hands, which always seemed like they should belong on a beefier body. He held it out sort of in between Zerbrowski and me, as if he wasn't sure who was in charge and didn't want to offend anyone. The last time I'd seen Malcolm he hadn't offered to shake hands. He'd known I wouldn't take it.

Tonight, I took his hand, because Zerbrowski was only human, and whatever I was, *only human* didn't cover it.

Malcolm hesitated in the middle of the handshake, as if I'd surprised him, but he recovered, smiling, his blue eyes glowing with pleasure at the opportunity to help the police. It was a lie. He didn't want us here. He certainly didn't want a murder involving his church. I felt nothing as our hands touched, except that he was cool, so he hadn't fed recently. Other than that, I felt nothing, because I was shielding. I'd gotten really good at shielding lately. I realized that I'd been shielding almost as hard as I could since Jean-Claude,

Richard, and I had bound ourselves together in that bed. It wasn't just guilt that had made me afraid. So Malcolm's hand was just a hand, cooler than human normal, but just a hand. Good.

I think we would have been fine if Malcolm hadn't tried a little vampire power on me. Maybe I was shielding too much, hiding too much of what I was, or maybe he was simply that arrogant. Whatever, he pulsed a little power down his hand into mine.

I was dizzy for a second, and he got an image of the dead girl in the apartment before I pushed back. I was still a little fuzzy on the whole psychic thing. I tend to overcompensate when I feel attacked. Yeah, I know, of course I overcompensated. It was so terribly me.

Malcolm stumbled back, and only my grip on his hand kept him on his feet. His eyes were wide, his mouth open in a little *O* of surprise. If he had just been some powerful vamp that tried to mind-fuck me, then I'd have taught him his lesson, and we'd have gone on about our investigation, but he was their master. I learned something in those few seconds, something I hadn't guessed. Every human in the Church had a mentor, and I'd assumed their vampire mentors were the ones that would bring them over when the time came. I knew the mentors took blood from their human trainees, but when push came to shove, Malcolm did those last three bites. Malcolm had brought over most of those hundreds, personally. Which meant when I shoved my power into him, it went through him like some huge sword. Through him and into the rest.

It was as if I could suddenly touch them, as if my hand shot through Malcolm's palm, through him, and into their bodies. I felt their pulses, some hearts, some wrists, some necks. I felt the pulse of all those vampires, felt it sluggish and oh, so slow. So long, so long since some of them had fed as they were meant to feed. He didn't let them hunt. He didn't even let them go to the clubs and take willing food there. I saw an endless stream of Church members garbed in white, like virgin sacrifices, offering their necks. Only taking a little blood, just enough blood, never enough to be satisfied, just enough not to die.

I saw the thick viscous punch in the parish hall, and I knew that it contained just a little blood from at least three different vamps. Malcolm made sure of that. He didn't want to accidentally blood oath them to someone else. But he never used his own blood, for fear of what it would mean.

Malcolm jerked away from me, but it was too late. I didn't need him anymore.

I looked past him at a girl with long dark hair and glasses. It was the first vampire I'd ever seen with glasses. She grabbed her chest, and I knew why. Her heart was beating. But I saw other things. I saw that once she'd been human here, and she'd knelt and given herself over, but it was a thing of chaste hands on her covered shoulders. No one had ever held her close, gripped her against their bodies, fed so powerfully that her body bucked against them, and sex was a pale thing compared to it.

'Stop it,' Malcolm said, 'stop it, let them go!'

I turned slowly to look at him, and whatever he saw in my face made him take a step back. 'You gave them to me,' I said, and my voice had a slow, honeyed feel to it. Power, such power. I'd learned only last night that vampires could act as a sort of witch's familiar to me. I'd thought it needed to be a vampire that I had some connection with, but I was wrong. I could feed on them all, use them like some kind of giant undead battery.

Zerbrowski came up close to me, though even he shivered when he was close enough to whisper, 'Anita, what's happening?'

'He tried to use vampire powers to find out what I knew,' I said in that same slow, luxurious voice. It was as if my voice was something you could hold in your mouth and suck, like candy. Jean-Claude's trick, and the thought was enough. He was suddenly aware of me, and what was happening. But most of what was happening, he needed to know. He was the Master of the City, not Malcolm. He had tolerated the treaty that the old master had made before her death, but now . . . well, we'd see. But that was for another night. This night was about murder.

'Are you hurt?' Zerbrowski asked. He sounded like he didn't think so, but knew something was wrong.

'No,' I said, 'no, I'm not hurt.' I thought, *if I can feel some of their emotions, if I can look into their faces and see memories, what else can I do?*

I thought, *Avery, Avery, where are you?* I felt an answer, like a small play of wind against my face. I turned toward that wind, and the left-hand side of pews. 'Avery, Avery, Avery.' I spoke his name, each time a little louder, not yelling, but with force in it.

A vampire stood up in the middle of a row. He was average height, with short brown hair, and a face that was handsome in a soft, unfinished way, as if he'd been barely legal when they killed him.

I held out my hand to him. 'Avery, come to me, come to me, Avery, come to me.'

He started to push his way through the crowd of other people. A hand grabbed his wrist, a human woman shaking her head, saying, 'Don't go.'

He jerked away from her, and I heard his voice as if he'd been standing next to me. 'I have to go, she's calling me.' And he turned eyes to me that were lost in vampire light, burning like brown glass in the sun, but the look on his face was one I'd only seen on humans. Humans that were bespelled by vampires. Humans that couldn't say, no.

Malcolm's rich voice filled the room. 'Children, stop him, stop him from answering her call. She's is the Master of the City's whore. She will corrupt our Avery.'

I have to say the whore comment pissed me off. I turned to Malcolm, and I let my anger fill my voice. '*I'll* corrupt them? My God, you've ruined them all. You stole their mortal lives, for what, Malcolm? *For what?*' I yelled the last, and the words held heat like the wind from some great fire.

All those little vampires that were still held on the lines of my power cried out. I'd hurt them, and I hadn't meant to. I tried to make it up to them, and the problem was that the anger was mine, but I wasn't very good at comforting people. But Jean-Claude was, in a way. It was that old, old problem of his and his line of vampires. If the only tool you have is a hammer, all your problems begin to look like nails. If the only tools you have are seduction and terror, and you're trying to be nice . . . well, there you go.

65

I COULD TASTE their pulses on my tongue. Not just one, but hundreds, as if I'd suddenly had a truckload of candy shoved in my mouth. Candy that was hard and sweet and melted slow across my tongue, but it wasn't just cherry, or grape, or root beer. It was like a thousand different flavors filled my mouth, so that instead of being delicious, it was overwhelming.

I couldn't pick one flavor, one pulse to follow. I literally couldn't pick just one, because I couldn't sort them out. I was choking on too many choices. Until I could choose one thread to follow, I couldn't swallow any of them. I collapsed to my knees, drowning in a thousand different scents, different skins. I could smell their skin, that wonderful smell at the side of the neck where the skin smells sweetest when you're in love. But it was a different scent for each neck: aftershave, perfume, cologne, soap, sweat. It was as if I'd walked up to each of them and put my face just above their skin – close enough to kiss – and breathed in the scent of them.

Zerbrowski was beside me, his gun out, but not pointed at anyone, sort of ceilingward. 'Anita, what's wrong? Did he hurt you?'

Who, I thought? Who was *he*? There were so many 'hes.' Which one did he mean?

I tried to swallow past all those pulses in my mouth, but I couldn't. I couldn't get this bite down. It was too much.

Jean-Claude's voice was in my head. '*Ma petite*, you must choose.'

I managed to think, 'Can't.'

'Who did you go there to find?' he asked.

Who did I go there to find? That was a good question. Who? It all went back to who.

Zerbrowski grabbed my arm, hard. 'Anita! I need you here. What's happening?'

He needed me. I saw Smith and Marconi both with weapons drawn. They needed me, because they couldn't feel it. I had to function, to think, to speak, or things were going to get out of hand. I was a federal marshal tonight, I had to remember that. I remembered something else, something that had been washed away in all that scent.

Avery, I needed Avery. I thought the name, and just like that, it was his pulse on my tongue. His skin smelled like cologne, something expensive so that it was powdery and sweet, almost like good perfume, but underneath that was sweat. He hadn't showered tonight. The thought made me wonder what else besides sweat he hadn't washed away. It was as if I was close to him again, as if my face passed down his body just above his skin. My breath was warm against his skin and helped blow the scents back from his skin to my nose, my mouth. I didn't simply smell the scents down his body, I tasted them. A faint taste, as if smell was the more important, but smell and taste were aligned differently than ever before. More intimately, somehow. That part wasn't Jean-Claude's power, but Richard's and I fought not to think of him, not to open the links between us farther than they were already. I did not want Richard in my head right now.

Jean-Claude let me know without words, or if with words, it was too quick to register, like a kind of telepathic shorthand, that he would guard me from Richard. He would not let me drown in still more sensation. But it was thanks to closer ties with Richard that I could smell and taste my way down Avery's body and enjoy it, or rather not be disgusted by it. Wolves, like dogs, do not think of scent and taste as a human does. They like it when we smell like live things. Avery had had sex and hadn't cleaned up afterward. I wasn't disturbed by that, more curious, because, thanks to Jean-Claude's marks and my own power, I knew Avery was as neat and meticulous in his person as he was in his housekeeping.

Zerbrowski squeezed my arm hard enough to bruise. 'Anita, damn it, we can't shoot him. The warrant doesn't have our name on it. We're not executioners. Anita, wake up!'

I blinked at him and saw Avery standing just on the other side of him. Marconi had stepped up and had his gun pressed against Avery's chest. Avery wasn't doing anything threatening, just standing and trying to walk forward against the press of the gun. He was trying to come to me. His face wasn't empty like a zombie's, in fact he was smiling, and so very present in his skin, but I'd called him, and even a gun barrel against his heart hadn't stopped that order.

'Stop,' I said.

Avery stopped trying to move forward and just stood there, waiting. He stared down at me with a look that only your best boyfriend should have given you, but I didn't mind. I wanted to pull his shirt out of his pants and rub his skin along mine. It was sexual, true, but it was also that urge that makes dogs roll in smelly stuff. It just smelled so good, and I could carry the scent with me and explore it at my leisure. I knew in that moment that wolves and dogs collect scents the way people collect rocks or houseplants – just because they like them, and they think they're pretty. Some smells just make you happy like a favorite color; the fact that sweat and stale sex was 'pretty' to that part of me that was Richard was a puzzle for another day. Now, I just tried not to question it too closely and not to do physically what I'd already done metaphysically.

'I'm alright, Zerbrowski.' But my voice was distant and lazy with power. That I couldn't help, but when he pulled me to my feet, I was able to stand. Yea for me. I took a step forward and said, 'It's okay, Marconi, I told him to come to me.'

Marconi had a funny look on his face. 'Not out loud you didn't.'

I shrugged. 'Sorry about that.' But I wasn't looking at Marconi, I was looking at Avery. I was looking at him like you'd gaze on a lover, but it was all tied up with food, and smell, and things that were so nonhuman that I was having trouble processing them. I wanted to scent mark him. He was mine. I wanted to wrap his scent on my body and think about those smells and what they meant. It was as if scent was like a photograph of a murder scene. I could carry it around and 'look' at it over and over again, think about it. The sense of smell had jumped from somewhere near the bottom of my sensory list to just behind visual, and the only thing that kept it lower than sight was that I was too much a primate to trust my nose that much.

'Put up your guns,' Zerbrowski said, 'welcome to the wide world of weird vampire shit.' He didn't sound happy, but I didn't look to see what face went with the tone, because that would have meant looking away from Avery, and I didn't want to do that.

He was a little clean-cut for my taste. His hair was a soft, medium brown, cut short the way a father or grandfather would cut it. The male hairstyle that has never really gone out of style for fifty years. His eyes matched his hair – a soft brown. His eyebrows were darker than his hair and arched in that way that men's eyebrows will, perfectly, while most women have to pluck for that line above the eye. He didn't have enough eyelashes, but they seemed thicker than they were because they were dark. His face was a soft oval, only the dark scattering of beard stubble saving him from looking even younger than he was. He was almost six feet, but seemed shorter, though I wasn't sure why. Everything about him said that here was someone who'd never had anything too bad happen to him. It wasn't just his face and coloring that was soft and undramatic; it was him. He had that flavor in my head of someone who'd never really been tested. How did you get to be a vampire and not lose that soft edge?

I got sadness from him, but he didn't feel like someone who had just killed a woman, on purpose, or by accident. Was I wrong? Or had he not been the only vampire in that spotless apartment?

Avery stood in front of me with a look that was sad, so sad. Did he know? Had he done it?

There was a knock on the church doors. The sound startled all of us, I think. You just didn't knock on the doors of a church. You came in, or you didn't, but you didn't knock. A voice called, 'Sergeant Zerbrowski?'

Zerbrowski went to the door and peeked out. When he came back through the door, he had a piece of paper in his hand. It was thicker than it used to be, but most of the additions were things that would keep me out of jail and wouldn't do a damn thing for Avery's health.

Zerbrowski came toward me holding out the paper. I opened it up and read it, though I already knew what it was. It was my warrant of execution. The days when any vampire hunter would kill someone without seeing the warrant first were past, but I'd gotten cautious sooner than some. I'd also never been successfully sued. One of our fellow hunters was still in prison for doing his job before the paperwork came through. Everyone who worked with me knew that without this little piece of paper, there was no vampire hunt. With it, I had almost carte blanche.

I scanned it. It was pretty standard. I could legally hunt down and execute the vampire, or vampires, responsible for – I read the names of the victims. It helped me focus. Helped me remember why I was doing this kind of work – and any other murder victims that might follow. I was empowered to use any force necessary to find and stop the murderers of these people. I was further empowered to do anything within my abilities to execute this warrant with all due haste. The bearer of this warrant is allowed to enter any and all buildings in pursuit of the suspects. Any person, or persons, human or otherwise that stand in the way of the lawful execution of my duty, forfeit their rights under the Constitution of these United States and the State of Missouri. There was other legalese, but what it all boiled down to was that I could have turned back to Avery, put a gun to his head, pulled the trigger, and not only would the police not stop me, but legally, they had to help me carry out my duty.

The entire idea of warrants of execution was drafted when

vampires had first gotten legal rights, and you couldn't kill them on sight just for being vampires. The warrant had seemed like a step up once, now I looked at it, and thought, *Huh*. What if Avery hadn't done it? What if he was innocent?

I looked at Zerbrowski, and he knew me well enough to frown. 'I don't the like that look. It always means you're about to complicate my job.'

I smiled at him and nodded. 'Sorry, but I'd like to make sure that I'm serving the warrant on the right vampires.'

Malcolm came forward. 'I would like to see that warrant, if it concerns my church and my followers.'

I fished it out, flung it open, but held on to it.

His eyes flicked down the page, and he shook his head. 'And you call *us* monsters.'

'Don't take it personally, Malcolm, some of my best friends are monsters.' I folded the warrant up and tucked it away.

'How can you make jokes, when you have come here to kill one of us?'

The congregation stirred and started to stand. There were hundreds of them and only a handful of us. This could get out of hand, and I didn't want that. Legally, if anyone interfered, then I could kill them, too. The last thing I wanted on my hands was a church full of martyrs.

It was as if Malcolm read my mind, or I read his, because he moved toward the door. Marconi stopped him with a hand up, not quite touching.

'We don't want any trouble,' Zerbrowski said, 'and you don't either, Malcolm.'

'Am I supposed to simply let you escort one of my congregation out of here, knowing that you could make him kneel in the parking lot and execute him? What kind of person would I be to simply stand by and let that happen?'

Shit, I thought.

'Who are you here for?' Avery said, and his voice was like the rest of him – soft, uncertain. Was it an act?

'You for starters,' I said.

His brown eyes went wide. 'Why?'

'If you try to take him, we will stand in front of the door. You will have to climb over our bodies to take him with you.'

I glanced at Malcolm, and I knew that he didn't mean it. He was gambling. Gambling that we wouldn't be willing to climb over the bodies of church members to execute this warrant here and now. Gambling that we'd go away and get Avery some other time. Usually I like having the warrant fast, but tonight it would have worked better to get it later, and not in front of the undead Billy Graham and his flock.

Zerbrowski looked at me. 'You're the vampire hunter, Anita, it has to be your call.'

'Thanks,' I said, but I had an idea. I could still taste Avery. He hit my radar as innocent, could I find out? Malcolm had tried to pull specific knowledge from me, and I'd turned it back on him. I'd gained knowledge from his vampires. I'd gotten very specific images about how they fed, and lived. Could I concentrate and get something even more specific? It felt like I could. It felt like, if I touched Avery, I could know anything in his head, his body, his soul. That if I touched him, he'd be mine, mine in a way that until tonight I hadn't wanted. Suddenly it wasn't such a bad thought.

I leaned into Zerbrowski and whispered, 'I can feel him in my head. I think I can find out what he saw last night.'

'How?'

I shrugged. 'Weird necromancy stuff, metaphysics, magic, whatever you want to call it.'

'The warrant does not allow you to use magic on my people.'

I looked at Malcolm; it was beginning not to be a friendly look. 'I am allowed to use whatever force or abilities I deem necessary. So, yeah, I can do magic, if it gets the job done.'

'I will not allow you to bespell him.'

'Has it occurred to you that I don't want to kill him if he didn't do it? If I take his heart and his head, then we find out he's innocent tomorrow, what am I supposed to do, say, "Sorry, oops"?' I was getting angry again. I took a deep breath and counted slowly to five. I didn't have the patience for ten. 'I don't want to kill him, Malcolm.' That last wasn't angry, that last sounded almost like a plea.

Malcolm looked at me, and it was a look I hadn't seen before. He was trying to decide if I was lying. 'I feel your regret, Anita. You grow tired of the killing, just as I did.'

See, that's the problem with vampires, you let them into your head an inch, and they take a metaphysical mile. I didn't like that he could read me like that, especially not with my shields up. Of course, I wasn't sure how far up my shields were. Had I dropped them to taste the vampires? I thought about my shields, and yeah, they'd dropped, or had been breached under a wave of smells and tastes and blood flowing in sluggish veins. I started to raise the shields back up, but I had something to do first.

I looked at Malcolm. 'I'm going to touch Avery. I'm going to look inside him and see what I can see. I am not going to hurt him, not on purpose. I want the truth, Malcolm, that's all. Give me your word that if he's guilty, you'll let me take him.'

'How will I know what you discover from him?'

I smiled, and again it wasn't a pleasant smile. 'When I tell you to, *if* I tell you to, touch me, and you'll know what I know.'

He looked at me, and I looked at him. We had one of those moments of unspoken questions. I knew that he'd tried to get information about a vampire murder when he shook my hand. There were states where that alone would get him put on a short list, a list of vampires that were getting dangerous. I knew what he'd done, and I had a warrant that allowed me enough leeway that I could pretend he was trying to hide his own involvement with the killings. I mean, there'd never be a trial. I would never have to prove my suspicions in court.

Malcolm took a breath deep enough to make his shoulders rock up and down. He nodded, once, short, curt, and almost awkwardly, as if he wasn't sure it was a good idea, but he was going to do it anyway. 'You may touch Avery, if he wishes you to touch him. You may use your marks with Jean-Claude to try and find the truth.'

I didn't correct him that it was my own necromancy more than Jean-Claude's powers that I was about to use. Everyone needed a few illusions, even master vampires.

I turned to Avery. 'Do you agree to what I'm about to do?'

He frowned and looked puzzled. I was beginning to wonder if he wasn't as bright as he looked, and wouldn't that be a shame. 'What do you want to do?'

'Touch you,' I said.

His lips curved upward, the barest of smiles, but it filled his eyes with more laughter than showed on his lips. 'Yes,' he said, 'yes, please.'

I held my hands out to him and smiled. 'Come to me, Avery.' And just like that, he took those few steps forward. He went to his knees in front of me without being asked. He raised his face up to me, and there were two things in his face, eagerness, and a complete and utter trust. It wasn't him who wasn't bright, it was me. I'd rolled him. I'd rolled him the way a master vampire could roll a mortal. In that moment before I touched him, I wondered, if I'd drawn a gun and put it to his head would he have flinched or stared at me with those trusting eyes, while I pulled the trigger?

66

HIS SKIN WAS soft, even the beard stubble was softer than it looked, so black against this white skin. Just by touching the beard, I knew his hair would be soft, that nothing on his body would be harsh or wiry. He was . . . soft.

He smiled up at me, and it was beatific, as if he saw something wondrous. Since he was looking at me, I knew it wasn't wondrous, because it was me. I was a lot of things, but wondrous wasn't one of them. Movement made me look up away from Avery's face. There were other vampires out of their seats. Some were standing in the pews looking confused, as if they weren't sure why they were standing up. A handful of them were already in the main aisle, but they'd stopped, as if they'd known where they were going, but now they weren't sure. But there were others, a dozen or so, that were in the main aisle who didn't look confused. They looked at me the way that Avery looked at me, as if I was the answer to a prayer. It made me nervous to see that look on anyone's face, but this many, all vampires, all strangers . . . Nervous didn't describe how it felt. Scared maybe, yeah, scared about covered it.

'You have bespelled them,' Malcolm said. He sounded angry.

'Like you do humans?' I said.

'I do not use my powers on humans.'

'Are you saying you don't use any power to make yourself prettier to the humans, or even the lesser vampires?'

He blinked the blue eyes at me, set into a face that was a good face, but it wasn't the face that he'd shown me the first few times

I'd met him. 'That would be vanity,' he said, at last, in a very quiet voice.

He hadn't denied it, but I let it go. My main concern about the 'vanity' was if he was using vamp powers to look better, what else was he using them for? But that was a problem for another night.

Avery laid his cheek against my hand, not rubbing like the wereleopards did, but reminding me he was still there. I looked down at him, then up at the other vampires waiting in the aisle. It was almost a line, as if once I finished with Avery, it would be someone else's turn. I hadn't done this on purpose, and I didn't know how to undo it.

I thought, Jean-Claude. His whisper ran through me, shivered along my skin, and that shiver ran through my hand and into the vampire at my feet. It made Avery close his eyes and almost sway.

I whispered, 'That didn't help, Jean-Claude. I want to stop this, not make it worse.'

'I have no talent for reading another's thoughts and feelings, *ma petite*, not to this degree. It is not my power that you are borrowing.'

'Then whose?'

'My surmise is Malcolm. For he used it on you first.'

'And just like that, it's mine for keeps?'

'Perhaps not for keeps, as you say, but for now. Use it quickly, *ma petite*, for it may fade.'

'What about the attraction thing?'

'Gain your information from this one, then I will help you tame that particular power. For now, I will withdraw, so I do not make it worse.' And he was as good as his word, he was just gone. Once his leaving would have cured the attraction problem, but not now. Now, I was still left with Avery at my feet and the others still staring at me, still waiting, still wanting. Wanting what? What in the name of God was I supposed to do with them? I took a deep breath and let it out slow. One problem at a time. One disaster at a time, or you get overwhelmed.

I looked down into Avery's pale brown eyes, and thought, *What happened in your apartment last night?* I got a glimpse of a woman, the dead woman, but alive this time. I got a glimpse of another woman, but I couldn't see her clearly. As if part of the image was misty.

Avery pressed his face against my hand, and the mist lifted a little, but I still couldn't see the other woman. I was borrowing Malcolm's power, but most of what was in me, was a much more intimate kind of magic. I put my other hand up and cradled Avery's face between my hands, and the mist thinned even more, but it was like watching a movie where part of the screen was scratched. I was so busy trying to see the other part of the 'screen' that I wasn't really watching the rest. Avery and the very alive woman were getting up close and very personal. Either my ability to be embarrassed was lessening, or when I'm working, I'm working. I was working.

I knew vamps could make people forget hours, or even days, but I'd never known anyone that could make just their part of a memory fuzzy. That was a level of control on their power that was new to me. Scary new.

Touching his face more had helped, because, like it or hate it, Jean-Claude's power and mine grew with physicality. I leaned over Avery's face, leaned into him with my hands framing him. He didn't close his eyes as I came in to kiss him, but I closed mine. I always closed mine. My lips touched his, and the woman on the other side of the bed had brown hair. The kiss grew into a press of mouths, and the woman's hair was soft brown waves that filled Avery's hand, softer even than it looked. Her face turned to his eyes, and that mist settled over his vision again. I couldn't see her face. Fine, I thought, *Her name, Avery, give me her name*, but there was a roaring silence in his head, as if there, too, whatever she'd done to him kept her safe, or at least anonymous.

The memory wasn't like a camera view, it was from Avery's eyes. I had a glimpse down his body, that he was nude, that both women were nude, but still her face . . . I couldn't see her face.

I slid to my knees, still kissing him. His hands wrapped around my body, and when he pressed us together, I let myself melt into the feel of his arms, his body. I gave myself to the kiss, the embrace, and it was like a stroke of lightning cut through the memory. The colors were brighter, I knew what Sally Cook's mouth tasted like. I could smell perfume, one that was sharper, more alcohol content, and the other that powdery musk of something expensive. The vampire's face was like crystal in my head, in his head. Her name was Nellie, and she was a master vampire, and she had met him at the strip clubs, not at the church. She'd brought the stripper, who Avery knew as Morgana.

It was like I suddenly had access to everything that Nellie had said to him, as if I'd unlocked a computer file, and suddenly the information poured in. She'd talked about her master, whom Avery had never met. Her master, who was a real master vampire, not like Malcolm. Someone who knew how to hunt, how to feed, how to be a true predator. Avery had tried to distance himself from her, but she'd pursued him hard. The thought led to a memory of Nellie and another woman vampire. The second vampire looked enough like Nellie to be her sister, almost twin. Her name was Nadine, and she was much younger, much weaker. But they looked alike, and the moment I saw that, I realized that they looked like Avery. They all had the same soft, brown hair, the same soft, oval faces, pale brown eyes. They could have been siblings. Nadine and Nellie had fought after they had had sex with him. Nadine didn't want to share Nellie on a regular basis.

Avery had used that as an excuse to distance himself again, but then Nellie showed up that night at the club, and she had Morgana in tow, and they offered, and he didn't say no. I tasted his guilt. It was real enough. He'd broken so many rules of the church. The club, the stripper, and Nellie was dangerous, he knew that, just not how dangerous.

He'd fed on the woman, fed at her neck, then had sex with Nellie.

He thought the evening was over, but Nellie started to go down on the other woman. She wanted him to feed from her thigh. Feed in that most intimate of places, but something about it panicked him. Maybe it was the look in the other vampire's eyes. Soft brown in color, but what we both saw in those eyes was hard, and he knew that if he didn't get up and go, that she would talk him into anything, everything.

He grabbed his clothes, fled the bedroom, dressed in the living room, and left Morgana alive and happy in bed with Nellie. He went to the church and took one of the coffins they had in the basement for emergencies. He'd been working up to telling Malcolm about Nellie and her scary offer, about a master vampire who knew how to hunt. A master who was actively recruiting church members for his scary little group. But Avery had been waiting until after church services. Then I had come, and plans changed.

I broke the kiss, the way you'd break the surface of a pool, fast and hard, when you've been too long under water and you need to breathe. It brought me gasping away from his mouth, and left me inches from his face, so that we were left staring into each other's wide eyes. If I'd been thinking clearly, I'd have tried to get the next question answered the same way I'd asked the rest, by touch and vampire trickery, or would that be necromancer trickery? Whatever, staring at his face from inches away, and seeing something close to devotion on a stranger's face, threw me. Jean-Claude might have been used to it, but I wasn't, and so I did what I always do when I'm scared by some new bit of metaphysics. I resorted to something human and ordinary. I spoke, out loud.

'Is there anyone in the church tonight that joined Nellie and her master?'

'Yes,' he said, in a voice that was still whispery from the kiss, 'Jonah, Nellie said, Jonah had met her master and liked him. She offered a three-way with Jonah and me and her. I said no.' I was still hooked up enough to know that he said that last defensively. The idea being, of course, he wouldn't go to bed with another man, not even with a woman in the same bed at the same time. If he thought that was going to win points with me, he was wrong. I liked men who were secure enough in their manhood to share me with another man, in fact, lately, it was damn near a prerequisite for dating me.

Avery was frowning at me, as if he'd gotten some of what I was thinking. But I didn't have time to worry about it, because Zerbrowski was yelling, 'He's running for it!'

I was on my feet in time to see one of the vampires bounding over the backs of the pews. His feet barely touching the wood, using it to bounce himself farther away. Almost levitation, but not quite. He didn't know how to fly yet. I like the young ones, they're easier to catch.

He couldn't fly, so he wouldn't try for the tall windows. I didn't chase him. I ran to the aisle against the far wall. There was a door that led into their parish hall. He couldn't fly. He needed a door.

I had my gun out. I hit the safety with my thumb and chambered a round as I ran. The vampire leapt off the back of the last pew and landed light as air on the floor. He took one step toward the far door, and I yelled, 'Stop, or I shoot.' I had the gun aimed at him two-handed. It's hard to walk forward and keep a bead on someone, but I was farther away than I wanted to be in a crowded church. Yeah, the innocent people were nicely to one side, but bullets are determined little things, once you pull the trigger they will hit something. I wanted to be close enough to be secure enough to pull that trigger, and not endanger anyone else. Of course, once the guns came out, people panicked. Usually they panic sooner, but for some strange reason I was in the far aisle and had a clean shot, before the crowd started screaming and scattering. Some of them scattered the wrong damn way. I suddenly had civilians screaming and hesitating between me and the vampire I was chasing.

I yelled, 'Get down, damn it, get down! Catch him, damn it!' He made the door, because I couldn't risk the shot.

But there were two vampires just behind him. They were two of the ones that had been in the aisle. Had I done that when I said, catch him? Were they being good citizens, or was it my fault? Shit.

I started through the screaming crowd with Zerbrowski at my back, and Marconi and Smith just behind. My gun was pointed at the ceiling, as I tried to get through them. They screamed at the guns, they screamed at me. They screamed because they could.

I heard Zerbrowski behind me giving the uniforms at the back door a heads-up and a description of our bad vamp. We'd almost waded through the panicked civilians. I heard different yelling over the high-pitched screams. Men yelling, but not screaming. I brought my gun up as I cleared the side of the door, with as little of my body showing as possible. No, I did not stand in the fucking middle of the doorway and make myself a perfect target. That kind of shit is great for movies, but in real life, take cover, worry about looking like a hero later, after you've survived.

There was a fight at the end of the hallway. Our civvies, one dark and one blond, had caught up with the bad guy. They seemed to be winning. They had him on the ground, though the dark-haired civie was on the ground, too. I cleared the door, gun in a two-handed grip, with Zerbrowski right behind me. He yelled, 'Police, every-body freeze!'.

The civilians hesitated in the fight, because they were upstanding citizens. Upstanding citizens tend to listen to the cops. It wasn't much of a hesitation, they just stopped fighting as hard, and they glanced at us. That was it, then they turned right back to the bad guy, but he was a bad guy, and he hadn't looked at us, or hesitated in the fight. After all, he had nothing to lose. I already had a warrant that let us kill his ass.

The two vampires had him down, but when they hesitated, one of them must have loosened their grip, just a fraction. I saw some-thing silver glint in the bad guy's hand. I yelled, 'Knife!' but it was too late. The blade hit the dark one in the chest. Something about that blow seemed to stagger the blond, because he went to his knees beside his friend. Maybe he thought we had the bad guy covered. He knelt and reached for his fallen friend, and if the bad guy had done the usual and stood up and run through the door, we'd have had clean shots at him. But he didn't, he pushed the door wide with his hand, and half-crawled, half-rolled through the door. The two civilians were blocking our shots completely.

I yelled, 'Fuck!' and started to run.

67

WE CLEARED THE far door, me going low, Zerbrowski high. Marconi and Smith a weight at our backs waiting for a clear angle. We were in the parish hall, and in the middle of all those long tables was the vampire. He was using his leather jacket to shield his face from the white-hot glow of the two uniforms' crosses. They had their guns in one hand, and the crosses in the other, almost like you'd hold flashlights, so that they were able to maintain a two-handed grip and still show the crosses. Training will tell.

I yelled, 'He's got a knife!'

I saw one of the men's eyes flick to me, but only for a second. 'We'll cover him, you pat him down.'

'Don't be a wussy, Roarke,' Smith said, from behind me.

'Call me a wussy when you're standing this close to him.'

I kept my gun on the vampire and walked slowly toward him. I talked while I moved, 'Slowly, drop the knife.'

The vampire didn't move, except to cower behind his jacket.

I stopped moving and looked down the barrel of my gun at him. I felt myself going quiet inside, slipping away inside my head to that distant strangely peaceful place I went when I killed, and had time to rev up for it. 'I'll ask one more time, Jonah. Drop the knife, or I put a bullet in you. I won't . . . ask . . . again.' All the air slid out of me, and my body went as still and peaceful as my head. I didn't hear that white noise tonight, that static, it was just quiet. The world had narrowed down to the crouching figure and nothing else. I wasn't really aware of the police, Zerbrowski behind me, even the glow of the crosses had pulled back, so that my vision was sharpened down to the man I was about to shoot.

Something dropped from that dark figure, something silver that glinted in the white glow, but it didn't really register. I didn't think knife. I had passed the point of no return. I was committed.

Zerbrowski's voice brought me back. 'Knife, Anita, he dropped the knife.' His voice was gentle, as if he understood that I was on the edge. The edge where a sharp voice might have pressed that trigger for me.

My breath came back in a sharp hiss of air. I pointed the gun at the ceiling, because I had to stop pointing it at the man. I had to point it elsewhere, or I was going to shoot him. Legally, I could have done it, but we needed him to talk to us. The dead, the true dead, aren't a chatty bunch.

'I've got him,' Zerbrowski said. He had his gun nice and steady on the vampire.

I nodded and pressed the back of my gun to my forehead. It didn't feel cool, it was warm. Warm from being tucked up under my arm, wedged next to my breast. If I wore the wrong bra I scraped the edge of my breast as I drew, so I'd learned that all those minimizer bras that spread the breast to the side are not my friend wearing a shoulder holster. Push-up bras actually keep your breasts up and out of the way. You just had to make sure that the bra actually covered the front of you, so you could run without falling out of it. Why was I thinking about bras when we had a double murdering vampire still to be subdued? Because I'd almost killed him. I'd almost shot into the mass of his body, not because it was time, but because that's what I did. I rarely looked down the barrel of a gun without being able to pull the trigger.

I'd almost killed him before we tried to question him. I'd almost killed him, because my body and mind fell into it. Fall into this is what we do. We look down the barrel of a gun, and we pull the trigger, and we shoot to stop. Dead is stop.

'Anita, how you doing?' Zerbrowski asked.

I nodded and lowered the gun to point at the floor. I trusted Zerbrowski to get a shot off and slow the vamp down. I trusted me to get my gun up in time to finish it. I wasn't sure in that moment that I trusted me to stand there with a bead on the vampire. Funny, but I didn't.

'I'm fine, Zerbrowski.'

He kept his eyes on the vampire along with his gun. 'Okay. It's your warrant.'

'Yeah,' I said, 'my dime.' I looked at the vampire, still hiding behind his leather jacket, and felt nothing. He was just something that I wanted information from. I couldn't offer him a deal for it. The law didn't allow deals with vampires who had murdered. But that was a problem for another hour.

'Slowly, put your hands on your head and lace your fingers. Now!'

His voice came strangely muffled. 'Have them put the crosses up.'

'Do you want to die right this second?'

He was quiet for a moment, then his voice again, 'No.'

'Then do what you're told. Hands on head, fingers laced, right fucking now. Now!'

He tried to keep his face hidden in the jacket, eyes squeezed tight shut as his arms came up and he put his hands on top of his head.

'Lace the fingers.'

He did.

'Now, on your knees.'

'Can I use my hands?'

I had my gun back up and pointed. 'You are beginning to get on my nerves. Drop to your fucking knees.'

He did it. Goodie.

'Cross your ankles.'

'What?'

'One ankle over the other, cross your ankles.'

He did it. Which meant it was time to actually pat him down. I hate patting down someone who's alive, so much easier to search the dead for weapons. How can you tell when you've been killing maybe a little too much? When you think it's a pain in the ass having to pat down someone who can still move.

I put the barrel of my gun against his head. 'If you move, I shoot. Is that clear?'

'Yes,' he said in a strained voice.

The other nice thing about only touching them after they're dead is that you don't hear the fear in their voices, or feel that fine tremble in their hands and arms. You don't have to know that what they're afraid of is you. You don't have to think about the fact that the person you're touching is going to have to die, and that nothing they can do, or you can do will stop it. The law isn't about justice or mercy. The law is about the law, and law didn't give Jonah NoLastName, or me, options.

He had another knife, this one was at the small of his back in a sheath on the inside of his belt. He had a wrist sheath, empty, and a larger sheath at his neck, hidden by the jacket's collar. I'd never known a vampire to carry that many weapons. When he dropped the knife, I thought I'd been wrong about seeing the knife in the other vamp's chest, but no, the bastard had stabbed him and had plenty of knives left. I remembered the knife like an exclamation point in the vamp's chest.

It made me wonder. I looked at one of the knives, hefted it, touched the flat of it with my thumb. 'Shit, it's silver.' I didn't run back to the vampire. I waited and helped them get Jonah the vampire hand-cuffed, though I knew that they would only slow him down, if he really wanted free. We just hadn't come up with anything that could hold up against a vampire's strength. It was one of the reasons that they were killed instead of held over for trial. One state had tried cross-wrapped coffins, but it had been shot down as cruel and unusual. If I'd been asked, I would have asked the legislators that decided the coffins were too cruel, if they, themselves would rather be held in a small confined space until trial, or just killed. I'd have bet they'd have chosen the coffin, but then, no one asked me. I'd been invited to speak before a Senate subcommittee on undead rights, but the date kept being switched, or the committee chairperson kept changing, or . . . it was almost as if someone didn't want the committee to finish its report. Probably political, but whatever, I hadn't been called. I'd just been asked, a date to be specified later. Funny, but I think the committee would have liked my testimony better if they'd let me come talk when they first issued the invitation. Lately, I had nothing comforting to say.

'Sit him in a chair. If he tries anything funny, shoot him.'

'Where are you going?' Zerbrowski asked.

'The knives are silver.'

'So?'

'So, our good Samaritan vampire may be dead, or dying.' I was already moving for the door. 'If he's going to survive, we've got minutes to save him.'

'Save him how?' Zerbrowski asked.

I just shook my head and went for the door.

'Go with her, Smith.'

Smith just changed his grip on his gun so it was pointed two-handed at the floor. 'I got your back.'

I didn't argue with Smith coming along. Zerbrowski and I were partnering tonight. We trusted each other to watch the bad vamp, but I had to check on the wounded vamp, so Zerbrowski stayed on the suspect and gave me backup. Because neither of us trusted anyone else to cover Jonah the vampire. Zerbrowski got the murderer, and I got the hero. Life had been so much simpler when vampires didn't come in hero-flavor.

68

I COULDN'T SEE our hero for the broad back of his friend. The blond was still kneeling there, holding his hand. The blond's shoulders were slumped, and he turned a tear-stained face up to me. Faint reddish-pink tracks down his face where the blood in his own tears had marked him. The tears made me fear the worst, until I moved around the feet of the other vamp. The hero lay on his back, but he blinked wide gray eyes up at me. The eyes were the only thing pale about him. Longish dark hair, and the beginnings of a beard around a wide mouth. I almost said out loud what I was thinking, *Oh, good, you're not dead*, but I managed not to. Point for me.

I knelt on the other side of him, across from his friend. The knife was sticking out of his chest like an exclamation point. I'd stabbed my share of vamps in my time, and I knew a heart blow when I saw one. Blood welled out around the blade, soaking into the dark-haired one's clothing. It was bleeding a lot. Which meant either he'd fed tonight, or it was a bad injury, or both.

'I didn't realize the knife was silver until we disarmed him. I'd have come back sooner.'

Smith said, 'We got company.'

'Sooner or later,' a voice said behind us, 'it matters not.' Malcolm was behind us. Other church members were behind him. You always get gawkers, I guess.

'It matters,' I said.

'He is dying, Anita, and nothing we can do will save him.'

I looked back at the hurt man and caught the look in his friend's blue eyes. Blue eyes framed by the blue of his shirt collar. 'I've seen vampires survive worse.'

'You have seen master vampires survive worse. He is not a master.'

'He gets power from his line, his master,' I said, 'it isn't always about personal power.'

'Truth and Wicked have no masters, do you?'

The blond looked at Malcolm, and there was such hopelessness in his face. I couldn't even make remarks about the names. I mean, who gets named Truth and Wicked? But in the face of such raw pain, I couldn't do anything but say, 'If you have something important to say, Malcolm, say it.'

'They are masterless, Anita. The master that made them died, and the *sourdre de sang* that created their line was destroyed, too. They survived the destruction of their line, but it weakened them.'

I looked up at the blond's face, Truth or Wicked, I didn't know which he was. He was staring at Malcolm, but the look in his eyes said it was the truth. 'If you had blood-oathed them, they'd have a master right now.'

'I allowed them into my church. Most masters would kill them.'

'Why?'

The vampire on the ground answered, 'They fear us,' in a strangled voice.

The blond said, 'Don't talk, brother, I will talk for you. They fear that if other vampires knew we survived the slaying of our entire bloodline, then others might wonder if they could kill those that enslave them, too, and survive.'

'Brother?' I said.

The blond looked up at me, fresh tears giving his blue eyes a reddish cast. 'Truth is my brother.'

Shit, I thought. 'Is Malcolm right, if we remove the knife will . . . Truth not heal it?'

'Once, yes, but the death of our line did weaken us. When a silver weapon is used, we heal like a human.'

I looked down at the hilt sticking out of the vampire's chest. 'If he was human, he'd be dead already, he's not.'

'He is dying, Anita, can you not feel it?' Malcolm said.

I put my hand on the vampire's chest, near the blade, in the cooling blood in his clothes, and I concentrated. I felt his energy, for lack of a better word, *fading*.

He took a deep gasping breath and had trouble getting the next breath.

'Shit, he's bleeding to death.' He was losing so much blood his body was beginning to shut down. Shit. I looked at the blond. 'If we just sit here, he will die. If we pull the blade out, I may be able to save him.'

'How?' the blond asked. I just couldn't think of anyone as Wicked, not as a name.

How? That was the question. If Jean-Claude were here, we could blood-oath him. Of course, now with the marks wide open between us, Truth could take my blood and be bound. Primo had found that out by accident, now it had possibilities.

'I'm going to contact my master, the Master of the City. If he agrees, I've got an idea.' I called in my head, 'Jean-Claude.'

I had a sense of movement around him. He was in the club. '*Oui, ma petite*, you rang?'

I didn't use words, I let him riffle through my head in a kind of shorthand. We ended with him feeling amazed. 'The Wicked Truth here in America.'

'You know them?'

'They are the only vampires in our history to purposefully hunt down their line and murder them.'

That threw me. 'What, why?'

'I knew their master, and his master, the *sourdre de sang*. They were warriors, *ma petite*, such warriors. They were to battle what Belle Morte is to sex.'

'So, are they too dangerous to bring on board?'

'Do you know what happens when the source of a line goes mad?'

It seemed like a trick question, but I said, 'Something bad.'

He laughed inside my head, and it made me shiver. 'All in their line suddenly began to slaughter people without pay, without politics, or motive of any kind. I was still with Belle at the courts. I know that the council was planning on sending assassins, but two of the vampires in the line took action. They saved us from coming to attention in England, and for that the council was grateful, but they slew their source of bloodline, their creator, and that is a death sentence among us.'

'So why aren't they dead?'

'Because some on the council interceded. I do not know why, or even entirely who, only that Belle voted for them to live, but they were masterless and sent to roam as they would with the hand of any master that met them turned against them. If they could slay their fountain of blood and survive, then most considered them too dangerous to survive.'

'How do you feel?'

'What are you offering, *ma petite*?'

'Remember what happened with Primo?'

'You will feed Truth, and he will be bound to me and to you, is that it?'

'Yeah.'

'They are not the brutes of the Dragon's line, but they are warriors that have survived centuries with every hand turned against them. I met them once when their master came to the courts. They were men of honor.'

'What does he say?' Wicked asked.

I held up a hand. 'He's thinking about it.'

'No one will risk it,' Truth said in that horribly strained voice.

Jean-Claude breathed through my mind, shivered over my skin. I moved my hand back from the wounded vampire, so the effect didn't spread. I opened the marks between us wide, and he filled me.

He spilled through my body, over my skin. His power hit mine, and it was like flame laid into some huge waiting bonfire. It spilled my head back, bowed my spine, and spilled out from my skin. It went out and out and out, and I could feel every vampire in the hallway. Feel them like individual lights in the dark, as if with closed eyes I would know them all.

'Back, my children,' Malcolm's voice came distant, as if he were talking through the roaring in my head, 'we must leave this place to her black magic.'

I opened my eyes and knew instantly that my eyes had bled to brown fire edged with black.

'What's about to happen?' Smith asked.

I looked up at him, and he let out a surprised yelp. He licked his lips and stared at me, pale and frightened.

'If you don't want to watch, then go back to Zerbrowski.'

Smith shook his head. 'I'll stay.'

'You won't like it,' I said.

He was fighting not to hug himself, and I remembered that he could sense the energy of shapeshifters. Nothing like being a little psychic in the middle of a metaphysical event. 'I don't like it now, but I've got your back, at least against anything that a gun will stop.' That last made me think he might be more sensitive than I'd thought. He knew there were dangerous things in the hallway now, but nothing that guns could help with. That was almost too smart. I'd have to be careful around Smith with the metaphysics; he might figure out more than I wanted him to know.

I turned back to the two vampires. 'I am Jean-Claude's human servant. We truly are blood of my blood to each other.'

'What do you propose?' Wicked asked.

'The knife comes out, then I let Truth feed, and we blood-oath him to Jean-Claude.'

'He would truly take us?'

'He said yes.'

Wicked looked down at his brother. 'Do you agree to this? To being bound to another master?'

'Felt her power, her call,' he had another of those gasping fits, 'if this is servant, then the master must be more.'

'Is that a yes?' I asked.

Wicked nodded. 'But if you take my brother, you have to take me, too.'

I simply knew that Jean-Claude was okay with that. There was no need to ask. 'Agreed, though whether I can feed you both tonight is a different question.'

'We have fed already this night. For Truth it will need to be a true feeding, but for me a taste will do.'

'Okay,' I said. I thought, *will this work*, and Jean-Claude's answer was almost certain. He was almost certain that it would work. 'Would it work better to blood-oath him, then take the knife out?' I asked.

'Perhaps, *ma petite*, but the silver may also interfere with the process. We are hoping to bring him back to health, and this will not happen with the silver still in his body.'

I blinked and looked at Wicked. With the eyes gone all vampire, his bone structure was very clear, and I realized that he was very manly-man handsome. Very masculine, and when I looked at his brother, I could trace that same bone structure underneath all the facial hair. How had I not seen the resemblance before?

'We need to take the knife out first, then he feeds.' I looked down at my wrists. My left was still healing from Primo and the zombie last night. I was not offering up my right wrist. Never injure your gun hand if you can avoid it. I touched my neck. Requiem's bite was still there, though almost healed. Damian's bite was faintest. I wasn't taking my top off, so breast was out. Neck it was. I was going to end up looking like a vampire junkie, always carrying a fresh bite mark. Oh, well.

'Sorry, I'm going over all the injuries. Right side of the neck for feeding.'

'He cannot sit up.'

'I'll lay down.' I gave my gun to Smith.

His eyes widened. 'What's this for?'

'I'm going to let Truth feed on my neck. I'd rather not have to worry about whether he can touch my gun or not.'

'You don't trust us,' Wicked said.

'I don't trust anybody.' I started to lie down on top of Truth, but the knife was very much in the way.

Jean-Claude said inside my head, 'The knife first, *ma petite.*'

I knelt back and looked at the brother. 'Do you want to do it, or do I do it?'

He seemed to understand without extra talk – nice for a change. 'I will do it.' He took his free hand, because the other was still wrapped around his brother's hand. He gripped the hilt of the blade and hesitated.

'It's time, brother,' Truth said.

I moved my hair to one side so the right side of my neck stretched clean. Once the knife was out, we had a minute, maybe, to make him live, or let him die. Wicked stayed immobile, hand on his brother and the hilt.

'Do you want me to do it?' I asked.

He shook his head, but still didn't move.

'Either you do it, or I do it . . . Wicked. We're running out of time.'

'Do it,' Truth whispered, 'do it.'

Wicked's arm tensed. 'Forgive me, brother,' he said, and pulled the blade out in one harsh jerk.

Blood welled up from the wound, thick, red. His body spasmed. I did what I said I'd do. How do you lay your body on top of a wounded man? The same way you do any man, if you don't want to roll off. I laid myself on top of him, legs on either side of his body, while he spasmed under me, and fought for his life.

I laid my neck in front of his face, and he couldn't control his body enough to feed. 'Oh, shit!' I looked up and met his brother's eyes. 'Help me.'

'How?'

'Hold him up enough so he can feed.'

Wicked didn't argue, he just moved around behind his brother, and raised his head and shoulders just enough off the ground. The spasming was growing less, but that wasn't good, that wasn't good at all.

Jean-Claude breathed through my body, 'Kiss him.'

'What?' I said out loud.

'What is it?' Wicked asked.

'Give him enough energy to feed.'

'How?'

He was just in my head, not words, not exactly images, I just suddenly understood, because he understood. The vampires had a kiss of life long before we humans had artificial respiration. Once I'd thought you had to be a *sourdre de sang*, or the person who made a vamp, to share energy like this, but I'd proven that it wasn't true. If Jean-Claude hadn't been so certain that it would work, I would have argued. I'd only done something similar to this once, and that had been with Asher, who was our sweetie, and who had fed on me before. This vampire was a stranger to me, and not one of our line, but Jean-Claude's certainty filled me, as if it were my own.

I looked into Truth's face, and his eyes were beginning to glaze, as his body went still. I called power, or maybe Jean-Claude did, or we both did. It was hard to tell where one magic ended and the other began. I leaned over the vampire's face.

'What are you doing?' Wicked asked.

There was no time to explain. I pressed my lips to the other vampire's mouth. His lips were so still against mine. I kissed him, and felt his death. Felt that spark flickering like a match in the wind. I breathed power into his mouth. I forced it inside him the way you force air into the dying. I breathed into his mouth and thought, *Wake*.

Wake to us, Truth, wake to our magic. Jean-Claude used me to thrust power like a sword down the line of his body. It was sharp and painful even to me. It brought Truth gasping, sitting up off the floor, yelling. Yelling something in a language I'd never known.

'Feed,' I said, and it was Jean-Claude's words. But it was my hand that swept my hair to the side and bared my neck to him.

He grabbed me, his hands digging into my shoulders. I saw his head coming forward, but the rest was lost to my sight. He bit me. Sudden, hard, fangs tearing my flesh. I yelled, because it hurt. There was no mind trick or sex to soften it. It just hurt.

I heard a startled male voice in the direction of the closest door. 'Shit, another one!'

'She volunteered,' Smith said, 'to save his life.'

'He's a fucking corpse, you can't save his life.'

'Marshal Blake made the decision, Roarke, go back to the others.'

'Shit,' he said again.

I couldn't say anything, couldn't help explain. My hands were on Truth's arms. I think I was going to start struggling. It just fucking hurt.

Jean-Claude was there, harder in my head. 'Relax, *ma petite*, do not fight him.'

'I'm not fighting,' I thought.

'Yes, you are. You are fighting his powers, you must lower your shields not just between yourself and me, but between him and yourself. Quickly, *ma petite*, quickly, or we will lose him.'

I dropped my shields, the ones that kept out all the other vamps. The ones that were so automatic that I didn't usually notice them. The shields that I had naturally as a necromancer. They fell down, and suddenly . . . it didn't hurt anymore.

It was like suddenly being thrown into that part of sex where pain is pleasure, where the bite that you'd have slugged someone for is just the best thing you've ever felt.

I'd let him feed on my neck, but I'd been straining away from him, now I relaxed into him. It was like melting into a kiss that caught you off-guard, and suddenly you give in to it. You stop thinking it to death, and just let it be.

I gave myself to the feel of his mouth on my neck, the strength of his hands on my back, the press of his body against mine. His hand slid lower, down to my lower back, and farther, so that he cupped my ass. He pressed us together, bowing his neck and shoulders to keep his mouth sealed to my neck, and pressed our lower bodies tight against one another. Tight enough that I could feel him hard and thick against the front of his body.

I'd lowered my shields, all my shields. The only miracle had been that the *ardeur* hadn't tried to rise sooner. But it rose now, rose with the press of his body, the sucking of his mouth. Rose through my body, across my skin and into him.

He drew back from my neck with an exclamation, 'Mother of Darkness save us, it's Belle Morte!'

I met that wide-eyed gaze. His eyes were bluer now than they had been, or seemed so. 'Not Belle, Truth, just me, just Jean-Claude, just us.' I whispered the last against his lips. The *ardeur* wanted me to kiss him, to press our mouths together and feed, energy for energy. I spoke with my mouth almost touching his, 'Jean-Claude, help me, help me put the genie back in the bottle. Help me stop this.'

'If I help you shield, the *ardeur* may spread here in the club, where I am.'

'Then feed like you did last night. Feed on the willing, but let this cup pass me by tonight. I need to catch a murderer, not fuck everyone we bring over.'

'Help us,' Truth said, 'help us, master.'

I felt Jean-Claude's surprise thrill along my skin, as if curiosity was a touch. 'Does he want to stop?' His question came out of my mouth, in my voice.

'Yes,' Truth breathed it against my lips, so that I could smell my blood on his breath, 'yes, help us stop this.'

'Why?' Jean-Claude asked.

This question I stopped, because I'd had enough. 'Satisfy your curiosity about him later, Jean-Claude. I've got police waiting in the other room. I need this over with.'

'Very well, *ma petite*.' It wasn't like he reached out to me, he was already in me almost as deep as he could go. But *reaching* was the only word I had for it. He didn't shield me or Truth. He didn't shield anything or anyone. He took the *ardeur* that was rising in us, and did two things at once. He swallowed the *ardeur*, and he shut down the link between him and me, tight and final, like slamming a door between us.

I was left alone pressed against Truth's body, our faces still inches apart, but suddenly it was just us. We both let out a breath in shaking unison, as if we'd both been holding our breath.

He moved his arms away, so I could get out of his lap. There was no teasing, no sense of loss from him at the touch of the *ardeur* and its going away. He seemed as relieved as I did. If I'd had time and could have figured out a way to ask why he was relieved, without sounding like my pride was hurt, I would have. But I had work to do, so I stood up and swayed, and only Truth's hand on my arm kept me from bumping a wall.

'Are you alright?' Smith and Wicked asked at the same time. Smith glared at the vampire, but Wicked's face was neutrally handsome.

'Just been donating a little too much blood lately. I'm fine.' To prove it, I stepped back from Truth's hand. I took a few deep breaths, and I was steady. But I was really going to have to see if I could go at least a night without opening a vein.

'I felt your master's power,' Wicked said. 'My brother is bound to him, but I am not. You promised you would take us both.'

'I will, Jean-Claude will, but not tonight. This blood bank is closed for the night.'

Wicked gave me a look that said he neither believed nor trusted me. His brother was simply standing beside him, as if he'd levitated to his feet. Maybe he had. He hugged Wicked one-armed across the shoulders. 'She'll do what she promised.' Truth was smiling.

'Why, because she helped you fight off the *ardeur*?'

'Partly.'

Wicked shook his head. 'You must be even better than that felt, for Truth to trust you this much.'

'I saved his life, that tends to impress people.'

'Not him, not Truth.'

'Fine, but I've got to go question a murder suspect, right now.'

'We'll go with you,' Truth said.

'Sorry, police business. Thanks for trying to catch the bad guy.'

'Your power called to us when you touched Avery,' Truth said.

'So when I said, catch him, you had to do it?'

They both nodded.

'Sorry about that.'

'I'm not,' Truth said.

Wicked gave me another cynical look. 'I'll let you know. I'm not sorry, yet.'

'Look, I give you my word that as soon as humanly possible I will give you to Jean-Claude.'

'Give me?'

I frowned. 'I give my word that as soon as humanly possible I will see that you will be bound to our Master of the City, good enough?'

'Promise me that you will bind me as you bound my brother.'

'I just did.'

'No, you didn't. For all I know you could pass me off to someone else in your master's household. My brother and I go together. To go together, we must go in the same way.'

I wished I'd had Jean-Claude to ask, was there a problem with this promise, but he was busy making all the customers at Guilty Pleasures happy. I thought about what he'd asked, and I couldn't see the problem with it, so, I said, 'Okay, I promise that I'll bind you like I did your brother. Happy now?'

He gave a small nod, with an even smaller smile.

'Then leave a card or number at one of Jean-Claude's clubs, and we'll arrange another meeting.'

'We'll be there,' Wicked said.

'Yes,' Truth said, 'yes, we will be there.'

I turned toward the door and the other room. Smith came at my back. I reached my hand out to him. 'Gun,' I said.

He handed me my gun. I holstered it and kept walking toward the other room and the waiting bad guy and police. I had a vague feeling that I'd missed something just now with Wicked and Truth. 'The Wicked Truth' Jean-Claude had called them, why? Just because they killed their bloodline? Or had I missed something. Something I'd regret missing later. I ran it over in my head, and all I had promised was to let Wicked take my blood and bind himself to Jean-Claude and me. That's all I'd promised, so why did I feel like the brothers were going to expect more than I'd offered. I thought, *Jean-Claude, what did I just do?*

To my surprise, he answered carefully, as if he were shielding me. 'We have our warriors, *ma petite*, just as you wished.'

'You can't be done feeding the *ardeur*, yet.'

'*Non*, but I remember Wicked, of old, and I thought it foolish not to check on you one more time.'

'You're holding the *ardeur* in check while you talk to me mind-to-mind, in a room full of lusty women?'

'*Oui.*'

'Nice to know our little three-way gained you something.'

'You make it sound as if you gained nothing, *ma petite*. It is you who called the Wicked Truth to us, to you, before they came to my hand. You said only last night that we needed people that could fight, not merely seduce, and less than forty-eight hours later, you have called two of our most legendary warriors to you. That, *ma petite*, is not just impressive, it is frightening.'

I ignored the frightening comment and concentrated on the other part. I didn't remember wishing for fighters, or warriors. I remembered thinking we needed more muscle.

'Then we have more muscle, just as you wished.'

I couldn't argue with him, but I'd have to be more careful what I wished for. Lately, it seemed I was getting it, no matter what I wished. Suddenly, the phrase *be careful what you wish for* had taken on a whole new meaning. I guess I'd just have to be damned careful what I wished for.

69

OF COURSE, WHAT I was wishing the second I entered the next room was that we could catch our serial killers before they killed again. I was pretty secure with that wish. It seemed like a wish we could all live with. They had sat the vampire in the chair with his hands cuffed through the rungs, again, just a delay, but if it went really wrong, a second delay could save lives. I stared at the vamp's face. His hair was darker than Avery's, a brunette that some would have said was black if I hadn't been standing in the room. His eyes were brown and dark. He was good looking in a standard haven't-I-seen-a-hundred-faces-just-like-that-way, but that wasn't what made me stare. I knew him. At first it was just a niggling in the back of my head, that his face was familiar, then suddenly it came full blown.

'You're Jonah Cooper. I got interviewed about how I felt that one of my fellow vampire hunters had been slain by the vampires. What was that, nearly two years ago now, three?'

His look, which had been neutral, went to hostile. 'Four.' He said that last word like it was a bad one.

'They're legal now, Cooper, why didn't you come out of the closet and tell people you didn't die in that fire?'

He looked down, then up, and his eyes had gone dark, sparkling with anger and vampire powers. I leaned into him with a smile. I knew what smile I was giving him, it was the cold one that left my eyes dead. My gun was pressed, not too hard to his chest, just over his heart. 'Or is it that you let, what was it, six policemen die in the fire?'

'Anita, what's going on?' Zerbrowski asked.

I told him. I didn't have to look up to know that Zerbrowski's face wouldn't be friendly. Nothing pisses off the cops like someone who kills one of their own. 'How'd you survive, Cooper?' I asked.

He glared up at me. 'You know how.'

'You sold them to the vampires you were hunting, didn't you?'

He just looked at me, but he didn't deny it. That was enough.

'He took money to betray cops?' Marconi asked.

'No,' I said, 'not money.'

'No,' Cooper said, 'not money.'

'What then?' Smith asked.

'Immortality,' I said, 'right, Cooper?'

'Not just that.'

'What, then?' I said.

'You're the Master of the City's human servant, you know what else.'

I blinked at him, not sure what to say, but I leaned back enough so that I wasn't pressing a gun into his chest. I knew what it was like to finally be seduced by the thing you hunted. Mine just happened to be a more traditional seduction. Okay, at least I was still among the living.

'What does he mean?' Smith asked.

Malcolm's rich voice filled the parish hall with its tables and punch bowl. Everything was all set out for cookies and punch, though the punch looked a little red for my tastes, a little thick. 'Power, Officer, power and sex, that is what Jean-Claude offers.'

'Be careful about the stones you throw, Malcolm, sometimes they get thrown back.'

'Is that a threat?'

'No, just a friendly warning that only the pure of motive should cast stones.'

'Ask your friend there. Ask him, was it sex with one of us that lured him. I have watched mortals come to this life for centuries for the sake of sex.'

'First,' I said, 'he's not my friend. Second, it doesn't matter why, only that he did it.' I'd touched Cooper while I searched him for weapons, and I'd gotten no flashes of information. No images. I hadn't acquired Malcolm's ability to see through touch, I'd only borrowed it. I wanted to borrow it again.

I guess I should at least pretend to try to do it the normal way. I turned to Cooper. 'Where is your master? Where is he now?'

'Feeding, most likely.'

'Where is the daytime lair?'

He shook his head, with something like a smile on his face. 'I won't tell you anything, Anita Blake. I would no more betray my master than you would yours.'

'But see, my master doesn't ask me to butcher helpless unarmed women, like yours does.'

He shook his head again. 'I will not betray him.'

Now, technically the vampire had no more rights. I could have put a bullet in his brain now, legally. The warrant read that I could use the force I deemed necessary. No one talked about it much, but I knew, and the rest of us legal hunters knew, that some of us used that part of the warrant to justify torture. I didn't like torture, not on either side of the chains. Besides, Cooper had had a reputation for being tough. We didn't have the time for him to be tough. We needed to know where his master lived.

I walked over to Malcolm. He didn't look happy to see me that close to him. 'What do you want, Ms Blake? You have your villain, take him and go.'

I lowered my voice so only we and the soon-to-be-dead Cooper would hear. 'Try to read my mind by touch again.'

'I did not . . .'

'If you deny it, I'll make sure that all those people that you've done negotiations with over the years know exactly how you outsmarted them. A shake of the hand, and you had them.'

'I did not bespell anyone.'

'No, but you read their minds, took knowledge from them, against their will. That's illegal.'

'Is that a threat again, Ms Blake?'

'Negotiation is simple with me, Malcolm. If you use your little clairvoyant powers on me now, it's our little secret. If you don't, then it won't be our little secret. See? Very simple.'

'How can I trust you?'

'Maybe you can't, but what choice do you have?'

I felt his power then, like water filling the room. Once, I'd worried I'd drown in his power. Now, I knew I could swim in it, or simply ignore it. 'Grandstanding won't win you any points with me.'

'I will do this, but not because you forced me. I want these killings stopped, and if we habored vipers among us, unbeknownst, then I want to know who they are. I will not have such things done in my church, or by my church members.'

'Fine.' I held my hand out to him. 'Talk is cheap.'

He frowned at me, but he gave me his hand, and the moment his fingers touched mine, I felt him riffle through my head. I felt him get a second image of the dead woman. A more complete image. I thrust my power outward like a defending blade. He was prepared this time. He simply drew his hand away and stepped back. 'May it give you all the joy it has given me over the centuries.'

It sounded like some kind of blessing turned curse, but I ignored it. Malcolm and I could squabble later. I had to use his gift while I still had it. I turned back to the vampire that was still cuffed to the chair.

He'd heard at least part of what Malcolm and I had said. His face was angry, defiant. 'I won't talk.'

'I won't ask you to.'

'What's happening, Anita?' Zerbrowski asked.

'I'm going to find out what we want to know.'

'How?' He looked positively suspicious.

It made me laugh. 'God, Zerbrowski, what do you think I'm about to do?'

'I don't know.'

That made the laughter fade, and the smile went with it. It's always hard to see your friends look at you like they don't trust you not to be monstrous. 'I'm not going to do anything you haven't seen me do already tonight.'

He widened eyes at me. 'This guy doesn't like you, the other one did.'

'It won't matter.'

He made a small gesture as if to say, help yourself, but he looked like he'd believe it when he saw it. I guess I couldn't blame him. I reached out toward Cooper's face.

'Don't touch me.'

'Would you rather I shoot you?'

He just glared at me.

'Then hold still.' If I hadn't been afraid that he'd either try to hurt me with his hands or his teeth, I'd have touched him from behind, but he was a vampire, and you don't cuddle one if you aren't sure about your safety. I touched him from the side, so if he tried to bite me I'd feel it, and could move. I touched the side of his face. He was clean shaven, but he was also cold. He hadn't fed tonight.

I thought, *Who is your master?*

He fought me. He tried to think random thoughts. I got chaotic images. I saw the second stripper, the one from last night. I saw her alive and dancing on the stage. I saw a cloaked figure huddled by her stage.

'No!' he jerked his head away from me.

I pressed my hip against his arm and put a hand on either side of his head. His hair was soft, but not as soft as Avery's. Cooper's hair had the texture of someone who, if they let it grow out at all, it would have body and wave to it.

'Don't,' he said, but it wasn't a shout this time. He tried to think of anything, everything. But somewhere in those confused images, I recognized a face. A woman's face. I remembered her at a banquet table. I remembered her at Belle's court. It wasn't my memory.

I thought, *Jean-Claude.* He whispered through me, and this time I got a sense that he was busy, or about to be. 'Do you need me to come to you, *ma petite?* I can put this off.'

I said it out loud, but for his ears, though more heard it. 'Who is she?'

'Gwenyth, Vittorio's lovely Gwennie.'

'Vittorio,' I said, and I had a face with the name. He was darkly handsome, and I doubted he'd started life with an Italian name. He looked very dark, Arabic maybe. 'Vittorio.' I must have whispered it out loud, because Cooper screamed and stood up. He stood up still cuffed to the chair. He stood up, and the last thing I got from him was a very clear thought. *I'll make them kill me.*

I was the closest, but I'd had to put my gun up to do my little hand trick. I did the first thing I thought of, I hit him. I hit him as hard and fast as I could. I hit him the way I'd been trained for years in martial arts. You don't try to throw someone to the floor, you aim for three feet below the floor. My target wasn't his cheek, it was the other side of his face. When I was merely human, it was just a way to concentrate, to get the maximum punch out of your body. Now, suddenly, aiming to punch a hole through someone had a whole new meaning.

Blood spattered, and his cheek gave under my fist. I thought I heard his jaw break. The blow spun him around, and he fell onto his side, chair and all. He fell on the floor and didn't get back up.

'Jesus,' one of the uniforms said, 'Jesus, you broke his neck.'

Had I? I stood there for a second with my right hand covered in blood, and I realized that my hand hurt. I'd cut myself on his teeth. 'He's not dead,' I said, and my voice was hoarse.

Everyone was staring at me, and not in a good way. More like I'd sprouted a second head, and it was a big, scary one. I looked at Malcolm. 'Does this work while he's unconscious?'

Malcolm just nodded.

I knelt beside the fallen vampire. I touched his hair and tried not to look at what I'd done to his face. I hadn't literally punched a hole through him, but I'd split the skin away from his teeth, as if I'd used a dull blade. I closed my eyes, and thought, *Daytime retreat, where is the daytime retreat?*

He couldn't fight me now. His thoughts came like smooth silk, and I knew in that moment that Malcolm could read people easier in their sleep. I let the thought go and followed Cooper's thoughts, images. It was a big building, a condo. A fucking modern condo. I wanted to see the front of the building. I saw it. I had the address. Wait, number and name on the condo, and I was looking at the little boxes with all the names and numbers. I was looking at it from higher up than I would have seen it. *Street*, I thought, *what street are we on?*

I said the address out loud, street and name that the condo was under. 'Got it,' Zerbrowski said.

I opened my eyes and took my hands off of Cooper. His eyes fluttered open. He made a sound, a low groan. The look he flashed up at me as I stood over him was one of surprise and fear. I was as surprised as anyone, but I couldn't let anyone see that. I'd known that joining with Jean-Claude and Richard would up the metaphysics, but hadn't thought what it would mean to the physical. If Cooper had been human, my punch would have snapped his neck. Shit.

Zerbrowski was already on his phone.

'Who are you calling?' I asked.

'Mobile Reserve. We'll want the fire power.'

'Wait,' I said.

Zerbrowski hit the button on his phone, killed it. 'Wait for what?'

'If we give them the address, they may go in tonight. We don't want that.'

'We want to catch these bastards,' Smith said.

'Yeah, but they're out hunting now. They won't be home, or at least most of them won't be. We'll miss some of them, or all of them, and once we've got that many police around the place, they'll know it. They'll never come back to the place again, and we won't know where to look for them.'

'We can't withhold the address,' Roarke said, 'not if we're asked.'

'If the address leaves this room, more women are going to die. If the address leaves this room, maybe cops are going to die. His master is someone so powerful that no master vamp in this city sensed him. That means he's really, really good. Mobile Reserve is who I want in a firefight, but they aren't immune to vampire powers. They go in at night when he's at his best, and they may all die.'

Everyone was looking at me, except Zerbrowski. He had already moved on and didn't need convincing. Marconi would be cool, it was the uniforms and Smith I had to convince.

'Zerbrowski, call Mobile Reserve, get me Captain Parker.'

Zerbrowski raised an eyebrow at me. 'You sure that's a good idea?'

'No, but he knows me. And he's the man in charge of Mobile Reserve. Get him for me.'

Zerbrowski made a face. 'Your funeral.'

'Let's hope not,' I said.

I looked down at Jonah Cooper, vampire, ex-vamp executioner. He blinked up at me. He'd have probably had something to say to me, but a broken jaw cuts down on the chit-chat.

Zerbrowski clicked his phone shut. 'I've left a message. He'll get back.'

I nodded. I looked down at Jonah again. I had everything he knew, all of it. I'd seen him helping murder women. I'd seen his own memory of it. I sighed.

'While we wait for the call back, help me move our prisoner outside.'

Zerbrowski gave me a look. I gave him one back. It was his turn to sigh. 'Smith, take his other arm. We're going to escort him outside.'

Smith was looking at us sort of funny, but he helped Zerbrowski lift the vampire to his feet. Cooper made small protesting noises and hissed curses under his breath. Maybe I hadn't broken his jaw, or at least not badly.

Zerbrowski and Smith got him on his feet and started him for the door. I got my gun out and followed them. One of the uniforms said, 'What are they going to do?'

'Go outside if you want to see the show,' Marconi said, 'I've seen it.' He sounded tired.

Roarke and the other uniform, whose name I couldn't remember, followed me. It was like a parade. I've got over eighty kills. Most of them actually legal. But I usually whack the bad guys when they're dead to the world. I usually haven't had to question them, touch them. I usually don't know who they were in life, or if I do, I feel like I'm putting them out of their misery, or did once, when I believed vampires were truly dead. Jonah Cooper had been what I am, and he had betrayed everything he stood for. He'd sacrificed law enforcement officers that had gone in as his backup. He'd murdered innocent women for kicks. I knew all that, but I'd have liked it better if I didn't know that his hair had nice texture, or that he'd gotten a hero's funeral. There's a reason that executioners through history usually only come in at the end when it's time to kill. If he'd run for it or fought, then the other cops could have shot him, killed him for me. But he wasn't going to run now, and no one else here had the legal authority to do what I was about to do.

We were outside in a small side area near the far parking lot. Cooper had figured out what was happening, because even with an injured jaw he was trying to talk to me. The words started out stiff, but got faster as he talked. Fear will override pain. 'You're Jean-Claude's human servant. How is what I'm doing any different from that?'

'I haven't killed innocent civilians because my master doesn't like strippers.'

'I killed more people as a hunter than I've killed as a vampire,' he said. He tried to turn around and look at me, but apparently that hurt too much.

We were on a plot of grass, with flowers to one side and the parking lot to the other. 'Good enough,' I said.

Zerbrowski turned, and Smith moved with him. They turned the vamp around so I could see his face. 'I kill because the law says I can, not because I want to,' I said.

'Liar.'

'Knees,' I said.

He fought them, and I didn't blame him. I shot him in the leg, and he collapsed to the ground. I hadn't expected to have to shoot him so soon, or for wounding. The echo of the gun up my arm thrilled through my body, like the gun was where all the adrenaline came from, tingling up my arm.

Smith looked pale. Zerbrowski grim. But they still had his arms, even with him on the ground.

'I can make this quick, Cooper, or I can make it slow. Your choice.' My voice was empty. Nothing showed on my face. I just looked at him and knew that if he struggled I would shoot him by inches, until he was too wounded to get away, and I could let Zerbrowski and Smith move away without risking Cooper getting away.

He struggled, and I shot him again.

Smith let go of the arm. 'I can't do this. This isn't right.'

'Then get the fuck away from him,' I said, and there was anger in my voice now, because I agreed with Smith. 'Zerbrowski.'

'Yeah.' His voice was very careful.

I had the gun on Cooper, and my body had gone quiet, the anger sliding away on the nice white static in my head. 'Move.'

He moved. Cooper tried to levitate. I figured he would. I put two shots into the center of his body, and he collapsed back to earth. He hadn't been able to fly in the church when he was healthy, I hadn't expected him to get better wounded. He didn't.

I walked up to him, gun in a two-handed grip, aimed on the center of his forehead. 'You're enjoying this,' he said, and he made a sound in his throat. There was blood on his lips, his blood.

'No,' I said, 'I'm really not.'

'Liar,' he said again, and tried to spit blood at my feet, but apparently his jaw hurt too much, and it made him writhe on his knees.

'I don't want to kill you, Cooper, and I don't enjoy it.'

He looked up at me, puzzled. 'You feel empty inside. I enjoyed killing.'

'Bully for you,' I said, and I knew I should have pulled the trigger, should have ended it. Never let them talk.

'You really don't enjoy this, do you?' he asked.

'No,' I said, looking into those brown eyes.

'Then how do you stay sane?'

I let all the air ease from my body, as the world narrowed down to the center of his forehead. But I could still see his eyes, so alive, so . . . real. I answered him, 'I don't know.' I squeezed the trigger, and the impact knocked him backward. He fell on his side, and I moved up on him, gun still held two-handed, because whether he was dead or whether he wasn't, I wasn't done.

He had a smallish hole in the middle of his forehead above his surprised eyes. I fired into his forehead until the top of his head exploded in brains and bone. Decapitation was nice, but spilling the brains all over the grass works, too. I switched my aim to his chest, and fired until my gun emptied. Then I got a second clip from my belt, reloaded and fired into his chest until I could see light through his body. Legally I could not carry my vamp executioner kit in the car unless I had a current warrant. I'd left home without a warrant, so my sawed-off shotgun was at home with my stakes and machete. Handguns will do the job, but it takes longer, and it wastes a hell of a lot of ammo.

The last gun shot echoed into the night. My ears were full of that ringing silence that happens when you've fired that many shots from that close a range without ear protection. I was standing over the body, one foot on its shoulder, pinning it to the ground. I must have kicked him over onto his back sometime during the chest shots. I didn't remember doing it, but shooting into the ground was a hell of a lot safer than shooting out into the night. Not all the bullets would stop in his body, not when you were trying to punch a hole through the person.

The first sound that came back was the sound of my blood in my ears, the pulse of my own body. Then some sound made me turn. Malcolm had brought his flock to watch, or maybe they had come on their own, and he couldn't stop them, so he'd come with them. Whatever, they were there held back by the uniforms. The vampires and the few humans among them stood staring at me. There was a little girl in front, and for a second I thought, *what the fuck are her parents thinking*, then I realized she was a vamp. I had trouble concentrating, but she was old. Older than the woman holding her hand and pretending to be her mommy.

I popped the clip in my gun and checked how much ammo I had left. I couldn't remember how many shots I'd fired. I'd only brought two clips with me. Silly me. I needed to load up. I needed my Jeep, or home. I put the clip back in and slammed it home with my hand. Some of the vamps jumped at the small sound it made. Somehow with all of them standing there staring at me, I didn't want to put the gun up. I didn't think they'd really rush us, but it was definitely not a friendly crowd.

Zerbrowski came up to me. 'Let's get you out of here,' he said, and either he whispered, or my hearing wasn't all the way back. But I didn't argue. I let him take me to his car, and I let Smith and Marconi watch our backs.

I saw Avery in the crowd as we moved. He didn't look happy to see me anymore. Guess the honeymoon was over. Zerbrowski got me into the passenger seat. Movement caught my eye. It was Wicked and Truth. They were by the entrance to the church. They didn't look upset. Truth gave me a nod, and Wicked kissed the tip of one finger in my direction.

I buckled my seat belt, raised a hand in their direction.

'You made some new friends tonight,' Zerbrowski said, as he put the car in gear and drove us slowly forward. We had to ease close to the waiting group of vampires. They watched us with blank, empty faces.

'Yeah, I make friends wherever I go.'

He gave a small, dry laugh. 'Jesus, Anita, did you have to blow a hole clean through his chest?'

'Yes, as a matter of fact, I did.' My voice wasn't the least bit friendly.

'I'd stay away from the church for awhile, if I were you. They're going to remember what you did tonight.'

I put my head back against the seat and closed my eyes. 'Yeah, me, too.'

'You alright with this?'

'No. Did Parker call back yet?'

'Yeah. I told him you were blowing a hole through a vampire's chest. He said you could call him back.'

I opened my eyes and looked at him. 'Is that really what you told him?'

He grinned at me. 'Yeah.'

I shook my head. 'Give me your damn phone.'

He handed it to me. 'Just hit this button, it'll ring him back.'

I hit the button, and the phone started to ring. I was numb. I felt nothing, but a vague shockiness. Parker answered on the second ring, and I started to talk about business. About solving murders, and saving lives. I concentrated on the fact that we were trying to save lives, but my mind kept jumping around. It kept jumping over a vision of Jonah Cooper's eyes, and his question, how do you stay sane? The answer, the real answer, was, you don't.

70

AN HOUR LATER, I was home. I had a date with Mobile Reserve for just after dawn. Captain Parker had told me to get some sleep, as if I sounded like I needed it. He'd even agreed to letting me go in with them. I was to their vampire raids what Haz-Mat was to their meth lab raids. An expert who could help them stay alive and not accidentally blow themselves to hell. Vampires wouldn't blow up like some of the chemicals used in methamphetamine labs, but lack of knowledge could make you just as dead. I would be their Johnny-on-the-spot expert, and no you don't want to know how much arguing I had to do to get both the invitation to go in with them and to keep the address until I met them at dawn.

I sat at my kitchen table sipping coffee and staring off into space. The coffee was sloshing against the sides of my cup, like it was trying to escape. That shouldn't be happening.

Micah was suddenly at my side. He put his hand on my coffee mug. 'You're going to drop it.'

I stared up at him and didn't know what he meant. It must have shown on my face, because he explained, 'Your hands are shaking. I'm afraid you're going to drop the cup.' He eased it out of my hands and set it on the table.

I stared at my hands, and he was right. They were shaking. Not a fine tremble, but a full-blown quaking, as if from the wrist down I was having a fit. I stared at my hands like they belonged to someone else.

Micah knelt in front of me, he put his hands on mine, held them tight between his. 'Anita, what happened?'

It felt good for him to hold my hands. It helped the shaking to slow, but it didn't go away. What happened? What had happened? What made this one different? Everything, nothing. It took me two tries to talk. 'I had to talk to him.'

'Him who?'

'The vampire I killed tonight.' The trembling was quieting under the press of his hands. My voice didn't show the trembling at all, it was empty.

'Why did you have to talk to him?'

'Interrogation, had to interrogate him.'

Micah touched my face, and it startled me, but it made me look at him. His eyes were very green in the dimness of the kitchen, with that yellow around his pupils more like light gathering around a single point. 'Did you learn what you needed to know?'

I nodded, still staring at his eyes.

'And why couldn't you wait until dawn to kill him?'

I shook my head. 'He was one of our serial killers. Couldn't risk him getting away and warning them.'

'Then you had to kill him.' He put his hand on the side of my face, and that made me look at him more, not just fascinate on his eyes. I saw him now, all of him, saw Micah. I'd known he was there, but it was as if I was only getting pieces of things. I looked at that face that was at once so familiar to me that I knew every curve and line, and yet, I was still surprised sometimes to look at him and realize that he was mine. That this was my sweetie. It still caught me off-guard sometimes, like a really good surprise. As if he was too good to be real, and I kept expecting him not to be there. Why should he be different?

He reached up to me, and I slid off the chair and into his arms. I wrapped myself around his waist, his chest, his shoulders. I hugged him as tight and close as I could with legs and arms, and he got to his feet with me still wrapped around him. We were the same height and weighed within fourteen pounds of each other. If he'd been human, he might not have been able to do it, but he wasn't human, and he stood up and began to walk through the darkened house. I knew where we were going, and I couldn't think of anything better than crawling under the covers and letting him hold me.

The phone rang. Micah kept walking. The machine caught it, and Ronnie's voice came on. ' 'Nita this is Ronnie. I need help.' Micah froze, because it didn't sound like Ronnie.

I hopped down to the floor and was running for the phone while she was still slurring her words. 'Ronnie, Ronnie, it's me. What's happened?'

'Anita, it's you.'

'Ronnie, what's happened?' My pulse was thudding in my throat again. Adrenaline had chased the shock and the numbness away.

'I'm drunk,' she said happily.

'What?'

'I'm at a club across the river. I am watching men take their clothes off.'

'What club?'

'Something Dreams.'

'Incubus Dreams,' I said.

'That's it,' and she slurred her *S*.

'Why are you at a strip club getting drunk?' I asked. The adrenaline was easing away.

'Louie won't live with me. He says marriage or nothin', and I said nuthin'.'

'Oh, Ronnie.'

'I am drunk, and the bartender says I need a ride. Can I have a ride?'

Micah was standing close enough that he'd caught some of it. 'I'll go get her.'

'Anita, why are men such bastards?'

I wasn't sure that men were such bastards, but I knew better than to argue. 'I'll come get you, just stay there, and don't do anything you'll regret when you wake up tomorrow.'

She giggled; Ronnie never giggled. 'Oh, I want to do something that Louie will regret tomorrow.'

Shit. 'Sit tight, don't do anything stupid. We'll be there as soon as we can.' She hung up, still laughing.

I filled Micah in on the parts he'd missed. 'You need to rest, Anita. I'll go get her.'

'First, she's in the men-are-bastards mind-set, and she's wanting to do something that Louie will regret tomorrow. I think you alone wouldn't be a good idea, besides she's my friend. But I'm letting you come with me.'

He was frowning at me.

I touched his arm. 'Going to bed with you beside me is the best idea in the world right now, but going to bed without you is like the worst idea in the world. I think alone my head's going to turn ugly. Maybe going out is exactly what I need.'

He frowned harder. 'You can just call her a taxi.'

'Ronnie and I just made up from a fight that's lasted for months. I don't want to lose her again.'

'I'm not going to talk you out of this, am I?'

'No.'

He smiled then, though his eyes still weren't happy. 'Then let's go.'

I smiled at him. 'Thank you.'

'What for, not arguing?'

'Yeah.'

'But I'm driving.'

I didn't argue. I did get my vampire hunter kit and my equipment bag. The equipment bag was new, but it held more weapons. It carried lots of guns, lots of ammo, pointy weapons, and it all looked like a medium sized black duffel bag, luggage thing.

Micah didn't argue about the extra firepower. He just held the door for me, since I had a bag in each hand. We met Nathaniel coming up the sidewalk. He grinned at me, until he saw my face and the bags. 'What's wrong? What's happened?'

I looked at Micah, and he looked at me. 'She's got a warrant, so she can carry her entire kit with her.'

'You aren't going to catch vampires with her, are you?'

I sighed. 'Right now, we're going to go rescue Ronnie. She's drunk as a skunk over the river at Incubus Dreams. The bartender took her keys.'

Nathaniel's eyebrows went up. 'Why go to that dump?'

I laughed and dropped a bag so I could hug him. He hugged me back. 'Come with us, and we'll discuss it in the car. I want to get there before she does something stupid.'

'You mean like get drunk at a strip club where I know the dancers will do a lot more than just strip for money?'

I looked at him, and my eyes were wide. 'Tell me you don't mean . . .'

He shrugged. 'That's the rumor, and I believe the person who told me.'

'Oh, shit.' I started to run for the Jeep, because having sex with a prostitute stripper would qualify nicely as something Louie would regret in the morning. The trouble with that kind of revenge is that you regret it so much more than whoever you're trying to hurt. I threw the bags in the back. Micah drove, and Nathaniel got in the back. We were off to try to save Ronnie from a fate worse than death, or something like that.

71

INCUBUS DREAMS SITS by itself in the middle of an open field, a distant stand of trees, and a gravel parking area. It sits by itself, partly by accident and partly because it is the only all-male show on this side of the river. Bright multicolored neon surrounded the entrace. There was a large printed sign on the door that read, 'All-Male Dancers.' It was a last chance for the drunks to make sure that this was what they wanted to see, and they weren't about to stumble into the wrong club.

The three of us stepped into the foyer, or whatever you call an open space with an empty display case and a little desklike area. There was no one behind it, no one to ask if we wanted to check our coats. I was actually the only one wearing a coat. It was mild for October, and lycanthropes tend to run warm. I had the short leather jacket on, mostly to hide the gun under my arm, more than to protect against the autumn chill. But whatever bouncer was supposed to check people out at the door wasn't at the door. We entered the club unmolested and unchecked out. Bad security, no cookie.

Of course, maybe they were counting on you being deafened and stunned for a moment by the music. It was so loud you could feel the bass in your bones, and not in a good way. You literally stood a moment on the raised area inside the doors, just trying to adjust your senses to the damn music. Who needs security when the music is like a blow against the side of your head? A headache started almost instantly, faint, but promising to be a real bitch. I went over how much money I had on me, and how much it would cost to get them to turn the music down. Twenty dollars, it'd be cheap at twenty dollars. Of course, the DJ in his raised booth would probably be offended. I tried to ignore the music and looked around the room, trying to spot Ronnie. How many tall, leggy blond women could there be here? More than you'd think. The room was packed. Shit.

We must have hesitated too long, because the DJ leaned down over his booth wall, which happened to be above us and to the left. He yelled, 'Pay at the bar.'

'What?' I yelled back.

He repeated himself, still yelling.

I took the opportunity to ask if he could turn the music down. He smiled, shook his head, and vanished behind his wall. I started to reach for my pocket, and Nathaniel touched my arm. He leaned in so that his face was almost touching my ear. 'Don't offer money for him to turn it down, you might offend him.'

I yelled back from an inch away, 'Like I care.'

Nathaniel smiled and yelled, 'He could turn it louder.'

I gave him wide eyes and let my hand fall back away from my jacket pocket. I didn't really think the music could get any louder, but just in case, I wouldn't tempt fate.

There was a dance floor to the right, and several small raised stages with shiny poles in their centers. A pool table to the left and little tables scattered around hither and yon. Bathrooms were strangely prominent against the far left wall. There seemed to be no door to the men's room, and no doors on any of the stalls, so even standing at the door you could see directly into it. That seemed weird. The bar was, of course, at the far side of the room.

There seemed to be a large group of women clustered around the nearest stage, though the stage itself was empty at the moment. But other than that one group of women, the rest of the customers were men. There were three blondes who could have been Ronnie, but when they turned, I realized they were so not Ronnie. The last blond was a man, who either liked the way he looked, or nature had been cruel. He'd have made a lovely women, but junior high must have been hell for him.

Micah got us both moving down the little steps and into the crowd, a hand on either of our arms. We threaded our way through the happy, mostly drunken crowd, and finally made it all the way across the room to the bar. We paid our cover charge, mostly by pantomime, because the bar was too wide to get close enough to yell in the guy's ear.

I tried to ask him where Ronnie was, but he just smiled, shook his head, and managed to hold an empty glass up, asking if we wanted a drink. Since I didn't have a blonde to hold up to ask if he'd seen one of those, I just shook my head, and we moved far enough away from the bar so that we weren't blocking those that did want a drink.

A man wearing only loose boxers and socks came out of a black-draped area to the side of the bar. That must be the dressing rooms.

We huddled, and I yelled, 'Bathroom. I'll check the bathroom.'

They both nodded, and we began to work our way around the bar toward the women's bathroom, which had a large piece of cloth suspended from the ceiling, covering the door. Maybe it was to hide the fact that the women's bathroom had a door, so the men wouldn't feel cheated.

There was a commode in the middle of the room across from the sink. It was just sitting there, in the middle of the floor, no stall, no nothing. It held water, and seemed to work, but it was just sitting there. There were two stalls against the wall, one had an 'out of order' sign. There was also a line. None of the women in there was Ronnie. The walls must have been thicker than they seemed, because I could hear myself, say, 'Ronnie, are you in here?'

No answer. I finally turned to a tall brown-haired woman and said, 'My friend called me for a ride home. Five feet eight, blonde, gray eyes, attractive. Too drunk to talk right.'

The woman shook her head. A woman's voice from inside the

stall yelled, 'Hell, that could be almost every blonde we've seen tonight.'

I explained that I'd seen the blondes in the bar, and they weren't Ronnie and asked whether they'd seen her earlier. No one had. One of the women was using the commode in the middle of the floor as I left. Oh, well. I opened the door, and either the music had actually been turned down a notch, or I was getting used to it or going deaf.

Micah and Nathaniel were where I'd left them, but they'd been joined by a man I didn't know. He was taller than either of them, but so thin all over that he looked smaller somehow. He had short, curly brown hair and was wearing a T-shirt, shorts, and socks. No shoes. Interesting.

Nathaniel took my hand as soon as I got close enough to be touched. The stranger touched Micah's shoulder and let his hand linger there, just a second too long. He was smiling and asked, 'Do the two of you like dick?'

I kept Nathaniel's hand and moved up in front of them both, so that it forced the man to step back from us. He actually reached around me and touched Micah's shoulder again. I had to let go of Nathaniel's hand, but I moved up two more steps. For a moment the man was almost pressed up against me. He started to smile at me, then saw my eyes, and the smile faltered, and he stepped back.

I don't know what look was on my face, but he stumbled a little over his words, 'They said they liked dick.'

'I said, I liked my own,' Micah said.

'If anyone else asks,' Nathaniel said, 'just say no.'

I said, 'We've had a misunderstanding here.'

The man nodded. 'Sorry.' He started to move away.

I said, 'We're trying to find our friend. She called drunk, needs a ride home.' I described her.

He gave me nervous eyes. He knew something, and I'd been scary, so he didn't want to tell me. I should really learn to tone down the whole silent threat thing, but damn, I've just gotten so good at it.

Nathaniel's hand snaked acround my shoulder. The hand had a twenty-dollar bill in it. He said, 'Ask again.'

I took the twenty and creased it down the middle. The man watched me do it. He seemed less nervous, but I could tell he still didn't like me or what was happening. Things hadn't gone the way they were supposed to go, and it had thrown him.

'Do you know where our friend is?' I held the twenty up.

'Maybe,' he said, and his voice sounded rough.

Nathaniel leaned over my shoulder. His voice was low and calm. 'We want to find her before she does something she'll regret. She had a fight with her boyfriend, they'll make up, but not if she crosses too many lines, do you understand me?'

'This will get you a lap dance, a good one. I have to do something for the money, or he'll know I told on him. He wouldn't like that, and he'd make sure I didn't like it.'

'Who?' I asked.

Nathaniel was standing so close to me I felt him sigh. 'Ronnie is already in the back, Anita.'

'The back?' I asked.

'Wherever they go, she's already back there.'

Shit. 'Take us to her,' I said.

'Dallas would kill me. We don't get that many beautiful women in here.'

'We could just start asking where Dallas is,' I said.

Something close to real fear went through his eyes. 'Don't do that, please.'

I hate when I start feeling sorry for them. 'What's your name?'

'Owen,' Nathaniel said, 'he said his name was Owen.'

'Alright, Owen, we don't want to get you hurt, but if you keep us talking and something bad happens . . .'

Micah said, 'Give him another twenty, then he can take us to the back.'

I looked at him.

'We can find her on our own, and he can pretend that he took us to the back for business.'

My look said it all.

He shrugged. 'He won't get hurt, and we'll all get what we need.'

I wanted to argue, but Nathaniel's hand had already appeared with another twenty in it. 'I had a good night,' he said. What did that mean? A good night? Good tips? Or did Nathaniel do lap dances when he wasn't on stage? I'd never asked. I hadn't wanted to know, hell, I still didn't want to know. I took the twenty and folded it together with the first one.

'Take us to the back, Owen.'

Another dancer appeared in what I finally realized was the outfit; loose shorts, T-shirt, and socks. This one had more meat on him and was cute in a boyish, unfinished sort of way. 'Need another hand?'

It was Nathaniel who moved up, hugging me from behind, smiling, suddenly. 'We've got all the men we need, don't we, Owen?'

Owen nodded, and I watched his face remold itself, so that when he turned to his coworker, he was smiling and at ease. He took the forty dollars from my hand and tucked it into the top of his white socks. He made the movement strangely graceful and more feminine than it should have been, as if in his mind he was tucking a hundred dollars into the tops of silk stockings. It was a good moment and made me think better of him in the job he'd chosen. Before that one movement, I'd wondered what the hell he was doing here. Of course, with Guilty Pleasures as my measuring rod, everyone here looked too thin, too fragile, not muscular enough, not anything enough.

I didn't manage a smile, but I kept my face pleasant and unreadable. 'Yeah, we have enough men.'

'We don't have women here,' the other dancer said. There was something in his eyes, something about the way he glanced at Owen, as if he didn't believe us.

'We brought our own,' Nathaniel said, and moved up between Owen and me, so he could drape an arm around us both. He was smiling. His lavender eyes shown with eagerness. It was an Oscar-worthy performance, and the other dancer seemed to buy it.

He did glance back at Micah. 'What's he going to be doing?'

'Watching, silly,' Owen said, and began to guide us around the other man. We threaded our way through the tables, with Micah trailing behind. I swear, I could feel the other dancer's eyes on us, as if he still didn't buy it. Or maybe he was jealous, God alone knew, because I didn't want to. Ronnie was so going to owe me for this one.

A dancer stepped out onto the bar as we passed it. He was so not in shape, not fragile, sort of like a computer geek, or accountant. He had glasses and short hair that didn't flatter his face. He was ordinary and so didn't look like anyone that should be stripping. I wondered what he was doing here, like this, then he grabbed a set of bright chrome bars that were suspended above the bar and proceeded to roll his entire body up and through his own arms, proving that he was every bit as double-jointed as Nathaniel. Okay.

The audience screamed behind us, and I couldn't help it, I glanced in that direction. The dancer was tall, thin, and a brunette and wearing only the white socks. He grabbed the bar in the center of the stage and began to writhe around it. I turned away, fast, and found that the dancer at the bar was nude now, too. I came almost face-to-face with the other reason he was stripping here; he was well-endowed. I nearly tripped us all trying to get some room between us and the bar. Owen laughed, a high girlish laugh, and Nathaniel joined it with a masculine chuckle. Micah followed silent, and I waited to stop blushing. They did total nudity across the river, how could I have forgotten? What I wanted to do was run screaming, but instead I let Owen maneuver us toward the black-draped area across from the bar. Nathaniel was plastered between us, still smiling, still laughing. If Nathaniel could keep playing nice, so could I. I glanced back to check on Micah and saw the dancer at the bar proving that it wasn't just his shoulders that could bend in amazing ways. A woman was holding up money. Micah was staring straight ahead, as if, if he didn't look, it would all just go away. It wasn't just me that Ronnie was going to owe.

Owen parted the black drapes, and in we went.

72

THERE WAS A small open area just inside the drapes. A man was leaning against the far wall. He straightened up as we came through the curtain. He was wearing a muscle shirt, exercise pants, and white socks. The clothes were slightly different, but the socks gave it away. He was another dancer. There was more muscle under the shirt, and he had a body closer to the kind I expected from a stripper. 'Need a hand?' he asked. It was exactly what the other dancer had asked. Coincidence, or code for something? Didn't know, wasn't sure I cared.

'No, thanks, we got it covered,' Owen trilled. He clung to Nathaniel's arm, and Nathaniel let him.

I tried to help. I said, 'Sorry, but I think I'm at my limit for men for the night. After three, don't they make you throw one back?'

The new guy laughed, shook his head, and motioned us toward a hallway that seemed to stretch the length of the club. Owen moved us all down that narrow corridor. There wasn't actually room for us to walk three abreast, so Nathaniel dropped ahead, and kept his arm around Owen. Owen must have taken that for a good sign, because he was suddenly draped around Nathaniel like some kind of tall, thin fashion accessory. Micah caught up with me, his arm sliding around my waist like I was his new security blanket. I guess I couldn't blame him, I wasn't exactly comfy myself.

There were small booths on either side, with curtains that could be drawn in front of them, though not everyone seemed to be bothering to pull curtains. Most of it was perfectly legal, a private lap dance. Rules for a lap dance are: The customer keeps their hands to themselves. The dancer does the touching, and even then, there are rules about what kind of touching can be done. Funny how living with a stripper and dating someone who owned a strip club had made me pay attention to things I never thought I'd want, or need, to know. But once you go in private, it's a negotiation between the dancer and customer. I don't mean just sex. Jason had one woman who wanted to lick the back of his knees, and was willing to pay fifty dollars for the privilege. Not my idea of fun, but not sexual, not legally. Or by most people's standards, at all.

I hadn't really thought how to find Ronnie once we were back here. Most of the booths were closed. I couldn't just start yelling her name without maybe getting Owen in trouble with this Dallas person. Shit.

But I didn't have to find Ronnie, I damn near tripped over her leg when it shot out from underneath a drape. I thought I knew the leg, but I was sure of the voice. 'I fell down, God, I'm drunk.' A man's voice murmured, and I think he was helping her to her feet.

I fought the urge to knock and said, 'Ronnie, is that you?' Though I knew it was, sometimes you just have to say the stupid shit. Giggling was the only answer she offered. I took a deep breath and pulled the drape aside.

Ronnie was on her knees in the back of the booth. There was a flash of pale breasts, her shirt was up, and there was no bra in sight. A man was leaning over her breasts like he owned them. The dancers are allowed to touch, but not that much. If the management found out, he'd be booted out, or at least that was the theory.

'I'll wait down the hallway,' Micah said.

I nodded. 'Yeah.'

Nathaniel took Owen by the arm and said, 'I'll look after Micah.' I was left alone with my friend and her friend.

Ronnie giggled and drew him up for a kiss. I don't think she realized that the curtain was open. If she'd been sober, I'd have turned on my heel and left her to it. She's over twenty-one, but she was drunk and depressed and confused and my friend. So I moved a little into the booth, close enough that she could see me over his shoulder.

She smiled up at me. 'Anita, why are you here?'

'You called me to give you a ride home, remember?'

She frowned up at me, as if to say, no, she didn't remember.

The man who was on his knees in front of her turned and looked up at me. 'You want to join us? I won't charge extra.'

'I'll just bet you won't. Come on, Ronnie, let's go home.'

'I don't want to go home. Not yet. I just found Dallas. We're having a private dance.'

'I see that,' I said, 'but if you'd planned on doing private dancing, you shouldn't have called me. I need to get to bed, and so do you.'

'But isn't he cute?' She put her hands on either side of his face and turned him to face me again. Truthfully, he was okay, but the face wasn't the show. He had the first body I'd seen since we got to the place that looked like a man's body and not that of a preadolescent boy. He had broad shoulders, nice waist, hips, muscles in his arms and legs that showed he lifted weights. The tattoo on his arm was a Marine tattoo. What was an ex marine doing in a place like this?

'Yeah, he's cute, now let's go.' I reached for her arm. Dallas didn't touch me, or try to keep her by force, he was sneakier than that, and smarter, too. He buried his face in her chest and nibbled gently on the edge of her breast. Ronnie threw her head back and made a noise that I never wanted to hear my friend make while I was in the same room.

Micah called, not quite a yell, 'Anita, what's taking so long?'

'Ronnie doesn't want to leave.'

'Then, let's go.' Something in his voice made me want to see what was happening with him.

'I'll be right back, don't do anything that you can get arrested for.' Dallas gave me a look that said plainly he was going to try and do just the opposite, but it was the best I could do, unless I wanted to drag Ronnie out of the booth by her hair. I wanted to see why Micah's voice sounded the way it did.

Micah was very politely, but firmly, saying to an older gentleman, 'Thank you, but no, we're waiting for a friend.'

'I'll be your friend,' the man said. He flashed a wad of bills about waist height, so you wouldn't see it from farther into the club. The bill that showed was a twenty, leaving the implication that it was a roll of twenties.

Micah shook his head.

The man peeled off two twenties.

'No,' Micah said.

I was almost up to them, when the man peeled off two more twenties – eighty bucks – and held it up to Micah. 'No one else is going to offer you more tonight.'

'Oh, I don't know,' I said, 'I'm throwing in room and board, and sex with a girl.' I put my arm around Micah's waist, and he did the same to me.

The man's eyes flicked to me, then back to Micah, then to me. 'You're his friend?'

I nodded.

'You really were waiting for a friend,' the man said.

'I did tell you that,' Micah said.

The man frowned and started folding his money away. 'I didn't think you meant this kind of friend.'

'He did,' I said, and gave him the smile that was bright and cheerful and never reached my eyes. I looked around for Nathaniel and found that I could barely see him around the backs of a couple that had him backed into a corner. He raised a hand, so I'd be sure to see him. Or maybe he was asking for help, like a drowning man.

I took Micah's hand and brought him with me. I think safety in numbers was our best bet. 'Excuse me, boys and girls,' I said.

The couple turned and looked at me. The man was tall and dark, the girl was a little taller than me and blond. She was wearing a halter dress that needed to be lined better. Her nipples were dark imprints against the pale fabric. I carefully kept my gaze above her waist, not even wanting to know if there were other dark imprints lower down. I don't mean to give the idea that they were cheap looking, they weren't. The girl was wearing a diamond in her engagement ring big enough to choke a puppy, and her bracelets were gold and more diamonds. Her makeup was artful, which meant she looked like she was wearing almost none but was actually wearing a lot. The man was dressed in a suit that had been tailored to his body and had probably come from the same shop that Micah and Nathaniel got theirs from. It had the look.

'I'm sorry, but we were talking to the gentleman first,' the man said.

I took in a lot of air through my nose and let it out slow. The woman's perfume was powdery and expensive. 'Actually, I was talking to him first, because I brought him here.'

They gave each other surprised looks.

Nathaniel started trying to ease past them. 'Sorry,' he said, 'I did tell you I came with somebody.' When he was safely beside me, and I was holding both Micah's and Nathaniel's hands, I figured we were safe from any more propositions. Silly me.

The woman went up on tiptoe, and the man bent down so she could whisper. I didn't care anymore. I started trying to maneuver us back to Ronnie. The area was just a little narrow for three people to move easily.

'Wait,' the woman said.

I turned back, because that's what you do when someone speaks to you.

'All three of you with us,' she said.

I blinked at her, the long blink that gave me time to process information when I just didn't believe what I'd just heard. Once upon a time, I'd have asked her what she meant, but I'd grown up since then, and I knew the answer. 'No,' I said, and sort of pushed Micah in front of me and pulled Nathaniel behind. We came to an abrupt halt, because Nathaniel stopped moving.

I knew what I was going to see before I turned back. I was half right, the man had grabbed Nathaniel's arm. I'd thought it would be the woman. Again, silly me.

I moved up beside Nathaniel. 'Let go of him, now,' and I put a lot of force in the 'now.'

He dropped Nathaniel's arm. 'My wife really likes your friend.'

'I'm happy for her, but it's not my problem. Don't touch him again. Don't touch any of us again, is that clear?'

'You're here for the same thing we are,' he said, 'let's go back to our place. We've got a bathtub big enough for all of us.' He stepped a little closer to us. 'I just know that you'll look even better out of your clothes than you do in them.'

I gave him the look, the one that makes bad guys flinch at twenty paces and the weaker ones run for their mommies.

His wife was smarter than he was, she pulled on his arm, and said, 'Honey, I don't think they want to play.'

'Listen to your wife, she's the smart one.' I thought that was a nice parting shot, and we turned to go, and again, Nathaniel stopped moving. I turned back and found that the man had grabbed Nathaniel's braid. That was it, no more nice.

I brought my badge out and shoved it at his face. He had to back up to look at the badge, as if he should have been wearing glasses but wasn't. But it made him let go of Nathaniel's hair.

He laughed. 'I've got one at home. If you want to play cops and robbers, we're into that.'

I had the badge in my left hand, so I had to use just my fingertips of the same hand to spread my jacket wide enough that I showed him the gun in its shoulder holster. 'You got one of these?' I asked.

The woman was pulling at his arm. 'Don't, honey, I think she's for real.'

He glared down at me. 'Who are you?'

'Federal Marshal Anita Blake, asshole, back it up and leave us alone.'

The look on his face said, clearly, he didn't believe me. Maybe he was one of those men who just didn't believe women in authority, or maybe he just wanted to see Nathaniel's hair spread all over his bed so badly, that he didn't want to believe it. I'd been willing to buy that it was his wife that liked Nathaniel, right up to the point where he'd been the one that grabbed his arm, touched his hair. His wife might like Nathaniel, who wouldn't? But it wasn't her who had a serious hard-on about it.

I let my jacket fall back into place and used my body to sort of push Nathaniel between Micah and me. No way was I leaving him at the end of the line by Mr Touchie. I put the badge up and started moving us down the narrow hallway, but I moved sort of backward, so I could keep an eye on the couple. Alright, on one half of the couple.

The wife was pulling at his arm trying to get him to move away. He jerked away from her and just kept looking at me. It was not a friendly look. In fact, there was enough heat in his eyes to cross that line to hate. I hadn't done anything to make him hate me, except tell him no. There are men that see no as the ultimate insult, but usually it takes more than a rejection during a bar pickup attempt to get this level of reaction. I kept my attention on him until we were swallowed by one of the curtains that hid the deeper rooms.

'That was just creepy,' I said.

'I know him,' Nathaniel said in a small voice.

I looked at him. 'How?'

He licked his lips, and his eyes looked haunted. 'When I was on the streets. He used to pick up the older boys, the ones that were almost too old for the trade.'

'Too old?' I asked.

'Most of the men that came down there weren't looking for men, Anita. They wanted boys. Once you looked too grown-up you had to move where you worked. A different clientele.' He said the last with a bitter little twist of his mouth. 'He's older now, and he didn't recognize me, but I remember him. I remember one of the older boys warned me about him.'

'Warned you?'

Nathaniel nodded. 'Yeah.'

'Did he hurt them?'

'Not yet, but sometimes everyone gets a feeling about a customer. He can ask for really standard stuff, but after awhile everyone just gets creeped. It's like you can smell the sickness on them, like you just know that it's only a matter of time before they hurt someone.'

I touched his face, and he looked at me, and his eyes held that sadness that he'd come to me with. That look that said he'd seen it all, done it all, and it had destroyed something inside him. I put my hands on either side of his face and kissed him gently. It helped chase some of that lostness away, but not all of it. Some of it clung around the edges.

Micah made a sound. 'Anita, she's your friend, but . . .'

I turned and found that Dallas the dancer was on the floor with Ronnie on top of him. She was still dressed from the waist down, but he wasn't. Her shirt was unbuttoned, and if she'd started the night with a bra, it was gone now.

I'd had enough. Enough of strangers pawing my boyfriends. Enough of Ronnie dragging our asses down here. Enough of her self-destructive indulgence. I got enough of that kind of shit from Richard, I didn't need it from her.

'Veronica Marie Simms,' I said.

She blinked up at the voice and the sound of all three of her names. 'Who are you, my mother?'

I grabbed the belt of her jeans and lifted her bodily off of the man. It startled her, and me, because I didn't have to fight to lift her. She was bigger than I was, taller, just bigger, and I lifted her like she weighed nothing. I got her stumbling to her feet.

Dallas said, 'Hey, we weren't finished.'

I showed him my badge. 'Yeah, you were.' I kept the badge in my left hand and threw Ronnie over my shoulder. I had to bounce her once up in the air to get her settled better, then we were fine. I walked down the hallway, Nathaniel got the curtain and followed us, Micah brought up the rear.

She didn't struggle, but she argued, 'Anita, put me down!'

The creepy couple was not waiting for us in the little area in front of the rooms. I was glad. I had my badge out, but I'd have to throw Ronnie on the floor to go for my gun. I scanned the room as we entered it, and the couple was nowhere in sight. Even better.

'Anita, I am not a fucking child. Put me down!'

The bouncer came our way, and I flashed my badge at him. He held his hands up, as if to say, no trouble here. We kept walking for the door. The music was still blaring loud enough that it hurt my skull, but the people noise died down as they watched us pass. I don't know if it was the badge, the fact that a girl was carrying a girl, the fact that Ronnie was probably flashing breast to the entire room, or everybody was mourning the fact that I was taking the two best looking men in the room with me. Whatever, we walked in a strange well of stillness, as everyone stopped dancing, stopped talking, stopped drinking, stopped and watched us.

I had to use my badge hand to help steady Ronnie as I went up the steps to the platform in front of the door, but we made it just fine. Nathaniel went ahead and got the door that led into the cloak-room. Micah went through the door and hurried in front of me to get the outside door. We went out into the cool autumn air. The door shut behind us, and the silence left my ears ringing.

'Put me the fuck down.' This time she struggled, not well, not like she could have, but I'd lost patience. She wanted down, I put her down. I dumped her on the gravel on her ass.

I think she might have yelled at me, but a funny look crossed her face, and she was suddenly scrambling to her feet and running, stumbling toward the grassy field that edged the parking area. She fell onto all fours and started to retch.

'Shit,' I said, softly and with feeling. I started walking toward her, and the men came at my back. I motioned them to stay by the last line of cars, as I waded out into the grass to Ronnie. The dry autumn grass made that whish-whish sound against my jeans.

Ronnie was still on all fours. The sour sweet smell of vomit reached me before I reached her. She had to be my friend, because I went to her, and I swept her hair back from her face and held it like you do a child. Only true friendship would have kept me there while she threw up everything she'd drunk that night.

I was trying to think of something else, anything else, while I stood there. I'm not good around people who are throwing up. Something about the sound of it and the smell of it leave me fighting not to throw up, too. I looked out across the field, trying to find something else to think about. Nothing was interesting enough, until I looked almost straight out from where I was standing. At first I thought it was a deadfall, a tree, but my eyes made more sense out of it, and I realized it was a person. A pale line of arm, one hand pointing skyward, as if it was propped on something I couldn't see. It didn't have to be a dead body. Someone could have come out here and passed out.

I looked back at Micah and Nathaniel, I motioned them over. Ronnie was starting to slow down. She'd reached the dry heaves, at least.

'Stay with her.' I knew that by walking up to it, I might be destroying evidence, but I also knew that it could be a mannequin, or someone passed out. I had to be sure before I called in the cavalry. What did it say about my life that I thought *dead, murder*, before anything else? That I'd worked on homicides too long.

I walked through the dry grass, and I was moving slower, watching where I put my feet. The grass didn't make a sound against my jeans, because I was creeping along. If there was a weapon anywhere I didn't want to step on it.

The more I saw of the body, the more I thought, *dead*. The skin had that paleness in the distant halogen lights and the cold light of the stars. It was a man, lying on his back, with that one arm propped up against a dead tree branch. If the hand hadn't been propped up, I might not have seen it so quickly. Like the girl's hair at the first scene, someone had taken a little extra effort to say, hey, look at me. Yeah, it was a man instead of a woman, but he was wearing a leopard skin thong that had been pulled aside so we wouldn't miss the fact that he was shaved, very shaved. The chances of him not being a stripper that worked at Incubus Dreams were almost nil. Vegas wouldn't take those odds.

The fang marks on his neck were black against his skin. More at the bend of his arm, his wrist. I didn't touch him to move his head to see if he had matching marks on the other side of his neck. I didn't move his legs and see if they'd marked him low. I just squatted down beside him, trying not to touch the ground anymore than I had to, and touched his arm. Yeah, I'd like to say I was searching for a pulse, but that wasn't really it. He was cold to the touch, but his arm moved when I pressed, oh so gently. Rigor had either not set in, or it had come and gone. Different things can affect that, but I was betting that he'd died earlier tonight. That they'd been killing him while we questioned Jonah Cooper at the Church of Eternal Life. Looking at the dead man, boy almost, he looked so young, I didn't feel so bad about killing Cooper. Funny.

I stood up and fished in my jacket pocket for my cell phone. I dialed a number I knew by heart.

'Zerbrowski here.'

'I hope you're not at home,' I said.

'Why?' and he sounded positively suspicious.

'Because I'm over the river and through the strip clubs, looking at another damn body.'

'No one notified us.'

'I'm notifying you.'

'Are you telling me that you found the body?' he asked.

'Yep.'

'Tell me what happened.'

I told him a short version. I didn't leave out that the bartender had told Ronnie to get a ride home, just that she was shit-faced about breaking up with Louie. I left out the creepy couple, but that was it.

'Shit,' he said, 'I've got to call this in. The Staties or the local sheriff are going to get there before we do. The sheriff didn't like you much.'

'I remember,' I said.

I could almost feel him thinking on his end of the phone. 'I'd almost say send your people home, but we'll need them to corroborate your story.'

'You don't believe me?'

'I do, but I won't be first on the scene, Anita. Do you understand?'

'I think so, I'm going to need an alibi to explain how I just happened to find the next murder victim when they've got people patrolling all the clubs. They're going to think that someone tipped me to it.'

'Yeah,' he said.

'You believe me, Zerbrowski.'

'Yeah, but I know you. If any woman could go out to a strip club trolling for guys and accidentally find a murder victim, it's you.'

'I was not trolling for guys,' I said.

'Oh, yeah, I'll be sure and tell all the guys here at RPIT that you were just doing a favor for a friend.'

'You bastard, don't tease me about this.'

'Would I do that?'

'Fuck you, Zerbrowski.'

'I'd say yes, but what would Katie say?' His voice got serious all of a sudden. 'I'll put the call in, tell them that one of our people is on the scene, but if the sheriff gets there first, be nice.'

'I'm always nice,' I said.

He laughed. 'Yeah, and hell is cool in the summertime. Just try to behave until we can get there to back you up.'

'I'll behave, if he does,' I said.

'Great. I'll be there as soon as I can, Anita.'

'I know you will.'

'Long damn night,' he said.

'Yeah,' I said.

He hung up. I hung up and started walking. I heard sirens before I even made it back to the parking area. I had time to give Nathaniel and Micah a thumbnail sketch of what had happened and what was about to happen. Ronnie was sitting on the ground, moaning and holding her head. I'm not sure she would have heard me even if I'd tried to talk to her. Then cars squealed into the gravel parking lot, and in the lead car was Sheriff Melvin Christopher. There wasn't a state cop in sight. Perfect.

73

THE EMTS, EMERGENCY medical techs, had given Ronnie a blanket. They seemed to think she was suffering from shock. That wasn't it. She was sobering up. Sobering up in the middle of a murder investigation, when she'd drunk more in one night than she'd consumed in the entire six years I'd known her. They had her sitting in the open back of their ambulance. I think partly it gave them something to do. It's good to keep busy.

Physically Ronnie felt the worst, but none of us were having a good time. Sheriff Melvin Christopher's opening shot to me had been, 'Almost didn't recognize you with more clothes on, Miss Blake.'

I smiled sweetly and said, 'That's Marshal Blake to you, sheriff, and you are awfully interested in women's clothing for a hetero-sexual man in a rural area.' It had gone downhill from there. I even admit that part of it was my fault. I shouldn't have made the comment about women's clothing, or questioned his sexual orientation, but, hey, his face got all the way to this awful maroon color before he started yelling at me. For a second, I thought I'd given him a stroke or something. Deputy Douglas had to separate us and take his boss for a little walk around the parking lot.

It gave me time to go check on Micah and Nathaniel. Micah was saying calmly, patiently, but in a tone that said it wasn't the first time he'd said it, or the second, 'I do not work at this club.'

The deputy who was questioning him was too tall for his body, as if his joints and hands and feet hadn't had a chance to catch up yet. He was either well under twenty-five, or needed to eat more. 'What club do you work at, then?'

Micah looked at me. The look said, help me.

I tried. 'Deputy,' I said.

He looked at me. His eyes flicked to the badge in my hand, but since his boss hadn't been too impressed with the badge, it was hard for him to be impressed, either. The boss sets the tone. He had pale bluish eyes. They weren't friendly, almost mean. 'I'm questioning a witness here.'

I smiled and tried to push it all the way up into my eyes, but probably didn't manage it. 'I see that, but, Deputy,' and I read his name tag, 'Patterson, the witness has answered your question several times.'

'He won't tell me where he works.'

'You never asked where I worked,' Micah said.

Deputy Patterson looked back at him, pale eyes narrowed in what he probably thought was a hard look. It wasn't. 'I did ask where you worked, and you won't answer.'

'You asked what club I work for, I do not work at a club of any kind. I do not strip for a living, is that clear enough?' Micah asked. His voice had an edge of impatience. He was one of the most easy-going people I knew. What had Patterson been saying to put that tone in Micah's voice?

Patterson's face showed that he didn't believe it. He was really going to have to work on the blank cop face, right now everything he thought spilled across his face. 'Then what were you doing inside this place?' A look of near evil joy crossed his face. 'Oh, I get it. You like to look at other people's beans and weinies.'

'Beans and weinies,' I said, 'what the fuck does that mean?'

'Dick and balls,' he said, with a tone that implied everyone knew that.

Micah looked at me, and even through the dark glasses, I could picture the look. I was beginning to see what had gotten on his nerves.

'Patterson, I allowed you to question my friends out of courtesy. This is my crime scene, not yours, and if you can't ask a single question that could help us solve this crime, then you need to go somewhere else.'

I don't know what he would have said, but I felt Sheriff Christopher coming up behind me, even before I saw the look of satisfaction on the deputy's face. His look said clearly that the sheriff would sort me out, and he'd enjoy a ringside seat.

Patterson said, 'He won't tell me where he works, Sheriff. Says he's not a stripper. Says he just came to watch a little fag wag.'

I made a small sound in my throat. 'I'm going to say this just one more time. We got a call from my friend Veronica Simms that the bartender at this club told her she was too drunk to drive and she needed a ride home. Micah came along so that he could help me with her.'

'And what about the other one?' Patterson asked. 'He says he's a stripper at Guilty Pleasures.'

'Nathaniel came along to keep us company,' I said.

Sheriff Christopher gave me a flat cop look. It was a real look. He might be a prejudiced, woman-hating, good ol' boy, but he was a cop, too. Underneath all the crap was someone who could be good at the job, when his personal agenda wasn't getting in the way. It made me feel better, that look, but of course, his personal agenda was raining all over us.

'Why'd you need two friends,' and he stressed the friends, 'to help pick up one drunk girlfriend?'

'Nathaniel had just gotten off work, and we hadn't gotten to talk, so he came along, so we could visit.'

Sheriff Christopher frowned at me. 'You said you were home.'

'I was.'

'I thought this one was your boyfriend.' He pointed at Micah.

'He is.'

'So what's that one?' he asked, pointing a thumb in Nathaniel's direction. Nathaniel was talking to the last deputy. He seemed to be having an easier time of it than Micah or me, maybe his deputy was smarter, or just less prejudiced.

'My boyfriend,' I said.

'They're both your boyfriends?'

I took in air, let it out slow. 'Yes.'

'Well, my, my,' he said.

I said a small prayer that Zerbrowski would get here soon. 'We've got another victim, Sheriff, or don't you care?'

'Yeah, that's another thing,' he said, and he put those hard cop eyes on me. If he thought it was going to make me flinch, he was wrong, but it was still a good look. 'You just accidentally found our serial killer's next vic.'

'Yes,' I said.

'Bullshit, bullfuckingshit.'

'Believe what you want, Sheriff. I've told you and your people the absolute truth. I could make stuff up, if it would make you happier.'

He looked past me to Micah. 'I like to see a man's eyes when I talk to him, take off the glasses.'

Shit. Micah looked at me, and I looked at him. I shrugged. 'Patterson has never actually asked what Micah does for a living. He's been too busy trying to get Micah to admit that he's a stripper, or a homosexual, to worry much about the facts.'

'Fine, I'm askin' what do you do for a living, Mr Callahan?'

'I am the coordinator for the Coalition for Better Understanding between Lycanthrope and Human Communities.'

'You're the what?' Patterson said.

'Shut up, Patterson,' Christopher said. 'So you're one of the bleeding heart liberals that think the animals deserve equal rights.'

'Something like that, Sheriff.'

Christopher was giving Micah all his attention suddenly. 'Take off the glasses, Mr Coordinator.'

Micah took off the glasses.

Patterson backed up, and his hand actually touched his gun butt. Not good. The sheriff just stared into Micah's kitty-cat eyes and shook his head. 'Beastiality and coffin-bait, that is pretty damn low for a white woman.'

And the 'white woman' comment took care of any worries I might have had about what other prejudices the sheriff happened to be carrying around. He was an equal opportunity bigot. He hated everybody that wasn't male and white and straight. What a terribly stark and empty worldview.

'My mother was Hispanic, from Mexico, does that help?'

'Half spic,' he said.

I smiled, and it went all the way to my eyes. 'Perfect,' I said, 'just perfect.'

'You look awfully happy for someone who's about to have a really bad night.'

'And how is this night supposed to get any worse, Sheriff?'

'You knew the body would be here, because your boyfriend and his people did it. That's how you found it.'

'And why did I bring my boyfriends, and how did I arrange for my friend to be here getting drunk?'

'You were going to move the body, hide it. That's why you needed this many people. There's something about this one that will lead to your fag vampire friends.'

I wondered how Jean-Claude and Asher would like being referred to as my fag vampire friends. Better not to know. I shook my head. 'How many lawsuits do you have against your department?'

'None,' he said.

I laughed, but it wasn't a happy laugh. 'I find that hard to believe.'

'I get the job done, and that's all people care about.'

It wasn't my business, but I had to wonder how many of his arrests were people not white, not straight, not like him. I would have bet almost any amount of money, most of his arrests fell into those categories. I hoped I was wrong, but I doubted I was.

'You know the line that if all you have is a hammer, all your problems begin to look like nails?'

He frowned at me, not sure where I was going. 'Yeah, I like Mr Ayoob's writings.'

'Yeah, so do I, but my point is this. If all you're looking at is the monsters, then that's all you're going to see.'

He frowned harder. 'I don't follow.'

Why was I even trying? 'You're so busy hating me and everyone with me, that you've done almost no real police work, or don't you care about this one? Is that it, sheriff? Is this just some little fag stripper that got himself killed, so it's not as important as the white women earlier?'

Something flinched through his eyes, if I hadn't been staring right at him, I'd have missed it. 'You must really hate this club.'

His eyes were cool and unreadable when he said, 'My experience has been that what goes around, comes around, Marshal. You engage in high-risk behavior, and it catches up with you, and payback's a bitch.'

I shook my head. 'No one so blind as those that will not see.'

'What?' he said.

'Nothing, Sheriff, just wasting my breath.'

The radios on the black and whites crackled to life, and what we heard was enough to stop the squabbling. 'Officer down, officer down.'

Location was just down the road at the first strip bar that the vampires hit. Ambitious bastards. I yelled to Micah and Nathaniel, 'Take Ronnie's car and go home.' I was already opening the Jeep's driver's side door.

'Anita . . .' Micah started.

'I love you,' I said, and I slid behind the wheel. I backed up and had to wait for one of the other police cars to get out of my way. Nathaniel was still leaning against the car where the deputy had questioned him. I hit the button for my driver's side window. I blew him a kiss. He smiled and blew one back. Then I was in line between two of the black and whites, and we were gone. Officer down, was it the vampires? Or had some drunk gotten lucky? No way to know until we got there. The only bright spot was that I wouldn't be alone with just the sheriff and his men for long. Police would come from all over for this one. Officers that wouldn't normally have any business or jurisdiction here would be driving up within minutes.

The ambulance was behind us, with its lights and sirens going. They could have been simply following the police's lead, but I took it for a good sign. EMTs only do the full cherry, when they know there's someone hurt but still alive. I said a quick prayer and concentrated on driving. The sheriff was a bigoted asshole, but he knew the roads, and I didn't. Here's hoping I didn't end up in a ditch.

74

WE WERE THE first officers on the scene, because we'd been less than ten minutes away. The sound of sirens wailed off into the night. More help coming. There was an Illinois State Trooper car standing in the parking lot with one door open, and the officer slumped, sitting by the door. His face was just a white blur, one arm looked injured, and his gun was clasped awkwardly in his other hand. There was blood on the shoulder of his uniform.

The black and whites hit their doors, and they took cover behind the doors, or the engine block while they looked around. No one just ran straight at the injured trooper. We all took cover, we all had our weapons out, we all assessed the situation before we ran in. You never know about bad guys, sometimes they use bait. I hugged the front of my Jeep with my back, gun out, pointed skyward. I had the engine block at my back, so no matter what the bad guys were using I was okay, as long as I was on the right side of the Jeep. There were so many things to think about, and no time to think deep, you had to let training and experience do some of the thinking for you.

The sheriff did something with his arm, and suddenly all the sirens cut off. The silence was suddenly loud, just the strobing of the lights to let people know something was wrong.

We were all scanning the parking lot and the surrounding area. There was a privacy fence behind the dumpsters. There were other buildings within a few yards. The parking lot was packed. The bad guy could be hiding behind any of the cars, or they could have fled when they heard the sirens. No way to be sure.

Nothing moved, except the trooper who blinked at us. He was

alive, and I wanted him to stay that way. We had to move up. As if
Sheriff Christopher had read my mind, he moved up. He kept low,
which with his stomach and his height was impressive. A lot more
limber than he looked.

I pointed my gun not at anything in particular, but in the direc-
tions I could cover that might potentially have someone hiding who
wanted to shoot at the sheriff. A white plastic bag rolled near the
Dumpster, pushed by the wind. Nothing else moved.

Sheriff Christopher gave the all clear. His men all stood up, broke
cover, and converged on him. I was more cautious, scanning the area
as I moved to join them, my gun pointed at the ground, but held
two-handed, ready to go back up. There was a crowd starting at the
door to the club. Until I stood up, I couldn't see the doors over the
hood of my Jeep, but I was betting the crowd had been there all
along. People have no sense. Or they knew something we didn't.
Naw.

I heard, 'Get the EMTs up here.'

Patterson trotted off to let the medics know it was safe to come
up. Sheriff Christopher glared up at me. 'It was one of your vampire
friends.'

'Looks like a knife wound to me, how do you know it was a
vampire?'

The trooper spoke in a voice that was strained low with pain and
shock, 'Bastards flew off with her. Flew up like fucking birds, straight
up.'

Okay. 'Alright, vampires. Who did they take?'

'One of the dancers,' the trooper said. 'I was making a drive-
through, like we're supposed to. Saw her come out, and saw
them just come out of the shadows, one on either side of her. She
started screaming. I got out, pulled my gun. But there was another
one, I didn't see him. I don't know why, but it was like he just
appeared behind me. He put the knife to my throat, told me to
watch. Then the others just flew away with the girl. They fucking

flew away.' He closed his eyes and looked like he was struggling with the pain.

The EMTs were there, pushing us all back.

The trooper opened his eyes, and he looked at the sheriff. 'He had the knife at my throat, why didn't he kill me? He swtiched the blade, drove it into my shoulder. Why? Why didn't he kill me?'

I answered, while the medics went to work on him. 'He wanted you alive, so you could tell us what you saw.'

'Why?' he asked, and he looked at me.

'It's a message.'

'What message?'

I shook my head. 'They want us to come and save her. They want to force us to move tonight, while they're strong, not wait until dawn when the advantage is ours.'

Sheriff Christopher stood up and reached out for me, but seemed to think better of it, and just motioned for me to follow him. I followed him. 'Last I knew we didn't know where these bastards are hiding. You sound like you know.'

I blinked up at him and thought, *What can I tell him that won't get us all in trouble?* 'I've got a date with Mobile Reserve for just after dawn, but if they've got a hostage, we can't wait until dawn.' I dug my cell phone out of my jacket pocket and dialed Zerbrowski's cell. 'Give me Captain Parker's number, Zerbrowski.'

'Why?'

'The vamps took a stripper, alive. They even made sure we had a wounded but living state trooper to tell us about it.'

'Jesus, Anita, it's a trap.'

'Probably, but give me the number anyway.'

He gave me the number, and I punched it in. Captain Parker came on the line with Sheriff Christopher watching me. I gave Parker the rundown.

'Is it a trap?' he asked.

'Maybe, or maybe they know we're coming, and they're just

trying to rush us, so we will come in at night when they've got the upper hand. But yeah, it's probably a trap.'

'I don't want to send my men in to die, Blake.'

'I'm not wild about it either, but she was alive when they took her, and if we wait for dawn, she won't be. Of course, she may already be dead, I don't know.'

'It's a trap, and the woman is bait,' Parker said.

'I know,' I said.

'You still demanding to go in with us?'

'Wouldn't miss it for the world.'

He gave a small dry chuckle. 'You argued your way into this operation, I hope you don't regret that.'

'I regret it now, but if you're really going in at night, then you're going to need me more than ever.'

'Are you really that much better with vamps than we are?'

'Yes, Captain, yes I am.'

'I hope you're as good as advertised, Marshal Blake.'

'Better,' I said.

'Then get over here, we're going to hit the target in less than thirty minutes, if you're late, we go without you.' He hung up.

I cursed as I folded the phone shut. I started walking for my Jeep. 'Where the hell are you going?'

'To take the bait,' I said.

He frowned. 'The stripper.'

I nodded, and was still walking with him dogging me.

'Mobile Reserve is really taking you in with them.'

'If you don't believe me, call Captain Parker yourself.' I was at the door to the Jeep.

He caught the door edge before I could close it. 'Isn't this a conflict of interest for you, shooting up your boyfriend's vampires?'

'These are bad guys, Sheriff, they don't belong to anybody.' I shut the door, and he let me. I didn't exactly peel out, but close. I knew Parker, and I knew how Mobile Reserve operated, if I didn't make the time schedule, they would leave without me. The vampires wanted us to go in tonight. They knew we had the address. They knew we were planning on hitting them. They assumed that we meant to hit them after sunrise, and they were forcing our hand. They wanted us in there on their terms. That meant tonight. But why not run? If they knew we had their location, why not just vacate it? Why not just run, and find another daytime retreat? Why take a hostage and go to such elaborate lengths to make sure we knew about it? It was a trap, but even knowing that's what it was, we still had to go.

75

THE DRY ERASE board was covered with diagrams. Sergeants Hudson and Melbourne had done a recon of the area before the rest of us got set up in our nice, safe, block-away location. They'd covered the whiteboard with entries and exits, lights, windows, and all the minutiae that I would never have noticed, or rather I'd have seen it, but I wouldn't have been able to make use of it. I could have reported what I'd seen, but one of them would have had to interpret it for everybody else. I simply hadn't had the training. My way of doing it would have been to do a front entry and kill everything that moved. It wouldn't have occurred to me to get a diagram of the condo's interior, or have the landlord of the building there tell us what he knew of the woman who owned the apartment. They'd already evacuated the condos adjoining ours, and they had the nearest neighbor, again, give us information about the interior and the owner. It was useful to know that there was almost no furniture in the condo, because the owner, Jill Conroy, was waiting for a shipment that had been delayed twice. That she worked as a lawyer in a large downtown firm and had just made partner. Fascinating, but I didn't see that it was useful. They were still trying to find someone who would answer the phone at her job, to find out when she was last at work. No one at work at nearly two in the morning, fucking slackers. It was all interesting, but our victim was in there, alone with vampires who had murdered at least ten people in three states. I wanted to get her out, and I was having trouble concentrating on the trivia. It must have shown, because Sergeant Hudson said, 'We boring you, Blake?'

I blinked up at him, from where I'd finally curled up on the street.

I was tired and didn't see a reason not to sit down, some of the Mobile Reserve guys were kneeling. 'A little,' I said.

The two men closest to me, Killian of the white, buzz cut, and Jung, who was the only green-eyed Asian American I'd ever met, both moved away from me, as if they didn't want to be too close when the blood started to fly. I noticed that Melbourne stayed where he was next to Hudson, as if he expected the blood flow to be one-sided.

'There's the street, Blake, start walking.'

'You asked the question, Sergeant. If you didn't want an honest answer, you should have warned me.'

Someone laughed, low enough that I wasn't sure who'd done it, and neither, apparently, was Hudson, because he didn't try to find out who'd laughed, he just used it as an excuse to be more pissed at me.

Hudson took a step toward me. I stood up.

'If we're boring you, Blake, then go home. We don't need your attitude, we got enough of our own.' His voice was low and even, and every word was very carefully enunciated. I knew that oh-so-careful tone. It was the voice you used instead of screaming or hitting something.

'Dawn Morgan may still be alive in there,' I said. 'But every minute we wait cuts her chances of survival. You can hate that your captain let me come, you can fucking hate me, I don't care, but let's get this done. I'd like to get to Dawn before it's too late, Sergeant Hudson. Just once, I'd like not to be the cleanup crew and be there early enough to have something left to rescue.'

He blinked solid brown eyes at me that matched the mustache and close-cropped hair. My own hair was back in a ponytail. They had handed me a helmet, and hair nearly to your waist just didn't fit in helmets without being pulled back in some fashion. I'd have cut my hair months ago, but Micah said if I cut mine, he'd cut his, the threat had left me with the longest hair of my life. I looked like a short, curvy hippie among the militaryesque haircuts and very masculine figures around me. Even stuffing me into one of their vests couldn't hide that I so didn't match everyone else. There are moments when I suddenly feel awkward again, not a cop, not a man, not part of this great brotherhood. Just a girl, just a voodoo dabbler, who no one trusts at their back. It had been years since I'd felt this bad about it. Maybe it was the borrowed equipment, which didn't really fit, or maybe it was Arnet and Dolph being mad at me, or maybe it was just that I believed what was in Hudson's eyes. I didn't belong here. I wasn't a tactical anything. I didn't know how they did business. I wasn't part of their team, and part of me understood that no matter how many friends I had that were cops, and no matter that I had a badge, that there would always be more cops that thought I didn't belong than ones who did. I would always and forever be the outsider, no matter what I did. Part of it was gender, part of it was my day job, part of it was fucking the monsters, and part of it was just simply that I didn't belong. I didn't follow orders, or keep my mouth shut, or play the political game. I would have never survived as a real policeperson, I just couldn't play the game by anyone else's rules. Police, real police, understand and live by the rules. I spent most of my life going, rules, what rules? I stood there and looked at Hudson, held his gaze, his anger, and I just wasn't angry. Too much of me agreed with his anger for me to get angry back.

'A badge doesn't make you a cop, Blake. You have no discipline. If you get any of my people killed because you were hotdogging it, you will not like the next talk we have.'

I wasn't really enjoying this talk very much, but I didn't say that out loud either. I was getting smarter, or more tired, or maybe I just didn't care enough anymore. Who the hell knew? I stood my ground, and I felt nothing. My voice was empty of all the emotion his was carrying when I said, 'What if you get your people killed because you didn't let me do my job to the best of my ability? Do I get to have a talk with you then?'

All the men around me just moved back, in unison, as if minimum safe distance was suddenly a real concern. He spoke through his teeth, and the anger turned his brown eyes nearly black. 'And what exactly is your job, Blake?'

'I'm a vampire hunter.'

He came toward me slowly, and Melbourne actually touched his shoulder, as if it was getting out of hand. Hudson just looked at the hand, and the hand went away. Everyone was treating Hudson like he was a very scary guy. He wasn't the biggest, or the most muscled, or anything, but he wore his authority like some sort of invisible coat; it was just there. If he hadn't hated me, I'd have respected it, but he made it impossible for me to see him as anything but an obstacle. He spoke from inches in front of me, each word pushed into my face, careful as a blow, 'You-are-a-fuck-ing-assassin.'

I looked up into his face, almost close enough to kiss, and said, 'Yeah, sometimes, sometimes, I am.'

He blinked at me, puzzlement filling his eyes, chasing back the anger. 'That was an insult, Blake.'

'I try never to get insulted by the truth, Sergeant.' I gave him mild eyes and willed myself to feel nothing, because if I let myself feel anything I was going to be sad, and if I teared up, or worse, cried, that would be it. They wouldn't let me play, not if I cried. I'd cried because Jessica Arnet thought I was corrupting Nathaniel. I'd cried because of having to kill Jonah Cooper. What the fuck was wrong with me tonight? Usually the only thing that made me cry was Richard.

He shook his head. 'You will just slow us down, Blake.'

'I'm immune to vampire powers,' I said.

'We will clear this entire structure in less than a minute. We know not to make eye contact, and we are cleared to treat all approaching vampires inside as hostiles. There won't be time for them to do any tricks on us.'

I nodded, as if I really understood how they could possibly clear an entire condo, the size of a small house, in less than a minute. 'Fine, you don't think you need me to help with the vampires, fine.'

He blinked again, and he couldn't hide the fact that I'd caught him off guard a second time in almost as many minutes. 'You'll wait outside?'

'What happens to your speed record, if you have to treat the vampires like human beings?' I asked.

'They're legal citizens, that makes them human beings.'

'Yeah, but can you clear the place in less than a minute if you have to take the time to subdue maybe upwards of seven vampires, at least one a master? If you think I'll slow you down, Hudson, trust me, they'll slow you down a lot more than I will.'

Melbourne spoke over Hudson's shoulder, 'We've been green-lighted. Everything vampire in there is target.'

I shook my head and looked at Melbourne, as if Hudson wasn't still looming over me. 'When warrants of execution first came into exis-tence, one of the main concerns was that they would turn the police of this country into nothing more than fucking assassins, so the warrants are worded very carefully. If the legal executioner is with you and we are in danger then you may use any and all means to execute this warrant, but if the legal executioner is not with you, then the warrant is not in effect.' I turned back to look at Hudson, and I was beginning to get a little angry, at last. Good, that was better than tears. 'Which means if you go in without me and shoot any damn body, that you'll be up on review, or leave, or some motherfucking shit. Hesitate against vampires, and you risk your life and the lives of your men. Don't hesitate against the vampires, and you may lose your job, your pension, or even see jail time. Depends on the judge, the lawyer, the political climate of the city at the time of the incident.' I was almost smiling, because I was telling the absolute truth.

Hudson gave a smile that was more snarl than anything. 'Or we can just sit this one out and let you take the order of execution all on your own little shoulders. How'd that be? You go in by yourself.'

I laughed, and it surprised him again, made him back up. 'Killian,' I said, turning to look for him. He came up to me, sort of hesitating, glancing at his sergeant. Killian was only an inch or two taller than me, it was one of the main reasons that his extra gear had nearly fit me. 'Help me out of this, I don't want to mess up your gear. Thanks for the loan.'

'Why are you taking off the gear?' Hudson asked.

'If I go in without you, I don't need the vest, or the helmet, or the damn radio that's attached to it. I go in alone, like normal, I get to take the equipment I want to take, not that I'm ordered to take.' I started looking at the straps. 'Help me out here, Killian, you helped me get into it.'

Hudson shook his head and Killian backed up. 'Ms Blake . . .'

'That's Marshal Blake to you, Sergeant Hudson.'

He took in a deep breath, and let it out slow. 'Marshal Blake, we can't let you go in there alone.'

'This is my damn warrant, not yours. I shared my information with you guys, not the other way around. None of you would have even known where to look for this woman without me.'

'Do you know what they're saying you did to get this information, Marshal?'

Just the way he said it, I knew I didn't want to know, but I said, 'No, what?'

'That you fucked the suspect. Fucked him in front of other officers, and he told you everything, then you blew his brains out with a gun. De-fucking-capitated him, you shot him so many times.'

I laughed again. 'Jesus, I'd love to know who made that one up.'

'You're saying it's a lie?'

'That I fucked him, yeah, wishful thinking on someone's part, but I did vamp it out of him, as in vampire, not whore. And yeah, I did shoot him until his head wasn't there anymore, because I didn't have my vampire hunting kit with me. The handgun was all I had, so it's what I used.'

I shook my head and felt that faint anger fade away. 'This warrant is my damn party, Sergeant Hudson. I invited you to the dance, not the other way around. I would like you to try and remember that, when we're dealing with each other.'

He looked at me, really looked at me. I don't think he'd seen me until that moment. I'd been some woman, some zombie queen slut, forced on him by the upper brass. I'd been a civilian with a badge, but I hadn't been real to him, not a person. Now he looked at me, and he saw me, and I watched that unreasoning anger fade.

'You really would go in there alone, wouldn't you?'

I sighed and shook my head. 'I'm a vampire executioner, Sergeant, I'm usually alone, just me and the bad guys.'

He gave a small smile, barely more than a flex of his mustache. 'Not tonight, Marshal, tonight, you go in with us.'

I smiled at him, it was a good smile, not flirting, though some men take it that way, just a good, open, honest, happy to have you smile. He smiled back, he couldn't seem to help it. 'Good, great,' I said, 'but can we move it along? We're burning moonlight.'

He gave me a look like he wasn't sure how to take me, then he laughed. The moment he laughed, all the other men relaxed, I could feel it, like a sort of psychic sigh of relief. 'You are a pushy damn woman.'

'Yes,' I said, 'yes, I am.'

He gave a smaller laugh. 'You'll follow orders once we're inside, yes?'

I sighed. 'I'll try.'

He shook his head.

'If I just say yes, it'll be a lie, but I will do my utmost to do what I'm told. I promise.'

'That's the best I'm going to get, isn't it?'

I nodded. 'Yep, unless you want me to lie to you.'

'No, truth from a federal agent is downright refreshing.'

'Well, then I am just going to be a breath of fresh air.'

He looked at me, shook his head, and started back toward the dry erase board. 'Now that I do believe Marshal, that I do believe.' They went back to their briefing, and I went back to counting the minutes and wondering if there was going to be anything alive in the condo by the time we hit the door.

76

AT MY SUGGESTION they put the sniper where he could see the windows, not at the front door. One, we didn't know what they looked like, so the sniper couldn't just drop the people coming out the front. There might be law-abiding vampire citizens in the building, so the sniper couldn't even just shoot vampires. If he could tell for dead certain they were vamps. Even I wouldn't want to say yes or no on the vamp question through a scope. I mean, what if you're wrong? High silver content, there would be no apology. But anyone that flew out of the windows of our condo, they would be bad guys, and the sniper could drop them with impunity. Green-light city.

The rest of us were huddled around the van. In the movies the van is sleek and roomy. In real life, it's narrow, cluttered, and looks like a cross between a plumber's van and the Good Humor truck, if it sold guns instead of ice cream. There wasn't room for us and the guns. Hell, as empty as it got, most of us wouldn't have fit. It was an equipment van, not a transport vehicle. I was still in the vest, even though I'd pointed out that nothing we were about to go up against would be shooting at us, and vests were useless for stabbing or tearing. I'd run into this before with both military and law enforcement. They just couldn't wrap their heads around the fact that the body armor, their best defense, didn't help against someone that could crush steel. It was like going up against Superman, and thinking Kevlar would keep you safe. Finally, Sergeant Melbourne said what few special tactical units will ever admit out loud, 'We're using bullets. Bullets can ricochet, and we'd just feel better if we knew you were safe from friendly fire.' The microphone was integral to the vest and attached to a little earpiece, like the Secret Service wear. They showed me the button for the mike in the center of the vest, near your gun when you were holding it. They made sure the mike worked, someone patted me on top of my helmet, and I was good to go. Or as good as it was going to get. Not going in would have been the good thing, but the vamps had kidnapped that option away from us.

The woman they'd taken was Dawn Morgan, twenty-two, and had only worked at the club about three weeks. They had a picture of her up on their Web site and we'd all seen it. It was a publicity shot for a stripper bar, so we tried to look at her face. Brown hair, about shoulder length, and enough makeup that it was hard to really see her face. She was all blue eyes and red pouting lips. I didn't ask if the men had a harder time looking at her face than I did. She was covered by hands and a few well-placed pieces of cloth, but the illusion was that more skin was showing than really was. Distracting, and meant to be. I'm sure if Ms Morgan had been told she'd be kidnapped by murderous vampires, she'd have left us a nice, less glamorous face shot. But you just don't plan for these kinds of things. We memorized the face of the hostage so we wouldn't accidentally shoot her during the action. Yeah, that would be bad.

I think that if I hadn't had my own dangerous toys to play with they would have taken me in unarmed. Most of the tactical team seemed to think I was a civilian and treated me that way. They weren't rude, just didn't like the idea of me having a loaded gun at their backs. I guess I couldn't blame them. I hadn't had their training. They'd never seen me use a gun. They'd never seen me do this kind of work. They seemed to consider me almost more dangerous than the vampires.

My biggest problem with the vest was that it made it impossible for me to carry the Browning and the Firestar in their current holsters and have any hope of drawing them. Officer Derry had thrown me a thigh holster with velcro straps. 'It'll hold the Browning and an extra clip.' Derry looked as Irish as his name, except for his coloring, which was dark.

I had to take the vest off to thread the upper part of the thigh holster through my belt, then the other straps went around my leg. The thigh holster wasn't bad actually, though I wouldn't have wanted to try it unless I had pants on to protect my thighs. My thighs rub together when I walk, thank you very much. But with jeans it wasn't bad. It was a different draw though, not just the angle, or where the gun was, but the actual hand movement was different. I wouldn't be as quick, because I'd have to think about it. Of course, for tonight's work, the handguns were secondary.

I had a new Mossberg 590A1 Bantam. Thirteen-inch length-of-pull, lighter weight overall. It meant more recoil, but, once you adjusted for it, it was the shotgun of my dreams. No more heavy barrel out there hanging while you tried to aim, leaving me feeling top heavy. I had a sawed-off that had started life as an Ithica 37, but now was just used for in-close vampire blasting. The Ithica had a strap fitted for it, so that it fitted across my body sort of like an awkward purse. To keep it from moving around until I wanted it for in-fighting, Edward, my friend and the only person I'd ever seen use a flamethrower, had helped me rig velcro to the thigh holster on my left thigh. That thigh holster was mine, but it was for extra ammo, not for holding guns. The velcro strap fit over the Ithica's shortened barrel, so that it was held tight against my leg, but not at an angle where if something went terribly wrong I'd shoot my kneecap off. One quick, hard pull, and the sawed-off would be in my hands, and it would be time to be very, very close with the vamps. The Mossberg had an Urban Ops sling from U.S. Tactical Supply. It had become my preferred sling for the bigger guns. Unfortunately, you couldn't carry two guns on two different Urban slings, because the sling was designed for switching hands, ease of movement. Which meant the gun would move around more. Edward, who was truly the assassin

Hudson had accused me of being, wasn't as fond of the Urban sling as I was, but then he didn't do as much close in undercover work with the monsters. Most of the time he went in like a one-man demolition team. The sling also worked better if you had a heavier jacket over the sling to keep it from sliding off your shoulder. If I'd had broader shoulders, it would have stayed put better, and since most of the people who test this stuff are male, and thus have broader shoulders, I couldn't really complain much. It was still a sweet piece of equipment.

I had a stock mag attached to the butt of the Mossberg. I'd started carrying extra ammo in a thigh holder, but the Browning was on that thigh. I'd found that if I wore the extra ammo on my left thigh, it was harder to get to. It cost me a second, or three. If I couldn't have my right thigh for it, then the stock mag was the next best thing. I went ahead and put extra ammo in the left thigh holder. You know that old saying, I'd rather have it and not need it, than need it and not have it. That applied to ammo better than anything else I knew.

Derry said, 'That's almost the exact same thigh holder as I gave you for your Browning. If you had it already, you didn't need to borrow ours.'

'I have two set up for ammo. I don't have one for handguns. If it's comfortable I might get one.'

'So glad Mobile Reserve could help you try out some new toys.' He smiled at me.

I smiled back.

'He gives you a lousy holster, and you flirt with him. I loan you my whole second rig and nothing,' Killian said.

'That wasn't flirting, Killian. When I flirt, you'll know it.'

'Ooh,' Derry said.

Hudson came up, in full gear. 'You going to keep distracting my men, Marshal, or are you ready to execute that warrant of yours?'

'I'm through distracting, if you're through planning.'

'I'm through,' he said.

'Then me, too. Let's go kill some vampires.'

'Not hunt, just kill?' he asked.

'Hunting vampires isn't a catch-and-release sport, Sergeant.'

He laughed, a short surprised sound. 'Either you're getting funnier, or it's fucking late.'

'It's fucking late,' I said. 'There are dozens of people who'll say that I'm not funny at all.' I made him laugh again, and when you're about to risk your life together, there are worse ways to begin.

77

IT WAS ONE of those buildings downtown that had been rehabbed until outside it was an architectural wonder that had been saved from demolition, but inside it was ultramodern, ultrasleek, with carpet and almost empty halls, as if once they agreed on the two-tone paint job, they couldn't agree on anything else. The building still had vacancies, but was mostly full. Good news for the investors, but bad news for us. If the building had been mostly empty the chances of having collateral damage would have been less. *Collateral damage*, isn't that a nice phrase. It was why they'd had to evacuate so many people. There was no way the vamps didn't know something was up.

We were outside the condo. It still belonged to Jill Conroy. It felt like we'd learned that hours ago, but actually only about an hour had passed from the first recon to us being here in the hallway. We'd finally gotten a number for one of her fellow lawyers. Jill had been AWOL from her job for five days. Three of those days she'd called in sick, but the fourth day she hadn't answered the phone. Hmm, three days home sick, then no answer. I was betting that Jill Conroy had become the undead. The evil, wicked undead, not a member of the Church of Eternal Life, and I knew not Jean-Claude's people. The fact that we had a third player in town and neither of the other sides had figured it out, was bad. It showed either the master of these guys was very powerful, or we'd become careless.

I would have liked to have pushed my power through their walls and checked out how many were in there. I was capable of doing that now, but if they were as good as I feared, they'd sense it. I feared they'd try more vampire tricks if they knew I, or someone with my skills, was with the cops. If they thought it was just cops, they might rely on speed and strength. If they did, my money was on us. So I had to go in blind, again, shit.

I'd done a lot of vampire lairs in my day, but never with Mobile Reserve or any police tactical unit. In some ways, it was very different, and in some ways, it was very the same. Difference one, I wasn't in front. Hudson was the guy in charge once we hit the building. He'd been in charge before, as far as I was concerned, but he'd had to answer to his chain of command. Incident commander, negotiation commander, tactical commander, but none of them was going in with us, and it was all about who was willing to pick up a gun and put their shoulder next to yours.

Hudson went third in the line order, though it wasn't going to be a true single line. 'You will move when I move, Blake. You are my fucking shadow until I tell you different. You will follow my direct orders once we're inside, or I will cuff you and leave you with a guard. Is that clear?'

'Crystal,' I said. I think he liked me as a person, but we were about to do his job. The job wasn't personal, and professionally, he didn't know me at all. No amount of charm could offset that he didn't really trust me at his back. I hadn't earned it yet.

They brought up a huge metal body shield with a little window in it. Officer Baldwin carried the shield. He wasn't the bulkiest of the men, that was Derry, but Baldwin had height, and since everyone was going to be crouching behind the shield, height counted, like tall people trying to crouch under a short person's umbrella.

I expected them to use one of those big metal rams, but they didn't. Ms Conroy had paid extra for a solid metal door with a lock that made it true security. All that looking at specs of the building and interviewing people had paid off. They put a small explosive charge on the lock and blew it.

The flash bang grenade went first, then in we went in the wake of the stunning noise and blinding light. When the searing light faded, the only light came from the sweeps of the men's flashlights mounted to their guns. Then it was chaos. Not the chaos of a fight, because no one was in the first room, but the chaos of trying to shuffle behind the shield and not trip or trip someone else. They shuffled as a unit, but it was so quick, like running inside a shell of bodies. While you're doing what amounts to dancing or gymnastics as a unit, you're also searching the dark, keeping track of the gun in your hand, and looking for something to shoot at.

Thanks to the briefing, I knew the layout of this condo almost better than my own house. The big empty living room, the small enclosed kitchen, the hallway beyond with the guest bathroom left and the guest room right. It was a straightforward layout, thank God.

Hudson spoke in the mike in my ear, a whisper even with me standing right behind him with my hand touching his back, 'Mendez, Derry, kitchen.' They peeled off wordlessly, the back of our little conga line lighter. Jung moved up, and I felt his hand against my back. Nice to know I wasn't the only one who needed a steadying hand.

Radio in my ear: 'Vic, female, not Morgan.' I think it was Derry.

'Vamp bites.'

'Yes.'

'Blake, check it out.'

I stumbled, made Jung stumble, we were like dominoes. I remembered to press my button. 'What?'

'Check out the body.'

I could have argued but there was no time. I knew he was doing it to get rid of me. Maybe I really had slowed them down, but he was definitely getting me out of the way before the main shit hit the fan.

I peeled off like they had shown me and went for the kitchen. I followed his order, even though I didn't agree. I went to check out the body, because the sergeant had told me to. Damn it.

I double-timed it to the kitchen, because if I hurried, I might still get to trail in for the main fight. Light shown through the louvered door of the kitchen. I smelled the blood before I touched the door.

Light washed over me, then dimmed, as my eyes adjusted. Derry was heading for the door as I was coming in. Hudson's voice, sounding strained but clear, hit the radio: 'Stay with Blake until she's checked the body.' Radio silence.

Derry's shoulders slumped, saying he was disappointed, but he didn't argue.

Derry just moved up with me, rifle still at the ready. I went with him, though I pointed my shotgun a little to one side. The room wasn't that wide, and I just wasn't sure there was enough room for all of us pointing guns in, without risking crossing someone's body. One of my goals tonight was not to do that.

I knew some of what we'd find, because I could smell it. Not just the blood, old blood, but that meaty, fluid smell, and a stale whiff of sex. Male sex. It helped me steel myself for what I was about to see.

She lay spread-eagle on the small four-seater table. Her legs had folded over the edge of the table, and her groin was splayed in a line for the door, so the view was painfully clear. She'd been raped, and for that much damage, probably not just with someone's body. Or at least not just with a penis. I was glad when I could look away. She was wearing what looked like a silver sequined bikini, but she had pantyhose on under it. Though I might not have realized that if the clothes on her lower body hadn't been ripped away. The pantyhose told me she was a stripper from this side of the river. The laws on the books in St Louis for strippers are odd. Jean-Claude's club gets around it on a grandfather clause, because as a vampire he was here before the laws went into effect, but anyone else had to abide by the rules. One of the rules was that the girls had to wear pantyhose, not just hose, under their outfits. The rules were designed by people who wanted to make sure that St Louis could not have 'those kinds' of clubs. There's no one so self-righteous as someone policing someone else's morality.

Her head was back, so that her eyes were staring at the far wall of the small but expensive-looking kitchen. Her hair was brown and must have been at least to her waist. I'd become pretty good at judging hair length when people were lying down. The hair was real, not a wig, so it wasn't our missing stripper. This was indeed someone else. How many people had they kidnapped tonight?

Either Mendez or Derry had used flex cuffs on her wrists. It was standard op on intact bodies. Officers had been killed by 'dead' bodies. Better safe than sorry.

Mendez squatted down. He was peering under the table. 'What is that?'

I squatted, because I was closer to the ground. Derry kept an eye on the room, gun sort of at the ready, but careful to not point out toward us. It was nice to work with professionals.

There was a long cylindrical object under the table. It was black with dried blood on it. It was so caked with blood that for a second I couldn't tell what it was, then it was like one of those abstract pictures that suddenly snap into place, and you know. I swallowed hard, against the burn of nausea. I took a slow breath through my nose and let it out easy through my mouth. My voice sounded odd even to me, when I said, 'Bottle, wine bottle.'

Mendez said, 'God.' He must have hit his button by accident, because Hudson heard him.

'What is it, Mendez?' Hudson asked over the headsets.

'Sorry, sir, just, Jesus, this was a bad way to die.'

'Steady, Mendez.'

'That didn't kill her,' I said, and stood up.

Mendez moved with me. His eyes flashed white through his mask and gear.

I pointed with one hand at her neck, her breast, her arms. 'They bled her to death.'

'Before?' he asked, sort of hopefully. Never a good sign when the police are asking you to please make this not as horrible as it looks.

I shook my head. 'But multiple bites means she's dead, she can't be a vampire. The body is checked out, guys. Can I join you, or am I on permanent baby-sit duty?'

Derry moved for the door of the kitchen. Oh, goody, I wasn't the only one who wanted out of here. I followed Derry, and Mendez brought up the rear. I'd have moved to the back of the line, but no one complained, so I stayed where I was. The sound of gunfire and yelling and screaming was ahead. I wanted to run, but Derry moved at a jog. If his body was tight with adrenaline, and his pulse thundering, it didn't show. Mendez followed Derry's lead, and so did I.

A woman's scream came high and shrill, from deeper into the apartment. Her screams were accompanied by sounds that were more animal than human. Thick, wet, sucking sounds. The vampires were feeding, and Dawn Morgan was still alive. We did the only thing we could. We rushed into the hallway. We rushed off to save her. We jogged into the trap, because the bait was screaming.

78

THE ONLY LIGHT was the sweep of flashlights ahead and behind. Because I didn't have a light, it ruined my night vision, but didn't really help me. Derry jumped over something, and I glanced down to find that there were bodies in the hallway. The glance down made me stumble over the third body. I only had time to register that one was our guy, and the rest weren't. There was too much blood, too much damage. I couldn't tell who one of them was. He was pinned to the wall by a sword. He looked like a shelled turtle, all that careful body armor ripped away, showing the red ruin of his upper body. The big metal shield was crushed just past the body. Was that Baldwin back there? There were legs sticking out of one of the doors. Derry went past it, trusting that the officers ahead of him hadn't left anything dangerous or alive behind them. It was a level of trust that I had trouble with, but I kept going. I stayed with Derry and Mendez, like I'd been told.

There was a vamp near the end of the hallway with most of the top of his head missing. His mouth was wide, showing fangs in the flash of someone's light. Derry hit the doorway and hugged the wall to the left. I followed him. Mendez went right. Only when Mendez didn't follow me, did I realize that I should have peeled off to the other wall with him. Hell, there were too many rules. I stayed with Derry, because there wasn't time to correct the mistake, if it was a mistake. If we lived, I'd ask someone.

The holy objects had blazed to life, so bright, white and blue like captive stars. They were ruining everyone's night vision. Made it hard to shoot. My cross was safely tucked away, for just that reason.

By the thin flashlight beams and the incandescent flare of holy fire I saw what there was to see.

If I'd been there from the beginning, my mind would have been slow and taking it all in with that artificial sense that you have more time to do things, decide things, than you actually do. But sometimes when you step into the middle of it, you see things in strobe effect, an image here, there, but never the large picture, as if to see it all at once would overwhelm you. Hudson yelling, MP5 to his shoulder. Bodies on the ground between him and the big bed. A glimpse of pale, naked flesh on the bed – female. Two other vampires riding two of the men. One rode him to the floor, so he had to be lost to sight from Hudson and Killian's position. The other man was trapped against the wall, still firing his gun into the chest of the vamp, while the body bucked and wouldn't die. The vamp was pressed tight to the white glow of something that looked like a luminous rosary.

Mendez with his rifle, trying to find a shot in the mess. Stepping around giving his back to the bed, so he could pin the gunbarrel against the back of the vamp's head. The vamp never lifted from Jung's neck. The gunshot, like all the others, was loud, but not nearly as loud as it could have been.

It was wrong, all wrong. No vamp, except the most powerful, could stand up to holy objects like this. Only revenants, mindless newbies would feed while you pushed a gun to their head and blew their brains out. You can't be ancient and a newbie, which meant, we were missing someone, someone that was standing right fucking here.

I dropped my shields, and I looked not toward the fighting, but away from it. Either he was better than I was, and he was invisible, which meant he was farther into the room, or he was hiding somewhere that the team hadn't gotten to yet, or both.

I found the energy of him in the far corner in plain sight. Even knowing he was there, I couldn't see him. Which meant either I was wrong, or he was good enough that he could stand wrapped in

shadows and darkness and be invisible. The only other vamp I'd
ever known that was that good had never been human. I think I
could have stripped him of it using my necromancy, or Jean-Claude's
marks, but I had the Mossberg in my hands. Why waste magic, when
you've got technology?

I tightened my brace of the butt against my shoulder, sighted down
the barrel, and pulled the trigger. The shot didn't kill him, but it
brought him stumbling away from the wall. Suddenly everyone could
see him. His hands were holding his stomach where I'd shot him.
He looked surprised. Tall bastard, I'd been aiming for his chest.

I hit him again, and there was an echo, two echoes. His body
slammed back against the wall. I yelled into the mike, 'I want to see
the wall through his chest.'

No one argued. Derry had moved over to help Mendez. I was
betting that Hudson had sent him, while I was concentrating on
vampire stuff. Hudson, Killian, and I shot the master vampire, until
there was a pale smear of wall through his chest. He slid down the
wall like a broken puppet, painting the wall dark with blood. Hudson
and Killian stopped firing, but I didn't. I put a shot into the head,
and had a second shot in before they joined me, but they did join
me. With three of us, it didn't take long to explode most of his head
like a melon thrown against a wall. When most of his head was gone
from his shoulders, I lowered my gun enough to look around and
see how everyone else was doing.

Now that the master was dead, the newbie vamps were cringing
away from the holy objects, just like they're supposed to. Well, the
one vamp that was still alive cringed. She pressed her bloody face
against the corner behind the bed, her small hands held out as if to
ward it off. At first it looked like she was wearing red gloves, then
the lights shone in the blood, and you knew it wasn't opera-length
gloves, it was blood all the way to her elbows. Even knowing that,
even having Melbourne motionless on the floor in front of her, still
Mendez didn't shoot her. Jung was leaning against the wall, like he'd

fall down if he didn't concentrate. His neck was torn up, but the blood wasn't gushing out. She'd missed the jugular. Let's hear it for inexperience.

I said, 'Shoot her.'

The vampire made mewling sounds, like a frightened child. Her voice came high and piteous, 'Please, please, don't hurt me, don't hurt me. He made me. He made me.'

'Shoot her, Mendez,' I said into the mike.

'She's begging for her life,' he said, and his voice didn't sound good.

'Shit,' I said and started across the room. Something grabbed my ankle. Reflex pointed the shotgun downward. One of the 'dead' vampires hissed up at me, with a hole in its forehead, but it still had my ankle, and it was still going to bite me. From less than two feet away, the sawed-off would have been better, but there was no time. I emptied my gun into its head and back, until it let go of me and blood and other things leaked out of the body. 'Hudson, dead is at least half their brains spilled, and daylight through their chests.'

He didn't argue, just stepped up close to the other vamp and started pegging away at it. I guess making invisible vampires visible had earned me some credits with the sergeant.

I peeled shotgun shells out of the stock holder and fed them into the gun, as I walked toward Mendez and the vampire. She was still crying, still begging, 'They made us do it, they made us do it.'

The woman on the bed was naked, and her eyes had started to glaze. Shit. But the room had to be secured before we could see to the victim. Secured in my line of work meant something different than for most officers of the law. Secured meant that everything in the room that wasn't on my side was dead.

Killian was moving up by the bed to check on our victim. I hoped he could help her, because it seemed worse to lose people who were trying to save someone that didn't get saved. Jung was trying to hold pressure on his own neck wound. Melbourne's body lay on its side, one hand outstretched toward the cringing vampire. Melbourne wasn't moving, but the vampire still was: That seemed wrong to me. But I knew just how to fix it.

I had the shotgun reloaded, but I let it swing down at my side. At this range the sawed-off was quicker, no wasted ammo.

Mendez had glanced away from the vamp to me, then farther back to his sergeant. 'I can't shoot someone who's begging for her life.'

'It's okay, Mendez, I can.'

'No,' he said, and looked at me, his eyes showed too much white. 'No.'

'Step back, Mendez,' Hudson said.

'Sir . . .'

'Step back and let Marshal Blake do her job.'

'Sir . . . it's not right.'

'Are you refusing a direct order, Mendez?'

'No, sir, but—'

'Then step back, and let the marshal do her job.'

Mendez still hesitated.

'Now, Mendez!'

He moved back, but I didn't trust him at my back. He wasn't bespelled, she hadn't tricked him with her eyes. It was much simpler than that. Police are trained to save lives, not take them. If she'd attacked him, Mendez would have fired. If she'd attacked someone else, he'd have fired. If she'd looked like a raving monster, he'd have fired. But she didn't look like a monster as she cringed in the corner, hands as small as my own held up trying to stop what was coming. Her body pressed into the corner, like a child's last refuge before the beating begins, when you run out of places to hide and you are literally cornered, and there's nothing you can do. No word, no action, no thing that will stop it.

'Go stand by your sergeant,' I said.

He stared at me, and his breathing was way too fast.

'Mendez,' Hudson said, 'I want you here, now.'

Mendez obeyed that voice, as he'd been trained to, but he kept glancing back at me and the vampire in the corner.

She glanced past her arm, and because I didn't have a holy item in sight, she was able to give me her eyes. They were pale in the uncertain light, pale and frightened. 'Please,' she said, 'please don't hurt me. He made us do such terrible things. I didn't want to, but the blood, I had to have it.' She raised her delicate oval face to me. 'I had to have it.' The lower half of her face was a crimson mask.

I nodded and braced the shotgun in my arms, using my hip and arm instead of my shoulder for the brace point. 'I know,' I said.

'Don't,' she said, and held out her hands.

I fired into her face from less than two feet away. Her face vanished in a spray of blood and thicker things. Her body sat up very straight for long enough that I pulled the trigger into the middle of her chest. She was tiny, not much meat on her, I got daylight with just one shot.

Mendez's voice came over the mike, 'We're supposed to be the good guys.'

'Shut up, Mendez,' Jung said in a voice that was choked and thicker than it should have been.

I knelt by Jung. 'Check Mel,' he whispered.

I didn't argue with him, though I was pretty sure that it was useless. I reached for the big pulse in his neck and found torn, bloody meat. The carpet around him was spongy with blood. They hadn't even fed on him. They'd just torn his throat out, not to feed, just to kill.

'How is he?' Jung asked.

'Hudson,' I said.

Hudson was there, and I got up and let him tell Jung the bad news. Not my job to break the news to the wounded. Not my job. I walked out into the middle of the room. There was movement in the hallway, and it took everything I had not to shoot the medics as they came through. Hudson had had to call on the headsets, but I hadn't heard him. Hell of a night.

They descended on the wounded with their bags and boxes, and I walked farther into the room, because there was nothing I could do. I had no power over human mortality. Vampires, some shapeshifters, but not straight humans. I didn't know how to save them.

'How could you look her in the eyes and do that?'

I turned and found Mendez by me. He'd taken off his mask and helmet, though I was betting that was against the rules until we left the building. I covered my mike with my hand, because no one should learn about someone's death by accident. 'She tore Melbourne's throat out.'

'She said the other vampire made her do it, is that true?'

'Maybe,' I said.

'Then how could you just shoot her?'

'Because she was guilty.'

'And who died and made you judge, jury, and ex—' He stopped in midsentence.

'Executioner,' I finished for him. 'The federal and state government actually.'

'I thought we were the good guys,' he said, and it had that note of a child who finally realizes that sometimes good and evil aren't so much opposites, as two sides of a coin. You toss it one way, and it looks good, another way, and it's evil. Sometimes it just depends on which end of the gun you're on.

'We are.'

He shook his head. 'You aren't.'

I have no excuse for what I said next, other than he hurt my feelings, and he said out loud something I'd began wonder about. 'If you can't take the heat, Mendez, get out of the fucking kitchen. Get a desk job. But whatever you do, right now, get the fuck away from me.'

He stared at me.

Hudson said, 'Mendez, go get some air. That's an order.'

Mendez gave us both a glance, then he went for the door. Hudson watched him go, then looked back at me. 'He didn't mean that.'

'Yeah, he did.'

'He doesn't understand what you do.'

I sighed. 'Sure.'

'In the movies, the vampires look peaceful. Nothing here looks peaceful.'

'I don't bring peace, Sergeant, I bring death.'

'You save more lives than you take.'

'Pretty to think so,' I said.

He clapped me on the back, the closest he'd ever get to hugging one of his people, but I took it for the compliment it was. 'You did good tonight, Blake, don't let anyone take that away from you.'

I nodded. 'Thanks.'

'You don't sound convinced,' he said.

'Let's just say that after awhile you get tired of having to shoot people who are begging for their lives.'

'They're vampires, they're already dead,' he said.

I shook my head and smiled. 'I wish I believed that, Sergeant Hudson, I do surely wish I believed that.' I watched them start taking out the wounded. They left Melbourne where he lay, but took the girl from the bed. They were triaging, taking the ones they could save; the dead aren't going anywhere. Well, none of the dead in this room.

79

I WAS HAVING an argument with Sergeant Hudson. We were doing it quietly at the back of the equipment van, so the media that had descended on us wouldn't get us on camera, but it was still an argument.

'It isn't them, Sergeant,' I said.

'So there was an extra vamp or two than the bite marks on the earlier victims. They made more.'

'The master vamp of this group is strong enough to hide his power from both the Church of Eternal Life and the Master of the City, nothing we killed up there had that kind of power.'

'We lost three men up there, I think that's plenty powerful enough.'

I shook my head. 'Most of these were babies, almost brand-new. What I saw at the earlier crime scenes wasn't a feeding frenzy, it was methodical. The vampires up in that condo were still more like animals than thinking beings. They were too wild to be taken on an organized hunt.'

'I don't know what you're talking about, an organized hunt. You make it sound like killing humans is like hunting deer, or rabbit.'

'To some of the vampires, it is.'

He shook his head, hands on hips, and started to pace in a tight circle, but the open door of the van stopped his pacing. 'It's the right number of vamps. They had one dead stripper, and one that they nearly killed. That's good enough.'

'They took her and left a state trooper as a witness, so we'd know. They wanted us to come here tonight. Why?'

'They ambushed us in the hallway, Blake. I think we were just better at killing them than they planned for us to be.'

'Maybe, but what if it wasn't a trap to kill us? What if it was a trap to kill the vampires?'

'That's just . . . that makes no sense.'

'You're ready to close the case. You're ready to declare them dead, defeated. We kill a few vampires, find a few dead humans in the condo, and you're ready to believe it's our serial killers.'

'And who else would it be? Are you saying we've got copycats?'

'No, I'm saying that if we close this case, then they can just move on to the next town. They can start over.'

'You're saying they left us some of their baby vampires so we'd kill them and think it was them? They sacrificed their own people for this?'

'Yeah, that's what I'm saying.'

'You know what I think, Blake?'

'No, what?'

'I think you just can't let it go. I think you want it not to be over.'

It was my turn to try to pace, but I was smaller, and standing a little farther out from the doors, so I got almost a full circle out of my pacing. It didn't help. 'I want this over with, Hudson, more than you do. Because if these vampires were left up there as sacrificial lambs, then they used me to kill them. They used all of us as a sort of a weapon, their weapon.'

'Go home, Blake, go home to your husband, or boyfriend, or fucking dog, but go home. Your job is done here. Do you understand that?'

I looked up at him and tried to think how to explain it. I finally tried something I didn't like admitting to the police at large. 'I saw inside the memories of one of the vampires at the church earlier tonight. I saw some faces. I got some names. Those faces aren't up there. Those names aren't going to belong to any of the dead.'

'This case is closed, Blake, which means your warrant has been fulfilled. You're done. Go home.'

'Actually, Sergeant, I have sole discretion on whether a warrant is finished or not. Mark me on this, if we don't get these guys in St Louis, they'll move shop. We got some of them tonight, but not all of them, and we sure as hell missed the big guy, and if you don't kill the main master, he just moves somewhere else and starts making new vampires. It's like going in for cancer surgery, if you don't get it all, then it keeps spreading.'

'I thought you were dating a vampire,' he said.

'I am,' I said.

'For someone who's dating one of them, you have a damned dark view of them.'

'Ask me how I feel about human beings sometimes. I've gotten called in on too many serial killer cases, where they want it to be a monster, because they don't want to believe that one human being could do shit like that to another human being.'

'How long you been doing this, hunting vamps, doing the bad crimes?'

'Six years, why?'

'Most violent crime units rotate their people about every two to five years. Maybe you need to see something a little less bloody for awhile.'

I didn't know what to say to that, so I sort of side-stepped it. 'Up there, the master vampire that was hiding in the corner, none of you could see him, right?'

'Until you shot him.'

'I could feel him. I knew exactly where he was. He was controlling the others in the bedroom. If he hadn't died, then the others would have kept attacking, even with the holy objects visible. We'd have lost more people.'

'Maybe, but what's your point?'

'My abilities with the dead are genetic, it's like a psychic gift. No amount of training or practice will teach you how to see the invisible. There are less than twenty people in the entire country that have abilities even close to mine.'

'There are a hell of a lot more than twenty people in the new federal marshal's program,' he said.

I nodded. 'Yeah, and some of them are good. Some of them would have sensed his power, but I don't know if any of the rest would have known exactly where to shoot.'

'You're saying that you're the only one who can do your job?'

I shrugged.

'Look, Blake, take some advice from someone who's been doing this longer than you have. You're not God, you can't save every-body, and the police work in this town has been running just fine without you to baby-sit. You aren't the only cop in this city, and you aren't the only one who can do this job. You've got to let go of that idea, or you'll go crazy. You'll start blaming yourself for not being there twenty-four-seven. You'll start thinking, if only I'd been there, this bad thing, or that bad thing, wouldn't have happened. It's a lie. You're just a person, with some good abilities, and good judgment, but don't try and carry the weight of the whole fucking world. It'll crush you.'

I looked up into his brown eyes, and there was something in his face that said he was giving advice that had been hard-won. If I'd been a girl-girl, I'd have said something like, you sound like you're talking from experience, but I'd hung around with the boys' club too long not to know my manners. Hudson was opening up, and he didn't have to, he was trying to help me; asking him personal shit would have made me an ungrateful wretch. 'I've been the only one for so long.'

'Did you go up in that condo by yourself?' he asked.

I shook my head.

'Then stop acting like you did. Do you have anyone waiting for you at home?' His voice was gentler than it had been when he'd first told me to go home to my husband or boyfriend.

'Yeah, I got someone waiting.'

'Then go home. Call him from the car, let him know that the officer down calls weren't you.' They never released names of the downed officers to the media until all the families had been contacted, better for the bereaved, but hell on all the other families with police officers out and about tonight. They were all waiting for the phone to ring, or worse, the doorbell. No one with a police officer in the family wanted to see another cop on their doorstep tonight.

I thought about how I'd left Micah and Nathaniel standing in the parking lot. How I'd told them to take Ronnie home. How I hadn't kissed either of them goodbye. My eyes were hot, and my throat hurt.

I nodded, maybe a little too rapidly. My voice was only a little shaky. 'I'll go home. I'll call home.'

'Get some sleep if you can, you'll feel better tomorrow.'

I nodded, but didn't look at him. I'd taken a couple of steps when I turned back and said, 'I'll bet you almost anything, Hudson, that the crime lab is going to agree with me. The DNA in the bites from the first vics aren't going to match most of the vamps upstairs.'

'You just won't let this go, will you?'

I shrugged. 'I don't know how to let go, Sergeant.'

'Take it from someone who knows, Blake. You better start learning, or you're going to burn out.'

I looked at him, and he looked back, and I wondered what he'd seen in me tonight for him to feel that I needed the 'burnout' lecture. Was he right? Or were we all just tired? Him, me, all of us.

80

I DROVE HOME thinking about vampires. Not the fun ones. The ones we'd just killed. It was nearly three in the morning, mine was almost the only car when I pulled out onto the highway. Eight dead vamps, plus one human cohort. My bet was a human servant, because he was the one that had killed Officer Baldwin with a sword. That spoke of long ago skills. Not many modern humans are good enough with a blade to take out a tactical officer armed with an MP5. Eight was enough to account for all of them, but I knew we'd missed Vittorio. He just hadn't been there.

The night was clear and bright, and as I left the city proper behind, stars studded the sky like someone had spilled a bag of diamonds across the velvet of it. I felt surprisingly good. I wasn't sure why and didn't look at it too closely, just in case it was fragile, and too much poking would have broken the mood. I felt good, and I was going home, and I'd saved everyone I could, and killed everyone I could. I was out of it for the night.

There'd been enough dead females to account for Nadine and Nellie, the pair that had seduced Avery Seabrook. There'd even been an extra that could have been Gwenyth, Vittorio's sweetheart, but I thought it long odds that all three of them would just let us shoot them without much of a fight. By the standards I was used to, it hadn't been much of a fight. Not for what this group had been capable of. At least one of them, or more, should have tried to fly out a window, to escape. The sniper had had nothing to do tonight.

It wasn't until I was turning off onto 55 South that I realized the Circus of the Damned would have been much closer, and gotten me to bed sooner. Now it was too late, as long or longer to backtrack as go forward. But I wanted my own bed tonight. I wanted a certain stuffed toy penguin. I wanted Micah and Nathaniel, and right at that moment I didn't really want to see another vampire. It wasn't the vampire vics that made me not want to face another vampire tonight, it was my victims. It was the flash pictures in my head of the girl who'd begged for her life, and Jonah Cooper, and the silent crowd watching me at the church. I tried to hide behind the shield of the horrible things they'd done to the woman in the kitchen. It had been horrible. Once I'd justified it for myself, by thinking that I was the good guy, that there were things I wouldn't do, lines I wouldn't cross. Lately, the lines seemed blurry, or gone. I agreed with Mendez. You didn't shoot someone begging for their life, not if you were a good guy. But a lot of them begged. A lot of them were sorry, once they were looking down the wrong end of a gun. But they weren't sorry while they were killing people, torturing people, no, they were having a good time, until they got caught.

What got me tonight, was her saying, 'He made us do it.' Had he? Had Vittorio so controlled them that they could not disobey him? I knew from the fallout with the London vamps that we'd adopted that you were legally bound to follow your master, almost morally bound, because he was like your liege lord. But was it more than that? Could vampires make other vampires do things they did not want to do? I'd ask Jean-Claude, but not tonight. Tonight I was tired.

The highway stretched black and empty. My only company was a semi truck pulling some all-night load across the country off in the distance. The truck and I had the road to ourselves.

I was betting that wherever Vittorio was, that's where we'd find the women. The crime lab would check the dead vamps' DNA against the bite marks in the first few victims, and we'd know how many we'd missed. As far the St Louis police were concerned, it was over. We'd executed most of them and chased the survivors out of town.

Trouble was, serial killers don't stop killing, they just move on and start again somewhere else. Sergeant Hudson and his men were done with it, and they'd paid a high price to be done. But my badge said federal, which meant that I might not be done with Vittorio and his people. I pushed the thought away. For now we'd driven him and his surviving members out of town. That had to be enough, at least for tonight.

I was off the highway now, on the smooth, more narrow road that led farther into Jefferson County and my house. Trees blocked the view, so the stars seemed farther away. I pulled into my driveway and saw the faint shine of lights against the living room drapes. Micah or Nathaniel had waited up. It was after three A.M., and someone had waited up. I felt guilty, happy, and apprehensive. Nothing good had ever come of my father and Judith waiting up for me. I still wasn't completely used to living with anyone, so sometimes old reactions crept up, like I was seventeen again, and there was a light on. I told myself I was being silly, but this would be the first call-out like this one since Nathaniel had the right to make more demands on me. I wasn't sure, yet, what all of those demands might be. So I was a little nervous as I put my key in the door. Was I being silly? Only one way to find out.

They were sitting on the couch. I thought Nathaniel was asleep with his head in Micah's lap, but he turned as I came through the door, and I caught the flash of his eyes in the light from the television. A look of such naked relief crossed Micah's face before he managed to hide it behind a smile. He was back to his usual smiling neutrality, back to making as few demands on me as possible, but I'd seen that first look. That look that said more than any words, that he'd wondered if he'd ever see me again. I hadn't kissed him good-bye. I had forgotten to call from the car, tell them the officer down calls weren't me. The thought cut deep like some guilty knife.

Nathaniel got to me first, then slowed, before he actually touched me. The look on my face, maybe, or the fact that I just stood there halfway between the couch and the door. The look on his face was so disappointed. I got a flash of emotion from him. So sad. He thought I was drawing back, away, too scared to really be with him, with them. That wasn't what I was scared of.

You can't shoot someone from less than three feet away with a sawed-off and not get blowback. I had blood in my hair, on my arms. I'd gotten some of it with the wet wipes I kept in the car, but not all of it. I wasn't clean. If I'd been just a cop, and the dead woman just a human, then I'd have worried about blood-borne disease. She could have AIDS, or hepatitis, but she was a vampire, so she couldn't carry anything, unless you counted vampirism. Yeah, I guess that counted, but Nathaniel and Micah couldn't get that either. But maybe I could. If I killed humans, then I was in more danger from disease, but vamps were cleaner. It was too weird for me tonight, too much thinking.

'Anita, are you alright?' Micah asked, and got off the couch to move up beside Nathaniel.

I jerked out of reach. 'I've got blood on me, other people's blood.' I was shaking my head over and over. 'God knows what I brought home with me.'

'We can't catch anything,' Nathaniel said, 'not even a cold.' He didn't look lost anymore, he looked worried.

'Blood can't hurt us,' Micah said.

They were right. I was being silly about contagion, but . . . 'Do you really want to touch me while I've still got the blood of my victims on me?'

'Yes,' Nathaniel said, and moved to hug me.

I moved back, just enough that he stopped. I was afraid if I let them hug me that I would lose it. I would just sink into their arms and sob.

'Victims?' Micah said. 'Anita, this doesn't sound like you.' But he came with Nathaniel; he tried to hug me.

I moved back until the door hit me, and I was shaking my head. 'If I let you hold me, I'm going to cry. Damn it, I hate to cry.'

Micah gave me a look. 'That's not it.'

I closed my eyes and let the equipment bag fall to the floor. He was right, that wasn't it, not completely. I tried to be honest. I tried to say what I felt. 'If I get any sympathy, I'm going to fall apart.'

'Maybe that's what you need to do,' Micah said, and he moved just a little closer, 'maybe just for a little while, let us take care of you.'

I kept shaking my head. 'I'm afraid.'

'Of what?' he asked, voice soft.

'Of letting go.'

Micah touched my shoulder, gently. I didn't pull away. He moved slowly, gently, easing me away from the door, and into his arms. I stayed stiff and unyielding for a moment, then my breath came out in a long wavering line, and I let myself fold around him. My hands grabbed at his shirt, handfuls of cloth, as if I couldn't get close enough, or hold on hard enough. I wanted him naked, not for sex, though that would probably come, but because I just wanted as much of him pressed against as much of me as possible.

'I'll go run the bath,' Nathaniel said.

I reached out for him, caught his shirt, and drew him into us. 'I'm sorry,' I said.

'What about?' he asked, and he and Micah exchanged a look.

The first tear squeezed out, traitorous bastard. My voice was almost steady when I said, 'I didn't kiss you goodbye, either of you. I just drove off. I'm sorry.'

They both kissed me, soft, chaste, a mere touch of lips. Micah brushed the tear off my cheek. 'We understood.' He looked at Nathaniel. 'Run the bath.'

'I'd rather have a shower and get to bed.'

They exchanged another look, but with a nod from Micah, Nathaniel went for the bathroom. I looked at Micah's face. The only man in my life I didn't have to look up to to meet his eyes. 'What's happened? What have I missed?'

He smiled, but it wasn't a happy smile. It was the smile he'd had

819

when I first met him. A smile that held sadness, self-deprecation, mocking, and something else, something that sadness was too light a word for. I'd almost broken him from that smile.

I grabbed his arms, almost shook him. 'What happened?'

'Nothing, I swear, everything's fine, but Jean-Claude warned us not to let you get in the shower. He said, and I quote, 'not between glass walls.' '

I frowned at him. 'What are you talking about? Why should Jean-Claude care about how I clean up?'

The phone rang. I jumped like I'd been stabbed. I said what I was thinking. 'If it's another murder scene tonight, I can't do it.' Even saying it, I knew I'd do it. If they needed me, I'd go. But what I'd said was true, I'd go, but I wasn't sure I could handle it tonight. Admitting that even to myself scared me. It was my job. I had to be able to do it.

Micah went for the phone, while I stood in the darkened living room and prayed for it not to be the police. He called, 'It's Jean-Claude.'

'Why is he calling on the phone?'

'Come and find out,' Micah said.

I walked to the lights of the kitchen. It was only the lights over the sink, not that much light, but I blinked like a deer in headlights. I took the receiver from Micah, while he tried not to give me worried eyes. 'What's up?' I asked.

'*Ma petite*, how do you feel?'

His voice was the joy for me it usually was, but tonight even that voice left me flat and empty. 'Like shit, why?'

'How long has it been since you fed?'

I leaned my forehead against the wall and closed my eyes. 'I ate some peanuts and chips in the last day, why?' Nathaniel had put some munchies in my glove compartment.

'I am not referring to food, *ma petite*.'

Suddenly the emptiness spilled away, replaced by panic. 'Jesus, Damian.'

'He is well. I have seen to it.'

'How can he be well, he started to die if I went just a few hours over six. I've gone almost twenty-four hours. God, I cannot believe this, so stupid.'

'And when in the last twenty-four hours could you have fed the *ardeur*, and who on?'

The question stopped the self-recriminations and helped me think. I guess there were worse things than forgetting about the *ardeur* during a police investigation. Like maybe, not forgetting the *ardeur* during a police investigation. Several horrible scenarios went through my head, like the *ardeur* rising in the van with Mobile Reserve, or Zerbrowski in his car. I was suddenly cold, and it had nothing to do with my earlier pangs of conscience.

'*Ma petite*, I can hear your sweet breath, but I need to hear your sweet voice.'

'Jesus, Mary, and Joseph, how did you keep it from getting me?'

'By shielding in every way between us, and Richard, and helping the others do so, as well.'

'That's why you're calling me on the phone, not mind-to-mind.'

'*Oui.*'

'How did you keep me from draining Damian and Nathaniel?'

'I fed the *ardeur* at the club, as we discussed, and I shared with Damian. It is only when he is drained that your triumvirate would begin to pull upon our bad kitty.'

'One feeding through you took care of it, for this long?'

He sighed, and he sounded tired, because he was still shielding too hard for me to feel it. '*Non, non, ma petite*. We have done your six-hour feedings for you.'

'Who's we?'

'Richard and Damian, and myself. Nathaniel had fed you last, and I was not a hundred-percent certain that I could control the feeding, so I did not use him.'

'Richard got a taste of the *ardeur* from the other side?'

'He did.'

'What'd he think of it?'

'He has new respect for our ability to not go mad.'

I wanted to ask who Richard had fed on, but it was none of my business. I wasn't monogamous, and neither was he. I was still leaning against the wall, but my eyes were open. 'Damian fed the *ardeur* not as the eatee, but as the eater?'

'It was not hard to raise it in him.'

'Is this permanent? I mean do Richard and Damian need to feed now, too?'

'*Non*, *ma petite*. Desperate measures, but not permanent ones.'

'How can you be sure?' I asked.

'Because I can feel it growing in me again, not just my need, but yours. I parceled it out, shared it among those I could, but it is time again, *ma petite*.'

I turned around and stared blindly out into the kitchen. 'Are you saying you borrowed my *ardeur* for the last few hours?'

He seemed to think about that. 'That will do for an explanation. *Oui*.'

'So I could hunt bad guys and not lose control in the middle of it all.'

'Yes.'

I didn't know what to say, so I said what I could, 'Thank you.'

'You are most welcome, *ma petite*, put dawn is near, and when I sleep, the *ardeur* will return home. I would prefer to give it back to you before then, so I might feel how tempestuous that return will be.'

'You're worried.'

'*Oui*.'

'You asked me how I felt, why?'

'The *ardeur* comes with a price, as all the hungers do, but they have their rewards, as well. I do not speak of the pleasure, but of the strengths that they give us. In effect, by stealing away your *ardeur*, I weakened you tonight. If I hadn't feared contacting you mind-to-mind, I would have asked your permission first, or warned you.'

'I didn't feel weak.' Then I thought about it. 'I'm really bugged by the vampires I killed tonight. I mean, more than normal. I'm sort of shaky, and wondering if I'm the good guy after all.'

'Such self-doubt is not like you.'

'I do have some self-doubt,' I said.

'But not too much, you could not be who you are if you doubted too much.'

'Are you saying that I draw some of my bravery, or my coldness, from the *ardeur*?'

'I am saying that the *ardeur* may feed that part of you that keeps you safe in your own mind, your own heart.'

I shook my head. 'This is too complicated for me, Jean-Claude. Just let me have it back, and we'll see if I feel any better.'

'I would rather you be alone with Micah when that happens. We have very carefully left him untouched while we sought to feed, so that you might feed on him yourself.'

I didn't feel the least bit sexy. I just wanted a quick shower and to sleep. 'I'm too tired for sex, Jean-Claude. Too tired for much of anything.'

'As I feared, I took too much, or the *ardeur* has become attached to your own natural drives.'

'What are you talking about?'

'Long before the *ardeur* found you, *ma petite*, I found that you were seldom too tired for sex.'

I thought about blushing, but found that even that seemed like too much effort. 'What do you want me to do?' What little excitement had crept back into my voice had vanished. Nothing seemed quite real, as if I was already asleep. Asleep on my feet.

'If you intend to clean up . . .'

'I've got other people's blood in my hair, so yeah.'

'Fine, go to the bathroom then, but take Micah with you. Hang up the phone, go to the bathroom, take Micah with you, and sometime before you have filled the bathtub with water, I will give back to you that which is yours.'

'Nathaniel is filling the tub now. Micah said you warned us not to use the shower. Something about glass.'

'The return may be more violent than I would like, *ma petite*. I would feel better if you and Micah were not surrounded by glass walls.'

'Do you know this is going to be bad, or are you just worried?'

'Let us say, that I have not lived so long, or courted you successfully, without thinking worst-case scenarios.'

'*Courting*, is that what you call it nowadays?'

'I am hanging up now, *ma petite*. I suggest you do as I have bid.' He hung up.

I put the receiver back in its cradle and started walking out of the kitchen. Micah was standing by the table, watching with careful kitty-cat eyes. I understood now how much he held back behind that careful face. But tonight I didn't pry. I had enough horrors of my own without borrowing. 'You know about what Jean-Claude's been doing with the *ardeur*?' I asked.

'Yes, Jean-Claude had me keep an eye on Nathaniel, so that if he started to get weak, I could call for help.'

I shook my head. 'I endangered him, all of you.' I felt numb again, even the self-recrimination felt like just words. Later, when there was more of me, I'd feel bad, but right now, I'd felt about as bad as I was able. There just wasn't enough of me left to worry about it.

'Anita.' Micah was in front of me and I hadn't seen him move. 'Anita, are you alright?'

I shook my head. The answer was no, but out loud I said, 'I want to be cleaned up before the *ardeur* comes back. I want to get this shit off of me.' I started for the bathroom. Micah trailed after me.

Nathaniel was bending over the bath tub, his pony tail trailing around his naked upper body. He'd stripped down to silk boxers.

The sight of him like that should have moved me, but it didn't. Cold, I felt so cold inside.

He gave me worried eyes as he moved toward me. 'What can I do to help?'

I flung myself on him hard enough he staggered. He held me against the warmth of his body. He held me tight and hard, responding to my desperation. I wanted to bury myself in his flesh, wrap him up around me, but I couldn't. I'd endangered him, risked his life, by simply not paying attention to the *ardeur*. If Jean-Claude had not helped out . . .

I tried to push the thought away, but Jonah Cooper's body flashed in my head. His body on the ground, my foot on his shoulder and grass showing through his chest. 'You feel the draw of them, I know you do,' he'd said.

I was on my knees and only Nathaniel's hands had kept me from hurting myself on the edge of the tub. 'Anita . . .'

I pulled away from Nathaniel and reached for Micah. He took my hand and said, 'Go, Nathaniel, go, before the *ardeur* comes.'

'I don't think . . .' he started to say.

I screamed, 'Go, please go! God, go!'

I didn't see Nathaniel go, or stay, because Jean-Claude dropped his shielding. I don't know what I'd expected. He'd made it sound like he borrowed my favorite coat, or book, and now he'd give it back, but a coat doesn't want to come back to you, a book doesn't care who reads it. He didn't hand it back to me, his shields dropped, and it roared home like a train that he had fought to hold back, to keep still, but it had strained against his hold. It had hungered to come home. It was like being caught on the tracks at night, and the first hint you have that disaster is here, is a bright light, and the tracks vibrating under your feet, then the world becomes noise, light, as if thunder and lightning could be forged into metal, and it's all coming straight through you, and you can't get off the tracks. You can't run. You can't hide, because your body is the tracks, and the train is a piece of yourself that wants to come home.

81

THE *ARDEUR* FELL on us, and we fell into the water. It took us almost a minute to remember we couldn't breathe under water. We came up, gasping for air, laughing almost as soon as we could breathe enough for it. Clothes had vanished in the first rush. We were naked in the water. How had we managed to get out of the jeans that fast? A piece of jean cloth floated by me. Oh, that's how.

'No missionary position, we'll both drown,' I said.

His curls were plastered to his head, and his hair looked black in the candlelight. The laughter died from his face, his eyes, and left something darker, more basic, behind. A look that made me shiver. All he said was, 'Okay.' He moved us to the edge of the tub, pressing my back against the smooth side of it. He pressed himself up against me, pinning me between the tub and his body. The feel of him hard and firm against the front of my naked body made me close my eyes for a moment. I had some vague memory of clothes being ripped away, but I wasn't sure when, or even which of us had done it. I was getting better at thinking when the *ardeur* rose, but there were moments when thinking was not what I did.

He moved back from my body so he could caress the front of himself. Just watching his hand play over that thick, firm flesh made me shiver. He angled himself downward so he could push between my thighs. He felt incredibly large sliding between my legs. He didn't try to angle upward, or enter me. He simply pushed himself between my thighs, so that the thickness of him brushed against all of me. He rubbed himself back and forth, using his body like another hand, to caress and play between my legs. But it was a thick, hard rubbing, with none of the delicacy of fingers. You'd think water would help everything be slippery, but water makes some parts less wet, less slick, so that though it felt good, it also was rougher than it would have been if I'd been wet with something other than water.

'Not wet enough,' he said, and his voice was thick and strangely hoarse, strangled with desire.

I would have liked to argue, because the *ardeur* wanted to argue, wanted to say, take me, take me now. If I'd been with almost any other man in my life, we could have done just that without hurting me, or him, but Micah was the exception to a lot of rules in my life. It wasn't the length that was the problem, it was the width. We'd found this out the hard way, and had had the rubby spots to prove it.

I managed to say, 'No, not wet enough.'

He leaned his forehead against mine and said a heartfelt, 'Shit.'

I nodded my head against his, wordless assent, because I didn't trust my voice. Micah wasn't the only one strangling on need. He drew his body from between my legs, and even that drew a small sound from me. His hands went to my waist and he just suddenly lifted me up, up so that I was perched on the edge of the tub. If his hand hadn't been on my leg I would have overbalanced and fallen back into the water, but he steadied me. One hand stayed on my leg, but the other hand moved up the line of my thigh. I thought he was going to do me by hand, but his finger slid inside me. It was unexpected, and even one finger felt tight and good. So good that I lay back along the raised tile around the tub. I felt the heat before I actually lay down on one of the candles, but the heat of it pressed against my skin. I sat up so abruptly that he had to move his hands and spill me back into the water.

'Did you get burned?' he asked.

I shook my head. 'No, not this time.' I'd caught my hair on fire once. I laughed, sort of shakily. 'Stupid.'

Micah looked at me, and there was something in that look.

'What?' I asked.

'The *ardeur* is gone.'

I thought about it, felt around for it, and found no, no, not gone, but receded. Not receded like when I fought it, but more like me getting almost burned had help me think again. Or maybe even the *ardeur* bows to physical survival. But I could feel it like a storm that had moved offshore, but was still coming.

'I thought I'd caught myself on fire.'

'Again,' he said.

I frowned at him. 'Yes, again. Is it my fault that you're so amazing that you make me forget everything, even physical safety?'

He shook his head. 'Not me, the *ardeur*. The *ardeur* makes everything better, Anita.'

There was something about the way he said it, something serious and a little sad, that made me say, 'What's wrong?'

He kissed me on the tip of the nose. 'Later.'

I might have argued with him, but the *ardeur* decided that it had given us enough time. It hit me like a train and threw me into his arms, made my hands move over his body as if I was hungry to touch him, as if no touch, no caress, nothing would be enough. We kissed the same way, as if we were hungry for each other. It was as if we could have we would have climbed into each other's skins, wrapped ourselves through each other, closer than skin or flesh could survive.

One minute my mouth was trying to climb inside Micah's, the next my beast rose, swimming up, up through my body, coming out of that metaphysical place, and climbing up my body. Micah drew back from my mouth enough to say, 'Anita . . .'

I used hands and body to press his mouth back to mine. His beast began to spill up through his body in a line of breath-stealing heat. It rose fast and faster as if it had to catch up with mine. They raced up our bodies, raced through that dark water, raced, and raced, faster and faster until they hit the surface. It wasn't about changing shape, it was about changing bodies. It was about that need to wrap as much of him around as much of me, as tight, and close as I could. It was as if the very essence of our bodies had responded to that desire. Our beasts spilled out of our mouths, and brushed metaphysical furred sides down each other, as we spilled inside each other's bodies. It was closer than sex. Closer than anything I'd ever felt. It was as if for a blinding, shattering moment, we were in each other's bodies. Not in our minds, not merely our thoughts, or feelings, not even memories, but for a breath or two, a part of me slipped inside him, and a part of him slipped inside me. They weren't parts that could think and feel like a human being. There was none of that, wow, so this is how it feels to be Micah. There was only a sense of burrowing down, down deep inside him, of finding that metaphysical hiding place where the beast lay and having my beast curl up, for a moment, inside his most secret space, while his beast did the same in me.

In that moment, the *ardeur* fed. Fed on that warm, living power, fed on the sensation of being deeper inside Micah's body than I'd ever been inside any man's before. The *ardeur* fed, and left us quieter, calmer, happier.

The beasts didn't turn and go back up the way they'd come. One moment that piece of me was curled warm and safe inside him, and the sensation of him inside me was like when we made love, as if even his beast were bigger and took up more room than mine. That warm, living energy didn't come back up our throats, it was as if the two energies spilled out the fronts of our bodies, out our skin, so that for a heartbeat it felt as if we'd burst our skins, and two great furred shapes were passing through us, then it was as if the two beasts dropped back into place. I swear I felt as if something physical with true weight was dropped down the center of my body, and hit the end of me. As if instead of falling from the height, I was the height, and could feel the body falling through me, and hitting my floor.

We broke from the kiss, laughing, breathless. I found my voice first, 'Wow.'

He looked happier than I'd ever seen him, relaxed, more . . . more at home somehow, as if some great weight had gone from him. 'You know,' he said, still breathing hard, 'you're not supposed to be able to do that, if one of you is human.'

'I didn't know you were supposed to be able to do that at all,' I said.

'If you are both powerful, and a true mated pair, then it's possible.'

'You say it, like it has a name.'

'Shiva and Parvati, or simply Maithuna, it's Sanskrit for union, or coupling.'

'Shiva, who would destroy the world with his energy if Parvati didn't constantly have sex with him and spill off the energy.'

He nodded. 'World religion class from college again?'

I shook my head. 'A few years back we found a naga, a real live one that had been a crime victim. It made me go look up Hindu religion. I mean, if you get one type of supernatural being, you might get others from the same place.'

'Did you?'

'Nope.' I thought about it. 'Well, not yet.' I put my arms behind his head, and drew him down for a kiss. He didn't fight, but he kept himself just above my face. 'You fed the *ardeur*.'

'I still want a kiss.'

He kissed me, and it was gentle at first, then grew until we were feeding at each other's mouths again. He drew back, laughing and breathless. 'I thought we'd done this already.'

I wasn't sure how to explain it. We'd had metaphysical sex, and like sometimes happens after regular sex I was pumped, energized. I could feel him still hard and thick pressed between our bodies. I wanted him inside me. I wanted him as close physically as I'd had him metaphysically.

I kept one hand behind his neck, but let the other trace down his body, until I could cup him in my hand. He closed his eyes and swallowed hard. I moved my hand up and wrapped my fingers around him. He was so hard, so thick, so solid in my hand that it made me close my eyes, made my breath shudder from my body.

I opened my eyes and knew that my focus was already soft. 'I want this inside me.'

He tried for amusement, but his face was raw with the beginnings of that need. His voice was hoarse again when he said, 'Even without the *ardeur*?'

I squeezed him tight enough to flutter his eyes back into his head. When he could see again, I said, 'It's not the *ardeur* that makes me want you, Micah.'

His voice was a harsh whisper, as if he were having trouble talking, 'We'll never top what we've already done tonight.'

I stroked my hand up the long, hard shaft of him. 'It's not about being better, just being as good.'

He shook his head. 'It won't be as good without the *ardeur* or our beasts, and this close to full moon, I don't think we want to keep trying the beasts. It could get out of hand.'

It was my turn to shake my head. 'Just us, Micah, just us.'

'From the moment we touched, it's never been just us. There's always someone, or something else, never just us.' He looked so serious.

I cupped one hand under the soft wetness of his testicles, and gently played with them, while I played my other hand over the head and shaft of him. 'Then we're past due, don't you think?'

He swallowed hard, laughed, then gave a small nod. 'You're wetter after you feed the *ardeur*, but we ended up back in the water, so you won't be wet enough or open enough for this,' he wrapped his hand around mine where I still held him, he squeezed our hands together until his head went back, eyes closed, and he shuddered hard enough to make the water slosh against the sides of the tub. He looked down at me and slipped his hand between my legs, searching, until he could slip a finger inside me. He managed two fingers inside me before my head went back, and my eyes fluttered shut. 'To go in there,' he whispered.

When I could talk, I said, 'Oh, darn, then you'll have to make me wet, and open.'

He shoved the two fingers fast and hard inside me, stopped my voice along with my breath. 'I can do that,' he said, and he had that look, that look that said he knew I wanted him, and that I wouldn't say no. I didn't say no, I said yes, over and over again. I said yes, until he worked me open with his fingers, and finally with his mouth, so he could push himself inside me. So we could finally put that in there, and it was wet and tight, and hard, and everything I wanted it to be. When I screamed his name and raked my nails down his back, when his body thrust one last time inside mine, thrust so far and so deep that it made me cry out again and arched his body above mine on the bathroom tile. Painted his body in flame and shadow above me, sent our hands into the candles, and spilled the candles into the water, to smoke and die, when all that was done, he looked down at me. Eyes not quite focused, face still slack with orgasm.

I said, in a voice breathy and panting, 'Metaphysics, we don't need no stinking metaphysics.'

It took him a blink to get the joke, but once he did, he started to laugh, and since he was still inside me, that made me writhe, which made him thrust inside me again, which made me writhe again, which made him writhe, which . . . He finally slid off to one side, onto a small candle-free slice of tile still laughing. We laughed until tiredness pulled at us like some giant hand dragging us under. It was as if the entire twenty-four hours caught up with me at once, and I was just done. Done for the day. Done for the night. Done for the year. Done.

We dried our hair as best we could. I insisted on at least running an oiled cloth over the knives that I'd dunked in the bathtub. Micah helped me gather up the big knife and the two handguns. I got the big equipment bag from the living room, but Micah begged me to just put it in the bedroom with us instead of putting everything into their various gun safes. 'Just one night, it'll be okay. I promise,' he said.

I had to agree that I didn't want to go upstairs to the long rifle safe, then downstairs to the ammo safe, then . . . well, you get the idea.

We dragged ourselves to bed carrying more weapons than clothes. I let the equipment bag drop beside the bed, softly. Nathaniel lay on his side, curled into a little ball, like he always lay when no one was in the bed but him. I laid the knives on the bedside table on his side of the bed, again, trying to be quiet.

He opened his eyes just enough to see me, then they closed, and his breathing deepened. He didn't wake completely, but his body responded to me climbing in beside him. He was so warm, almost hot, feverish, or maybe that was just how cool our skin was, from the bath, and the sex in the open air. I put the Browning in its homemade holster in the head of the bed. Micah put the Firestar on the bedside table by him. Nathaniel relaxed into the curve of my body, pressing as much of him against as much of me as he could. It was only then that I realized we were all nude. Nathaniel hadn't worn anything to bed, and neither had we. I let Micah come to bed nude if he wanted to, but never Nathaniel, and never me. It hadn't even occurred to me to get clothes on first. I'd just wanted to go to bed, to sleep, to cuddle between them both. Micah settled in against my back, and I let myself sink into the sensation of being held between them. I'd slept with Micah pressed naked to my back, but never Nathaniel. I'd had his ass pressed into the curve of my stomach and groin for months, but never without clothes, never just skin-to-skin. I pressed my breasts against the warmth of his back, one arm up and over his head so I could touch his hair. My other hand went around his waist. In his sleep, he pulled my hand closer to his body, lower, so that my fingers brushed areas I'd made very sure stayed covered.

'What's wrong?' Micah whispered, as if he'd felt some tension in me.

I touched the silky warmth of the skin just inside Nathaniel's hip, that soft pocket of flesh that frames the groin. Nathaniel's hand on mine, holding me close to him, as his breathing evened back into deep sleep. I snuggled in against him, until my breath danced along his neck, and he snuggled harder against me. 'Nothing,' I whispered, 'nothing at all.'

Micah spooned himself in at my back. His arm going underneath my pillow, and a little under Nathaniel's. Micah's other arm went over my waist, and because Nathaniel was so close to me, his hand ended up resting on Nathaniel's hip. 'Ah,' he whispered, 'no clothes.'

'No clothes,' I said.

He whispered against the back of my neck, and it half-tickled. 'That a problem?'

'No,' I said, and moved my head a fraction down my pillow so I could breathe in the scent of Nathaniel's neck.

'You sure?'

'Yeah.' And I was, because it felt too right to be wrong.

82

THE RAID ON the vampire condo got national attention. A mixed blessing. Headlines ranged from 'Condo of Death,' to 'Police Raid Ends Vampire Serial Killer's Rampage,' or the most popular, 'Vampires turned serial killers, next on Channel . . .' The reports were so similar it didn't much matter what local channel it was on. I just stopped answering my phone for a few days. The interview requests were national, and a few international. I wondered if anyone on Mobile Reserve was getting this much attention. If they were, I hoped they were enjoying it more than I was.

DNA came back, and my worst fears were confirmed. Three of the vamps killed matched the earlier victims' bites, but that left us with five unaccounted for. Five serial killers still at large. Serial killers don't stop killing, not unless they're locked up, or permanently dead.

They'd fled St Louis, the way they fled New Orleans, and Pittsburgh before that. They'd killed policemen in all three towns. Their kill count was more than twenty, and they were still out there.

There'd been a gap of of nearly three months between the killings in Pittsburgh and the killings in New Orleans. Barely a month between New Orleans and St Louis. They were escalating, less time between killing sprees, more victims of choice, though St Louis had managed to get away with the fewest dead among our police. How did we get so lucky? Jean-Claude got a letter.

The writing was beautiful, calligraphy, on heavy vellum paper with a watermark. The note was from Vittorio's Gwennie:

Jean-Claude, Master of the City of St Louis,

I have left Vittorio. His madness has grown beyond anything that I can excuse or take part in. I cannot live as he lives anymore. If he finds me, he will kill me. I have fled with another younger vampire of our kiss, Myron, and Vittorio will not forgive the betrayal. Vittorio is seeking another city now. You have driven him out, but he will find another hunting ground. His madness does not let him rest for long now. His only release seems to come when he kills the people that he sees as taunting him. I saw your Asher at Belle's Court after the church was done with him; let me say only that Vittorio was not so lucky. He is a ruin of a man now. No, he is a monster. He has let the holy water that ate his body eat his mind, as well. Everything I loved in him is gone, lost to this mind sickness.

I hope you found the little that Myron and I could do to assist the police, helpful. We moved the bodies so that they would be found sooner. It was all we could do with Vittorio so close. Myron was the one who left the policeman alive, so you would know that the girl was taken. Myron was also in the church as one of our spies. He knew that you had the address from Cooper before he died. He did not tell anyone, but me, for the rest are trapped in Vittorio's evil dream. We did all we could to help you, and your human servant. Please believe that. If we survive, I will try to contact you again. I truly expect that Vittorio will find us before the year is out. But sometimes it is better to live a short good life, than an evil long one.

Most Sincerely Yours,
Gwen

The letter solved some of the mystery, but it left the biggest part unanswered. Where was Vittorio? How long until he found another city to stalk? I was a federal officer, that meant when he resurfaced, I'd get to see it, if I wanted to, or if the local vampire hunter called me in on it. Denis-Luc St John is still in the hospital in New Orleans. I talked to him on the phone, let him know what happened to the vampires that nearly killed him. He wants a piece of them when they resurface. Good for him, I'm kind of hoping to be left out of it. Is that cowardly? Maybe. If I thought I was the only one who could track them down and save the world, I'd do it, but I'm not the only cop in the country. I'm not even the only vampire executioner with a badge in the country. Let someone else have the fun for a change. I'd had about as much fun in the last few years as I could take. I'll go if I'm asked, but I'm not volunteering. There are always more bad guys, always. There's no way to win the war. You can win a battle here and there, but the war is always ongoing. You kill one villainous bastard, and another one just as bad, or worse, crops up. It never seems to end.

We have a meeting set up to talk to Malcolm about the blood-oath situation. Unfortunately, the no-blood-oath policy is countrywide, not just in St Louis. A fucking disaster waiting to happen. Several of the vamps that were at the church the night I killed Cooper have approached Jean-Claude to change masters from Malcolm to him. Avery Seabrook and Wicked and Truth are among those jumping ship.

Marianne did another tarot reading that duplicated the last one. It being identical means we're still working through it. I still don't know who's supposed to help me, someone from my past. Everyone that is helping seems very much my present and future.

The Dragon has given Primo permission to stay in St Louis and would like to talk to us at a later date about council business. A mixed blessing that.

I've contacted the police working on the Browns' case. They've agreed to have an officer fly down with some of the boy's personal effects, which means they are stumped. Evans has agreed to look at the stuff. Barbara Brown sent me a card saying how sorry she was she hurt me.

I can't fix the world, but I'm making progress on my life. Some nights it's enough to come home alive and crawl into bed beside someone you love, who loves you back.

I found orchids that were the same greenish-gold as Micah's eyes. A bouquet of them is sitting on the coffee table in our living room. Micah says he's never gotten flowers before. Nathaniel got a frilly white apron, like no one's mother ever really wore, and a string of pearls. I found him lying on the bed running the pearls over and over through his fingers.

For Jean-Claude pure white orchids in a simple but elegant black vase. He put them on the coffee table in his living room. Yellow roses for Asher, though they paled beside the gold of his hair. Richard and I aren't back to the flower-giving stage yet. And, truthfully, he never did see much point in he, himself, getting flowers from anyone.

Damian nearly started a riot at Danse Macabre the first night he went to work after we became a true triumvirate. He seems to have gained powers that are more Belle Morte's line of vampire than Moroven's line. He's enjoying his new-found sex appeal. I'm not sure Damian is exactly in the boyfriend category, but he is my vampire servant, and he deserves better than he's been getting from me. I gave him an envelope with a gift certificate in it. A certificate to a furniture store. He can decorate the basement as his room until we can have an apartment built over the garage for him. We had a basement-cleaning party one night; Nathaniel's idea. Basically invite a lot of friends over and make them do grunt work, then feed them pizza afterward. Well, okay, the wereleopards, werewolves, wererats, and humans got pizza. The vampires got something a little less solid. No, Jean-Claude did not come help clean up the basement, but surprisingly, Asher did. So did Richard. He behaved himself all the way up to refreshments, then he couldn't stand me opening a vein for Asher. He didn't argue, he just left. He's trying.

We're all trying. I'm trying to remember what I thought I was doing when I started hunting vampires and helping the police. I used to think I was doing something noble. That there was a reason and a purpose to it. I used to know that I was the good guy. But lately, it feels like I'm just shoveling one pile of shit, so another one can takes its place. Like the bad guys are an avalanche, and I'm trying to stay ahead of it, by shoveling. Maybe I'm just tired, or maybe I'm wondering if Mendez was right. Maybe you can't be one of the good guys, if you spend most of your time shooting people to death. I don't know what bothers me more, that I can shoot someone in the face who's begging for their life, or that legally there's no other option. I don't mind killing to defend my life and the lives of others. I don't mind killing if the person has truly earned it. I'd cap Vittorio in a heartbeat. But what if the girl in the condo had told the truth? What if because her master told her to do something, she had no choice? What if away from the bad guy, she's not a bad guy? Oh, hell, I don't know. The only thing I know for certain is that it isn't my job to worry about how the poor bastard turned into a killer. It's my job to make sure they never kill anyone else again. That's what I do. I am the executioner. Murder someone in my town, and I'm the one that you get to see. Once.

It's time to satisfy your bloodlust . . .

Turn the page for a preview of the next sensational novel featuring Anita Blake.

LAURELL K. HAMILTON

MICAH

AND

STRANGE CANDY

An Anita Blake,
Vampire Hunter, Novel

headline

I

IT WAS HALF past dawn when the phone rang. It shattered the first dream of the night into a thousand pieces so that I couldn't even remember what the dream had been about. I woke gasping and confused, asleep just long enough to feel worse but not rested.

Nathaniel groaned beside me, mumbling, 'What time is it?'

Micah's voice came from the other side of the bed, his voice low and growling, thick with sleep. 'Early.'

I tried to sit up, sandwiched between the two of them where I always slept, but I was trapped. Trapped in the sheets, one arm tangled in Nathaniel's hair. He usually braided it for bed, but last night we'd all gotten in late, even by our standards, and we'd just fallen into bed as soon as we could manage it.

'I'm trapped,' I said, trying to extract my hand from his hair without hurting him or tangling worse. His hair was thick and fell to his ankles; there was lots of it to tangle.

'Let the machine pick up,' Micah said. He'd raised up on his elbows enough to see the clock. 'We've had less than an hour of sleep.' His hair was a mass of tousled curls around his face and shoulders. His face was dim in the darkness of the blackout curtains.

I finally got my hand free of Nathaniel's warm, vanilla-scented hair. I lay on my side, propped on my elbow, waiting for the machine to kick in and let us know whether it was the police for me or the Furry Coalition hotline for Micah. Nathaniel, as a stripper, didn't get emergency calls much. Just as well; I wasn't sure I wanted to know what a stripper emergency call would be. The only ideas I could come up with were either silly or nefarious. Ten rings, and the machine finally kicked on. Micah spoke over the sound of his own voice on the machine's message. 'Who set the machine on the second phone line to ten rings?'

'Me,' Nathaniel said. 'It seemed like a better idea when I did it.'

We'd put in the second phone line because Micah was the main help for a hotline that new wereanimals could call and get advice or a rescue. You know, *I'm at a bar and I'm about to lose control, come get me before I turn furry in public.* It wasn't technically illegal to be a wereanimal, but new ones sometimes lost control and ate someone before they came to their senses. They'd probably be shot to death by the local police before they could be charged with murder. If the police had silver bullets. If not . . . it could get very, very bad.

Micah understood the problems of the furred, because he was the local Nimir-Raj, their leopard king.

There was a moment of breathing on the message, too fast, frantic. The sound made me sit up in bed, letting the sheets pool into my lap. 'Anita, Anita, this is Larry. You there?' He sounded scared.

Nathaniel got the receiver before I did, but he said, 'Hey, Larry, she's here.' He handed me the receiver, his face worried.

Larry Kirkland – fellow federal marshal, animator, and vampire executioner – didn't panic that easily anymore. He'd grown, or aged, since he'd started working with me.

'Larry, what's wrong?'

'Anita, thank God.' His voice held more relief than I ever wanted to hear in anyone's voice. It meant he expected me to do something important for him. Something that would take some awful pressure or problem off their hands.

'What's wrong, Larry?' I asked, and I couldn't keep the worry out of my own voice.

He swallowed hard enough for me to hear it. 'I'm okay, but Tammy isn't.'

I clutched the receiver. His wife was Detective Tammy Reynolds, member of the Regional Preternatural Investigation Squad. My first thought was that she'd been hurt in the line of duty. 'What happened to Tammy?'

Micah leaned in against me. Nathaniel had gone very quiet beside me. We'd all been at their wedding. Hell, I'd been at the altar on Larry's side.

'The baby. Anita, she's in labor.'

It should have made me feel better, but it didn't, not by much. 'She's only five months pregnant, Larry.'

'I know, I know. They're trying to get the labor stopped, but they don't know . . .' He didn't finish the sentence.

Tammy and Larry had been dating for a while when Tammy ended up pregnant. They'd married when she was four months pregnant. Now the baby that had made them both change all their plans might never be born. Or at least not survive. Shit.

'Larry, I'm . . . Jesus, Larry, I'm so sorry. Tell me what I can do to help.' I couldn't think of anything, but whatever he asked, I'd do it. He was my friend, and there was such anguish in his voice. He'd never mastered that empty cop voice.

'I'm due on an eight a.m. flight to raise a witness for the FBI.'

'The federal witness who died before he could testify,' I said.

'Yeah,' Larry said. 'They need the animator that brings him back to be one of us who's also a federal marshal. Me being a federal marshal was one of the reasons the judge agreed to allow the zombie's testimony.'

'I remember,' I said, but I wasn't happy. I wouldn't turn him down or chicken out, not with Tammy in the hospital, but I hated to fly. No, I was afraid to fly. Dammit.

'I know how much you hate to fly,' he said.

That made me smile, that he was trying to make me feel better when his life was about to break apart. 'It's okay, Larry. I'll see if the flight has some empty seats. If not I'll get a later flight, but I'll go.'

'All my files on the case are at Animators, Inc. I'd stopped by the office to get them and load up the briefcase when Tammy called. I think my briefcase is just sitting on the floor in our office. I got all the files in it. The agent in charge is . . .' And he hesitated. 'I can't remember. Oh, hell, Anita, I can't remember.' He was panicking again.

'It's okay, Larry. I'll find it. I'll call the Feds and tell them there's been a change of cast.'

'Bert's going to be pissed,' Larry said. 'Your rates are almost four times what mine are for a zombie raising.'

'We can't change the price in midcontract,' I said.

'No –' and he almost laughed – 'but Bert is going to be pissed that we didn't try.'

I laughed, because he was right. Bert had been our boss, but he'd been reduced to business manager because all the animators at Animators, Inc. had gotten together and staged a palace coup. We'd offered him business manager or nothing. He'd taken it when he realized his income wouldn't be affected.

'I'll get the files from the office. I'll get a flight. I'll be there. You just take care of yourself and Tammy.'

'Thanks, Anita. I don't know what I . . . I've got to go – the doctor's here.' And he was gone.

I handed the phone to Nathaniel, who placed it gently in the cradle.

'How bad is it?' Micah said.

I shrugged. 'I don't know. I don't think Larry knows, not really.' I started to crawl out of the covers and the nest of warmth that their bodies made.

'Where are you going?' Micah asked.

'I've got a plane to schedule and files to find.'

'Are you thinking of going out of town on a plane by yourself?' Micah asked. He was sitting up, knees tucked to his chest, arms encircling them.

I looked back at him from the foot of the bed. 'Yeah.'

'When will you be back?'

'Tomorrow, or the day after.'

'Then you need to book at least two seats on the plane.'

It took me a moment to understand what he meant. I raised the dead and was a legal vampire executioner. That's what the police knew for certain. I was a federal marshal because all the vamp executioners who could pass the firearms test had been grandfathered in so that the executioners could both have more powers and be better regulated. Or that was the idea. But I was also the human servant of Jean-Claude, the master vampire of St Louis. Through ties to Jean-Claude I'd inherited some abilities. One of those abilities was the *ardeur*. It was as if sex were food, and if I didn't eat enough I got sick.

That wasn't so bad, but I could also hurt anyone that I was metaphysically tied to. Not just hurt, but potentially drain them of life. Or the *ardeur* could simply choose someone at random to feed from. Which meant the *ardeur* raised and chose a victim. I didn't always have a lot of choice in who it chose. Ick.

So I fed from my boyfriends and a few friends. You couldn't feed off the same person all the time, because you could accidentally love him to death. Jean-Claude held the *ardeur* and had had to feed it for centuries, but my version was a little different from his, or maybe I just wasn't as good at controlling it yet. I was working on it, but my control wasn't perfect, and it would be a bad thing to lose control on an airplane full of strangers. Or in a van full of federal agents.

'What am I going to do?' I asked. 'I cannot take my boyfriend on a federal case.'

'You aren't going as a federal marshal, not really,' Micah said. 'It's your skills as an animator that they want, so say that I'm your assistant. They won't know any different.'

'Why do you get to go?' Nathaniel asked. He lay back on the pillows, the sheets just barely covering his nakedness.

'Because she fed on you last,' Micah said. He moved enough to touch Nathaniel's shoulder. 'I can feed her more often than you can without passing out or getting sick.'

'Because you're the Nimir-Raj and I'm just a regular wereleopard.' There was a moment of sullenness in his voice, and then he sighed. 'I don't mean to be a problem, but I've never stayed here with both of you gone.'

Micah and I looked at each other and had one of those moments. We'd all been living together for about six months. But he and Nathaniel had both moved in at the same time. I'd never dated either of them alone, not really. I mean I'd gone out with them individually, and sex wasn't always a group activity, but the sleeping arrangements were.

Micah and I both had a certain need for personal time, alone time, but Nathaniel didn't. He didn't much like being alone.

'Do you want to stay at Jean-Claude's place while we're gone?' I asked.

'Will he want me there without you?' Nathaniel asked.

I knew what he meant, but . . . 'Jean-Claude likes you.'

'He won't mind,' Micah said, 'and Asher won't mind at all.'

There was something about the way he said that last that made me look at him. Asher was Jean-Claude's second in command. They'd been friends, enemies, lovers, enemies, and shared a woman that they both loved for a few decades of happiness in centuries of unhappiness.

'Why'd you say it like that?' I asked.

'Asher likes men more than Jean-Claude does,' Micah said.

I frowned at him. 'Are you saying that he made a pass at you or Nathaniel?'

Micah laughed. 'No, in fact, Asher is always very, very careful around us. Considering that we've both been naked in a bed with Asher, Jean-Claude, and you more than once, I'd say that Asher's been a perfect gentleman.'

'So why the comment about Asher liking men more than Jean-Claude?' I asked.

'It's the way Asher watches Nathaniel when you aren't looking.'

I looked at the other man in my bed. He appeared utterly at home half-naked in my sheets. 'Does Asher bother you?'

He shook his head. 'No.'

'Have you noticed him looking at you the way Micah just said?'

'Yes,' Nathaniel said, face still peaceful.

'And that doesn't bother you?'

He smiled. 'I'm a stripper, Anita. I get a lot of people looking at me like that.'

'But you don't sleep naked in a bed with them.'

'I don't sleep naked in a bed with Asher either. He takes blood from me so he can fuck you. It may be sensual, but it's not about sex; it's about blood.'

I frowned, trying to think my way through the tangle that had become my love life. 'But Micah's implying that Asher sees you as more than food.'

'I'm not implying,' Micah said. 'I'm stating that if Asher didn't think you and Jean-Claude would be pissed, he'd have already asked Nathaniel to be more than friends.'

I stared from one to the other of them. 'He would?'

They both nodded in unison, as if they'd practiced.

'And you both knew this?'

They nodded again.

'Why didn't you tell me?'

'Because you, or I, were always there to protect Nathaniel,' Micah said. 'Now we won't be.'

I sighed.

'I'll be okay,' Nathaniel said. 'If I'm really that worried about my virtue, I'll bunk in with Jason.' He smiled even wider.

'What's so funny?' I asked. I sounded angry, because I had totally missed the whole Asher-liking-Nathaniel thing. Sometimes I felt slow, and sometimes I felt totally unprepared for dealing with the men in my life.

'The look on your face, so worried, so surprised.' He bounced up off the bed, leaving the sheet behind him. He crawled toward me, naked and beautiful. I was at the end of the bed and had nowhere to go. But he came at me so fast that I tried to back up and ended up falling off the bed. I sat naked on the floor, trying to decide if I had any dignity left to save.

Nathaniel leaned over the bed and grinned at me. 'If I tell you that was really cute, will you be mad at me?'

'Yes,' I said, but I was fighting not to smile.

He leaned his upper body off the bed, toward me. 'Then I won't say it,' he said. 'I love you, Anita.' He leaned down, but if we were going to kiss I'd have to come to my knees and meet him halfway.

I moved into the kiss he was offering and whispered against his lips, 'I love you, too.'

'Tell me what city we're flying to,' Micah said from the bed, 'and I'll see about flights.'

I broke the kiss enough to mumble, 'Philadelphia.'

Nathaniel leaned in to me again, one hand holding on to the bedpost to keep him in place. The muscles of his arm flexed effortlessly as he used the other hand to smooth hair away from my face. 'I'll miss you.'

'I'll miss you, too,' I said, and I realized that I meant it. But one 'assistant' I might be able to explain to the FBI, not two. Two and they'd begin to wonder who they were and exactly what they were assisting me with. Or that's what I told myself. Staring into the startling lavender of Nathaniel's eyes, I wondered if I cared what the FBI thought of me enough to leave him behind. Almost not. Almost.

Guilty Pleasures

An Anita Blake, Vampire Hunter, Novel

Laurell K. Hamilton

'I don't date vampires. I kill them.'

My name is Anita Blake. Vampires call me the Executioner. What I call them isn't repeatable.

Ever since the Supreme Court granted the undead equal rights, most people think vampires are just ordinary folks with fangs. I know better. I've seen their victims. I carry the scars . . .

But now a serial killer is murdering vampires – and the most powerful bloodsucker in town wants me to find the killer.

978 0 7553 5529 7

headline

Skin Trade

An Anita Blake, Vampire Hunter, Novel

Laurell K. Hamilton

'I'd worked my share of serial killer cases, but none of the killers had ever mailed me a human head. That was new.'

My name is Anita Blake and my reputation has taken some hits. Not on the work front, where I have the highest kill count of all the legal vampire executioners in the country, but on the personal front. No one seems to trust a woman who sleeps with the monsters. Still, when a vampire serial killer sends me a head from Las Vegas, I know I have to warn Sin City's local authorities what they're dealing with.

Only it's worse than I thought: several officers and an executioner have been slain paranormal style. When I get to Las Vegas, I'm joined by three other federal marshals. Which is a good thing because I need all the back up I can get when hunting a killer this powerful and dangerous.

978 0 7553 5255 5

headline

Now you can buy any of these bestselling
books by **Laurell K. Hamilton** from your bookshop
or *direct from her publisher.*

FREE P&P AND UK DELIVERY
(Overseas and Ireland £3.50 per book)

Guilty Pleasures	£7.99
The Laughing Corpse	£7.99
Circus of the Damned	£7.99
The Lunatic Cafe	£7.99
Bloody Bones	£7.99
The Killing Dance	£7.99
Burnt Offerings	£7.99
Blue Moon	£7.99
Obsidian Butterfly	£7.99
Narcissus in Chains	£7.99
Cerulean Sins	£7.99
Incubus Dreams	£7.99
Skin Trade	£7.99

TO ORDER SIMPLY CALL THIS NUMBER

01235 400 414

or visit our website: www.headline.co.uk
Prices and availability subject to change without notice.